$23.95

D1117003

WHO GOES THERE

A BIBLIOGRAPHIC DICTIONARY

Being a guide to the works of authors who
have contributed to the literature of fantasy
and science fiction, and who have published some
or all of their work pseudonymously.

Compiled by

James A. Rock

JAMES A. ROCK & CO.

BLOOMINGTON, INDIANA

1979

The first great post-industrial literary movement occurred in the mid-twentieth century. Designated "science fiction" by its members, it exhibited all of the characteristics that have since defined the term literary movement, including the development of a socio-literary framework which included authors, publishers, editors, and readers, each group interacting with the others. Criticism developed and published by the reader, a blurring of distinction between author and reader, and extensive collaboration between editors, readers, and authors were all developed in this period. The Science Fiction movement was the first to use increased communication potentials and access to widely available printing materials [*History of Printing*: mimeograph (archaic), photo-copy, offset] to develop a continuous dynamic relationship of critical interaction between authors and readers. Social structures were also developed which provided direct and personal contact between writers and readers, centered in literary conventions known as "cons." These meetings frequently lasted for several days and at their height saw the meeting of as many as four to five thousand readers [designated "fans"], authors, editors, and publishers (obs.), for socio-literary interaction.

Collaboration between authors, between editors and authors, and between authors and readers became commonplace within the socio-literary milieu of the movement and reader involvement often reached the modern stage of symbiosis with the author typified by the statement "fan-dom is a way of life."

Within fifty years (1926-1976) the Science Fiction movement had developed a complete literary structure which sustained its development through the end of the 20th century, and was supplying fifteen percent of the fiction published in its main North American center [see *United States of America: Cultural Development*]. Early non-movement criticism provided, for the most part, by pre-industrial literary institutions offers insight into the ancient "critical" coteries which dominated pre-literary cultures. [see under *History of Literature*: Literary Critic (obs.), Academic respectability (archaic)] RELATED ARTICLES: Gernsback and Campbell, Fathers of Modern Literature. Ancient Literary Movements: Bloomsbury, The Algonquin Circle, Greenwich Village—literary isolation among the ancient authors; or the absence of Ego-boo and its effects on Ancient Literature.

From the article Modern Literary Movements: The Development of Our Socio-literary Heritage. Encyclopedia Intergalactica (31st Tellurian Edition) 2790AD

PREFACE

Many influences help to determine the form of a reference book such as this. The final product is the result of a very personal response to those influences. At one point in the compilation of this book I called a well-known book dealer and author in order to check some points in his entry. He was very gracious, but at some point in the conversation he asked a very perplexing question, to wit, "Just what is it you are trying to do?" My answer was a rather disjointed set of mumbles, which I am sure left him more perplexed than ever.

The answer to the question is, simply put, that I am trying to remove certain irritations. Over the past twenty years I have often read reference books and biographical sketches of authors in which one of the following phrases would appear: "well-known in the mystery field under a variety of pseudonyms," or, "a prolific writer who has used a dozen pseudonyms both in and outside the fields of fantasy and science fiction." For years I assumed that a reference book existed which would tell me exactly what books in what fields and under what names a given author had written. As I became a more avid collector, and then a dealer, I acquired more and more reference books related to the field. I found that many books dealt with the writings of authors in the areas of fantasy and science fiction but ignored the works of these authors outside these fields. Conversely, I found a number of reference books that mentioned important writers outside their fields but ignored their works of fantasy or science fiction. The most frustrating books were those that did not completely ignore an author's work in other fields but gave one only a hint of the existence of those works. These books often gave no hints as to how one might discover what these works were or where they had appeared—especially if they had been written pseudonymously.

What I have tried to do, then, is to produce a reference book which treats authors who have written fantasy and science fiction holistically. If a reader or researcher is interested in an author covered in this book, that author's entry is designed to give information which will open up the entire range of the author's literary output—under whatever name. It seems important to me that a writer of interest be considered not just for his output in one field or even two. Fantasy and science fiction writers have often been varied and prolific in their output. I believe that it is both fascinating and important to present them as complete literary entities. I hope the reader will find my efforts useful and my format congenial.

J. A. R.
July 1979

The arrangement and form of *Who Goes There* is unique and is the result of many decisions made in the attempt to present in a simple form diverse information about authors who have often made it their avocation to be complicated and misleading. Comments and suggestions about the format as well as any information concerning errors of fact would be greatly appreciated by the compiler. It would be immeasurably helpful if comments about errors of fact or omissions were accompanied by explicit source citations. All correspondence should be addressed to James A. Rock & Co., P.O. Box 1431, Bloomington, Indiana 47402.

FIAWOL

This book is dedicated to all of us when we were ten.

ACKNOWLEDGEMENTS

Grateful acknowledgements to the following people:

Lynne Rock, my wife, who lived, ate, breathed, and typeset *Who Goes There* for the past two years. There is no more perfect wife, friend, or helpmate.

Sue Tatum (also known as Pseu) who worked prodigiously, often fifty or sixty hours a week, proofreading, encouraging, nagging, etc.

Donald R. Wilds, who laid out, pasted up, proofread, and stayed calm, again for many sixty-hour weeks.

Without these people there would be no *Who Goes There*.

My thanks also to Anita Kulman, who helped with the initial checking of reference books through many hot summer afternoons in an un-airconditioned house; to Arthur Jackson and Janis Starcs, who took over many of my day to day duties in our used book store, allowing me time for research; Paul Smedberg, who helped in typesetting and layout and to the many authors and editors who gave me information which was otherwise unobtainable. A final word of gratitude to the staff of the main library reference room at Indiana University for their help during the many evenings and weekends I spent ploughing through their reference books and to Bill Cagle, the librarian at the Lilly Library of Indiana University for the use of that library's facilities, and to the many others too numerous to mention.

GUIDE TO USAGE

In compiling this dictionary clarity has been the major consideration rather than absolute uniformity in arrangement or rigid consistency in mechanical details. Consequently, some adaptations of the basic patterns of arrangement will be noted where such adaptation has been called for by the nature of the material.

The basic pattern of arrangement and the principal mechanical devices are described and illustrated below.

Basic Pattern of Arrangement

Principal author entries in the main body of the dictionary are in **UNIVERSE BOLD** and are arranged alphabetically by the author's latest known complete legal name.

Information appears, as known, at the beginning of each entry in the following order: titles held by author; birth and death dates; name at birth (if it has been legally changed by other means than marriage); nationality; place of birth; biographies or autobiographies; and bibliographies. Following this introductory information are sub-entries arranged alphabetically, each headed by a name used by the author.

Sub-headings appear in the following formats:

as John Doe

This sub-heading indicates that the author wrote the works cited under this sub-heading *alone* using this name.

as John Doe [in collaboration with Mary Smith]

This sub-heading indicates that the author wrote the works cited under this sub-heading in *collaboration with* Mary Smith and that only the name **John Doe** appeared on the works cited.

IMPORTANT NOTE: *Credited collaborations* are indicated within all sub-headings by placing the co-author's name preceded by the word *with*, in parentheses preceding the title of the work. Such names are given in the form in which they appear on the work.

as John Doe
(with Mary Smith) *book title,* date, etc.

Under each sub-heading information is arranged as follows:

1. EARLY (USUALLY FIRST) PUBLICATION IN A PERIODICAL UNDER THIS NAME.

In some cases several magazine publications have been acknowledged because of the importance of the work or the lack of availability of the work in book form.

Additional citations from periodicals are sometimes given when an author has contributed to periodicals of different types. This allows the reader to have an indication of the various markets in which that name appeared on the author's stories.

When more than one periodical citation appears they are listed chronologically.

Periodical citations include: title of story, name of publication, and date appearing on publication.

2. FANTASY AND SCIENCE FICTION PUBLICATIONS IN BOOK FORM UNDER THIS NAME.

First edition information on titles has been cited as follows: book title, place of publication, publisher, year of publication, page numbers, illustrations (if any), and whether bound in paper wrappers.

Where more than one city of publication appears on the title page the first listed has been given.

Names of publishers have often been shortened to the first name in the firm.

When brackets [ ] surround the date of publication this indicates that the year does not appear on the title page, although it may appear on the copyright page or elsewhere. Note that the lack of brackets does not indicate that the year *does* appear on the title page. In point of fact, most unbracketed years on post World War II paperbacks probably do not have the year on the title page as it has not been the practice to put a year on the title pages of these publications.

Page numbers indicate the last numbered page in the book cited.

Additional information which would aid in the identification of the first edition is given in ( )'s at the end of the book entry.

Abbreviations in italics at the end of book entries indicate format (i.e. *ss col* for short story collection, etc.).

Book entries are given for first publication under the original title. Later publications under different titles are not given unless significant textual changes have occurred in the new edition.

Fantasy and science fiction book entries are listed chronologically within each sub-entry.

3. AT THE END OF THE CHRONOLOGICAL LISTING OF FANTASY AND SCIENCE FICTION BOOKS IN EACH SUB-ENTRY FOUR SYMBOLS (WITH CORRESPONDING ENTRY INFORMATION) WILL BE FOUND: □, ■, ✔, ●.

□ precedes listing of representative fiction outside the fields of fantasy and science fiction. Citations in this section are normally shortened to title and year of publication. Some important works are given full citation. Titles in this section are sometimes grouped by subject or format and when this is done the group is preceded by an identifying heading (i.e. MYSTERY, SCREENPLAY, WESTERN, etc.). The grouping is terminated by a period. Comments about subject or format of individual books in this section follow the year of the book (i.e. *Title,* date (mystery)).

> NOTE: There are a number of titles listed as general fiction in the dictionary which may be fantasy or science fiction titles. These are often books which I have not been able to peruse. Any information on books which are listed as general fiction, but which contain fantasy or science fiction content would be greatly appreciated.

■ precedes listing of representative non-fiction works.

✔ precedes listing of *confirmed* pseudonyms, about which no bibliographic information has been ascertained. Confirmed means that a number of usually reliable sources have indicated, such that there is little doubt, that the author has used this name on some published work(s).

● precedes listing of *unconfirmed* pseudonyms. Unconfirmed means that someone, somewhere, sometime indicated that the author used this pseudonym. The listings after the bullets are advisory only and are to be considered totally *unsubstantiated.* [Bullets are sometimes placed in front of stories, and occasionally elsewhere, to indicate that the information is unconfirmed.]

GENERAL NOTES

The term *pseudonym*, used in the title and introduction to the dictionary, is an imprecise and misleading designation for many of the entries in this book. Titles such as Lord Dunsany and Mrs. James Mason, surnames which are legal names for a given period in a person's life, and old legal names which have been discarded are not pseudonyms. Consequently, except for the term "house pseudonym," the word pseudonym is not used in the body of the dictionary. Each main entry is the fullest form of the last legal name known to the compiler. Each sub-heading is a name or title used by this person and is given in the form of the word "as" followed by the name or title used on the works cited within that sub-entry to identify the author.

Cultural conventions with regard to women's names: taking of a husband's last name, use of a previous husband's or an original surname, and use of titles-by-marriage are confusing and subject to change through time.

The following conventions have been used for dealing with these inconsistencies:

1. If there is evidence that a woman took her husband's surname for legal purposes, then that name is the name under which she is alphabetized. If she produced work under her original surname it is listed under a sub-heading.

2. If a woman has been divorced or widowed and she has reassumed her original surname, she is alphabetized under that name. If she produced work under her previous married surname it is listed in a sub-heading.

3. The term Mrs. followed by the husband's first name and surname is not regarded as a name but as a title-by-marriage. If a woman produced work under this title it is listed under a sub-heading.

   Pamela Mason (p. 99) is a good example of this convention. She is divorced from James Mason, but still uses the surname Mason. Before she was married she used her original surname, writing as Pamela Kellino. While married she was often referred to in print by the title "Mrs. James Mason."

No book of this type can ever hope to be complete or completely up to date. There are obviously going to be numerous authors whose pseudonymous subterfuges have escaped my attention and, even as I write, new pseudonyms are being concocted by editors and authors across the country and around the world.

In an attempt to be comprehensive I have obviously gone far beyond the area in which I could claim total competence for the job at hand. No one compiler can be intimately familiar with the body of work represented by the almost 1400 authors covered in this work. In recognition of this fact all information has been checked as carefully and as completely as the various reference tools and collections at my disposal have allowed. I can only hope that the flaws are such that they will be forgiven by those who use the dictionary.

It is meet that I point out to the reader certain inconsistencies and flaws in this work which, while not exactly intentional, are, shall we say, studied. The information on place of birth, nationality, biographies, bibliographies, etc., was not in the original design for the book. However, I came across so much of this type of information which was not included in reference books covering the fields that I have cited whatever came my way. There was no attempt, however, to be complete in this respect or specifically to seek this information. I am sure, therefore, that there are many more biographies, bibliographies, and checklists extant on the authors covered in this dictionary than those I have cited.

With regard to completeness of book entries within the field I can only say that my work on this book coincided with the greatest publishing boom the fields of fantasy and science fiction have ever seen. Rather than select an arbitrary cut-off date for inclusion, I have simply listed as much information about recent publications as I could obtain. If I only know a title and year for a recent book, I have cited it. This, of course, will give the reader more book information than if I had simply stopped at 1970 or 1972. The reader should be aware, however, that living writers who have books listed in the mid- and late 1970's could easily have others of which I am unaware.

Criteria used to determine pseudonym(s)

1. Admission of the use of the pseudonym by the author.
2. Attribution of a pseudonym to an author by either the *National Union Catalogue* or the *British Museum Catalogue* and one other standard reference work.
3. Attribution of a pseudonym to an author by two standard reference books.
4. Attribution of a pseudonym to an author by *Webster's Biographical Dictionary* or *Contemporary Authors*.
5. Attribution in a full fledged bibliography of a given author's work.

Abbreviations/Symbols/Terms

Br. - British
c. - *circa*
col. - collection (as in stories, novellas, etc.)
cop. - copies
crit./lit. crit. - criticism/literary criticism
ed. - editor, edited by/edition (as context dictates)
ff - and following
fl - flourished
F.P.C.I. - Fantasy Publishing Company, Inc.
front. - frontispiece
ill. - illustrated
incl. - including
juv. - juvenile
n.d. - no date given
n.p. - no place (of publication) given
nr - near
NY - New York City
paper - paperback or paper wrappers
pp. - pages
pre. - previous
pub. - published/publication (as context dictates)
SF - (used occasionally) science fiction
ss col - short story collection
trans. - translated (by)/translator (as context dictates)
vol. - volume(s)

Signed - term indicating book(s) signed by author

numbered - indicates this work had a limited press run and copies were individually numbered

boxed - books which come with a special fitted "box" to protect them—often decorative

fanzine - a magazine or newsletter published by a science fiction fan(s), often containing fiction. Fanzines offer no payment for material used, other than copies of the fanzine itself—this distinguishes them from "prozines," the fan name for magazines which do pay authors for their work

ABBOTT, EDWIN A(bbott) (1838-1926) *English.*
British clergyman, schoolmaster, and biographer. Headmaster, City of London School, 1865-69.
as Edwin A. Abbott
■ *A Shakespearian Grammar,* 1870; *Francis Bacon,* 1885; *The Anglican Career of Newman,* 1892.
as A. Square
Flatland; A Romance of Many Dimensions. Boston: Roberts Bros., 1885, 155pp.
anonymous
Flatland, a romance of many dimensions with illustrations by the author, a square. London: Seeley, 1884, 100pp., ill.

ABRAHAMSEN, CHRISTINE
as Cristabel
The Cruachan and the Killane. NY: Curtis, [1970], 287pp., paper.
The Mortal Immortal. NY: Walker, [1971], 271pp.
□ *The Golden Olive,* 1972.
● Kathleen Westcott

ACKERMAN, FORREST J(ames) (1916-   ) *U.S.*
Born: Los Angeles, California
Autobiography: *Forrest J. Ackerman and Friends,* [c. 1970].
A famous personality in organized U.S. science fiction fandom. ████████████████████ First editor of *Famous Monsters of Filmland* magazine.
as Sgt. Ack Ack
Byline on publications while stationed at Fort McArthur, California, early 1940s.
as Forrest J. Ackerman
(with Francis Flagg) Earth's Lucky Day. *Wonder Stories,* March 1936.
■ "*I Bequeath,*" 1946.
as Dr. Acula
The Terror from Transylvania. *A Book of Weird Tales #1,* Jan 1960   *article*
as Jacques de Forrest Erman
(with Wilfred Owen Morley) Dhactwhu!—Remember? *Super Science Stories,* April 1949.
as Jack Ermann
Fan name in the 1940s
as Geoffrey Giles [in collaboration with Walter Gillings]
Fantasy's Prodigy. *Fantasy Review,* Summer 1949 (Br.) (*article* on Ray Bradbury)
as Alden Lorraine
The Micro Man. *New Worlds #2,* 1946 (Br.)
as Spencer Strong
Fan name in the 1940s
as Claire Voyant
Fan name in the 1940s
as Hubert George Wells
Earth Can Be Fair. *Other Worlds,* Oct 1950
as Weaver Wright
Micro Man. *Fantasy Book #1,* [1947]
↙ Forry Ackerman, Silvestre Aldeano, Les Angeleno, Nick Beal, Carl F. Burke, Morris Chapnik, Walter Chinwell, J. Forrest Eckman, 4e, Aime Merritt, Fisher Trentworth

ACKERMAN, WENDAYNE [*nee* Tilly Porjes] *naturalized U.S.*
Born: Frankfurt-am-Main, Germany
Fan personality during the 1940s. Later married to Forrest J. Ackerman.

as Mrs. Forrest J. Ackerman
Photo in *New Worlds,* Autumn 1951
as Wendayne Ackerman
(Translator) *Hard To Be a God,* by Arkadi and Boris Strugatski. Seabury, 1973.
as Wendayne Mondelle
Fan name during the late 1940s
● W. N. Dane

ADAMS, J.
as Skelton Kuppord
The Uncharted Island. London: Nelson, 1899 [1898] 350pp., ill.
A Fortune from the Sky. London: Nelson, 1903, 230pp., ill.
□ *Hammond's Hard Lines,* 1894; *The Fifteen Stamps,* 1895; *The Rickerton Medal,* 1896.

ADDIS, ERIC ELDRINGTON   *English*
as Peter Drax
Murder by Chance. London: Hutchinson, [1936], 287pp.
□ MYSTERY: *Murder by Proxy,* 1937; *Death by Two Hands,* 1937; *Crime within a Crime,* 1938; *Tune to a Corpse,* 1938; *Crime to Music,* 1939; *Sing a Song of Murder,* 1944.

ADDIS, HAZEL IRIS WILSON (Mrs. E. E.) (1900-   ) *British*
as Hazel Adair
(with Ronald Marriott) *Stranger from Space.* London: Weidenfeld & Nicolson, 1953, 191pp., ill.
□ *Wanted: A Son,* 1935; *Mistress Mary,* 1936; *All the Trumpets,* 1937; *Sparrow Market,* 1938.
as H. I. Addis
■ Books for Boy Scouts, e.g., *Duty To God in the Wolf Cub Pack,* 1951.
as A. J. Heritage
□ *The Happy Years,* 1938.
● Mao

AIKEN, JOAN (1924-   ) *English*
Born: Rye, Sussex
Daughter of author Conrad Aiken. Much of her fantasy is for juveniles and/or is humorous.
as Joan Aiken
All You've Ever Wanted, and Other Stories. London: Jonathan Cape, 1953, 190pp., ill. *ss col*
More Than You Bargained For, and Other Stories. London: Jonathan Cape, 1955, 190pp., ill. *ss col*
Trouble with Product X. London: Gollancz, 1966, 189pp.
The Crystal Crow. Garden City: Doubleday, 1968 [1967], 263pp.
Night Fall. London: Pan, [1969], 125pp., paper.
A Small Pinch of Weather and Other Stories. London: Jonathan Cape, 1969, 190pp., ill. *ss col*
The Windscreen Weepers and Other Tales of Horror and Suspense. London: Gollancz, 1969, 256pp. *ss col*
The Whispering Mountain. Garden City: Doubleday, [1969], 237pp., ill.
Smoke from Cornwell's Time and Other Stories. Garden City: Doubleday, 1970, 163pp. *ss col*
The Cuckoo Tree. London: Jonathan Cape, 1971, 250pp., ill.
The Green Flash, and Other Tales of Horror, Suspense, and Fantasy. NY: Holt, [1971], 163pp.
□ MYSTERY: *The Silence of Herondale,* 1965; *Beware of the Bouquet,* 1966; *The Ribs of Death,* 1967; *Hate Begins at Home,* 1967.
↙ Nicholas Dee, Rosie Lee

AITKEN, ROBERT (1872- ?) [of Gray's Inn]
as Robert Aitken
The Golden Horseshoe. NY: McBride, [1907], 348pp.
Beyond the Skyline. London: Murray, 1909, 309pp. *ss col*

The Lantern of Luck. London: Murray, 1910, 341pp.
The Man in the Mirror; or, The Purple Emperor and the Painted Lady. Weybridge, Surrey: R. Aitken, 1910, 302pp.
as Hudson Douglas
A Million a Minute; A Romance of Modern New York and Paris. NY: W. J. Watt, [1908], 304pp.
The Lantern of Luck. NY: W.J. Watt, [1909], 377pp., ill.
The Man in the Mirror. NY: W.J. Watt, [1910], 302pp.
The White Blackbird. Boston: Little, Brown, 1912, 366pp., ill.

ALDISS, BRIAN W(ilson) (1925-   ) *English*
Born: Dereham, Norfolk
Bibliography: *Item 83—Brian W. Aldiss, A Bibliography 1954-1972,* compiled by Margaret Aldiss.
Aldiss is a past president of the British Science Fiction Association (1960). He is noted for his editing as well as his books. *Billion Year Spree,* listed below, is a history of science fiction.
as Brian W. Aldiss
On Writing Science Fiction. *Authentic,* May 1954 (Br.) *article*
Criminal Record. *Science Fantasy,* July 1954 (Br.)
The Brightfount Diaries. London: Faber, 1955, 200pp., ill.
Space, Time and Nathaniel. London: Faber, 1957, 208pp., ill.
Non-Stop. London: Faber, [1958], 252pp.
Vanguard from Alpha. NY: Ace, [1959], 109pp., paper. (Ace Double D 369)
No Time Like Tomorrow. NY: Signet, [1959], 160pp., paper. *ss col*
The Canopy of Time. London: Faber, [1959], 222pp. *ss col*
Bow Down to Nul. NY: Ace, [1960], 145pp., paper. (Ace Double D443)
Galaxies Like Grains of Sand. NY: Signet, [1960], 144pp. paper. *ss col*
Male Response. NY: Beacon/Galaxy, [1961], 188pp., paper.
The Primal Urge. NY: Ballantine, [1961], 190pp., paper.
The Long Afternoon of Earth. NY: Signet, 1962, 192pp., paper.
Hothouse. London: Faber, 1962, 253pp.
The Airs of Earth. London: Faber, 1963, 256pp. *ss col*
Starswarm. NY: Signet, [1964], 159pp., paper. *ss col*
The Dark Light Years. London: Faber, 1964, 190pp.
Greybeard. London: Faber, 1964, 237pp.
Earthworks. London: Faber, 1965, 155pp.
Best SF Stories of Brian W. Aldiss. London: Faber, 1965, 253pp. *ss col*
The Saliva Tree and Other Strange Growths. London: Faber, [1966], 232pp. *ss col*
An Age. London: Faber, [1967], 224pp.
Report on Probability A. London: Faber, [1968], 176pp.
Barefoot in the Head: A European Fantasia. London: Faber, [1969], 281pp. *ss col & poems*
A Brian Aldiss Omnibus. London: Sidgwick & Jackson, 1969, 191 & 191 & 126pp. *col*
Intangibles, Inc. & Other Stories. London: Faber, 1969, 198pp. *ss col*
The Moment of Eclipse. London: Faber, [1970], 215pp.
The Book of Brian Aldiss. NY: DAW #29, 1972, 191pp., paper.
The Comic Inferno. London: New English Library, 1973, 159pp.
Frankenstein Unbound. London: Jonathan Cape, [1973], 184pp.
The Eighty-Minute Hour; a Space Opera. London: Jonathan Cape, [1974], 286pp.
The Malacia Tapestry. London: Jonathan Cape, 1976, 313pp., ill.
Brothers of the Dead, London: 1978.
□ *The Hand-Reared Boy,* 1970; *A Soldier Erect: being further Adventures of the Hand-Reared Boy,* 1971.
■ *The Shape of Further Things,* 1970; *The Billion Year*

Spree, 1973; *Hell's Cartographers* (edited with Harry Harrison), 1975.
as Jael Cracken
Lazarus. *Science Fantasy #65,* June/July 1964 (Br.)
The Impossible Smile. *Science Fantasy #72 and #73,* May and June 1965 (Br.)
as Peter Pica
Series of articles about life in a bookshop in *The Bookseller,* 1954-55 (British); see *The Brightfount Diaries* as B. W. Aldiss
as John Runciman
Unauthorized Persons. *Science Fantasy #65,* June/July 1964 (Br.)
as C. C. Shackleton
Give Me Excess of It, That Something Snaps. *SF Horizons 1,* Spring 1964 (Br.)
● **Arch Mendicant**

ALEXANDER, R(obert) W(illiam) (1905-   ) *English*
as R. W. Alexander
The Path of the Sun, a romance. London: Unwin, 1927, 272pp.
as Joan Butler
Deep Freeze. London: Stanley Paul, [1952], 256pp.
Space To Let. London: Stanley Paul, 1955, 191pp.
□ *The Heavy Husband,* 1930; *Mixed Pickle,* 1934; *Double Figures,* 1946; *Paper Money,* 1954.
as Ralph Temple
Cuckoo Time. London: Nicholson & Watson, [1944], 320pp.

ALFVEN, HANNES OLOF GOESTA (1908-   ) *Swedish*
Born: Norrkoeping
as Hannes Alfven
■ *Cosmological Electrodynamics,* 1950; *On the Origin of the Solar System,* 1954; *Worlds-Antiworlds, Antimatter in Cosmology,* 1966.
as Olof Johannesson
The Tale of the Giant Computer (translated by Naomi Wallford). NY: Coward-McCann, 1968, 126pp.

ALGER, LECLAIRE GOWANS (1898-   )
as Leclaire Alger
Jan and the Wonderful Mouth-organ. NY: Harper, 1939, 177pp., ill.
Dongal's Wish. NY: Harper, 1942, 244pp., ill.
The Golden Summer. NY: Harper, [1942], 205pp., ill.
as Sorche Nic Leodhas
Heather and Broom: Tales of the Scottish Highlands. NY: Holt, 1960, 128pp., ill. *ss col*
Gaelic Ghosts. NY: Holt, 1963, 110pp., ill.
Ghosts Go Haunting. NY: Holt, 1965, 128pp.

ALLEN, CHARLES GRANT BLAIRFINDIE (1848-1899)
Canadian/British
Born: Kingston, Ontario
Allen received his B.A. from Oxford (1871) and was professor of mental and moral philosophy at Jamaica College for Negroes in the mid-1870s. He returned to England in 1876 to pursue his literary career.
as Grant Allen
Strange Stories. London: Chatto & Windus, 1884, 356pp. *ss col*
(with May Cotes) *Kalee's Shrine.* Bristol: Arrowsmith, 1886, 196pp.
The Beckoning Hand and Other Stories. London: Chatto & Windus, 1887, 341pp. *ss col*
The White Man's Foot. London: Hatchards, 1888, 216pp. ill.
The Jaws of Death. London: Simpkin, Marshall, 1889, 110pp.
The Great Taboo. London: Chatto & Windus, 1890, 280pp.
Ivan Greet's Masterpiece. London: Chatto & Windus, 1893, 330pp. *ss col*

Mr. Grant Allen's New Story "Michael Crag." London: Leadenhall, 1893, 194pp.

The British Barbarians, A Hill Top Novel. London: John Lane, 1895, 202pp.

Twelve Tales with a headpiece, a talepiece, and an intermezzo. London: G. Richards, 1899, 351pp. *ss col*

Hilda Wade, A Woman with Tenacity of Purpose. NY: Putnam, 1900, 383pp., ill.

The Backslider. London: Lewis, Scribner's, 1901, 380pp. *ss col*

□ *The Woman Who Did,* 1895. MYSTERY: *The African Millionaire,* 1897; *Miss Cayley's Adventures,* 1899.

■ *Physiological Aesthetics,* 1876; *Anglo-Saxon England,* 1881; *Belgium; Its Cities,* 1884; *Force and Energy,* 1885.

as Cecil Powers

□ *Philistia.* London: Chatto & Windus, 1884, 3 vols.

as Olive Pratt Rayner

□ *The Type-writer Girl.* London: Pearson, 1897, 261pp.

✔ Martin Leach Warborough

● J. Arbuthnot Wilson

[This name seems to exist only as a cross reference to a non-existent entry in the British Museum Catalogue and as a notation as co-author of a London edition of *Strange Stories* (1885) listed in the National Union Catalogue but not the BMC.]

ALLEN, HENRY FRANCIS   *U.S.*

as Henry Allen

■ *Labor Reform. An Address Before the St. Louis Section of International Workingmen,* [c.1872], 13pp.

as Pruning Knife

The Key to Industrial Co-operative Government. St. Louis, Missouri: the author, 1886, 133pp., ill.

A Strange Voyage . . . An Interesting and Instructive Description of Life on the Planet Venus. St. Louis, Missouri: Monitor Publishing Co., 1891, 226pp.

ALLEN, HENRY WILSON (1912-   ) *U.S.*

as Henry (Wilson) Allen

Genesis Five. NY: Morrow, 1968, 256pp.

as Clay Fisher

□ WESTERN: *Red Blizzard,* 1951; *The Big Pasture,* 1955; *The Brass Command,* 1955.

as Will Henry

□ WESTERN: *Journey to Shiloh,* 1960; *Mackenna's Gold,* 1963; *Custer's Last Stand,* 1966.

ALTER, ROBERT EDMOND (1925-1965)   *U.S.*

Born: San Francisco, California

as Robert Edmond Alter

Coup de Grace. Bizarre Mystery Magazine, Oct. 1965

□ *The Dark Keep,* 1962.

as Robert Retla

The Mariner's Ghost. Bizarre Mystery Magazine

✔ Robert Raymond

ALTSHULER, HARRY

as Alexander Faust

The Witch in the Fog. Weird Tales, Sept. 1938

ALVAREZ-DEL REY (Y De Los Uerdes), RAMON F(elipe San Juan Mario Silvio Enrico Smith Heathcourt-Brace Sierra Y) (1915-   ) *U.S.*

Born: Minnesota

Editor of Ballantine's science fiction line issued as "Del Rey Books." Books listed as written in collaboration with Paul W. Fairman may be ghost-written by Fairman according to some sources.

as John Alvarez

Fifth Freedom. Astounding, May 1943

as R. Alvarez

Anything. *Unknown,* Oct 1939

Publisher of *Science Fiction Adventures* magazine Nov 1952*ff.*

as Ramon F. Alvarez del Rey

Letters to the editor. *Astounding,* 1935*ff.*

as Lester del Rey

The Faithful. Astounding, April 1938

"*. . . And Some Were Human.*" Philadelphia: Prime Press, 1948, 331pp., ill.

Marooned on Mars. Philadelphia: Winston, [1952], 210pp. *juv*

Attack from Atlantis. Philadelphia: Winston, [1953], 207pp. *juv*

Step to the Stars. Philadelphia: Winston, [1954], 210pp. *juv*

Mission to the Moon. Philadelphia: Winston, [1956], 207pp. *juv*

Nerves. NY: Ballantine 151, [1956], 153pp., paper and hardback

Robots and Changelings. NY: Balantine 246, [1957], 157pp., paper and hardback *ss col*

Day of the Giants. NY: Avalon, 1959, 224pp.

Moon of Mutiny. NY: Holt, 1961, 217pp.

The Eleventh Commandment. NY: Regency, 1962, 159pp., paper.

The Sky is Falling & Badge of Infamy. NY: Galaxy/Magnabook #1, 1963, 158pp., paper. *2 novellas*

Outpost of Jupiter. NY: Holt, [1963], 191pp.

Mortals and Monsters. NY: Ballantine, [1965], 188pp., paper *ss col*

Rocket from Infinity. NY: Holt, [1966], 191pp.

The Infinite Worlds of Maybe. NY: Holt, 1966, 192pp.

Psalemate. NY: Putnam, 1971, 190pp.

Gods and Golems. NY: Ballantine, [1973], 246pp., paper. *ss col*

The Early del Rey. Garden City: Doubleday, [1975], 424pp. *ss col*

(with R. F. Jones) *Weeping May Tarry.* NY: Pinnacle, 1978.

□ *A Pirate Flag for Monterey,* 1952.

■ *Rockets Through Space,* 1957; *The Mysterious Earth,* 1960; *The Mysterious Sea,* 1961; *The Mysterious Sky,* 1964.

as Lester del Rey [in collaboration with Paul W. Fairman]

The Runaway Robot. Philadelphia: Westminster, [1964], 176pp.

The Scheme of Things. NY: Belmont, [1966], 157pp., paper.

Siege Perilous, The Man without a Planet. NY: Lancer, [1966], 157pp., paper.

Tunnel Through Time. Philadelphia: Westminster, [1966], 153pp.

Prisoners of Space. NY: Westminster, [1968], 142pp.

as Cameron Hall

Editor of *Fantasy Fiction,* Nov. 1953*ff.*

as Marion Henry

The Renegade. Astounding, July 1943

Associate editor of *Fantasy Magazine,* Feb.-March 1953*ff.*

as Philip James [in collaboration with James H. Beard]

Carillion of Skulls. Unknown, Feb 1941

as Wade Kaempfert

Route to the Planets. *Rocket Stories,* July 1953 *article*

Editor of *Rocket Stories,* April 1953–Sept. 1953

as Edson McCann [in collaboration with Frederik Pohl]

Preferred Risk. *Galaxy,* June 1955

Preferred Risk. NY: Simon & Schuster, 1955, 248pp.

as Henry Marion

Possibly books on gardening

as Philip St. John

Unto Him That Hath. Space SF, Nov. 1952

Rocket Jockey. Philadelphia: Winston, 1952, 207pp.

Rocket to No Where. Philadelphia: Winston, 1954

as Charles Satterfield [house pseudonym] [in collaboration with Frederik Pohl]

No More Stars. Beyond, July 1954

as Eric Van Lhin

Moon Blind. *Space SF*, Sept. 1952

Battle on Mercury. Philadelphia: Winston, 1953, 207pp. *juv*

Police Your Planet. NY: Avalon, 1956, 224pp.

as John Vincent

Associate editor, *Rocket Stories*, April-Sept. 1953

Associate editor, *Fantasy Fiction*, Feb./March 1953-Nov. 1953

Associate editor, *Science Fiction Adventures*, Nov. 1952-May 1953

Associate editor, *Space SF*, Sept 1952–Sept 1953

as Kenneth Wright

The Mysterious Planet. Philadelphia: Winston, [1953], 209pp.

AMES, ELEANOR MARIA EASTERBROOK (Mrs.)
(1831-1908) *U.S.*

Born: Brooklyn, New York

as Eleanor Kirk

Libra: An Astrological Romance. Brooklyn, New York: E. Kirk, [1896], 270pp., ill.

The Christ of the Red Planet. NY: Publishers' Printing Co., [c.1901], 138pp.

☐ *Up Broadway and Its Sequel*, 1870.

■ *Beecher as a Humorist*, 1887; *Perpetual Youth*, 1895; *The Bottom Plank of Mental Healing*, 1899.

AMIS, KINGSLEY W(illiam) (1922-   ) *English*

Born: London

as Kingsley Amis

Something Strange. *Spectator*, 1960 (Br.) *Magazine of Fantasy and Science Fiction*, July 1961.

The Anti-Death League. London: Gollancz, 1966, 325pp.

The Green Man. London: Jonathan Cape, 1969, 253pp.

The Alternation. NY: Viking, 1977.

☐ *Lucky Jim*, 1954; *That Certain Feeling*, 1955; *Take a Girl Like You*, 1960; *I Want It Now*, 1968; *Girl, 20*, 1971.

■ *New Maps of Hell*, 1960.

as Robert Markham

Colonel Sun: A James Bond Adventure. London: Jonathan Cape, 1968, 255pp.

ANDERSON, POUL (1926-   ) *U.S.*

Born: Bristol, Pennsylvania

as Poul Anderson

(with F. N. Waldrop) Tomorrow's Children. *Astounding*, March, 1947.

Logic. *Astounding*, July 1947

Vault of the Ages. Philadelphia: Winston, [1952], 210pp.

Brain Wave. NY: Ballantine 80, [1954], 164pp., paper.

The Broken Sword. NY: Abelard-Schuman, 1954, 274pp.

No World of Their Own. NY: Ace, [1955], 158pp., paper. (Ace Double D 110)

Planet of No Return. NY: Ace, [1956], 105pp., paper. (Ace Double D199)

Starways. NY: Avalon, 1957, 224pp.

(with Gordon Dickson) *Earthman's Burden.* NY: Gnome, 1957, 184pp., ill.

The Snows of Ganymede. NY: Ace, [1958], 96pp., paper. (Ace Double D303)

The War of the Wing Men. NY: Ace, [1958], 160pp., paper. (Ace Double D 303)

Virgin Planet. NY: Avalon, 1959, 224pp.

War of Two Worlds. NY: Ace, [1959], 108pp., paper. (Ace Double D 335)

We Claim These Stars. NY: Ace, [1959], 125pp., paper. (Ace Double D407)

The Enemy Stars. Philadelphia: Lippincott, 1959 [c.1958], 189pp.

The High Crusade. Garden City: Doubleday, 1960, 192pp.

Guardians of Time. NY: Ballantine, [1960], 140pp., paper. *ss col*

Earthman, Go Home. NY: Ace, [1960], 110pp., paper. (Ace Double D 479)

Twilight World. NY: Torquil, [1961], 181pp.

Mayday Orbit. NY: Ace, [1961], 126pp., paper. (Ace Double F104)

Three Hearts and Three Lions. Garden City: Doubleday, 1961, 191pp.

Strangers from Earth. NY: Ballantine, [1961], 144pp., paper.

Orbit Unlimited. NY: Pyramid, [1961], 158pp., paper.

After Doomsday. NY: Ballantine 579, [1962], 128pp., paper.

The Makeshift Rocket. NY: Ace, [1962], 97pp., paper. (Ace Double F139)

Un-Man and Other Novellas. NY: Ace, [1962], 158pp., paper. (Ace Double F 139) *col*

Shield. NY: Berkley, [1963], 158pp., paper.

Let the Spacemen Beware! NY: Ace, [1963], 98pp., paper. (Ace Double F209)

Time and the Stars. Garden City: Doubleday, 1964, 249pp.

Trader to the Stars. Garden City: Doubleday, 1964, 176pp.

Three Worlds To Conquer. NY: Pyramid, [1964], 143pp., paper.

The Star Fox. Garden City: Doubleday, 1965, 274pp.

Agent of the Terran Empire. Philadelphia: Chilton, [1965], 201pp.

Flandry of Terra. Philadelphia: Chilton, [1965], 225pp.

The Corridors of Time. Garden City: Doubleday, 1965, 209pp.

The Trouble Twisters. Garden City: Doubleday, 1966, 189pp.

Ensign Flandry. Philadelphia: Chilton, 1966, 203pp.

(with Christian Molbech) *The Fox, the Dog, and the Griffin.* Garden City: Doubleday, 1966, 62pp., ill.

World Without Stars. NY: Ace, [1966], 125pp., paper.

The Horn of Time. NY: Signet, [1968], 144pp., paper. *ss col*

Seven Conquests. NY: Macmillan, [1969], 224pp.

Beyond the Beyond. NY: Signet, [1969], 263pp., paper. *ss col*

Tales of the Flying Mountains. NY: Macmillan, 1969.

Satan's World. Garden City: Doubleday, 1969, 204pp.

The Rebel Worlds. NY: Signet, [1969], 141pp., paper.

Tau Zero. Garden City: Doubleday, 1970, 208pp.

A Circus of Hells. NY: Signet, [1970], 160pp., paper.

The Byworlder. NY: Signet, [1971], 160pp., paper.

The Dancer from Atlantis. Garden City: Doubleday, [SF Book Club, 1971], 183pp.

The Broken Sword. NY: Ballantine, [1971], 207pp., paper.

Operation Chaos. Garden City: Doubleday, 1971, 232pp.

A Chapter of Revelation. The Day the Sun Stood Still, Nashville: T. Nelson, 1972, 240pp.

There Will Be Time. Garden City: Doubleday [SF Book Club, 1972], 181pp.

The Day of Their Return. Garden City: Doubleday [SF Book Club, 1973], 182pp.

Hrolf Kraki's Saga. NY: Ballantine, [1973], 261pp., paper.

The People of the Wind. NY: Signet, [1973], 176pp., paper.

The Queen of Air and Darkness. NY: Signet, [1973], 149pp., paper. *ss col*

Fire Time. Garden City: Doubleday, 1974, 210pp.

The Many Worlds of Poul Anderson. Radnor, Pennsylvania: Chilton, [1974], 324pp. *ss col*

The Worlds of Poul Anderson. NY: Ace, [1974], paper.

A Midsummer Tempest. Garden City: Doubleday, 1974, 207pp.

A Knight of Ghosts and Shadows. Garden City: Doubleday [SF Book Club, c.1974], 184pp.

(with Gordon R. Dickson) *Star Prince Charley.* NY: Putnam, 1975.

Homeward and Beyond. Garden City: Doubleday, 1975, 204pp.

The Winter of the World. Garden City: Doubleday, [SF Book Club, 1975], 182pp., maps.

Homebrew. New England SF Association Press, 75pp.,

ill. *miscellany* (500 copies)
The Best of Poul Anderson. NY: Pocket Books, [1976], 287pp., paper. *ss col*
Mirkheim. NY: Berkley/Putnam, 1977, 218pp.
The Earth Book of Storm Gate. NY: Berkley/Putnam, 1978.
□ MYSTERY: *Perish by the Sword*, 1959; *Murder in Black Letter*, 1960; *Stab in the Back*, 1960; *Murder Bound*, 1962; HISTORICAL FICTION: *The Golden Slave*, 1960; *Rogue Sword*, 1960.
■ *Thermonuclear Warfare*, 1963; *Is There Life on Other Worlds*, 1963.
as A. A. Craig
Witch of the Demon Seas. *Planet Stories*, Jan. 1951.
as Michael Karageorge
In the Shadow. *Analog*, March 1967.
as Winston P. Sanders
Wherever You Are. *Astounding*, April 1959

ANDERSON, STELLA BENSON (Mrs. J. C. O'Gorman) (1892-1933)
as Stella Benson
Living Alone. London: Macmillan, 1919, 263pp.
The Awakening, a Fantasy. San Francisco: Lantern Press, 1925, 15pp.
The Far Away Bride. NY: Harper, 1930, 445pp.
Christmas Formula and Other Stories. London: Joiner & Steele, 1932, 67pp. *ss col*
Collected Short Stories. London: Macmillan, 1936, 303pp. *ss col*
□ *Goodbye Stranger*, 1926. PLAY: *Kwan-yin*, 1922.

ANDERSON, WILLIAM CHARLES (1920-) *U.S.*
Born: La Junta, Colorado
as Andy Anderson
(with Barrie Fletcher) From Bad To Verse. *Startling Stories*, Aug. 1952.
The Valley of the Gods. Baraboo, Wisconsin: Andoll Publishing Co., 1957.
as William C. Anderson
Five, Four, Three, Two, One—Pfff. NY: Ace, [1960], 157pp., paper.
Penelope. NY: Crown, 1963, 215pp.
Adam M-1. NY: Crown, 1964, 255pp.
Pandemonium on the Potomac. NY: Crown, 1966, 245pp.

ANGOFF, CHARLES (1902-) *naturalized U.S.*
Born: Russia
as Charles Angoff
Adventures in Heaven. NY: Ackerman, 1945, 120pp.
Advisory editor, *Magazine of Fantasy and Science Fiction*, Sept. 1952–Aug. 1954.
Associate editor, *Magazine of Fantasy and Science Fiction*, Sept. 1954–May 1956.
□ *Journey to the Dawn*, 1951; *In the Morning Light*, 1953; *The Sun at Noon*, 1955.
■ *A Literary History of the American People*, 1931; *Palestrina; Savior of Church Music*, 1944; *A Handbook of Libel, A Practical Guide for Editors and Authors*, 1946.
as Richard W. Hinton
(ed) *Arsenal for Skeptics*. NY: Knopf, 1934, 370pp.
□ Editor of *American Mercury* magazine in the 1930s.

APPLETON, VICTOR [house pseudonym]
see **HOWARD GARIS** and **EDWARD STRATEMEYER**

ARCHER, LEE [house pseudonym]
unattributed
Lease to Doomsday. *Amazing*, Sept 1956
Peter Merton's Private Mint. *Fantastic*, Oct 1956

by Harlan Ellison
Escape Route. *Amazing*, March 1957

ARLEN, MICHAEL (*ne* Dikran Kouyoumdjian) (1895-1956) *British*
Born: Roustchouk, Bulgaria
as Michael Arlen (legal name after 1922)
These Charming People, London: Collins, (1923), 265pp. *ss col*
May Fair. London: Collins, (1925), 319pp., ill *ss col*
Man's Mortality. Garden City: Doubleday, 1933, 307pp.
Hell!, Said the Duchess, A Bedtime Story. Garden City: Doubleday, 1934, 241pp.
□ *The London Venture*, 1920; *The Green Hat*, 1924; *The Crooked Coronet*, 1937; *Flying Dutchman*, 1939.

ARMOUR, R. COUTTS
as Coutts Brisbane
A Matter of Gravity. *serial, The Red Magazine* (London), Jan. 1, 1913*ff*.
Beyond the Orbits. *The Red Magazine* (London), Feb. 15, 1914.
Take It As Red. *The Red Magazine* (London), Feb. 15, 1918.
Earthwise. *The Red Magazine* (London), April 1, 1918.
All Briny. *The Red Magazine* (London), June 1918.
Under the Moons. *The Red Magazine* (London), July 15, 1919
When It Was Dark, *The Yellow Magazine* (London), Dec. 16, 1921.
as Reid Whitney
The Dominant Factor, *The Red Magazine* (London), June 1, 1913.

ARMSTRONG, CHARLES WICKSTEED (1871- ?) *English*
as Charles Wicksteed Armstrong
Paradise Found; or, Where the Sex Problem Has Been Solved (a story from South America). London: Bale, 1936, 211pp.
■ *The Survival of the Unfittest*, 1927.
as Charles Strongi'th'arm
The Yorl of the Northmen; or, the Fate of the English Race. Being Romances of a Monarchical Utopia. London: Reeves & Turner, 1892, 127pp.

ARMSTRONG, TERENCE IAN FYTTON (1912-1970) *English*
Born: London
as T. I. F. Armstrong
(ed) *Full Score*. London: Rich & Cowan, (1933), 295pp. *ss col*
as John Gawsworth
(ed) *Strange Assembly*, London: Unicorn Press, 1932 336pp.
(ed) *Thirty New Tales of Horror*. London: Hutchinson, 1935.
(ed) *Crimes, Creeps, and Thrills*. London: The Daily Express, (1936), 735pp., ill.
(ed) *Twenty Tales of Terror*. Calcutta: Siesil Gupta, 1945.
□ *Confession*, 1931 (poetry).
as Orpheus Scrannel
An Unterrestrial Pity. Being Contributions towards a biography of the late Pinchbeck Lyre. Fiern Barnet: Blue Moon Press, 1931.
□ *Snowballs*, 1922 (poetry)

ARNETTE, ROBERT [house pseudonym]
unattributed
Empire of Evil. *Amazing*, Jan 1951
Death By Degrees. *Amazing*, Aug 1951
Matter of Stupidity. *Amazing*, Nov 1951
Moon of the Twelve Gods. *Amazing*, Dec 1952
The Involuntary Enemy. *Fantastic Adventures*, Feb 1953
Growing Pains. *Fantastic*, Aug 1956
by Roger P. Graham

The Unfinished Equation. *Fantastic Adventures*, April 1952
by Robert Silverberg
Cosmic Kill. *Amazing*, April/May 1957

AROUET, FRANCOIS-MARIE (1694-1778) *French*
Born: Paris
Best known as satirist and writer of philosophical fiction, also noted for his defense of religious tolerance.
as Mr. le Docteur Ralph
Candide, ou l'Optimisme. Traduit de l'Allemande de Mr. le Docteur Ralph. (London?): 1759, 299pp.
as Francois de Voltaire
Memnon. Histoire orientale. Londres [Paris]: 1747, 172pp.
Le Micromegas de Mr. de Voltaire, avec une Histoire des Croisades un Nouveau plan de l'Histoire de l'espirit humain. Londres: J. Robinson, 1752, 257pp.
Micromegas: A Comic Romance. Being a severe satire upon the philosophy, ignorance, and self-conceit of Mankind. Together with a detail of the Crusades: and a new plan for the History of the Human Mind. London: D. Wilson, 1753, 252pp.
Candid: or, All for the Best, London: J. Nourse, 1759, 132pp.
La Princesse de Babilone. Geneve: 1768, 184pp.
The Princess of Babylon. London: Bladen, 1768, 184pp.
Le Taureau Blanc. Traduit du syriaque par M. Voltaire. Memphis [Paris]: 1774.
The White Bull, an oriental history. From an ancient Syriac manuscript communicated by Mr. Voltaire. Cum notis editoris et valiorum: sc. clarrissimmi: Philoterasti Phantophagi (trans. J. Bentham). London: J. Ben, 1774, 2 vol.
Le Taureau Blanc: or, the White Bull. From the French. the second edition trans. from the Syriac by M. de Voltaire, London: Murray, 1774, 75pp.
☐ *Brutus,* 1730; *Zaire,* 1732; *Merope,* 1743; *Zadig,* 1747; *Irene,* 1778.
■ *Philosophic Dictionary,* 1764; *Rights of Man,* 1768.

ARROW, WILLIAM [house pseudonym]
by Don Pfeil
Escape from Terror Lagoon. NY: Ballantine, [1976], paper.
by William Rotsler
Visions of Nowhere. NY: Ballantine, [1976], paper.
Man the Hunted Animal. NY: Ballantine, [1976], paper.

ASHBEE, CHARLES ROBERT (1863-1942) *British*
Born: Isleworth
Founder and director of the Guild of Handicraft.
as C.R. Ashbee
The Building of Thelema, London: Dent, 1910, 361pp.
Kingfisher Out of Egypt; a dialogue in an English garden. London: H. Milford, Oxford U. Press, 1934, 51pp., ill.
☐ *Echoes from the City of the Sun,* 1905. (poetry) (250 cop)
■ *An Endeavor Towards the Teaching of John Ruskin and William Morris,* 1901; *Should We Stop Teaching Art,* 1911.
anonymous
(as edited by C. R. Ashbee) *Peckover, The Abbottscourt Papers 1901-1931.* London: The Astrolat Press, 1932, 208pp., ill. (350 cop)
■ *The Private Press, A Study In Idealism,* 1909.

ASHBY, R(ubie) C(onstance) (1899-   ) *British*
as R. C. Ashby
He Arrived at Dusk. London: Hodder & Stoughton, (1933), 318pp. *ss col*
Out Went the Taper. London: Hodder & Stoughton, 1934, 320pp.
☐ MYSTERY: *Death on Tiptoe,* 1930; *One Way Traffic,* 1933.

● Ruby Freugon

ASHKENAZY, IRWIN
as Irwin Ashkenazy
The Headless Miller of Kohold's Keep. *Avon Fantasy Reader #14* [c.1950].
as G. Garnet
The Headless Miller of Kohold's Keep. *Weird Tales,* Jan 1937

ASHTON, WINIFRED (1888-1965) *British*
Born: Blackheath, London
as Winifred Ashton
■ *Approaches to Drama,* 1961.
as Clemence Dane
The Babyons. London: Heinemann, [1927], 380pp.
Fate Cries Out, Nine Tales. London: Heinemann, [1935], 307pp. *ss col*
(ed) *100 Enchanted Tales.* London: M. Joseph, 1937, 685pp. *ss col*
The Moon Is Feminine. London: Heinemann, [1938], 282pp.
The Arrogant History of White Ben. NY: Doubleday, Doran, [1939], 363pp.
The Saviors. NY: Doubleday, Doran, 1942, 302pp. *play*
(dramatized by Clemence Dane) *Alice's Adventures In Wonderland, Through the Looking Glass,* by Lewis Carroll with music by Richard Addinsell. London: Samuel French, [1948], 63pp., paper.
The Godson, a fantasy. London: M. Joseph, [1964], 47pp., ill.
☐ *Regiment of Women,* 1917; *Legend,* 1919; *Wandering Stars,* 1924, PLAYS: *A Bill of Divorcement,* 1921; *Will Shakespeare,* 1921; *Manners,* 1926; *Moonlight In Silver,* 1934.
■ *The Woman's Side,* 1927 (Essay); *Tradition and Hugh Walpole,* 1930.
● Diana Cortes

ASHTON-GWATKIN, FRANK TRELAWNY ARTHUR (1889-   )
as Frank T. A. Ashton-Gwatkin
■ *The British Foreign Service,* 1950
as John Paris
The Island Beyond Japan. London: Collins, [1929], 276pp.
☐ *Kimono,* 1922; *Sayonara,* 1924; *Banzai (Hurrah!)* 1926; *Matsu,* 1932; *A Japanese Don Juan and Other People,* 1932 (poetry).

ASHWELL, PAULINE
as Paul Ash
Big Sword. *Astounding,* Oct 1958
as Pauline Ashwell
Unwillingly To School. *Astounding,* Jan 1958

ASIMOV, ISAAC (1920-   ) *naturalized U.S.*
Born: Petrovichi, Russian S.F.S.R.
Autobiography: *In Memory Yet Green (1920-1954).* Garden City: Doubleday, 1979, 732pp.
Bibliography: *Isaac Asimov: A Checklist of Works Published in the U.S., March 1939-May 1972,* Compiled by Marjorie M. Miller, Kent, Ohio: 1972.
Dr. Asimov has been active in the science fiction field since boyhood; first as a fan in New York, and later as one of the most respected writers for *Astounding* and *Galaxy* magazines in the 1940s and 1950s. His non-fiction books, which number almost 200, deal with an awesome range of subject matter. He is best known outside of the science fiction field as a popularizer of science for the layman. Dr. Asimov holds a Ph.D. in chemistry and was formerly a Professor of Bio-Chemistry at the Boston University School of Medicine. In recent years he has published some well regarded work in the mystery field.

as Dr. A.
■HUMOR: *The Sensuous Dirty Old Man*, 1971.
as Isaac Asimov
Marooned Off Vesta. *Amazing*, March 1939
Pebble In the Sky. Garden City: Doubleday, [1950], 223pp.
I, Robot. NY: Gnome, [1950], 253pp. *ss col*
The Stars, Like Dust. Garden City: Doubleday, [1951], 218pp.
Foundation. NY: Gnome, [1951], 255pp.
The Currents of Space. Garden City: Doubleday, [1952], 217pp.
Foundation and Empire. NY: Gnome, [1952], 247pp.
Second Foundation. NY: Gnome, [1953], 210pp.
The Caves of Steel. Garden City: Doubleday, [1954], 224pp.
The Martian Way. Garden City: Doubleday, [1955], 222pp.
The End of Eternity. Garden City: Doubleday, [1955], 191pp.
The Naked Sun. Garden City: Doubleday [1957], 187pp.
Earth Is Room Enough. Garden City: Doubleday, [1957], 192pp. *ss col*
Nine Tomorrows. Garden City: Doubleday, [1959], 239pp. *ss col*
The Rest of the Robots. Garden City: Doubleday, [1964], 556pp. *ss col*
Fantastic Voyage. Boston: Houghton-Mifflin, [1966], 239pp.
Through A Glass Clearly. London: New English Library, [1967], 124pp., paper. *ss col*
Night Fall and Other Stories. Garden City: Doubleday, [1969], 343pp. *ss col*
The Gods Themselves. Garden City: Doubleday, [1972], 288pp.
Have You Seen These. Boston: NESFA Press (A Boskone Book), 1974, 94pp. (500 cop.) *ss col*
Buy Jupiter. Garden City: Doubleday, [1975], 206pp. *ss col*
The Heavenly Host. NY: Walker, [c.1975], 79pp., ill.
The Bicentennial Man & Other Stories. Garden City: Doubleday, [1976], 211pp. *ss col*
Good Taste: A Story. Topeka, Kansas: Apocalypse Press, [c.1976], 36pp., ill. (1012 copies of which 500 are signed)
☐ MYSTERY: *The Death Dealers*, 1958; *Asimov's Mysteries*, 1968; *Tales of the Black Widowers*, 1974; *Murder At the A. B. A.*, 1976.
■ *Biochemistry and Human Metabolism*, 1952; *The Chemicals of Life*, 1954; *Inside the Atom*, 1956; *Chemistry and Human Health*, 1956; *Building Blocks of the Universe*, 1957; *Words of Science*, 1959; *The Intelligent Man's Guide to Science*, 1960; *View From A Height*, 1963; *Asimov's Biographical Encyclopedia of Science and Technology*, 1964; *Adding A Dimension*, 1964; *The Human Brain*, 1964; *The Greeks*, 1965; *An Easy Introduction to the Slide Rule*, 1965; *The Moon*, 1966; *The Neutrino*, 1966; *The Genetic Effects of Radiation*, 1966; *The Egyptians*, 1967; *The Roman Empire*, 1967; *Photosynthesis*, 1968; *Asimov's Guide to the Bible*, 1968/69; *Twentieth Century Discovery*, 1969; *The Shaping of England*, 1969; *Great Ideas of Science*, 1969; *Opus 100*, 1969; *Asimov's Guide To Shakespeare*, 1970; *Uncertain, Coy, and Hard to Please*, 1970; *Treasury of Humor*, 1971; *Where Do We Go From Here*, 1971; *The Left Hand of the Electron*, 1972; *The Tragedy of the Moon*, 1973; *Jupiter, the Largest Planet*, 1973; *The Shaping of North America*, 1974; *Science Past, Science Future*, 1975; *Of Matters Great and Small*, 1975; *The Planet That Wasn't*, 1976; *Opus 200*, 1979.
as George E. Dale
Time Pussy. *Astounding*, April 1942
as Paul French
David Starr, Space Ranger. Garden City: Doubleday, 1952.
Lucky Starr and the Pirates of the Asteroids. Garden City: Doubleday, 1953.
Lucky Starr and the Oceans of Venus. Garden City: Doubleday, 1954.
Lucky Starr and the Big Sun of Mercury. Garden City: Doubleday, 1956.
Lucky Starr and the Moons of Jupiter. Garden City: Doubleday, 1957.
Lucky Starr and the Rings of Saturn. Garden City: Doubleday, 1958.

ATHANAS, W(illiam V(erne) (1918-1962)
as Verne Athanas
☐ WESTERN: *The Proud Ones*, 1952; *Rogue Valley*, 1953.
as W. V. Athanas
The Madcap Metalloids. *Planet Stories*, Summer 1949.
✔ Bill Colson

ATKEY, PHILIP (1908-) *English*
Born: New Forrest, Wiltshire
as Philip Atkey
Heirs of Merlin. London: Cassell, 1945, 192pp.
☐ MYSTERY: *Blue Water Murder*, 1935; *Juniper Rock*, 1952.
as Pat Merriman
☐ MYSTERY: *Night Call*, 1937.
as Barry Perowne
A Singular Conspiracy. Indianapolis: Bobbs-Merrill, 1974.
☐ *Arrest These Men*, 1932; *Raffles Revisited*, 1974.

ATKINS, FRANK *British*
as Fenton Ash
A Son of the Stars. serial *Young England* (London) vol. 29, 1907-1908
Caught By A Comet. *The Red Magazine* (London), May 1, 1910
The Radium Seekers; or, the Wonderful Black Nugget. London: I. Pitman & Sons, 1905, 348pp.
A Trip to Mars. London: W. & R. Chambers, Ltd., 1909, 318pp., ill.
By Airship to Ophir. London: John F. Shaw, [1910], 320pp.
The Black Opal. London: John F. Shaw, [1915], 320pp., ill.
as Fred Ashley
A Queen of Atlantis. *Argosy*, Feb 1899
A Temple of Fire. London: I. Pitman, 1905, 332pp.
as Frank Aubrey
The Devil Tree of El Dorado. London: Hutchinson, 1896, 392pp.
A Studio Mystery. London: Jarrold & Sons, 1897, 195pp.
Strange Stories of the Hospitals. London: C. A. Pearson, 1898, 139pp. *ss col*
A Queen of Atlantis: A Romance of the Caribbean Sea. London: Hutchinson, 1899, 391pp.
King of the Dead; A Weird Romance. London: J. Macqueen, 1903, 292pp.

AUSTIN, MARY HUNTER (Mrs. Stafford W.) (1868- ?) *U.S.*
Born: Carlinville, Illinois
Autobiography: *Earth Horizon*. Boston: Houghton Mifflin, 1932, 381pp.
as Mary (H.) Austin
The Basket Woman. Boston: Houghton Mifflin, 1904, 220pp. *ss col*
Lost Borders. NY: Harper, 1909, 298pp., ill. *ss col*
The Green Bough: A Tale of the Resurrection. Garden City: Doubleday, 1913, 40pp.
☐ PLAYS: *The Arrow Maker*, 1911; *The Man Who Didn't Believe in Christmas*, 1916.
■ *Character and Personality Among American Indians*, 1933.
as Gordon Stairs
Outland. London: Murray, 1910, 311pp.

AVALLONE, MICHAEL (Angelo), JR. (1924-　) *U.S.*
Born: New York, New York
as Michael Avallone, Jr.
The Man Who Walked On Air. *Weird Tales,* Sept 1953
□MYSTERY: *The Tall Dolores,* 1953; *The Brutal Kook,*
1964; *Birds of A Feather Affair,* 1966; *Fallen Angel,*
1974; *Devil, Devil,* 1974.
■ (ed) *The Third Degree,* house organ, Mystery Writers
of America
as Nick Carter [house pseudonym]
□ *MYSTERY: Run, Spy, Run,* 1964; *China Doll,* 1964.
as Priscilla Dalton
□ *90 Gramercy Park,* 1965.
as Mark Dane
The Stop At Nothing. *Tales of the Frightened,* Spring 1957
□ *Felicia,* 1964.
as Dorothea Nile
□ *Mistress of Farrondale,* 1966; *Vampire Cameo,* 1968.
as Edwina Noone
(ed) *Edwina Noone's Gothic Sampler.* NY: Award, 1967,
159pp., paper *ss col*
□ *Corridor of Whispers,* 1965; *Dark Cypress,* 1965.
as John Patrick
□ *The Main Attraction,* 1963.
as Sidney Stuart
□ *The Night Walker,* 1964.
● Troy Conway, Jean-Anne De Pre, Steve Michaels, Stuart
Sidney, Vance Stanton

AVICE, CLAUDE (1925-　) *French*
Born: Le Mans, France
as Pierre Barbet
Baphomet's Meteor. NY: DAW #35, [1972], paper.
Games Psyborgs Play. NY: DAW #83, [1973], paper.
The Enchanted Planet. NY: DAW #156, [1975], paper.
The Napoleons of Eridanus. NY: DAW #199, [1976], paper.
The Joan-of-Arc Replay. NY: DAW #287, [1978], paper.
as David Maine
Les Disparus du club Chronos. Paris: M. Albin, 1972.
Guerillero galactique, Paris: M. Albin, 1976.
as Oliver Sprigel
Crepuscule du Future. Paris: Masque, 1976.

AYCOCK, ROGER D(ee) (1914-　) *U.S.*
as Roger Dee
Ultimatum. Planet Stories, Spring 1950
An Earth Gone Mad. NY: Ace, [1954], 144pp., paper.
(Ace Double D84)
as John Starr
Grim Green World. *Planet Stories,* Nov 1951.

BACHELDER, JOHN
as A Former Resident of the Hub
A.D. 2050. Electrical Development At Atlantis. San
Francisco: Bancroft, 1890, 83pp.

BAHL, FRANKLIN [house pseudonym]
unattributed
The Justice of Tor. *Fantastic Adventures,* Jan 1951
by Roger P. Graham
Face Beyond the Veil. *Fantastic Adventures,* April 1950
Lady Killer. *Amazing,* Feb 1953

BAKER, RACHEL MADDUX (Mrs. King) (1912-　) *U.S.*
Born: Wichita, Kansas
as Rachel Maddux
Turnips Blood, in the *Flying Yorkshire Man.* NY: Harper,
1938.
□ *The Green Kingdom,* 1957; *Abel's Daughter,* 1960; *A
Walk in the Spring Rain,* 1966.

BALCHIN, NIGEL MARLIN (1908-1970) *British*
as Nigel Balchin
No Sky. London: H. Hamilton, [1934], 314pp.
The Small Back Room. London: Collins, 1943, 192pp.
Kings of Infinite Space. London: Collins, 1967, 256pp.
□ *Last Recollections of My Uncle Charles,* 1954; *Seen
Dimly Before Dawn,* 1962.
■ *The Anatomy of Villainy,* 1950.
as Mark Spade
■ HUMOR: *How To Run A Bassoon Factory, or Business
Explained,* 1934. *Business for Pleasure,* 1935.

BALDWIN, OLIVER RIDSDALE (2nd Earl)　(1899-　)
British
Autobiography: *The Questing Beast.* London: Grayson
& Grayson, [1932], 243pp.
as Oliver Baldwin
■ *Six Prisons and Two Revolutions,* 1925; *Conservatism
and Wealth, a radical indictment,* 1929; *Unborn Son,*
1933; *Oasis,* 1936; *The Englishman,* 1940.
as Martin Hussingtree
Konyetz. London: Hodder & Stoughton, [1924], 320pp.

BALFOUR, FREDERIC H(enry)
as Frederic Henry Balfour
□ *Cherryfield Hall, episodes in the career of an Adventuress,* 1895.
■ *Idiomatic Dialogues in the Peking colloquial,* 1883;
(ed) *Taoist Texts, ethical, political, and speculative,*
1884; *Unthinkables Discussed: How to believe in
nothing, etc.,* 1897; *The Higher Agnosticism,* 1907.
as Ross George Dering
Dr. Mirabel's Theory. London: Richard Bentley, 1893, 3 vol.
[NY: Harper, 1893, 340pp.]
□ *Giraldi; or, the Curse of Love,* 1889; *The Virgin's
Vengeance, or How The Irish Got Home Rule,* 1889.

BALFOUR, MARGARET MELVILLE
as M. Melville Balfour
*The Vanishing Mayor of Padstow and Other Truthful
Narratives.* London: Faber, [1938], 233pp., ill. *ss col*
□ POETRY: *London Pride,* 1927; *The Long Robe,* 1930.

BALL, BRIAN N. (1932-   ) *English*
Born: Cheshire
as B. N. Ball
The Pioneer. *New Worlds #115*, Feb 1962 (Br.)
☐ has written juvenile fiction under this name.
as Brian N. Ball
Sundog. London: Dobson, [1965], 216pp.
Timepiece. London: Dobson, [1968], 144pp.
Timepivot. London: Dobson, 1970.
Timepit. London: Dobson, [1971], 188pp.
Lesson For the Damned. London: New English Library, 1971, paper.
The Probability Man. NY: DAW #3, [1972], 175pp., paper.
Night of the Robots. London: Sidgwick & Jackson, 1972.
Planet Probability. NY: DAW #40, [1973], paper.
Singularity Station. NY: DAW #84, [1973], 176pp., paper.
The Space Guardians: Space 1999 #3. NY: Pocket Books, [1975], paper.
as Brian Kinsey-Jones
☐ *Lay Down Your Wife for Another,* 1971.

BALLINGER, WILLIAM S(anborn) (1912-   ) *U.S.*
as Bill S. Ballinger
49 Days of Death. Los Angeles: Sherbourne Press, [1969], 214pp.
☐ MYSTERY: *The Body In the Bed,* 1948; *The Body Beautiful,* 1949; *Portrait in Smoke,* 1950; *The Heir Hunters,* 1966.
as William S. Ballinger
The Fourth of Forever. NY: Harper, [1963], 204pp.
as Frederick Freyer
☐ MYSTERY: *The Black, Black Hearse,* 1955.
as B. X. Sanborn
The Doom Maker, NY: Dutton, 1959, 188pp.

BALTER, E.
as Arthur Cooke [in collaboration with Cyril Kornbluth, Robert W. Lowndes, John Michel and Donald A. Wollheim]
The Psychological Regulator. *Comet Stories,* March 1941

BANGS, JOHN KENDRICK (1862-1922)   *U.S.*
Born: Yonkers, New York
Biography: *John Kendrick Bangs, Humorist of the Nineties,* by F. H. Bangs, NY: Knopf, 1941.
as John Kendrick Bangs
Roger Camerden. A Strange Story. NY: G. J. Coombes, 1887, 102pp.
Tiddledywink Tales. NY: R. H. Russell, 1891, 236pp., ill. *ss col*
Toppleton's Client: or, A Spirit In Exile. NY: C. L. Webster, 1893, 269pp.
The Water Ghost and Others. NY: Harper, 1894, 296pp., ill. *ss col*
A Houseboat on the Styx. NY: Harper, 1895, 171pp., ill.
Mr. Bonaparte of Corsica. NY: Harper, 1895, 265pp.,ill.
The Bicyclers and Three Other Farces. NY: Harper, 1896, 176pp., ill. *ss col*
The Pursuit of the Houseboat. NY: Harper, 1897, 204pp. ill.
Ghosts I Have Met and Some Others. NY: Harper, 1898, 190pp., ill.
The Dreamers: A Club. NY: Harper, 1899, 246pp., ill.
The Enchanted Typewriter. NY: Harper, 1899, 170pp., ill.
The Booming of Acre Hill. NY: Harper, 1900, 265pp., ill.
Mr. Munchausen. Boston: Noyes, Platt & Co., 1901, 180pp., ill.
Over the Plum Pudding. NY: Harper, 1901, 244pp., ill.
Bikey the Skicycle and Other Tales of Jimmieboy. NY: Rigg Publishing Co., 1902, 321pp., ill. *ss col*
Mollie and the Unwiseman. Philadelphia: H. T. Coates & Co., [1902], 198pp., ill.

Olympian Nights. NY: Harper, 1902, 223pp., ill.
(with C. R. Macauley), *Emblemland.* NY: R. H. Russell, 1902, 164pp., ill.
The Inventions of the Idiot. NY: Harper, [1903], 185pp.
Mrs. Raffles. NY: Harper, 1905, 179pp., ill.
The Worsted Man; A Musical Play for Amateurs. NY: Harper, 1905, 85pp., front.
Andiron Tales. Philadelphia: J. Winston, [1906], 101pp., ill.
Alice In Blunderland, An Iridescent Dream. NY: Doubleday, 1907, 124pp., ill.
The Autobiography of Methuselah. NY: B. W. Dodge, 1909, 185pp., ill.
Jack and the Check Book. NY: Harper, 1911, 235pp., ill.
☐ *R. Holmes & Co.,* 1906; *Sherlock Holmes; His Posthumous Memoirs,* 1973 (300 cop.)
■ *Coffee and Repartee,* 1893; *Cobwebs from A Literary Corner,* 1899; *From Pillar to Post,* 1916.
as Two Wags [in collaboration with Frank Sherman]
New Waggings of Old Tales. Boston: Ticknor, 1888, 165pp., ill. *ss col*
as Anne Warrington Witherup
(collected by John K. Bangs) *Peeps at People.* NY: Harper, 1899, 184pp., ill.

BANIM, JOHN (1798-1842)   *Irish*
Born: Kilkenny, County Kilkenny
as John Banim
Revelations of the Dead-Alive. London: Simpkin & Marshall, 1824, 376pp.
☐ *The Denounced,* 1829.
■ *The Anglo-Irish,* 1838.
as The O'Hara Family
The Ghost-Hunter and His Family. Philadelphia: Carey, Lea & Blanchard, 1833, 269pp.
[John Banim's brother Michael claimed, at various times, to have written some, most, or all of the "O'Hara Family" Tales.

BANIM, MICHAEL (1796-1874)   *Irish*
Born: Kilkenny, County Kilkenny
as Michael Banim
■ *Father Connell,* 1842; *Clough Fion,* 1852; *Town of the Cascades,* 1864.
as The O'Hara Family
The Ghost-Hunter and His Family. Philadelphia: Carey, Lea & Blanchard, 1833, 269pp.
[see **JOHN BANIM**]

BARBER, MARGARET FAIRLESS (1869-1901)   *British*
Born: Rastrick, Yorkshire
Biography: *Michael Fairless, Her Life and Writings,* by Palmer (Dowson) and Haggard. London: Duckworth, 1913.
as Michael Fairless
The Roadmender. London: Duckworth, 1902, 158pp.
The Complete Works of Michael Fairless. London: Duckworth, [1931], 356pp. *col*

BARCLAY, FLORENCE LOUISA CHARLESWORTH (Mrs.) (1862-1921)   *British*
Born: Limpsfield, Surrey
as Florence Barclay
Returned Empty. London: Putnam, 1920, 154pp.
☐ *The Rosary,* 1909; *Mistress of Shenstone,* 1910; *The Broken Halo,* 1913; *White Ladies of Worchester,* 1917.
as Brandon Roy
☐ *Guy Mervyn,* 1891

BARCLAY, GABRIEL [house pseudonym]
by Cyril M. Kornbluth
Hollow of the Moon. *Super Science Stories,* May 1940

by Manly Wade Wellman
Elephant Earth. *Astonishing*, Feb 1940.

BARFIELD, ARTHUR OWEN (1898-   ) *English*
Born: London
as Owen Barfield
The Silver Trumpet. London: Faber & Gwyer, 1925, 142pp.
Unancestral Voices. London: Faber, [1965], 163pp.
■ *History in English Words*, 1926; *Poetic Diction, a study in meaning*, 1928; *Romanticism Comes of Age*, 1944; *Greek Thought In English Words; Saving the Appearances, a study in Idolatry*, 1957; *Worlds Apart*, 1963.
as G. A. L. Burgeon
This Ever Diverse Pair. London: Gollancz, 1950, 144pp.

BARGONE, FREDERIC CHARLES PIERRE EDOUARD (1876-1957) *French*
as Claude Farrere
La Maison des Hommes Vivants. Paris: Librairie des Annales politiques et litteraires, [c.1911], 299pp.
Les condamnes a mort. Paris: 1920, 79pp., ill & map.
The House of the Secret. NY: Dutton, [1923], 234pp. (1500 cop.)
Useless Hands. NY: Dutton, [1926], 300pp.
□ *The Man Who Killed*, 1917; *Thomas, the Lambkin*, 1924.

BARHAM, RICHARD H(arris) (1788-1845) *English*
Born: Canterbury, Kent
Biography: *The Life and Letters of the Rev. Richard Harris Barham*, by his son. London: R. Bentley, 1870.
as Thomas Ingoldsby
The Ingoldsby Legends, or, Mirth and Marvels [1st series]. London: R. Bentley, 1840, 338pp., ill. (12 copy edition & trade edition)
The Ingoldsby Legends, or, Mirth and Marvels [2nd series]. London: R. Bentley, 1842, 288pp., ill.
The Ingoldsby Legends, or, Mirth and Marvels [3d series]. London: R. Bentley, 1847, 364pp., ill.
□ *The Ingoldsby Lyrics*, 1881.
as Scriblerus Oxoniensis, editor
Martin's Vagaries; Being A Sequel to "A Tale of A Tub," recently discovered at the University of Oxford. London: A.H. Bailey, 1843, 48pp., ill.

BARKER, LEONARD N(oel) (1882-   )
as L. Noel
The Golden Star; A Love Story of Tomorrow. London: S. Paul, [1935], 288pp.
□ *Wings of Fate*, 1928; *Flames of Desire*, 1928. MYSTERY: *Mystery Street*, 1930.

BARLOW, JAMES WILLIAM (1826-1913) *Irish*
as James William Barlow
The Immortals' Great Quest: Translated from an unpublished manuscript in the library of a continental university. London: Smith, Elder, 1909, 177pp.
as Antares Skorpios
History of A Race of Immortals Without a God. Dublin: William McGee, 1891, 177pp.

BARNARD, MARJORIE FAITH (1897-   ) *Australian*
as Marjorie Faith Barnard
□ *The Persimmon Tree and Other Stories*, 1943.
■ HISTORY: *Macquarie's World*, 1941; *Australian Outline*, 1949.
as M. Barnard Eldershaw [in collaboration with F. S. P. Eldershaw]
Tomorrow and Tomorrow. Melbourne: Georgian House, 1947, 466pp.
□ *A House is Built*, 1929; *Green Memory*. 1931.

BARNES, ARTHUR KELVIN (1911-1969) *U.S.*
Born: Bellingham, Washington
as Arthur K. Barnes
Lord of the Lightning. *Wonder Stories*, Dec 1931
Interplanetary Hunter. NY: Gnome, [1956], 231pp.
as Dave Barnes
The House That Walked. *Astounding*, Sept 1936
as Kelvin Kent [in collaboration with Henry Kuttner]
Roman Holiday. *Thrilling Wonder Stories*, Aug 1939
Science Is Golden. *Thrilling Wonder Stories*, April 1940
as Kelvin Kent [alone]
Knight Must Fall. *Thrilling Wonder Stories*, June 1940
The Greeks Had A War For It. *Thrilling Wonder Stories*, Jan 1941
DeWolfe of Wall Street. *Thrilling Wonder Stories*, Feb 1943
Grief of Baghdad. *Thrilling Wonder Stories*, June 1943
[other stories under this name are by Henry Kuttner alone]

BARR, ROBERT (1850-1912) *British*
Born: Glasgow, Scotland
as Robert Barr
In A Steamer Chair and Other Shipboard Stories. London: Chatto & Windus, 1892, 264pp. ss col
From Whose Bourne. London: Chatto & Windus, 1893, 277pp.
The Face and The Mask. London: Hutchinson, 1894, 304pp. ss col
Revenge! London: Chatto & Windus, 1896, 344pp. ss col
□ *A Woman Intervenes*, 1896; *Jennie Baxter, Journalist*, 1899; *A Woman Wins*, 1904; *Tales of Two Continents*, 1920. MYSTERY: *The Triumphs of Eugene Valmont*, 1906.
as Luke Sharp
Detective Stories Gone Wrong: The Adventures of Sherlew Kombs. *The Idler*, May 1892 [a Sherlock Holmes spoof. Reprinted in *The Face and The Mask*, see under **ROBERT BARR** above.]
Strange Happenings. London: Dunkerley, 1883, 128pp., ill.
□ MYSTERY: *Sunshine Johnson, Murderer*, 1893.

BARRETT, ALFRED W(alter) (1869- ?)
as R. Andom
● *The Strange Adventures of Roger Williams & Other Stories.* London: Tylston & Edwards, 1895, 280pp., ill. [Not in NUC or BMC, sometimes listed in bibliographies as *The Strange Adventures of Roger Wilkins.*]
The Identity Exchange, A Story of Some Odd Transformations. London: Jarrolds, 1902, 286pp., ill.
The Enchanted Ship: A Story of A Mystery with a lot of Imagination. London: Cassell, 1908, 279pp., ill.
The Magic Bowl and the Blue Stone Ring, oriental stories. London: Jarrolds, [1909], 312pp., ill. (2d ed) ss col
□ *We Three and Troddles*, 1894.

BARSTOW, EMMUSKA ORCAY (Mrs. Montagu W.) (1865-1947) *British*
Born: Tarna-Ors, Hungary
as Baroness Orczy
By the Gods Beloved. London: Greening, 1905, 310pp.
□ MYSTERY: *The Case of Miss Elliott*, 1905; *The Scarlet Pimpernel*, 1905; *The Old Man In the Corner*, 1908; *Lady Molly of Scotland Yard*, 1910; *Unravelled Knots*, 1925.

BARTLE, L. E.
as Richard Lawrence
One In Every Port. *Science Fantasy*, Spring 1953 (Br.)
as Francis Richardson [in collaboration with Frank Parnell]
The Trojan Way. *Science Fantasy #7*, Spring 1954 (Br.)

BARTLETT, ALICE ELINOR BOWEN (Mrs. J. M. D. Bartlett) (1848-1920)
as Birch Arnold

A New Aristocracy. NY: Bartlett Pub. Co., 1891, 316pp.
Birch Leaves, 1905 (poetry)
as Mrs. J. M. D. Bartlett
  □ *Until the Day Breaks,* 1877.

BARTON, EUSTACE ROBERT (Dr.) (1854— ?)
as Robert Eustace
  (with L. T. Meade) *A Master of Mysteries.* London:
    Ward, Lock, [1898], 279pp.
  (with L. T. Meade) *The Brotherhood of the Seven Kings.*
    London: Ward, Lock, 1899, 373pp.
  (with L. T. Meade) *The Sanctuary Club.* London: Ward,
    Lock, 1900, 300pp., ill.
  A Human Bacillus. The Story of A Strange Character.
    London: J. Long, 1907, 318pp.
  □ MYSTERY: (with Dorothy L. Sayers) *The Documents
    in the Case,* 1930.

BARUCH, HUGO (1907-   ) *English*
  Autobiography: *Jack Bilbo; An Autobiography.* London:
    The Modern Art Gallery, [1948], 453pp., ill.
as Jack Bilbo
  Out of My Mind. London: The Modern Art Gallery,
    [1946], 124pp., quarto, ill. *ss col*

BASSETT, EDWARD BARNARD
as Beta
  *The Model Town; or, the Right and Progressive Organ-
    ization of Industry for the Production of Material and
    Moral Wealth.* Cambridge, England: Printed for the
    Author, 1869, 104pp.

BASSLER, THOMAS J.
as T. J. Bass
  Star Seeder. *If,* Sept 1969
  The Godwhale. London: Eyre Methuen, 1975, 306pp.
    [possibly not 1st]
  Half Past Human. NY: Ballantine, [c. 1971], paper.

BATES, HARRY (1900-   )
as Harry Bates
  Editor—*Astounding Stories:* Jan 1930–March 1933
    A Matter of Size. *Astounding,* April 1934
as Anthony Gilmore [in collaboration with D. W. Hall]
  The Tentacles from Below. *Astounding,* Feb 1931
  Space Hawk. NY: Greenberg, [1952], 274pp.
as Anthony Gilmore [alone—the only story thus]
  The Return of Hawk Carse. *Amazing,* July 1942
as A. R. Holmes
  The Slave Ship From Space. *Astounding,* July 1931
as ¿Quien Sabe?
  The City of Eric, *Amazing Stories Quarterly,* Spring 1929
as H.G. Winter [in collaboration with D.W. Hall]
  The Hands of Aten. *Astounding,* July 1931

BATES, H(erbert) E(rnest) (1905-   ) *English*
  Born: Rusden, Northampton
as H. E. Bates
  Seven Tales and Alexander. London: Scholastic Press, 1929,
    166pp. (1000 cop) *ss col*
  The Woman Who Had Imagination, and Other Stories.
    London: Jonathan Cape, 1934, 288pp.
  □ *Two Sisters,* 1926; *The Black Boxer,* 1932; *Beauty's
    Daughters,* 1935; *Fair Stood the Wind for France,* 1944;
    The Darling Buds of May, 1958; *The Day of the Tortoise,*
    1961.
  ■ *Down The River,* 1937; *Country Life,* 1943; *The Modern
    Short Story,* 1949.
as Flying Officer "X"
  ■ *The Greatest People in the World,* 1942; *How Sleep
    the Brave,* 1943.

BAUM, L(yman) FRANK (1856-1919) *U.S.*
  Born: Chittenango, New York
as Floyd Akers
  □"The Boy Fortune Hunters" series. e.g. *The Boy Fortune
    Hunters in Alaska, 1908.*
as Laura Bancroft
  *Twinkle and Chubbins; Their Astonishing Adventures In
    Nature's Fairy Land.* Chicago: Reilly & Britton, [1911],
    348pp., ill.
  □*Prince Mud-Turtle,* 1906; *Policeman Bluejay,* 1907;
    Babes In Birdland, 1911.
as L. Frank Baum
  The Wonderful Wizard of Oz. Chicago: G. M. Hill & Co.,
    1900, 259pp., ill.
  A New Wonderland. NY: R. H. Russell, 1900, 189pp., ill.
  American Fairy Tales. Chicago: Kennedy & Hall, 1901,
    [unpaged], ill.
  The Master Key. An Electrical Fairy Tale. Indianapolis:
    Bowen-Merrill, [1901], 245pp., ill.
  The Enchanted Island of Yew. Indianapolis: Bobbs-
    Merrill, [1903], 242pp., ill.
  *The Surprising Adventures of the Magical Monarch of Mo
    and His People.* Indianapolis: Bobbs-Merrill, [1903],
    236pp., ill.
  The Marvelous Land of Oz. Chicago: Reilly & Britton,
    [1904], 287pp., ill.
  Queen Zixi of Ix; or, the Story of the Magic Cloak. NY:
    Century, [1905], 303pp., ill.
  John Dough and the Cherub. Chicago: Reilly & Britton,
    [1906], 314pp., ill.
  Ozma of Oz. Chicago: Reilly & Britton, [1907], 270pp., ill.
  *Baum's American Fairy Tales; Stories of Astonishing Ad-
    ventures.* Indianapolis, Bobbs-Merrill, [1908], 222pp.,
    ill.
  The Road to Oz. Chicago: Reilly & Britton, [1909],
    261pp., ill.
  The Sea Fairies. Chicago: Reilly & Britton, [1911], 239pp., ill.
  Sky Island. Chicago: Reilly & Britton, [1912], 287pp., ill.
  The Patchwork Girl of Oz. Chicago: Reilly & Britton,
    [1913], 340pp., ill.
  Tik-Tok of Oz. Chicago: Reilly & Britton, [1914], 271pp. ill.
  Little Wizard Stories of Oz. Chicago: Reilly & Britton,
    [1914], 198pp., ill.
  The Scarecrow of Oz. Chicago: Reilly & Britton, [1915],
    288pp., ill.
  Rinkitink in Oz. Chicago: Reilly & Britton, [1916], 314pp., ill.
  The Lost Princess of Oz. Chicago: Reilly & Britton, [1917],
    312pp., ill.
  The Tin Woodsman of Oz. Chicago: Reilly & Britton,
    [1918], 287pp., ill.
  The Magic of Oz. Chicago: Reilly & Lee, [1919], 265pp., ill.
  Glinda of Oz. Chicago: Reilly & Lee, [1920], 279pp., ill.
  (enlarged and expanded by Ruth P. Thompson) *The Royal
    Book of Oz.* Chicago: Reilly & Lee, [1921], 312pp., ill.
as Hugh Fitzgerald
  □JUVENILE: *Sam Steele's Adventures On Land and
    Sea,* 1906; *Sam Steele's Adventures In Panama,* 1907.
as Suzanne Metcalf
  □*Anabel, A Novel for Young Folks,* 1906.
as Schuyler Staunton
  □*The Fate of A Crown,* 1905; *Daughters of Destiny,* 1906.
as Edith Van Dyne
  □ "Aunt Jane's Nieces" series, e.g., *Aunt Jane's Nieces,*
    1906; *Aunt Jane's Nieces Abroad,* 1907; etc.
  ✔ **John Estes Cooke**

BAXTER, JOHN MARTIN (1939-   ) *Australian*
  Born: Sydney
as John Baxter
  (editorial) View From the Underground. *New Worlds,* Sept
    1962 (Br.)
  Vendetta's End. *Science Fiction Adventures #29,* Nov 1962

The Off Worlders. NY: Ace, 1966, 127pp., paper.
as Martin Loran [in collaboration with Ronald Loran Smith]
An Ounce of Dissension. *Analog,* July 1966

BAYLEY, B(arrington) J.
as Michael Barrington [in collaboration with Michael Moorcock]
Peace on Earth. *New Worlds #89,* Dec 1959 (Br.)
as Barrington J. Bayley
Kindly Travellers. *Authentic,* July 1955 (Br.)
The Star Virus. NY: Ace, [1970], 120pp., paper. (Ace Double)
The Annihilation Factor. NY: Ace [1972], 134pp., paper. (Ace Double 33710)
Empire of Two Worlds. NY: Ace [1972], 157pp., paper.
Collision Course. NY: DAW, [1973], 174pp., paper.
The Fall of Chronopolis. NY: DAW, [1974], 175pp., paper.
Soul of the Robot. Garden City: Doubleday, 1974, 206pp.
The Garments of Caen. Garden City: Doubleday, 1976, 189pp.

BEARD, JAMES H.
as James H. Beard
Five Fathoms of Pearls. *Unknown,* Dec 1939
(with Theodore Sturgeon) The Hag Seleen. *Unknown,* Dec 1942
as Philip James [in collaboration with R. Alvarez-del Rey]
Carillion of Skulls. *Unknown,* Feb 1941

BEAUMONT, EDGAR (Dr.)
as Clifford Halifax
(with L.T. Meade) *Stories From the Diary of A Doctor.* [first series]. London: G. Newnes, 1894, 370pp.
(with L. T. Meade) *Stories From the Diary of A Doctor.* [second series]. London: Bliss, Sands, 1896, 357pp.

BECHDOLT, JOHN ERNEST (1884-   ) *U.S.*
as Jack Bechdolt
The Torch. *Argosy,* 24 Jan 1920
The Lost Vikings. NY: Cosmopolitan, 1931, 267pp., ill.
The Vanishing Hounds. London: Oxford University Press, 1941, 153pp.
The Torch. Philadelphia: Prime Press, 1948, 229pp., ill.

BECK, ELIZA LOUISA (Moresby) ADAMS (Mrs.)
(? -1931) *English*
as E. Barrington
□ HISTORICAL FICTION: *The Divine Lady,* 1924; *Glorious Apollo,* 1925.
as Lily Adams Beck
The Ninth Vibration and Other Stories. NY: Dodd, Mead, 1922, 313pp. *ss col*
The Key of Dreams; A Romance of the Orient. NY: Dodd, Mead, 1922, 351pp.
The Perfume of the Rainbow, and Other Stories. NY: Dodd, Mead, 1923, 324pp. *ss col*
The Treasure of Ho, A Romance. London: Collins, [1923], 290pp.
The Way of Stars, A Romance of Reincarnation. NY: Dodd, Mead, 1925, 408pp.
Dreams and Delights. NY: Dodd, Mead, 1926, 317pp. *ss col*
The House of Fulfillment, the Romance of A Soul. London: T. Fisher Unwin, 1927, 278pp.
The Garden of Vision. NY: Cosmopolitan, 1929, 421pp.
The Openers of the Gate. NY: Cosmopolitan, 1930, 368pp. *ss col*
as L(ouis) Moresby
Captain Java. NY: Doubleday, Doran, 1928, 368pp.
The Glory of Egypt; A Romance. London: T. Nelson, [1926], 281pp.

BEDFORD-JONES, H(enry) (James O'Brien) (1887-1949) *naturalized U.S.*
Born: Napanee, Ontario, Canada

as Donald F. Bedford [in collaboration with Kenneth Fearing and Donald Friede]
John Barry. NY: Creative Age Press, [1947], 418pp.
as H. Bedford-Jones
The Opium Ship. *The Thrill Book,* July 1919
The Drums of Damballa. NY: Covici-Friede, 1929, 295pp.
as Allan Hawkwood
The Seal of Solomon. London: Hurst & Blackett, [1925], 283pp.
as John Wycliffe
Against The Tide. NY: Dodd, Mead, 1924, 279pp.
✔ **Montague Bris(s)ard, Cleveland B. Chase, George Souli de Mourant, Paul Ferval, Capt. Bedrod-Foran** [in collaboration with **Capt. W. Robert Foran**]**, Michael Gallister, Gordon Keyne, M. Lassez, Louis Pamjean, Margaret Love Sangerson, David Seabrooke, Gordon Stuart, Torquay Trevision.**
[no book information has been unearthed, these were most likely used on non fantasy and science fiction stories in the pulps between 1900 & 1930.]
as Elliott Whitney [in collaboration with H. L. Sayler]
□ *The Blind Lion of the Congo,* 1912; *The White Tiger of Nepal,* 1912; *The King Bear of Kadiak* [sic] *Island,* 1912.

BEESLEY, DOROTHY GLADYS SMITH (Mrs. Alec Macbeth)
(1896-   ) *English*
Born: Whitefield, Lancashire
as C. L. Anthony
□ PLAYS: *Autumn Crocus,* 1930; *Service,* 1932; *Touch Wood,* 1933; *Call It A Day,* 1935.
as Dodie Smith
The Starlight Barking. NY: Simon & Schuster, 1967, 156pp., ill.
□ *One Hundred and One Dalmations,* 1956.

BEFFROY DE REIGNY, LOUIS ABEL (1757-1811) *French*
as Cousin-Jacques
Nicodeme dans la Lune, ou, La Revolution Pacifique. Folie en Prose et en Trois Actes. Avignon: Garrigan, 1791, 56pp.
La Constitution de la Lune, Reve Politique et Moral. Paris: Chez Froulle, 1793, 302pp.

BEGBIE, HAROLD (1871-1929)
as Harold Begbie
The Day That Changed the World. London: Hodder & Stoughton, [1914], 289pp.
as Caroline Lewis
Clara In Blunderland. London: Heinemann, 1902, 150pp., ill.

BEITH, JOHN HAY (Sir) (1876-1952) *British*
as Ian Hay
Half A Sovereign; An Improbable Romance. Boston: Houghton Mifflin, 1926, 307pp.
□ *A Safety Match,* 1911; *Housemaster,* 1936; *Stand At Ease,* 1940; (with P. G. Wodehouse) *Admirals All,* 1934.
as K(1), The Junior Subaltern
□ *The First Hundred Thousand,* 1915.

BELASCO, DAVID (1859-1931) *U.S.*
Born: San Francisco, California
as David Belasco
The Return of Peter Grimm. NY: Published by the Author, 1911, 44 & 56 & 17pp. (3 acts bound in folios) *typescript*
The Return of Peter Grimm. [In *Representative Plays by American Dramatists* (edited by Montrose J. Moses)] NY: Dutton, 1918, ill.
□ PLAYS: *May Blossom,* 1884; *Lord Chumley,* 1887; *The Heart of Maryland,* 1895; *The Girl of the Golden West,* 1905; *Laugh, Clown, Laugh,* 1923.
as David Belasco [actually ghost written completely by Albert Payson Terhune] (novelization of play of 1911)

The Return of Peter Grimm. NY: Dodd, Mead, 1912, 344pp., ill.

BELFOUR, HUGO JOHN   (1802-1827)
as St. John Dorset
  The Vampire; A Tragedy in 5 Acts & Verse. London: C. & J. Ollier, 1821, 108pp.
  □ POETRY: *Montezuma, A Tragedy,* 1822.

BELL, ERIC TEMPLE   (1883-1960)   *naturalized U.S.*
  Born: Aberdeen, Scotland
  He came to the U.S. in the early 1900s. He became Professor of Mathematics at the California Institute of Technology in 1927, a post he held until retirement in 1953. Professor Bell served a term as President of the Mathematics Association of America. He was noted for his books on mathematics for the layman.
as Richard C. Badger
  Copyright holder of *The Singer,* see J.T.
as Eric Temple Bell
  ■ *The Cyclotomic Quinary Quintic,* 1912; *Algebraic Arithmetic,* 1927; *Debunking Science,* 1930; *The Search for Truth,* 1934; *The Handmaiden of the Sciences,* 1937; *Men of Mathematics,* 1937; *The Developement of Mathematics,* 1940; *Mathematics, Servant of Science,* 1952; *The Last Problem,* 1961.
as J. T.
  Recreations. Boston: Gorham Press, 1915, 151pp. (poetry)
  The Singer. Boston: Gorham Press, 1916. (poetry)
as John Taine
  The Ultimate Catalyst. *Amazing Stories Quarterly,* Winter 1930
  The Purple Sapphire. NY: Dutton, [1924], 325pp.
  Quayle's Invention. NY: Dutton, [1927], 451pp.
  The Gold Tooth. NY: Dutton, 1927, 436pp.
  Green Fire. NY: Dutton, 1928, 313pp.
  The Greatest Adventure. NY: Dutton, [1929], 258pp.
  The Iron Star. NY: Dutton, [1930], 356pp.
  Before the Dawn. Baltimore: Williams & Wilkins, 1934, 247pp.
  The Time Stream. Buffalo, New York: Buffalo Book Co., 1946, 251pp.
  The Forbidden Garden. Reading, Pennsylvania: Fantasy Press, 1947, 278pp., ill.
  The Cosmic Geoids and One Other. Los Angeles: FPCI, 1949, 179pp., ill.
  Seeds of Life. Reading, Pennsylvania: Fantasy Press, 1951, 255pp.
  The Crystal Horde. Reading, Pennsylvania: Fantasy Press, 1952, 254pp.
  G. O. G. 666. Reading, Pennsylvania: Fantasy Press, 1954, 256pp.
as James Temple
  Used on early poetry pieces

BELL, JOHN KEBLE   (1875-1928)   *English*
  Autobiography: *My Motley Life, A Tale of Struggle,* by Keble Howard. London: E.Benn, 1927.
as Keble Howard
  The Peculiar Major; An Almost Incredible Story. London: Hutchinson, [1919], 246pp.
  □ PLAYS: *The God In The Garden,* 1904; *Compromising Martha,* 1906; *Martha Plays the Fairy,* 1907; *Martha the Soothsayer,* 1909; *The Cheerful Knave,* 1913.

BELLIN, EDWARD J. [house pseudonym]
unattributed
  No Place To Go. *Cosmic Stories,* May 1941
by Henry Kuttner
  The Touching Point. *Stirring Science Stories,* April 1941

BENEDICT, STEVE   (1899-   )   *U.S.*
as Steve Benedict
  Stamp From Moscow. *Astounding,* Jan 1953
  □ *Gabee of the Delta,* 1953; *The Little House on Wheels,* 1953.
as Marius
  Vandals From the Moon. *Amazing,* July 1928

BENJAMIN, LEWIS SAUL   (1874-1932)   *U.S.*
as Lewis Melville
  (ed) (with Reginald Hargreaves) *Great German Short Stories.* NY: Liveright, [1929], 1012pp. *ss col*
  (ed) (with Reginald Hargreaves) *Great English Short Stories.* NY: Viking, 1930, 1047pp.
  ■ *The Life of William Makepeace Thackeray,* 1899; *Victorian Novelists,* 1926; *Horace Walpole,* 1930; *In the Days of Queen Anne,* 1929.

BENNETT, GEOFFREY MARTIN   *British*
as Sea-Lion
  Phantom Fleet. London: Collins, 1946, 192pp.
  This Creeping Evil. London: Hutchinson, 1950, 176pp.
  The Invisible Ships. London: Hutchinson, [1950], 208pp.
  □ *Sink Me the Ship,* 1946; *When Danger Threatens,* 1949; *The Stolen Cipher,* 1955.

BENNETT, GERTRUDE BARROWS   (1884-1939?)   *U.S.*
  Born: Minneapolis, Minnesota
as Francis Stevens
  The Nightmare. *All Story Weekly,* 14 April 1917
  The Heads of Cerberus. *The Thrill Book,* 15 Aug 1919
  The Heads of Cerberus. Reading, Pennsylvania: Polaris Press, 1952, 190pp. (1500 cop)
  Claimed. NY: Avalon [1966], 192pp.
  The Citadel of Fear. NY: Ballantine, [c.1971], paper.

BENNETT, W(illiam) E(dward)   (1898-   )   *English*
as Warren Armstrong
  The Authentic Shudder. London: Elek, 1965, 176pp.
  ■ *Battle of the Oceans,* 1943; *Freedom of the Seas,* 1943; *Salt Water Tramp,* 1944.

BENSON, ALLAN INGVALD
as Allan Ingvald Benson
  The Psychopathic Martian. *Super Science Stories,* Aug 1941
as Victor Valding [in collaboration with John Victor Peterson]
  Atmospherics. *Astounding,* Sept 1939

BENSON, EDWIN [house pseudonym] real name used in error.
by Richard Shaver
  Marai's Wife. *Other Worlds,* March 1950

BERCKMAN, EVELYN DOMENICA   (1900-   )   *U.S.*
  Born: Philadelphia, Pennsylvania
as Evelyn Berckman
  The Evil of Time. NY: Dodd, Mead, 1954, 197pp.
  Heir of Starvelings. Garden City: Doubleday, 1967, 235pp.
  □ MYSTERY: *The Beckoning Dream,* 1955; *The Strange Bedfellow,* 1956; *Lament for Four Brides,* 1959; *Stalemate,* 1966.
  ■ *Nelson's Dear Lord; a Portrait of St. Vincent,* 1962.
  ● Joanna Wade

BERESFORD, LESLIE   *British*
as Leslie Beresford
  The Second Rising. London: Hurst & Blackett, 1910, 328pp.
  The Great Image. London: Oldhams, [1920], 288pp.
  Mr. Appleton Awakes. London: J. Long, [1924], 254pp.
  The Venus Girl. London: J. Long, [1925], 318pp.
as "Pan"
  Three Fairy Tales. London: Griffith, 1884.

The Kingdom of Content. London: Mills & Book, 1918, 278pp.

☐ *The Furnace*, 1920; *The Orchard of Dreams*, 1921; *Flame*, 1935.

BERINGTON, SIMON   (1680-1755)
as Simon Berington
■ *Dissertation on the Mosaical Creation, Deluge, Building of Babel, and Confusion of Tongues, etc.* 1750.
as Signor Gaudentio di Lucca
The Memoirs of Signor Gaudentio di Lucca: being the substance of his examination before the fathers of the Inquisition, at Bologna in Italy, giving an account of an unknown country in the midst of the desarts (sic) of Africa, etc. London: T. Cooper, 1737, 355pp.

BERRY, BRYAN   (1930-1955)   *English*
as Bryan Berry
Aftermath. Authentic #24, Aug 1952 (Br.)
And The Stars Remain. London: Panther, 1952, 112pp., paper.
Dread Visitor. London: Panther, 1952, paper.
Born In Captivity. London: Hamilton, 1952, 198pp.
From What Far Star. London: Hamilton, 1953, 143pp.
The Venom Seekers. London: Hamilton, 1953, 160pp.
as Rolf Gardner
The Resurgent Dust. London: Hamilton, 1953, 160pp.
The Immortals. London: Hamilton, 1953, 158pp.
The Indestructible. London: Hamilton, 1954, 159pp.

BERTIN, EDDY C.   (1944-   )   *Belgian*
Born: Altona, Germany
as Eddie C. Bertin
A Taste of Rain and Darkness. Bizarre Fantasy Tales, Fall 1970
as Eddy C. Bertin
The Whispering Thing. Weird Terror Tales, Winter 1969
Horror House. Dertlien Macabre Verhalen. St. Amendsberg, Gent: Helmut Gaus, 1968 [1969].
De Achtjaarlykse God, 1971.
✔ Edith Brendall, Doriac Greysun.

BESSIERE, RICHARD   *French*
as F. Richard Bessiere [in collaboration with Francois Richard]
used for novels in the Fleuve Noir Anticipation Series (Fr.)

BESTER, ALFRED   (1913-   )   *U.S.*
as Alfred Bester
The Broken Axiom. Thrilling Wonder Stories, April 1939
The Demolished Man. Chicago: Shasta, [1953], 250pp. (100 sgnd & numbered)
Tiger, Tiger! London: Sidgwick & Jackson, [1956], 231pp.
The Stars My Destination. NY: Signet, [1956], 197pp., paper.
Starburst. NY: Signet, 1958, 160pp., paper. *ss col*
The Dark Side of the Earth. NY: Signet, [1964], 160pp., paper. *ss col*
☐ *Who He?,* 1953.
■ *La Traviata, A New Libretto,* 1942; *The Life and Death of A Satellite,* 1966.
as Sonny Powell
The Black Nebula. Magazine of Fantasy and Science Fiction, Sept 1959

BICKERSTAFFE-DREW, FRANCIS BROWNING
(Monsignor Count)   (1858-1928)   *English*
as John Ayscough
Prodigals and Sons. London: Chatto & Windus, 1913, 320pp.
☐ *Rosemary,* 1900; *Dromina,* 1909; *Fastula,* 1912; *A Prince in Petto,* 1919; *The Foundress,* 1921; *Dobachi,* 1922.

■ *Discourses and Essays,* 1922.

BIERCE, AMBROSE (Gwinnett)   (1842-1914?)   *U.S.*
Born: Meigs County, Ohio
Biography: *Ambrose Bierce: The Devil's Lexicographer.* Norman, Oklahoma: U. of Oklahoma Press, 1951, by P. Fatout.
Bibliography: *Ambrose Bierce, A Bibliography,* by Vincent Starrett. Philadelphia: Centaur Book Shop, 1929, 117pp., ill. (300 copies)
as Ambrose Bierce
Tales of Soldiers and Civilians. San Francisco: E. L. G. Steele, 1891, 300pp. (brown cloth)
(with G. A. Danziger) *The Monk and the Hangman's Daughter.* Chicago: F.J. Schulte, 1892 [c.1891], 166pp., ill.
In The Midst of Life. London: Chatto & Windus, 1892, [c.1891], 244pp.
Can Such Things Be? NY: Cassell, [c.1893], 320pp. *ss col*
Fantastic Fables. NY: Putnam, 1899, 194pp. [1st ad. at end for "By Anne Fuller" in 1st state]
A Son of the Gods and A Horseman In the Sky. San Francisco: P. Elder, [c.1907], 47pp. (1,000 copies)
A Horseman In the Sky; A Watcher by the Dead; The Man and The Snake. San Francisco: Bookclub of California, 1920, 53pp. (400 copies)
☐ *Black Beetles In Amber,* 1892 (poetry); *Shapes of Clay,* 1903 (poetry); *The Cynic's Word Book,* 1906.
■ *The Shadow On the Dial,* 1909; *Battle Sketches,* 1931.
as Dod Grile
The Fiend's Delight. London: John Camden Hotten, [1872], 197pp., front. [author's first book]
(collected by J. Milton Sloluck) *Nuggets and Dust, Panned Out In California.* London: Chatto & Windus [1872], 175pp.
Cobwebs: Being Fables of Zambri and Parsee. London: "Fun" Office, [1873], 215pp., ill.
Cobwebs From An Empty Skull. London: Routledge, 1874, 215pp., ill.
as William Herman [in collaboration with Thomas A. Harcourt]
A Dance of Death. San Francisco: H. Keller & Co., 1877, 131pp.
as J. Milton Sloluck
(collector of) *Nuggets and Dust Panned Out In California by Dod Grile.* London: Chatto & Windus, [1872], 175pp.

BIGNON, JEAN PAUL, Abbe   (1662-1743)   *French*
as M. de Sandisson
Les Aventures d'Abdalla, Fils d'Hanif, Envoye par le Sultan des Indes a la Decouverte de L'Ile de Borico. . . avec la Relation du Voyage de Rouschen, Dame Persane, dans l'Ile Detournee. Paris: Chez Pierre Witte, 1712-1714, 2 vol.
as William Hatchett
The Adventures of Abdulla, Son of Hanif, Sent by the Sultan of the Indies, to Make A Discovery of the Island of Borico, Where the Fountain Which Restores Past Youth Is Supposed to Be Found. Also an Account of the Travels of Rouschen, a Persian Lady, to the Topsy-Turvey Island, Undiscover'd to This Day. . . Done into English by William Hatchett, Gentleman. London: T. Worrall at the Judge's Head, 1729, 169pp., ill.

BINDER, EARL ANDREW   (1904-   )   *U.S.*
Born: Bessemer, Michigan
as Eando Binder [in collaboration with Otto Oscar Binder]
The First Martian. Amazing, Oct 1932 [see Otto Oscar Binder]
Anton York, Immortal. NY: Belmont, [1965], 158pp., paper.
Adam Link, Robot. NY: Paperback Library [1965], 174pp., paper.
as John Coleridge [in collaboration with Otto Oscar Binder]
Martian Martyrs. Science Fiction, March 1939
Martian Martyrs. NY: Columbia Publications, [c.1940],

paper. (SF Classics #1)

The New Life. NY: Columbia Publications, [c.1940], paper. (SF Classics #4)

as Dean D. O'Brien [in collaboration with Otto Oscar Binder]
Guyon 45X. *Super Science Stories,* March 1940

BINDER, OTTO OSCAR (1911-) *U.S.*
Born: Bessemer, Michigan

as Eando Binder [in collaboration with Earl A. Binder]
[all stories before 1935 are collaborations]
The First Martian. *Amazing,* Oct 1932
[all known collaborations in magazines after 1934 are are listed below]
The Robot Aliens. *Wonder Stories,* Feb 1935
The Chemical Murder. *Amazing,* April 1937
Blue Beam of Pestilence. *Amazine,* Dec 1937
The Space Pirate. *Amazing,* June 1938
Anton York, Immortal. NY: Belmont, [1965], 158pp., paper.
Adam Link, Robot. NY: Paperback Library, [1965], 174pp., paper.

as Eando Binder [alone]
Set Your Course By the Stars. *Astounding,* May 1935
[all stories after 1934 not listed above are attributed to Otto Oscar Binder alone]
Lords of Creation. Philadelphia: Prime Press, [1949], 232pp.

as Otto Binder
The Ring Bonanza. *Startling Stories,* July 1947
The Avengers Battle the Earth Wrecker. NY: Bantam, [1967], 122pp., paper.

as John Coleridge [in collaboration with Earl A. Binder]
Martian Martyrs. *Science Fiction,* March 1939
Martian Martyrs. NY: Columbia Publications, [c.1940], paper. (SF Classics #1)
The New Life. NY: Columbia Publications, [c.1940], paper. (SF Classics #4)

as Will Garth [house pseudonym]
Rays of Blindness. *Thrilling Wonder Stories,* April 1938

as Gordon A. Giles
Diamond Planetoid. *Astounding,* May 1937

as Dean D. O'Brien [in collaboration with Earl A. Binder]
Guyon 45X. *Super Science Stories,* March 1940

BIRKIN, CHARLES L(loyd) (1907-) *English*
Born: Nottingham

as Charles (L.) Birkin
Devil's Spawn. London: G. Allen, 1936, 251pp. *ss col*
The Smell of Evil. London: Tandem, 1965, 188pp., paper. *ss col*
Where Terror Stalked. London: Tandem, 1966, 192pp., paper. *ss col*
My Name Is Death and Other New Tales of Horror. London: Panther, 1966, 139pp., paper. *ss col*
Dark Menace. London: Tandem, 1968, 188pp., paper. *ss col*
So Pale, So Cold. London: 1970

● Charles Lloyd [may have been used on stories published in pre-war "Creeps Library" (Br.) book series— unconfirmed]

BIRON, HENRY CHARTRES (1863- ?)
as Chartres Biron
■ *Pious Opinions,* 1923; *Without Prejudice,* 1936.

as Hyder Ragged
King Solomon's Wives; or, the Phantom Mines. London: Vizetelly, 1887, 125pp., ill.

BISHOP, ZEALIA BROWN REED (Mrs. D. W.)
as Zealia B. Bishop
The Curse of Yig. *Weird Tales,* Nov 1929
The Curse of Yig and Others. Sauk City, Wisconsin: Arkham House, 1953, 175pp. *ss col* (1217 cop)
■ *H.P. Lovecraft, A Pupil's View; A Wisconsin Balzac:*

A Profile of August Derleth.
as Hazel Heald
The Man of Stone. *Wonder Stories,* Oct 1932
The Horror In the Museum. *Weird Tales,* July 1933

BIXBY, DREXEL JEROME LEWIS (1923-) *U.S.*
Born: Los Angeles, California

as Jerome Bixby
Tubemonkey. *Planet Stories,* Winter 1949
Devil's Scrapbook. NY: Brandon, 1964, 158pp., paper. *ss col*
Space By The Tale. NY: Ballantine, [1964], 159pp., paper. *ss col*

as Jay B. Drexel
The Crowded Colony. *Planet Stories,* Fall 1950

as Thornecliff Herrick [house pseudonym] [used in Planet Comics - late 1940s]

as D.B. Lewis
Vengeance on Mars! *Planet Stories,* Sept 1951

as Alger Rome [in collaboration with Algirdas J. Budrys]
Underestimation. *Rocket Stories,* Sept 1953

✔ **Harry Neal**

BLADE, ALEXANDER [house pseudonym]
[Alexander Blade has been the most widely used pseudonym in the science fiction magazines. Stories were written under this name by David Vern, who originally used it as a personal pseudonym and by Howard Browne, Millen Cooke, Gordon Randall Garrett, Chester S. Geier, Roger P. Graham, Edmond Hamilton, Heinrich Hauser, Berkeley Livingston, Herb Livingston, William P. McGivern, David Wright O'Brien, Louis H. Sampliner, Richard S. Shaver, Robert Silverberg, David Vern, Don Wilcox, Leroy Yerxa, and probably others. Many of the unattributed stories below are probably by the authors listed above.]

unattributed
Vignettes of Famous Scientists, [appeared regularly in *Amazing* (Jan 1943-Aug 1948) and *Fantastic Adventures* (Dec 1942-July 1948)]
The Strange Adventures of Victor MacLeigh. *Amazing,* May 1941
The Man Who Wasn't Himself. *Amazing,* Dec 1941
Return of A Demon. *Fantastic Adventures,* May 1943
Scientist of the Air. *Amazing,* May 1943 *article*
Professor Cyclone. *Fantastic Adventures,* Dec 1943
Diamond of Doom. *Fantastic Adventures,* July 1945
Death Seems So Final. *Amazing,* Jan 1947
Death Wears a Rose. *Fantastic Adventures,* Jan 1947
Vanishing Spaceman. *Amazing,* July 1947
The Monster from Mars. *Amazing,* April 1948
The Valley of Madness. *Amazing,* June 1948
The Plotters. *Amazing,* Dec 1948
Beyond the Veil of Science. *Amazing,* Jan 1949
The Insane Planet. *Amazing,* Feb 1949
The Mermaid of Maracot Deep. *Fantastic Adventures,* March 1949
War of the Giant Apes. *Fantastic Adventures,* April 1949
The Jinx. *Amazing,* May 1949
Lamp of No Light. *Fantastic Adventures,* May 1949
Dynasty of the Devil. *Amazing,* June 1949
The Man Who Laughed at Time. *Fantastic Adventures,* Aug 1949
The World Is Dead. *Amazing,* Aug 1949
The Octopus of Space. *Fantastic Adventures,* Oct 1949
Prometheus' Daughter. *Amazing,* Nov 1949
The Laughing Death. *Amazing,* July 1950
Mr. Lahr Says His Prayers. *Amazing,* Oct 1950
The Man Who Hated Tuesday. *Fantastic Adventures,* Feb 1951
A Man Called Meteor. *Fantastic Adventures,* Feb 1953
Gambit On Ganymede. *Fantastic Adventures,* March 1953
Zero Hour. *Imagination,* April 1956

Flight of the Ark II. *Imaginative Tales,* July 1956
The Man With the Golden Eyes. *Imagination,* Aug 1956
The Cosmic Destroyer. *Imaginative Tales,* Sept 1957
Blacksheep's Angel. *Other Worlds,* Sept/Oct 1957
The Cheat. *Fantastic,* May 1958
Come Into My Brain! *Imagination,* June 1958
The Deadly Mission. *Space Travel,* Sept. 1958
by Howard Browne
Carbon-Copy Killer. *Amazing,* July 1943
by Gordon Randall Garrett & Robert Silverberg
in collaboration
The Alien Dies At Dawn. *Imagination,* Dec 1956
Wednesday Morning Sermon. *Imaginative Tales,* Jan 1957
The Ambassador's Pet. *Imagination,* Oct 1957
by Roger P. Graham
Brainstorm. *Fantastic Adventures,* Dec 1948
Warrior Queen of Mars. *Fantastic Adventures,* Sept 1950
by Edmond Hamilton
Battle for the Stars. *Imagination,* June 1956
The Cosmic Kings. *Imaginative Tales,* Nov 1956
The Tattooed Man. *Imaginative Tales,* March 1957
The Sinister Invasion. *Imagination,* June 1957
The Cosmic Looters. *Imagination,* Feb 1958
by Heinrich Hauser
The Brain. *Amazing,* Oct 1948
by Herb Livingston
The Silver Medusa. *Fantastic Adventures,* Feb 1948
by Louis H. Sampliner
Dr. Loudon's Armageddon. *Amazing,* Sept 1941
by Richard S. Shaver
Flesh Against Spirit. *Amazing,* March 1948
by Robert Silverberg
The Android Kill. *Imaginative Tales,* Nov 1957
3117 Half-Credit Uncirculated. *Science Fiction Adventures,* June 1958
by Don Wilcox
The Eye of the World. *Fantastic Adventures,* June 1949
by Leroy Yerxa
Is This the Night? *Amazing,* March 1945

BLAIR, ANDREW
as Tenth President of the World Republic
Annals of the Twenty-ninth Century; or, the Autobiography of the Tenth President of the World Republic. London: Tinsley, 1874, 3 vol. [it is not clear from references in the NUC, but Blair's name may appear on the book]

BLAIR, ANDREW J(ames) F(raser)   (1872-1935)
as Hamish Blair
1957. Edinburgh: Blackwood, 1930, 354pp.
Governor Hardy. Edinburgh: Blackwood, 1931, 303pp.
The Great Gesture. Edinburgh: Blackwood, 1931, 295pp.
■ *India! the Eleventh Hour,* 1934.

BLAIR, ERIC ARTHUR   (1903-1950)   *British*
Born: Bengal, India
Autobiography: *Such, Such Were The Joys,* 1953.
as George Orwell
Animal Farm; A Fairy Story. London: Secker & Warburg, 1945, 91pp.
1984. London: Secker & Warburg, 1949, 312pp.
□ *Down and Out in Paris and London,* 1933; *Burma Days,* 1934; *Keep Aspidistra Flying,* 1936.
■ *The Road To Wigan Pier,* 1937; *Homage To Catalonia,* 1938; *Shooting An Elephant,* 1950 (essays).

BLAND, EDITH NESBIT   (1858-1924)
as Fabian Bland [in collaboration with Hubert Bland]
□ *The Prophet's Mantle,* 1885.
as E(dith) Nesbit
Something Wrong. London: Innes, 1893, 158pp. *ss col*
Grim Tales. London: Innes. 1893, 167pp. *ss col*

The Five Children and It. London: Unwin, 1902, 301pp. *juv*
The Phoenix and the Carpet. London: Macmillan, 1904, 257pp., ill. *juv*
The Story of the Amulet. NY: Dutton, 1907, 374pp., ill. *juv*
The Enchanted Castle. NY: Harper, 1908, 296pp., ill. *juv*
Fear. London: S. Paul, 1910, 318pp. *ss col*
The Wonderful Garden; or, The Three C's. London: Macmillan, 1911, 402pp., ill.
Dormant. London: Methuen, [1911], 312pp.
□ *The Red House,* 1903; *The Lark,* 1922. JUVENILE: *The Wouldbegoods,* 1901; *New Treasure Seekers,* 1904; *The Railway Children,* 1904.

BLASSINGAME, WYATT RAINEY   (1909-   )   *U.S.*
Born: Demopolis, Alabama
as Wyatt Blassingame
The Horror At His Heels. [c.1936].
Appointment With A Lady. *Strange Stories,* Feb 1941
■ *Great Trains of the World,* 1953; *The Navies' Frogmen in WWII,* 1963
as W. B. Rainey
[titles unknown, possibly used for non-fiction, as the two titles above.]

BLAUSTEIN, ALBERT P(aul)   (1921-   )   *U.S.*
Born: New York, New York
as Albert P. Blaustein
■ (with C. O. Porter and C. T. Duncan) *The American Lawyer; a Summary of the Survey of the Legal Profession,* 1954.
as Allen De Graeff
(ed) *Human and Other Beings.* NY: Collier, 1963, 319pp.

BLISH, JAMES (Benjamin)   (1921-1975)   *U.S.*
Born: Orange, New Jersey
as William Atheling, Jr.
Reviews in various genre (SF) magazines 1952–1963
The Issue at Hand. Chicago: Advent, 1964, 136pp. *review col*
More Issues at Hand. Chicago: Advent, 1970, 154pp. *review col*
as James Blish
Emergency Refueling. *Super Science Stories,* March 1940
Jack of Eagles. NY: Greenberg, [1952], 246pp.
The Warriors of Day. NY: Galaxy SF Novel #16, [1953], 125pp., paper.
Earthman, Come Home. NY: Putnam, [1955], 239pp.
They Shall Have The Stars. London: Faber, 1956, 181pp.
The Seedling Stars. NY: Gnome, [1957], 185pp.
The Frozen Year. NY: Ballantine, [1957], 155pp., paper.
The Triumph of Time. NY: Avon, [1958], 158pp., paper.
A Case of Conscience. NY: Ballantine, [1958], 188pp., paper.
VOR. NY: Avon, [1958], 159pp., paper.
(with Robert Lowndes) *The Duplicated Man.* NY: Avalon, [1959], 222pp.
Galactic Cluster. NY: Signet, [1959], 176pp., paper. *ss col*
The Star Dwellers. NY: Putnam, [1961], 192pp.
So Close To Home. NY: Ballantine, [1961], 142pp., paper. *ss col*
Titan's Daughter. NY: Berkley, [1961], 142pp., paper.
The Night Shapes. NY: Ballantine, [1962], 125pp., paper.
A Life For the Stars. NY: Putnam, [1962], 188pp.
Doctor Mirabilis. London: Faber, [1964], 287pp.
Mission To The Heart Stars. NY: Putnam, [1965], 158pp.
(with Norman L. Knight) *A Torrent of Faces.* Garden City: Doubleday, 1967, 270pp.
Star Trek #2. NY: Bantam, [1968], 122pp., paper.
The Vanished Jet. NY: Weybright & Talley, [1968], 177pp.

Welcome To Mars. NY: Putnam, [1968], 159pp.

Black Easter, or Faust Aleph Null. Garden City: Doubleday, 1968, 165pp.

Anywhen. Garden City: Doubleday, 1970, 168pp. *ss col*

The Day After Judgement. Garden City: Doubleday, 1971, 166pp.

as Donald Laverty [in collaboration with Damon Knight]
No Winter, No Summer. *Thrilling Wonder Stories,* Oct 1948

as Marcus Lyons
non-fantasy and science fiction, titles unknown.

as John MacDougal [in collaboration with Robert W. Lowndes]
Chaos, Co-ordinated. *Astounding,* Oct 1946

as Arthur Merlyn
Sunken Universe. *Super Science Stories,* May 1942

as Luke Torley
non fantasy and science fiction, titles unknown

BLIXEN-FINECKE, KAREN CHRISTENTZE DINESEN
(Baroness) (1885-1962) *Danish*
Born: Rungsted, Zealand
Biographies: *Titania,* by P. Migel. London: M. Joseph, 1967; *The Life and Destiny of Isak Dinesen,* by Svendsen and Lassen. NY: Random House, 1970.

as Pierre Andrezel
□ MYSTERY: *The Angelic Avengers.* London: Putnam, [1946], 303pp. [originally published as *Gengaedelsens Veje.* Copenhagen, 1944.]

as Karen Blixen
Out of Africa. London: Putnam, 1937, 416pp., ill.
Breve Fra et Land I Krig. Copenhagen: Heretica, 1948.

as Tania Blixen
Africa, Dunkel Lockende Welt. Stuttgart, Germany: Deutsche Verlag-Anstalt, [1954], 326pp.

as Karen Blixen-Finecke
Sandhedens Haevn. Copenhagen: Tilskuerens Redakion, 1926. *play*

as Isak Dinesen
Seven Gothic Tales. NY: Smith & Haas, 1934, 420pp. *ss col*
[printed as *Syv Fantasticke Fortaellinger.* Copenhagen: 1935 (trans. by the author)]
Winter's Tales. London: Putnam, 1942, 313pp., *ss col*
Last Tales. London: Putnam, 1957, 405pp. *ss col*
Anecdotes of Destiny. NY: Random House, [1958], 244pp.
Carnival: Entertainments and Posthumous Tales. Chicago: U. of Chicago Press, [1977], 338pp. *ss col*

as Osceola
Eneboerne. *Tilskuerens Redakion* (Copenhagen), Aug 1907

as Titania
nickname among family members and friends.

BLOCH, ROBERT (Albert) (1917-   ) *U.S.*
Born: Chicago, Illinois

as Robert Bloch
Lilies. *Marvel Tales,* Winter 1934
The Feast In the Abbey. *Weird Tales,* Jan 1935
The Secret in the Tomb. *Weird Tales,* May 1935
A Visit with H.P. Lovecraft. Belleville, New Jersey: [1937], 58pp. [The Science-Fantasy Correspondent #2, Jan-Feb 1937]
The Secret of the Observatory. *Amazing,* Aug 1938
Sea Kissed. London: Utopian Publications, [c.1945], 39pp.,
The Opener of the Way. Sauk City, Wisconsin: Arkham House, 1945, 309pp. (2065 cop) *ss col*
The Sea Witch. London: Utopian Publications, [c.1945], paper.
The Scarf. NY: Dial Press, 1947, 247pp.
Blood Runs Cold. NY: Simon & Schuster, 1953, 246pp. *ss col*
Ladies Day and This Crowded Earth. NY: Belmont, [1958], 172pp., paper. (Belmont Double Novel)
Shooting Star. NY: Ace, [1958], paper. (Ace Double D-265)
Psycho. NY: Simon & Schuster, 1959, 185pp.

Pleasant Dreams—Nightmares. Sauk City, Wisconsin: Arkham House, 1960, 233pp. (2060 cop) *ss col*
More Nightmares. NY: Belmont, [1962], 173pp., paper. *ss col*
Terror. NY: Belmont, [1962], 157pp., paper. *ss col*
Yours Truly, Jack the Ripper. NY: Belmont, [1962], paper. *ss col*
Atoms and Evil. Greenwich, Connecticut: Fawcett Gold Medal, [1962], 160pp., paper. *ss col*
Horror 7. NY: 1963. *ss col*
Bogey Man. NY: Pyramid, [1963], 159pp., paper. *ss col*
The House of the Hatchet. 1965.
Tales In A Jugular Vein. NY: Pyramid, [1965], 144pp., paper. *ss col*
The Skull of the Marquis de Sade and Other Tales. NY: Pyramid, [1965], 157pp., paper. *ss col*
Dragons and Nightmares. Baltimore: Mirage, 1968, 185pp., ill. (1000 cop) *ss col*
Fear Today, Gone Tomorrow. NY: Award Books, [c.1971], 159pp., paper. *ss col*
It's All In Your Mind. NY: Modern Library, 1971, 128pp., paper. *ss col*
The King of Terrors: Tales of Madness and Death. 1977. (250 cop signed)
Cold Chills. Garden City: Doubleday, 1977, 178pp. *ss col*
Such Stuff as Screams Are Made Of. NY: Ballantine, [1979], 287pp., paper.
□ *The Kidnapper,* 1954; *Spiderweb,* 1954; *Night World,* 1972; *American Gothic,* 1974.
■ *The Eighth Stage of Fandom, Selections from 25 Years of Fan Writing.* Chicago: Advent, 1962, 176pp., ill.

as Tarleton Fiske
The Sorcerer's Jewel. *Strange Stories,* Feb 1939

as Nathan Hindin
(with Robert Bloch) Fangs of Vengeance. *Weird Tales,* April 1937
(with Robert Bloch) Death Is An Elephant. *Weird Tales,* Feb 1939

as Collier Young
□ MYSTERY: *The Todd Dossier,* 1969.

✓ **Wilson Kane, John Sheldon**

BLOW, MARYA MANNES (Mrs. Richard) (1904-   ) *U.S.*
Born: New York, New York

as Marya Mannes
Message From A Stranger. NY: Viking, 1948, 246pp.
They. NY: Doubleday, 1968, 215pp.

BLOWER, ELIZABETH (1763-   ?   ) *English*
as Author of "George Bateman"
Maria, A Novel. London: Cadell, 1785, 2 vol.

BLYTH, HARRY (1852-1898) *British*
as Harry Blyth
□ *The Old Bailey,* 1879; *The Secret of Sinclair's Farm,* 1887; *The Black Pirate,* 1893.
■ *Eat, Drink, and Be Merry,* 1877.

as Hal Meredith
The Missing Millionaire. The Half-Penny Marvel #6, 1893, 16pp. (Br) [first appearance of the detective character Sexton Blake.]
□ *The Gold Fiend. A Story of South African Mystery.* The Half-Penny Marvel #2, 1893, 16pp. (Br)

BOAISTUAL DE LAUNAY, PIERRE (?   -1556) *French*
as Pierre Boaistual
■ *Bref Discovrs de l' Excellence et Dignite de l'Homme,* 1559; *Le Theatre du Monde,* 1561.

as Chelidonius Tigurinus
L'Histoire de Chelidonius Tigurinus sur l' Institution des Princes Chrestiens et Origine des Royaumes. Paris: Estienne Groulleaux, 1556, 143pp.

as E. Fenton [real name of translator]
■ *Certaine Secrete Wonders of Nature, Containing a Description of Sundry Strange Things, Seming Monstrous in Our Eyes and Iudgement, Bicause we are not Privie to the Reasons for Them. . .,(sic), 1569.*

BOEX, JOSEPH HENRI HONORE (1856-1940) *French*
Born: Paris
Autobiography: *Memoirs de la vie litteraire: L'Academie Goncourt, etc.* by J. H. Rosny-Aine. Paris: G. Cres, 1927, 239pp.
as Enacryos
La Flute de Pan. Paris: Librairie Borel, 1897, 45pp., ill.
as J. H. Rosny [alone—pre 1893]
Les Xipehuz. Paris: A. Savine, 1888 [1887], 84pp.
as J. H. Rosny [in collaboration with Justin Boex, 1893-1907]
□ *L'Autre Femme,* 1895; *Un Autre Monde,* 1898; *Les Ames Perdues,* 1899; *Le Crime du Docteur,* 1903.
as J. H. Rosny-Aine [after 1907]
Le Mort de la Terre; roman suivi de Contes. Paris: Plon-Nourrit, 1912, 362pp.
La Force Mysterieuse. Paris: Plon-Nourrit, [1914], 320pp.
The Giant Cat; or, The Quest of Aoun and Zouhr. NY: McBride, 1924, 242pp.
Les Autres vies et les Autres Mondes. Paris: G. Cres et Cie, 1924, 327pp. (1850 cop)
La Vampire de Bethnal Green. Paris: Editions Albert, [c.1935], 204pp.
■ *Les Sciences et la Pluralisme,* 1922.

BOEX, SERAPHIN JUSTIN FRANCOIS (1859-1948)
French
Born: Paris
as J. H. Rosny [in collaboration with J. H. H. Boex]
[see J. H. H. Boex]
as J. H. Rosny-Jeune [after 1907]
□ *L'Argentine,* 1931; *Le Banquet de Platon,* 1942.
■ *Les Amours d' Elisabeth d' Angleterre,* 1929.

BOLAND, BERTRAM J(ohn) (1913-   ) *English*
Born: Birmingham
as John Boland
Herma. Science Fantasy #20, Dec 1956 (Br.)
White August. London: M. Joseph, 1955, 239pp.
No Refuge. London: M. Joseph, 1956, 254pp.
Operation Red Carpet. London: Boardman, 1959, 192pp.
□ *The Gentlemen Reform,* 1961; *The Counterpol,* 1963; *The Catch,* 1964; *The Disposal Unit,* 1966; *Breakdown,* 1968; *The Shakespeare Course,* 1969; *The Big Job,* 1970; *The Trade of Kings,* 1972.
■ *Short-Story Writing,* 1960.

BOLITHO, HENRY HECTOR (1897-1974) *British*
Born: New Zealand
as Hector Bolitho
The House in Half Moon Street, and Other Stories. London: Cobden-Sanderson, [1935], 303pp. *ss col*
□ *Judith Silver,* 1929; *The Flame on Ethirdova,* 1930.
■ *The Islands of Wonder,* 1920; *The New Zealanders,* 1928. BIOGRAPHY: *Victoria,* 1934; *Edward VIII,* 1937; *A Century of British Monarchy,* 1951.

BOND, NELSON S(lade) (1908-   ) *U.S.*
Born: Scranton, Pennsylvania
as Nelson (S.) Bond
The Word of Power. Parade, Spring 1936
Down the Dimensions. Astounding, April 1937
Mr. Mergenthwirker's Lobblies and Other Fantastic Tales. NY: Coward-McCann, 1946, 243pp. *ss col*
The 31st of February. NY: Gnome, 1949, 272pp. (of which 112 copies were numbered, signed and boxed)

Exiles of Time. Philadelphia: Prime Press, 1949, 183pp. (of which 112 copies were numbered, signed and boxed; also prepublication edition of 25 in paper)
The Remarkable Exploits of Lancelot Biggs: Spaceman. Garden City: Doubleday, 1950, 224pp.
No Time Like The Future. NY: Avon, [1954], 221pp., paper. *ss col*
Mr. Mergenthwirker's Lobblies, A Fantastic Comedy in Three Acts. NY: S. French, 1957, 93pp. *play*
State of Mind, A Comedy in 3 Acts. NY: S. French, 1958. *play*
(adapted from Orwell) *Animal Farm; A Fable in Two Acts.* NY: S. French, 1964, 57pp. *play*
Nightmares and Daymares. Sauk City, Wisconsin: Arkham House, 1968, 269pp. (2040 cop) *ss col*
■ *The Postal Stationery of Canada, A Reference Catalogue,* 1953.
as George Danzell
The Castaway. Planet Stories, Winter 1940
as Hubert Mavity
The Message From the Void. Dynamic Stories, Feb 1939

BOND, STEPHEN
as Stephen Bond
Rock and Roll on Pluto. Fantastic Universe, June 1957
as Stephen Lloyd
Flying Saucer of the Seas. New Worlds, March 1960 (Br.)

BOREL, MARGUERITE (Appell) (1883-   ) *French*
as Camille Marbo
Le Survivant, roman. Paris: A. Fayard & Cie [1918], 258pp.
The Man Who Survived. NY: Harper, [1918], 190pp.

BOTT, HENRY
as Henry Bott
High Vacua. Astounding, Nov 1941 *article*
as Charles Recour
Amoeba 'Roid. Amazing, July 1948
That We May Rise Again. Amazing, July 1948

BOUNDS, SYDNEY JAMES (1920-   ) *English*
Born: Brighton
as Sydney Bounds
Too Efficient. New Worlds #5, 1949 (Br.)
The Moon Raiders. London: Foulsham, 1955, 160pp.
as Wes Saunders
used on westerns, no titles known
↙ James Marshal

BOWER, JOHN G(raham) (1886-   ) *British*
as John Graham Bower
□ *On Patrol,* 1919.
as Klaxon
H. M. S. _____. London: Blackwood, 1918, 327pp.
□ *Heather Mixture,* 1922; [with "Euphan"] *Stories of the Coronations,* 1937.
■ *The Story of Our Submarines,* 1919; *Dead Reckoning, A Story of Our Submarines,* 1933.

BOYD, LYLE G(ifford) (Mrs. William C.) *U.S.*
as Lyle G. Boyd
Verb Sap?. Magazine of Fantasy and Science Fiction, Feb 1956
■ (with William C. Boyd) *An Attempt To Determine The Blood Groups of Mummies,* 1934.
as Boyd Ellanbee [in collaboration with William C. Boyd]
A Toothache on Zenob. If, Oct 1958
as Boyd Ellanby [in collaboration with William C. Boyd]
Category Phoenix. Galaxy, May 1952

BOYD, WILLIAM C(louser) (1903-   ) *U.S.*
as William C. Boyd

Living Fossils In Print. *Astounding,* April 1958 *article*
■ *Fundamentals of Immunology,* 1943; *Genetics and the Races of Man,* 1950; (with Isaac Asimov) *Races and People,* 1955; [see **LYLE G. BOYD**].

as Boyd Ellanbee [in collaboration with Lyle G. Boyd]
A Toothache on Zenob. *If,* Oct. 1958

as Boyd Ellanby [in collaboration with Lyle G. Boyd]
Category Phoenix. *Galaxy,* May 1952

BRADBURY, RAY (Douglas) (1920-   ) *U.S.*
Born: Waukegan, Illinois
Bibliography & Literary Biography: *The Ray Bradbury Companion,* by William F. Nolan. Detroit: Gale Research, 1975, 339pp., ill.
Bradbury wrote extensively in fan publications before his professional career began.

as Guy Amory
Is It True What They Say About Kuttner? *Futuria Fantasia #2* (fanzine), Fall 1939. *fan article*

as D. R. Banat
Corpse Carnival. *Dime Mystery,* July 1945

as Edward Banks
The Dead Man [probable title]. *Weird Tales,* July 1945 (Can.)

as Ray Bradbury
(with Henry Hasse) Pendulum. *Super Science Stories,* Nov 1941
Eat, Drink and Be Wary. *Astounding,* July 1942
The Candle. *Weird Tales,* Nov 1942
Dark Carnival. Sauk City, Wisconsin: Arkham House, 1947, 313pp. (3112 cop) *ss col*
The Martian Chronicles. Garden City: Doubleday, 1950, 222pp. *ss col*
The Illustrated Man. Garden City: Doubleday, 1951, 251pp. *ss col*
Golden Apples of the Sun. Garden City: Doubleday, 1953, 250pp., ill. *ss col*
Fahrenheit 451. NY: Ballantine, 1953, 199pp., ill., paper. (4500 of which were case bound; 200 of these were bound in an asbestos material with exceptional resistance to pyrolysis and signed by the author)
Switch On the Night. NY: Pantheon, 1955, 52pp., ill. *juv*
The October Country. NY: Ballantine, [1955], 306pp., paper. *ss col*
Sun and Shadow. Berkeley, California: Quenian Press, 1957, 19pp. (90 cop)
Dandelion Wine. Garden City: Doubleday, 1957, 281pp.
A Medicine For Melancholy. Garden City: Doubleday, 1959, 240pp. *ss col*
Something Wicked This Way Comes. NY: Simon & Schuster, 1962, 317pp.
R Is for Rocket. Garden City: Doubleday, 1962, 233pp. *ss col*
The Anthem Sprinters and Other Antics. NY: Dial Press, 1963, 159pp. *play col*
The Machineries of Joy. NY: Simon & Schuster, 1964, 256pp. *ss col*
The Pedestrian. Glendale, California: Roy A. Squires, [1964], 16pp., paper. (280 cop)
The Vintage Bradbury. NY: Vintage, [1965], 329pp., paper. *ss col*
The Autumn People. NY: Ballantine, [1965], 189pp., ill., paper. (reprint of comic book adaptations)
Tomorrow Midnight. NY: Ballantine, [1966], 188pp., ill., paper. (reprint of comic book adaptations)
S is for Space. Garden City: Doubleday, 1966, 238pp.
I Sing The Body Electric. NY: Knopf, 1969, 305pp. *ss col*
Old Ahab's Friend, and Friend to Noah, Speaks His Piece. Glendale, California: Roy A. Squires, Apollo Year Two [1971], 16pp., paper. (485 copies of which 40 were numbered and signed by the author)
The Wonderful Ice Cream Suit and Other Plays. NY: Bantam Pathfinder, 1972, 161pp., paper.

Madrigals for the Space Age: For Mixed Chorus and Narrator. music by L. Schifrin, NY: Associated Music Publishers, [1972], 43pp., paper.
When Elephants Last In the Dooryard Bloomed. NY: Knopf, 1973. *poetry*
That Son of Richard III . . . Glendale, California: Roy A. Squires, 1974, paper. (issued in envelope, 400 copies, numbered)
Pillar of Fire and Other Plays for Today, Tomorrow, and Beyond. NY: Bantam, [1975], 113pp., paper. *play*
Long After Midnight. NY: Knopf, 1976, 271pp. *ss col*
That Ghost, That Bride of Time. 1976, paper. (150 copies, issued in d. j. with envelope)
Twin Hieroglyphs That Swim the River Dust. 1978.
□ SCREENPLAYS: *It Came From Outer Space,* 1953; (with John Huston) *Moby Dick,* 1956; *An American Journey,* 1964.
■ *The Essence of Creative Writing,* 1962; *Zen and the Art of Writing,* 1973, (250 cop).

as Anthony Corvais
Return From Death. *Futuria Fantasia #2* (fanzine), Fall 1939

as Cecil Claybourne Cunningham
Fan pseudonym

as E. Cunningham
Fan pseudonym

as Leonard Douglas
Love Contest. *Saturday Evening Post,* May 23, 1952

as Brian Eldred
How To Run A Successful Ghost Agency. *D' Journal* (fanzine), March 1939 *article*

as William Elliott
Her Eyes, Her Lips, Her Limbs. *The Californian,* June 1946
Electrocution. *The Californian,* Aug 1946

as Hollerbochen
Hollerbochen's Dilemma. *Imagination* (fanzine), Jan 1938

as Omega
As I Remember. *Futuria Fantasia #3* (fanzine), Winter 1940 *essay*

as Ron Reynolds
Don't Get Technatal. *Futuria Fantasia #1* (fanzine), Summer 1939

as Doug Rogers
Satan's Mistress. *Futuria Fantasia #2* (fanzine), Fall 1939 *verse*

as Douglas Spaulding
(with E. Boyd) *Picasso Summer.* Warner/Seven Arts, 1972 *screenplay*

as Leonard Spaulding
The Highway. *Copy,* Spring 1950

as Brett Sterling [house pseudonym]
Referent. *Thrilling Wonder Stories,* Oct 1948

as D. Lerium Tremaine
Tremonstrous. *Le Zombie* (fanzine), Jan 30, 1940 *verse*

BRAINERD, CHAUNCEY COREY   (1874-1922) *U.S.*
as E. J. Rath [in collaboration with Edith Brainerd]
Once Again. NY: G. H. Watt, 1929, 312pp.
□ *The Sixth Speed,* 1908; *Sam,* 1915; *Too Much Efficiency,* 1917; *Too Many Crooks,* 1918; *The Sky's the Limit,* 1929.

BRAINERD, EDITH RATHBONE (Jacobs) *U.S.*
as E. J. Rath [in collaboration with Chauncey Brainerd]
see CHAUNCEY BRAINERD

BRA[I]THWAIT[E], RICHARD   (1588?-1673) *English*
Braithwaite's name appeared on his books as variously: Braithwait, Brathwait, Braithwayt, Brathwayte, and Brathwayt.
as Richard Braithwaite (and variations)

The Honest Ghost; or, A Voice From the Vault. London: Hodginsonne, 1658, 326pp.

□ *Love's Labyrinth; or, the True-Lovers,* 1615; *Essaies Upon the Five Senses, with a Pithie One Upon Detraction,* 1620; *The English Gentleman,* 1630.

as Corymboeus

Barnabee's Journall, 1638.

as Hesychius Pamphilus

■ *The History of Moderation,* 1669.

as Musaeus Palatinus

□ *The Two Lancashire Lovers,* 1640.

as Philogenes Panedonius

□ *Ar't Asleepe Husband? A Boulster Lecture,* 1640.

as Castalio Pomerano

Panthalia; or the Royal Romance. A Discourse Stored With Infinite Variety in Relation to State Government... London: Williamson, 1659, 303pp.

BRANSBY, EMMA LINDSAY SQUIER (Mrs. John)
(1892-) *U.S.*
Born: Marion, Indiana
as Emma Lindsay Squier
The Wild Heart. NY: Cosmopolitan, 1922, 220pp., ill.
On Autumn Trails and Adventures In Captivity. NY: International Fiction Library, [1923], 239pp. *ss col*
Child of the Twilight. NY: Cosmopolitan, 1926, 257pp.
The Bride of the Sacred Well and Other Tales of Mexico. NY: Cosmopolitan, 1928, 275pp., ill.
■ *Gringa; An American Woman In Mexico,* 1934.

BRASH, MARGARET MAUD (1880-) *British*
as M(argaret) M. Brash
□ *Jannock,* 1928; *The Rooftree Rides,* 1929; *Over the Windmills,* 1932.
as John Kendall
Unborn To-Morrow. London: Collins, [1933], 319pp.

BREBNER, PERCY (1864-1922)
as Percy Brebner
The Ivory Disc. NY: Duffield, 1920, 254pp.
□ MYSTERY: *Mr. Quixley, of the Gate House,* 1904; *Princess Maritza,* 1906; *Christopher Quarles, College Professor and Master Detective,* 1911; *The Master Detective,* 1916; *A Gallant Lady,* 1919; *The Fountain of Green Fire,* 1923.
as Christian Lys
The Fortress of Yadasara. London: F. Warne, 1899, 432pp. ill.

BREEN, MARION ELEANOR ZIMMER BRADLEY
(Mrs. Walter) (1930-) *U.S.*
Born: Albany, New York
as Marion Zimmer Bradley
Keyhole. Vortex #2, 1953
Women Only. Vortex #2, 1953
Centaurus Changeling. Magazine of Fantasy & Science Fiction, April 1954
The Door Through Space. NY: Ace, [1961], 131pp., paper. (Ace Double F117)
Seven From the Stars. NY: Ace, [1961], 120pp., paper. (Ace Double F127)
The Planet Savers. NY: Ace, [1962], 91pp., paper. (Ace Double F153)
The Sword of Aldones. NY: Ace, [1962], 164pp., paper. (Ace Double F153)
The Colors of Space. NY: Monarch, [1963], 124pp., paper.
The Dark Intruders and Other Stories. NY: Ace, [1964], 124pp., paper. (Ace Double F273) *ss col*
The Falcons of Narabella. NY: Ace, [1964], 127pp., paper. (Ace Double F273)
The Bloody Sun. NY: Ace, [1964], 191pp., paper. (Ace Double F303)

Star of Danger. NY: Ace, [1965], 160pp., paper. (Ace Double F350)
The Brass Dragon. NY: Ace, [1969], 125pp., paper. (Ace Double 37250)
The World Wreckers. NY: Ace, [1971], 189pp., paper.
Dark Satanic. NY: Berkley, [c.1972], 224pp., paper.
Darkover Landfall. NY: DAW, [c.1972], 160pp., paper.
Hunters of the Red Moon. NY: DAW #71, [1973], 176pp., paper.
The Spell Sword. NY: DAW, [c.1974], 158pp., paper.
Endless Voyage. NY: Ace, [1975], 189pp., paper.
The Shattered Chain. NY: DAW #191, [1976], 287pp., paper.
The Forbidden Tower. NY: DAW #256, [1977], 364pp., paper.
□ *The Drums of Darkness.*
■ (with Gene Damon) *A Complete Cumulative Checklist of Lesbian, Variant, and Homosexual Fiction in English. . . for the use of collectors, students, and librarians,* 1960.
● Brian Morley, Dee O'Brien

BRENGLE, WILLIAM [house pseudonym]
unattributed
Your Rope Is Waiting. Fantastic Adventures, Aug 1950
by Howard Browne
Return to Lilliput. Fantastic Adventures, May 1943
The Star Shepherd. Fantastic Adventures, Aug 1943

BRETNOR, REGINALD (1911-) *naturalized U.S.*
Born: Vladivostok, Russia
as Reginald Bretnor
Maybe Just A Little One. Harper's Magazine, Aug 1947
The Gnurrs Come From the Voodvork Out. Magazine of Fantasy and Science Fiction, Winter/Spring 1950
■ (ed) *Modern SF: Its Meaning and Its Future,* 1953; (ed) *Science Fiction Today and Tomorrow,* 1974.
as Grendel Briarton
Through Time and Space with Ferdinand Feghoot. Magazine of Fantasy and Science Fiction, May 1956
Through Time and Space with Ferdinand Feghoot. Berkeley, California: Paradox Press, 1962, 111pp.

BRIDGES, THOMAS (of Hull) (fl1759-1775)
as The Author of "Homer Travestie"
The Battle of the Genie. A Fragment, in three cantos. Taken from an ancient Erse Manuscript... [A Burlesque of Book 6 of Paradise Lost] London: S. Hooper, 1765, 63pp.
as Cotton, Junior
□ *Homer Travestie: Being A New Translation of the First Four Books of the Illiad,* 1762.
anonymous
The Adventures of A Bank Note. London: T. Davies, [c.1770], 4 vol [vol I & II published in 1770, vol III & IV published in 1771]

BRIDGES, THOMAS C(harles) (1868- ?) *British*
as Christopher Beck
The Crimson Aeroplane. London: C. A. Pearson, 1913, 256pp.
The Brigand of the Air. London: C. A. Pearson, 1920, 224pp.
The People of the Chasm, etc. London: C. A. Pearson, [1924], 256pp.
□ *Strong-Hand Saxon,* 1910; *Sons of the Sea,* 1914.
as Thomas C. Bridges
Martin Crusoe: A Boy's Adventure On Wizard Island. London: Harrap, 1920, 255pp.
Men of the Mist. London: Harrap, 1923, 251pp.
Death Star. London: Collins, [1940], 288pp.
■ *The Book of Inventions,* 1925; *Kings of Commerce,* 1928; *Master Minds of Modern Science,* 1930.

BRIGHT, MARY CHAVELITA DUNNE (Mrs. Reginald G.)
(1860-1945) *British*
Born: Melbourne, Victoria, Australia
as George Egerton
Fantasias. London: J. Lane, 1898, 156pp. *ss col*
☐ *Key Notes*, 1893; *Discords*, 1894; *The Wheel of God*,
1898; *Flies In Amber*, 1905; (translator) *Hunger*, by
Knut Hamsun, 1920; *Camilla States Her Case*, 1925.
(play)

BRINEY, ROBERT E(dward) (1933-   ) *U.S.*
as Robert E. Briney
(ed) *Shandu; a collection of Fantasy*. North Tonawanda,
New York: SSSR Publications, [1953], 101pp., ill. *ss col*
as Andrew Duane
(with Brian G. McNaughton) *The Black Tower* (in the short
story collection *Shandu*). North Tonawanda, New York:
SSSR Publications, [1953], 101pp., ill.

BRIUSOV, VALERI YAKOVLEVICH (1873-1924) *Russian*
as Valeri Briussov
The Fiery Angel, A 16th Century Romance. London:
H. Toulmin, [1930], 392pp.
as Valery Brussof
The Republic of the Southern Cross and Other Stories.
London: Constable, [1918], 162pp. *ss col*

BROCKIES, ENID FLORENCE (1911-   )
as Countess Helene Magriska
Ten Poplars. London: Constable, [1937], 321pp.

BRONTE, ANNE (1820-1849) *English*
as Acton Bell
Agnes Grey. London: T. C. Newley, 1847, 363pp.
(states "vol III" issued as third volume of *Wuthering
Heights* by Ellis Bell [Emily Bronte])
☐ *Poems, by Currer, Ellis, and Acton Bell*, 1848 [1846]
(poetry); *The Tenant of Windfell Hall*, 1848.

BRONTE, CHARLOTTE (1816-1855) *English*
Born: Haworth, Yorkshire
as Currer Bell
Villette. London: Smith, Elder, 1853, 3 vol.
☐ *Jane Eyre: An Autobiography*, 1847; *Shirley*, 1849;
The Professor, 1857.
as Charlotte Bronte
The Four Wishes, a Fairy Tale. London: Privately Printed
by C. Shorter, 1918, 13pp. (20 cop)
The Twelve Adventures and Other Stories. London:
Hodder & Stoughton, 1925, 214pp. (1000 cop) *ss col*
*Legends of Angia, Compiled from the Early Writings of
Charlotte Bronte*. London: Oxford University Press,
1933, 322pp., ill.

BRONTE, EMILY (Jane) (1818-1848) *English*
as Ellis Bell
Wuthering Heights: A Novel. London: T. C. Newley, 1847,
3 vol. (of which the third is *Agnes Grey*, by Acton Bell
[Anne Bronte])

BROOKS, EDWY SEARLES (1889-*c*.1965) *British*
Born: Hackney, London
as Edwy Searles Brooks
The Strange Case of the Antlered Man. London: Harrap,
[1935], 327pp.
☐ MYSTERY: *The Grouser Investigates*, 1936.
as Robert W. Comrade
Ghost Gold. London: Rich & Cowan, [1935], 282pp.
as Berkeley Gray
☐ MYSTERY: *Mr. Mortimer Gets the Jitters*, [1938];
Miss Dynamite, 1939; *Conquest Marches On*, 1939;
Leave It To Conquest, 1944.

as Victor Gunn
wrote mysteries under this name, no titles known.

BROSTER, D(orothy) K(athleen) (1877-1950)
as D. K. Broster
A Fire of Driftwood. London: Heinemann, [1932], 347pp.
(with Forester G. Broster) *World Under Snow*. London:
Heinemann, [1935], 276pp.
Couching at the Door. London: Heinemann, [1942], 130pp.
[a shorter version appeared in Dorothy Sayers' *3rd
Omnibus of Crime*, 1935]
☐ *Chantemerle*, 1911; *The Flight of the Heron*, 1926;
The Sea Without A Haven, 1941; *The Gleam In the
North*, 1949.

BROWN, FREDRIC (1926-1972) *U.S.*
Born: Cincinnati, Ohio
Bibliography: "A Fredric Brown Checklist," by Newton
Baird, in *The Armchair Detective Magazine*.
as Fredric Brown
The Moon For A Nickel. *Detective Story*, 1936
Not Yet The End. *Captain Future*, Winter 1941
What Mad Universe. NY: Dutton, 1949, 255pp.
Space On My Hands. Chicago: Shasta, [1951], 224pp. *ss col*
The Lights In The Sky Are Stars. NY: Dutton, 1953,
254pp.
Angels and Spaceships. NY: Dutton, 1954, 224pp. *ss col*
Martians, Go Home. NY: Dutton, 1955, 189pp.
Rogue In Space. NY: Dutton, 1957, 189pp.
Honeymoon In Hell. NY: Bantam, [1958], 170pp., paper.
ss col
The Mind Thing. NY: Bantam, [1961], 149pp., paper.
Nightmares and Geezenstacks. NY: Bantam, [1961], 137pp.,
paper. *ss col*
Daymares. NY: Lancer, [1968], 317pp., paper. *ss col*
Paradox Lost, and Twelve Other Great SF Stories. NY:
Random House, 1973, 211pp. *ss col*
The Best of Fredric Brown. Garden City: Doubleday SF
Book Club, 1977. *col*
☐ MYSTERY: *The Fabulous Clip Joint*, 1947; *Dead Ringer*,
1948; *The Bloody Moonlight*, 1949; *The Screaming Mimi*,
1949, *Compliments of A Fiend*, 1950; *Here Comes A
Candle*, 1950; *Night of the Jabberwock*, 1950; *We All
Killed Grandma*, 1952; *One For The Road*, 1958; *The
Shaggy Dog and Other Murders*, 1963. *ss col*
as Felix Graham
The Hat Trick. *Unknown*, Feb 1943

BROWN, J(ohn) MACMILLAN (1846-1935) *British*
Born: Irvine, Scotland
as John Macmillan Brown
■ *The Merchant of Venice, A Study*, 1894; *Maori and
Polynesian*, 1907; *The Riddle of the Pacific*, 1924;
Peoples and Problems of the Pacific, 1924.
as Godfrey Sweven
Riallaro: The Archipelago of Exiles. NY: Putnam, 1901,
420pp.
Limanora: The Island of Progress. NY: Putnam, 1903,
711pp.

BROWN, MORNA DORIS (MacTaggart) (1907-   )
British
Born: Rangoon, Burma
as E. X. Ferrars
☐ MYSTERY: *Murder of A Suicide*, 1941; *Alibi For A
Witch*, 1952 (U.S.)
as Elizabeth Ferrars
☐ MYSTERY: *Give A Corpse A Bad Name*, 1940; *Alibi
For A Witch*, 1952 (Br.)

BROWN, ZENITH JONES (Mrs. Ford K.) (1898-   ) *U.S.*
Born: Smith River, California

as Leslie Ford
- ☐ MYSTERY: *By the Watchman's Clock*, 1932; *The Sound of Footsteps*, 1933; *The Clue of the Judas Tree*, 1933.

as David Frome
- ☐ MYSTERY: *The Man From Scotland Yard*, 1932; *Scotland Yard Can Wait*, 1933; *Mr. Pinkerton Finds A Body*, 1934.

BROWNE, F. G. (1870-1954) *U.S.*
as Robert A(mes) Bennet
The Bowl of Baal. *New Story Magazine* (serial) Nov 1916–Feb 1917
Thyra; A Romance of the Polar Pit. NY: Holt, 1901, 258pp., ill.
- ☐ *The Shogun's Daughter*, 1910; *The Two Gun Man*, 1924; *White Buffalo*, 1935.

as Lee Robinet
The Forest Maiden. Chicago: Browne & Howell, 1913, 349pp.

BROWNE, HABLOT KNIGHT (1815-1882) *English*
as Phiz
Illustrator for many 19th century books, including works by Charles Dickens and Charles Lever.

BROWNE, HELEN DE GUERRY SIMPSON (Mrs. Denis) (1897-1940) *British*
as Helen (de Guerry) Simpson
Pan In Pimlico; A Fantasy in One Act. Oxford: Blackwell, 1926, 26pp. *play*
Boomerang. London: Heinemann, [1932], 506pp.
The Woman On the Beast. London: Heinemann, [1933], 492pp.
- ☐ *Acquittal*, 1925; *Henry VIII*, 1934; *Saraband for Dead Lovers*, 1935; *Maid No More*, 1940.
- ■ *A Woman Among Wild Men*, 1938; *The Women of New Zealand*, 1940.

BROWNE, HOWARD (1908-   ) *U.S.*
Born: Omaha, Nebraska
Served as editor of *Amazing Stories* and *Fantastic Adventures* in the 1940s, and was first editor of *Fantastic Magazine*, all Ziff-Davis publications.
as Alexander Blade [house pseudonym]
Carbon-Copy Killer. *Amazing*, July 1943
as William Brengle [house pseudonym]
Return To Lilliput. *Fantastic Adventures*, May 1943
The Star Shepherd. *Fantastic Adventures*, 1943
as Howard Browne
Warrior of the Dawn. *Amazing*, Dec 1942
Warrior of the Dawn, the Adventures of Tharn. Chicago: Reilly & Lee, [1943], 286pp.
Return of the Tharn. Providence, Rhode Island: Grandon, 1956, 253pp. (500 cop)
as H. B. Carleton [house pseudonym]
They Gave Him A Rope. *Fantastic Adventures*, March 1943
as Lawrence Chandler
Forgotten Worlds. *Fantastic Adventures*, May 1948
[all stories under this name probably by Browne]
as John Evans
- ☐ *Andrew's Harvest*, 1933. MYSTERY: "Paul Pine" series of detective novels beginning with *Halo in Blood*, 1946; also *If You Have Tears*, 1947; *Halo for Satan*, 1948; *Halo in Brass*, 1949.
as Lee Francis [house pseudonym]
The Man From Yesterday. *Fantastic Adventures*, Aug 1948
as Peter Phillips [house pseudonym]
Field Study. *Galaxy*, April 1951
At No Extra Cost. *Marvel*, Aug 1951
She Who Laughs. *Galaxy*, April 1952
Lost Memory. *Galaxy*, May 1952

Criteria. *Planet Stories*, May 1952
University. *Galaxy*, April 1953
Lila. *Startling Stories*, April 1953
Sylvia. *Fantasy Magazine*, June 1953
The Warning. *Magazine of Fantasy and Science Fiction*, Sept 1953
c/o Mr. Makepeace. *Magazine of Fantasy and Science Fiction*, Feb 1954
First Man In the Moon. *Magazine of Fantasy and Science Fiction*, Sept 1954
Variety Agent. *Infinity*, June 1956
Next Stop the Moon. *New Worlds #67*, Jan 1958 (Br.)
as John X. Pollard [house pseudonym]
The Strange Mission of Arthur Pendran. *Fantastic Adventures*, June 1944

BROWNE, THOMAS A(lexander) (1826-1915) *Australian*
Born: London, England
as Rolfe Boldrewood
The Ghost Camp; or, The Avengers. London: Macmillan, 1902, 397pp.
- ☐ *Robbery Under Arms*, 1888; *The Squatter's Dream*, 1890; *Nevermore*, 1892; *In Bad Company*, 1901. *ss col*

BROWNELL, ANNA GERTRUDE (Hall) (Mrs.) (1863- ?) *U.S.*
Born: Boston, Massachusetts
as Gertrude Hall
Far From Today. Boston: Roberts Bros., 1892, 291pp.
Foam of the Sea and Other Tales. Boston: Roberts Bros., 1895, 299pp. *ss col*
The Hundred and Other Stories. NY: Harper, 1898, 255pp., ill. *ss col*
- ☐ *Age of Fairygold*, 1899 (poetry); *Aurora the Magnificent*, 1917; *Miss Ingalis*, 1918.

BROWNING, DAPHNE DU MAURIER (Mrs. Frederick A. M.) (1907-   ) *British*
Born: London
as Daphne du Maurier
The Progress of Julius. London: Heinemann, [1933], 304pp.
My Cousin Rachel. London: Gollancz, 1951, 352pp.
The Apple Tree. London: Gollancz, 1952, 264pp.
The House On the Strand, 1969.
Echoes from the Macabre, 1976.
- ☐ *The Loving Spirit*, 1931; *Jamaica Inn*, 1936; *Rebecca*, 1938; *Frenchman's Creek*, 1942.
- ■ *Gerald, A Portrait*, 1934; *The du Mauriers*, 1937.

BRUCE, KENNETH (1876-1916)
as Diedrick Crayon, Jr.
The Return of the Half-Moon. NY: Broadway Publishing Co., 1909, 147pp., ill.

BRUECKEL, FRANCIS J.
as Frank J. Bridge
The Mechanical Bloodhound. *Wonder Stories*, 1930
as Frank (J.) Brueckel, (Jr.)
The Moon Men. *Amazing*, Nov 1928

BRULLER, JEAN (Marcel) (1902-   ) *French*
Bruller's pseudonym is derived from his code name in the French resistance during World War II.
as Vercors
Les Animaux denatures. Paris: A. Michel, 1952.
You Shall Know Them. Boston: Little, Brown, 1953, 249pp.
Sylva. Paris: Editions Bernard Grasset, 1961.
Sylva. NY: Putnam, 1962, 256pp.
- ☐ *Put Out the Light*, 1942; *Guiding Star*, 1943.

BRUNNER, JOHN (Kilian Houston) (1934-   ) *British*
Born: Oxfordshire

as John Brunner

The Talisman. *Science Fantasy*, Sept 1955 (Br.)

Threshold of Eternity. NY: Ace, [1959], 148pp., paper. (Ace Double D 335)

The 100th Millenium. NY: Ace, [1959], 110pp., paper. (Ace Double D362)

The Brink. London: Gollancz, 1959, 192pp.

Echo In the Skull. NY: Ace, [1959], 94pp., paper. (Ace Double D385)

The World Swappers. NY: Ace, [1959], 153pp., paper. (Ace Double D 391)

Slavers of Space. NY: Ace, [1960], 118pp., paper. (Ace Double D421)

The Skynappers. NY: Ace, [1960], 117pp., paper. (Ace Double D 457)

The Atlantic Abomination. NY: Ace, [1960], 128pp., paper. (Ace Double D 465)

Sanctuary In the Sky. NY: Ace, [1960], 122pp., paper. (Ace Double D 471)

Meeting At Infinity. NY: Ace, [1961], 155pp., paper. (Ace Double D 507)

Secret Agent of Terra. NY: Ace, [1962], 127pp., paper. (Ace Double F133)

The Super Barbarians. NY: Ace, [1962], 160pp., paper.

Times Without Number. NY: Ace, [1962], 139pp., paper. (Ace Double F 161)

No Future In It. London: Gollancz, 1962, 192pp. *ss col*

The Dreaming Earth. NY: Pyramid, [1963], 159pp., paper.

Listen! The Stars! NY: Ace, [1963], 96pp., paper. (Ace Double F 215)

The Astronauts Must Not Land. NY: Ace, [1963], 148pp., paper. (Ace Double F 227)

The Space-Time Juggler. NY: Ace, [1963], 84pp., paper. (Ace Double F 227)

Castaways' World. NY: Ace, [1963], 127pp., paper. (Ace Double F 242)

The Rites of Ohe. NY: Ace, [1963], 129pp., paper. (Ace Double F 242)

To Conquer Chaos. NY: Ace, [1964], 192pp., paper.

Endless Shadow. NY: Ace, [1964], 97pp., paper. (Ace Double F 299)

The Whole Man. NY: Ballantine, [1964], 188pp., paper.

Enigma From Tantalus. NY: Ace, [1965], 102pp., paper. (Ace Double M 115)

The Repairman of Cyclops. NY: Ace, [1965], 150pp., paper. (Ace Double M 115)

The Altar on Asconel. NY: Ace [1965], 143pp., paper. (Ace Double M 123)

Now Then! London: Mayflower, [1965], 143pp., paper

The Day of the Star Cities. NY: Ace, [1965], 158pp., paper.

The Long Result. London: Faber, 1965, 204pp.

The Squares of the City. NY: Ballantine, [1965], 319pp., paper.

No Other Gods But Me. London: Compact, [1966], 159pp., paper. *3 novellas*

A Planet of Your Own. NY: Ace, [1966], 99pp., paper. (Ace Double G 592)

Out of My Mind. NY: Ballantine, [1967], 220pp., paper. *ss col*

The Productions of Time. NY: Signet, [1967], 139pp., paper.

Born Under Mars. NY: Ace, [1967], 127pp., paper. (Ace Double G 664)

Quicksand. Garden City: Doubleday, 1967, 240pp.

Not Before Time. London: 4 Square, 1968, 128pp., paper. *ss col*

Bedlam Planet. NY: Ace, [1968], 159pp., paper. (Ace Double G 709)

Into the Slave Nebula. NY: Lancer, 1968, 176pp., paper.

Father of Lies. NY: Belmont, [1968], paper. (Belmont Double)

Catch A Falling Star. NY: Ace, [1968], 158pp., paper.

Stand on Zanzibar. Garden City: Doubleday, 1968, 505pp.

The Jagged Orbit. NY: Ace, [c.1969], 343pp., paper.

Black Is The Color. NY: Pyramid, [c.1969], 189pp., paper.

The Evil That Men Do. NY: Belmont, [1969], 173pp., paper. (Belmont Double)

Time Scoop. NY: Dell, [1969], 156pp., paper.

The Avengers of Carrig. NY: Dell, [1969], 157pp., paper.

The Devil's Work. NY: Norton, [1970], 365pp.

The Wrong End of Time. Garden City: Doubleday, 1971, 204pp.

The Traveler In Black. NY: Ace, [1971], 222pp., paper.

From This Day Forward. Garden City: Doubleday, 1972, 238pp.

The Sheep Look Up. NY: Harper, 1972, 461pp.

Total Eclipse. Garden City: Doubleday, 1974, 187pp.

The Dramaturges of Yan. NY: Ace, [1972], 157pp., paper.

The Stone That Never Came Down. Garden City: Doubleday, 1973, 206pp.

From This Day Foreward. NY: DAW, [1973], 176pp., paper.

☐ *Life In A Explosive Forming Press,* 1970; MYSTERY: *A Plague on Both Your Causes,* 1969; *Honky In the Woodpile,* 1971.

as K. Houston Brunner

Brainpower. *Nebula #2,* Spring 1953 (Br.)

as John Loxmith.

Thou Good and Faithful. *Astounding,* March 1953

as Trevor Staines

Negative Proof. *Science Fantasy #17,* Feb 1956 (Br.)

as Keith Woodcott

No Future In It. *Science Fantasy #15,* Sept 1955 (Br.)

I Speak For Earth. NY: Ace, [1961], 120pp., paper. (Ace Double D 498)

The Ladder In the Sky. NY: Ace, [1962], 137pp., paper. (Ace Double F 141)

The Psionic Menace. NY: Ace, [1963], 108pp., paper. (Ace Double F 199)

The Martian Sphinx. NY: Ace, [1965], 149pp., paper.

BUCHAN, JOHN   (1st Baron Tweedsmuir [from 1935])
(1875-1940) *British*
Born: Perth, Scotland
Autobiography: *Pilgrim's Way,* 1940.

as John Buchan

Grey Weather. Moorland Tales of My Own People. London: Lane, 1899, 297pp. *ss col*

The Watcher By the Threshold and Other Tales. Edinburgh: Blackwood, 1902, 334pp. *ss col*

Prester John. London: T. Nelson, [1910], 376pp.

The Moon Endureth: Tales and Fancies. Edinburgh: Blackwood, 1912, 324pp. *ss col*

The Dancing Floor. Boston: Houghton & Mifflin, [1926], 311pp.

Witch Wood. London: Hodder & Stoughton, [1927], 380pp.

The Runagates Club. London: Hodder & Stoughton, [1928], 331pp. *ss col*

The Blanket of the Dark. Boston: Houghton & Mifflin, 1931, 301pp.

The Magic Walking Stick. NY: Houghton & Mifflin, 1932, 176pp., ill.

☐ *John Burnet of Barns,* 1898; *Greenmantle,* 1916; *John Macnab,* 1925. MYSTERY: *The 39 Steps,* 1915.

as Cadmus and Harmonia [in collaboration with Susan Buchan]

The Island of Sheep. London: Hodder & Stoughton, 1919, 193pp.

as Douglas Erskine

A Bit of Atlantis. Montreal: A. T. Chapman, 1900, 197pp. [ascribed by some bibliographies to John Buchan, unconfirmed]

BUCHAN, SUSAN (1882-   )
as Cadmus and Harmonia [in collaboration with John Buchan]
The Island of Sheep. London: Hodder & Stoughton, 1919, 193pp.

BUCK, JAMES S. (1812-1892) *U.S.*
as James S. Buck
☐ *An Historical Poem, Milwaukee's Early Days,* 1874 (poetry)
■ *Pioneer History of Milwaukee,* 1876-1886.
as Ichabod
The Address With Which Ichabod Explains His Post-Centennial Position. Milwaukee, Wisconsin, 1876.
as The Prophet James
The Chronicle of the Land of Columbia. Milwaukee, Wisconsin: F. W. Stearns, 1876, 112pp.

BUDRYS, ALGIRDAS JONAS (1931-   ) *naturalized U.S.*
Born: Konigsberg, East Prussia
as Algis Budrys
The High Purpose. Astounding, Nov 1952
False Night. London: Lion, 1954, 127pp., paper.
Man of Earth. NY: Ballantine, [1958], 144pp., paper.
Who? NY: Pyramid, [1958], 157pp., paper.
The Falling Torch. NY: Pyramid, [1959], 158pp., paper.
The Unexpected Dimension. NY: Ballantine, [1960], 159pp. paper. *ss col*
Rogue Moon. Greenwich, Connecticut: Fawcett Gold Medal, [1960], 176pp., paper.
Some Will Not Die. Evanston, Illinois: Regency, 1961, 159pp., paper. [*False Night* expanded]
Budrys' Inferno. NY: Berkley, 1963, 160pp., paper. *ss col*
The Amsirs and the Iron Thorn. Greenwich, Connecticut: Fawcett Gold Medal, 1967, 159pp., paper.
as David C. Hodgkins
Between the Dark and the Daylight. Infinity SF, Oct 1958
as Ivan Janvier
Thing. Fantastic Universe, March 1955
as Paul Janvier
Nobody Bothers Gus. Astounding, Nov 1955
as Robert Marner
There Ain't No Other Roads. Venture, March 1958
as Alger Rome [in collaboration with Drexel J. Bixby]
Underestimation. Rocket Stories, Sept 1953
as William Scarff
Fire God. Rocket Stories, July 1953
as John A. Sentry
Thunderbolt. Fantastic Universe, April 1955
as Albert Stroud
Contact Between Equals. Venture, July 1958
● Harold Van Dall

BULMER, H(enry) KENNETH (1912-   ) *English*
Born: London
● **as Alan Burt Akers**
Transit to Scorpio. NY: DAW #33, [1972], 190pp., paper.
The Suns of Scorpio. NY: DAW #49, [1973], 192pp., paper.
Warrior of Scorpio. NY: DAW #65, [1973], paper.
Swordships of Scorpio. NY: DAW #81, [1973], 191pp., paper.
Prince of Scorpio. NY: DAW #97, [1974], paper.
Man Hounds of Antares. NY: DAW #113, [1974], paper.
Arena of Antares. NY: DAW #129, [1974], paper.
Flyers of Antares. NY: DAW #145, [1975], paper.
Bladesman of Antares. NY: DAW #159, [1975], paper.
Avenger of Antares. NY: DAW #173, [1975], paper.
Armanda of Antares. NY: DAW #189, [1976], paper.
The Tides of Kregen. NY: DAW #204, [1976], paper.
Renegades of Kregen. NY: DAW #221, [1977], paper.
Krozair of Kregen. NY: DAW, [1977], paper
Secret Scorpio. NY: DAW #269, [1977], paper.
Savage Scorpio. NY: DAW #285, [1978], paper.
Captive Scorpio. NY: DAW, [1978], paper.
Golden Scorpio. NY: DAW #317, [1978], 207pp., paper.
as (H.) Ken(neth) Bulmer
First Down. Authentic, 1954
(with A. V. Clarke) *Space Treason.* London: Hamilton, 1952, 112pp., paper.
(with A. V. Clarke) *Cybernetic Controller.* London: Hamilton, 1952, 112pp., paper.
Encounter In Space. London: Panther, [1952], 128pp., paper.
The Stars Are Ours. London: Panther, [1953], 158pp., paper.
Space Salvage. London: Panther, [1953], 143pp., paper.
Galactic Intrigue. London: Panther, [1953], 160pp., paper.
Empire of Chaos. London: Panther, [1953], 158pp., paper.
Challenge. London: Curtis Warren, [1954], 160pp., paper.
World Aflame. London: Panther, [1954], 144pp., paper.
City Under the Sea. NY: Ace, [1957], 175pp., paper. (Ace Double D 255)
The Secret of Z. NY: Ace, [1958], 161pp., paper. (Ace Double D 331)
The Changeling Worlds. NY: Ace, [1959], 145pp., paper. (Ace Double D 369)
The Earthgods Are Coming. NY: Ace, [1960], 107pp., paper. (Ace Double D 453)
Beyond the Silver Sky. NY: Ace, [1961], 100pp., paper. (Ace Double D 507)
No Man's World. NY: Ace, [1961], 128pp., paper. (Ace Double F 104)
The Fatal Fire. London: Digit, [1962], 160pp., paper.
The Wizard of Starship Poseidon. NY: Ace, 1963, 124pp., paper. (Ace Double F 209)
The Million Year Hunt. NY: Ace, [1964], 133pp., paper. (Ace Double F 285)
Demon's World. NY: Ace, [1964], 139pp., paper. (Ace Double F 289)
Land Beyond The Map. NY: Ace, [1965], 136pp., paper. (Ace Double M 111)
Behold The Stars. NY: Ace, [1965], 120pp., paper. (Ace Double M131)
Worlds For the Taking. NY: Ace, [1966], 159pp., paper. (Ace Double F 396)
To Outrun Doomsday. NY: Ace, [1967], 159pp., paper. (Ace Double G 625)
The Key to Irunium. NY: Ace, [1967], 138pp., paper. (Ace Double H 20)
The Key to Venudine. NY: Ace, [1968], 122pp., paper. (Ace Double H 65)
The Doomsday Men. Garden City: Doubleday, 1968, 207pp.
The Star Ventures. NY: Ace, [1969], 124pp., paper. (Ace Double 22600)
The Ships of Durostorum. NY: Ace, [1970], 101pp., paper. (Ace Double 76096)
The Hunters of Jundagai. NY: Ace, [1971], 111pp., paper. (Ace Double 68310)
The Chariots of Ra. NY: Ace, [1972], 130pp., paper. (Ace Double 10293)
On the Symb-Socket Circuit. NY: Ace, [1972], 174pp., paper. (Ace Double 63165)
Roller-Coaster World. NY: Ace, [1972], 173pp., paper.
as Kenneth Johns [in collaboration with John Newman]
■ *The True Book About Space Travel,* 1960.
as Philip Kent
Mission To the Stars. London: Pearson, 1953.
Vassals of Venus. London: Pearson, 1953.
as Karl Maras
Zhorani. London: Comyns, 1953.
Peril From Space. London: Gaywood, 1955.

as Nelson Sherwood
Galactic Galapagos. *Science Fiction Adventures #6*, Jan 1959
as Tully Zetford
Whirlpool of Stars. NY: Pinnacle, [1975], paper.
The Boosted Man. NY: Pinnacle, [1975], paper.
Star City. NY: Pinnacle, [1975], paper.
The Virility Gene. NY: Pinnacle, [1976], paper.
● **Ernest Corley, H. Philip Stratford**

BURGH, JAMES   (1714–1775)
as J. Vander Neck
An Account of the First Settlement, Laws, Form of Government, and Police, of the Cessares, a People of South America: in Nine Letters, from Mr. Vander Neck, One of the Senators of that Nation, to His Friend in Holland. London: J. Payne, 1764, 121pp.
■ *The Dignity of Human Nature,* 1752; *The Art of Speaking,* 1761.

BURKE, JOHN FREDERICK   (1922–   )   *English*
Born: Rye, Sussex
as John (Frederick) Burke
□ *Swift Summer,* 1949; *The Outward Walls,* 1952 [1951]; *The Angry Silence,* 1961; *Beautiful Britain,* 1976.
as Jonathan Burke
Chessboard. *New Worlds #19,* Jan 1953 (Br.)
Dark Gateway. London: Hamilton, 1953, 223pp.
The Echoing Worlds. London: Panther, 1953, 159pp.
The Twilight of Reason. London: Panther, 1954, 159pp.
Hotel Cosmos. London: Panther, 1954, 142pp.
Pattern of Shadows. London: Museum Press, 1954, 128pp.
Revolt of the Humans. 1955.
Deep Freeze. 1955.
Alien Landscapes. 1955.
Pursuit Through Time. London: Ward, Lock, 1956, 187pp.
□ MYSTERY: *The Weekend Girls,* 1966.
● **Jonathan George, Joanna Jones, Robert Miall, Sara Morris, Martin Sands**

BURKHARDT, EVE (Mrs. Robert F.)
as Adam Bliss [in collaboration with Robert F. Burkhardt]
□MYSTERY: *The Camden Ruby Mystery,* 1931; *Murder Upstairs,* 1934; *Four Times A Widower,* 1936.
as Rob Eden [in collaboration with Robert F. Burkhardt]
□ *Heartbreak Girl,* 1931; *Fickle,* 1933; *Golden Goddess,* 1935; *Daughters Who Dare,* 1943.
as Rex Jardin [in collaboration with Robert F. Burkhardt]
The Devil's Mansion. NY: The Fiction League, 1931, 291pp.

BURKHARDT, ROBERT F(erdinand)   (1892–1947)
as Adam Bliss [in collaboration with Eve Burkhardt]
see **EVE BURKHARDT**
as Rob Eden [in collaboration with Eve Burkhardt]
see **EVE BURKHARDT**
as Rex Jardin [in collaboration with Eve Burkhardt]
The Devil's Mansion. NY: The Fiction League, 1931, 291pp.

BURKITT, FREDERICK EVELYN
as Author of "The Terror by Night"[in collaboration with G. C. S. Saben]
□ *The Co-Respondent,* 1912.
as Gregory Saben [in collaboration with G. C. S. Saben]
The Terror by Night. London: Newnes, [1912], 316pp.
The Sorcerer. London: J. Richmond, [1918], 316pp.
□ *Born of A Woman,* 1913.

BURKS, ARTHUR J.   (1898–1974)   *U.S.*
as Arthur J. Burks
Luisma's Return. *Weird Tales,* Jan 1925
Monsters of Mayen. *Astounding,* April 1930

The Great Amen. NY: Egmont Press, [1938], 231pp.
Look Behind You. Buffalo, New York: Shroud, 1954, 73pp., ill., paper. (650 cop) *ss col*
Black Medicine. Sauk City, Wisconsin: Arkham House, 1966, 308pp. (1952 cop)
□ (with Bess B. Loomis) *The Return of Benjamin Franklin.* 1955.
■ *Bells Above the Amazon,* 1951.
as Estil Critchie
Thus Spake the Prophetess. *Weird Tales,* Nov 1924
as Burke MacArthur
□ *Rivers Into Wilderness,* 1932.
✓ **Spencer Whitney**

BURRAGE, ALFRED M(c Lelland)   (1899–1956)   *British*
Born: Hillingdon, Middlesex
as A. M. Burrage
Some Ghost Stories. London: C. Palmer, [1927], 276pp. *ss col*
Seeker to the Dead. London: Swan, 1942, 188pp.
Don't Break the Seal. London: Swan, 1946, 159pp.
Between the Minute and the Hour. London: H. Jenkins, 1967, 221pp.
□ *The Golden Barrier,* 1925; *Poor Dear Esme,* 1925; *The Smokes of Spring,* 1926.
as Ex-Private X
Someone In the Room. London: Jarrolds, [1931], 285pp. *ss col*
□ *War is War,* 1930.

BURROUGHS, EDGAR RICE   (1875–1950)   *U.S.*
Born: Chicago, Illinois
Biography: *Edgar Rice Burroughs, the Man Who Created Tarzan,* by Irwin Porges, 1975.
Bibliography: *Golden Anniversary Bibliography of E. R. B.,* by Rev. H. Heins, 1964.
as Norman Bean
Under the Moons of Mars. *All Story Weekly,* Feb-July 1912.
as Edgar Rice Burroughs
Tarzan of the Apes. *All Story Weekly,* Oct 1912
Tarzan of the Apes. Chicago: McClurg, 1914, 400pp., front.
The Return of Tarzan. Chicago: McClurg, 1915, 365pp., ill.
The Beasts of Tarzan. Chicago: McClurg, 1916, 336pp., ill.
The Son of Tarzan. Chicago: McClurg, 1917, 394pp., ill.
A Princess of Mars. Chicago: McClurg, 1917, 326pp., ill.
Tarzan and the Jewels of Opar. Chicago: McClurg, 1918, 350pp., ill.
The Gods of Mars. Chicago: McClurg, 1918, 348pp., front.
The Jungle Tales of Tarzan. Chicago: McClurg, 1919, 319pp., ill. *ss col*
The Warlord of Mars. Chicago: McClurg, 1919, 296pp., front.
Thuvia, Maid of Mars. Chicago, McClurg, 1920, 256pp., ill.
Tarzan the Untamed. Chicago: McClurg, 1920, 428pp., ill.
Tarzan the Terrible. Chicago: McClurg, 1921, 408pp., ill.
The Mucker. Chicago: McClurg, 1921, 414pp., ill.
The Chessmen of Mars. Chicago: McClurg, 1922, 375pp., ill.
At the Earth's Core. Chicago: McClurg, 1922, 277pp., ill.
Tarzan and the Golden Lion. Chicago: McClurg, 1923, 333pp., ill.
Pellucidar. Chicago: McClurg, 1923, 322pp., ill.
The Land That Time Forgot. Chicago: McClurg, 1924, 422pp., ill.
Tarzan and the Ant Men. Chicago: McClurg, 1924, 346pp. front.
The Eternal Lover. Chicago: McClurg, 1925, 316pp., front.
The Cave Girl. Chicago: McClurg, 1925, 323pp., front.
The Moon Maid. Chicago: McClurg, 1926, 412pp., front.
The Mad King. Chicago: McClurg, 1926, 365pp.
The Tarzan Twins. Joliet, Illinois: P. F. Volland Co., [c.1927], 126pp., ill.

Tarzan, Lord of the Jungle. Chicago: McClurg, 1928, 377pp.

The Mastermind of Mars. Chicago: McClurg, 1928, 312pp., ill.

The Monster Men. Chicago: McClurg, 1929, 304pp.

Tarzan and the Lost Empire. NY: Metropolitan Books, 1929, 313pp.

Tarzan at the Earth's Core. NY: Metropolitan Books, [1930], 301pp., front.

Tanar of Pellucidar. NY: Metropolitan Books, [1930], 312pp., front.

A Fighting Man of Mars. NY: Metropolitan Books, [1931], 319pp., front.

Tarzan the Invincible. Tarzana, California: Burroughs, [1931], 318pp., front.

Tarzan Triumphant. Tarzana, California: Burroughs, [1932], 318pp.

Jungle Girl. Tarzana, California: Burroughs, [1932], 318pp., ill.

Tarzan and the City of Gold. Tarzana, California: Burroughs, [1933], 316pp., ill.

Tarzan and the Lion Man. Tarzana, California: Burroughs, [1934], 318pp., ill.

Pirates of Venus. Tarzana, California: Burroughs, [1934], 314pp., ill.

Tarzan and the Leopard Men. Tarzana, California: Burroughs, [1935], 332pp., ill.

Lost on Venus. Tarzana, California: Burroughs, [1935], 318pp., ill.

Swords of Mars. Tarzana, California: Burroughs, [1936], 315pp., ill.

Tarzan's Quest. Tarzana, California: Burroughs, [1936], 318pp., ill.

Back to the Stone Age. Tarzana, California: Burroughs, [1937], 318pp., ill.

The Lad and the Lion. Tarzana, California: Burroughs, [1938], 317pp., ill.

Tarzan and the Forbidden City. Tarzana, California: Burroughs, [1938], 315pp., ill.

Carson of Venus. Tarzana, California: Burroughs, [1939], 312pp., ill.

Tarzan the Magnificent. Tarzana, California: Burroughs, [1939], 318pp., ill.

Synthetic Men of Mars. Tarzana, California: Burroughs, [1940], 315pp., ill.

The Land of Terror. Tarzana, California: Burroughs, [1944], 319pp.

Escape On Venus. Tarzana, California: Burroughs, [1946], 347pp., ill.

Tarzan and the Foreign Legion. Tarzana, California: Burroughs, [1947].

Llana of Gathol. Tarzana, California: Burroughs, [1948], 317pp., ill.

Beyond Thirty and the Man Eater. South Ozone Park, NY: Science & Fantasy Publications, 1957, 229pp.

At the Earth's Core. NY: Canaveral, 1962, 159pp., ill. (reprint)

Back to the Stone Age. NY: Canaveral, 1963, 318pp., ill. (reprint)

Savage Pellucidar. NY: Canaveral, 1963, 274pp., ill. (reprint)

Tarzan and the Tarzan Twins. NY: Canaveral, 1963, 192pp., ill. (reprint)

Beyond the Farthest Star. NY: Ace, [1964], 125pp. paper.

John Carter of Mars. NY: Canaveral, [1964], 208pp., ill.

Tarzan and the Madman. NY: Canaveral, [1964], 236pp., ill.

Tales of Three Planets. NY: Canaveral, [1964], 283pp., ill.

☐ *The Girl From Hollywood,* 1923; *The Bandit of Hell's Bend,* 1925; *Apache Devil,* 1933; *The Oakdale Affair, the Rider,* 1937; *The Deputy Sheriff of Comanche County,* 1940; *I Am A Barbarian,* 1967.

⌐ **John Tyler McCulloch**

BURROUGHS, WILLIAM S(eward) (1914-   ) *U.S.*
as William S. Burroughs

The Naked Lunch. Paris: Olympia, 1959, paper. (on back cover "francs: 1,500)

The Soft Machine. Paris: Olympia, 1961, paper. (on back cover "15 NF")

The Ticket That Exploded. Paris: Olympia, 1962, paper.

Nova Express. NY: Grove, 1964, 187pp.

as William Lee

Junkie. NY: Ace, 1953, paper. (Ace Double with *Narcotics Agent* by M. Helbrand)

BURSTENBINDER, ELISABETH (1838-1918) *German*
as E. Werner

Vineta, The Phantom City. NY: Dodd Mead, [1876].

The Fairy of the Alps. NY: G. Munro, [1889], 285pp.

☐ *"Good Luck!"* 1874; *No Surrender,* 1881; *A Judgement of God,* 1889; *The Master of Ettersberg,* 1891; *The Stolen Veil,* 1892.

BURTON, ALICE ELIZABETH (1908-   ) *British*
Born: Cairo, Egypt
as Elizabeth Burton

☐ *Cling To Her, Waiting,* 1939.

as Susan (Alice) Kerby

Miss Carter and the Ifrit. London: Hutchinson, [1945], 160pp.

The Roaring Dove. NY: Dodd, Mead, 1948, 260pp.

Mr. Kronion. London: Laurie, [1949], 223pp.

☐ *Fortnight In Frascati,* 1940; *Fortune's Gift,* 1947.

BURTON, RICHARD FRANCIS (Sir) (1821-1920) *British*
as Richard Francis Burton

(translator) *Vikram and the Vampire; or, tales of Hindu Deviltry.* London: Longmans, Green & Co., 1870.

■ *Scinde; or, the Unhappy Valley,* 1851; *Wit and Wisdom from West Africa,* 1865; *Zanzibar,* 1872.

as F. B.

The Kasidah of Haji Abdu al-Yazdi, 1880.

BURTON, ROBERT (1577-1640) *English*
as Democritus Junior

The Anatomy of Melancholy. Oxford: Printed by Iohn Lichfield and Iames Short for H. Cripps, 1621, 783pp. (contains "An Utopia of My Own")

BYRNE, S(tuart) J(ames) *U.S.*
as John Bloodstone

The Land Beyond the Lens. *Amazing,* March 1952

as S(tuart) J. Byrne

The Music of the Spheres. *Amazing,* Aug 1935

as Howard Dare

The Ultimate Death. *Other Worlds,* July 1952

as Marx Kaye [house pseudonym]

Mystery of the Peruvian Giants. *Amazing,* June 1947 article

CABET, ETIENNE (1788-1856) *French*
Born: Dijon, Cote-d'Or
as Francis Adams
Voyage et Aventures de Lord Williams Garisdall en Icarie, Traduits de Francis Adams, Par Th. Dufruit. Paris: Souverain, 1840, 2 vol. [the translator is apocryphal]
as Etienne Cabet
Voyage en Icarie. Paris: J. Mallet, 1842, 566pp.
■ *Colony, or Republic of Icaria in the United States of America, Its History.* Nauvoo, Illinois: Icarian Printing Office, 1852, 19pp.; *Colonie Icarienne aux Etats-Unis d' Amerique. Sa constitution ses lois, sa situation materielle et morale, apres le premier semestre 1855.* Paris: Chez l'auteur, 1856, 239pp.

CALLENBACH, FRANZ (1663-1743)
as Vermelio Wurmsaam
Wurmland nach Lands-Art, Regiment, Religion, Sitten und Lebens-Wandel. . . Im Gast-Haus zum Regenwurm [Nuremberg]: Im Jahr da es Wurmstichig War [1710?], 127pp.

CAMERON, ELIZABETH DOROTHEA COLE BOWEN (Mrs. Alan C.) (1889-1973) *Irish*
Born: Dublin
as Elizabeth Bowen
Encounters. London: Sidgwick & Jackson, 1923, 203pp. *ss col*
Joining Charles and Other Stories. London: Constable, [1929], 216pp. *ss col*
The Cat Jumps and Other Stories. London: Gollancz, [1934], 285pp. *ss col*
Look At All Those Roses. London: Gollancz, [1941], 263pp. *ss col*
The Demon Lover, and Other Stories. London: Jonathan Cape, [1945], 189pp. *ss col*
Stories By Elizabeth Bowen. NY: Vintage, 1959, 306pp., paper. *ss col*
□ *The Hotel,* 1927; *The Last September,* 1929; *To the North,* 1932; *Death of the Heart,* 1938.
■ *Anthony Trollope,* 1946; *Collected Impressions,* 1950.

CAMPBELL, JOHN RAMSEY (1946-   ) *English*
Born: Liverpool
as (J.) Ramsey Campbell
The Church In High Street. in *Dark Mind, Dark Heart* edited by August Derleth. Sauk City, Wisconsin: Arkham House, 1962, 249pp. (2493 cop)
The Inhabitant of the Lake and Less Welcome Tenants. Sauk City, Wisconsin: Arkham House, 1964, 207pp. (2009 cop) *ss col*
Demons By Daylight. Sauk City, Wisconsin: Arkham House, 1973, 153pp. (3500 cop) *ss col*
The Doll Who Ate His Mother. Indianapolis: Bobbs-Merrill, [c.1976], 209pp.
The Height of the Scream. Sauk City, Wisconsin: Arkham House, 1976, 229pp.
as Carl Dreadstone
The Wolfman. 1977.
Bride of Frankenstein. 1977.
Dracula's Daughter. 1977.

as Errol Undercliffe
probable fantasy pseudonym in Fanzine *Spirited*
✓ **Montgomery Comfort**

CAMPBELL, JOHN W(ood) (Jr.) (1910-1971) *U.S.*
Born: Newark, New Jersey
as John W. Campbell, (Jr.)
When The Atoms Failed. *Amazing,* Jan 1930
The Mightiest Machine. Providence, Rhode Island: Hadley, [1947], 228pp., ill.
Who Goes There? Chicago: Shasta, 1948, 230pp. *ss col*
The Incredible Planet. Reading, Pennsylvania: Fantasy Press, [1949], 344pp.
The Moon Is Hell. Reading, Pennsylvania: Fantasy Press, 1951, 256pp.
The Cloak of Aesir. Chicago: Shasta, [1952], 254pp.
The Black Star Passes. Reading, Pennsylvania: Fantasy Press, [1953], 254pp.
Islands of Space. Reading, Pennsylvania: Fantasy Press, [1956], 224pp.
Invaders from the Infinite. Reading, Pennsylvania: Fantasy Press, [1961], 189pp. (300 cop)
The Planeteers. NY: Ace, [1966], 150pp., paper. (Ace Double G 585)
The Ultimate Weapon. NY: Ace, [1966], 106pp., paper. (Ace Double G 585)
■ *The Atomic Story,* 1947; *Collected Editorials From Analog,* 1966.
as Arthur McCann [for non-fiction]
Stress Fluid. *Astounding,* June 1937 *article*
as Don A. Stuart
Twilight. *Astounding,* Nov 1934
Who Goes There? *Astounding,* Aug 1938
as Karl Van Campen
The Irrelevant. *Astounding,* Dec 1934

CANADY, JOHN
● **Mathew Head**

CANEDO, ALEJANDRO
as Alejandro
Covers for *Astounding,* 1946-1949

CAPLIN, ALFRED GERALD (1909-   )
as Al Capp
L'il Abner in The Time Capsule. *Satellite,* Aug 1957
□ *Life and Times of Shmoo,* 1948; *Fearless Fosdick,* 1956; *Al Capp's Bald Iggle,* 1956.

CAPPS, CARROLL M. (1917-1971)
as Carroll M. Capps
The Judas Bug. *Analog,* Oct 1967
Secret of the Sunless World. NY: Dell, 1969, paper.
as C.C. MacApp
A Pride of Islands. *If,* May 1960
Omha Abides. NY: Paperback Library, 1968, 160pp., paper.

CARAS, ROGER ANDREW (1928-   ) *U.S.*
Born: Methuen, Massachusetts
as Roger Caras
■ NATURE: *Creatures of the Night,* 1972; *The Boundary: Land and Sea,* 1972; *Going to the Zoo with Roger Caras,* 1973; *The Wonderful World of Mammals,* 1973, *The Venomous Animals,* 1974; *The Bizarre Animals,* 1974; *Skunk For A Day,* 1976.
as Roger Sarac
The Throwbacks. NY: Belmont, 1965, 140pp., paper.

CARLETON, H. B. [house pseudonym]
unattributed
Hard Guy. *Amazing,* Nov 1942

by Howard Browne
They Gave Him A Rope. *Fantastic Adventures*, March 1943

CARR, JOHN DICKSON (1906-   ) *U.S.*
Born: Uniontown, Pennsylvania
as John Dickson Carr
The Other Hangman. *Mysterious Traveler Magazine*, Nov 1951
The Burning Court. London: Hamilton, [1937], 318pp.
The Devil In Velvet. London: Hamilton, 1951, 352pp.
The Men Who Explained Miracles. NY: Harper, [1963], 182pp.
Most Secret. NY: Harper & Row, [1964], 235pp.
□ MYSTERY: *It Walks By Night*, 1930; *Poison In Jest*, 1932; *Hag's Nook*, 1933; *Scandal At High Chimneys*, 1959.
■ (with Adrian Conan Doyle) *The Life of Sir Arthur Conan Doyle*, 1949.
as Carr Dickson
□ *The Bowstring Murders*, 1933.
as Carter Dickson
The Department of Queer Complaints. London: Heinemann, 1940, 238pp.
Fear Is the Same. London: Morrow, 1956, 284pp.
□ *The Plague Court Murders*, 1934; *The Unicorn Murders*, 1935; *The Third Bullet*, 1937.
as Roger Fairbairn
□ HISTORICAL FICTION: *Devil Kinsmere*, 1934.

CARR, TERRY (1937-   ) *U.S.*
Born: Grant's Pass, Oregon
as Carl Brandon
Stanley Toothbrush. *Magazine of Fantasy and Science Fiction*, July 1962
as Terry Carr
Startling. *Startling Stories*, Dec 1952 *verse*
Who Supps With the Devil. *Magazine of Fantasy and Science Fiction*, May 1962
Warlord of Kor. NY: Ace, [1963], 97pp., paper. (Ace Double F 177)
as Norman Edwards [in collaboration with Theodore White]
Invasion from 2500. NY: Monarch, [1964], 126pp., paper.

CARREL, FREDERIC
as Author of "The Adventures of John Johns"
2010. London: Laurie, [1914], 249pp.
□ *The King and Isabella*, 1908.
as Frederic Carrel
The Adventures of John Johns. London: Laurie, 1897, 302pp.
□ *The Progress of Pauline Kessler*, 1900; *The Methods of Mr. Ames*, 1908.

CARRINGTON, HEREWARD HUBERT LAVINGTON
(1880-   ) *naturalized U.S.*
Born: Jersey, Channel Islands, England
as Hereward Carrington
(ed) *Week-End Book of Ghost Stories.* NY: Ives Washburn, 1953, 280pp.
■*Death Deferred*, 1912; *Modern Psychical Phenomena*, 1919; *Haunted People, Stories of the Poltergeist Down the Centuries*, 1951; *Psychic Oddities*, 1952; *Haunted People*, 1952; *The Case For Psychic Survival*, 1958; *The Phenomenon of Astral Projection*, 1961.
● **Nandor Fodor, Hubert Lavington.**

CARTER, JOHN FRANKLIN (1897-   ) *U.S.*
Born: Fall River, Massachusetts.
Autobiography: *The Rectory Family*, by John F. Carter. NY: Coward, McCann, 1937, 275pp.
as John Carter
■ *Conquest, America's Painless Imperialism*, 1928; *Man*

Is War, 1926.
as Diplomat
□ MYSTERY: *Murder In the State Department*, 1930; *The Corpse on the White House Lawn*, 1932; *Death In the Senate*, 1933.
as Jay Franklin
Champagne Charlie. NY: Duell, Sloan, Pearce, 1950, 190pp.
The Rat Race. Los Angeles: Fantasy Publishing Co., Inc. (FPCI), 1950, 371pp.
■ "We The People," Syndicated Newspaper Column; *La Guardia, A Biography*, 1937; *Remaking American*, 1942.
as Unofficial Observer
■ *The New Dealers*, 1934; *American Messiahs*, 1935.

CARTER, JOHN L(ouis) J(ustin) (1880-   )
as John L. Carter
□ *Dust*, 1917; *Come Day, Go Day*, 1922.
as Compton Irving
Daughter of Egypt. London: P. Allan, [1937], 253pp. [The NUC lists these names and titles as above. The BMC lists this author's real name as Compton Irving Carter, with the pseudonym of John L. Carter. The BMC does *not* list Compton Irving as a pseudonym of Compton Irving Carter. However, Compton Irving is listed, as though it were a real name, and with the entry for *Daughter of Egypt*. Compton Irving is also credited with a play (in the BMC) with the same name as one of the novels listed in the BMC for John L. Carter, i.e. *His Lady's Secretary.*]

CARTER, LIN(wood) (Vrooman) (1930-   ) *U.S.*
Born: St. Petersburg, Florida
as Lin Carter
(with Gordon Randall Garrett) Masters of the Metropolis. *Magazine of Fantasy and Science Fiction*, April 1957
The Wizard of Lemuria. NY: Ace, [1965], 127pp., paper.
Thongor of Lemuria. NY: Ace, [1966], 127pp., paper.
The Star Magicians. NY: Ace, [1966], 124pp., paper. (Ace Double G 588)
The Man Without A Planet. NY: Ace, [1966], 113pp., paper.
(with David Grinnell) *Destination Saturn.* NY: Avalon, 1967, 192pp.
The Flame of Iridar. NY: Belmont, [1967], 99pp., paper.
(with Robert E. Howard) *King Kull.* NY: Lancer, [1967], 223pp., paper. *ss col*
Thongor Against The Gods. NY: Paperback Library, [1967], 157pp., paper.
(with Robert E. Howard and L. Sprague de Camp) *Conan.* NY: Lancer, [1968], 221pp., paper. *ss col*
The Thief of Thoth. NY: Belmont, [1968], 85pp., paper. (Belmont Double)
(with Robert E. Howard and L. Sprague de Camp) *Conan of the Isles.* NY: Lancer, [1968], 189pp., paper.
Tower At the Edge of Time. NY: Belmont, [1968], 141pp., paper.
Thongor In the City of Magicians. NY: Paperback Library, [1968], 160pp., paper.
(with Robert E. Howard & L. Sprague de Camp) *Conan the Wanderer.* NY: Lancer, [1968], 222pp., paper.
The Purloined Planet. NY: Belmont, [1969], paper.
Beyond the Gates of Dream. NY: Belmont, [1969], 157pp. paper.
Giant of World's End. NY: Belmont, [1969], paper.
(with Robert E. Howard & L. Sprague de Camp) *Conan of Cimmeria.* NY: Lancer, [1969], 189pp., paper.
Lost World of Time. NY: Signet, [1969], 128pp., paper.
Tower of the Medusa. NY: Ace, [1969], 106pp., paper.
Star Rogue. NY: Lancer, [1970], 190pp., paper.
Thongor Fights the Pirates of Tarakus. NY: Berkley, [1970], 160pp., paper.

Thongor at the End of Time. NY: Paperback Library, [1970], paper.

(with Robert E. Howard & L. Sprague de Camp) *Conan the Buccaneer.* NY: Lancer, [1971], 191pp., paper.

Outworlder. NY: Lancer, [1971], 175pp., paper.

Black Legion of Callisto. NY: Dell, [1972], paper.

Under the Green Star. NY: DAW #30, [1972], paper.

The Quest of Kadji. NY: Belmont, [1972], 188pp., paper.

The Black Star. NY: Dell, [1973], 235pp., paper.

Jandar of Callisto. NY: Dell, [1973 (1972)], 224pp., paper.

The Man Who Loved Mars. Greenwich, Connecticut: Fawcett Gold Medal, [1973], 157pp., paper.

Sky Pirates of Callisto. NY: Dell, [1973], 189pp., paper.

When the Green Star Calls. NY: DAW #62, [1973], paper.

The Valley Where Time Stood Still. Garden City: Doubleday, [1974], 179pp.

Time War. NY: Dell, [1974], paper.

By the Light of the Green Star. NY: DAW #110, [1974], paper.

The Warrior of World's End. NY: DAW #125, [1974], paper.

The Nemesis of Evil (Zarkon—Lord of the Unknown). Garden City: Doubleday, 1975, 172pp.

Invisible Death (Zarkon—Lord of the Unknown). Garden City: Doubleday, 1975, 173pp.

Dreams from R'lyeh. Sauk City, Wisconsin: Arkham House, 1975, 72pp.

Mad Empress of Callisto. NY: Dell, [1975], paper.

Mind Wizard of Callisto. NY: Dell, [1975], paper.

Lankar of Callisto. NY: Dell, [1975], paper.

As the Green Star Rises. NY: DAW #138, [1975], paper.

The Enchantress of World's End. NY: DAW #150, [1975], paper.

The Volcano Ogre (Zarkon—Lord of the Unknown). Garden City: Doubleday, 1976, 177pp.

In the Green Star's Glow. NY: DAW #180, [1976], paper.

The Immortal of World's End. NY DAW #210, [1976], paper.

The Barbarian of World's End. NY: DAW #243, [1977], paper.

(with Robert E. Howard & L. Sprague de Camp) *Conan of Aquilonia.* NY: Ace, [1977], paper.

Ylana of Callisto. NY: Dell, [1977], paper.

The City Outside the World. NY: Berkley, [1977], paper.

Renegade of Callisto. NY: Dell, [1978], paper.

The Wizard of Zao. NY: DAW #293, [1978], paper.

The Pirate of World's End. NY: DAW #310, [1978], 173pp., paper.

■ *Tolkien: A Look Behind "The Lord of the Rings,"* 1969; *Lovecraft: A Look Behind the "Cthulhu Mythos,"* 1972.

CARTER, MARGERY LOUISE ALLINGHAM (Mrs. Phillip Y.) (1904-1966) *English*
as Margery Allingham
The Mind Readers. London: Chatto & Windus, 1965, 265pp.
□ MYSTERY: *The Crime at Black Dudley,* 1929; *Mystery Mile,* 1929; *Police At the Funeral,* 1931; *Flowers for the Judge,* 1936; *The Fashion In Shrouds,* 1938; *Traitor's Purse,* 1941; *The Casebook of Mr. Campion,* 1947 (ss col); *The Tiger In the Smoke,* 1952; *The China Governess,* 1962.

CARTER, PAUL A.
as Paul A. Carter
Unbalanced Equation. Magazine of Fantasy and Science Fiction, Jan 1956
as Philip Carter
Ounce of Prevention. Magazine of Fantasy and Science Fiction, Summer 1950

CARTMELL, ROBERT (1877- ?)
as Robert Tarnacre
Beyond the Swamps. London: J. Lane, 1929, 324pp.

CARTMILL, CLEVE (1908-1964) *U.S.*
Born: Plattsville, Wisconsin
as Cleve Cartmill
Oscar. Unknown, Feb 1941
as Michael Corbin
Guardian. Unknown, Feb 1943

CASELEYR, CAMILLE AUGUST MARIE (1909-)
Australian
Born: Antwerp, Belgium
as Jack Danvers
The End of It All. London: Heinemann, 1962, 231pp.

CASEY, RICHARD [house pseudonym]
unattributed
Pearl-Handled Poison. Fantastic Adventures, Dec 1943
Horn O'Plenty. Fantastic Adventures, June 1944
Valley of Delirium. Amazing, March 1945
Dragons Behind Us. Fantastic Adventures, April 1945
Don't Look Behind You. Fantastic Adventures, Sept 1945
Fingerprints of Fear. Fantastic Adventures, Oct 1945
Lark On the Ark. Fantastic Adventures, Feb 1946
Carrion Crypt. Fantastic Adventures, July 1947
The Miracle of Herbert Plunk. Fantastic Adventures, Nov 1947
My World Died Tonight. Fantastic Adventures, May 1948
Tomorrow I Die. Fantastic Adventures, Aug 1948

CASSIDAY, BRUCE BINGHAM (1920-) *U.S.*
as Carson Bingham
Gorgo. Derby, Connecticut: Monarch, [1960], 141pp., paper.
□ *It Happened In Hawaii,* 1961.
as Bruce Cassiday
□ *Blast Off!,* 1964; *Guerrilla Scout,* 1965; *The Wild One,* 1969.
■ *Practical Home Repair For Women,* 1966; (with Doris Cassiday) *Fashion Industry Careers,* 1977.
✔ **Max Day**

CASWELL, EDWARD A.
as Myself and Another
Toil and Self. Chicago: Rand McNally, [1900], 154pp.

CAVE, HUGH B(arnett) (1910-) *naturalized U.S.*
Born: Chester, Cheshire, England
as Hugh B. Cave
Corpse on the Grating. Astounding, Feb 1930
The Door of Doom. Strange Tales, Jan 1932
The Brotherhood of Blood. Weird Tales, June 1932
The Witching Lands, Tales of the West Indies. London: Redman, [1962], 260pp. ss col
Murgunstrumm and Other Stories. Chapel Hill, North Carolina: Carcosa House, 1977, 500+pp., ill. ss col
□ *The Cross On the Drum,* 1959; *Black Sun,* 1960.
■ *Haiti, Highroad to Adventure,* 1952.
● **Allen Beck, Justin Case, Geoffrey Vace**

CHANDLER, A. BERTRAM (1912-) *British*
Born: Aldershot, Hampshire
as A. Bertram Chandler
This Means War! Astounding, May 1944
The Rim of Space. NY: Avalon, [1961], 220pp.
Bring Back Yesterday. NY: Ace, [1961], 173pp., paper. (Ace Double D 517)
Rendezvous on A Lost World. NY: Ace, [1961], 124pp., paper. (Ace Double F117)
Beyond the Galactic Rim. NY: Ace, [1963], 114pp.,

paper. (Ace Double F 237)

The Ship From Outside. NY: Ace, [1963], 108pp., paper. (Ace Double F 237)

The Hamelin Plague. NY: Monarch, [1963], 126pp., paper.

The Deep Reaches of Space. London: H. Jenkins, 1964, 190pp.

Glory Planet. NY: Avalon, [1964], 190pp.

Into the Alternate Universe. NY: Ace, [1964], 128pp., paper. (Ace Double M 107)

The Coils of Time. NY: Ace, [1964], 128pp., paper. (Ace Double M 107)

The Alternate Martians. NY: Ace, [1965], 129pp., paper. (Ace Double M 129)

Empress of Outer Space. NY: Ace, [1965], 127pp., paper. (Ace Double M 129)

Space Mercenaries. NY: Ace, [1965], 131pp., paper. (Ace Double M 133)

Contraband From Outer Space. NY: Ace, [1967], 104pp., paper. (Ace Double G 609)

Nebula Alert. NY: Ace, [1967], 121pp., paper. (Ace Double G 632)

The Road to the Rim. NY: Ace, [1967], 117pp., paper. (Ace Double H 29)

False Fatherland. NY: Horwitz, [1968], 161pp., paper.

Catch the Star Winds. NY: Lancer, [1969], 222pp., paper.

Spartan Planet. NY: Dell, [c.1969], paper.

To Prime the Pump. NY: Modern Literary Edition, [1971], 157pp.

Alternate Orbits. NY: Ace, [1971], 136pp., paper.

The Dark Dimension. NY: Ace, [1971], 117pp., paper.

The Hard Way Up. NY: Ace, [1972], 112pp., paper.

To Keep the Ship. NY: DAW, [1978], 175pp., paper.

as Bertram (A.) Chandler

It Started With Sputnik. *Amazing*, Aug 1958

as George Whitley

One Came Back. *Thrilling Wonder Stories*, Fall 1945

✔ Andrew Dunstan

CHAPMAN, MARGARET STORM (Jameson) (Mrs. Guy P.) (1897-   ) *British*

as (M.) Storm Jameson

In The Second Year. London: Cassell, [1936], 300pp.

Then We Shall Hear Singing; A Fantasy in C Major. London: Cassell, [1942], 232pp.

The Moment of Truth. NY: Macmillan, 1949, 179pp.

☐ *Happy Highways*, 1920; *Fairwell to Youth*, 1928; *Here Comes A Candle*, 1938; *The Black Laurel*, 1947.

■ *The Decline of Merry England*, 1930; *Modern Drama in Europe*, 1920.

CHATRIAN, ALEXANDRE (1826-1890) *French*
Born: Pfalzburg

as Erckmann-Chatrian [in collaboration with Emile Erckmann]

Stories of the Rhine. London: Lock & Tyler, [1875], 217pp. *ss col*

The Man Wolf and Other Tales. London: Ward, Lock & Tyler, [1876], 252pp. *ss col*

Strange Stories. NY: Appleton, 1880, 190pp., *ss col*

The Polish Jew and Other Tales. London: Ward, Lock, [c.1890], 229pp., ill. *play & ss col*

The Wild Huntsman and Other Tales. London: Ward, Lock, 184pp. *ss col*

CHETWOOD, WILLIAM RUFUS (? -1766) *English*

as Author of "The Lover's Opera"

☐ *The Generous Free-Mason, or, the Constant Lady*, 1729 (musical play).

as Capt. Robert Boyle

The Voyages and Adventures of Captain Robert Boyle, in Several Parts of the World. London: J. Watts, 1726, 374pp.

as Rufus Chetwood

■ *A General History of the Stage*, 1749; *The British Theatre*, 1750.

CHILDERS, ROBERT ERSKINE (1870-1922) *Anglo/Irish*
Born: London

as Erskine Childers

The Riddle of the Sands. London: Smith, Elder, 1903, 336pp., ill.

■ *The Times History of the South African War*, 1903; *The Framework of Home Rule*, 1911.

CHILDS, EDMUND BURTON

as Edmund Burton

The Radium King. Worthing, England: Lloyd Cole, [1943], 66pp.

The Quest of the Golden Orchid. Worthing, England: Lloyd Cole, [1943], 80pp.

Peril of Creation. London: UTB, [c.1941-5], 33pp., paper.

CIARDI, JOHN (1916-   ) *U.S.*

as John Anthony

The Hypnoglyph. *Magazine of Fantasy and Science Fiction*, July 1953.

as John Ciardi

Love Letter From Mars. *Magazine of Fantasy and Science Fiction*, Jan 1965 (verse)

☐ POETRY: *Homeward To America*, 1940; *Other Skies*, 1947; *As If*, 1955; *I Marry You*, 1958; *39 Poems*, 1959; (with Isaac Asimov) *Limericks Too Gross*, 1978.

■ *How Does A Poem Mean?*, 1959; *Dialogues With An Audience*, 1963.

CLARK, CHARLES H(eber) (1841-1915)

as Max Adeler

Out of the Hurly-Burly; or Life In An Odd Corner. Philadelphia: G. Maclean, 1874, 398pp. *ss col*

Random Shots. NY: J. W. Lovell, [1878], 326pp.

An Old Fogey and Other Stories. London: Ward, Lock, [1881], 372pp., ill. *ss col*

The Fortunate Island and Other Short Stories. Boston: Lee & Shepard, 1882, 333pp., ill. *ss col*

Transformations, Containing Mrs. Shelmire's Djinn. London: Ward, Lock, [1883], 122pp. *ss col*

A Desperate Adventure and Other Stories. London: Ward, Lock, [1883], 122 & 255pp., ill. boards, ill. *ss col*

☐ *Frictional Electricity, A Tale*, 1905.

■ *Elbow Room*, 1876; *Things Generally*, 1902.

as Charles Heber Clark

By the Bend of the River; Tales of Connock Old and New. Philadelphia: J. C. Winston, [1914], 307pp. *ss col*

☐ *Captain Bluitt, A Tale of Old Turley*, 1901.

■ *Ethics of the Tariff System*, 1885; *How Shall the Revenues of the Federal Government Be Reduced?*, 1887.

CLARK, CYNTHIA CHARLOTTE (Moon) (1829-1895)

as Charles M. Clay

How She Came Into Her Kingdom; A Romance. Chicago: Jansen, McClurg, 1878, 337pp.

☐ *The Modern Hagar*, 1882.

CLARKE, ARTHUR C(harles) (1917-   ) *English*
Born: Minehead, Somersetshire
Autobiographical: *The View From Serendip*. NY: Random House, [1977], 273pp.

as Arthur C. Clarke

Man's Empire of Tomorrow. *Tales of Wonder*, Winter 1938 article

Loophole. *Astounding*, April 1946

Prelude To Space. NY: Galaxy Novel #3, 1951, 160pp., paper.

Sands of Mars. London: Sidgwick & Jackson, 1951, 219pp.

[NY: Gnome, 1952, 216pp.]

Islands In the Sky. Philadelphia: Winston, 1952, 209pp.

Childhood's End. NY: Ballantine, [1953], 214pp., paper/ hardback.

Against the Fall of Night. NY: Gnome, [1953], 223pp.

Expedition to Earth. NY: Ballantine, [1953], 165pp., paper/ hardback. *ss col* (contains "The Sentinel" short story on which *2001: A Space Odyssey* is based)

Earthlight. NY: Ballantine, [1955], 155pp., paper/hardback.

Reach for Tomorrow. NY: Ballantine, [1956], 166pp., paper/hardback. *ss col*

The City and the Stars. NY: Harcourt, Brace, [1956], 310pp. [a rewrite of *Against the Fall of Night*]

The Deep Range. NY: Harcourt, Brace, 1957, 238pp.

Tales From the White Hart. NY: Ballantine, [1957], 151pp., paper. *ss col*

The Other Side of the Sky. NY: Harcourt, Brace, 1958, 245pp. *ss col*

Across the Sea of Stars. NY: Harcourt, Brace, 1959, 584pp. *col*

A Fall of Moondust. London: Gollancz, 1961, 224pp.

From the Oceans, From the Stars. NY: Harcourt, Brace, 1961, 515pp. *col*

Tales of Ten Worlds. NY: Harcourt, Brace, 1962, 245pp. *ss col*

Dolphin Island. NY: Holt, 1963, 187pp.

Prelude To Mars. NY: Harcourt, Brace, 1965, 497pp. *col*

The Nine Billion Names of God. NY: Harcourt, Brace, 1967, 288pp. *ss col*

2001: A Space Odyssey. NY: New American Library, [1968], 221pp., paper.

The Lion of Comarre & Against the Fall of Night. NY: Harcourt, Brace, [1968], 214pp.

The Wind From the Sun. NY: Harcourt, Brace, [1972], 193pp. *ss col*

Rendezvous With Rama. NY: Harcourt, Brace, [1973], 214pp.

Imperial Earth. NY: Harcourt, Brace, [1976], 303pp.

The Fountains of Paradise. NY: Harcourt, Brace, [1978], 261pp.

■ *Interplanetary Flight,* 1950; *The Exploration of Space,* 1951; *The Making of A Moon,* 1957; *The Challenge of the Sea,* 1960; *Profiles of the Future,* 1962; *The Promise of Space,* 1968; *Report on Planet Three and Other Speculations,* 1972.

as E. G. O'Brien

The Fires Within. *Fantasy,* Aug 1947 (Br.)

as Charles Willis

Castaway. *Fantasy,* April 1947 (Br.)

CLARKE, F(rancis) H.

as Francis H. Clarke

Morgan Rockefeller's Will; A Romance of 1991-92. Portland, Oregon: Clarke-Cree Publishing Co., 1909, 306pp. [some bibliographies have listed Zebina Forbush, the author of *The Co-opolitan; A Story of the Co-operative Commonwealth of Idaho.* Chicago: C. H. Kerr, 1898, 170pp. (Library of Progress No. 26) as a pseudonym of Francis H. Clarke. This seems to be an error.]

CLARKE, GEORGE S(ydenham) (1st Baron Sydenham of Combe) (1848-1933) *British*

Autobiography: *My Working Life,* by Colonel Lord Sydenham of Combe. London: Murray, 1927, 456pp.

as George S(ydenham) Clarke (Lord Sydenham)

■ *Practical Geometry and Engineering Drawing,* 1875; *On the Defense of Plevna in 1877-78,* 1881; *Fortification,* 1890; *Imperial Defense,* 1897; *India and the War,* 1915; *Naval and Military Defense,* 1917; *The Jewish World Problem,* 1921; *The "Shakespeare Myth,"* 1924; *Studies of An Imperialist,* 1928.

as A. Nelson Seaforth

The Last Great Naval War. An Historical Retrospect. London: Cassell, [1890], 120pp., maps. [preface is dated 1920 in 1st ed, 1930 in later editions] [BMC states in error 20pp. — other sources, including the NUC, state 120pp., which is correct]

CLAYTON, RICHARD HENRY MICHAEL (1907-   )
British

as William Haggard

Slow Burner. London: Cassell, [1958], 192pp.

□ SPY THRILLERS: *Closed Circuit,* 1960; *The Arena,* 1961; *The Unquiet Sleep,* 1962; *The High Wire,* 1963.

CLEMENS, SAMUEL L(anghorne) (1835-1910) *U.S.*
Born: Hannibal, Missouri

as Huck Finn

□ (edited by Mark Twain) *Tom Sawyer Abroad,* 1894.

as Mark Twain

[this pseudonym was originally used by Isaiah Sellers (?1802-1864) writing in the *New Orleans Picayune,* Samuel L. Clemens adopted it for most of his work]

A Connecticut Yankee In King Arthur's Court. NY: C. L. Webster, 1889, 575pp., ill.

The £1,000,000 Bank-Note; and Other New Stories. NY: C. L. Webster, 1893, 260pp. *ss col*

Extracts From Adam's Diary. NY: Harper, 1904, 89pp., ill.

Eve's Diary (translated from the original manuscript). NY: Harper, 1906, 109pp.

Extract From Captain Stormfield's Visit To Heaven. Harper, 1909, 120pp., front.

The Mysterious Stranger. NY: Harper, 1916, 150pp.

The Curious Republic of Gondour and Other Whimsical Sketches. NY: Boni and Liveright, 1919, 140pp.

The Mysterious Stranger and Other Stories. NY: Harper, 1922, 323pp.

Report From Paradise. NY: Harper, 1952, 94pp., ill.

Letters From The Earth. NY: Harper [1962], 303pp.

□ *The Celebrated Frog of Calaveras County and Other Sketches,* 1867; *The Adventures of Tom Sawyer,* 1876; *The Prince and the Pauper,* 1881; *The Stolen White Elephant,* 1882; *The Adventures of Huckleberry Finn,* 1884.

■ *The Innocents Abroad,* 1869; *Life On the Mississippi,* 1883; *English As She Is Taught,* 1900; *Editorial Wild Oats,* 1905.

CLERY, WILLIAM E.   *British*

as Austin Fryers

The Devil and the Inventor. London: C. A. Pearson, 1900, 272pp.

□ *A New Lady Audley,* 1891; *A New Rip Van Winkle,* (18-?); *A Pauper Millionaire,* 1899; (with A.W.Barrett) *The Man With the Opals,* 1906; *Mrs. Alison's Engagement; A Fantastic Love Story,* 1906 (play); *The Babylonian Diamond,* 1907; *The Uncreated Man,* 1912.

■ *A Guide to the Stage,* 1904.

CLINTON, ED(win) M. JR. (1926-   )

as Edwin M. Clinton Jr.

Overload. *Startling Stories,* Oct 1953

as Anthony More

Puzzle Box. San Francisco: Trover Hall, 1946, 111pp. *ss col*

CLOUTIER, CHARLES

as Charles Cloukey

Sub-Satellite. *Amazing,* March 1928

COBBE, FRANCES POWER (1822-1904) *British*
Born: Ireland

as Frances Power Cobbe

■ *Friendless Girls,* 1861; *Female Education,* 1862; *Broken*

Lights, 1864; *Criminals, Idiots, Women, and Minors. Is the Classification Sound? A Discussion On the Laws Concerning the Property of Married Women,* 1869; *Darwinism In Morals,* 1872; *The Moral Aspects of Vivisection,* 1876; *The Duties of Women,* 1881.
as Merlin Nostradamus
The Age of Science: A Newspaper of the 20th Century. London: Ward, Lock, [1877], 50pp.
anonymous
■ *The Theory of Intuitive Morals,* 1855.

COCHRAN, WILLIAM E.
as S. Kye Boult
Solo Kill. NY: Berkley, 1977, paper.

COCKBURN, FRANCIS CLAUDE (1904-) *British*
as Claude Cockburn
The Incredulity of Colonel Mumph. *Magazine of Fantasy and Science Fiction,* April 1956
as James Helvick
Overdraft on Glory. London: Boardman, 1955, 285pp.
□ *Beat the Devil,* 1953
as Frank Pitcairn
■ *Reporter in Spain,* 1936

COHEN, CHESTER
as Chester Cohen
Flower Girl. *Rocket Stories,* Sept 1953
as Chester B. Conant
Forbidden Flight. *Future,* Oct 1941

COLE, LES(ter)
as Les(ter) Cole
Unborn of Earth. *Science Fantasy #10,* Sept 1954 (Br.)
as Colin Sturgis [in collaboration with Melvin Sturgis)
Conversion Factor. *Magazine of Fantasy and Science Fiction,* Nov 1957

COLES, CYRIL HENRY (1899-1965) *British*
Born: London
as Manning Coles [in collaboration with Adelaide Frances Oke Manning]
The Emperor's Bracelet. London: U. of London Press, 1947, 234pp., ill.
Brief Candles. Garden City: Doubleday, 1954, 252pp.
The Far Traveller. Garden City: Doubleday, 1956, 224pp.
□ MYSTERY: "Tommy Hambleton" starting with *Drink To Yesterday,* 1940 and *Pray Silence,* 1940.
as Francis Gaite [in collaboration with Adelaide Frances Oke Manning]
Brief Candles. London: Hodder & Stoughton, 1954, 189pp.
Family Matter. London: Hodder & Stoughton, 1956, 192pp.
Come and Go. London: Hodder & Stoughton, 1958, 192pp.
□ *Duty Free,* 1959.

COLLIN DE PLANCY, JACQUES SIMON (1794-1881)
ne Jacques A. S. Collin *French*
as J. A. S. C*** de P***
■ *Dictionnaire de la Folie et la Raison,* 1820.
as J. Collin de Plancy
Voyage du Centre de la Terre. . . au Pole Nord et dans le Pays Inconnus, Traduit de l'anglais de Sir Homidas-Peath par M. Jacques de St. Albin. Paris: 1821. [probably 3 vol]
as J. A. S. Collin de Plancy
■ *Dictionnaire infernal, ou, Recherches et anecdotes, sur les demons, les espirits, les fantomes, les spectres, les revenants, les loups-garoux, les possedes, les sorciers, le Sabbat, les magiciens, les salamandres, les sylphes, les gnomes, etc; les visions, les songes, les prodiges, les charmes, les malefices, les secrets merveilleux, les talismans, etc; en un mot, sur tout ce qui tient aux*

apparitions a la magie, au commerce de l'enfer, aux divinations, aux sciences secretes, aux superstitions, aux choses mysterieuses et surnaturelles, etc, etc, etc. Par J. A. S. Collin de Plancy. Paris, P. Mongie aine, 1818.
as le Docteur Ensenada
■ *L'Art de Vivre Cent ans et au dela, etc.,* 1868.
as Baron de Glanaville
■ *Un Million d'Anecdotes Suisses, Plaisanteries, etc.,* 1861.
as Sir Homidas-Peath
[see above entry under J. Collin de Plancy]
as Jacques Loyseau
□ *Les Fabliaux du Moyen Age. . .,* 1846.
as Baron de Nilinse
□ *La Vie de Saint Adelaide,* 1847.
as J. S. C. de Saint-Albin
■ *Les Contes Noirs; ou, Les frayeurs populaires, nouvelles, contes aventures merveilleuses, bizarres et singulieres, anecdotes, inedites, etc., sur les apparitions, les diables, les spectres, les revenans, les fantomes, les brigands, etc.* Paris, 1818.

COLLINS, EDWARD JAMES MORTIMER (1827-1886)
English
Born: Plymouth, Devonshire
Biography: *Mortimer Collins: His Letters and Friendships, with Some Account of His Life,* ed. by Frances Collins. London: 1877.
as Mortimer Collins
The British Birds: A Communication from the Ghost of Aristophanes. London: Publishing Co., 1872, 75pp. *poem*
Transmigration. London: Hurst & Blackett, 1874, 3 vol.
□ *Who Is the Heir?,* 1865; *Sweet Anne Page,* 1868; *The Ivory Gate,* 1869; *The Vivian Romance,* 1870; *The Marquis and the Merchant,* 1871; *Two Plunges for A Pearl,* 1872; *Blacksmith and Scholar and From Midnight to Midnight,* 1876 [1875].
as Robert Turner Cotton
□ *Mr. Carington. A Tale of Love and Conspiracy,* 1873, 3 vol.

COLLINS, J. L.
as Jonquil
Queen Krinaleen's Plagues; or, How A Simple People Were Destroyed. A Discourse in the Twenty-second Century. NY: American News Company, 1874, 151pp.
□ *Was She Engaged?,* 1871.

COLLINS, (William) WILKIE (1824-1889) *British*
Born: London
as Wilkie Collins
Basil: A Story of Modern Life. London: R. Bentley, 1852, 3 vol.
After Dark. London: Smith, Elder, 1856, 2 vol.
The Queen of Hearts. London: Hurst & Blackett, 1859, 3 vol.
A Woman In White. A Novel. London: Sampson, Low, 1860, 3 vol.
Armadale. London: Smith, Elder, 1866, 2 vol., ill.
The Haunted Hotel, A Mystery of Modern Venice. London: Chatto & Windus, 1878, 341pp., ill.
The Ghost's Touch and Other Stories. NY: Harper, 1885, 198pp. *ss col*
Little Novels. London: Chatto & Windus, 1887, 3 vol.
□ *Hide and Seek,* 1854; *The Dead Secret,* 1857; *No Name,* 1862; *The Moonstone,* 1868; *The Evil Genius,* 1886.

COMBE, WILLIAM (1741-1823) *English*
Born: Bristol, Gloucestershire
Combe was a famous ne'er-do-well. He worked as a bookseller's hack, private soldier, waiter, cook, and law student. He spent most of his life after 1780 in King's Bench debtors' prison.

as W(illiam) Combe
  ☐ *Clifton, a poem. In Imitation of Spencer,* 1775 (poetry).
as William Coomb
[various bibliographies sometimes use this spelling]
as Dr. Syntax
  ☐ *Tour of Dr. Syntax, In Search of the Picturesque,* 1812; *The Second Tour of Dr. Syntax, In Search of Consolation,* 1820; *The Third Tour of Dr. Syntax, in Search of A Wife, a poem,* 1821 (poetry).
anonymous
  The Devil Upon Two Sticks In England. London: Logographic (?) Press, 1790, 4 vol.
  The Devil Upon Two Sticks In England. London: A. K. Newman, 1817, 6 vol.
  ☐ *The Diaboliad, a poem. Dedicated to the worst man in His Majesty's Dominions,* 1776. (poetry)

COMPTON, D(avid) G(uy) (1930-   ) *English*
Born: London
as D. G. Compton
  It's Smart To Have An English Address. *Impulse,* Feb 1967
  The Quality of Mercy: A Novel of 1979. London: Hodder & Stoughton, 1965, 157pp.
  Farewell Earth's Bliss. London: Hodder & Stoughton, 1966, 191pp.
  The Silent Multitude. NY: Ace, [1966], 189pp., paper.
  Synthajoy. London: Hodder & Stoughton, 1968, 190pp.
  Chronocules. London: 1970.
  The Steel Crocodile. NY: Ace, [1970], paper.
  The Missionaries. London: 1972.
  The Unsleeping Eye. NY: DAW, [1974], paper.
  ☐ MYSTERY: *Too Many Murders,* 1962; *Medium for Murder,* 1963; *Dead On Cue,* 1964.
as Frances Lynch
  A Dangerous Magic, 1978.

CONKLIN, EDWARD GROFF (1904-1968)
as Groff Conklin
  Editor of numerous science fiction, fantasy and horror anthologies.
as W. B. deGraeff
  Congress Is Too Busy for the Atom. *Astounding,* Sept 1946 *article*

CONNELL, ALAN
as Alan Conn
  Fate. *Wonder Stories,* March 1936
as Alan Connell
  The Reign of the Reptiles. *Wonder Stories,* Aug 1935

CONQUEST, (George) ROBERT (Acworth) (1917-   ) *English*
Born: Malvern
as J. E. M. Arden
  ■ *Where Do Marxists Go From Here?,* 1958.
as Robert Conquest
  The Veteran. *Analog,* Oct 1965
  A World of Difference. London: Ward, Lock, 1955, 192pp.
  ☐ POETRY: *Poems,* 1955; *Between Mars and Venus,* 1962; *Arias From A Love Opera,* 1969.
  ■ *The Soviet Deportation of Nationalities,* 1960; *Common Sense About Russia,* 1960; *Courage of Genius; the Pasternak Affair,* 1961; *Marxism Today,* 1964; *The Politics of Ideas in the U.S.S.R.,* 1967; *The Soviet Police System,* 1968; *The Human Cost of Soviet Communism,* 1971; *V. I. Lenin,* 1972.

CONWAY, GERARD (F)
as Gerard (F.) Conway
  The Midnight Dancers. NY: Ace, 1971, paper.
  Mindship. NY: DAW #90, [1973], 191pp., paper.

as Wallace Moore
  The Bloodstone. NY: Pyramid, paper.
  The Caves of Madness. NY: Pyramid, [1975], paper.
  The Lights of Zetar. NY: Pyramid, [1975], paper.

COOK, CHRISTINE CAMPBELL THOMSON (Mrs. Oscar) (1897-   ) *British*
Born: London
Autobiography: *I Am A Literary Agent: Memoirs Personal and Professional,* by Christine Campbell Thomson. London: S. Low, 1951, 230pp.
as Dair Alexander
  non fantasy and science fiction, fiction
as Molly Campbell
  juveniles
as Christine Hartley
  ■ *The Western Mystery Tradition,* 1968; *A Case For Reincarnation,* 1972.
as Flavia Richardson
  Out of the Earth. *Weird Tales,* 1927.
as C(hristine) C(ampbell) Thomson
  editor of the "Not At Night" series of short story collections beginning with *Not At Night,* 1925.
  [this series contains many 1st book publications of short stories from *Weird Tales*]
  ☐ *Bourgoyne of Goyne,* 1921; *The Incredible Island,* 1924; *His Excellency,* 1927; *Hawk of the Sahara,* 1939.

COOK, MABEL C(ollins) (Mrs. Kenningsgate) (1851-1927)
as Mabel C. Collins
  The Idyll of the White Lotus. London: Reeves & Turner, 1884, 141pp.
  The Blossom and the Fruit; A True Story of a Black Magician. NY: J. W. Lovell, 1889, 290pp. (Lovell's Occult Series no. 1)
  Suggestion. NY: Lovell, Gestefeld, [1892], 276pp.
  Morial the Mahatma. NY: Lovell, Gestefeld, [1892], 270pp.
  The Star Sapphire. Boston: Roberts Bros., 1896, 311pp.
  The Story of Sensa. London: Theosophical Pub. Society, [1911], 95pp.
  ☐ *The Prettiest Woman In Warsaw,* 1886; *The Confessions of A Woman,* 1890; *Illusions,* 1905.

COOKE, JOAN CONQUEST (Mrs. Leonard)
as Joan Conquest
  Leonie of the Jungle. London: Laurie, [1921], 253pp.
  The Reckoning. NY: Macauley, [1931], 343pp.
  ☐ *Desert Love,* 1920; *The Hawk of Egypt,* 1922; *Forbidden,* 1927; *Love's Curse,* 1932; *The Sleeping Woman,* 1936; *Yashmak,* 1938.
  ■ *Strange Beds; Life Story of Love, Thrills, and Adventure,* 1937.

COOPER, EDMUND (1926-   ) *English*
as Richard Avery
  The Death Worms of Kratos. Greenwich, Connecticut: Fawcett Gold Medal, 1975, 191pp., paper.
  The Rings of Tantalus. Greenwich, Connecticut: Fawcett Gold Medal, 1975, 192pp., paper.
  The War Games of Zelos. Greenwich, Connecticut: Fawcett Gold Medal, 1975, 176pp., paper.
  The Venom of Argus. Greenwich, Connecticut: Fawcett Gold Medal, 1976, paper.
as Edmund Cooper
  The Jar of Latakia. *Authentic #49,* Sept 1954 (Br.)
  Deadly Image. NY: Ballantine, 1958, 190pp., paper.
  Tomorrow's Gift. NY: Ballantine, 1958, 164pp., paper. *ss col*
  Seed of Light. NY: Ballantine, 1959, 159pp., paper.
  Voices In the Dark. London: Digit, 1960, 157pp., paper. *ss col*

Tomorrow Came. London: Panther, 1963, 123pp., paper.
  ss col
Transit. London: Faber, 1964, 232pp.
All Fool's Day. London: Hodder & Stoughton, 1966, 192pp.
A Far Sunset. London: Hodder & Stoughton, 1967, 189pp.
News From Elsewhere. London: Mayflower, 1968, 128pp.
  paper. *ss col*
Five to Twelve. London: Hodder & Stoughton, 1968,
  187pp.
The Square Root of Tomorrow. London: Hale, 1970,
  192pp.
The Firebird [in *Double Phoenix* edited by Roger L. Green]
  NY: Ballantine, [c.1971], 210pp., paper [may not be 1st
  edition]
Who Needs Men? A Novel. London: Hodder & Stoughton,
  1972, 192pp.
The Cloud Walker: A Novel. London: Hodder & Stoughton,
  1973, 223pp.
The Tenth Planet; A Novel. NY: Putnam, [1973], 214pp.
  [may not be 1st edition]
Prisoner of Fire. London: Hodder & Stoughton, 1974,
  191pp.
The Slaves of Heaven. NY: Putnam [1974], 185pp. [may
  not be 1st edition]

COOPER, JAMES FENIMORE (1789-1851) *U. S.*
  Born: Burlington, New Jersey
as An American
  ■ *Gleanings In Europe: England, France, Italy, etc.,*
    1837–1838. [a series of travel descriptions]
as Author of "The Prairie," "The Red Rover," "The Pilot," etc.
Mark's Reef; or, the Crater. London: Bentley, 1847, 3 vol.
as Author of "The Spy," "The Pilot," etc...
The Monikins. A Land of Civilized Monkeys. London:
  Bentley, 1835, 3 vol. [Philadelphia: Carey, Lea &
  Blanchard, 1835, 2 vol.]
as Author of "Miles Wallingford," etc.
The Crater, or, Vulcan's Peak. NY: Burgess, Stringer &
  Co., 1847, 2 vol. in one. [same as Mark's Reef above]
as James Fenimore Cooper
  □ *The Deerslayer*, 1841.
  ■ *History of the Navy of the U.S.,* 1839; *The Battle
    of Lake Erie,* 1843.
as Jane Morgan
  □ *Tales for Fifteen; or, Imagination and Heart,* 1823
    (ss col).
anonymous or as "Author of ———"
  □ *Precaution,* 1820; *The Spy,* 1821; *The Pioneers,* 1823;
    The Pilot, 1823; *The Last of the Mohicans,* 1826;
    The Prairie, 1827; *The Red Rover,* 1828; *The Wept of
    Wish-ton-Wept,* 1829; *The Water Witch,* 1831; *The
    Pathfinder,* 1840.

COPPEL, ALFREDO JOSE DE MARINI Y, JR. (1921-   )
  U.S.
  Born: Oakland, California
as Alfred Coppel
The Age of Unreason. Astounding, Dec 1947
Dark December. Greenwich, Connecticut: Fawcett Gold
  Medal, [1960], 208pp., paper.
  □ *Hero Driver,* 1954; *Night of Fire and Snow,* 1957;
    A Certainty of Love, 1966; *The Gate of Hell,* 1967;
    The Land Locked Man, 1972; *Thirty-Four East,* 1974;
    The Dragon, 1977.
as Sol Galaxan
The Flight of the Eagle. Planet Stories, Sept 1953
as Robert Cham Gilman
The Rebel of Rhada. NY: Harcourt, Brace, [1968], 192pp.
The Navigator of Rhada. NY: Harcourt, Brace, [1968,
  (c.1969)], 223pp.
The Starkhahn of Rhada. NY: Harcourt, Brace, [1970], 190pp.
as Derfla Leppoc

Love Affair. Vortex #1, 1953
as A. C. Marin
  □ *Rise With the Wind,* 1969; *A Storm of Spears,* 1971.
● **Alfred Marin**

CORBETT, ELIZABETH B(urgoyne) (Mrs. George)
  (1846- ?) *British*
as E. B. Corbett
New Amazonia; A Foretaste of the Future. London: Power
  Publishing Co., [1889], 146pp.
*Secrets of A Private Enquiry Office, Being Tales Weird
  and Tales Ghostly, etc.* London: Routledge, 1891, 256pp.
  □ *The Missing Note,* 1884; *Cassandra,* 1884; *Mrs. Grundy's
    Victims,* 1893; *When the Sea Gives Up Its Dead, A
    Thrilling Detective Story,* 1894.
as G. Corbett
  □ *A Young Stowaway,* 1910 (school edition).

CORNWELL, DAVID JOHN MOORE (1931-   )
as John Le Carre
  □ MYSTERY AND SPY THRILLERS: *Call For the Dead,*
    1961; *A Murder of Quality,* 1962; *The Spy Who Came
    In From the Cold,* 1963; *The Looking Glass War,* 1965;
    A Small Town In Germany, 1968; *The Naive and
    Sentimental Lover,* 1971.

CORSTON, MICHAEL GEORGE (1932-   ) *English*
  Born: Kenton, Middlesex
as George Corston
Aftermath. London: Hale, 1968, 206pp.

CORY, MATILDA WINIFRED MURIEL (Graham) (Mrs.)
  Autobiography: *That Reminds Me,* 1945 (vol. 1); *Obser-
    vations,* 1947 (vol. 2); and *I Introduce,* 1948 (vol. 3)
as Winifred Graham
Angels, and Devils, and Man. London: Cassell, 1904, 344pp.
The Needlewoman. London: Mills & Boon, 1911, 313pp.
The Gods of the Dead. London: Rider, [1912], 316pp.
The Pit of Corruption. London: Stanley Paul, 1913, 318pp.
Hallomas Abbey. London: Hutchinson, [1935], 304pp.
The Frozen Death. London: Hutchinson, [1938], 280pp.
  □ *The Great House of Castleton and Patricia,* 1898;
    The Zionists, 1902; *The Enemy of Woman,* 1910; *Eve
    and the Elders,* 1924; *The Diamond Heels,* 1926; *Vacant
    Possession,* 1932; *Tongues in Trees,* 1934; *Glenvirgin's
    Ghost,* 1938.

CORY, VIVIAN *British*
as Victoria Cross
The Beating Heart. London: Daniel, 1924, 280pp. *ss col*
Martha Brown, M. P., A Girl of Tomorrow. London: T. W.
  Laurie, [1935], 256pp.
  □ *To-Morrow,* 1904; *Daughters of Heaven,* 1920 (ss col);
    Eclectic Love, 1929; *The Girl In the Studio; The Story
    of Her Strange, New Way of Loving,* 1934.
as Victoria Crosse
  □ *The Woman Who Didn't.* London: J. Land, 1895,
    159pp. (cover and title page by A. Beardsley) [a satire
    of Grant Allen's "The Woman Who Did," see Charles
    Grant Allen]

CORYELL, JOHN RUSSELL (1848-1924) *U.S.*
as Nick Carter (a.k.a. Sgt. Ryan and Nicholas Carter)
  [John Russell Coryell in collaboration with Ormond G. Smith
    wrote the original story under this pseudonym in the
    New York Weekly, 18 Sept 1886. It has since been
    used by countless hacks, and some good writers, for
    thousands of pulp stories and novels and hundreds of
    books. A few of those attributed to Coryell are listed
    below.]
  □ MYSTERY: *The American Marquis; or, Detective For
    Vengeance,* 1889; *Among the Fire Bugs,* 1895; *Among*

the Nihilists, 1898; *Lady Velvet,* 1900.
as John R. Coryell
☐ *A Woman's Hand,* 1890; *Adventures for Schoolboys,* 1911 (ss col)
■ *Sex Union and Parenthood,* 1906.
as Julia Edwards
☐ *Prettiest of All,* 1889; *Beautiful But Poor,* 1890; *The Little Widow,* 1890.
as Geraldine Fleming
☐ *A Terrible Secret,* 1885; *Entrapped. A Love Story,* 1886; *$5,000 Reward; or, the Missing Bride,* 1887.
as Margaret Grant
☐ *A Child of Love; A Startling Story of the Struggles of A Girl Born Out of Wedlock Against the Sins and Perversions of Today,* 1904.
✓ **Bertha M. Clay**

COSTELLO, P.F. [house pseudonym]
unattributed
[All but those two below, many stories under this name written before 1950 are probably by Chester Geier.]
by Roger P. Graham
Secret of the Flaming Ring. *Fantastic Adventures,* March 1951.
Space Is For Suckers. *Amazing,* June 1958

COULSON, JUANITA RUTH WELLONS (Mrs. Robert S.) (1933-   ) *U.S.*
Born: Marion, Indiana
as Juanita Coulson
A Helping Hand. *If,* Nov 1970
Crisis on Cheiron. NY: Ace, [1967], 129pp., paper. (Ace Double H 27)
The Singing Stones. NY: Ace, [1968], 132pp., paper. (Ace Double H 77)
☐ *The Secret of Seven Oaks,* 1972; *Door Into Terror,* 1972; *Stone of Blood,* 1975; *Fear Stalks the Bayou,* 1976.
as John Jay Wells
(with Marion Zimmer Bradley)   Another Rib. *Magazine of Fantasy and Science Fiction,* June 1963.

COULSON, ROBERT S.
as Robert Coulson
(with Gene DeWeese) *Gates of the Universe.* NY: Laser Books #4, [1975], 190pp., paper.
(with Gene DeWeese) *Now You See It/Him/Them . . .* Garden City: Doubleday, 1975, 157pp.
(with Gene DeWeese) *Charles Fort Never Mentioned Wombats.* Garden City: Doubleday, 1977, 173pp.
✓ **Thomas Stratton** [in collaboration with Gene DeWeese]

COVE, JOSEPH WALTER (1891-   ) *U.S.*
as Lewis Gibbs
Excursion to Lilliput. London: Dent, [1933], 244pp.
Parable for Lovers. London: Dent, [1934], 245pp., front.
Late Final. London: Dent, 1951, 216pp.
☐ *Michael and His Angels, A Chronicle History,* 1936.
■ *Sheridan, His Life and Theatre,* 1948.

COX, ANNE *British*
as Author of "Margaret Dunbar"
'*Twixt Shade and Shine.* London: Tinsley, 1883 [1882], 3 vol.
as Annabel Gray
☐ *A Romance of Regent Street,* 1881; *Through Rifted Clouds,* 1891; *Comrades,* 1896; *The Mystic Number Seven,* 1900.
■ *War's Harvest: The Kaiser's Aftermath,* 1915.

COX, A(nthony) B(erkeley) (1893-1970) *British*
as Anthony Berkeley
☐ MYSTERY: *The Poisoned Chocolate Case,* 1929; *The Pic-*

adilly Murder, 1929; *Murder In the Basement,* 1932; *Trial and Error,* 1937.
as A. B. Cox
The Family Witch, An Essay In Absurdity. London: Jenkins, 1925, 312pp.
The Professor On Paws. London: Collins, [1926], 306pp.
☐MYSTERY: "Holmes and The Dasher" in *Jugged Journalism,* 1925 (Sherlock Holmes parody); *Mr. Priestley's Problem,* 1927.
as Francis Iles
☐ Mystery Critic for the (London) *Daily Telegraph* and *Sunday Times,* 1930s-on. MYSTERY: *Malice Aforethought,* 1931; *Before the Fact,* 1932; *As For the Woman,* 1939.

COX, ARTHUR JEAN
as Ralph Carghill
The Question. *Fantastic Story Magazine,* Sept/Fall 1952
as Arthur Jean Cox
Linguistics and Time. *Astounding,* Aug 1950 *article*
as Jean Cox
The Sea Change. *Magazine of Fantasy and Science Fiction,* March 1967

COXE, EDWARD D.
as A Fugitive
The Fool Killer. Chicago: American Publisher's Association, 1885, 316pp.

COXON, MURIEL (Hine) (Mrs. Sidney) *British*
as Muriel Hine
The Seven Lovers and Other Stories. London: J. Lane, [1927], 293pp. *ss col*
☐ *Half In Ernest,* 1912; *The Man With the Double Heart,* 1914; *The Hidden Valley,* 1919; *Torquil's Success,* 1921; *The Spell of Siris,* 1923; *Ten Days' Wonder,* 1930; *A Man's Way,* 1934.

CRAIGIE, DOROTHY M. *British*
as David Craigie
The Voyage of Luna I. London: Eyre & Spottiswoode, [1948], 272pp., ill. *juv*
Dark Atlantis. London: Heinemann, [1952], 220pp., ill. *juv*

CRAIK, DINAH MARIA MULOCK (Mrs. George L.) (1826-1887) *English*
Born: Stoke-on-Trent, Staffordshire
as Author of "John Halifax, Gentleman"
Romantic Tales. London: Smith, Elder, 1859, 406pp., ill.
The Adventures of A Brownie, as Told to My Child. London: S. Low, [c.1872], 114pp., ill.
The Little Lame Prince and His Traveling Cloak. London: Daldy, Isbister, 1875, 169pp., ill.
☐ *A Brave Lady,* 1870.
■ *A Woman's Thoughts About Women,* 1858.
as Author of "Olive"
Avillion and Other Tales. London: Smith, Elder, 1853, 3 vol. *ss col*
☐ *Agatha's Husband,* 1852.
as Miss Mulock
The Italian's Daughter. NY: G. Munro, [c.1880], 26pp. *ss col*

CRANSTON, RUTH (Mrs.)
as Author of "Mastering Flame"
■ *My Cosmopolitan Year,* 1913.
as Ruth Cranston
■ *The Story of Woodrow Wilson,* 1945; *World Faith, the Story of the Religions of the United Nations,* 1949.
as Anne Warwick
The Shrieking Hands and Other Mixed Shorts. London: Gandy, [1926], 183pp. *ss col*
☐ *Compensation,* 1911; *The Unknown Woman,* 1912; *Victory Law,* 1914; *The Chalk Line,* 1915; *The Unpretenders, 1916.*

CRAWFORD, MARGARET (Mrs. William L.) *U.S.*
as Garret Ford [in collaboration with William L. Crawford,
  Forrest J. Ackerman, and others]
  Editor of *Fantasy Book*, published by FPCI, Los
  Angeles, California, first issue *c.* 1947
  [This is not the same Margaret Crawford who wrote the
  article "Pig-Sticking in Bengal" in *Modern Pig-Sticking*
  [1914], edited by A. E. Wardrop.]

CRAWFORD, WILLIAM L. *U.S.*
as William L. Crawford
  Editor of *Spaceways Magazine*— all issues
as Garret Ford [in collaboration with Margaret Crawford,
  Forrest J. Ackerman, etc.]
  Editor of *Fantasy Book*, published by FPCI, Los Angeles,
  California, first issue *c.* 1947.

CREASEY, JOHN (1908-1973) *British*
Born: Surrey
Bibliography: *John Creasey; Master of Mystery.* NY:
  Harper & Row, 1972.
as Gordon Ashe
  □ MYSTERY: *The Speaker,* 1939.
as John Creasey
  The Flood. London: Hodder & Stoughton, 1956, 191pp.
  The Blight. London: Hodder & Stoughton, 1968, 192pp.
  □ MYSTERY: "Dr. Palfrey" series; "Dept. Z" series;
    "Inspector West" series; the "Toff" series.
  ■ *Heroes of the Air,* 1943.
as Norman Deane
  □ *I Am the Withered Man,* 1971.
as Robert Caine Frazer
  □ MYSTERY: The "Mark Kilby" series.
as Michael Halliday
  □ *Cat and Mouse,* 1955; *Death of A Stranger, 1957.*
as Kyle Hunt
  □ MYSTERY: *Kill Once, Kill Twice,* 1956; *Cunning As A
    Fox,* 1965.
as J. J. Marric
  □ MYSTERY: "Gideon" series
as Anthony Morton
  □ MYSTERY: The "Baron" series, e.g. *Alias the Baron,*
    1939.
as William K. Riley
  □ WESTERN: *War On the Lazy-K,* 1946.
as Jeremy York
  □ MYSTERY: *So Soon To Die,* 1955; *Come Here and Die,*
    1957.
✔ Margaret Cooke, Henry St. John Cooper, Elise Fecamps,
Patrick Gill, Charles Hogarth, Brian Hope, Colin Hughes,
Abel Mann, Peter Manton, James Marsden, Richard Maitin,
Rodney Matheson, Ken Ranger, Tex Riley, Henry St. John,
Jimmy Wilde.

CRELLIN, HORATIO (Nelson) *British*
as Al Arawiyeh
  Tales of the Caliph. London: Unwin, 1888, 234pp.
as H. N. Crellin
  Romances of the Old Seraglio. London: Chatto & Windus,
  1894.

CRICHTON, MICHAEL (1942-   ) *U.S.*
as Michael Crichton
  The Andromeda Strain. NY: Knopf, 1969, 295pp., ill.
  The Terminal Man. NY: Knopf, 1972, 247pp., ill.
  Westworld. NY: Bantam, [1974], 107pp., paper.
  □ *The Great Train Robbery,* 1975; *Eaters of the Dead,*
    1976.
  ■ *Five Patients, the Hospital Explained,* 1970.
as Michael Douglas [in collaboration with Douglas Crichton]
  □ *Dealing; or, the Berkeley-to-Boston Forty-Brick Lost-Bag
    Blues: A Novel.* NY: Knopf, 1971 [*c.*1970], 222pp.

as Jeffery Hudson
  □ MYSTERY: *A Case of Need.* NY: World, 1968, 309pp.
as Joan Lange [erroneous]
  ■ [The National Union Catalogue 1968-72 lists the
    *Conitivity Paradox, an Inquiry Into the Claims of
    Philosophy,* 1970, by Joan Lange, under Michael Crichton.
    This book was actually written by a real **JOHN LANGE**
    (born: 1931) and has nothing to do with **MICHAEL
    CRICHTON.**]
as John Lange
  □ *Zero Cool,* 1969; *The Venom Business,* 1969; *Binary,*
    1972; *Scratch One,* 1974.

CROCKER, SAMUEL (1845-1921) *U.S.*
as Sam Crocker
  ■ *The Political Separation of Capital and Labor,* 1883;
    Our Next Republic, 1887.
as Theodore Oceanic Islet
  That Island, a political romance. . . Kansas City, Missouri:
    Press of the Sidney F. Woody Printing Co., [*c.*1892],
    156pp.

CROLY, HERBERT DAVID (1869-1930) *U.S.*
as Herbert (David) Croly
  Founder of *The New Republic,* 1914 and its editor 1914-
  1930.
  □ *The Promise of American Life,* 1909; *Marcus Alonzo
    Hanna,* 1912; *Progressive Democracy,* 1914; *The "New
    Republic" Idea,* 1932.
● as William Herbert
  *The World Grown Young. Being A Brief Record of
  Reforms Carried Out from 1894-1914 by the Late Mr.
  P. Adams, Millionaire and Philanthropist.* London: W. H.
  Allen & Co., [1892], 304pp.
  ■ *Houses for Town or Country,* 1907.

CRONIN, BERNARD CHARLES (1884-   ) *Australian*
as Dennis Adair
  □ *Death Rides the Desert,* 1940.
as Bernard Cronin
  Toad. London: Hodder & Stoughton, [1929], 320pp.
  □ *Timber Wolves,* 1920; *Salvage,* 1923; *Dragonfly,* 1928;
    Bracken, 1931.
as Eric North
  Three Against the Stars. Argosy, 2 July 1938
  The Ant Men. Philadelphia: Holt, 1955, 216pp.
  □ *A Chip On My Shoulder,* 1956; *The Name is Smith,*
    1957; *Nobody Stops Me,* 1960.

CROOK, COMPTON N.
as Stephen Tall
  The Stardust Voyages. NY: Berkley, 1975, paper.
  The Ramsgate Paradox. NY: Berkley, 1976, paper.

CROSBY, HARRY C. *U.S.*
as Christopher Anvil
  The Prisoner. Astounding, Feb 1956
  The Day the Machines Stopped. NY: Monarch, 1964, 124pp.
    paper.
  Strangers in Paradise. NY: Tower, [*c.*1969], 170pp., paper.
  Pandora's Planet. Garden City: Doubleday, 1972, 233pp.
  Warlord's World. NY: DAW #168, [1975], 207pp., paper.

CROSS, JOHN KEIR (1914-1967) *Scottish*
as John Keir Cross
  The Other Passenger. London: Westhouse, 1944, 274pp.,
    ill. *ss col*
  The Angry Planet. London: P. Lunn, 1945, 200pp., ill.
  The Owl and the Pussycat. London: P. Lunn, 1946,
    158pp., ill. *juv*
  The Flying Fortunes, In An Encounter With Rubberface.

London: F. Muller, [1952], 216pp. *juv*

The Red Journey Back. NY: Coward-McCann, [1954], 252pp. ill.

S. O. S. From Mars. London: Hutchinson, 1954, 216pp. [American title: *The Red Journey Back*]

☐ *The White Magic*, 1947; *The Man In Moonlight*, 1947; *Juniper Green*, 1952 (Br. edition); *The Dancing Tree*, 1955.

as Stephen MacFarlane

☐ *Blackadder, A Tale of the Days of Nelson*, 1950.

as Susan Morley

☐ *Mistress Glory*, 1948; *Juniper Green*, 1953 (U.S. edition).

CROSSEN, KENDELL F(oster) (1910-) *U.S.*

as M. E. Chaber

☐ MYSTERY: *Hangman's Harvest*, 1952; *As Old As Cain*, 1954; *Born to Be Hanged*, 1973.

as Ken(dell) F. Crossen

The Boy Who Cried Wolf 359. *Amazing*, Feb 1951

Restricted Clientele. *Thrilling Wonder Stories*, Feb 1951

Once Upon A Star. NY: Holt, 1953, 237pp.

Year of Consent. NY: Dell, [1954], 224pp., paper.

as Richard Foster

The Rest Must Die. Greenwich, Connecticut: Fawcett Gold Medal, 1959, 176pp., paper.

☐ MYSTERY: *Blond and Beautiful*, 1951.

as Christopher Monig

The Green Earth Forever. *Spaceway*, June 1954

☐ MYSTERY: *The Burned Man*, 1956; *Abra-Cadaver*, 1958.

as Clay Richards

☐ MYSTERY: "Grant Kirby" series; including *Death of An Angel*, 1963; *The Gentle Assassin*, 1964; and other mysteries, e. g. *Who Steals My Name*, 1964.

● Bennet Barlay, H. R. C. Lorac, Kent Richard

CROUCH, NATHANIEL (1632?-1725?) *English*

as Robert Burton

[later editions of the work below, as well as other works]

as R.B., Author of "The History of the Wars of England, &c.", and "Remarks of London, &c."

■ *Admirable Curiosities, Rarities and Wonders in England, Scotland, and Ireland. Or, an account of many remarkable persons, and places, and likewise of the battels [sic], sieges, prodigious earthquakes, tempests, inundations, thunders, lightenings, fires, murders, and other considerable occurrences, and accidents for several hundred years past. Together with the natural and artificial rarities in every country and many other observable matters; as they are recorded by the most authentick and credible historians of former and latter ages; adorned with the lively description of several memorable things therein contained, ingraven on copper plates*. London: 1682, 12mo., 232pp.

[A title that oozes a sense of wonder earns this non-fiction work an entry. Had there been science fiction writers, as such, in 1682, the book would have been a standard reference and repository of story-lines, it still might not be a bad idea . . .]

CROWN, PETER J.

● Pete Lewis

CROWNINSHIELD, MARY BRADFORD (Mrs. Schuyler) (? -1913)

as (Mrs. Schuyler) Crowninshield

Latitude 19°: A Romance of the West Indies in the Year of Our Lord Eighteen Hundred and Twenty. NY: Appleton, 1898, 418pp., ill.

☐ *The Ignoramuses*, 1887; *Plucky Smalls*, 1889; *San Isido*, 1900; *The Mysterious Miss Dacres*, 1901 (ss col).

CRUGER, JULIA GRINNELL (Storrow) (Mrs. Van Rensselaer) (18 ? -1920)

Born: France

as Mrs. Van Rensselaer Cruger

■ TRAVEL: *From Fog to Sun*, 1911.

as Julien Gordon

Vampires; Mademoiselle Reseda. Philadelphia: Lippincott, 1891, 299pp. *2 novels*

☐ *A Diplomat's Diary*, 1890; *A Puritan Pagan*, 1891; *Marionettes*, 1892; *A Wedding and Other Stories*, 1896 (ss col); *Eat Not Thy Heart*, 1897.

■ *Abraham Lincoln and His Relations to Women*, 1894.

CULLEN, STEPHEN

as Author of "The Haunted Priory," &c., &c.

The Castle of Inch Valley: A Tale—Alas! Too True. Hackney, [London]: S. & J. Cave for W. Evans, 1820, 522pp., ill.

anonymous

The Haunted Priory; or, The Fortunes of the House of Rayo. A Romance Founded Partly on Historical Fact. Dublin: W. Jones, 1794, 262pp.

The Castle of Inch Valley: A Tale—Alas! Too True. . . London: J. Bell, 1796, 3 vol.

CUMMINGS, MONETTE A.

as M. A. Cummings

The Brides of Ool. *Planet Stories*, Summer 1955

Exile and Other Tales of Fantasy. NY: Flagship, 1968, 160pp., paper. *ss col*

CUMMINGS, (Mrs. Ray) *U.S.*

as Gabriel Wilson [in collaboration with Ray Cummings]

Earth-Venus 12. *Thrilling Wonder Stories*, Dec 1936

CUMMINGS, RAY(mond) KING (1887-1957) *U.S.*

Born: New York, New York

as Ray Cummings

The Girl In the Golden Atom. *All Story Weekly*, 15 Mar 1919

The Girl In the Golden Atom. London: Methuen, [1922].

The Girl In the Golden Atom. NY: Harper, 1923, 341pp.

The Man Who Mastered Time. Chicago: McClurg, 1929, 351pp.

The Sea Girl. Chicago: McClurg, 1930, 302pp.

Terrano, The Conqueror. Chicago: McClurg, 1930, 345pp.

Brigands of the Moon. Chicago: McClurg, 1931, 386pp.

The Shadow Girl. London: Swan, [1946], 186pp., paper.

The Man On the Meteor. London: Swan, [c.1946], 125pp. paper.

The Princess of the Atom. NY: Avon, [1950], 158pp., paper. (Avon Fantasy Novels No. 1)

Beyond the Vanishing Point. NY: Ace, [1958], 95pp., paper. (Ace Double D 331)

Wandl the Invader. NY: Ace, [1961], 135pp., paper. (Ace Double D 497)

Beyond the Stars. NY: Ace, [1963], 160pp., paper. (Ace Double F 248)

A Brand New World. NY: Ace, [1964], 158pp., paper.

Exile of Time. NY: Avalon, [1964], 192pp.

Explorers Into Infinity. NY: Avalon, 1965, 192pp.

Tama of the Light Country. NY: Ace, 1965, 124pp., paper.

Tama Princess of Mercury. NY: Ace, 1966, 128pp., paper.

The Insect Invasion. NY: Avalon, [1967], 191pp.

as Gabriel Wilson [in collaboration with Mrs. Ray Cummings]

Earth-Venus 12. *Thrilling Wonder Stories*, Dec 1936

CURTIES, T. J. HORSLEY

as T. J. Horsley Curties

Ancient Records; or, the Abbey of St. Oswythe. A Romance. London: W. Lane, 1801, 4 vol.

The Monk of Udolpho. London: J. F. Hughes, 1807, 4 vol.

☐ *The Scottish Legend; or, the Isle of St. Clothair*, 1802

4 vol.; *The Watch Tower; or, The Sons of Uthona,*, 1803-04, 5 vol; *St. Botolph's Priory; or, the Sable Mask,* 1806, 5 vol.

as T. J. Horsley

Ethelwina; or, The House of Fitz Auburne. London: W. Lane, 1799, 3 vol.

CURZON-HERRICK, (Maud) KATHLEEN (Cairnes) (Plantagenet), (Lady) (1893-   ) *British*

as Maud Cairnes

Strange Journey. London: Cobden-Sanderson, [1935], 356pp.

as Lady Herrick

☐ *The Disappearing Duchess,* 1939.

DAHLGREN, SARAH MADELEINE (Vinton) (Mrs. John A.) (1825-1898)   *U.S.*

Born: Gallipolis, Ohio

as Madeleine (Vinton) Dahlgren

South-Mountain Magic, A Narrative. Boston: J. R. Osgood, 1882, 218pp.

The Woodley Lane Ghost and Other Stories. Philadelphia: D. Biddle, 1899, 474pp., ill. *ss col*

☐ *Idealities,* 1859; *South Sea Sketches,* 1881; *Divorced,* 1887; *The Secret Directory. A Romance of Hidden History,* 1896.

■ (translator) *Catholicism, Liberalism, and Socialism* by Donoso Cortes; *Thoughts On Female Suffrage,* 1871; *Social Life In Washington,* 1873.

DAKERS, ELAINE KIDNER (Mrs. Andrew)   (1905-   )

as Jane Lane

A State of Mind. London: Muller, [1964], 203pp.

☐ HISTORICAL FICTION: *England For Sale,* 1943; *Gin and Bitters,* 1945; *Fortress In the Forth,* 1950; *Dark Conspiracy,* 1952; *The Phoenix and the Laurel,* 1954; *Wind Through the Heather,* 1965.

■ *Puritan, Rake, and Squire,* 1950; *The Reign of King Covenant,* 1956.

DALEY, BERNARD JOHN

as John Bernard Daley

The Gun. *Fantastic,* Feb 1955

DANIEL, GLYN E(dmund) (1914-   )   *Welsh*

Born: Lampeter

as Glyn E(dmund) Daniel

■ *Myth or Legend?* NY: Macmillan, 1955, 125pp., ill. [non-fiction of SF interest]

■ *A Hundred Years of Archaeology,* 1950; *The Prehistoric Chamber Tombs of England and Wales,* 1950; *Lascaux and Carnac,* 1955.

as Dilwyn Rees

☐ MYSTERY: *The Cambridge Murders,* [1945].

DANIEL, YULI MARKOVICH (1925-   )   *Russian*

as Nikolai Arzhak

used in Russian language publications

as Yuli Daniel (Nikolai Arzhak)

This Is Moscow Speaking and Other Stories. London: Collins, 1968, 159pp. *ss col*

as Yuli Daniel

☐ *Prison Poems,* 1971 (poetry).

DANNAY, FREDERIC (1905-   )   *ne* Daniel Nathan   *U.S.*

Born: Brooklyn, New York

as Daniel Nathan

☐ *The Golden Summer,* 1953. [autobiographical fiction]

as Ellery Queen [in collaboration with Manfred Lee]

☐ MYSTERY: *The Roman Hat Mystery,* 1929; *The Adventures of Ellery Queen,* 1934 (ss col); *The Door Between,* 1937; *The Devil To Pay,* 1938; *Calamity Town,* 1942; *The Case Book of Ellery Queen,* 1945 (ss col); *Cat of Many Tails,* 1949; *The Origin of Evil,* 1951; *The Scarlet Letters,* 1953; *The Finishing Stroke,* 1958; *And On the Eighth Day,* 1964; *A Study in Terror* (British title: *Sherlock Holmes vs. Jack the Ripper)*, 1966; *Q. E. D.: Queen's Experiments in Detection*, 1968 (ss col); *The Last Woman in His Life*, 1970; *A Fine and Private Place*, 1971.

as Barnaby Ross [in collaboration with Manfred Lee]
  □ MYSTERY: "Drury Lane" series: *Tragedy of X*, 1932; *Tragedy of Y*, 1932; *Tragedy of Z*, 1933; *Drury Lane's Last Case*, 1933.

D'APERY, HELEN (Burrell) (Mrs.)   (1842-1915)   *U.S.*
as Olive Harper and another
  The Sociable Ghost. Being the Adventures of A Reporter. NY: J. S. Olgilvie, 1903, 235pp., front.
  □ *What Do You Think*, 1895; *The Show Girl*, 1902; *Bertha, the Sewing Machine Girl*, 1906; *Caught In Mid Ocean*, 1911. [Many of Olive Harper's novels were novelizations of plays]

DAUKES, SIDNEY HERBERT   (1879-   )
as S(idney) H(erbert) Daukes
  ■ *Barrier Charts for Health Officers*, 1921; *The Medical Museum*, 1929.
as Sidney Fairway
  The Long Tunnel. London: S. Paul, [1935], 320pp.
  □ *The Doctor's Defense*, 1931; *The Yellow Viper*, 1931; *A Cuckoo on Harley Street*, 1932; *Thanks to Dr. Molly*, 1937; *Quack's Paradise*, 1938; *A Late Recovery*, 1940.

DAVIES, HOWELL   *British*
● **as Andrew Marvell**
  Minimum Man; or, Time to Be Gone. London: Gollancz, 1938, 350pp.
  Three Men Make A World. London: Gollancz, 1939, 286pp.
  Congratulate the Devil. London: Gollancz, 1939, 285pp.

DAVIES, M(ary) C(atherine)
as M. C. Davies
  Adventures With the Mermaids. Sydney, Australia: S. Wood, 1930, 128pp., ill.

DAVIS, HORACE CHANDLER   (1926-   )   *U.S.*
  Born: Ithaca, New York
as Chan Davis
  The Nightmare. *Astounding*, May 1946
as Horace Chandler Davis
  Associate Editor, *Mathematical Reviews* [professional journal]

DAVIS, JAMES   (1853-1907)   *British*
as Owen Hall
  "*Eureka.*" London: Chatto & Windus, 1899, 308pp.
  □ *An Artist's Model*, 1895 (play).
  [Owen Hall was noted as a librettist]

DAY, EMILY FOSTER   (Mrs. Frank R.)   *U.S.*
as Emily Foster Day
  □ *Goliath; or, At the Break of the Market* [n.d. unproduced] (play)
  ■ *The Menehunes*, 1905.
as Mrs. Frank R. Day
  Princess of Manoa and Other Romantic Tales From the Folk-Lore of Old Hawaii. San Francisco: P. Elder & Co., [1906], 85pp., ill. *ss col*

DAY-LEWIS, C(ecil)   (1904-1972)   *British*
  Born: Ireland
  Biographical Study: *C. Day-Lewis*, by Clifford Dyment, 1955.
  Bibliography: *C. Day-Lewis, the Poet Laureate.* Compiled by G. Handley-Taylor and T. Smith, London: St. James Press, 1968.

as Nicholas Blake
  The Smiler With the Knife. NY: Harper, 1939, 303pp.
  □MYSTERY: *A Question of Proof*, 1935; *Thou Shell of Death*, 1936; *There's Trouble Brewing*, 1937; *The Beast Must Die*, 1938; *Malice in Wonderland*, 1940; *The Case of the Abominable Snowman*, 1941; *Minute for Murder*, 1947; *Head of A Traveller*, 1949; *The Dreadful Hollow*, 1953; *The Whisper in the Gloom*, 1954; *A Tangled Web*, 1956; *End of Chapter*, 1957; *A Penknife In My Heart*, 1958; *A Widow's Cruise*, 1959; *The Worm of Death*, 1961; *The Deadly Joker*, 1963; *The Sad Variety*, 1964; *The Morning After Death*, 1966; *The Private Wound*, 1968.
as C. Day(-)Lewis
  The Antique Heroes. *Magazine of Fantasy and Science Fiction*, Feb 1957 *poetry*
  □ POETRY: *Beechan Vigil*, 1925; *From Feathers to Iron*, 1931; *The Magnetic Mountain*, 1933.
  ■ *A Hope For Poetry*, 1934; *Revolution In Writing*, 1935; *The Poetic Image*, 1946; *A Need For Poetry?*, 1968.

DE BANZIE, ERIC(h)
as Gregory Baxter [in collaboration with John Ressich]
  The Narrowing Lust. London: Selwyn & Blount, 1928, 287pp.
  □ MYSTERY: *Blue Lightning*, 1926; *The Ainceworth Mystery*, 1930; *Death Strikes at Six Bells*, 1930; *Murder Could Not Kill*, 1932.

DE BURY, F. BLAZE (Mademoiselle)
as F. Dickberry
  The Storm of London: A Social Rhapsody. London: J. Long, 1904, 313pp.
  □ *The Nymph*, 1906; *Phantom Figures*, 1907; *Stephen Ormond. A Man's Life*, 1913.

DE CAMP, CATHERINE CROOK (Mrs. L. Sprague)
as Catherine C. de Camp
  Windfall. *Astounding*, July 1951
  ■ All with L. Sprague de Camp: *Ancient Ruins and Archaeology*, 1964; *Spirits, Stars, and Spells*, 1966; *The Story of Science In America*, 1967; *Darwin and His Great Discovery*, 1972. ALONE: *The Money Tree, a New Guide to Successful Personal Finance*, 1972; *Teach Your Child to Manage Money*, 1974.

DE CAMP, L(yon) Sprague (1907-   )   *U.S.*
  Born: New York, New York
as L. Sprague de Camp
  The Isolinguals. *Astounding*, Sept 1937
  Lest Darkness Fall. NY: Holt, [c.1941], 379pp., ill.
  (with Fletcher Pratt) *The Incomplete Enchanter.* NY: Holt, [c.1941], 326pp.
  (with Fletcher Pratt) *The Land of Unreason.* NY: Holt, [1942], 260pp.
  Divide and Rule. Reading, Pennsylvania: Fantasy Press, 1948, 231pp.
  (with Fletcher Pratt) *The Carnelian Cube.* NY: Gnome, 1948, 230pp.
  The Wheels of If. Chicago: Shasta, 1948 [1949], 223pp. *ss col*
  (with Fletcher Pratt) *The Castle of Iron.* NY: Gnome, [1950], 224pp.
  (with P. Schuyler Miller)   *Genus Homo.* Reading, Pennsylvania: Fantasy Press, 1950, 225pp.
  Rogue Queen. Garden City: Doubleday, 1951, 222pp.
  The Undesired Princess. Los Angeles: FPCI, 1951, 248pp.
  The Continent Makers and Other Tales of the Viagens. NY: Twayne, [1953], 272pp. *ss col*
  (with Fletcher Pratt) *Tales From Gavagan's Bar.* NY: Twayen, [1953], 228pp., ill. *ss col*
  The Tritonian Ring. NY: Twayne, [1953], 262pp.

Cosmic Man Hunt. NY: Ace, [1954], 128pp., paper. (Ace Double D 61)

(with Robert E. Howard) *Tales of Conan.* NY: Gnome, [1955], 218pp.

Solomon's Stone. NY: Avalon, [1957], 224pp.

(with Robert E. Howard and B. Nyberg) *The Return of Conan.* NY: Gnome, 1957, 191pp.

The Tower of Zanid. NY: Avalon, [1958], 220pp.

(with Fletcher Pratt) *Wall of Serpents.* NY: Avalon, 1960, 223pp.

The Glory That Was. NY: Avalon, [1960], 223pp.

The Search for Zei. NY: Avalon, [1962], 224pp.

A Gun for Dinosaur. Garden City: Doubleday, 1963, 359pp. *ss col*

The Hand of Zei. NY: Avalon, [1963], 222pp.

(with Robert E. Howard) *Conan the Adventurer.* NY: Lancer, [1966], 224pp., paper.

(with Robert E. Howard) *Conan the Usurper.* NY: Lancer, [1967], 256pp., paper.

(with Robert E. Howard and Lin Carter) *Conan.* NY: Lancer, [1968], 221pp., paper. *ss col*

(with Robert E. Howard) *Conan the Freebooter.* NY: Lancer, [1968], 223pp., paper.

(with Robert E. Howard and Lin Carter) *Conan the Wanderer.* NY: Lancer, [1968], 222pp., paper.

(with Robert E. Howard and B. Nyberg) *Conan the Avenger.* NY: Lancer, [1968], 192pp., paper.

(with Robert E. Howard and Lin Carter) *Conan of the Isles.* NY: Lancer, [1968], 189pp., paper.

The Goblin Tower. NY: Pyramid, [1968], 253pp., paper.

(with Lin Carter and Robert E. Howard) *Conan of Cimmeria.* NY: Lancer, [1969], 189pp., paper.

The Golden Wind. Garden City: Doubleday, 1969, 288pp.

Demons and Dinosaurs. Sauk City, Wisconsin: Arkham House, 1970 [1969], 72pp. (500 cop)

The Reluctant Shaman and Other Fantastic Tales. NY: Pyramid, [1970], 190pp., paper. *ss col*

(with Robert E. Howard and Lin Carter) *Conan the Buccaneer.* NY: Lancer, [1971], 191pp., paper.

(edited with George Scithers) *The Conan Grimoire.* Baltimore: Mirage, 1972 [1971], 261pp. (1500 cop) *nonfiction collection*

Phantoms and Fancies. Baltimore: Mirage, 1972, 107pp., ill.

Scribblings. Boston: 1975. (A Boskone Book).

Literary Swordsmen and Sorcerers: The Makers of Heroic Fantasy. Sauk City, Wisconsin: Arkham House, 1976, 313pp.

(with Robert E. Howard and Lin Carter) *Conan of Aquilonia.* NY: Ace, [1977], paper.

□ HISTORICAL NOVELS: *An Elephant for Aristotle*, 1958; *The Dragon of Istar Gate*, 1961; *Arrows of Hercules*, 1965.

■ *Inventions and Their Management*, 1937; *The Evolution of Naval Weapons*, 1947; (with Willy Ley) *The Lands Beyond*, 1952; *Science Fiction Handbook*, 1953 (revised c.1975); *The Ancient Engineers*, 1963.

[for non-fiction written with Catherine Crook de Camp see her entry]

(introduction to) *Al Azif (The Necronomicon)* by Abdul Al Hazred. Philadelphia: Owlswick Press, [c. 1974], 196pp., (348 cop).

[text consists of seeming repetition of eight pages of manuscript (perhaps a cruel jest of the Old Ones), in seeming Syriac script. Is untranslatable, and probably best so (see Howard P. Lovecraft.)]

as Lyman R. Lyon

Employment. *Astounding*, May 1939

as J. Wellington Wells

book reviews in *Unknown*.

DE CASTRO, GUSTAF ADOLF DANZIGER (1859?-1959)
U. S. [also given in NUC as 1866-1959]

as Adolphe Danziger

□ *The Children of Fate, A Story of Passion*, 1905; *After the Confession*, 1908 (poetry); *In the Garden of Abdullah and Other Stories*, 1916 (ss col); *The Painter's Dream*, 1940.

■ *Jewish Forerunners of Christianity*, 1903.

as G(ustav) A. Danziger

(with Ambrose Bierce) *The Monk and the Hangman's Daughter.* Chicago: F.J. Schulte, 1892 [c.1891], 166pp., ill.

In the Confessional and The Following. NY: Western Authors' Pub. Assn., 1893, 283pp. (on cover "Western Authors' Series No. 2") *ss col*

as Adolf de Castro

The Last Test. *Weird Tales*, Nov 1928

DE LA MARE, WALTER J(ohn) (1873-1956) *English*
Born: Charlton, Kent
Biography: *Walter de la Mare*, by Leonard Clark. London: 1960.

as W. J. D.

The Powder Monkey Bob. *The Choristers' Journal* [c.1890]. (Br.)

A Moonlight Skate. *The Choristers' Journal*, [c.1890], (Br.)

as Walter (J.) de la Mare

Henry Brocken. London: Murray, 1904, 202pp.

The Three Mulla-Mulgars. London: Duckworth, 1910, 312pp., ill.

The Return. NY: Putnam, 1911, 354pp.

Crossings: A Fairy Play. London: Beaumont, [1921], 131pp.

The Riddle and Other Tales. London: Selwyn and Blount, 1923, 303pp. *ss col*

Broomsticks and Other Tales. London: Constable, 1925, 378pp., ill. (278 cop, signed & numbered) *ss col*

Two Tales: The Green Room & The Connoisseur. London: Bookman's Journal, [1925], 128pp. (250 cop)

The Connoisseur and Other Stories. London: Collins, 1926, 357pp. *ss col*

Seaton's Aunt. London: Faber & Gwyer, [1927], 40pp.

On the Edge. London: Faber, 1930, 289pp., ill. *ss col*

The Lord Fish. London: Faber, [1933], 289pp., ill.

The Nap and Other Stories. London: Nelson, [1936], 197pp. *ss col*

The Wind Blows Over. London: Faber, [1936], 326pp.

Best Stories of Walter de la Mare. London: Faber, 1942, 397pp. *ss col*

Collected Stories. NY: Knopf, 1950, 467pp. *ss col*

Beginning and Other Stories. London: Faber, 1955, 256pp. *ss col*

Ghost Stories. London: Folio Society, 1956, 234pp., ill. *ss col*

Some Stories. London: Faber, 1962, 192pp., paper. *ss col*

Eight Tales. Sauk City, Wisconsin: Arkham House, 1971, 108pp. *ss col*

□ POETRY: *Poems*, 1906; *The Listeners and Other Poems*, 1912.

as Walter Ramal

Kismet. *The Sketch*, Aug 7, 1895

A Mote. The Village of Old Age. *Cornhill Magazine*, [c.1896] *short story*

□ POETRY: *Songs of Childhood*, 1902.

DE MILLE, JAMES (1837-1880)

as (Prof.) James De Mille

□ *The Cryptogram*, 1870; *Lost In the Fog*, 1870; *The Lady Of the Ice*, 1870; *A Comedy of Terrors*, 1872; *Among the Brigands*, 1872; *The Living Link*, 1874; *A Castle In Spain*, 1878.

as Gilbert Gaul

A Strange Manuscript Found In A Copper Cylinder. NY: Harper, 1888, 291pp., ill.

DEMING, RICHARD
as Richard Deeming
Margin of Error. *If,* March 1953
as Richard Deming
The Shape of Things That Came. *Magazine of Fantasy and Science Fiction,* Oct 1951
☐ MYSTERY: *Tweak the Devil's Nose,* 1953; *Whistle Past The Graveyard,* 1954.
as Max Franklin
☐ MYSTERY: *Justice Has No Sword,* 1953; *Hell Street,* 1954. (compiler) *Anthology of Wit and Humor,* 1923.

DE MORGAN, JOHN   *U.S.*
as Author of "He"
King Solomon's Treasures. NY: N. L. Munro, 1887, 200pp.
King Solomon's Wives. NY: N. L. Munro, 1887, 239pp.
as Author of "King Solomon's Wives," "King Solomon's Treasures," "He," "It," etc.
"Bess:" A Companion to "Jess." NY: N.L. Munro, 1887, 234pp.
as John De Morgan
In Unknown Worlds, or, A Trip to A Mystery Land. NY: Street & Smith, [1927], 214pp.
anonymous
"He," A Companion to She. NY: N. L. Munro, [1887], 234pp.
"It" A Wild Weird History. NY: N. L. Munro, [1887], 242pp.

DENNIS, WALTER L.   *U.S.*
as Walter Dennis
(with Ernest Tucker) The Gladiators. *Startling Stories,* Jan 1943
as Dennis Mc Dermott [in collaboration with Paul McDermott and P. Schuyler Miller]
The Duel on the Asteroid. *Wonder Stories,* Jan 1932.

DENT, LESTER   (1904–   ) *U.S.*
Born: La Plata, Missouri
as Lester Dent
The Derelict of Skull Shoal. *Doc Savage Magazine,* March 1944
☐ Pirate Cay. *Top Notch Magazine,* Sept 1929
Dead At the Take-Off, 1946; *Lady Afraid,* 1948.
as Kenneth Roberts
The Man of Bronze. *Doc Savage Magazine,* March 1933
as Kenneth Robeson
The Land of Terror. *Doc Savage Magazine,* April 1934
The Man of Bronze. NY: Street & Smith, [1933], 252pp.
The Land of Terror. NY: Street & Smith, [1933], 252pp.
✔ Maxwell Grant [house pseudonym], Tim Ryan

DE REYNA, DIANE DETZLER   (Mrs.) (1930–   ) *U.S.*
Born: Ridgeford, Connecticut
as Jorge de Reyna
The Return of the Starships. NY: Avalon, 1968, 192pp.
as Diane Detzler
The Tomb. *Science Fiction Stories,* Nov 1958
The Planet of Fear. NY: Avalon, 1968, 190pp.
as Adam Lukens
The Sea People. NY: Avalon, [1959], 221pp.
Conquest of Life. NY: Avalon, [1960], 221pp.
Sons of the Wolf. NY: Avalon, [1961], 224pp.
The Glass Cage. NY: Avalon, [1962], 223pp.
The World Within. NY: Avalon, [1962], 222pp.
Alien World. NY: Avalon, [1963], 192pp.
Eevalu. NY: Avalon, [1963], 192pp.

DERLETH, AUGUST W(illiam)   (1909-1971) *U.S.*
Born: Sauk City, Wisconsin
Bibliography: *One Hundred Books by August Derleth.*

Sauk City, Wisconsin: Arkham House, 1962, 121pp., ill. (1225 cop)
Derleth founded the first of the successful modern fantasy and science fiction small presses in 1939, with Donald Wandrei. Arkham House promoted the works of H.P. Lovecraft and became publisher for some of the best *genre* writers.
as August (W.) Derleth
Bat's Belfrey. *Weird Tales,* May 1926
Mrs. Carter Makes Up Her Mind. *Fantastic Adventures,* May 1942
Someone In the Dark. Sauk City, Wisconsin: Arkham House, 1941, 335pp. (1145 cop) *ss col*
Something Near. Sauk City, Wisconsin: Arkham House, 1945, 274pp. (2054 cop) *ss col*
(with H. P. Lovecraft) *The Lurker At the Threshold.* Sauk City, Wisconsin: Arkham House, 1945, 196pp. (3041 cop)
Oliver the Wayward Owl. Sauk City, Wisconsin: Stanton and Lee, 1945, 84pp., ill. (3089 cop) *juv*
Not Long For This World. Sauk City, Wisconsin: Arkham House, 1948, 221pp. (2067 cop) *ss col*
(with H. P. Lovecraft) *The Survivor and Others.* Sauk City, Wisconsin: Arkham House, 1957, 161pp. (2096 cop) *ss col*
The Mask of Cthulhu. Sauk City, Wisconsin: Arkham House, 1958, 201pp. (2051 cop) *ss col*
Lonesome Places. Sauk City, Wisconsin: Arkham House, 1962, 198pp. (2201 cop) *ss col*
Trail of the Cthulhu. Sauk City, Wisconsin: Arkham House, 1962, 248pp. (2470 cop) *ss col*
(with Mark Schorer) *Colonel Markesan and Less Pleasant People.* Sauk City, Wisconsin: Arkham House, 1966, 285pp.
Harrigan's File. Sauk City: Wisconsin: Arkham House, 1975.
☐ SAC PRAIRIE SERIES: *Place of Hawks,* 1935; *Still Is the Summer Night,* 1937; *Wind Over Wisconsin,* 1938; *Any Day Now,* 1938; *Restless Is the River,* 1939. POETRY: *Hawk On the Wind,* 1938; *Here On A Darkling Plain,* 1940. MYSTERY: "Judge Peck" series including: *The Man On All Fours,* 1934; *Murder Stalks the Wakely Family,* 1934; *Sign of Fear,* 1935; *Sentence Deferred,* 1939; *The Narracong Riddle,* 1940; *No Future for Luana,* 1945; *Fell Purpose,* 1953; and "Solar Pons" series including: *In Re: Sherlock Holmes,* 1945; *Memoirs of Solar Pons,* 1951; *Three Problems for Solar Pons,* 1952.
as Stephen Grendon
A Gentleman From Prague. *Weird Tales,* Nov 1944
A Bishop's Gambit. *Avon Fantasy Reader #3*
Mr. George and Other Odd Persons. Sauk City, Wisconsin: Arkham House, 1963, 239pp. (2546 cop) *ss col*
as Eldon Heath
Joliper's Gift. *Strange Stories,* April 1940
as Tally Mason
Lord of Evil. *Weird Tales,* April 1939
☐ *Consider Your Verdict,* 1937.
as Michael West
Hector. *Weird Tales,* Nov 1951
✔ Kenyon Holmes

DE WEESE, GENE   *U.S.*
as Gene De Weese
(with Robert Coulson) Gates of the Universe. NY: Laser Books #4, [1975], 190pp., paper.
(with Robert Coulson) *Now You See It/Him/Them. . .* Garden City: Doubleday, 1975, 157pp.
(with Robert Coulson) *Charles Fort Never Mentioned Wombats.* Garden City: Doubleday, 1977, 173pp.
as Jean De Weese
☐ GOTHIC ROMANCE: *Web of Guilt,* 1976; *The Doll With the Open Eyes,* 1976; *Cave of the Moaning Wind,* [c.1977].
✔ Thomas Stratton [in collaboration with Robert Coulson]

DE WEINDECK, WINTELER
as Capt. George Z. Fighton
The Ghost of Passy; A Sensational Novel. London: Hutchinson, 1889, 131pp.

DIFFIN, CHARLES WILLARD
as Charles Willard Diffin
Spawn of the Stars. *Astounding,* Feb 1930
□ AMERICAN INDIAN TALES: *Gray Smoke, the Coyote of El Coronel,* 1940; *The Secret of Sun-God's Cave,* 1942.
as C. D. Willard
Out of the Dreadful Depths. *Astounding,* June 1930

DIKTY, JULIAN CHAIN MAY (Mrs. Theodore)   (1931-   ) U.S.
as Julian Chain
Success Story. *Astounding,* May 1951
as J. C. May
Dune Roller. *Astounding,* Dec 1951
as Julian (C.) May
Star of Wonder. *Thrilling Wonder Stories,* Feb 1953
■ *There's Adventure in Atomic Energy,* 1957 (juv).

DINGLE, AYLWARD EDWARD   (1874-   )
as Brian Cotterell
□ *Sinister Eden,* 1934.
as Capt. Dingle
□ *Wide Waters,* 1924; *Fathomless,* 1929; *Seaworthy,* 1930; *Spin A Yarn Sailor,* 1935.
as Sinbad
The Age-Old Kingdom. London: Hutchinson, [1947], 176pp.
□ *Pipe All Hands,* 1935; *Pirates May Fly,* 1943.
■ *Rough Hewn; the Autobiography of A Modern Sinbad,* 1933.

DISCH, THOMAS M.   (1940-   ) U.S.
Born: Des Moines, Iowa
as Thom Demijohn [in collaboration with John T. Sladek]
Black Alice. Garden City: Doubleday, 1968.
as Thomas M. Disch
The Double Timer. *Fantastic,* Oct 1962
The Genocides. NY: Berkley, [1965], 143pp., paper.
Mankind Under the Leash. NY: Ace, [1966], 140pp., paper. (Ace Double G 597)
One Hundred and Two H Bombs. London: Compact, 1966, 192pp. ss col
Echo Round His Bones. NY: Berkley, [1967], 144pp., paper.
Camp Concentration. London: Hart-Davis, 1968, 177pp.
Under Compulsion. London: Hart-Davis, 1968, 220pp. ss col
Fun With Your New Head. Garden City: Doubleday, 1968, 216pp.
334. London: Mac Gibbon & Kee, [1972], 201pp.
Getting Into Death. London: Hart-Davis, [1973], 206pp. ss col
□ (with Marilyn Hacker and Charles Platt) *Highway Sandwiches,* 1970 (poetry); *The Right Way to Figure Plumbing,* 1972.
as Leonie Hargrave
□ *Clara Reeve,* 1975.

DISRAELI, BENJAMIN   (1st Earl of Beaconsfield) (1804-1881'   British
Born: London
as Author of "Vivian Grey"
The Voyage of Captain Popanilla. London: H. Colburn, 1828, 243pp.
The Wondrous Tale of Alroy. London: Saunders and Otley, 1833, 3 vol.
□ *The Tragedy of Count Alarcos, 1839.*
as Benjamin Disraeli (Lord Beaconsfield)

Ixion in Heaven. London: Routledge, 1847.
□ *Vivian Grey,* 1826; *Sybil,* 1845; *Lothair,* 1870; *Endymion,* 1880.
■ *Speeches On the Conservative Policies of the Last Thirty Years,* 1869.

DITZEN, RUDOLF   (1893-1947) German
as Hans Fallada
Sparrow Farm, the Tale of the City Clerk Who Flew Into the Country For A Holiday. London: Putnam, [1937], 239pp.
□ *Little Man, What Now?,* 1933; *The World Outside,* 1934; *Wolf Among Wolves,* 1937; *Iron Gustav,* 1940; *The Drinker,* 1952.

DIVER, KATHERINE HELEN MAUDE (Marshall) (Mrs.)   (1867-1945) British
as Maude Diver
But Yesterday. London: Murray, 1927, 384pp.
□ *The Great Amulet,* 1908; *Lilamani, A Study In Possibilities,* 1911; *Strange Roads,* 1918; *Strong Hours,* 1919; *Siege Perilous and Other Stories,* 1924. (ss col)
■ *The English Woman In India,* 1909; *Royal India,* 1942.

DIVINE, ARTHUR DURHAM   (1904-   ) South African
Born: Capetown
as Arthur D. Divine
Dark Moon. London: Methuen, [1913], 329pp.
They Blocked the Suez Canal. NY: Green Circle, 1936, 252pp.
Tunnel From Calais. London: W. Collins, 1942, 192pp.
□ *Admiral's Million,* 1936; *Fire In the Ice,* 1938.
■ *Dunkirk,* 1945; *Navies In Exile,* 1944; *Road to Tunis,* 1944.
as David Divine
Atom at Spithead. London: R. Hale, 1953, 186pp.
□ *The King of Fassarai,* 1950; *The Golden Fool,* 1954; *Boy On A Dolphin,* 1955.
as David Rame
Tunnel From Calais. NY: Macmillan, 1943, 246pp. [see British edition under Arthur D. Divine]
□ *Wine of Good Hope,* 1939; *The Sun Shall Greet Them,* 1941.

DOCKWEILER, JOSEPH HAROLD   (c.1920-c.1948) U.S.
Biography: Sketch in *The Early Pohl,* by Frederik Pohl. Garden City: Doubleday, 1976.
[possibly changed name legally to Dirk Wylie]
as Paul Dennis Lavond [house pseudonym] [in collaboration with Frederik Pohl and Robert W. Lowndes]
Something From Beyond. *Future,* Dec 1941
as Paul Dennis Lavond [house pseudonym] [in collaboration with Frederik Pohl]
Star of the Undead. *Fantasy Book #2,* [c.1948]
as Dirk Wylie [in collaboration with Frederik Pohl]
Asteroid of the Damned. *Planet Stories,* Summer 1942
Sky Test. *Super Science Stories,* Nov 1942
Outpost of the Eons. *Astonishing,* April 1943
as Dirk Wylie [in collaboration with F. Pohl and C. Kornbluth]
Vacant World. *Super Science Stories,* Jan 1941
as Dirk Wylie
(with Frederic Arnold Kummer, Jr.) When Time Went Mad. *Thrilling Wonder Stories,* Feb 1950
[Frederik Pohl wrote at least one story: Highwayman of the Void. *Planet Stories,* Fall 1944, alone as Dirk Wylie]

DODGSON, CHARLES L(utwidge)   (1832-1898) English
Born: Daresbury, Cheshire
as Lewis Carroll
Alice's Adventures In Wonderland. London: Macmillan, 1865, ill.
Alice's Adventures In Wonderland. London: Macmillan,

1866 [1865], ill.

Phantasmagoria. London: Macmillan, 1869, 202pp.

Through the Looking Glass and What Alice Found There. London: Macmillan, 1872, 224pp., ill.

The Hunting of the Snark; An Agony In Eight Fits. London: Macmillan, 1875, 53pp., ill. *verse*

Rhyme? and Reason? London: Macmillan, 1883, 214pp., ill.

A Tangled Tale. London: Macmillan, 1885, 152pp., ill.

Sylvie and Bruno. London: Macmillan, 1889, 395pp., ill.

Sylvie and Bruno Concluded. London: Macmillan, 1893, 411pp., ill.

as Charles L(utwidge) Dodgson

■ *An Elementary Treatise on Determinants,* 1867; *Euclid and His Modern Rivals,* 1879; *Curiosa Mathematica,* 1888; *Symbolic Logic,* 1896.

DONNELLY, IGNATIUS (1831-1901) *U.S.*

Born: Philadelphia, Pennsylvania

Biography: *Donnelly, The Portrait of A Politician,* by M. Rudge. Chicago: U. of Chicago Press, 1962.

as Edmund Boisgilbert, M.D.

Caesar's Column: A Story of the Twentieth Century. Chicago: F. J. Schulte, [c.1890], 367pp.

as Ignatius Donnelly

Doctor Huguet. Chicago: F. J. Schulte, [1891], 309pp.

The Golden Bottle; or, The Story of Ephraim Benezet of Kansas. NY: D. D. Merrill, 1892, 313pp.

■ (editor) *The Anti-Monopolist* (Weekly Journal), 1874-1879; *Atlantis, the Antediluvian World,* 1882; *Ragnarok: The Age of Fire and Gravel,* 1884[1882]. SHAKESPEARE/BACON CONTROVERSY: *The Great Cryptogram: Francis Bacon's Cipher in the So-called Shakespeare Plays,* 1888; *The Cipher in the Plays and on the Tombstone,* 1899.

DOUGLAS, GEORGE BRISBANE SCOTT (5th Baronet) (1856-1935) *Scottish*

as George Douglas

(ed) *Scottish Fairy and Folk Tales.* London: W. Scott, [1893], 301pp. *ss col*

The New Border Tales. London: W. Scott, [c.1895], 283pp., ill. *ss col*

■ *A History of the Border Counties,* 1899; (with W. S. Crockett) *Robert Burns,* 1904; *Scottish Poetry,* 1911 (lectures).

[Several bibliographies have ascribed *The New Border Tales* to George Douglas Brown (1869-1902), another Scottish author whose pen name was George Douglas and whose most famous book was *The House With The Green Shutters* (1901). The National Union Catalogue compounds the error by ascribing some of Sir George Douglas' other work, notably his biographical sketch of James Hogg, to George Douglas Brown. The NUC also attributes a novel written by Lady Gertrude Douglas, *Brown As A Berry,* to George Douglas Brown. It was published when Mr. Brown was five years old—it makes me wonder about the howlers *you* are going to find in my bibliography...]

DOUGLAS, GEORGE NORMAN (1868-1952) *British*

as Norman Douglas

They Went. London: Chapman and Hall, 1920, 250pp.

In the Beginning. Florence, Italy: The Author, 1927, 259pp.

Nerinda. Florence, Italy: Orioli, 1929, 137pp.

■ *On the Herpetology of the Grand Duchy of Baden,* 1894; *Siren Land,* 1911; *Old Calabria,* 1915; *Southwind,* 1917; *Paneros: Some Words On Aphrodisiacs and the Like,* 1930.

as Normyx

Unprofessional Tales. London: Unwin, 1901, 247pp. *ss col*

DOUGLASS, ELLSWORTH *British*

as Isaiah Werner

Pharaoh's Broker; The Very Remarkable Experiences In Another World of Isidore Werner. London: C. A. Pearson, 1899, 316pp.

[This title has been ascribed to Elmer Dwiggens, unconfirmed]

DOWDING, A. L. *British*

as Lewis Ramsden

The Temple of Fire. London: Collins' Clear Type Press, [1905], 360pp., ill.

□ *The Quest of the Luck,* 1904; *Red Cavalier,* 1907.

DOWNEY, EDMUND (1856- ?)

as F. M. Allen

Through Green Glasses. London: Ward & Downey, 1887, 236pp., ill. *ss col*

The Voyage of the Ark, As Related by Don Banim. London: Ward & Downey, 1888, 128pp.

Brayhard. The Strange Adventures of One Ass and Seven Champions. London: Ward & Downey, 1890, 308pp., ill.

The Round Tower of Babel. London: Ward & Downey, 1891, 121pp.

Green As Grass. London: Chatto & Windus, 1892, 240pp. *ss col*

The Little Green Man. London: Downey, [1895], 152pp., ill. *ss col*

Pinches of Salt. London: Downey, 1896, 246pp. *ss col*

London's Peril. London: Downey, [1900], 96pp.

□ *From the Green Bag,* 1889.

as Edmund Downey

The Brass Ring. The Extravagant Adventures of A City Clerk. London: Simpkin & Marshall, 1904, 152pp.

The Land Smeller and Other Yarns. London: Ward & Downey, 1893, 272pp. *ss col*

□ *A House Full of Tears,* 1888; *Clashmore,* 1903; *Morrissey,* 1924.

■ *Charles Lever: His Life In His Letters,* 1906 (2 vol.)

DRAPER, WARWICK HERBERT (1873- ?)

as Warwick Herbert Draper

The New Britain. London: Headley Bros., 1919, 143pp. [same as *The Tower* below]

■ *Alfred the Great. A Sketch,* 1901; *Chiswick,* 1923.

as Watchman

The Tower. London: Headley Bros., 1918, 143pp.

DRIANT, EMILE A(ugustin) (Cyprien) (1855- ?) *French*

as Captain Danrit

The Sunken Submarine. London: G. Richards, [1910], 294pp., ill.

as Captaine Danrit

La Guerre en Ballon. Paris: Flammarion, [1893], 2 vol., ill.

La Guerre Fatale, France—Angleterre. Paris: Flammarion, [c.1904], ill, maps.

L'Aviateur du Pacifique. Paris: Flammarion, [c.1909], 512pp., ill. maps.

Un Dirigeable au Pole Nord. Paris: Flammarion, [1909], 282pp.

Robinson de l'Air. Paris: Flammarion, [1909], 352pp., ill.

L'Alerte. Paris: Flammarion, [c.1910], 454pp., ill. maps.

Au-dessus du Continent Noir. Paris: Flammarion, [c.1911], 472pp., ill. maps.

□ *Evasion d'Empereur,* 1905; *De Samarcande a Lhassa,* 1907; *La Guerre en Rase Campagne,* 1917.

DRUSSAI, GAREN

as Garen Drussai

Extra-Curricular. *Magazine of Fantasy and Science Fiction,* Aug, 1952

⌐ Milo Kirkman

DU BOIS, EDWARD   (1774-1850)   *English*
as Author of "The Rising Sun," &c.
The Tarantula; or, the Dance of Fools, 1809.
as Count Reginald de Saint Leon
St. Godwin: A Tale of the Sixteenth, Seventeenth, and Eighteenth Century. London: P. Wogan, 1800, 218pp. [Satire on William Godwin's novel *Saint Leon: A Tale of the Sixteenth Century.*]
anonymous
[supposed translator] *The Fairy of Misfortune; or, the Loves of Octar and Zulima. An Eastern Tale.* London: J. Bell, 1799, 193pp.

DUCASSE, ISIDORE L(ucien)   (1846-1870)
as Compte de Lautreamont
The Lay of Maldoror. London: Casanova Society, 1942, 319pp. (1000 cop)
[Manuscript left without final editing at author's death. Many French language editions precede this first English translation. Ten copies were issued to the author in 1869. Printed by A. LaCroix, Verboeckhoven et Cie [Brussels] 332pp. They state on title page: *Les Chants de Maldoror* par Le Compte de Lautreamont. Paris: En vente chez tous les Libraires, 1869. Some of these sheets were issued in 1874 with the fictitious imprint "Typ. de. E. Wittmann" on verso of half-title and new imprint on title page "Paris et Bruxeles, 1874"]

DUCHACEK, IVO MARIA RUDOLF (Duka)   (1913-   )
naturalized U.S.
Born: Prostejov, Moravia (later Czechoslovakia)
as Ivo (D.) Duchacek
■ *The Strategy of Communist Infiltration: Czechoslovakia 1944-1948,* 1950; *Nations and Men: International Politics Today,* 1969; *Comparative Federalism; The Territorial Dimension of Politics,* 1970.
as Ivo Duka
(with Helena Kolda) *The Secret of the Two Feathers.* NY: Harper, [1954], 88pp., ill. *juv*
(with Helena Kolda) *Martin and His Friend From Outer Space.* NY: Harper, 1955, 95pp., ill. *juv*

DUNKERLEY, WILLIAM A(rthur)   (1852-1941)   *British*
[possibly changed name legally to Oxenham—unconfirmed]
as John Oxenham
The Man Who Would Save the World. London: Longmans, Green, 1920, 210pp.
The Cedar Box. London: Longmans, Green, 1924, 43pp., front.
□ *God's Prisoner,* 1899; *Bondman Free,* 1902; *The Very Short Memory of Mr. Joseph Scorer,* 1903 (ss col); *Barbe of Grand Bayou,* 1903; *Carette of Sark,* 1907; *The Song of Hyacinth and Other Stories,* 1908 (ss col); *The Coil of Carne,* 1911; *Maid of the Mist,* 1914; *"Policeman X,"* 1914; *The Loosing of the Lion's Whelps,* 1917 (ss col); *The Recollections of Roderick Fyfe,* 1927; *The Hawk of Como,* 1935. POETRY: *Bees In Amber,* 1913; *"All Clear,"* 1919.

D'URFEY, THOMAS   (1653-1723)   *English*
as Tom D'Urfey
A Common-Wealth of Women: A Play. London: R. Bentley, 1686, 55pp. *play*
[said to be a reworking of *The Sea Voyage,* ascribed to John Fletcher (1579-1625)]
Wonders In the Sun; or, the Kingdom of the Birds (A Comick Opera). London: J. Tonson, 1706, 69pp. *play*
□ PLAYS: *The Siege of Memphis,* 1676; *The Fond Husband,* 1676; *Madam Fickle,* 1677; *The Virtuous Wife, or, Good

Luck At Last, 1680; *Campaigners,* 1698.
■ *Wit and Mirth; or, Pills to Purge Melancholy,* 1719-1720 (6 vol.) (songs).

ECCLES, CHARLOTTE O'CONOR *British*
as Author of "The Rejuvenation of Miss Semaphore"
□ *Aliens of the West*, 1904.
as Charlotte O'C(onor) Eccles
□ *The Matrimonial Lottery*, 1906.
as Hal Godfrey
The Rejuvenation of Miss Semaphore; A Farcical Novel.
London: Jarrold, 1897, 239pp.

EDGAR, ALFRED
● **as Barre Lyndon**
The Man In Half Moon Street. London: Hamish, Hamilton,
1939, 189pp. *play*

EDMONDS, HELEN WOODS (Mrs. Stuart) (1904-1968)
British
Born: Cannes, France
as Helen Ferguson
□ *A Charmed Circle*, 1929; *The Dark Sisters*, 1930;
Let Me Alone, 1930; *A Stranger Still*, 1935.
as Anna Kavan
Asylum Piece and Other Stories. London: Jonathan Cape,
1940, 212pp. *ss col*
I Am Lazarus. London: Jonathan Cape, [1945], 146pp.
ss col
[the two books above combined in one volume form *Asylum*.
NY: 1946]
The House of Sleep. Garden City: Doubleday, [1947], 223pp.
Ice. London: P. Owen, 1967, 158pp.
□ *Change the Name*, 1941.

EDWARDS, FREDERICK A(nthony) (1896-   )
as Charman Edwards
Fear Haunts the Roses. London: Ward, Lock, [1936],
314pp.
□ *The Yellow Wagon*, 1932; *Peking Madness*, 1934;
Passenger to Peking, 1935; *No Coffins In China*, 1937.
as J. Van Dyke
□ *Chinese Lovesong*, 1933; *Chinese Chapter*, 1934; *Chinese
City*, 1946.

EIDE, EDITH
Well known fan personality during the 1940's.
as Tigrina
Last Act: October. *Phantom*, July 1958
[reprinted in *Magazine of Horror*, May 1964]

ELDERSHAW, FLORA SYDNEY PATRICIA (1897-   )
as M. Barnard Eldershaw [in collaboration with Marjorie
Faith Barnard] see **MARJORIE FAITH BARNARD**

**ELISABETH, QUEEN-CONSORT OF CHARLES I KING OF
RUMANIA** (*nee* Pauline Elisabeth Ottilie Luise)
(1843-1916) *Rumanian*
Born: Castle Monrepos, Neuwied, Germany
as Elisabeth, Queen of Roumania
A Real Queen's Fairy Tales. Chicago: Davis, 1901, 229pp.
Dreamer of Dreams. London: Hodder & Stoughton, [1915],
181pp., ill. (illustrations by Edmund Dulac)
as Carmen Sylva
Pilgrim Sorrow. A Cycle of Tales. London: Unwin, 1884,
262pp.

□ *Pelesch Marchen*, 1883; *Astra*, 1886; *Lieder aus dem
Dimbovitzathal*, 1889; *Defizit*, 1890; *Geflusterte Worte*,
1903.
✔ **Dito und Idem** [in collaboration with Mme. Mite Kremnitz],
Princess of Wied

ELLET, ELIZABETH FRIES (Lummis) (Mrs.) (1818-1877)
U.S.
Born: Sodus Point, New York
as (Mrs.) E(lizabeth) (F.) Ellet
Evenings at Woodlawn. NY: Baker & Scribner, 1849,
348pp.
□ *Poems, Original and Selected*, 1835. (poetry)
■ *The Character of Schiller*, 1839; *Pioneer Women of the
West*, 1852; *Queens of American Society*, 1867; *Women
of the American Revolution*, 1848-1850 (3 vol.)

ELLIK, RON(ald) (D.) (1938-1968) *U.S.*
as Frederick Davies [in collaboration with Steve Tolliver]
Some of the novels in the "Man From U.N.C.L.E." series
as Ron Ellik
■ (with Bill Evans) *The Universes of E. E. Smith.*
Chicago: Advent, 1966, 272pp., ill.

ELLIS, CRAIG [house pseudonym]
by Lee Rogow
Dr. Varsag's Experiment. *Amazing*, Jan 1940
by David Vern
Dr. Varsag's Second Experiment. *Amazing*, Aug 1943

ELLISON, HARLAN (Jay) (1934-   ) *U.S.*
Born: Cleveland, Ohio
Bibliography: *Harlan Ellison: A Bibliographical Checklist*,
by Leslie Kay Swigart, 1973.
as Lee Archer [house pseudonym]
Escape Route. *Amazing*, March 1957
as C. Bird
Song of Death. *Fantastic Universe*, July 1957
as Cordwainer Bird
"You Can't Get There From Here," for *The Flying Nun*,
11 April 1968. *screenplay*
"Phoenix Without Ashes," for *Starlost*, 22 Sept 1973.
screenplay
as Cortwainer Bird
Invasion Footnote. *Super-Science Fiction*, Aug 1957
as Jay Charby
(with Henry Slesar) The Kissing Death! *Sure-Fire*, April
1957
as Robert Courtney
One Thousand Miles Up. *Science Stories*, April 1954
as Price Curtis
□ The Gal With the Horizontal Mind. *Mermaid*, Vol. 1., #6,
1958
as John Doyle
□ The Girl in the Red Room, *Pix*, Vol. 1, #4, 1964
as Wallace Edmondson
Children's Hour. *Fantastic Universe*, July 1958
as Landon Ellis
□ Hit and Run. *Trapped*, June 1957
as Harlan Ellison
Glowworm. *Infinity*, Feb 1956
World of Women. *Fantastic*, Feb 1957
The Man With Nine Lives. NY: Ace, [1959], 133pp.,
paper. (Ace Double D 413)
A Touch of Infinity. NY: Ace, [1959], 123pp., paper.
(Ace Double D 413)
The Juvies. NY: Ace, [1961], 189pp., paper. *non sf*
Ellison Wonderland. NY: Paperback Library, [1962], 191pp.,
paper. *ss col*
Paingod and Other Delusions. NY: Pyramid, [1965], 157pp.,
paper. *ss col*

I Have No Mouth and I Must Scream. NY: Pyramid, [1967], 175pp., paper. *ss col*

Doomsman. NY: Belmont, [1967], 74pp., paper. (Belmont Double Novel)

From the Land of Fear. NY: Belmont, 1967, 176pp., paper. *ss col*

Love Ain't Nothing But Sex Misspelled. NY: Trident, [1968], 382pp.

All Harlan Ellison Issue. Science Fiction Greats #14, Spring 1969

The Beast That Shouted Love At the Heart of the World. NY: Avon, [1969], 245pp., paper. *ss col*

Over The Edge: Stories From Somewhere Else. NY: Belmont, [1970], 191pp., paper. *ss col*

Alone Against Tomorrow. NY: Macmillan, 1971, 312pp. *ss col*

Partners In Wonder: Harlan Ellison In Collaboration with... NY: Walker, 1971, 471pp. *ss col*

Approaching Oblivion. NY: Walker, 1974, 238pp. *ss col*

(with Edward Bryant) *Phoenix Without Ashes.* Greenwich, Connecticut: Fawcett Gold Medal, [1975], 192pp., paper.

Deathbird Stories. NY: Harper, [1975], 334pp. *ss col*

No Doors, No Windows. NY: Pyramid, 1975, 223pp. *ss col*

☐ *Rumble*, 1958; *The Deadly Streets*, 1958; *Gentleman Junkie, and Other Stories of the Hung-up Generation*, 1961. (ss col)

■ *Memos From Purgatory; Two Journeys of Our Time*, 1961; *The Glass Teat*, 1970 (essays on television).

as Sley Harson [in collaboration with Henry Slesar]
☐ He Disappeared! *Guilty*, March 1957

as Ellis Hart
But Who Wilts The Lettuce? *Amazing*, Sept 1956
☐ The Big Rumble. *Trapped*, Aug 1956

as E. K. Jarvis [house pseudonym]
The Moon Stealers. *Fantastic*, Oct 1957
If This Be Utopia. *Fantastic*, Dec 1957

as Ivar Jorgensen [house pseudonym]
Children of Chaos. *Amazing*, Nov 1957

as John Magnus
☐ Dead Wives Don't Cheat. *Crime and Justice Detective Story Magazine*, March 1957

as Paul Merchant
☐ Sex Gang. *Cad*, March 1969

as Clyde Mitchell [house pseudonym]
The Wife Factory. *Fantastic*, Nov 1957

as Pat Roeder
☐ Someone Is Hungrier. *Rogue*, March 1960

as Jay Solo
☐ The Big Needle. *Nightcap*, Vol. 2, No. 4, 1963; Again The Cat Prowls. *Adam*, Oct 1967.

as Derry Tiger
☐ A Blue Note for Bayou Betty. *Mermaid*, Vol. 1, No. 6, 1958

✔ Phil "Cheech" Beldone, Ivar Jorgenson [house pseudonym], **Al Maddern, Nalrah Nosille, Bert Parker, Ellis Robertson** [in collaboration with Robert Silverberg]
● Hal Ellson

ELY, GEORGE H(erbert)
as Herbert Strang [in collaboration with C. J. L'Estrange]
King of the Air; or, To Morocco On An Airship. London: Hodder & Stoughton, 1908, 272pp.

Lord of the Seas. London: Hodder & Stoughton, 1909, 238pp.

Swift and Sure. The Story of a Hydroplane. London: Hodder & Stoughton, 1910, 242pp.

Round the World In Seven Days. London: Hodder & Stoughton, 1911 [1910], 295pp.

The Cruise of the Gyro-car. London: Hodder & Stoughton, 1911, [1910], 243pp.

The Flying Boat. London: Hodder & Stoughton, 1912, 271pp.

A Thousand Miles An Hour. London: H. Milford, [1924], 160pp.

The Heir of a Hundred Kings. London: H. Milford, [1924], 160pp.

EMANUEL, VICTOR ROUSSEAU (1879-1960) *naturalized U.S.*
Born: London

as H. M. Egbert
My Lady of the Nile. London: Hodder & Stoughton, [1923], 286pp.
Draught of Eternity. London: J. Long, [1924], 254pp.
The Sea Demons. London: J. Long, 1924, 254pp.
Eric of the Strong Heart. London: J. Long, 1925, 254pp.
Mrs. Alladin. London: J. Long, [1925], 254pp.

as V. R. Emanuel
☐ *Wooden Spoil*, 1919; *The Story of Paul*, 1923; *The Selmans*, 1925.

as Victor Rousseau
The Sea Demons. *All Story Weekly*, 1 Jan 1916
The Fruit of the Lamp. serial. *Argosy*, Feb 2-23, 1918
The Curse of Amen Ra. *Book of Weird Tales #1*, 1960.
The Messiah of the Cylinder. Chicago: McClurg, 1917, 319pp., ill.
☐ *Derwent's Horse*, 1901; *The Big Muskeg*, 1921.
● Clive Trent

EMERSIE, JOHN
● **as Mrs. Ansel Oppenheim**
Evelyn: A Story of the West and Far East. NY: Broadway, 1904, 385pp., front.

EMSHWILLER, ED(mund) (Alexander) (1925-   ) *U.S.*
Born: Lansing, Michigan
as EMSH
On science fiction art, especially on magazines in the U.S. during the 1950's.
● Ed Alexander, Emsler, Willer

ERCKMANN, EMILE (1822-1899) *French*
Born: Pfalsbourg, Alsace
as Erckmann-Chatrian [in collaboration with Alexandre Chatrian, see Alexandre Chatrian]

ERIE, PAUL *French*
as Paul d'Avoi
The Laughing Death. serial. *All Story Cavalier's Weekly*, March 27, 1915-April 17, 1915

ERNST, PAUL FREDERICK (1900-   ) *U.S.*
as Paul (Frederick) Ernst
The Temple of Serpents. *Weird Tales*, Oct 1928
Marooned Under the Sea. *Astounding*, Sept 1930
Dr. Satan. Oaklawn, Illinois: 1974.
as Kenneth Robeson
a number of the "Avenger" lead stories in 1939
as Paul Frederick Stern
The Way Home. *Weird Tales*, Nov 1935

ERNSTING, WALTER (1920-   ) *German*
Born: Koblenz
✔ Clark Darlton, F. MacPatterson

ERSKINE, THOMAS (1st Baron Erskine of Restormel) (1750-1823) *Scottish*
as T.E.
Armata, A Fragment. London: J. Murray, [1816], 210pp.
The Second Part of Armata. London: J. Murray, 1817, 209pp.

ESMENARD, JEAN D' (Vicomte) (1893-   ) *French*
as Jean D'Esme
The Red Gods, A Romance. NY: Dutton [1924], 365pp.

ESTIVAL, IVAN LEON
as "Estival"
 Mandragora. London: Staples, 1952, 239pp.

EVANS, E. E(verett) (1893-1958) *U.S.*
as E. E(verett) Evans
 Guaranteed. *Startling Stories,* Jan 1948
 Man of Many Minds. Reading, Pennsylvania: Fantasy
  Press, [1953], 222pp.
 Alien Minds. Reading, Pennsylvania: Fantasy Press, [1955],
  223pp.
 The Planet Mappers. NY: Dodd, Mead, 1955, 242pp.
as Henry Gardener
 Visitor From Kos. *Vortex SF #1,* 1953
as H. E. Verett [in collaboration with Thelma Hamm Evans]
 Best Man. *Vortex SF #1,* 1953
 ✔ **E. Verett**

EVANS, MARGUERITE FLORENCE HELENE JERVIS (Mrs.
  Caradoc) (1894-) *British*
 Autobiography: *Full and Frank, the Private Life of A*
  Woman Novelist, by Oliver Sandys. London: Hurst &
  Blackett, 1941, 207pp.
as Countess Barcynska
 The Golden Snail and Other Stories. London: Hurst &
  Blackett, [1927], 287pp. *ss col*
 ☐ *The Honey-pot,* 1916; *Sanity Jane,* 1919; *We, Women!,*
  1923; *Mint Walk,* 1926; *A Certified Bride,* 1928;
  Fantoccini, 1930.
as Oliver Sandys
 The Sorceress, The Tale of A Vamp. London: Hurst &
  Blackett, 1927, 284pp.
 ☐ *Tilly-Make-Haste,* 1924; *Blinkeyes,* 1925; *Misty Angel,*
  1931; *Squire,* 1932; *Crinklenose,* 1938.
 ■ *Caradoc Evans,* 1946.

EVANS, T(helma) D. Hamm (Mrs. E. Everett)
as T. D. Hamm
 The Last Supper. *If,* Sept 1952
as Thelma D. Hamm
 Gallie's House. *Magazine of Fantasy and Science Fiction,*
  Sept 1953
as H. E. Verett [in collaboration with E. Everett Evans]
 Best Man. *Vortex SF #1,* 1953
 ● **Hamm Edwards**

EVERETT, H. D. (Mrs.) *British*
as Julia Douglas
 ☐ *Deerhurst; or, The Rift In the Cloud,* 1893.
as Theo Douglas
 Iras; A Mystery. Edinburgh: Blackwood, 1896, 281pp.
 Nemo. London: Smith, Elder, 1900, 344pp.
 One or Two; A Romance. London: Brown & Langham &
  Co., 1907, 320pp.
 A White Witch. London: Hurst & Blackett, 1908, 331pp.
 ☐ *Behind A Mask,* 1898; *Windygap (A Tale),* 1898;
  A Legacy of Hate, 1899; *Three Mysteries,* 1904.
as Mrs. H. D. Everett
 The Grey Countess. London: Cassell, 1913, 311pp.
 Malevola. London: Heath, Cranston, [1914], 314pp.
 The Death Mask and Other Ghosts. London: P. Allen,
  [1920], 321pp. *ss col*
 ✔ **Julia**

FAIRBURN, EDWIN   *British*
as Mohoao
 The Ships of Tarshish; A Sequel to Sue's "Wandering
  Jew." London: Hall, 1867, 32+104pp. [preface fictitiously
  dated 1884]

FAIRMAN, PAUL W. (1916-) *U.S.*
as Adam Chase [in collaboration with Milton Lesser]
 The Final Quarry. *Imaginative Tales,* May 1956
 The Golden Ape. NY: Avalon, 1959, 221pp.
as Lester del Rey [in collaboration with R. Alvarez-del Rey]
 The Runaway Robot. NY: Westminster, [1965], 176pp.
 The Scheme of Things. NY: Belmont, [1966], 157pp., paper.
 Siege Perilous. NY: Lancer, [1966], 157pp., paper.
 Tunnel Through Time. NY: Westminster, [1966], 153pp.
 Prisoners of Space. NY: Westminster, [1968], 142pp.
as Paul W. Fairman
 No Teeth For the Tiger. *Amazing,* Feb 1950
 City Under the Sea. London: Digit, 1963, 158pp., paper.
 The World Grabbers. NY: Monarch, 1964, 126pp., paper.
 I The Machine. NY: Lancer, 205pp., paper.
 The Forgetful Robot. NY: Holt, [1968], 163pp. *ss col*
 ☐ *Five Knucklebones,* 1972.
as Clee Garson [house pseudonym]
 Nine Worlds West. *Fantastic Adventures,* April 1951
as E. K. Jarvis [house pseudonym]
 Never Trust A Martian. *Amazing,* Jan 1951
as Ivar Jorgenson [house pseudonym]
 Deadly City. *If,* March 1953
 ● **Robert Eggert Lee, F. W. Paul, Mallory Storm**

FANTA, HOLLY ROTH (Mrs. Joseph) (1916-1964) *U.S.*
 Born: Chicago, Illinois
as K. G. Ballard
 ☐ MYSTERY: *The Coast of Fear,* 1958; *Bar Sinister,* 1960;
  The Gauge of Deception, 1963.
as P. J. Merrill
 ☐ MYSTERY: *The Slender Thread,* 1959.
as Holly Roth
 The Mask of Grass. NY: Vanguard, 1951, 221pp.
 ☐ MYSTERY: *The Content Assignment,* 1954; *Button,*
  Button, 1966.

FANTHORPE, R(obert) L(ionel) (1935-) *English*
 Born: Dereham, Norfolk
 [R. Lionel Fanthorpe's output, though prodigious, is
 largely undocumented in standard reference books. The
 B.M.C. and N.U.C. list no books by him. The titles listed
 below are probably all from one firm in Britain which
 publishes under the imprints of Badger and Arcadia House.
 Some of Fanthorpe's books seem to have been issued twice
 with the same title under different names, while others may
 have been issued with different titles. Some of the titles have
 seen U.S. reprint, not necessarily under their original name
 or with their original pseudonym. Most titles are probably
 paperback firsts under the "Badger" imprint. All
 information in this entry is of an advisory nature and is
 considered unconfirmed by the compiler. Although I have
 seen a number of these titles I have found no way to check
 my instincts as to their pedigree.]
as Neil Balfort
 stories about the supernatural
as Erle Barton
 The Planet Seekers, [1964].

as Lee Barton
The Unseen, 1963; *The Shadow Man.* 1966.
as Othello Barton
stories about the supernatural
as Thornton Bell
Space Trap, 1964; *Chaos*, [1964].
as Leo Brett
Exit Humanity, [1960]; *The Microscopic Ones*, [1960]; *The Faceless Planet*, [1960]; *March of the Robots*, [1961]; *Black Infinity*, [1961]; *Mind Force*, 1961; *Nightmare*, [1962]; *Face In the Night*, 1962; *The Immortals*, 1962; *They Never Come Back*, [1963]; *The Forbidden*, 1963; *From Realms Beyond*, 1963; *The Alien Ones*, 1963; *Power Sphere*, 1963.
as Bron Fane
Juggernaut, [1960]; *Last Man On Earth*, [1960]; *Rodent Mutation*, [1961]; *The Intruders*, [1963]; *Somewhere Out There*, 1963; *Softly By Moonlight*, 1963; *Unknown Destiny*, [1964]; *Nemesis*, [1964]; *Suspension*, 1964; *The Macabre Ones*, [1964]; *Blue Juggernaut*, [1965]; *U.F.O. 517*, 1965.
as R. Lionel Fanthorpe
The Waiting World, 1958; *Alien From the Stars*, 1959; *Hyperspace*, 1959; *Doomed World*, 1960; *The Man Who Couldn't Die*, 1960; *Out of the Darkness*, 1960; *Asteroid Man*, 1960; *Werewolf At Large*, 1960; *Hand of Doom*, 1960; *Flame Mass*, 1961; *Fingers of Darkness*, 1961; *Face In the Dark*, 1961; *Devil From the Depths*, 1961; *Centurion's Vengeance*, 1961; *The Golden Chalice*, 1961; *The Grip of Fear*, 1961; *Chariot of Apollo*, 1962; *Hell Has Wings*, 1962; *Graveyard of the Damned*, 1962; *The Darker Drink*, 1962; *Curse of the Totem*, 1962; *Space Fury*, 1962; *Goddess of the Night*, 1963; *Twilight Ancestor*, 1963; *Sands of Eternity*, 1963; *Negative Minus*, 1963; *Death Has Two Faces*, 1964; *The Shrouded Abbot*, 1964; *Neuron World*, 1965; *Bitter Reflection*, 1965; *The Triple Man*, 1965; *Call of the Wild*, 1965; *Vision of the Damned*, 1965; *The Unconfined*, 1966; *Watching World*, 1966.
as Mel Jay
Orbit One, [1966].
as Marston Johns
The Venus Venture, [1965]; *Beyond Time*, [1965].
as Oben Lerteth
stories about the supernatural
as Robert Lionel
Time Echo, [1964]; *The Face of X*, [1965].
as John E. Muller
A 1,000 Years On, 1961; *The Ultimate Man*, 1961; *The Uninvited*, 1961; *Crimson Planet*, 1961; *The Venus Venture*, 1961; *The Return of Zeus*, 1962; *Perilous Galaxy*, 1962; *The Eye of Karnak*, 1962; *The Man Who Conquered Time*, 1962; *Orbit One*, 1962.
as Elton T. Neef
stories about the supernatural
as Phil Nobel
The Hand From Gehema, 1964.
as Peter O'Flinn
stories about the supernatural
as Lionel Roberts
Discovery. Futuristic Science Stories #7, 1952 (Br.)
Time Echo, 1959; *The In-World*, 1960; *The Face of X*, 1960; *The Last Valkyrie*, 1961.
as Rene Rolant
stories about the supernatural
as Deutero Spartacus
stories about the supernatural
as Robin Tate
stories about the supernatural
as Neil Thanet
Beyond the Veil, 1964; *The Man Who Came Back*, 1964.

as Trebor Thorpe
Five Faces of Fear, 1960; *Lightning World*, 1960.
as Pel Torro
Frozen Planet, 1960; *World of the Gods*, 1960; *The Phantom Ones*, 1961; *Legion of the Lost*, 1962; *The Strange Ones*, 1963; *Galaxy 666*, 1963; *Formula 29X*, 1963; *The Timeless Ones*, 1963; *Through the Barrier*, 1963; *The Last Astronaut*, 1963; *The Face of Fear*, 1963; *The Return*, 1964; *Space No Barrier*, 1964; *Force 97X*, 1965; *Exiled In Space*, 1969; *Beyond the Barrier*, 1969.
as Olaf Trent
Roman Twilight, 1963. [also, stories of the supernatural]
as Karl Zeigfield
Gods of Darkness, 1962; *Walk Through Tomorrow*, 1962; *Android*, 1962; *Atomic Nemesis*, 1962; *Zero Minus X*, 1962; *Escape To Infinity*, 1963; *Radar Alert*, 1963; *World of Tomorrow*, 1963; *The World That Never Was*, 1963; *Project Infinity*, 1964; *No Way Back*, 1964; *World of the Future*, 1964; *Barrier 346*, 1965; *Girl From Tomorrow*, 1965.

FARGUS, FREDERICK J(ohn) (1847-1885) *British*
as Hugh Conway
Bound Together: Tales. London: Remington & Co., 1884, 2 vol. *ss col*
Carriston's Gift and Other Tales. NY: Holt, 1885, 239pp., ill. *ss col*
Circumstantial Evidence; and Other Stories. NY: International Book Co., [1890], 149pp. *ss col*
☐ MYSTERY: *Called Back*, 1884; *Dark Days*, 1884; *A Family Affair*, 1885; *A Cardinal Sin*, 1886; *Living or Dead*, 1886.

FARJEON, J(oseph) J(efferson) (1883-1955) *British*
[Brother of writer Eleanor Farjeon (1881- ?) and composer Herbert Farjeon (1878-1948)
as J. J(efferson) Farjeon
The Invisible Companion and Other Stories. London: Polybooks, [1946], 62pp., paper. *ss col*
Death of A World. London: Collins, 1948, 192pp.
☐ *No. 17*, 1925 (play); *After Dark*, 1926; *The Green Dragon*, 1929; *Philomel*, 1932; *The Judge Sums Up*, 1942; *Green Mask*, 1944.
as Anthony Swift
☐ MYSTERY: *Murder At A Police Station*, 1942 (Br.).

FARMER, PHILIP JOSE (1918-) *U.S.*
Born: North Terre Haute, Indiana
Bibliography: *The First Editions of P. J. Farmer*, by Lawrence J. Knapp, 1976.
as Philip Jose Farmer
The Lovers. *Startling Stories*, Aug 1952
The Green Odyssey. NY: Ballantine, 1957, 152pp., paper.
Strange Relations. NY: Ballantine, [1960], 190pp., paper. *ss col*
A Woman A Day. NY: Beacon/Galaxy Novel #43, [1960], 160pp., paper.
Flesh. NY: Beacon/Galaxy, [1960], 160pp., paper.
The Lovers. NY: Ballantine, [1961], 160pp., paper.
The Alley God. NY: Ballantine, [1962], 176pp., paper.
Cache From Outer Space. NY: Ace, [1962], 139pp., paper. (Ace Double F 165)
The Celestial Blue Print. NY: Ace, [1962], 114pp., paper. (Ace Double F 165)
Inside Outside. NY: Ballantine, [1964], 156pp., paper.
Tongues of the Moon. NY: Ballantine, [1964], 143pp., paper.
Dare. NY: Ballantine, [1965], 159pp., paper.
The Maker of Universes. NY: Ace, [1965], 191pp., paper.
Night of Light. NY: Berkley, [1966], 160pp., paper.
The Gate of Time. NY: Belmont, [1966], 176pp., paper.

The Gates of Creation. NY: Ace, [1966], 159pp., paper.
A Private Cosmos. NY: Ace, [1968], 192pp., paper.
The Image of the Beast. North Hollywood, California: Essex House, 1968, 255pp., paper.
A Feast Unknown. North Hollywood, California: Essex House, [1969], 286pp., paper.
Behind the Walls of Terra. NY: Ace, [1970], 188pp., paper.
The Mad Goblin. NY: Ace, [1970], 130pp., paper. (Ace Double 51375)
The Lord of the Trees. NY: Ace, [1970], 122pp., paper. (Ace Double 51375)
Lord Tyger. Garden City: Doubleday, [1970], 335pp.
The Stone God Awakens. NY: Ace, [1970], 190pp., paper.
Down In the Black Gang. Garden City: Doubleday, [1971], 215pp.
To Your Scattered Bodies Go. NY: Putnam, [1971], 221pp.
The Fabulous Riverboat. NY: Putnam, [1971], 253pp.
The Wind Whales of Ishmael. NY: Ace, [1971], paper.
Tarzan Alive. Garden City: Doubleday, [1972], 312pp. [fictional biography]
Time's Last Gift. NY: Ballantine, [1972], 201pp., paper.
The Other Log of Phileas Fogg. NY: DAW, [1973], 191pp., ill. paper.
The Book of Philip Jose Farmer. NY: DAW #63, [1973], 239pp., paper. *ss col*
Traitor to the Living. NY: Ballantine, [1973], paper.
Hadon of Ancient Opar. NY: DAW, [1974], 224pp., ill. paper.
Mother Was A Lovely Beast: A Feral Man Anthology. Radnor, Pennsylvania: Chilton, [1974].
The Adventure of the Peerless Peer. Boulder, Colorado: Aspen Press, [1974], 111pp.
Blown, or Sketches Among the Ruins of My Mind. London: Quartet, [1975], 208pp., paper.
Iron Castle. NY: DAW, [1976], paper.
Flight To Opar. NY: DAW, [1976], paper.
The Lavalite World. NY: Ace, [1977], 282pp., paper.
The Dark Design. NY: Berkley/Putnam, 1977, 412pp.
□ *Love Song*, 1970; *Fire and the Night*, 1972.
as Harry Manders
The Problem of the Sore Bridge—Among Others. *Magazine of Fantasy & Science Fiction*, Sept 1975
as Jonathan Swift Somers III
A Scarletin Study. *Magazine of Fantasy & Science Fiction*, March 1975
as Kilgore Trout
Venus on the Half-Shell. NY: Dell, [1975], 204pp., paper.

FARNESE, A.
as Franchezzo
A Wanderer In the Spirit Lands. London: W. J. Sinkins, 1896, 307pp.

FARNOL, JOHN JEFFERY (1878-1952) *British*
as Jeffery Farnol
The Shadow and Other Stories. London: S. Low, [1929], 313pp. *ss col*
Voices From the Dust. London: Macmillan, 1932, 369pp., ill. *ss col*
□ *The Broad Highway*, 1910; *The Amateur Gentleman*, 1912; *Beltane the Smith*, 1915; *Peregrine's Progress*, 1922; *The Quest of Youth*, 1927; *The Way Beyond*, 1933; *John O'the Green*, 1935; *The Lonely Road*, 1938; *Adam Penfeather, Buccaneer*, 1940; *Murder By Nail*, 1942; *Heritage Perilous*, 1946.
■ *Great Britain At War*, 1918.

FAST, HOWARD MELVIN (1914-   ) *U.S.*
Born: New York, New York
as E. V. Cunningham
Phyllis. Garden City: Doubleday, 1962, 214pp.

□ *Sylvia*, 1960; *Shirley*, 1964; *Lydia*, 1964; *Penelope*, 1965; *Helen*, 1966; *Maggie*, 1966; *Samantha*, 1967.
as Walter Ericson
□ *Fallen Angel*, 1952 [c.1951].
as Howard Fast
Wrath of the Purple. *Amazing*, Oct 1932
The Edge of Tomorrow. NY: Bantam, [1961], 120pp., paper. *ss col*
The Hunter and The Trap. NY: Dial, [1967], 214pp.
The General Zapped An Angel. NY: Morrow, [c.1969].
A Touch of Infinity. NY: Morrow, 1973.
□ *Strange Yesterday*, 1934; *The Children*, 1935; *The Last Frontier*, 1941; *The Unvanquished*, 1942; *Citizen Tom Paine*, 1943; *Freedom Road*, 1944; *The American*, 1946; *Spartacus*, 1951; *Moses, Prince of Egypt*, 1958; *April Morning*, 1961; *The Hill*, 1963.
■ *The Naked God; The Writer and the Communist Party*, 1957.

FAULKNER, DOROTHEA M.
as Dorothea M. Faulkner
A Weather Report From Mercury. *Thrilling Wonder Stories*, Oct 1951
as Rory Magill
The Last Gentleman. *If*, Jan 1953

FAUST, FREDERICK SCHILLER (1892-1945) *U.S.*
Born: Seattle, Washington
Bio-Bibliography: *Max Brand, The Man and His Works*, by Rev. D. C. Richardson, Los Angeles: FPCI, 1952.
as Frank Austin
□ WESTERN: *King of the Range*, 1935.
as George Owen Baxter
□ WESTERN: *Donnegan*, 1923; *Brother of the Cheyennes*, 1936.
as M. B.
□ *The Thunderer*, 1933 (950 cop).
as Max Brand
John Ovington Returns. *All Story Weekly*, June 8, 1918
Devil Ritter. *All Story Weekly*, July 13, 1918
□ *Alcatraz*, 1923; *Calling Doctor Kildare*, 1940. WESTERN: *The Untamed*, 1918; *Destry Rides Again*, 1930. MYSTERY: *Six Golden Angels*, 1937.
as Walter C. Butler
□ MYSTERY: *Cross Over Nine*, 1935; *The Night Flower*, 1936.
as George Challis
The Smoking Land. *Argosy*, May 29, 1937
□ HISTORICAL FICTION: *The Bait and The Trap*, 1935; *The Golden Knight*, 1937.
as Evan Evans
□ WESTERN: *The Border Bandit*, 1926.
as Frederick Faust
Convalescence. *All Story Weekly*, March 31, 1917
Dionysus In Hades. Oxford: Blackwell, 1931, 89pp. (500 cop)
as John Frederick
□ *The Bronze Collar*, 1925.
as Frederick Frost
□ *Secret Agent Number One*, 1936; *Spy Meets Spy*, 1937; *The Bamboo Whistle*, 1937.
as David Manning
□ WESTERN: *Bandit's Honor*, 1927.
as Peter (Henry) Morland
□ *Beyond the Outpost*, 1925; *Lost Wolf*, 1928.
✓ Lee Bolt, Peter Dawson, Martin Dexter, Evin Evan, Dennis Lawson, Dennis Lawton, Hugh Owen, Nicolas Silver, Henry Uriel, Peter Ward

FAWCETT, FRANK D(ubrez) (1893-   ) *British*
as F(rank) D(ubrez) Fawcett
Hole In Heaven. London: Sidgwick & Jackson, [1954],

244pp. (British SF Library No. 1)

■ *Dickens the Dramatist*, 1952; *Cyclopaedia of Initials and Abbreviations*, 1963; *A Dictionary of English Misusage*, 1965.

as Simpson Stokes

Down On the Farm. *Thrilling Wonder Stories*, April 1937

Air-Gods' Parade. London: A. Barron, [1935], 180pp., front.

FAWKES, F(rank) A(ttfield)

as F(rank) A(ttfield) Fawkes

Adventures of A Chemist . . . A Series of Unusual Detective Stories. London: Simpkin & Marshall, [1930], 177pp.

■ *Babies: How To Rear Them*, 1883; *Architects' Doors and Their Ornaments*, 1884; *Spiritualism Exposed*, 1920; *How To Organize Bazaars, Fetes, etc.*, 1924; *Shaping A New World, A Philosophy of Tools*, 1924.

as X

Marmaduke, Emperor of Europe. Being A Record of Some Strange Adventures In the Remarkable Career of A Political and Social Reformer Who Was Famous At the Commencement of the Twentieth Century. Chelmsford: E. Durrant, 1895, 271pp., front.

FEARING, KENNETH (1902-1961) *U.S.*

Born: Oak Park, Illinois

as Donald F. Bedford [in collaboration with Donald Friede and H. Bedford-Jones]

John Barry. NY: Creative Age Press, [1947], 418pp.

as Kenneth Fearing

Clark Gifford's Body. NY: Random House, [1942], 285pp.

The Loneliest Girl In the World. NY: Harcourt, Brace, [1951], 238pp.

□ MYSTERY: *The Hospital*, 1939; *Dagger of the Mind*, 1941; *The Big Clock*, 1946; *The Crozart Story*, 1960. POETRY: *Poems*, 1935; *Dead Reckoning*, 1938; *Afternoon Of A Pawnbroker*, 1943; *Stranger At Coney Island*, 1948.

FEARN, JOHN RUSSELL (1908-1960) *British*

Born: Worsley, Manchester

Bio-Bibliography: *The Multiman: A Biographical and Bibliographical Study of John Russell Fearn*, by Philip J. Harbottle, 1968.

as Geoffrey Armstrong

Superhuman. *Tales of Wonder #1*, [c.1937]

as Thornton Ayre

Penal World. *Astounding*, Oct 1937

as Hugo Blayn

□ MYSTERY: *Except For One Thing*, 1948; *The Five Match Boxes*, 1949; *Flashpoint*, 1952; *What Happened To Hammond?*, 1952; *The Silvered Cage*, 1955.

as Morton Boyce

Nemesis. *British Space Fiction Magazine*, Vol. 2, No. 1, 1955 (Br.)

as Dennis Clive

Valley of Pretenders. *Science Fiction*, March 1939

The Voice Commands. NY: Columbia Pub., [1949], paper.

as John Cotton

Outlaw of Saturn. *Science Fiction*, March 1939

as Poulton Cross

The Mental Ultimate. *Astounding*, Jan 1938

Other Eyes Watching. London: Pendulum, 1946, 120pp., paper.

□ WESTERN: *Stockwhip Sheriff*, [c.1948].

as Astron del Martia [this book only by Fearn, other writers who used this name unknown]

The Trembling World. London: Frances, [1949], 128pp., paper.

as Mark Denholm

Solar Assignment. *New Worlds No. 1*, 1946 (Br.)

as Douglas Dodd

Mars For Sale. *British Space Fiction Magazine*, Vol. 2, #5, 1955 (Br.)

as Sheridan Drew

Imperfect Crime. *British Space Fiction Magazine*, Vol. 2 #4, 1955 (Br.)

as Max Elton

Hero Worship. *British Space Fiction Magazine*, Vol. 2 #6, 1955 (Br.)

as John Russell Fearn

The Intelligence Gigantic. *Amazing*, June 1933

Intelligence Gigantic. Surrey: World's Work, 1943, 100pp.

The Golden Amazon. Surrey: World's Work, 1944, 117pp.

Liners of Time. Surrey: World's Work, [1947], 156pp.

Slaves of Ijax. London: Kaner Pub. Co., [1947], 80pp.

The Golden Amazon Returns. Surrey: World's Work, 1948, 133pp.

Operation Venus. London: Scion, [1950], 128pp., paper.

Emperor of Mars. London: Hamilton, 1950, 127pp., paper.

Warrior of Mars. London: Hamilton, 1950, 127pp., paper.

Red Men Of Mars. London: Hamilton, 1950, 127pp., paper.

Goddess of Mars. London: Hamilton, 1950, 126pp., paper.

The Golden Amazon's Triumph. Surrey: World's Work, 1953, 192pp.

The Golden Amazon's Diamond Quest. Surrey: World's Work, 1953, 174pp.

The Amazon Strikes Again. Surrey: World's Work, 1954, 175pp.

Twin of the Amazon. Surrey: World's Work, 1954, 159pp.

□ WESTERN: *The Avenging Ranger*, 1948; *Arizona Love*, 1950. MYSTERY: *Murder's A Must*, 1949.

as Vorsted Gridban

[this pseudonym used by E. C. Tubb on some earlier titles, *see* **E.C. TUBB**]

March of the Robots. *Vargo Statten SF Magazine #1*, 1954 (Br.)

Titles grouped below all: London: Scion, [1953], 128pp., paper.

Moons For Sale; The Dyno Depressant; The Magnetic Brain; Scourge of the Atom; A Thing of the Past; Exit Life; The Master Must Die.

Titles grouped below all: London: Scion, [1954], 128pp., paper.

The Purple Wizard; The Genial Dinosaur; The Frozen Limit; I Came—I Saw—I Wondered; The Lonely Astronomer.

as Malcolm Hartley

Out of the Past. *British SF Magazine #9*, 1954 (Br.)

as Timothy Hayes

□ WESTERN: *King of the Mesa*, 1953.

as Conrad G. Holt

Cosmic Exodus. London: Pearson's, 1953, 64pp., paper.

as Frank Jones

Arctic God. *Amazing*, May 1942

as Marvin Kayne

The Grey Avenger. *British Space Fiction Magazine*, Vol. 2, #2, 1955 (Br.)

as Herbert Lloyd

Murmuring Dust. *British SF Magazine #12*, 1955 (Br.)

as Paul Lorraine [this title only]

Dark Boundaries. London: Curtis, 1953, 159pp., paper.

as Dom Passante

Moon Heaven. *Science Fiction*, June 1939

as Francis (Frank) Rose

Saturnian Odyssey. *British SF Magazine #7*, 1954 (Br.)

as Laurence F. Rose

The Hell Fruit. London: Pearson's, 1953, 64pp., paper.

as Ward Ross

No Place On Earth. *British SF Magazine #8*, 1954 (Br.)

as Doorn Sclanders

□ WESTERN: *Canyon of Renegades*, 1953; *Cactus Hits the Trail*, 1955.

as Joan Seagar

☐ ROMANCE: *The Black Star*, 1950; *The Harvest Is Ours*, 1950.

as Brian Shaw [this title only]
Z Formations. London: Curtis, [1953], 159pp., paper.

as John Slate
☐ MYSTERY: *Black Maria*, 1944; *Maria Marches On*, 1945; *One Remain Seated*, 1946; *Thy Arm Alone*, 1947; *Framed In Guilt*, 1948; *Death In Silhouette*, 1950.

as Vargo Statten
Survivor of Mars. Science Adventure Books, Spring 1953
Titles grouped below all: London: Scion, [1950], 128pp., paper.
Annihilation; The Micro Men; Wanderer of Space; 2000 Years On; Inferno; The Cosmic Flame; Nebula X; The Sun Makers.
Titles grouped below all: London: Scion, [1951], 128pp., paper.
The Avenging Martian; Cataclysm; The Red Insects; Deadline To Pluto; The Petrified Planet; Born Of Luna.
Titles grouped below all: London: Scion, [1951], 112pp., paper.
The Devouring Fire; The Renegade Star; The Catalyst.
Titles grouped below all: London: Scion, [1952], 112pp., paper.
The Inner Cosmos; The Space Warp; The Eclipse Express; The Time Bridge; The Man From Tomorrow; The G-Bomb.
Titles grouped below all: London: Scion, [1952], 96pp., paper.
Laughter In Space; Across the Ages; The Last Martian; Worlds To Conquer; Decreation; The Time Trap.
Science Metropolis. London: Scion, [1952], 128pp., paper.
The Ultimate. London: Scion, [1952], 128pp., paper.
Titles grouped below all: London: Scion, 1953, 128pp., paper.
Ultra Spectrum; The Dust Destroyer; Black-Wing of Mars; Man In Duplicate; Zero Hour; The Black Avengers; Odyssey of Nine; Pioneer 1990; The Interloper; Man Of Two Worlds; The Lie Destroyer; Black Bargain; The Grand Illusion.
Titles grouped below all: London: Scion, [1954], 128pp. paper.
Wealth of the Void; A Time Appointed; I Spy; The Multi-Man.
The Creature From the Black Lagoon. London: Dragon, [1954], 176pp., paper. (movie adaptation)
1,000 Year Voyage. London: Dragon, 1954, 128pp., paper.
Earth 2. London: Dragon, 1955, 128pp., paper.

as Rosina Tarne
Prize winning critical letters to British film magazines in the late 1930's.

as K. Thomas
Knowledge Without Learning. *New Worlds #1*, 1946 (Br.)

as Earl Titan
The Gold of Akada. London: Scion, [1951], 128pp., paper.
Anjan the Mighty. London: Scion, [1951], 128pp., paper.

as Arthur Waterhouse [probable]
Invisible Impact. *Vargo Statten SF Magazine #2*, 1954 (Br.)

as John Werheim
The Copper Bullet. *Vargo Statten SF Magazine #1*, 1954 (Br.)

as Ephriam Winiki
Leeches From Space. *Science Fiction*, March 1939

FEDER, ROBERT ARTHUR (1909-1969) *U.S.*
as Robert Arthur
The Terror From the Sea. *Wonder Stories*, Dec 1931
Post Marked For Paradise. *Argosy*, June 15, 1940
Ghosts and More Ghosts. NY: Random House, [1963], 211pp., ill.
☐ MYSTERY: (all published in the "Alfred Hitchcock Mystery " series by Random House) *The Secret of Terror Castle*, 1964; *The Mystery of the Whispering Mummy*,

1965; *The Mystery of the Green Ghost*, 1965; *The Mystery of the Vanishing Treasure*, 1966; *The Secret of Skeleton Island*, 1966; *The Mystery of the Fiery Eye*, 1967; *The Mystery of the Silver Spider*, 1967.

FIELD, JULIAN OSGOOD (1849-1925) *British*
as Author of "Uncensored Recollections"
■ *Things I Shouldn't Tell*, 1924; *More Uncensored Recollections*, 1926.
as Julian Field
☐ *Little Hand and Muckle Gold*, 1899.
as Sigma
■ *Personalia; Intimate Recollections of Famous Men*, 1903.
as X. L.
Aut Diabolus aut Nihil and Other Tales. London: Methuen, 1894, 303pp. *ss col*
☐ *The Limb; an Episode of Adventure*, 1896.
anonymous
■ *Uncensored Recollections*, 1924.

FIGGIS, DARRELL (1882-1925) *Irish*
as Darrell Figgis
☐ *Broken Arcs*, 1911; *Queen Tara*, 1913 (play); *Children of the Earth*, 1918; POETRY: *A Vision of Life*, 1909; *The Crucibles of Time*, 1911.
■ *Shakespeare, A Study*, 1911; *AE (George W. Russell)*, 1916 (biography); *By-Ways Of Study*, 1918; *The Paintings of William Blake*, 1925; *Recollections of the Irish War*, 1927.
as Michael Ireland
The Return Of The Hero. London: Chapman and Dodd, 1923, 253pp.

FINNEY, WALTER BRADEN (1911-) *U.S.*
Born: Milwaukee, Wisconsin
as Jack Finney
The Third Level. *Magazine of Fantasy and Science Fiction*, Oct 1953
The Body Snatchers. NY: Dell, [1955], 191pp., paper.
The Third Level. NY: Rinehart, [c.1956], 256pp. *ss col*
I Love Galesburg In the Springtime. NY: Simon & Schuster, 1963 [c.1962], 224pp. *ss col*
The Woodrow Wilson Dime. NY: Simon & Schuster, [1968], 190pp.
Time and Again. NY: Simon & Schuster, [1970], 399pp., ill.
The Night People. Garden City: Doubleday, 1977, 215pp.
☐ *Five Against The House*, 1954; *Telephone Roulette*, 1956 (play); *The House Of Numbers*, 1957; *Assault On A Queen*, 1959; *Good Neighbor Sam*, 1963; *Marion's Wall*, 1973.
∠ **Walter Braden**

FIRTH, VIOLET M(ary) (1890-1946) *British*
as Violet M. Firth
☐ POETRY: *Violets*, 1904; *More Violets*, 1905; *The Machinery of the Mind*, 1922; *Avalon of the Heart*, 1934.
as Dion Fortune
The Secrets Of Doctor Taverner. London: N. Douglas, [1926], 253pp. *ss col*
The Demon Lover. London: N. Douglas, [1927], 286pp.
The Winged Bull. London: Williams & Norgate, [1935], 323pp.
The Goat-Foot God. London: Williams & Norgate, 1936, 382pp.
The Sea Priestess. London: By the Author, 1938, 316pp.
Moon Magic. London: Aquarian Press, 1956, 241pp.
■ *The Problem of Purity*, 1928; *The Esoteric Orders and Their Works*, 1929; *Sane Occultism*, 1929; *Psychic Self Defense*, 1930; *The Mystic Qabalah*, 1935; *Practical Occultism*, 1935.

FISCHER, MARGARET ANN PETERSON (Mrs. A. O.)
(1883-1933) *British*
Born: Bombay, India
as Glint Green
  ☐ *Poison Death*, 1933; *Beauty-A Snare*, 1933.
as Margaret Peterson
  Moonflowers. London: Hutchinson, [1926], 252pp.
  The Yellow People; or, Queen of Sheba's Tomb. London:
    Shaw, [1930], 320pp.
  ☐ *The Lure of the Little Drum*, 1913; *Blind Eyes*, 1914;
    The Death Drum, 1919; *Deadly Nightshade*, 1924;
    The Unknown Hand, 1924; *Twinkleface, The Merry Elf*,
    1926; *Pamela and Her Lion Man*, 1926; *The Thing That
    Cannot Be Named*, 1929; *Life-And-A-Fortnight*, 1929;
    Flame of the Forest, 1930; *The Eye of Isis*, 1931;
    Death In Goblin Waters, 1934.

FISH, ROBERT L. (1912-   ) *U.S.*
Born: Cleveland, Ohio
as Robert L. Fish
  Not Counting Bridges. *Magazine of Fantasy and Science
    Fiction*, April 1963
  ☐ MYSTERY: *The Fugitive, Isle of the Snakes*, 1963;
    The Shrunken Head, 1963; *The Incredible Schlock
    Homes*, 1966; *The Green Hell Treasure*, 1971; *The Mem-
    oirs of Schlock Homes*, 1974.
as A. C. Lamprey
  ☐ Police Procedurals
as Robert L. Pike
  ☐ MYSTERY: *Mute Witness*, 1963; *The Quarry*, 1964;
    Police Blotter, 1965.

FISHER, GENE
as Gene Lancour
  The Lerios Mecca. Garden City: Doubleday, 1973, 180pp.
  The War Machines Of Kalinth. Garden City: Doubleday,
    1977, 190pp.
  Sword For The Empire. Garden City: Doubleday, 1978.

FISHER, STEPHEN G(ould) (1912-   ) *U.S.*
as Stephen Fisher
  Saxon's Ghost. Los Angeles: Sherbourne Press, [1967],
    211pp.
as Steve Fisher
  Returned From Hell. *Unknown*, May 1939
  Destroyer. NY: Appleton-Century, 1941, 236pp.
  ☐ *Satan's Angel*, 1935; *The Night Before Murder*, 1939;
    I Wake Up Screaming, 1941; *City In Flames*, 1956
    (teleplay); *Image of Hell*, 1961; *The Big Dream*, 1970.
as Stephen Gould
  ☐ MYSTERY: *Murder Of The Admiral*, 1936; *Murder Of The
    Pigboat Skipper*, 1937; *Homicide Johnny*, 1940.
as Grant Lane
  ☐ MYSTERY: *Spend the Night*, 1935.

FITZPATRICK, BERNARD EDWARD BARNABY (2d Baron
Castletown) (1849-19?)
  Autobiography: *"Ego," Random Records Of Sport, Service
    and Travel In Many Lands.* London: J. Murray, 1923,
    245pp.
as Lord Castletown
  A Bundle Of Lies. London: Drane's, [1924], 192pp.
as Bernard Fitzpatrick
  ■ *The ABC of the Irish Land Question*, 1881; *Ireland's
    Brighter Prospects*, 1881.

FITZPATRICK, ERNEST H(ugh)
as Hugo Barnaby
  *The Marshall Duke of Denver; or, The Labor Revolution
    of 1920.* Chicago: Donohue & Henneberry, [c.1895], 208pp.
as Ernest H. Fitzpatrick
  The Coming Conflict of Nations; or, The Japanese-American

War; A Narrative. Springfield, Illinois: H. W. Rokker,
  [c.1909], 306pp.
  ☐ *Magdalene of France*, 1899 (play); *The Passing of
    William McKinley. A Poem*, 1901 (poetry); *True Gold of
    Tennessee*, 1922.
  ■ *Prohibition and Prussianism, A Parallel. Are We
    Americans, or, Are We Hottentots? Which?*, 1919.

FLACK, ISAAC H(arvey) (1912-   ) *British*
as Harvey Graham
  A Crab Was Crushed. London: Rich & Cowan, [1937],
    281pp.
  ■ *Surgeon's All*, 1939; *Eternal Eve. (A History of Gyne-
    cology & Obstetrics)*, 1950; *A Doctor's London*, 1952.

FLETCHER, J(oseph) S(mith) (1863-1935) *English*
Born: Halifax, Yorkshire
Biography: *Journalist*, by James W. Smith. London, 1928.
as J(oseph) S(mith) Fletcher
  The Wonderful City. London: T. Nelson, 1894, 185pp., ill.
  The Blue Bell Inn. Chicago: Rand, McNally, [1898], 203pp.
  The Three Days of Terror. London: J. Long, 1901, 307pp.
  The Air-Ship and Other Stories. London: Digby, Long,
    1903, 303pp. ss col
  The Ransom For London. London: Mason, 1927, 309pp.
  The Matheson Formula. NY: Knopf, 1929, 275pp.
  *The Man In No. 3, and Other Stories of Crime, Love,
    and Mystery.* London: Collins, [1931], 252pp. ss col
  ☐ HISTORICAL FICTION: *When Charles First Was King*,
    1892; *Mistress Spitfire*, 1896. POETRY: *Collected Verses
    (1881-1931)*, 1931. MYSTERY: *The Adventures of Archer
    Dawe*, 1909; *The Middle Temple Murder*, 1918; *The Char-
    ing Cross Mystery*, 1923; *Cobweb Castle*, 1928; *The
    Murder of the Ninth Baronet*, 1932; *"Casebook of Ronald
    Camberwell"* series beginning with *Murder At Wrides
    Park*, 1931; through *The Millhouse Murder*, 1937.
  ■ *A Book About Yorkshire*, 1908; *The Cisterians In York-
    shire*, 1918.
as "A Son of the Soil"
  newspaper articles

FOIGNY, GABRIEL DE (c.1650-1692) *French*
as Mr. (James) Sadeur
  *La Terre Australe Connue: C'est a Dire, la Description de
    ce Pays Inconnu Jusqu' Ici, de Ses Moeurs et de Ses
    Costumes.* Vannes, Switzerland, 1676, 267pp.
  *A New Discovery of Terra Incognita Australis, or, The
    Southern World.* London: J. Dunton, 1693, 186pp.

FOLEY, DAVE
as Gerald Hatch
  The Day the Earth Froze. Derby, Connecticut: Monarch,
    [1963], 125pp., paper.

FOOT, MICHAEL (Mackintosh) (1913-   ) *English*
as "Cassius"
  The Trial of Mussolini. London: V. Gollancz, 1943, 82pp.
  ■ *The Bretton Woods Plan (For World Domination by
    the U.S.A.); Blueprints for A Third World War*, 1947.
as Michael Foot
  ■ *Armistice 1918-39*, 1940; (with R. H. S. Crossman)
    A Palestine Munich?, 1946.

FORAN, W(illiam) ROBERT (Capt.) *British*
Autobiographical: *A Cuckoo In Kenya, the Reminiscences
  of A Pioneer Police Officer.* London: Hutchinson, 1936,
  360pp.
as W(illiam) Robert Foran
  ☐ *Drums of Sacrifice*, 1934.
  ■ *Kill: Or Be Killed; the Rambling Reminiscences of An
    Amateur Hunter*, 1934.
  ↙ Capt. Bedrod-Foran [in collaboration with H. Bedford-Jones]

FORD, D(ouglas) M(orley)
as Author of "A Time of Terror"
The Raid of Dover: A Romance of the Reign of Woman, A.D. 1940. London: King, Sell & Olding, 1910, 188pp.
as Douglas Morley Ford
□ *Kate Savage. A Novel,* 1873.
■ *Solicitors As Advocates,* 1881; *Matrimonial Law, and the Guardianship of Infants,* 1888; *The Law of Briefs,* 1904.
anonymous
A Time of Terror: The Story of A Great Revenge, A. D. 1910. London: Greening, 1906, 340pp.

FORD, FORD MADDOX (1873-1939) *ne* Hueffer *British*
Born: Merton, Surrey
Autobiography: *It Was the Nightingale.* London: Heinemann, 1934, 354pp.
as Daniel Chaucer
□ *The Simple Life Limited,* 1911; *The New Humpty-Dumpty,* 1912.
as Ford Maddox Ford
□ *No More Parades,* 1925; *No Enemy,* 1929; *When the Wicked Man,* 1931; *Collected Poems,* 1936 (poetry).
■ *New York Is Not America,* 1927; *The English Novel,* 1929; *Great Trade Route,* 1937; *The March of Literature,* 1938.
as Ford (H.) (Maddox) Hueffer
The Brown Owl. NY: Stokes, 1891, 165pp., ill. *juv* [London: Unwin, 1892]
The Queen Who Flew. London: Bliss, 1894, 118pp., ill.
(with Joseph Conrad) *The Inheritors; An Extravagant Story.* London: Heinemann, 1901, 323pp.
The 'Half Moon. A Romance of the Old World and the New. London: E. Nash, 1909, 346pp.
Ladies Whose Bright Eyes. London: Constable, 1911, 363pp.
□ *The Feather,* 1892 (juv); (with Joseph Conrad) *The Romance,* 1903; POETRY: *Poems For Pictures,* 1897; *From Inland & Other Poems,* 1907; *Collected Poems,* 1913.
■ *When Blood Is Their Argument. An Analysis of Prussian Culture,* 1915.

FORD, GARRET [house pseudonym]
Used at F.P.C.I. (Fantasy Publishing Company, Inc.) for editor of *Fantasy Book* and *Spaceway,* two magazines published by the firm. Used by F.P.C.I. publisher William L. Crawford, his wife Margaret Crawford, as well as others.
See WILLIAM L. CRAWFORD

FOSTER, E. M. (Mrs.) *British*
as E. M. F.
The Duke of Clarence; An Historical Novel. London: W. Lane, 1795, 4 vol.
anonymous or by the author of———
□ *Miriam. A Novel,* 1800 (2 vol); *Concealment, or, The Cascade of Llantwarryhn,* 1801; *Light and Shadow. A Novel,* 1803 (4 vol.).

FOSTER, GEORGE C(ecil) (1893-) *British*
as George C(ecil) Foster
Full Five Fathoms. London: Jenkins, 1930, 320pp.
The Lost Garden. London: Chapman & Hall, [1930], 266pp.
Awakening. London: Chapman & Hall, [1932], 307pp.
Walls Whisper. London: Chapman & Hall, [1932], 353pp.
□ *The Oldest Profession,* 1925; *The Thief of Time,* 1926; *Sunwards,* 1931; *Turkish Delight,* 1936; *Peace Among the Pelicans,* 1949.
as Seaforth
Cats In the Coffee. London: H. Jenkins, [1938], 285pp.

We Band of Brothers. London: H. Jenkins, [1939], 288pp., ill.
Diana Of Ephesus. London: H. Jenkins, [1939], 283pp.

FOULDS, ELFRIDA VIPONT (Brown) (1902-)
as Charles Vipont
□ *Blow the Man Down,* 1949.
as Elfrida Vipont
Terror By Night. London: H. Hamilton, 1966, 154pp. ss col
Ghosts' High Noon. NY: H. Z. Walck, 1967, 167pp.
□ *The Lark In the Morn,* 1948; *The Lark On the Wing,* 1951; *The Family At Dowbiggins,* 1955.
■ *Good Adventure, the Quest Music In England,* 1931; *The Story of Quakerism,* 1954; *The Birthplace of Quakerism,* 1955; *The Quaker Witness,* 1955; *Henry Purcell and His Times,* 1959; *Towards A High Attic, the Early Life of George Eliot,* 1970.

FOX, GARDNER F(rancis) (1911-) *U.S.*
Born: Brooklyn, New York
as Jefferson Cooper
□ *Arrow In the Hill,* 1955; *The Swordsman,* 1957.
■ *Custom Rifles,* 1957.
as Gardner F. Fox
The Weirds of the Woodcarver. *Weird Tales,* Sept 1944
The Last Monster. *Planet Stories,* Fall 1945
(with John Guinta, artist) Crom the Barbarian. *Out Of This World,* June 1950 *comic book*
Five Weeks In A Balloon. NY: Pyramid, [1962], paper.
Escape Across The Cosmos. NY: Paperback Library, [1964], 160pp., paper.
The Arsenal of Miracles. NY: Ace, [1964], 156pp., paper. (Ace Double F 299)
The Warrior of Llarn. NY: Ace, [1964], 160pp., paper.
The Hunter Out of Time. NY: Ace, [1965], 126pp., paper. (Ace Double F354)
The Thief of Llarn. NY: Ace, [1966], 158pp., paper.
Kothar—Barbarian Swordsman. NY: Belmont, [1969], 153pp., paper.
Kothar of the Magic Sword. NY: Belmont, [1969], 154pp., ill., paper.
Kothar and the Demon Queen. NY: Tower, [1969], 155pp., paper.
Kothar and the Wizard Slayer. NY: Belmont, [1970], paper.
Kothar and the Conjurer's Curse. NY: Belmont, [1970], paper.
Conehead. Ace, [1973] [?] paper.
Kyrik, Warlock Warrior. NY: Leisure Books, [1974].
Kyrik, Fights the Demon World. NY: Leisure Books, [1975].
Kyrik and the Wizard's Sword. NY: Leisure Books, [1975].
Kyrik and the Lost Queen. NY: Leisure Books, [1976].
□ Has been writing for comic books since the mid-thirties. *The Borgia Blade,* 1953; *Rebel Wench,* 1955.
as Simon Majors
The Druid Stone. NY: Paperback Library, 1967, 157pp., paper.
as Bart Somers
Beyond the Black Enigma. NY: Paperback Library, 1965, paper.
Abandon Galaxy. NY: Paperback Library, 1967, paper.
✓ Jeffrey Gardner, James Kendricks

FRANCIS, LEE [house pseudonym]
unattributed
[many of the following stories are probably by Howard Browne]
Shadow of the Spider. *Amazing,* March 1943
Daughter of Destiny. *Amazing,* April 1943

Citadel of Hate. *Fantastic Adventures*, June 1943
Stone Goddess of Yunan. *Amazing*, Aug 1943
Witch of Blackfen Moor. *Fantastic Adventures*, Dec 1943
Appointment With the Past. *Fantastic Adventures*, Feb 1944
Hitler's Right Eye. *Fantastic Adventures*, June 1944
Comet From Yesterday. *Amazing*, March 1945
Change For the Bitter. *Fantastic Adventures*, April 1945
Cursed Caverns of Ra. *Amazing*, Sept 1945
Sentimental Monster. *Amazing*, Dec 1946
When the Spirit Moves Me. *Fantastic Adventures*, May 1947
Terror On The Telephone. *Amazing*, Sept 1947
Hell Is A Circle. *Fantastic Adventures*, Nov 1947
Murder Solves A Problem. *Amazing*, Nov 1947
Zero A.D. *Fantastic Adventures*, March 1948
Flight Into Fog. *Fantastic Adventures*, April 1948
Forgotten Hades. *Amazing*, May 1948
Phantom of the Forest. *Amazing*, Nov 1948
Outlaws of Corpus. *Fantastic Adventures*, Dec 1948
The Chemical Vampire. *Amazing*, March 1949
Midgets and Mighty Men. *Fantastic Adventures*, May 1949
Coffin of Hope. *Amazing*, July 1949
Backward Passage. *Fantastic Adventures*, Sept 1949
The Man Who Could Not Die. *Fantastic Adventures*, Jan 1950
The Soul Snatchers. *Fantastic Adventures*, May 1952

by Howard Browne
The Man From Yesterday. *Fantastic Adventures*, Aug 1948

FRANKAU, JULIA (Davis) (Mrs.) (1864-1916)
as Frank Danby
Twilight. London: Hutchinson, 1916, 332pp.
☐ *Dr. Phillips, A Maida Vale Idyll*, 1887; *A Babe In Bohemia*, 1890; *Pigs In Clover*, 1903; *Baccarat*, 1904; *An Incompleat Etonian*, 1909; *Let the Roof Fall In*, 1910; *The Story Behind the Verdict*, 1915.

FRAZEE, CHARLES S(tephen) (1909-   ) *U.S.*
Born: Salida, Colorado
as Steve Frazee
The Sky Block. NY: Rinehart, [1953], 247pp., ill.
☐ WESTERN: *Lawman's Feud*, 1953; *The Gun-Throwers*, 1954; *Spur To the Smoke*, 1955.
as Dean Jennings
☐ WESTERN: *Range Trouble*, 1951.

FREEMAN, R(ichard) Austin (1862-1943) *English*
Born: London
as Clifford Ashdown [in collaboration with John James Pitcairn]
☐ MYSTERY: *The Adventures of Romney Pringle*, 1902.
as R(ichard) Austin Freeman
(with Ashdown Piers) By The Black Deep. *Winsor Magazine*, May 1903
The Mystery of 31, New Inn. London: Hodder & Stoughton, 1912, 311pp.
The Great Portrait Mystery. London: Hodder & Stoughton, [1918], 318pp.
☐ *The Uttermost Farthing: A Savant's Vendetta*, 1914.
☐ MYSTERY: "Dr. Thorndyke" series including: *Dr. Thorndyke's Cases*, 1909; *The Singing Bone*, 1912; *The Magic Casket*, 1927; *For the Defense: Doctor Thorndyke*, 1934.
■ *Travels and Life In Ashanti and Jaman*, 1898; *Social Decay and Regeneration*, 1921.

FRENCH, ALICE (1850-1934) *U.S.*
Born: Andover, Massachusetts
as Octave Thanet
Otto the Knight, and Other Trans-Mississippi Stories. Boston: Houghton-Mifflin, 1891, 348pp. ss col
The Missionary Sheriff. NY: Harper, 1897, 248pp., ill.
Stories That End Well. Indianapolis: Bobbs-Merrill, [c.1911], 340pp., ill.

☐ *Knitters In The Sun*, 1887; *Man of the Hour*, 1905; *The Lion's Share*, 1907; *By Inheritance*, 1910.
■ *An Adventure In Photography*, 1893.

FRIEDMAN, DAVID GERROLD *U.S.*
as David Gerrold
The God Machine. *Galaxy*, May 1970
When Harlie Was One. London: 1969? [unconfirmed]
(with Larry Niven) *The Flying Sorcerers.* NY: Ballantine, [1971], 316pp., paper.
When Harlie Was One. Garden City: Doubleday, [1972], 247pp.
Space Skimmer. NY: Ballantine, [1972], 218pp., paper.
With A Finger In My I. NY: Ballantine, [1972], 245pp., paper. ss col
Yesterday's Children. NY: Dell, [1972], 251pp., paper.
The Man Who Folded Himself. NY: Random House, [1973], 148pp.

FRIEND, OSCAR J(erome) (1897-1963) *U.S.*
as Oscar J. Friend
Of Jovian Build. *Thrilling Wonder Stories*, Oct 1938
The Kid From Mars. NY: Frederick Fell, [1949], 270pp.
The Star Men. NY: Avalon, [1963], 221pp.
☐ WESTERN: *The Round Up*, 1924; *Half-Moon Ranch*, 1931; *The Range Doctor*, 1950.
as Owen Fox Jerome
British Thermal Units. *Thrilling Wonder Stories*, June 1942
The Hand of Horror. NY: Clode, [1927], 309pp.
☐ MYSTERY: *The Red Kite Clue*, 1928; *Murder As Usual*, 1942; *The Corpse Awaits*, 1946.
as Ford Smith
Venusian Nightmare. *Thrilling Wonder Stories*, Winter 1944.
☐ WESTERN: *Range Doctor*, 1958.

FYFE, H(orace) B(rowne) (1918-   ) *U.S.*
Born: Jersey City, New Jersey
as Horace B. Fyfe
Locked Out. *Astounding*, Feb 1940
D—99. NY: Pyramid, [1962], 144pp., paper.
↙ **Andrew MacDuff**

GADE, HENRY [house pseudonym]
unattributed
Heroes Die Hard. *Fantastic Adventures,* Dec 1943
My Name Is Madness. *Fantastic Adventures,* Nov 1949
by Raymond A. Palmer
Pioneer — 1957. *Fantastic Adventures,* Nov 1939
Liners Of Space. *Amazing,* Dec 1939
The Invincible Crime Buster. *Amazing,* July 1941

GALBRAITH, ALEXANDER (1924-   ) *English*
as Sandy Wilson
This Is Sylvia: Her Lives Her Loves. NY: Dutton, 1955, 125pp.
☐ *The Boyfriend,* 1954 (musical comedy play).

GALLOWAY, JAMES M.
as James M. Galloway
Lock and Key. NY: G. W. Dillingham, 1899, 407pp. [2nd ed of title *John Harvey, etc.* see Anon Moore below.]
as Anon Moore
John Harvey; A Tale of the Twentieth Century. Chicago: C. H. Kerr, 1897, 407pp.

GALLUN, RAYMOND Z. (1910-   ) *U.S.*
Born: Beaver Dam, Wisconsin
as Arthur Allport
Gentle Brain. *Science Fiction, Quarterly,* Summer 1940
as William Callahan
The Machine That Thought. *Science Fiction,* March 1939
The Machine That Thought. NY: Columbia Pub., 1940.
as Dow Elstar
Avalanche. *Astounding,* Dec 1935
as Raymond Z. Gallun
The Space Dwellers. *Science Wonder Stories,* Nov 1929
The Crystal Ray. *Air Wonder Stories,* Nov 1929
People Minus X. NY: Simon & Schuster, 1957, 186pp.
The Planet Strappers. NY: Pyramid, [1961], 157pp., paper.
as E. V. Raymond
Nova Solis. *Astounding,* Dec 1935

GALOUYE, DANIEL F(rancis) (1920-   ) *U.S.*
Born: New Orleans, Louisiana
as Louis G. Daniels
. . . Do Us Part. *Imagination,* April 1953
as Daniel F. Galouye
Rebirth. *Imagination,* March 1952
Dark Universe. NY: Bantam, [1961], 154pp., paper.
Lords of the Psychon. NY: Bantam, [1963], 155pp., paper.
Simulacron—3. NY: Bantam, [1964], 152pp., paper.
Counterfeit World. London: Gollancz, 1964, 158pp.
The Last Leap and Other Stories of the Supermind. London: Corgi, 1964, 172pp., paper. *ss col*
The Lost Perception. London: Gollancz, 1966, 190pp.
Project Barrier. London: Gollancz, 1968, 207pp. *ss col*
A Scourge of Screamers. NY: Bantam, [1968], 172pp., paper.
The Infinite Man. NY: Bantam, [1973], 202pp., ill., paper.

GALSWORTHY, JOHN (1867-1933) *British*
Born: Coombe, Surrey
as John Galsworthy

Caravan. London: Heinemann, 1925, 950pp. *ss col*
☐ *Villa Rubein,* 1900; *A Man of Devon,* 1901; *The Man Of Property,* 1906; *The Patrician,* 1911; *Beyond, 1917; In Chancery,* 1920; *To Let,* 1921; *Swan Song,* 1928. PLAYS: *The Silver Box,* 1906; *Joy,* 1907; *Strife,* 1909; *The Skin Game,* 1920.
■ *The Inn of Tranquility,* 1912 (essays).
as John Sinjohn
☐ *From the Four Winds,* 1897 (ss col); *Jocelyn,* 1898; *A Bit O' Love,* 1915.

GANLEY, W. PAUL
as Toby Duane
The Fire Born, in *Shanadu* (ss col). Tonawanda, NY: SSR Publications, 1953, 101pp.

GARDNER, E. D.
as "Schire"
High Magic's Aid. London: Hodder & Stoughton, 1949, 352pp.

GARDNER, ERLE STANLEY (1889-1970) *U.S.*
Born: Malden, Massachusetts
Bibliography: *Erle Stanley Gardner: A Checklist,* by E.H. Mundell.
as A. A. Fair
☐ MYSTERY: *The Bigger They Come,* 1939; *Bats Fly At Dusk,* 1942; *Cats Prowl At Night,* 1943; *Crows Can't Count,* 1946; *Owls Don't Blink,* 1947.
as Erle Stanley Gardner
Rain Magic. *Argosy,* Oct 20, 1928
The Human Zero. *Fantastic,* Jan 1962
New Worlds. *Fantastic,* Sept 1962
☐ MYSTERY: "Perry Mason" series e.g. *The Case of the Velvet Claws,* 1933. and other mysteries e.g. *The D.A. Calls It Murder,* 1937.
■ *The Land of Shorter Shadows,* 1948; *Court of Last Resort,* 1952; *Hunting the Desert Whale,* 1960; *Hovering Over Baja,* 1961; *The Hidden Heart of Baja,* 1962.
as Carleton Kendrake
☐ MYSTERY: *The Clew of the Forgotten Murder,* 1934.
as Charles J. Kenny
☐ *This Is Murder,* 1935.
✔ Kyle Corning, Charles M. Green, Robert Parr, Les Tillray.

GARIS, HOWARD ROGER (1873-1962) *U.S.*
as Victor Appleton
All are entitled *Tom Swift:* and are listed chronologically. They are all NY: Grosset & Dunlap, appx. 212pp.: *and His Motor Cycle,* 1910; *and His Motor Boat,* 1910; *and His Airship,* 1910; *and His Submarine Boat,* 1910; *and His Electric Runabout,* 1910; *and His Wireless Messenger,* 1910; *Among the Diamond Makers,* 1911; *In the Caves of Ice,* 1911; *and His Sky Racer,* 1911; *and His Electric Rifle,* 1911; *In the City of Gold,* 1912; *and His Air Glider,* 1912; *In Captivity,* 1912; *and His Wizard Camera,* 1912; *and His Great Searchlight,* 1912; *and His Great Cannon,* 1913; *and His Photo Telephone,* 1914; *and His Aerial Warship,* 1915; *and His Big Tunnel,* 1916; *In the Land Of Wonders,* 1917; *and His War Tank,* 1918; *and His Air Scout,* 1919; *and His Undersea Voyage,* 1920; *Among the Fire Fighters,* 1921; *and His Electric Locomotive,* 1922; *and His Flying Boat,* 1923; *and His Great Oil Gusher,* 1924; *and His Chest of Secrets,* 1925; *and His Airline Express,* 1926; *Circling the Globe,* 1927; *and His Talking Pictures,* 1928; *and His House On Wheels,* 1929; *and His Big Dirigible,* 1930; *and His Sky Train,* 1931; *and His Giant Magnet,* 1932; (later stories under this name are products of the Stratemeyer syndicate, authorship unattributed).
as Marion Davidson
☐ *The Campfire Girls; or, The Secret of An Old Mill,*

1913; *The Campfire Girls On Ice,* 1913.

as Howard R. Garis

Tam of Fire Cave. NY: Appleton, 1927, 257pp. *juv*

Rocket Riders Over the Desert. NY: Burt, [1933], 250pp. *juv*

Rocket Riders Across the Ice. NY: Burt, [1933], 251pp. *juv*

Rocket Riders In Stormy Seas. NY: Burt, [1933], 246pp. *juv*

Rocket Riders In the Air. NY: Burt, [1934], 251pp. *juv*

□ "Buddy" series, "Curly Tops" series, "Larry Dexter, or, the Great Newspaper" series, "Rick and Ruddy" series, "Teddy" series, "Uncle Wiggily" series—all juveniles. *The King of Unadilla,* 1903.

GARRETT, EILEEN JEANETTE (Lyttle) (1893-   ) *U.S.*

Autobiographical: *My Life As A Search For the Meaning of Mediumship.* NY: Oquaga, 1939 and *Adventures In the Supernormal—A Personal Memoir.* NY: Creative Age Press, 1949, 252pp.

as Eileen J. Garrett

Telepathy; In Search of A Lost Faculty. NY: Creative Age Press, 1941, 210pp. (with selected bibliography) *non fiction*

Awareness. NY: Creative Age Press, 1943, 308pp.

The Sense and Non Sense of Prophecy. NY: Creative Age Press, 1950, 279pp. *non fiction*

Beyond the Five Senses. Philadelphia: Lippincott, 1957, 384pp. *non fiction*

■ (with A. Lamarque) *Man the Maker, A Pictorial History of Man's Inventiveness,* 1946.

as Jean Lyttle

□ *Today the Sun Rises,* 1942; *You are France, Lisette,* 1943; *Sheila Lacey,* 1944.

GARRETT, (Gordon) RANDALL (Philip) (David)   *U.S.*

as Gordon Aghill [in collaboration with Robert Silverberg]

Gambler's Planet. *Amazing,* June 1956

as Grandal(l) Barretton [Grandell Barretton (sic)]

Through Time and Space with Benedict Breadfruit - I. *Amazing,* March 1962 [a spoof on Reginald Bretnor's Ferdinand Feghoot series]

as Alexander Blade [house pseudonym] [in collaboration with Robert Silverberg]

The Alien Dies At Dawn. *Imagination,* Dec 1956.

Wednesday Morning Sermon. *Imaginative Tales,* Jan 1957

The Ambassador's Pet. *Imagination,* Oct 1957

as Walter Bupp

Vigorish. *Astounding,* June 1960

as Ralph Burke [in collaboration with Robert Silverberg] [other stories under this name are by Robert Silverberg alone]

No Trap For the Keth. *Imaginative Tales,* Nov 1956

The Incomplete Theft. *Imagination,* Feb 1957

as Gordon Garrett

The Absence of Heat. *Astounding,* June 1944

as Randall Garrett

The Waiting Game. *Astounding,* Jan 1951

(with Larry M. Harris) *Pagan Passions.* NY: Beacon, [1959], 158pp., paper.

The Unwise Child. Garden City: Doubleday, 1962, 215pp.

Too Many Magicians. Garden City: Doubleday, 1967, [1966], 260pp.

■ *Pope John XXIII, Pastoral Prince,* 1962; *A Gallery of the Saints,* 1963.

as David Gordon

By the Rule. *Other Worlds,* Oct 1950

as Richard Greer [house pseudonym] [in collaboration with Robert Silverberg]

The Great Kladnar Race. *Amazing,* Dec 1956

as Ivar Jorgensen [house pseudonym] [in collaboration with

Robert Silverberg]

Bleekman's Planet. *Imagination,* Feb 1957

Slaughter On Dornel IV. *Imagination,* April 1957

Pirates of the Void. *Imaginative Tales,* July 1957

as Darrel(l) T. Langart

What The Left Hand Was Doing. *Astounding,* Feb 1960

Anything You Can Do . . . Garden City: Doubleday, 1963, 192pp.

as Clyde T. Mitchell [house pseudonym] [in collaboration with Robert Silverberg]

The Mummy Takes A Wife. *Fantastic,* Dec 1956

Deadly Decoy. *Amazing,* Feb 1957

as Mark Phillips [in collaboration with Larry M. Harris]

That Sweet Little Old Lady. *Astounding,* Sept-Oct 1959

Brain Twister. NY: Pyramid, [1962], 144pp., paper.

The Impossibles. NY: Pyramid, [1963], 157pp., paper.

Supermind. NY: Pyramid, [1963], 192pp., paper.

as Robert Randall [alone]

(ed) *Infinity Magazine* [Oct 1956 issue only]

as Robert Randall [in collaboration with Robert Silverberg]

Vanishing Act. *Imaginative Tales,* Jan 1956

The Shrouded Planet. NY: Gnome, 1957, 188pp.

The Dawning Light. NY: Gnome, [1959], 191pp.

as Leonard G. Spencer [house pseudonym] [in collaboration with Robert Silverberg]

The Beast with 7 Tails. *Amazing,* Aug 1956

as S. M. Tenneshaw [house pseudonym] [alone]

Kill Me If You Can. *Imagination,* June 1957

as S. M. Tenneshaw [house pseudonym] [in collaboration with Robert Silverberg]

The Ultimate Weapon. *Imaginative Tales,* Jan 1957

The Man Who Hated Noise. *Imaginative Tales,* March 1957

House Operator. *Imagination,* Dec 1957

as Gerald Vance [house pseudonym] [in collaboration with Robert Silverberg]

The Judas Valley. *Amazing,* Oct 1956

GARRISON, CHARLES M.

as Charles MacDaniel

Murder On the Moon. NY: Vantage, [1968], 224pp.

GARSON, CLEE [house pseudonym] [possibly all by David Wright O'Brien, but others may have used this name]

Sharbeau's Startling Statue. *Fantastic Adventures,* Nov 1942

Madagascar Ghost. *Fantastic Adventures,* Dec 1942

Saunders' Strange Second Sight. *Fantastic Adventures,* Jan 1943

Direct Wire. *Amazing,* Jan 1943

Club of the Damned. *Fantastic Adventures,* Feb 1943

The Other Abner Small. *Fantastic Adventures,* March 1943

The Money Machine. *Amazing,* March 1943

The Merchant of Venus. *Fantastic Adventures,* April 1943

Let's Give Away Mars! *Amazing,* April 1951

The Spoilers Of Lern. *Fantastic Adventures,* Aug 1951

The Martian Cross. *Amazing,* Dec 1952

The Scavengers of Space. *Fantastic,* Oct 1955

by Paul W. Fairman

Nine Worlds West. *Fantastic Adventures,* April 1951

GARTH, WILL [house pseudonym]

unattributed

Bloodless Peril. *Thrilling Wonder Stories,* Dec 1937

Men Of Honor. *Captain Future,* Spring 1940

Memory Blocks. *Captain Future,* Spring 1941

by Otto Binder

Rays of Blindness. *Thrilling Wonder Stories,* April 1938

by Edmond Hamilton

The Great Illusion. *Thrilling Wonder Stories,* June 1938

by Henry Kuttner

Hands Across the Void. *Thrilling Wonder Stories*, Dec 1938
Dr. Cyclops. NY: Phoenix Press, [1940], 255pp.
by Mort Weisinger
Turnabout. *Startling Stories*, March 1939
Incident On Titan. *Thrilling Wonder Stories*, June 1941

GARTMANN, HEINZ (1917-1960) *German*
as Heinz Gartmann
■ *The Men Behind the Space Rockets*, 1956; *Man Unlimited; Technology's Challenge To Human Endurance*, 1957.
as Werner Wehr
Ich Lelte Im Jahr 3000; Roman Einer Moglichen Reise. Stuttgart, 1959, 295pp.

GASKO, GORDON
as Nathaniel Gordon
The Golden Judge. *Astounding*, Dec 1955

GEIER, CHESTER S. (1921-   ) *U.S.*
[It is probable that Chester S. Geier wrote the majority of stories appearing under the house pseudonyms below, in some cases he may have written all stories under a given name, but this is not confirmed.]
as Guy Archette
Not As Plotted. *Fantastic Adventures*, March 1947
as Alexander Blade [house pseudonym]
stories unknown [see unattributed stories under Alexander Blade]
as P. F. Costello [house pseudonym]
stories unknown [see unattributed stories under P. F. Costello]
as Chester S. Geier
A Length Of Rope. *Unknown*, April 1941
as Warren Kastel
Illusion On Callisto. *Amazing*, May 1948
    see **ROBERT SILVERBERG**
as S. M. Tenneshaw [house pseudonym]
stories unknown [see unattributed stories under S. M. Tenneshaw]
as Gerald Vance [house pseudonym]
stories unknown [see unattributed stories under Gerald Vance]
as Peter Worth [house pseudonym]
stories unknown [see unattributed stories under **PETER WORTH**]

GEISEL, THEODOR SEUSS (1904-   )
as Theo Le Sieg
□ *Ten Apples Up On Top!*, 1961 (juv reader)
as Dr. Seuss
Many children's fantasies including: *And To Think I Saw It On Mulberry Street*, 1937; *The Cat In the Hat*, 1957; *How the Grinch Stole Christmas*, 1957; and *Yertle the Turtle*, 1958.

GENTLEMAN, FRANCIS (1728-1784) *Irish*
as Francis Gentleman
□ PLAYS: *Narcissa and Eliza*, 1754; *The Stratford Jubilee*, 1769; *The Sultan*, 1770; *The Tobaconist*, 1771; *The Pantheonites*, 1773; *The Modish Wife*, 1774. POETRY: *The General*, 1764; *Royal Fables*, 1766.
■ *The Dramatic Censor*, 1770; *Introduction to Shakespeare's Plays*, 1774.
as Sir Humphrey Lunatic, Bart.
A Trip To The Moon. Containing An Account of the Island of Noibla. Its Inhabitants, Religious and Political Customs, &c. York: A. Ward for S. Crowder, etc. [London] 1764-1765, 2 vol.

GEORGE, PETER BRYAN (1924-1966) *Welsh*
as Peter Bryant
Two Hours to Doom. London: Boardman, 1958, 192pp.

as Peter George
Red Alert. NY: Ace, [1958], 191pp., paper. [retitling of *Two Hours to Doom*]
Dr. Strangelove, or, How I Learned to Stop Worrying and Love the Bomb. London: Corgi, [1963], 145pp.
Commander - 1. London: Heinemann, [1965], 252pp.
□ MYSTERY: *Come Blonde, Come Murder*, 1952; *The Final Steal*, 1962.
as Bryan Peters
□ MYSTERY: *Hong Kong Kill*, 1958; *The Big H*, 1963.

GERAHTY, DIGBY GEORGE
as Robert Standish
The Radio-Active General and Other Stories. London: P. Davies, [1959], 222pp. ss col
The Talking Dog and Other Stories. London: P. Davies, [1961], 215pp.
□ *The Three Bamboos*, 1942; *Bonin*, 1943; *The Small General*, 1945; *Mr. On Loong*, 1946; *The Gulf of Time*, 1947; *Elephant Walk*, 1948; *Gentleman of China*, 1949; *Follow the Seventh Man*, 1950; *Storm Centre*, 1951; *A Worthy Man*, 1952; *A Long Way From Pimlico*, 1954; *Private Enterprise and Other Stories*, 1954; *Blind Tiger*, 1956; *Hot Chestnuts and Other Stories*, 1964; *Elephant Law and Other Stories*, 1969.
■ *The Prince of Storytellers; the Life of E. Phillips Oppenheim*, 1957.

GERMANO, PETER B.
as Barry Cord
The Lost Planet. *Thrilling Wonder Stories*, March 1941
The Pyramids From Space. *Amazing*, Nov 1951
□ WESTERN: *Trail Boss From Texas*, 1948; *Cain Basin*, 1954; *Boss of Barbed Wire*, 1955; *Dry Range*, 1955.
as Jim Kane
□ WESTERN: *Spanish Gold*, 1963; *Tangled Trails*, 1963.

GERNSBACK, HUGO (1884-1967) *naturalized U.S.*
Born: Luxembourg
as Grego Banshuck
The Electronic Baby. *Science Fiction +*, May 1953
as Greno Gashbuck
The Cosmatomic Flyer. *Science Fiction +*, March 1953
as Hugo Gernsback
Ralph 124C41+. *Modern Electronics*, April 1911
Ralph 124C41+; A Romance of the Year 2660. Boston: Stratford, 1925, 293pp.
Tina In Phantaland. NY: [1948], 22pp., ill.
Ultimate World. NY: Walker Co., [1971], 187pp.
■ *The Wireless Telephone*, 1910; *Radio For All*, 1913.
as Gus N. Habergock
The Radio Brain. *Science Fiction +*, April 1953
as Baron Munchausen
Baron Munchausen's New Scientific Adventures. Series in the *Electrical Experimenter*, [c.1915].

GERVE(E), BARONTE(I?)
as (Princess) Gerve(e) Baronti
Eyes of India. NY: Macauley, [1925], 320pp.
□ *A Modern Phoenix*, 1917; *In the Red Years*, 1917 (poetry); *Dying Flame*, 1935; *More Truth Than Poetry*, 1944.
■ *You Have Lived Before*, 1936; *Your Previous Life On Earth*, 1938; *Twilight In India*, 1949.

GIBSON, AMANDA MELVINA THORLEY *Australian*
as Una Cooper Mathieson
A Marriage Of Souls: A Metaphysical Novel. Perth, Australia: Truth Seeker Publishing Co., 1914, 702pp.
■ *The Universal Health Restorer; or, the Great Physician Within*, 1929.

GIBSON, JOE
as John Bridger
I'm A Stranger Here Myself. *Amazing,* Aug 1950
as Carleton Furth
We're off to Mars! *Imagination,* Sept 1951
as Joe Gibson
I Like You, Too. *Thrilling Wonder Stories,* Oct 1948

GIBSON, WALTER B(rown) (1897-   ) *U.S.*
as Walter B. Gibson
The Day New York Ended. *Fantastic,* Aug 1952
The Return Of The Shadow. NY: Belmont, 1963, paper.
■ *The Bunco Book,* 1927.
as Maxwell Grant
The Living Shadow. *The Shadow Magazine,* Spring 1931
as Harry Houdini [ghost written]
■ *Houdini On Magic,* 1930.
✔ Howard Thurston

GIBSON (Mrs. Walter B.)
as Litzka Raymond
■ *How To Read Palms,* 1950.

GIDDY, ERIC CAWOOD GWYDDN (1895-   )
as (W.) Kobold Knight
The Fanatic. *Oriental Stories,* April 1931
The Doctor of Souls. London: Cassell, [1927], 320pp.
□ *The Monsoon Bird,* 1927.
■ *A Guide To Fiction Writing,* 1936.

GIFFARD, HARDINGE GOULBURN (2nd Earl of Halsbury)
(1880-   ) *British*
as Oliver Bath
□ *Naughty Nancy,* 1902 (play).
as Earl of Halsbury
1944. London: T. Butterworth, [1926], 302pp.
■ *The Principles and Practice of Prize Law,* 1914.

GILES, R. A.
as B. X. Barry
Pirates of Space. *Amazing,* Dec 1931.

GILLINGS, WALTER *British*
as Geoffrey Giles [alone]
Lost Planet. *Fantasy,* Dec 1946 (Br.)
as Geoffrey Giles [in collaboration with Forrest J. Ackerman]
[probably only on this article]
Fantasy's Prodigy. *Fantasy Review,* Summer 1949 (Br.)
[article on Ray Bradbury]
as Walter Gillings
The Moon Men. *Fantasy,* Dec 1946 (Br.)
as Thomas Sheridan
Going Down! *Fantasy,* Dec 1946 (Br.) *article*

GLEMSER, BERNARD (1908-   ) *British*
as Robert Crane
The Purple Fields, in *Star SF Stories #2* (pp. 98-110)
NY: Ballantine, [1952], 195pp., paper/hardback. *ss col*
Hero's Walk. NY: Ballantine, [1954], 196pp., paper/hardback.
as Bernard Glemser
□ *The Twins,* 1946; *High Moon,* 1949; *The Dove On His Shoulder,* 1953; *The Lieutenant,* 1958; *The 60th Monarch,* 1974; *Grand Opening,* 1976.
■ *All About the Human Body,* 1958; *All About Biology,* 1964; *Man Against Cancer,* 1969; *Mr. Burkitt and Africa,* 1970.
as Geoffrey Napier
□ *A Very Special Agent,* 1967.
as Geraldine Napier
□ *Girls In White Satin,* 1966.

GODWIN, FRANCIS (Bishop of Hereford) (1562-1633)
English
as Domingo Gonsales
The Man In the Moone: or, A Discourse Of A Voyage Thither. London: J. Kirton & T. Warren, 1638, 126pp., ill.
as F. G.
■ *A Catalogue of the Bishops Of England,* 1601; *Annales of England,* 1630 [1616].

GODWIN, WILLIAM (1756-1836) *English*
Born: Wisbeach,
Biography: *Shelley, Godwin, and Their Circle,* by Henry N. Brailsford. London: 1951.
as Edward Baldwin
■ *The History of England, For the Use Of Schools,* 1815; *New Guide To the English Tongue,* 1833.
as William Godwin
Things As They Are; or, The Adventures of Caleb Williams. London: B. Crosby, 1794, 3 vol.
Saint Leon: A Tale Of the Sixteenth Century. London: Robinson, 1799, 4 vol.
■ *Inquiry Concerning Political Justice,* 1793; *Memoirs Of the Author of A Vindication of Women's Rights [Mary Wollstonecraft Godwin],* 1798; *Life of Chaucer,* 1803; *Of Population,* 1820; *History of the Commonwealth,* 1824-1828.
as Theophilus Marcliffe
□ *The Looking Glass. A True History of the Early Years of An Artist,* 1805.

GOLD, EVELYN PAIGE (Mrs. Horace L.) *U.S.*
as Evelyn Paig
Asst. Editor. *Galaxy,* Oct & Nov 1951
as Evelyn Paige
Asst. Editor & Managing Editor of *Beyond*
Asst. Editor & Managing Editor of *Galaxy*

GOLD, H(orace) L(eonard) (1914-   ) *naturalized U.S.*
Born: Montreal, Canada
as Clyde Crane Campbell
Inflexure. *Astounding,* Oct 1934
as Dudley Dell
The Biography Project. *Galaxy,* Sept 1951
as Harold C. Fosse
Grifter's Asteroid. *Tops In SF,* Fall 1953
as H. L. Gold
A Matter of Form. *Astounding,* Dec 1938
The Old Die Rich and Other SF. NY: Crown, 1955, 250pp. *ss col*
(ed) *Galaxy,* Oct 1950-Oct 1961

GOMPERTZ, MARTIN LOUIS ALAN (1886-1951)
as Ganpat
Harilek, A Romance of Modern Asia. Edinburgh: Blackwood, 1923, 342pp.
Stella Nash. Edinburgh: Blackwood, 1924, 351pp.
Snow Rubies. Edinburgh: Blackwood, 1925, 335pp.
The Voice of Dashin. London: Hodder & Stoughton, [1926], 319pp.
High Snow. London: Hodder & Stoughton, [1927], 304pp.
Mirror of Dreams. London: Hodder & Stoughton, [1928], 319pp.
Dainra. London: Hodder & Stoughton, [1929], 317pp.
The Speakers In Silence. London: Hodder & Stoughton, [1929], 313pp., ill.
Walls Have Eyes. London: Hodder & Stoughton, [1930], 320pp.
The Three R's. London: Hodder & Stoughton, [1930], 316pp.

Marches of Honour. London: Hodder & Stoughton, 1931, 318pp.

Fairy Silver. London: Hodder & Stoughton, 1932, 320pp.

Out of Evil. London: Hodder & Stoughton, 1933, 319pp.

The Second Tigress. London: Hodder & Stoughton, [1933], 320pp.

Seven Times Proven. London: Hodder & Stoughton, 1934, 312pp.

The Snow Falcon. London: Hodder & Stoughton, 1935, 312pp., ill.

Wrexham's Romance. London: Hodder & Stoughton, 1935, 316pp.

The One Eyed Knave. London: Hodder & Stoughton, 1936, 316pp.

The War Breakers. London: Hodder & Stoughton, [1939], 295pp., ill.

as Major M. L. A. Gompertz
■ *Magic Ladakh; An Intimate Picture of A Land of Topsy-Turvy Customs,* 1928; *The Road to Lamaland,* 1926.

as Martin Gompertz
□ *The Sleeping Duke,* 1938.

GOODCHILD, GEORGE (1888-   ) *British*
as Alan Dare
The Eye of Abu. London: Jenkins, 1927, 312pp.
□ *The Isle of Hate,* 1924; *The Guarded Soul,* 1928; *Body and Soul,* 1929.

as George Goodchild
□ MYSTERY: "McLean of Scotland Yard" series including *McLean of Scotland Yard,* 1929; *McLean Investigates,* 1930; etc. Also, *The Alaskan,* 1921; *Captain Crash,* 1924; *The Emperor of Hallelujah Island,* 1930; *The Monster of Grammont,* 1930; *The Road to Marrakesh,* 1931; *Q33-Spy Catcher,* 1937.

as Wallace Q. Reid
□ *The Man From Peace River,* 1933.
● **Jesse Templeton**

GOODRICH, SAMUEL GRISWOLD (1793-1860)
as Peter Parley
The Balloon Travels of Robert Merry and His Young Friends, Over Various Countries In Europe. NY: J.C. Derby, 1855, 312pp.

Faggots For the Fireside; or, Fact and Fancy. NY: Appleton, 1855, 320pp.

Peter Parley's Thousand and One Stories of Fact and Fancy, Wit and Humor, Rhyme, Reason and Romance. NY: Derby, 1857, 751pp., ill. *ss col*

GOODWIN, H(arold) L(eland) (1914-   ) *U.S.*
as John Blaine [in collaboration with Peter J. Harkins]
The "Rick Brant" series incl:
The Rocket's Shadow. NY: Grosset & Dunlap, 1947, 209pp.
The Lost City. NY: Grosset & Dunlap, [1947], 209pp.
Sea Gold. NY: Grosset & Dunlap, [1947], 214pp., ill.
100 Fathoms Under. NY: Grosset & Dunlap, [1947], 209pp.

The Whispering Box Mystery. NY: Grosset & Dunlap, [1948], 216pp., ill.

The Phantom Shark. NY: Grosset & Dunlap, [1949], 206pp., ill.

Smuggler's Reef. NY: Grosset & Dunlap, [1950], 211pp.
The Caves Of Fear. NY: Grosset & Dunlap, [1951], 210pp.
Stairway to Danger. NY: Grosset & Dunlap, [1952], 210pp., ill.

The Golden Skull. NY: Grosset & Dunlap, [1954], 214pp., ill.

The Wailing Octopus. NY: Grosset & Dunlap, 1956, 209pp., ill.

The Electronic Mind Reader. NY: Grosset & Dunlap, 1957, 214pp., ill.

The Scarlet Lake Mystery. NY: Grosset & Dunlap, 1958, 178pp., ill.

The Pirates of Shan. NY: Grosset & Dunlap, 1958, 181pp., ill.

The Blue Ghost Mystery. NY: Grosset & Dunlap, 1960, 181pp., ill.

The Egyptian Cat Mystery. NY: Grosset & Dunlap, 1961, 182pp., ill.

The Flaming Mountain. NY: Grosset & Dunlap, 1962, 172pp., ill.

The Flying Stingaree. NY: Grosset & Dunlap, 1963, 176pp., ill.

The Ruby Ray Mystery. NY: Grosset & Dunlap, 1964, 176pp., ill.

The Veiled Raiders. NY: Grosset & Dunlap, 1965, 178pp., ill.

Rocket Jumper. NY: Grosset & Dunlap, 1966, 177pp., ill.

The Deadly Dutchman. NY: Grosset & Dunlap, 1967, 176pp., ill.

Danger Below! NY: Grosset & Dunlap, 1968, 178pp., ill.
■ *Rick Brant's Science Projects,* 1960.

as Hal Goodwin
□ *A Microphone For David,* 1942; *The Feathered Cape,* 1947.
■ (with Don Cook) *Aerial Warfare,* 1943; *The Real Book About Stars,* 1951; *The Real Book of Space Travel,* 1952; *The Science Book of Space Travel,* 1954.

GOWING, SIDNEY F(loyd) (1878-   )
as John Goodwin
The Spider Woman. London: Jenkins, 1920, 256pp.
□ *Without Mercy,* 1920; *The Man With the Brooding Eyes,* 1921; *The Sign of the Serpent,* 1923; *Let It Lie,* 1929; *Sealed Orders,* 1929; *The Shadow Man,* 1932.

GRAHAM, ROGER P(hillips) (1909-1965) *U.S.*
Born: Spokane, Washington
as Clinton Ames
Victims of the Vortex. *Amazing Stories,* July 1950
as Robert Arnette [house pseudonym]
The Unfinished Equation. *Fantastic Adventures,* April 1952
as Franklin Bahl [house pseudonym]
Face Beyond the Veil. *Fantastic Adventures,* April 1950
Lady Killer. *Amazing,* Feb 1953
as Alexander Blade [house pseudonym]
Brainstorm. *Fantastic Adventures,* Dec 1948
Warrior Queen of Mars. *Fantastic Adventures,* Sept 1950
as Craig Browning
Squeeze Play. *Amazing,* Nov 1947
as Gregg Conrad
The Mental Assassins. *Fantastic Adventures,* May 1950
as P.F. Costello [house pseudonym]
Secret of the Flaming Ring. *Fantastic Adventures,* March 1951
Space Is For Suckers. *Amazing,* June 1958
as Roger P. Graham
The Space. *Amazing,* Sept 1946
as Inez McGowan
In This Dark Mind. *Fantastic,* Sept 1958
as Rog Phillips
Let Freedom Ring. *Amazing,* Dec 1945
Time Trap. Chicago: Century, [1949], 158pp., paper.
Worlds Within. Chicago: Century, [1950], 159pp., paper.
The Worlds of If. Chicago: Century, [1951], 126pp., paper.
The Involuntary Immortals. NY: Avalon, 1959, 223pp.
as Melva Rogers
To Give Them Welcome. *Other Worlds,* Jan 1950
as Chester Ruppert
The Last Stronghold. *Amazing,* May 1949

as William Carter Sawtelle
Slaves of the Crystal Brain. *Amazing*, May 1950
as A. R. Steber [all stories after October 1950 are by Graham:
see **R. A. PALMER**]
A Man Named Mars. *Other Worlds*, Oct 1950
as Gerald Vance [house pseudonym]
The Cosmic Trap. *Fantastic*, Nov 1957
as John Wiley
Venus Trouble Shooter. *Other Worlds*, Nov 1949
as Peter Worth [house pseudonym]
The Robot and the Pearly Gates. *Amazing*, Jan 1949
I Died Tomorrow. *Fantastic Adventures*, May 1949
Window To the Future. *Amazing*, May 1949
Lullaby. *Amazing Annual*, 1950
Null F. *Fantastic Adventures*, Feb 1950
The Master Ego. *Fantastic Adventures*, March 1951
The Imitators. *Amazing*, June 1951

GRAINGER, FRANCIS E(dward)   (1857-1927)
as Headon Hill
The Divinations of Kala Persad and Other Stories. London:
Ward, Lock, 1895, 246pp. *ss col*
Seaward For The Foe. London: Ward, Lock, 1903, 378pp.,
ill.
□ *Zambra the Detective*, 1894; *Tracked Down*, 1902;
The One Who Saw, 1905; *The Thread of Proof*, 1912;
The Narrowing Circle, 1924.

GRANVILLE-BARKER, HARLEY G(ranville)   (1877-1946)
English
as Granville Barker
Souls on Fifth. Boston: Little, Brown, 1916, 61pp. *play*
□ PLAYS: *The Marrying of Ann Leete*, 1901; *The Voysey
Inheritance*, 1905; *Waste*, 1907; *The Madras House*,
1910; *Vote By Ballot*, 1917.
■ (with William Archer) *A National Theatre*, 1907; *The
Exemplary Theatre*, 1922; *Prefaces To Shakespeare*,
1923-1947; (with G. B. Harrison) *A Companion to
Shakespeare Studies*, 1934; *The Use of the Drama*, 1945.

GRAUTOFF, FERDINAND H(einrich)   (1871-1935)   *German*
as Parabellum
Bansai. Leipzig: Dieterich, 1908, 277pp.
Banzai! London: S. Paul, 1909, 332pp.
as Seestern
"1906" Der Zusammenbruch der Alten Welt. Leipzig:
Dieterich, [c.1905], 203pp.
Armageddon, 190—, London: Kegan Paul, 1907, 402pp.

GRAVES, CLOTILDE INEZ MARY   (1863-1932)   *Irish*
Born: County Cork
as Richard Dehan
The Cost of Wings and Other Stories. London: Heinemann,
[1914], 300pp. *ss col*
Off Sandy Hook, and Other Stories. London: Heinemann,
[1915], 322pp. *ss col*
Under the Hermes, and Other Stories. London: Heinemann,
1917, 341pp. *ss col*
The Eve of Pascua and Other Stories. London: Heinemann,
1920, 288pp., paper. *ss col*
The Villa of the Peacock and Other Stories. London:
Heinemann, 1921, 315pp. *ss col*
The Sower of the Wind. London: Butterworth, [1927],
446pp.

GRAYDON, ROBERT MURRAY   (? -1937)
as Murray Roberts
"Captain Justice" series in *Modern Boy* (Br.) pre 1937

GREBANIER, FRANCES (Vinciguerra)   (Mrs. Bernard D. N.)
(1900-   )
as Frances Winwar

Pagan Interval. Indianapolis: Bobbs-Merrill, [1929], 352pp.
Gallows Hill. NY: Holt, [1937], 292pp.
■ *Poor Splendid Wings, The Rosettis and Their Circle,*
1933; *Oscar Wilde and the Yellow Nineties,* 1940;
American Giant, Walt Whitman and His Times, 1941;
The Life of the Heart; George Sand and Her Times,
1945.

GREEN, ROLAND C.
as Jeffrey Lord [house pseudonym]
Monster of the Maze. NY: MacFadden-Bartell, 1972, paper.

GREENER, WILLIAM O(liver)   (1862- ?)
as Wirt Gerrare
Rufin's Legacy: A Theosophical Romance. London: Hutch-
inson, [1892], 312pp.
*Phantasms: Original Stories Illustrating Posthumous
Personality and Character.* London: Roxburghe Press,
1895, 234pp., front. *ss col*
The Warstock; A Tale of To-Morrow. London: W. W.
Greener, 1898, 218pp.
■ *A Bibliography of Guns and Shooting,* 1896; *The
Story of Moscow,* 1900; *Greater Russia,* 1903.
as William O. Greener
□ HISTORICAL FICTION: *The Men Of Harlech,* 1896.
■ *A Secret Agent In Port Authur,* 1905.

GREENWOOD, JULIA EILEEN COURTNEY
as Francis Askham
The Heart Consumed. London: J. Lane, [1944], 234pp.
□ *A Foolish Wind,* 1946.
■ *The Gay Delavals,* 1955.

GREER, RICHARD [house pseudonym]
unattributed
Calling Captain Flint. *Amazing*, Aug 1956
The Secret of the Shan. *Fantastic*, June 1957
by Gordon Randall Garrett and Robert Silverberg
The Great Kladnar Race. *Amazing*, Dec 1956

GRENNELL, DEAN A.
as Dean Grennell
Panacea. *Universe #5*, May 1954
■ (with Mason Williams) *Law Enforcement Handgun
Digest,* 1972; *The ABC's of Reloading,* 1974.
as Art Wesley
Dropper. *Universe #5*, May 1954

GRIBBON, WILLIAM LANCASTER   (1879-1940)   *naturalized
U.S.*
Born: Surrey, England
Bibliography: *The Talbot Mundy Bibliography,* by B.M.
Day, 1955.
as Talbot Mundy
King - of the Khyber Rifles. Indianapolis: Bobbs-Merrill,
[1916], 395pp., ill.
The Nine Unknown. Indianapolis: Bobbs-Merrill, [1924],
353pp., ill.
Om: The Secret of Ahbor Valley. Indianapolis: Bobbs-
Merrill, [1924], 392pp.
The Caves of Terror. Garden City: Doubleday, [1924], 118pp.
The Devil's Guard. Indianapolis: Bobbs-Merrill, [1926],
334pp.
Queen Cleopatra. Indianapolis: Bobbs-Merrill, [1929],
426pp.
Black Light. Indianapolis: Bobbs-Merrill, [1930], 315pp.
Jimgrim. NY: Century, [1931], 385pp.
The Mystery of Khufu's Tomb. London: Hutchinson,
[1933], 253pp.
All Four Winds: Four Novels of India. London: Hutch-
inson, 1934, 1232pp. (omnibus of 4 vol.)
Tros of Samothrace. NY: Appleton-Century, 1934, 949pp.

Full Moon. NY: Appleton-Century, 1935, 312pp.

Purple Pirate. NY: Appleton-Century, 1935, 367pp.

The Thunder Dragon Gate. NY: Appleton-Century, 1937, 335pp.

Old Ugly Face. London: Hutchinson, 1939, 608pp.

☐ *Rung Ho!,* 1914; *Winds of the World,* 1915; *The Ivory Trail,* 1919; *The Eye of Zeitoon,* 1920; *Told In the East,* 1920; *Guns of the Gods,* 1921; *The Marriage of Meldrum Strange,* 1930; *"C.I.D.,"* A New Chullunder Ghose Story, 1932; *Jungle Jest,* 1932; *The Lion of Petra,* 1933; *The Gunga Sahib,* 1934; *The King In Check,* 1934; *East and West,* 1937.

GRIFFIN, ANTHONY JEROME (1866-1935)

as Altair

Chaos; A Vision of Eternity. NY: D. C. McMurtrie, 1919, 55pp. *poetry*

as Hon. Anthony J. Griffin of N.Y., Member of House of Representatives

■ *McNary—Haugen Bill, Class Legislation Contrary to Democratic Principles,* 1927; *One Hundred and Forty Years of Tariff Tinkering,* 1929; *The Legislative Brain,* 1933.

GRIFFITH, MARY (Mrs.) (c.1800-1877) *U.S.*

Born: Charles Hope, New Jersey

as Author of "Our Neighborhood"

Camperdown; or, News From Our Neighborhood. Philadelphia: Carey, Lee & Blanchard, 1836, 300pp.

as Mary Griffith

Three Hundred Years Hence. Philadelphia: Prime Press, 1950, 131pp. [reprint of 1st Section of Camperdown]

☐ *Two Defaulters: Or, A Picture of the Times,* 1842.

anonymous

☐ *Our Neighborhood,* 1831.

GRIFFITH-JONES, GEORGE CHETWYND (1857-1906) *British*

Born: Plymouth

Bibliography: In *The Raid of "Le Vengeur,"* by George Locke. London: Ferret Fantasy Ltd., 1974.

as Levin Carnac

A Gamble With Destiny. Pearson's Weekly, Jan 27, 1894 (Br.)

as George Griffith

The Angel of the Revolution. Pearson's Weekly, Jan 21, 1893-Oct 14, 1893, 1893 (Br.)

The Angel of the Revolution. London: Tower, 1893, 393pp., ill.

Olga Romanoff; or, The Syren of the Skies. London: Tower, 1894, 377pp., front.

The Outlaws of the Air. London: Tower, 1895, 376pp., ill. front.

Valdar The Oft-Born. London: C.A. Pearson, 1895, 416pp., ill.

Briton or Boer. London: F. V. White, 1897, 304pp., ill. (pp. 297-304 are advertisements)

The Romance of the Golden Star. London: F. V. White, 1897, 284pp., ill.

The Gold Finder. London: F. V. White, 1898, 312pp., ill. front.

The Destined Maid. London: F. V. White, 1898, 314pp., front.

Gambles With Destiny. London: F. V. White, 1899, 232pp. *ss col*

The Great Pirate Syndicate. London: F. V. White, 1899, 302pp., front.

Captain Ishmael. London: Hutchinson, 1901, 344pp.

Denver's Double; A Story of Inverted Identity. London: F.V. White, 1901, 318pp.

A Honeymoon In Space. London: C. A. Pearson, 1901, 302pp., ill.

The White Witch of Mayfair. London: F. V. White,

1902, 312pp.

The World Masters. London: J. Long, 1903, 303pp.

The Lake of Gold; A Narrative of the Anglo-American Conquest of Europe. London: F. V. White, 1903, 319pp.

The Stolen Submarine. London: F. V. White, 1904, 320pp.

A Criminal Croesus. London: J. Long, 1904, 319pp.

A Mayfair Magician. A Romance of Criminal Science. London: F. V. White, 1905, 306pp.

The Great Weather Syndicate. London: F. V. White, 1906, 320pp.

The Mummy and Miss Nitocris; A Phantasy of the Fourth Dimension. London: T. W. Laurie, [1906], 311pp.

The World Peril of 1910. London: F. V. White, 1907, 320pp.

The Sacred Skull. London: Everett, 1908, 308pp.

The Lord of Labour. London: F. V. White, 1911, 318pp.

The Raid of "Le Vengeur." London: Ferret Fantasy, Ltd., [1974], 144pp., ill., paper. (900 cop)

☐ *A Heroine of the Slums,* 1894 (ss col); *Virgin of the Sun,* 1898; *Brothers of the Chain,* 1898; *Knaves of Diamonds,* 1899; *A Woman Against the World,* 1903.

■ *In An Unknown Prison Land,* 1901; *With Chamberlain Through South Africa,* 1903.

as Lara

☐ POETRY: *Poems,* 1883; *The Dying Faith,* 1894.

as Stanton Morich

☐ *Thou Shalt Not — —,* London: C. A. Pearson, 1900, 311pp.

GRIGSBY, ALCANOAN O.

as Jack Adams

Nequa; or, The Problem of the Ages. Topeka, Kansas: Equity Publishing Co., 1900, 387pp.

GROUSSET, PASCHAL (1844-1909) *French*

as Phillipe Daryl

■ *A Dictionary of Painters,* 1877; *Public Life In England,* 1884; *Ireland's Disease,* 1888.

as A(ndre) Laurie

The Conquest of the Moon; A Story of the Bayouda. London: S. Low, Marston, 1889, 334pp., ill.

New York to Brest in Seven Hours. London: S. Low, 1890, 302pp., ill.

The Secret Life of the Magian; or, the Mystery of Ecbatana. London: S. Low, 1892 [1891], 314pp., ill.

Axel Eberson, the Graduate of Upsala. London: S. Low, 1892, 286pp.

The Crystal City Under the Sea. London: S. Low, [1896], 293pp., ill.

☐ *Captain Trafalgar,* 1887; *Schoolboy Days In Russia,* 1892; *Schoolboy Days In Italy,* 1893; *Schoolboy Days In Japan,* 1895.

GUEZENEC, ALFRED (1823-1866) *French*

as Alfred (de) Brehat

The Black Sorcerers. A Tale of the Peasants' War. Chicago: Rand McNally, 1883, 303pp., ill. [title in later editions *A Dark Deed*]

Adventures of A Little French Boy. NY: Hurd, 1866, 237pp., ill. [later editions entitled *Jean Belin, the French Robinson Crusoe*]

GUIN, WYMAN WOODS (1915-   ) *U.S.*

Born: Wanette, Oklahoma

as Wyman Guin

Beyond Bedlam. Galaxy, Aug 1951

Living Way Out. NY: Avon, [1967], 208pp., paper.

The Standing Joy. NY: Avon, [1969], 224pp., paper.

as Norman Menasco

Trigger Tide. Astounding, Oct 1950

GULL, C(yril) A(rthur) Ranger   (1876-1923)   *British*
as (C)(yril) Ranger Gull
  The Soul Stealer. London: White, 1906, 312pp.
  Black Honey. A Novel. London: Greening, 1913, 320pp.
  The Enemies of England. London: T.W. Laurie, [1914], 292pp.
  When Satan Ruled. London: Greening, 1914, 304pp.
  The Air Pirate. London: Hurst & Blackett, [1919], 287pp.
  The City In the Clouds. London: Hurst & Blackett, [1921], 288pp.
  □ *The Cigarette Smoker, Being the Terrible Case of Uther Kennedy,* 1902 [1901]; *The Terror By Night,* 1909; *House of Torment,* 1911 [1910]; *The Ravenscroft Horror,* 1917; *Cinema City,* 1922.
as Leonard Cresswell Ingleby
  ■ *Oscar Wilde,* 1907 (Bio).
as Guy Thorne
  When It Was Dark, The Story of A Great Conspiracy. NY: Putnam, 1904, 391pp., ill.
  (with Leo Custance) *Sharks: A Fantastic Novel for Businessmen and Their Families.* London: Greening, 1904, 348pp.
  The Angel. London: Ward, Lock, 1908, 328pp. [NY: G. W. Dillingham, [1908], 356pp., ill.]
  The Cruiser On Wheels. London: Jack, 1915, 192pp.
  The Secret Sea-Plane. London: Hodder & Stoughton, 1915, 243pp.
  And It Came To Pass. London: Jarrolds, [1916], 345pp.
  The Secret Monitor. London: Skeffington, [1918], 192pp.
  Lucky Mr. Loder. London: Ward, Lock, 1918, 319pp., front.
  Doris More. London: Ward, Lock, 1919, 304pp.
  The House of Danger. London: Ward, Lock, 1920, 315pp.
  The Love Hater. London: Ward, Lock, 1921, 304pp.
  The Dark Dominion. London: Ward, Lock, 1923, 304pp.
  When the World Reeled. London: Ward, Lock, 1924, 317pp.
  □ *The Oven,* 1902; *The Drunkard,* 1912; *Not In Israel,* 1913; *The Hammers of Hate,* 1919; *Muriel Wins Through,* 1923; *The Mystery of St. Michael's,* 1923.

GUNN, JAMES E(dwin)   (1923-   )   *U.S.*
as James E. Gunn
  Paradox. *Thrilling Wonder Stories,* Oct 1949
  (with Jack Williamson) *Star Bridge.* NY: Gnome, 1955, 221pp.
  This Fortress World. NY: Gnome, [1955], 216pp.
  Station In Space. NY: Bantam, [1958], 156pp., paper.
  The Joy Makers. NY: Bantam, [1961], 160pp., paper.
  The Immortals. NY: Bantam, [1962], 154pp., paper.
  Future Imperfect. NY: Bantam, [1964], 137pp., paper.
  The Witching Hour. NY: Dell, [1970], 188pp., paper.
  The Immortal. NY: Bantam, [1970], 136pp., paper. [this is an adaptation of the T.V. series *The Immortal* which was based on *The Immortals* (1962) by James E. Gunn]
  Breaking Point. NY: Walker, [1972], 182pp. *ss col*
  The Listeners. NY: Scribner, [1972], 275pp., ill.
  Some Dreams Are Nightmares. NY: Scribner, [1974], 220pp., ill. *ss col*
  The End of the Dreams. NY: Scribner, [1975], 202pp. *ss col*
  The Magicians. NY: Scribner, [1976], 197pp.
  ■ *Alternate Worlds: The Illustrated History of Science Fiction,* 1975.
as Edwin James
  Communications. *Startling Stories,* Sept 1949

GUTHRIE, THOMAS A(nstey)   (1856-1934)   *British*
Born: London
  Autobiographical: *A Long Retrospect.* London: Oxford U. Press, 1936, 424pp.
  Bibliography: *A Bibliography of the Worlds of F. Anstey (Thomas Anstey Guthrie),* by Martin J. Turner. London: Stockwell, 1931, 44pp. (150 cop)
as F(rank) Anstey

  Vice Versa; or, A Lesson to Fathers. London: Smith, Elder, 1882, 364pp.
  The Giant's Robe. London: Smith, Elder, 1884, 439pp., ill.
  The Black Poodle and Other Tales. London: Longmans, Green, 1884, 269pp., ill. *ss col*
  The Tinted Venus, A Farcical Romance. London: Simpkin, Marshall, 1885, 192pp.
  A Fallen Idol. London: Smith, Elder, 1886, 334pp.
  Tourmalin's Time Cheques. Bristol: Arrowsmith, [1891], 172pp.
  The Talking Horse. NY: U.S. Book Co., [1891], 298pp. *ss col*
  The Statement of Stella Maberly. NY: Appleton, 1896, 230pp.
  The Brass Bottle. London: Smith, Elder, 1900, 312pp., front.
  Only Toys! London: Grant Richards, 1903, 260pp., ill.
  Salted Almonds. London: Smith, Elder, 1906, 312pp.
  In Brief Authority. London: Smith, Elder, 1915, 413pp.
  Humor and Fantasy. London: J. Murray, [1931], 1173pp. omnibus volume
  □ *Baboo Jabberjee, B. A.,* 1897; *The Man From Blankley's,* 1901 (play).
  ■ *Monopoly and Democracy,* 1906; *Red Europe,* 1920.

GUY, L.
as A Patriot
  An Englishman's Home. London: E. Arnold, 1909, 96pp.

HAGGARD, J. HARVEY
as J. Harvey Haggard
　　Faster Than Light. *Wonder Stories*, Oct 1930
as The Planet Prince
　　Poetry in *Amazing.*

HAHN, GEORGE R.
as George R. Hahn
　　Gangway for Homer. *Science Fiction Quarterly*, Spring
　　1942
as Cyril Mand [in collaboration with Richard Levin]
　　The Fifth Candle. *Weird Tales*, Jan 1939.

HALDEMAN, JOE W. *U.S.*
as Robert Graham
　　Attar's Revenge. NY: Pocket Books, 1975, paper.
　　War of Nerves. NY: Pocket Books, 1975, paper.
as Joe Haldeman
　　War Year. NY: Holt, 1972.
　　The Forever War. NY: St. Martin's, [1975 (c.1974)], 236pp.
　　Mindbridge. NY: St. Martin's, 1976, 186pp., ill.
　　All My Sins Remembered. NY: St. Martin's, 1977.
　　Planet of Judgement. NY: Bantam, [1977], paper.

HALE, EDWARD EVERETT (1822-1909) *U.S.*
　　Born: Boston, Massachusetts
as E(dward) E(verett) Hale
　　The Brick Moon. *Atlantic Monthly*, Oct 1869 - Dec 1869
　　Sybaris and Other Homes. Boston: Fields, Osgood, 1869,
　　206pp.
　　His Level Best and Other Stories. Boston: Roberts
　　Brothers, [1872], 293pp. *ss col* [contains *The Brick Moon*]
　　Crusoe In New York and Other Tales. Boston: Roberts
　　Brothers, 1880, 259pp. *ss col*
　　The Brick Moon and Other Stories. Boston: Little, Brown,
　　1899, 369pp. *ss col*
　　□ *Man Without A Country*, 1865 (mag. 1863); *In His
　　Name*, 1873.
　　■ *Letters On Irish Emigration*, 1852; *The State's Care of
　　Its Children*, 1855; *Stories of Invention*, 1885; *The Story
　　of Spain*, 1887; *History of the U.S.*, 1887; *Historic
　　Boston*, 1898.
as Frederic Ingham
　　Ten Times One Is Ten: The Possible Reformation.
　　Boston: Roberts Brothers, 1871, 148pp.

HALE, MARICE R(utledge) (Gibson) (Mrs.) (1884-　)
　　U.S.
as Marie Louise Goetchius
　　□ *Anne of Treboul*, 1910.
as Marice Rutledge
　　□ *Children of Fate*, 1917.
as Maryse Rutledge
　　The Silver Peril. NY: Fiction League, 1931, 320pp.
　　□ *The Sad Adventurers*, 1924.
as Marie Louse Van Saanen
　　□ *The Blind Who See*, 1911; *Wild Grapes*, 1913.

HALL, D(esmond) W(inter)
as Anthony Gilmore [in collaboration with Harry Bates]
　　The Tentacles From Below. *Astounding*, Feb 1931
　　Hawk Carse. *Astounding*, Nov 1931

　　Space Hawk. NY: Greenberg, [1952], 274pp.
as D. W. Hall
　　Werewolves of War. *Astounding*, Feb 1931
as H. G. Winter [in collaboration with Harry Bates]
　　The Hands of Aten. *Astounding*, July 1931

HALL, JOSEPH (Bishop of Exeter and Norwich) (1574-1656)
　　English
as Mercurio Britannico
　　*Mundus Alter et Idem Siue Terra Australis Ante Hac
　　Semper Incognita Longis Itineribus Peregrini Academici
　　Nuperrime Lustrata.* Auth: Mercurio Britannico. Franc-
　　ofurti [London c. 1605], 224pp., ill. maps.
as "An English Mercury"
　　*The Discovery of A New World, or, A Description of the
　　South Indies, Hetherto Unknowne. By an English
　　Mercury* (trans. by Joseph Healey). London: Blount &
　　Barrett, [c.1609], 244pp., ill., maps.

HALL, STEVE
as Steve Hall
　　Einstein's Universe. *Science Fiction Adventures #25*,
　　March 1962 (Br.)
as Russ Markham
　　Who Went Where? *New Worlds*, Nov 1962 (Br.)

HALSEY, HARLAN PAGE (1839?-1898)
as Tony Pastor
　　□ *The Swordsman of Warsaw; or, Ralph of the Iron
　　Arm*, 1889; *Tom and Jerry; or, the Double Detective*,
　　1889.
as Old Sleuth
　　Crusoe Harry; or, the Treasures of the Lost Ship. NY:
　　Olgilvie, [1896], 94+pp.
　　Creco, The Swordsman; or, The Man of Mystery. NY:
　　Olgilvie, [1897], 89pp.
　　*Allie Baird, the Settler's Son; A Weird Tale of the Wilder-
　　ness*. NY: Olgilvie, [1897], 83pp.
　　*An Amazing Wizard; or, The Further Adventures of Fire
　　Bomb Jack*. NY: Olgilvie, [1898], 82pp.
　　□ *Old Electricity, The Lightning Detective*, 1885; *Van
　　the Government Detective; or, The Base Metal Coiners*,
　　1888; *Mura, The Western Lady Detective*, 1891; *Cad
　　Metti, The Female Detective Strategist*, 1895; *Nimble
　　Ike's Mystery*, 1896; *Amzi the Detective*, 1897; *A
　　Plucky Girl*, 1897.
as Judson R. Taylor
　　□ *The Chosen Man; or, The Mystery of the Secret
　　Service*, 1888.

HAMILTON, CHARLES
as Frank Richards
　　Rub-A-Dub-Dub. *Imagination*, June 1953

HAMILTON, EDMOND MOORE (1904-1977) *U.S.*
　　Born: Youngstown, Ohio
as Alexander Blade [house pseudonym]
　　Battle For the Stars. *Imagination*, June 1956
　　The Cosmic Kings. *Imaginative Tales*, Nov 1956
　　The Tattooed Man. *Imaginative Tales*, March 1957
　　The Sinister Invasion. *Imagination*, June 1957
　　The Cosmic Looters. *Imagination*, Feb 1958
as Robert Castle
　　The Conqueror's Voice. *Science Fiction*, March 1939
as Hugh Davidson
　　Vampire Village. *Weird Tales*, Nov 1932
as Will Garth [house pseudonym]
　　The Great Illusion. *Thrilling Wonder Stories*, June 1938
as Edmond Hamilton
　　The Monster-God of Mamurth. *Weird Tales*, Aug 1926
　　The Comet Doom. *Amazing*, Jan 1928
　　Captain Future and the Space Emperor. *Captain Future*,

Winter 1940

The Horror On The Asteroid and Other Tales of Planetary Horror. London: P. Allen, 1936, 256pp. *ss col*

Quest Beyond the Stars. NY: Popular Library, [1941], paper.

● *Outlaws of the Moon.* NY: Popular Library, paper.

● *Planets In Peril.* NY: Popular Library, paper.

Outlaw World. NY: Popular Library, [c.1945], 126pp., paper.

Tiger Girl. London: Utopian, [1945], 36pp., paper.

Murder In the Clinic. London: Utopia, [1945], 36pp. paper. *2 short stories*

The Star Kings. NY: Fell, 1949, 262pp.

The Monsters of Juntonheim. London: Pemberton, 1950, 160pp., paper.

Tharkol, Lord of the Unknown. London: Pemberton, 1950, 160pp., paper.

City At World's End. NY: Fell, 1951, 239pp.

The Sun Smasher. NY: Ace, [1959], 110pp., paper. (Ace Double D 351)

The Star of Life. NY: Dodd, Mead, [1959], 192pp.

The Haunted Stars. NY: Dodd, Mead, [1960], 192pp.

Battle For the Stars. NY: Dodd, Mead, [1961], 206pp.

Outside the Universe. NY: Ace, [1964], 173pp., paper.

The Valley of Creation. NY: Lancer, 1964, 159pp., paper.

Crashing Suns. NY: Ace, [1965], 192pp., paper. *ss col*

Fugitive Of The Stars. NY: Ace, [1965], 116pp., paper. (Ace Double M 111)

Doomstar. NY: Belmont, [1966], 158pp., paper.

The Weapon From Beyond. NY: Ace, [1967], 158pp., paper.

Calling Captain Future. NY: Popular Library, [1967], 144pp., paper.

Captain Future and the Space Emperor. NY: Popular Library, [1967], 128pp., paper.

Galaxy Mission. NY: Popular Library, [1967], 128pp., paper.

Captain Future's Challenge. NY: 1968.

The Magician Of Mars. NY: Popular Library, [1968], 128pp., paper.

The Closed Worlds. NY: Ace, [1968], 157pp., paper.

World of the Starwolves. NY: Ace, [1968], 158pp., paper.

The Comet Kings. NY: Popular Library, [1969], paper.

The Galactic Hunters. NY: 1969.

Return To The Stars. NY: Lancer, [1969], 207pp., paper.

The Best of Edmond Hamilton. NY: Ballantine, [1977], 381pp., paper.

as Brett Sterling [house pseudonym]

The Star of Dread. *Captain Future,* Summer 1943

Magic Moon. *Captain Future,* Winter 1944

Red Sun Of Danger. *Startling Stories,* Spring 1945

Never the Twain Shall Meet. *Thrilling Wonder Stories,* Fall 1946

Danger Planet. NY: Popular Library, 1968, paper.

as S. M. Tenneshaw [house pseudonym]

Last Call For Doomsday! *Imagination,* Dec 1956

as Robert Wentworth

World Without Sex. *Marvel Tales,* May 1940

HAMILTON, LEIGH BRACKETT DOUGLASS (Mrs. Edmond) (1915-1978) *U.S.*

Born: Los Angeles, California

as Leigh Brackett

Martian Quest. *Astounding,* Feb 1940

Shadow Over Mars. Surrey: World's Work, 1951, 128pp., paper.

The Starmen. NY: Gnome, 1952, 213pp.

The Sword of Rhiannon. NY: Ace, [1953], 187pp., paper. (Ace Double D 36)

The Long Tomorrow. Garden City: Doubleday, 1955, 222pp.

The Big Jump. NY: Ace, [1955], 131pp., paper. (Ace Double D 103)

Alpha Centauri - or Die! NY: Ace, [1963], 121pp., paper. (Ace Double F 187)

People of the Talisman. NY: Ace, [1964], 128pp., paper. (Ace Double M 101)

The Secret of Sinharat. NY: Ace, [1964], 95pp., paper. (Ace Double M 101)

The Coming Of the Terrans. NY: Ace, [1967], 157pp. paper.

The Halfling and Other Stories. NY: Ace, [1973], 351pp., paper. *ss col*

The Ginger Star. NY: Ballantine, [1974], 186pp., paper.

☐ SCREENPLAYS: (with W. Faulkner) *The Big Sleep,* 1946; *The Long Goodbye,* 1972. MYSTERY: *No Good From A Corpse,* 1944; *An Eye For An Eye,* 1957; *The Tiger Among Us,* 1957; *Silent Partner,* 1969. WESTERN: *Follow the Free Wind,* 1963.

as George Sanders [ghost writer]

☐ MYSTERY: *Stranger At Home.* NY: Simon & Schuster, 1946, 228pp.

HAMMETT, (Samuel) DASHIELL   (1894-1961) *ne* Samuel Dashiell(?)

Born: St. Mary's County, Maryland

as Peter Collinson

☐ $106,000 Blood Money. *Black Mask,* Feb 1927 (mystery)

The Big Knockover. *Black Mask,* March 1927 (mystery)

Red Harvest. *Black Mask,* Nov 1927 (mystery)

The Dain Curse. *Black Mask,* Nov 1928 (mystery)

as Dashiell Hammett

(ed.) *Creeps by Night.* NY: Day, 1931, 525pp. *ss anthology*

☐ *Secret Agent X-9,* 1934; MYSTERY: *$106,000 Blood Money,* c.1927; *Red Harvest,* 1929; *The Dain Curse,* 1929; [the preceding mysteries have marginal fantastic themes or content]; *The Maltese Falcon,* 1930; *The Glass Key,* 1931; *The Thin Man,* 1934; *The Continental Op,* 1945.

■ (with Corporal Robert Colodny) *The Battle of The Aleutians: A Graphic History 1942-1943,* 1944.

HANKINSON, CHARLES J(ames)   (1866- ?)   *British*

as Clive Holland

An Egyptian Coquette. London: C. A. Pearson, 1898, 232pp. [in later editions changed to *The Spell of Isis*]

☐ *My Japanese Wife,* 1895; *The Lure of Fame,* 1896; *The Seed of the Poppy, A Tale,* 1898; *In the Vortex,* 1904; *The Hidden Submarine,* 1917.

■ "Things Seen In —" series including *Japan,* 1907; *Egypt,* 1907; *Belgium,* 1930. *How To Take and Fake Photographs,* 1901; *How To Use A Camera,* 1905.

● **HANSEN, LOUIS INGVALD**   (1904-   )

as L. Taylor Hansen

[stories submitted by L(ouise) Taylor Hansen, but probably written by her brother, Louis]

What the Sodium Lines Revealed. *Amazing Stories Quarterly,* Winter 1929

as Louis Ingvald Hansen

■ *The Synthesis of Alpha (ortho and para-methoxyphenyl) Propionic Acids and Related Compounds,* 1939.

HARCOURT, THOMAS A.

as William Herman [in collaboration with Ambrose Bierce]

A Dance of Death. San Francisco: H. Keller & Co., 1877, 131pp.

HARKINS, PETER J.

as John Blaine [in collaboration with H. L. Goodwin]

"Rick Brant" series   [see **H. L. GOODWIN**]

HARLAND, HENRY   (1861-1905)   *naturalized U.S.*

Born: St. Petersburg, Russia

as Henry Harland

☐ (ed) *The Yellow Book* [c.1890].

☐ *Two Women or One?,* 1890; *Two Voices,* 1890; *Grey*

Roses, 1895; *The Cardinal's Snuff Box,* 1900; *The Lady Paramount,* 1902; *My Friend Prospero,* 1903.

as Sidney Luska

As It Was Written; A Jewish Musician's Story. NY: Cassell, [c.1885], 253pp., front.

□ *Mrs. Peixada,* 1886; *My Uncle Florimond,* 1888; *Mr. Sonnenschein's Inheritance,* 1888; *Mea Culpa; A Woman's Last Words,* 1891; *Mademoiselle Miss; To Which Is Added, etc.,* 1893.

HARLEY, (Mrs. M.) (fl 1786-1797)

as Author of "Saint Bernard's Priory"

The Castle of Mowbray. An English Romance. London: Stalker, 1788, 256pp.

as Mrs. Harley

□ *The Prince of Leon,* 1794.

anonymous

Saint Bernard's Priory . . . Being the First Literary Production of A Young Lady. London: Printed for the Authoress, 1786, 117pp.

HARRIS, ARTHUR T. [house pseudonym]

unattributed

The Armageddon of Johann Schmidt. *Amazing,* Jan 1941

Mr. Duffy's Other Life. *Fantastic Adventures,* May 1941

Abner Schlap's Strange Insight. *Fantastic Adventures,* July 1941

The Throne of Valhalla. *Amazing,* Sept 1941

The Plastic Genie. *Thrilling Wonder Stories,* April 1942

The Traitor. *Fantastic Adventures,* July 1942

Caution: Dead Man at Work. *Amazing,* Feb 1947

Ernest's Evil Entity. *Fantastic Adventures,* Oct 1948

HARRIS, JOHN (Wyndham Parkes Lucas) B(eynon)
(1903-1971(1969?)) *British*

Born: Knowle, Warwickshire

as John B(eynon)

The Perfect Creature. *Tales of Wonder #1,* 1937 (Br.)

The Secret People. London: Newnes, [1935], 256pp.

Planet Plane. London: Newnes, [1936], 247pp.

□ MYSTERY: *Foul Play Suspected,* [c.1935].

as John B(eynon) Harris

Worlds To Barter. *Wonder Stories,* May 1931

The Mon Devils. *Strange Tales #2,* 1946 (Br.)

as Johnson Harris

Love In Time. London: Utopian, [1945], 36pp., paper.

as Wyndhame Parkes

Child of Power. *Fantasy #3,* 1939.

as John Wyndham

The Day of the Triffids. London: M. Joseph, [1951], 302pp. [Garden City: Doubleday, 1951, 222pp.; Greenwich, Connecticut: Fawcett Gold Medal, [1951], paper. [1st paper]]

The Kraken Wakes. London: M. Joseph, [1953], 288pp.

Jizzle. London: Dobson, 1954, 251pp. *ss col*

The Chrysalids. London: M. Joseph, [1955], 238pp.

The Seeds of Time. London: M. Joseph, 1956, 256pp. *ss col*

Tales of Gooseflesh and Laughter. NY: Ballantine, [1956], 150pp., paper. *ss col*

The Midwich Cuckoos. London: M. Joseph, [1957], 239pp.

The Trouble With Lichen. London: M. Joseph, [1960], 190pp.

Consider Her Ways and Others. London: M. Joseph, 1961, 223pp. *ss col*

Chocky. NY: Ballantine, 1968, 221pp., paper.

The Wanderers of Time. London: Coronet, 1973, 158pp., paper.

The Man From Beyond and Other Stories. London: M. Joseph, 1975, 283pp.

as John Wyndham and Lucas Parkes

The Outward Urge. London: M. Joseph, 1959, 192pp.

HARRIS, LARRY MARK (1933-) *U.S.*

Born: Brooklyn, New York

as Tom Beach

Who You Callin' a Monster? *Cosmos,* March 1954

as Larry Mark Harris

Expatriate. *Cosmos,* Nov 1953

(with Randall Garrett) *Pagan Passions.* NY: Beacon, [1959], 158pp., paper.

as William Logan

Mex. *Fantastic Universe,* Jan 1957

as Laurence M. Janifer

Love Story. *Fantastic,* May 1963

Slave Planet. NY: Pyramid, [1963], 142pp., paper.

The Wonder War. NY: Pyramid, [1964], 128pp., paper.

You Sane Men. NY: Lancer, [1965], 159pp., paper.

Impossible? NY: Belmont, [1968], 159pp., paper.

A Piece of Martin Cann. NY: Belmont, [1968], 141pp., paper.

(with S. J. Treibich) *Target: Terra.* NY: Ace, [1968], 104pp., paper. (Ace Double H 91)

Bloodworld. NY: Lancer, [1968], 159pp., paper. [retelling of *You Sane Men*]

(with S. J. Treibich) *The High Hex.* NY: Ace, [1969], paper.

(with S. J. Treibich) *The Wagered World.* NY: Ace, [1969], paper.

Power. NY: Dell, [1974], paper.

Survivor. NY: Ace, [1977], paper.

as Mark Phillips [in collaboration with Gordon Randall Garrett]

That Sweet Little Old Lady. *Astounding,* Sept - Oct 1959

Brain Twister. NY: Pyramid, 1962, 144pp., paper.

The Impossibles. NY: Pyramid, 1963, 157pp., paper.

Supermind. NY: Pyramid, 1963, 192pp., paper.

HARRIS-BURLAND, JOHN B(urland) (1870- ?) *British*

as Harris Burland

Dacoba; or, The White Priest of Akriman. London: Everett, 1903, 315pp.

The Princess Thora. Boston: Little, Brown, 1904, 360pp., ill.

The Financier. NY: Dillingham, [1906], 352pp.

□ *The House of the Soul,* 1909.

as J. B. Harris Burland

Workers In Darkness. London: Greening, 1908, 323pp.

as J(ohn) B. Harris-Burland

The Gold Worshippers. NY: Dillingham, [1906], 310pp., front.

Dr. Silex, etc. London: Ward, Lock, 1905, 344pp.

□ *The Broken Law,* 1908; *Love the Criminal,* 1908; *Lord of Irongray,* 1911; *The White Rook,'* 1918; *The Shadow of Malreward,* 1919; *The Poison League,* 1921.

HARRISON, HARRY MAX (1925-) *U.S.*

Born: Stamford, Connecticut

as Felix Boyd

An Artist's Life. *Rocket Stories,* Sept 1953

as Hank Dempsey

CWACC. *Astounding,* June 1966

as Cameron Hall

(ed) *Fantasy Magazine / Fantasy Fiction,* Nov 1953

as Harry Harrison

Rock Diver. *Worlds Beyond,* Feb 1951

Deathworld. NY: Bantam, [1960], 154pp., paper.

The Stainless Steel Rat. NY: Pyramid, [1961], 158pp., paper.

Planet of the Damned. NY: Bantam, [1962], paper.

War With the Robots. NY: Pyramid, [1962], 158pp., paper.

Deathworld 2. NY: Bantam, [1964], 151pp., paper.

Bill, The Galactic Hero. Garden City: Doubleday, 1965, 185pp.

Two Tales and Eight Tomorrows. London: Gollancz, 1965, 191pp. *ss col*

Plague From Space. Garden City: Doubleday, 1965, 207pp.

Make Room! Make Room! Garden City: Doubleday, 1966, 216pp.

Sense of Obligation. London: Dobson, [1967], 135pp.

The Technicolor® Time Machine. Garden City: Doubleday, 1967, 190pp.

The Man From P.I.G. NY: Avon, [1968], 120pp., paper.

Deathworld 3. NY: Dell, 1968, 188pp., paper.

Captive Universe. NY: Putnam, [1969], 185pp.

One Step From Earth. NY: Macmillan, [1970], 210pp. *ss col*

Spaceship Medic. Garden City: Doubleday, 1970, 142pp.

The Stainless Steel Rat's Revenge. NY: Walker, [1970], 185pp.

Tunnel Through the Deeps. NY: Putnam, [1972], 192pp.

Montezuma's Revenge. Garden City: Doubleday, 1972, 180pp.

(with Leon Stover) *Stonehenge.* NY: Scribner, [1972], 254pp.

The Stainless Steel Rat Saves the World. NY: Putnam, [1972], 191pp.

Star Smashers of the Galaxy Rangers. NY: Putnam, [1973], 212pp.

The California Iceberg. NY: Walker, 1975, 128pp., ill.

Skyfall. London: Faber, 1976, 270pp.

□ MYSTERY: *Queen Victoria's Revenge,* 1974.

■ *Great Balls of Fire: Sex In Science Fiction,* 1978.

HARRISON, MARY ST. LEGER (Kingsley) (Mrs. W.) (1852-1931) *British*
Born: Eversley, Hampshire
as Lucas Malet

The Carissima; A Modern Grotesque. London: Methuen, 1896, 295pp.

The Gateless Barrier. London: Methuen, 1900, 350pp.

The Tall Villa. NY: Doran, [1919], 256pp.

□ *Mrs. Lorimer,* 1882; *Colonel Enderby's Wife,* 1885; *The Wages of Sin,* 1890; *The History of Sir Roger Calmady,* 1901; *The Far Horizon,* 1906; *The Score,* 1909; *Adrian Savage,* 1911; *Damaris,* 1916; *Deaham Hard,* 1919; *The Survivors,* 1923; *The Dogs of Want,* 1924.

HARRISON, MICHAEL (1907-) *British*
as Quentin Downes
□ MYSTERY: *No Smoke, No Flame,* 1952; *Heads I Win,* 1955.

as Michael Egremont
The Bride of Frankenstein. London: Reader's Library Pub. Co., [1935], 252pp.

as Michael Harrison
Getaway. New Worlds #42, Dec 1955

The Higher Things. London: MacDonald, 1945, 187pp.

The Brain. London: Cassell, 1953, 287pp.

□ *The Exploits of Chevalier Dupin.* Sauk City, Wisconsin: Mycroft & Moran, 1968, 138pp.

■ *A New Approach To Stamp Collecting,* 1953; *Airborne At Kitty Hawk,* 1953; *Peter Cheyney: Prince of Hocum,* 1954; *In the Footsteps of Sherlock Holmes,* 1958; *London By Gaslight,* 1963; *Painful Details: Twelve Victorian Scandals,* 1962; *Fanfare of Strumpets,* 1971.

HART, HARRY (1907-) *U.S.*
as Pat Frank
Mr. Adam. Philadelphia: Lippincott, 1946, 252pp.

Forbidden Area. Philadelphia: Lippincott, [1956], 252pp.

Alas, Babylon. Philadelphia: Lippincott, [1959], 253pp.

□ *An Affair of State,* 1948; *Hold Back The Night,* 1952; *Seven Days to Never,* 1957.

■ *The Long Way Around,* 1953; *How To Survive the H-Bomb and Why,* 1962; (editor) *The Goldwater Cartoon Book,* 1964; *Rendezvous At Midway,* 1967.

HARTE, FRANCIS BRETT (c.1836-1902) *U.S.*
Born: Albany, New York
as Bret Harte
Colonel Starbottle's Client and Some Other People. Boston: Houghton, Mifflin, 1892, 283pp. *ss col*

The Ancestors of Peter Atherly and Other Tales. Boston: Houghton, Mifflin, [1900], 381pp. *ss col*

□ *The Lost Galleon, and Other Tales,* 1867 (poetry); *Condensed Novels and Other Papers,* 1867; *The Luck of Roaring Camp and Other Sketches,* 1870 (ss col); *Gabriel Conroy,* 1875; *The Deadwood Mystery,* 1877; *Jeff Briggs's Love Story,* 1880; *The Argonauts of North Liberty,* 1888.

HARTING, PIETER (1812-1885)
as Dr. Dioscorides
Anno 2065: Een Blik in de Toekomst. Utreckt: 1865.

Anno 2071. London: Tegg, 1871, 132pp.

HARTMAN, DARLENE
as Simon Lang
All the Gods of Eisernon. NY: Avon, [1973], 302pp., paper.

The Elluvon Gift. NY: Avon, [1975], paper.

HARTMANN, FRANZ (1838-1912)
as Franz Hartmann
The Talking Image of Urur. NY: Lovell, [1890], 307pp.

Among the Gnomes: An Occult Tale of Adventure In the Untersberg. London: T. F. Unwin, 1895, 272pp., ill.

■ *Magic, White and Black,* 1886; *The Principles of Astrological Geomancy,* 1889; *Buried Alive,* 1895.

as "A Student of Occultism"
An Adventure Among the Rosicrucians. Boston: Occult Pub. House, 1887, 181pp.

HASSE, HENRY
as Henry Hasse
(with A. Fedor) The End of Tyme. *Wonder Stories,* Nov 1933

He Who Shrank. *Amazing,* Aug 1936

(with Ray Bradbury) Pendulum. *Super Science Stories,* Nov 1941

The Stars Will Wait. NY: Avalon, 1968, 191pp.

as Henry Hasse [in collaboration with Emil Petaja - this story only]
Don't Come To Mars! *Fantastic Adventures,* April 1950

as Theodore Pine [in collaboration with Emil Petaja - this story only]
Secret of Satellite Seven. *Amazing,* Feb 1952

HATCH, DAVID PATTERSON (1846-1912)
as David P. Hatch
■ *Scientific Occultism,* 1905; *The Blood of Gods. A Monographic Treatise of the Temperance Question,* 1906.

as Paul Karishka
El Reshid, A Novel. Chicago: Rand McNally, [1900], 438pp.

■ *Some Philosophy of the Hermetics,* 1900 [1898 ed anonymous]; *The Twentieth Century Christ,* 1906; *Straight Goods In Philosophy,* 1910 (essays); *The Under World and Its Women,* 1910 (on prostitution).

anonymous
El Reshid, A Novel. Los Angeles: B. R. Baumgardt & Co., 1899, 438pp.

HAUSER, HEINRICH (1901-1955) *German*
as Alexander Blade [house pseudonym]
The Brain. *Amazing,* Oct 1948

as Heinrich Hauser
Agharti. Amazing, June 1946
☐ *Brackwasser,* 1928 (Ger.); *Donner uberm Meer,* 1929; *Bitter Water,* 1929; *Thunder Above the Sea,* 1931; *Last Port of Call,* 1938.
■ *Fair Winds and Foul; Ship, Crew, Sea, Horizon,* 1932; *Once Your Enemy,* 1936; *Battle Against Time; A Survey of the Germany of 1939 From the Inside,* 1939; *Hitler Versus Germany,* 1940; *The German Talks Back,* 1945; *After the Years of the Locust,* 1947.

HAVERS, THEODORA (1847-1889) [later (Mrs.) T. H. Boulger] *British*
Born: Norfolk County
as Theo Gift
Not For the Night Time. London: Roper & Drowley, 1889, 209pp. *ss col*
Fairy Tales From the Far East. London: Lawrence & Bullen, 1892, 200pp.
☐ *A Matter-Of-Fact Girl,* 1881; *Visited On the Children,* 1881; *Victims,* 1887; *An Island Princess,* 1893.
↙ Dora Havers

HAWKER, MARY ELIZABETH (1865-1908) *British*
as Author of "Mademoiselle Ixe"
The Hotel Angleterre and Other Stories. London: Unwin (Pseudonym Library), 1891, 196pp. *ss col*
as L. F.
☐ *Shoulder To Shoulder, A Tale,* 1891.
as Lanoe Falconer
Cecilia de Noel. London: Macmillan, 1891, 197pp.
☐ *The Hotel d'Angleterre,* 1891 (U.S. ed); *Mademoiselle Ixe,* 1891.

HAWKES, JESSIE JACQUETTA (Hopkins)
as Jacquetta Hawkes
A Woman As Great As the World and Other Fables. NY: Random House, [1953], 184pp. *ss col*
Providence Island, An Archaeological Tale. London: Chatto & Windus, 1959, 251pp.
☐ *King of the Two Lands,* 1957? [possibly 1966].
● Mrs. J(ohn) B(oynton) Priestley

HEAD, RICHARD (c. 1637-c. 1686)
as Frank Careless
The Floating Island: or, A New Discovery, Relating the Strange Adventure On A Late Voyage, From Lambethana to Villa Franca, Alias Ramallin, to the Eastward of Terra del Templo: By Three Ships viz: The Pay-Naught, The Excuse; The Least-In-Sight. Under the Conduct of Robert Owe-Much; Describing the Nature of the Inhabitants, Their Religion, Laws and Customs. London: 1673, 39pp.
as William Hamilton
O-Brazile, or the Inchanted Island: Being a Perfect Relation of the Late Discovery and Wonderful Dis-Inchantment of An Island On the North of Ireland: With An Account of the Riches and Commodities Thereof. London: 1660.
The Western Wonder; or, O Brazeel, An Inchanted Island Discovered. . . to Which Is Added, A Description of A Place, Called Montecapernia, Relating the Nature of the People, Their Qualities, Humours, etc. London: N.C., 1674, 40pp.
☐ *The Canting Academy, or, The Devil's Cabinet Opened,* 1673; *The Life And Death of Mother Shipton,* 1677.
as M. Latroon
News From the Stars: or, Erra Pater's Ghost. [London], 1673, 16pp., ill. [satire on Astrology]

HEARD, H(enry) F(itzgerald) (1889-1971) *naturalized U.S.*
Born: London
as Gerald Heard

The Marble Ear. Magazine of Fantasy and Science Fiction, Dec 1952
■ *Narcissus, An Anatomy of Clothes,* 1924; editor of *The Realist* (periodical), 1929; *The Ascent of Humanity,* 1929; *This Surprising World,* 1932; *Pain, Sex, and Time,* 1939; *A New Hypothesis of Evolution,* 1939; *Code of Christ,* 1941; *Human Venture,* 1955.
as H. F. Heard
The Collector. Magazine of Fantasy and Science Fiction, Aug 1951
A Taste for Honey. NY: Vanguard, [1941], 234pp.
Murder By Reflection. NY: Vanguard, [1942], 283pp.
Reply Paid. NY: Vanguard, [1942], 274pp.
The Great Fog and Other Weird Tales. NY: Vanguard, [1944], 238pp. *ss col*
The Doppelgangers; An Episode of the Fourth, the Psychological Revolution, 1997. NY: Vanguard, 1947, 281pp.
The Lost Cavern and Other Tales of the Fantastic. NY: Vanguard, [1948], 262pp. *ss col*
The Black Fox: A Novel of the Seventies. London: Cassell, [1950], 234pp.
Gabriel and the Creatures. NY: Harper, 1952, 244pp., ill.
☐ MYSTERY: *The Notched Hairpin,* 1949.

HEARN, (Patricios) Lafcadio (Tessima Carlos) (1850-1904) *ne Irish/Greek → naturalized U.S. → naturalized Japanese*
Born: Santa Maura, Ionia, Greece.
as Lafcadio Hearn
Stray Leaves From Strange Literatures. Boston: Houghton, Mifflin, 1883, 225pp. *ss col*
Some Chinese Ghosts. Boston: Roberts Brothers, 1887, 185pp. *ss col*
A Japanese Miscellany. NY: Little, Brown, 1901, 305pp., ill. *ss col*
Kotto. NY: Macmillan, 1902, ill. *ss col*
Kwaidan. Boston: Houghton, Mifflin, 1904, 240pp. *ss col*
The Romance of the Milky Way. Boston: Houghton, Mifflin, [1905].
Fantastics and Other Fancies. Boston: Houghton, Mifflin, 1914, 242pp. (550 cop) *ss col*
Karma. NY: Boni & Liveright, 1918, 183pp.
(with James, Chambers, et. al.) *Japanese Fairy Tales.* NY: Boni & Liveright, 1918, 160pp.
■ *Two Years In the French West Indies,* 1890; *Glimpses of Unfamiliar Japan,* 1894; *Exotics and Retrospectives,* 1898; *Japan, An Attempt At Interpretation,* 1904.
as Koizumi Yakumo
legal name after becoming a Japanese citizen.

HEARNE, MARY ANNE (1834-1909) *British*
Autobiography: *A Working Woman's Life; An Autobiography.* London: Clarke, 1907, 281pp., ill.
as Marianne Farningham
Nineteen Hundred? A Forecast and A Story. London: Clarke, 1892, 318pp.
☐ POETRY: *Poems,* 1869; *Songs Of Sunshine,* 1878. *Out of the Depths,* 1878 (ss col).
■ *Women and Their Work: Wives and Daughters of the Old Testament,* 1906.

HECHT, FRIEDRICH (1903-　) *German*
as Manfred Langrenus
Reich Im Mond. Utopisch-Wissenschaftlicher Roman aus Naher Zukunft und Jahrmillionenferner Vergangenheit. Leoben: F. Loewe, [1951], 545pp.

HEDGELAND, ISABELLA KELLY (Mrs.) (fl. 1794-1813) *English*
as Author of "Madeleine"
The Abbey of St. Asaph. London: Lane, 1795, 3 vol.
as Isabella Kelly

☐ *Joscelina*, 1797 (2 vol); *Eva*, 1799 (3 vol); *Ruthinglenne*, 1801(3 vol); *A Modern Incident*, 1803; *The Secret*, 1805; Jane de Dunstanville; or, Characters As They Are, 1813.

anonymous

Madeleine; or, the Castle of Montgomery, 1794 (3 vol).

HEILBRUN, CAROLYN G.   (1926-   )

as Amanda Cross

☐ MYSTERY: *In The Last Analysis*, 1964; *The James Joyce Murder*, 1967; *Poetic Justice*, 1970; *The Theban Mysteries*, 1971; *The Question of Max*, 1976.

as Carolyn G. Heilbrun

■ *Christopher Isherwood*, 1970 (essay & bibliography); *Towards A Recognition of Androgyny*, 1973 (Psychology of Literature monograph).

HEINLEIN, ROBERT A(nson)   (1907-   )   *U.S.*

Born: Butler, Missouri

Biographical (Literary): *Heinlein In Dimension*, by Alexei Panshin. Chicago: Advent, 1968, 204pp.

as Robert A. Heinlein

Life-Line. Astounding, Aug 1939

Rocket Ship Galileo. NY: Scribner, 1947, 212pp., ill.

Space Cadet. NY: Scribner, 1948, 242p., ill.

Beyond This Horizon. Reading, Pennsylvania: Fantasy Press, 1948, 242pp. ill.

Red Planet. NY: Scribner, 1949, 211pp., ill.

Sixth Column. NY: Gnome, 1949, 256pp. [title later changed to *The Day After Tomorrow*]

Waldo and Magic, Inc. Garden City: Doubleday, 1950, 219pp. *2 novellas*

The Man Who Sold The Moon. Chicago: Shasta, 1950, 299pp. *ss col*

Farmer In The Sky. NY: Scribner, 1950, 216pp., ill.

Between Planets. NY: Scribner, 1951, 222pp., ill.

The Green Hills of Earth. Chicago: Shasta, 1951, 256pp. *ss col*

Universe. NY: Dell, 1951, 54pp., paper.

The Puppet Masters. Garden City: Doubleday, 1951, 219pp.

The Rolling Stones. NY: Scribner, 1952, 276pp., ill.

Starman Jones. NY: Scribner, 1953, 305pp., ill.

Revolt in 2100. Chicago: Shasta, 1953, 317pp.

Assignment in Eternity. Reading, Pennsylvania: Fantasy Press, 256pp. *ss col*

The Star Beast. NY: Scribner, 1954, 282pp., ill.

Tunnel In the Sky. NY: Scribner, 1955, 273pp.

Double Star. Garden City: Doubleday, 1956, 186pp.

Time for the Stars. NY: Scribner, 1956, 244pp.

The Door Into Summer. Garden City: Doubleday, 1957, 188pp.

Citizen of the Galaxy. Garden City: Doubleday, [1957], 302pp., ill.

Methuselah's Children. NY: Gnome, [1958], 188pp.

Have Space Suit, Will Travel. NY: Scribner, 1958, 276pp.

Starship Troopers. NY: Putnam, 1959, 309pp.

The Menace From Earth. NY: Gnome, 1959, 255pp.

The Unpleasant Profession of Jonathan Hoag. NY: Gnome, 1959, 256pp. [later title *6XH*]

Stranger In A Strange Land. NY: Putnam, 1961, 408pp.

Podkayne of Mars. NY: Putnam, 1963, 191pp.

Glory Road. NY: Putnam, 1963, 288pp.

Orphans of the Sky. NY: Gollancz, 1963, 160pp. *2 novellas*

Farnham's Freehold. NY: Putnam, 1964, 315pp.

The Moon Is A Harsh Mistress. NY: Putnam, 1966, 383pp.

The Worlds Of Robert A. Heinlein. NY: Ace, [1966], 189pp., paper. *ss col*

The Past Through Tomorrow. NY: Putnam, 1967, 667pp. *col of "Future History" series*

I Will Fear No Evil. NY: Putnam, 1971.

Time Enough For Love. NY: Putnam, [1973], 605pp.

as Anson McDonald

Sixth Column. *Astounding*, Jan 1941

as Lyle Monroe

Heil. *Futuria Fantasia #4*, 1940 [Fanzine: published by Ray Bradbury]

Let There Be Light. *Super Science Stories*, May 1940

as John Riverside

The Unpleasant Profession of Jonathan Hoag. *Unknown Worlds*, Oct 1942

as Caleb Saunders

Elsewhere. *Astounding*, Sept 1941

✔ **Simon York** [probably mysteries]

HEMMING, N(ora) K(athleen)   (1927-1960)   *English*

Born: Ilford, Essex

as N. K. Hemming

Loser Take All. *Science Fantasy*, Winter 1951-1952

● **Paul de Wreder**

HENHAM, ERNEST G(eorge)   (1870- ?)   *English*

as Ernest G. Henham

Bonanza. A Story of the Outside. London: Hutchinson, 1901, 320pp.

as John Trevena

Furze the Cruel. London: A. Rivers, 1907, 391pp.

Heather. London: A. Rivers, 1908, 477pp.

Granite. London: A. Rivers, 1909, 488pp. (484-488 adverts) [*Furze the Cruel*, *Heather*, and *Granite* form a trilogy]

Written In the Rain. London: Mills & Boon, [1910], 344pp. *ss col*

The Reign of the Saints. London: A. Rivers, 1911, 376pp.

☐ *God, Man and The Devil*, 1897; *Arminel of the West*, 1907; *The Feast of Bacchus*, 1907; *By Violence*, 1918 (ss col); *Off the Beaten Track*, 1925; *Typet's Treasure*, 1929.

HENNEBERG ZU IRMELSHAUSEN WASUNGEN, CHARLES   (1899-1959)   *German/French*

as Charles Henneberg [in collaboration with Nathilie Henneberg zu Irmelshausen Wasungen]

The Blind Pilot. Magazine of Fantasy and Science Fiction, Jan 1960

Au Premier Ere Spatial. Paris: 1959.

La Rosee du Soleil. Paris: 1959.

Les Dieux Verts. Paris: 1961.

as N(athilie) C(harles) -Henneberg [in collaboration with Nathilie Henneberg zu Irmelshausen Wasungen]

Le Forleresse Perdue. Paris: 1962.

Le Mur de la Lumiere. Paris: A. Michel, [1972], 244pp. [original title *Au Premier Ere Spatial*, 1959]

La Plaie. Paris: A. Michel, 1974, 318pp.

Le Dieu Foudroye. Paris: A. Michel, 1976 [possibly by Nathilie alone].

HENNEBERG ZU IRMELSHAUSEN WASUNGEN, NATHILIE   (Mrs. Charles)

see **CHARLES HENNEBERG**

HENNISSART, MARTHA

as R. B. Dominic [in collaboration with Mary J. Latis]

☐ MYSTERY: *Murder, Sunny Side Up*, 1968; *Murder In High Places*, 1970; *There Is No Justice*, 1971.

as Emma Lathen [in collaboration with Mary J. Latis]

Murder To Go. NY: Simon & Schuster, [1969], 256pp.

☐ MYSTERY: *Banking On Death*, 1961; *A Place For Murder*, 1963; *Accounting For Murder*, 1964; *Murder Makes the Wheels Go 'Round*, 1966; *Death Shall Overcome*, 1966; *Murder Against The Grain*, 1967; *A Stitch In Time*, 1968; *Come To Dust*, 1968; *When In Greece*, 1969; *Pick Up Sticks*, 1970; *Ashes To Ashes*, 1971; *Murder Without Icing*, 1972; *Sweet and Low*, 1974; *By Hook Or By Crook*, 1975.

HERNHUTER, ALBERT
as Burt Ahearne
Red Chrome. *Vortex #1*, 1953
as Albert Hernhuter
The Smiler. *If*, July 1952
↙ Lee Jarvis

HERON-ALLEN, EDWARD (1861-1943) (His Oddship) (Necromancer To Ye Sette of Odd Volumes) *British*
Born: London
as Christopher Blayre
The Purple Sapphire and Other Posthumous Papers. London: P. Allen, [1921], 210pp. *ss col*
The Cheetah Girl. London: 99 pp. [pagination 209-308] [appx. 20 copies for private circulation]
The Strange Papers of Dr. Blayre. London: P. Allen, 1932, 271pp.
Some Women Of the University. Sorelle, Nessuno, Nubiana: [London: R. Stockwell], 1934, 171pp. [100 cop]
as Flavius
various stories printed in the *Anglo-French Review* before 1922
as Edward Heron-Allen
(with Selina Delaro) *The Princess Daphne.* London: H. J. Drane, 264pp., paper.
□ *Kisses of Fate*, 1888; *The Fatal Fiddle; The Commonplace Tragedy of A Snob*, [c.1889].
■ *The Ancestry of the Violin*, 1882; *Violin Making, As It Is and Was*, 1884; *A Manual of Cheirosophy*, 1885; *De Fidiculis Bibliographia: Being An Attempt Towards A Bibliography of the Violin and All Other Instruments Played with A Bow In Ancient and Modern Times*, 1890-94 (2 vol); *Practical Cheirosophy, A Synoptical Study of the Science of the Hand*, 1896; (with Arthur Earland) *An Experimental Study of the Foraminiferal Species Verneuilina, etc.*, 1919; (with Arthur Earland) *Foraminifera*, 1922; *Barnacles In Nature and Myth*, 1928.

HERRICK, THORNECLIFF [house pseudonym]
by Drexel J. Bixby
stories in *Planet Comics*

HERRON, EDNA (1904-)
as Ben Aronin
The Doubt. *Amazing*, May 1932
The Lost Tribe. NY: Simons Press, 1934, 352pp.
The Moor's Gold. Chicago: Argus, 1935, 270pp.
□ *The New Mother Goose*, 1943.
■ *The Birth Of the Jewish People*, 1951.

HERSEY, HAROLD (1892-)
Biography: "Pulpwood Editor" article in *The Golden Atom*, 1955. [First editor of *The Thrill Book*, magazine; also edited *Flying Aces, The Dragnet*, and *Underworld Magazine*. Publisher of *Miracle Science & Fantasy Stories*]
as C. Buxton
Marsa. *The Thrill Book*, May 15, 1919
as Harold Hersey
The Street Without A Name. *The Thrill Book*, June 1, 1919.
The Dead Book. *The Thrill Book*, July 15, 1919.
as H. Kemp
The Ballad of the Living Dead. *The Thrill Book*, July 15, 1919
as P. Kennedy
Flowerflight. *The Thrill Book*, April 1, 1919
as Roy Le Moyne
Lilth. *The Thrill Book*, March 1, 1919 *verse*
as Seymour Le Moyne

Living Dead. *The Thrill Book*, April 1, 1919
as Lerrovitch
The Twisted Tapers. *The Thrill Book*, March 1, 1919 *verse*
as A. Owens
My Lovely. *The Thrill Book*, March 15, 1919.
as A. Tyson
Freedom. *The Thrill Book*, April 15, 1919 *verse*
as V. Vernon
The King. *The Thrill Book*, April 15, 1919 *verse*
● C. Kiproy

HERZOG, EMILE SALOMON WILHELM (1885-1967)
French
Born: Elbeuf, France
Autobiographical: *Memoirs: 1885-1967*, trans. by D. Lindley. NY: Harper & Row, [1970], 439pp.
as Andre Maurois
The Next Chapter: The War Against the Moon. London: K. Paul, [1927], 74pp.
A Voyage to the Island of the Articoles. London: J. Cape, [1928], 63pp., ill.
Patapoufs et Filifers. Paris: Hartman, 1930, 96pp., ill. (325 cop)
The Weigher of Souls. London: Cassell, 1931, 125pp.
A Private Universe. NY: Appleton, 1932, 364pp., ill. *col* [contains "The Earth Dwellers"]
The Thought-Reading Machine. London: Harper, 1938, 217pp.
Les Mondes Impossibles. Paris: Gallimard, [1947], 305pp. *ss col*
The Weigher of Souls and The Earth Dwellers. NY: Macmillan, 1963, 187pp., ill.
Fattypuffs and Thinifers. NY: Knopf, [1969 (1968)], 87pp., ill.
□ *Les Silences du Colonel Bramble*, 1918; *Les Discours du Docteur O'Grady*, 1921.
■ *Ariel, The Life of Shelley*, 1924; *Vie de Disraeli*, 1927; *Aspects of Biography*, 1929; *Les Mondes Imaginaires* (Lit. Crit. on fantastic stories), 1929; *Byron*, 1930; *Voltaire*, 1932; *Dickens*, 1934; *Prophets and Poets*, 1935; *Histoire d'Angleterre*, 1937; *Chateaubriand*, 1938; *Seven Faces of Love*, 1944; *The Quest For Proust*, 1950; *The Metamorphosis of the God*, 1960; *An Illustrated History of the United States*, 1969.

HETTINGER, JOHN (1880-)
as J(ohn) Hettinger (Ph.D.)
■ *The Ultra-Perceptive Faculty; An Experimental Investigation.* London: Rider & Co., [1940], 204pp. [Ph.D. Dissertation, U. of London]
Telepathy and Spiritualism, Personal Experiments, Experiences, and Views, 1952.
as Johnhett
Our Glorious Future, A Novel In Two Parts: The Miracle Child, The Battle of the Spirits. London: C. W. Daniel, [1931], 308pp.

HEWELCKE, GEOFFREY
as Hugh Jeffries
The Dust of Death. *Weird Tales*, April-May 1931

HEYDON, J(oseph) K(entigern)
as J. K. Heydon
■ *Wage-Slavery*, 1924; *Fascism and Providence*, 1937; *The God of Reason*, 1939; *The God of Love*, 1944; *Freewill and Science*, 1944.
as Hal P. Trevarthen
(edited by J. K. Heydon) *World D. by Hal P. Trevarthen, Official Historian of The Superficies. Being A Brief Account of the Founding of Helioxenon.* London: Sheed & Ward, 1935, 320pp.

HILTON, JAMES (1900-1951 (1954?)) *British*
Born: Leigh, Lancashire
as James Hilton
Lost Horizon. London: Macmillan, [1933], 281pp.
 □ *Catherine Herself,* 1920; *Rage In Heaven,* 1932; *Knight Without Armour,* 1933; *Goodbye Mr. Chips,* 1934; *We Are Not Alone,* 1937; *Random Harvest,* 1941; *Nothing So Strange.* 1947.
as Glen Trevor
 □ MYSTERY: *Murder At School,* 1931 [U.S. Title: *Was It Murder,* 1933]

HIRD, JAMES D(ennis) (1850-1920)
as Lord Bottsford
Toddle Island: Being the Diary of Lord Bottsford. London: R. Bentley, 1894, 406pp.
as Dennis Hird
 □ *A Christian With Two Wives,* 1915.
 ■ *Pulpit Science; Is Immortality An Established Fact,* 1897; *Was Jesus Christ A Rationalist,* 1900; *An Easy Outline of Evolution,* 1903; *The Temperance Reader,* 1905; *From Brute to Brother,* 1907.

HOADLEY, H. O(rlo)
as H. Hoadley
Picture From Tokyo. *Astounding,* Jan 1944
as Gene Mitchell
 ■ Refraction and Lenses. *Astounding,* Aug 1944 *article*

HOAR, ROGER SHERMAN (1887-1963) *U.S.*
as Ralph Milne Farley
The Radio Man. *Argosy,* June 28, 1924
The Radio Beasts. *Argosy,* 1925
The Vanishing Man. *Amazing Detective Stories,* Aug 1930
The Immortals. London: Popular Pub., [1947], 95pp.
The Radio Man. Los Angeles: Fantasy Pub. Co. Inc., (FPCI), 1948, 177pp., ill.
The Hidden Universe. Los Angeles: FPCI, 1950, 134pp.
The Omnibus of Time. Los Angeles: FPCI, 1950, 315pp. *ss col*
The Radio Beasts. NY: Ace, [1964], 191pp., paper.
The Radio Planet. NY: Ace, [1964], 224pp., paper.
as Roger Sherman Hoar
 ■ *The Tariff Manual,* 1912; *Constitutional Conventions, Their Nature, Powers, and Limitations,* 1917; *A Course On Exterior Ballistics,* 1920; *Patents, What A Business Executive Should Know,* 1926; *Conditional Sales; Law and Local Practice,* 1929; *Unemployment Insurance In Wisconsin,* 1932.
as Lt. John Pease
The Invisible Bomber. *Amazing,* June 1938
 ↙ General "X", Bennington Orth

HODDER-WILLIAMS, (John) CHRISTOPHER GLAZEBROOK
 (1926-) *English*
as James Brogan
The Cummings Report. London: Hodder & Stoughton, [1958(1957)], 222pp.
as Christopher Hodder-Williams
Chain Reaction. London: Hodder & Stoughton, [1959], 224pp., ill.
The Main Experiment. London: Hodder & Stoughton, [1964], 224pp.
The Egg Shaped Thing. London: Hodder & Stoughton, 1967, 249pp.
Fist Full of Digits. London: Hodder & Stoughton, 1968, 288pp.
 □ *Final Approach,* 1960; *Turbulence,* 1961; *The Higher They Fly,* 1963.

HOGARTH, GRACE (Allen) (1905-)
as Grace Hogarth

 □ *As A May Morning,* 1958
as Allen Weston [in collaboration with Andre Norton]
 □ MYSTERY: *Murders For Sale.* London: Hammond & Hammond, [1954], 240pp.

HOGG, JAMES (1770-1835) *Scottish*
Born: Ettrick, Selkirk
as The Ettrick Shepherd
Tales and Sketches of the Ettrick Shepherd. Glasgow, Scotland: Blackie, [1836], ill. (6 vol)
as "A Justified Sinner"
The Private Memoirs and Confessions of A Justified Sinner: Written By Himself. London: Longmans, 1824, 390pp.
as James Hogg
The Long Pack; A Northumbrian Tale, An Hundred Years Old. Newcastle, Scotland?: J. Bell, 1817, 24pp.
The Brownie of Bodsbeck and Other Tales. Edinburgh: Blackwood, 1818, 2 vol. *ss col*
Winter Evening Tales. Edinburgh: Oliver, 1820, 2 vol *ss col*
 □ POETRY: *Donald M'Donald,* 1800; *Scottish Pastorals,* 1801; *The Mountain Bard,* 1807; *Forest Minstrel,* 1810; *The Queen's Wake,* 1813; *Pilgrims of the Sun,* 1815; *The Poetic Mirror,* 1816; *Queen Hynde,* 1826.

HOLBERG, LUDWIG (Baron) (1684-1754) *Danish*
 [*known as founder of Danish literature*]
Born: Bergen, Norway
Autobiographical: *Memoirs of Lewis Holberg.* London: Whittaker, 1830, 289pp.
as Nicolas Klimius
Nicolai Klimu Iter Subterraneum Novam Telluris Theoriam ac Historiam Quintae Monarchiae Adhuc Nobis Incognitae Exhibens e Bibliotheca B. Abelini. Hafniae et Lipsiae [Copenhagen and Leipzig]: Iacobi Preussii [Jacob Preuss], 1741, 380pp.
A Journey To the World Underground. London: T. Astley, 1742, 324pp.

HOLLY, JOAN CAROL (1932-) *U.S.*
Born: Lansing, Michigan
as J. Hunter Holly
Silence. *Fantastic,* June 1965
Encounter. NY: Avalon, [1959], 224pp.
The Green Planet. NY: Avalon, [1960], 222pp.
The Dark Planet. NY: Avalon, [1962], 224pp.
The Flying Eyes. NY: Monarch, [1962], 140pp., paper.
The Running Man. NY: Monarch, [1963], 142pp., paper.
The Gray Aliens. NY: Avalon, [1963], 192pp.
The Time Twisters. NY: Avon, [1964], 160pp., paper.
The Dark Enemy. NY: Avalon, [1965], 190pp.
The Mind Traders. NY: Avalon, [1966], 192pp.
The Assassination Affair. NY: Ace, [1967], paper.
Keeper. NY: Laser, [1976], paper.
Shepard. NY: Laser, [1977], paper.
Death Dolls of Lyra. NY: Manor, [1977], paper.

HOME-GALL, W. B.
as W. B. Home-Gall
 □ *Where Honour Sits,* 1884-85.
as Reginald Wray
Beyond the Northern Lights. London: Burleigh, 1903.

HOMPF, ALOIS
as Dr. Ali Homo
Neue Erde; den Volkern Gewidet. Homoneion, Unitas Magna Warmbrunn: Einheit Verlag, 1938, 98pp., 6 maps.
as Alois Hompf
 ■ *Reich und Religion,* 1933.

HOOD, ARCHER LESLIE
as Lilian Leslie [in collaboration with Violet Lilian Perkins]

The Melody From Mars. NY: Authors' International Pub. Co., [1924], 206pp.

HOOKE, CHARLES W(itherle) (1861-1929) *U.S.*
as Howard Fielding
The Mind Cure and Other Humorous Sketches. NY: Manhattan Therapeutic Co., [1888], 31pp., ill. *ss col*
Automatic Bridget, and Other Humorous Sketches. NY: Manhattan Therapeutic Co., [1889], 32pp., ill. *ss col*
☐ *The Housekeeper's Secret,* 1889; *Col. Evans From Kentucky and Other Humorous Sketches,* 1889 (ss col); *The Victim of His Clothes,* 1890; *Equal Partners,* 1901; *Straight Crooks,* 1927.

HOOKER, FANNY
as Miss Fanny Hooker
☐ *Captive Yet Conqueror: A Tale of the First Christian Century,* 1882.
as Erniest Hoven
The Man With Two Shadows. Philadelphia: Presbyterian Pub. Committee, [1869], 203pp., ill.

HOPF, ALICE MARTHA LIGHTNER (Mrs. Ernest Joachim) (1904-   )
Born: Detroit, Michigan
as Alice L. Hopf
☐ *Wild Traveler, The Story of A Coyote,* 1967.
■ *Monarch Butterflies,* 1965; *Earth's Bug-Eyed Monsters,* 1968; *Misunderstood Animals,* 1973; *Misplaced Animals, and Other Living Creatures,* 1975; *Biography of An Armadillo,* 1975.
as A. M. Lightner
A New Game. Boy's Life, 1959
A Great Day For the Irish. If, May 1960
The Rock of Three Planets. NY: Putnam, [1963], 157pp., ill.
The Planet Poachers. NY: Putnam, [1965], 184pp.
Doctor to the Galaxy. NY: Norton, [1965], 175pp.
The Galactic Troubadours. NY: Norton, [1965], 237pp.
The Space Plague. NY: Norton, [1966], 156pp.
The Space Olympics. NY: Norton, [1967], 211pp.
The Space Ark. NY: Putnam, [1968], 190pp., ill.
Day of the Drones. NY: Norton, [1969], 255pp.
The Thursday Toads. NY: McGraw-Hill, [1971], 189pp.
Gods or Demons? NY: Four Winds Press, [1973], 208pp.
Star Dog. NY: McGraw-Hill, [1973], 179pp.
The Space Gypsies. NY: McGraw-Hill, [1974], 216pp.
☐ *The Pillar and the Flame,* 1928 (poetry); *The Walking Zoo of Darwin Dingle,* 1969 (juv).

HOPKINS, ALICE K(imball) (Mrs.) (1839- ?)
as A. K. H.
A Daughter of the Druids. Boston: A Mudge, 1892, 297pp., ill.
as Lowell Choate
☐ *The Romance of A Letter,* 1887.
as Alice K. Hopkins
Mona the Druidess; or, The Astral Sciences of Old Britain. Boston: Eastern Publishing Co., 1904, 345pp., ill.

HORLER, SYDNEY (1888-1954) *British*
Born: Leytonstone, Essex
Autobiography: *Excitement. An Impudent Autobiography.* London: Hutchinson, 1933, 288pp.
as Peter Cavendish
☐ *Romeo and Julia,* 1928.
as Martin Heritage
The House of Wingate, A Novel. London: Hurst & Blackett, [1928], 285pp.
as Sydney Horler
The Mystery of No. 1. London: Hodder & Stoughton, [1925], 320pp.

The Curse of Doone. London: Hodder & Stoughton, [1928], 320pp.
The Screaming Skull and Other Stories. London: Hodder & Stoughton, 1930, 318pp. *ss col*
The Man Who Shook the Earth. London: Hutchinson, 1933, 288pp.
The Formula. London: J. Long, [1934], 286pp.
The Vampire. London: Hutchinson, [1935], 288pp.
Lord of Terror. London: Collins, [1935], 252pp.
The Evil Messenger. London: Hodder & Stoughton, 1938, 314pp.
Virus X. London: Quality Press, 1945, 159pp.
The Devil Comes To Bolobyn. London: Marshall, 1951, 255pp.
☐ *A Legend of the League,* 1922; *The Order of the Octopus,* 1926; *The House of Secrets,* 1926; *False-Face,* 1926; *A Life For Sale,* 1928; *Miss Mystery,* 1928; *The Evil Chateau,* 1930; *Horror's Head,* 1932; *The Menace,* 1933; *The Man Who Loved Spiders,* 1949.
■ *London's Underworld; the Record of A Month's Sojourn In the Crime Centres of the Metropolis,* 1934; *Malefactor's Row; A Book Of Crime Studies,* 1940; *I Accuse the Doctors,* 1949 (pro osteopathy tract).

HORN, PETER [house pseudonym]
by Henry Kuttner
50 Miles Down. Fantastic Adventures, May 1940
by David Vern
Vagabonds of the Void. Amazing, March 1940
Giants Out of the Sun. Amazing, May 1940

HORNIG, CHARLES D. (1916-   ) *U.S.*
Born: Jersey City, New Jersey
Noted editor of magazines in 1930's, e.g. *Wonder Stories.*
Helped to found Hugo Gernsback's Science Fiction League.
as Charles D. Hornig
Esperanto, Tongue of Tomorrow. Science Fiction, June 1939 *article*
as Derwin Lesser
The Fatal Glance. Wonder Stories, Feb 1935

HOUGH, RICHARD ALEXANDER (1922-   ) *English*
as Bruce Carter
The Perilous Descent Into A Strange World. London: Bodley Head, [1952], 179pp., ill.
☐ *Speed Six,* 1956; *Target Island,* 1956; *The Kidnapping of Kensington,* 1958; *The Gannet's Nest,* 1966.
as Richard (Alexander) Hough
■ *Six Great Railway Men,* 1955; *The Wright Brothers,* 1955; *The Potemkin Mutiny,* 1960; *Racing Cars,* 1966.

HOUGH, S(tanley) B(ennett) (1917-   ) *English*
Born: Preston, Lancashire
as Rex Gordon
Utopia 239. London: Heinemann, 1955, 208pp.
No Man Friday. London: Heinemann, 1956, 201pp.
First To the Stars. NY: Ace, [1959], 190pp., paper.
Beyond the Eleventh Hour. London: Hodder & Stoughton, 1961, 190pp.
First Through Time. NY: Ace, [1962], 160pp., paper.
Utopia Minus X. NY: Ace, [1966], 190pp., paper.
☐ *The Yellow Fraction,* 1969.
as S. B. Hough
Moment of Decision. London: Hodder & Stoughton, 1952, 190pp.
Extinction Bomber. London: Bodley Head, 1956, 192pp.
☐ *Sweet Sister Seduced,* 1968; *Fear Fortune, Father,* 1974.
● Bennett Stanley

HOWARD, ALBERT WALDO
as M. Auburre Hovorre

The Milltillionaire; or, Age of Bardization. Boston: Author, 1895, 30pp. [slightly different 1898 edition has "First installment March 9, 1895"]
■ *Beethoven and His Deafness; or, Is Deafness Essential to the Hearing of the Higher Harmonies and Symphonies of the Soul,* 1900.

HOWARD, JOHN HAYDEN
as Hayden Howard
It. *Planet Stories,* Jan 1952
The Eskimo Invasion. NY: Ballantine, [1967], 380pp., paper.

HOWARD, MARGHANITA LASKI (Mrs. John) (1915-) *English*
as Marghanita Laski
The Victorian Chaise-Longue. London: Cresset, 1953, 159pp.
□ *Love On The Super-Tax,* 1944 [1945]; (ed) *Victorian Tales For Girls,* 1947; *Toasted English,* 1948; *Tory Heaven; or, Thunder On the Right,* 1948.
■ *Mrs. Ewing, Mrs. Molesworth, and Mrs. Hodgson Burnett,* 1950.

HOWARD, ROBERT E(rwin) (1906-) *U.S.*
Born: Peaster, Texas
as Patrick Erwin
Alleys of Darkness. The Magic Carpet Magazine, Jan 1934
as Robert E. Howard [see also L. SPRAGUE DE CAMP and LIN CARTER]
Spear and Fang. *Weird Tales,* July 1925
The Phoenix On the Sword. *Weird Tales,* Dec 1932 [first Conan story]
(et.al.) *The Garden Of Fear by Robert E. Howard and Other Stories of the Bizarre and Fantastic.* Los Angeles: Crawford, [1945], 79pp. *ss col*
Skull Face and Others. Sauk City, Wisconsin: Arkham House, 1946, 472pp. (3004 cop) *ss col*
Conan the Conqueror. NY: Gnome, [1950], 255pp.
Sword of Conan. NY: Gnome, [1952], 251pp.
The Coming of Conan. NY: Gnome, [1953], 224pp.
King Conan. NY: Gnome, [1953], 255pp.
Conan the Barbarian. NY: Gnome, [1954], 224pp.
(with L. Sprague de Camp) *Tales of Conan.* NY: Gnome, [1955], 218pp., ill.
Always Comes Evening. Sauk City, Wisconsin: Arkham House, 1957, 86pp. (636 cop) *poetry*
The Dark Man and Others. Sauk City, Wisconsin: Arkham House, 1963, 284pp. (2029 cop) *ss col*
Almuric. NY: Ace, [1964], 157pp., paper., ill.
Red Shadows. West Kingston, Rhode Island: Donald M. Grant, 1968, 381pp., ill.
Wolfshead. NY: Lancer, [1968],190pp., paper.
Bran Mak Morn. NY: Dell, [1969], 192pp., paper.
Echoes From An Iron Harp. West Kingston, Rhode Island: Donald M. Grant, 1972, ill. *poetry*
Black Dawn. NP: 1972, 10pp. (234cop)
Marchers of Valhalla. West Kingston, Rhode Island: Donald M. Grant, 1972, 121pp., ill. *col*
Road To Rome. NP: [c.1972], 10pp. (217 cop)
Sowers of the Thunder. West Kingston, Rhode Island: Donald M. Grant, 1973, 285pp., ill. *col*
Worms Of The Earth. West Kingston, Rhode Island: Donald M. Grant, 1974, 233pp., ill.
The Lost Island of Iskander. West Linn, Oregon: FAX, 1974, 194pp., ill. *col*
People of the Black Circle. West Kingston, Rhode Island: Donald M. Grant, 1974, 149pp., ill.
The Incredible Adventures of Dennis Dorgan. West Linn, Oregon: FAX, [1974], 165pp., ill. *ss col*
Tigers of the Sea. West Kingston, Rhode Island: Donald M. Grant, 1974, 212pp., ill.

The Gold and the Grey. California: Roy A. Squires, 1974, [16]pp., paper. (218 cop)
A Witch Shall Be Born. West Kingston, Rhode Island: Donald M. Grant, 1975, 106pp., ill.
Almuric. West Kingston, Rhode Island: Donald M. Grant, 1975, ill.
Red Nails. West Kingston, Rhode Island: Donald M. Grant, 1975, 142pp., ill.
Black Vulmea's Vengeance and Other Tales Of Pirates. West Kingston, Rhode Island: Donald M. Grant, 1976, 223pp., ill. *ss col*
Swords of Shahrazar. West Linn, Oregon: FAX, [1976], 133pp., ill. *col*
The Devil In Iron. West Kingston, Rhode Island: Donald M. Grant, 1976, ill.
□ *A Gent From Bear Creek,* 1965; *Singers In the Shadows,* 1968 (poetry); (with T. S. Smith) *Red Blades of Cathay,* 1971.
as Sam Walser
□ Stories in *Spicy Adventure Stories*
✔ Patrick Howard, John Taveral, Robert Ward

HUBBARD, L(a Fayette) Ron(ald) (1911-) *U.S.*
Born: Tilden, Nebraska
as Winchester Remington Colt
□ Western stories for the pulps in the 1930's.
as Tom Esterbrook [house pseudonym]
□ used in Scientology publications, e.g. *The Auditor.*
as L. Ron Hubbard
The Dangerous Dimension. *Astounding,* July 1938
Final Blackout. Providence, Rhode Island: Hadley, [1948], 154pp., ill.
Death's Deputy. Los Angeles: FPCI, 1948, 167pp., ill.
Slaves of Sleep. Chicago: Shasta, 1948, 206pp.
Triton, and Battle of Wizards. Los Angeles: FPCI, 1949, 172pp.
The Kingslayer. Los Angeles: FPCI, 1949, 208pp. *col*
Typewriter In the Sky & Fear. NY: Gnome, 1951, 256pp.
Return To Tomorrow. NY: Ace, [1954], 157pp., paper.
Ole Doc Methuselah. Austin, Texas: Theta Press, [1970], 176pp.
□ *Buckskin Brigades,* 1937; *Hymn of Asia, An Eastern Poem,* 1974 (poetry).
■ *Dianetics; The Modern Science of Mental Health, A Hand Book of Dianetic Theory,* 1950; *Science of Survival; Simplified Faster Dianetic Techniques,* 1951; *A Key To the Unconscious; Symbological Processing, A Work Volume For Use In Counseling,* 1952; *Dianetics!,* 1955; *Scientology; A New Slant On Life,* 1965.
as Rene Lafayette
Old Doc Methuselah. *Astounding,* Oct 1947.
as Capt. B. A. Northrup
■ Fortress In the Sky. *Air Trails Magazine,* May 1947 [article on military use of satellites]
as Kurt Von Rachen
The Idealist. *Astounding,* July 1940
✔ Elron, Frederick Engelhardt

HUDLESTON, GILBERT ROGER (Dom) [Benedictine Priest] (1874-1936) *British*
Born: nr. Penrith, Cumberland
as (Philip) Roger Pater
Mystic Voices. London: Burns, Oates, 1923, 251pp.
My Cousin Philip: Being the Life Story of Philip Rivers Pater, etc. London: Burns, Oates, 1924, 259pp.

HUGHES, WALTER LLEWELLYN (1910-) *English*
Born: Bilston, Stafford
as Hugh Walters
Blast Off At Woomera. London: Faber, 1957, 202pp.
The Domes of Pico. London: Faber, 1958, 196pp.
Operation Columbus. London: Faber, 1960, 191pp.

Moon Base One. London: Faber, 1961, 189pp.
Expedition Venus. London: Faber, 1962, 160pp.
Destination Mars. London: Faber, 1963, 160pp.
Terror By Satellite. London: Faber, 1964, 159pp.
Journey to Jupiter. London: Faber, 1965, 156pp.
Mission To Mercury. London: Faber, 1965, 158pp.
Spaceship To Saturn. London: Faber, 1967.
□ *The Mohole Mystery,* 1968.

HUME, FERGUSON WRIGHT (1859-1932) *British*
as Fergus Hume
The Gentleman Who Vanished. London: F. V. White,
1890, 102pp.
*The Year of Miracle: A Tale of the Year One Thousand
Nine Hundred.* London: Routledge, [1891], 148pp.
Chronicles Of Fairyland. London: Griffith, 1892, 344pp.
ss col
The Island Of Fantasy; A Romance. NY: Lovell, Coryell,
[1892], 453pp.
Aladdin In London; A Romance. London: A. C. Black,
1892, 432pp.
The Harlequin Opal. Chicago: Rand McNally, [1893],
432pp.
The Dwarf's Chamber and Other Stories. London: Ward,
Lock, 1896, 386pp., ill. *ss col*
The Expedition Of Captain Flick. London: Jarrolds, 1896,
363pp., ill.
For the Defense. Chicago: Rand McNally, [1897], 254pp.
The Mother Of Emeralds. London: Hurst & Blackett,
1901, 337pp.
The Sacred Herb. London: J. Long, 1908, 319pp.
The Amethyst Cross. NY: Cassell, 1909, 304pp.
The Spider. London: Ward, Lock, 1910, 304pp., ill.
The Son Of Perdition; An Occult Romance. London: Rider,
1912, 403pp.
□ MYSTERY: *The Mystery Of the Hansom Cab,* 1886;
The Millionaire Mystery, 1906; *The Mystery of the
Shadow,* 1907; *Seen In the Shadow,* 1913.

HUNGERFORD, MARGARET WOLFE (Hamilton)
(Mrs. Thomas H.) (c.1855-1897) *Irish*
as The Duchess
The Haunted Chamber, A Novel. NY: J. W. Lovell,
[1886], 94pp.
□ *Airy-Fairy Lilian,* 1879.
as Margaret W. Hungerford
The Professor's Equipment. London: Chatto & Windus,
1895, 3 vol.

HUNTER, BLUEBELL M(atilda) (Mrs.) (1887-   )
as John Guildford
□ MYSTERY: *Death Dams the Tide,* 1932.
as Bluebell M. Hunter
□ *The Manchu Empress.*
as George Lancing
Fraudulent Conversion. A Romance of the Gold Standard.
London: Stanley Paul, [1935], 335pp.
□ *Infamous Conduct,* 1934; *Peking Glass,* 1939; *Lotus
Blossom,* 1939; *The Mating Of the Dragon,* 1946;
Dragon In Chains, 1947; *Phoenix Triumphant,* 1950.

HUNTINGTON, EDWARD S.
as Edward Stanton
Dreams of the Dead. Boston: Lee & Shephard, 1892,
268pp.

HUTCHINSON, ROBERT H(are) (1887-   )
as Robert Hare
The Hand Of the Chimpanzee. London: Hurst & Blackett,
[1934], 287pp.
□ *Spectral Evidence,* 1932; *The Crime In the Crystal,*
1933; *The Doctor's First Murder,* 1933.

as Robert H. Hutchinson
■ *The "Socialism" of New Zealand,* 1916.

HYDE, (Mrs. Nelson Waldorf) (1893-   )
as Thyra Samter Winslow
The Sex Without Sentiment. NY: Abelard-Shuman, [1954],
312pp.
■ *Be Slim—Stay Slim,* 1955; *The Winslow Weight
Watcher,* 1953.

HYMAN, SHIRLEY JACKSON (Mrs. Stanley Edgar) (1919-
1965) *U.S.*
Born: San Francisco, California
as Shirley Jackson
The Road Through The Wall. NY: Farrar, Straus, 1948,
271pp.
The Lottery. NY: Farrar, Straus, 1949, 306pp. *ss col*
The Bird's Nest. NY: Farrar, Straus, 1954, 276pp.
The Sundial. NY: Farrar, Straus, 1958, 245pp.
Haunting of Hill House. NY: Viking, 1959, 246pp.
We Have Always Lived In the Castle. NY: Viking, 1962,
214pp.
9 Magic Wishes. NY: Crowell-Collier, 1963, 45pp., ill.
juv
Famous Sally. NY: Harlin Quist, 1966, [46]pp. *juv*
Come Along With Me. NY: Viking, 1968, 243pp. *ss col*
□ *Hangsaman,* 1951.
■ *Life Among the Savages,* 1953; *The Witchcraft of Salem
Village,* 1956; *Raising Demons,* 1957; *The Bad Children,*
1959.

HYNAM, JOHN CHARLES (1915-   ) *British*
as John Kippax
Dimple. Science Fantasy, Dec 1954
(with Dan Morgan) *Thunder of Stars.* London: MacDonald,
1968, 159pp.

HYND, LAVINIA (Leitch) (Mrs. W. A.)
as Lavinia Leitch
A Vampire and Other Stories. Boston: Christopher Publishing House, [1927], 231pp. *ss col*

HYNE, C(harles) J(ohn) CUTLIFFE (Wright) (1865-1944)
English
Born: Bibury, Gloucestershire
Autobiography: *My Joyful Life.* London: Hutchinson,
1935, 281pp., ill.
as Weatherby Chesney
The Adventures of A Solicitor. London: Bowden, 1898,
268pp., ill.
The Baptist Ring. London: Methuen, 1903, 309pp.
as C. J. Cutliffe-Hyne
Beneath Your Very Boots. London: Digby, Long, [1889],
388pp.
The New Eden. London: Longmans, Green, 1892, 258pp.,
ill.
The Recipe for Diamonds. London: Heinemann, 1893,
241pp.
The Adventures of Captain Kettle. London: Pearson,
1898, 318pp. *ss col*
Further Adventures of Captain Kettle. London: Pearson,
1899, 315pp. *ss col*
The Lost Continent. London: Hutchinson, 1900, 368pp.
Captain Kettle, K.C.B. London: Pearson, 1903, 294pp., ill.
Atoms of Empire. London: Macmillan, 1904, 311pp. *ss col*
Empire of the World. London: Everett, [1910], 314pp., ill.
The Marriage of Captain Kettle. Indianapolis: Bobbs-
Merrill, [1912], 373pp., ill.
The Tale of An Anglo-German War. London: Newnes,
1915, 254pp.
Red Herrings. London: Methuen, 1918, 237pp. *ss col*

The Rev. Captain Kettle. London: Harrap, 1925, 245pp. *ss col*

Abbs, His Story Through Many Ages. London: Hutchinson, [1929], 287pp.

Captain Kettle, Ambassador. London: Ward, Lock, [1932], 318pp.

Man's Understanding; Short Stories. London: Ward, Lock, [1933], 287pp.

Ice Age Woman. 1936.

Ivory Valley. London: Ward, Lock, 1938, 315pp.

Wishing Smith. London: Hale, 1939, 282pp.

☐ *Honour of Thieves*, 1895; *The Derelict*, 1901 (ss col); *Mr. Horrocks, Purser*, 1909 (ss col); *The Escape Agents*, 1910; *Captain Kettle On the Warpath*, 1916; *Captain Kettle's Bit*, 1918; *Captain Kettle, K.C.B. (The Last Adventures)*, 1928; *President Kettle*, 1929; *Don't You Agree?*, 1936.

■ *Through Arctic Lapland*, 1898; *But Britons Are Slaves*, 1931.

IRELAND, M. J.
as Joslyn Maxwell
The Outpost On the Moon. *Wonder Stories*, Dec 1930.

IRELAND, WILLIAM HENRY   (1777-1835)   *English*
as H.C.
☐ *The Cottage Girl, A Poem*, 1810 (poetry).
as Cervantes
☐ *The Death Of Bonaparte; or, One Pound One*, 1812 (poetry).
as Charles Clifford
☐ *The Angler: A Didactic Poem*, 1804 (poetry).
as Baron Karlo Excellmans
■ *The Eventful Life of Napoleon Bonaparte*, 1828 (4 vol).
as Flagellum
☐ *All the Blocks!, or, An Antidote to "All the Talents,"* 1807.
as William Henry Ireland
Rimualdo; or, The Castle of Badajos. London: Longman & Rees, 1800, 4 vol.
Gondez the Monk, A Romance of the Thirteenth Century. London: Earle & Hucklebridge, 1805, 4 vol. [vol 3 imprint date misprinted 1085 in earlier copies]
☐ *The Abbess*, 1799; *Ballads In Imitation of the Antient* [sic], 1801; *The Catholic*, 1807; *The Woman of Feeling*, 1804.
■ *An Authentic Account of the Shakspearian MSS*; 1796 [c.1804].
as Arser Pen-Drag-On, Esq.
(as editor) *Scribbleomania; or, The Printer's Devil Polichronicon. A Sublime Poem*, 1815 (poetry).
as Satiricus Sculptor, Esq.
☐ *Chalcographimania; or, The Portrait-Collector and Print Seller's Chronicle, With Infatuations of Every Description. A Humorous Poem*, 1814 (poetry).
as William Shakspeare [forgeries]
☐ PLAYS: *Vortigern and Rowena*, 1795; *Henry II*, 1795.

IRVING, WASHINGTON   (1783-1859)   *U.S.*
Born: New York, New York
as Fray Antonio Agapida
■ *A Chronicle of the Conquest of Granada*, 1829 (U.S.)
as Author of the Sketch Book
The Alhambra: A Series of Tales & Sketches of the Moors and Spaniards. Philadelphia: Carey & Lea, 1832, 2 vol. *col*
The Crayon Miscellany No. 1. Philadelphia: Carey, Lea, & Blanchard, 1835, 274pp. *col*
The Crayon Miscellany No. 2. Carey, Lea, & Blanchard, 1835, 230pp. *col*
The Crayon Miscellany No. 3. Philadelphia: Carey, Lea, & Blanchard, 1835, 276pp. *col*
as Geoffrey Crayon
The Sketch Book of Geoffrey Crayon. NY: C. S. Van Winkle, 1819-1820, 7 parts.
Braceridge Hall, or, The Humorists. NY: C. S. Van Winkle, 1822, 2 vol.
Tales of A Traveller. Philadelphia: Carey, Lea, & Blanchard, 1824, 4 parts [1st part pub. 24 Aug 1824].
Tales of A Traveller. London: J. Murray, 1824, 2 vol. [pub. 25 Aug 1824].
as Washington Irving
Wolfert's Roost and Other Papers. NY: G. P. Putnam,

1855, 383pp.
■ *A History of the Life and Voyages of Christopher Columbus*, 1828; *A Chronicle of the Conquest of Granada*, 1829 (Br.); *Voyages and Discoveries of the Companions of Columbus*, 1831.

as Diedrich Knickerbocker
A History of New York. Inskeep & Bradford, 1809, 2 vol.

as Launcelot Langstaff
Salmagundi; or, the Whim Whams and Opinions of Launcelot Langstaff & Others. NY: Longworth, 1807-1808, 2 vol., (issued in 20 parts beginning Jan 24, 1807—ending Jan 25, 1808) [see **James K. Paulding**]

IRWIN, G. H. [house pseudonym]
unattributed
You Can Say That Again. *Fantastic Adventures*, Dec 1943
The Scarpein Of Delta Sira. *Other Worlds*, Nov 1952
by Raymond A. Palmer
The Vengeance of Martin Brand. *Amazing*, Aug 1942
The Justice of Martin Brand. *Other Worlds*, July 1950
by Richard S. Shaver
Lair of the Grimalkin. *Fantastic Adventures*, April 1948
Where No Foot Walks. *Other Worlds*, Nov 1949
Glass Woman of Venus. *Other Worlds*, Jan 1951

IRWIN, INEZ HAYNES GILLMORE (Mrs.)   (1873-   )
U.S.
Born: Rio de Janeiro, Brazil
as Inez Haynes Gillmore
Angel Island. NY: Holt, 1914, 351pp.
□ *June Jeopardy*, 1908; *The Native Sons*, 1919.
as Inez H. Irwin
Out of the Air. NY: Harcourt, Brace, 1921, 269pp.
□ *Confessions of A Business Man's Wife*, 1931; *Strange Harvest*, 1934.

JACKSON, JOHN
as William T. Silent
Lord of the Red Sun. NY: Walker, 1971.

JACOB, PIERS ANTHONY DILLINGHAM   (1934-   )
English
Born: Oxford, Oxon
as Piers Anthony
Possible To Rue. *Fantastic*, April 1963
Chthon. NY: Ballantine, [1967], 252pp., paper.
SOS the Rope. NY: Pyramid, [1968], 157pp., paper.
(with R. Margroff) *The Ring.* NY: Ace, [1968], 254pp., paper.
Omnivore. NY: Ballantine, [1968], 221pp., paper.
Macroscope. NY: Avon, [1969], 480pp., paper.
Orn. Garden City: Doubleday, [1970], 247pp.
Prostho Plus. London: Gollancz, 1971, 190pp.
Var the Stick. London: Faber, 1972, 191pp.
Race Against Time. NY: Hawthorn, [1973], 179pp.
Rings Of Ice. NY: Avon, [1974], 191pp., paper.
Triple Detente. NY: DAW, [1974], 175pp., paper.
Neq the Sword. London: Corgi, 1975, 191pp.

JAFFE, HYMAN   (1882-   )
as Alterego
Abdera, and the Revolt of the Asses. NY: Clarion, [1937], 199pp.

JAMES, G(eorge) P(ayne) R(ainsford)   (1799-1860)   *English*
Born: London
Biography & Bibliography: *The Solitary Horseman; or, The Life & Adventures of G. P. R. James*, by S. M. Ellis. Kensington: The Cayme Press, 1927, 303pp. (800 cop)
as Author of "Darnley"
The String of Pearls. London: Richard Bentley, 1832, 2 vol. *ss col*
□ HISTORICAL ROMANCE: *Richelieu*, 1829; *Philip Augustus*, 1831.
as F. De Lunatico
The Commissioner: or, De Lunatico Inquirendo. Dublin: Curry, Jun & Co., [1841—1843], 440pp. [issued in parts]
as G. P. R. James
The Commissioner; or, De Lunatico Inquirendo. London: Orr, 1842.
Eva St. Clair; and Other Collected Tales. London: Longman, Brown, Green, 1843, 2 vol. *ss col*
The Castle of Ehrenstein; Its Lords, Temporal and Spiritual; Its Inhabitants, Earthly and Unearthly. London: Smith, Elder, 1847, 3 vol.
The Last of the Fairies. London: Parry, [1847], 231pp., ill.
□ *De l'Orme*, 1830; *The Desultory Man*, 1836; (with M.B. Field) *Adrian; or, the Clouds Of the Mind*, 1852; *Agnes Sorel*, 1853.

JAMESON, ANNIE EDITH (Foster)   (1868-1931)
as J.E. Buckrose
Young Hearts. London: Hodder & Stoughton, [1920], 315pp.
□ *The Art of Living*, 1903; *Voices*, 1908; *The Wolf*, 1908; *A Golden Straw*, 1910; *Down Our Street*, 1911; *The Grey Shepherd*, 1916; *The Round-About*, 1916;

The Silent Legion, 1918; *The House With Golden Windows*, 1921; *A Knight Among Ladies*, 1922; *Sheep's Head*, 1932 (ss col).
■ *Rambles In the North Yorkshire Dales*, 1913; *What I Have Gathered*, 1924 (essays); *Aesop Dancing: or, The Heart of Oliver Goldsmith*, 1930.

JAMESON, MALCOLM (1891-1945) *U.S.*
as Malcolm Jameson
Eviction by Isotherm. *Astounding*, Aug 1938
Atomic Bomb. NY: Bond-Charteris, [1945], 128pp., paper.
Bullard of the Space Patrol. Cleveland, Ohio: World, [1951], 255pp.
Tarnished Utopia. NY: Galaxy SF Novel #27, 1956, 126pp., paper.
as Mary Mac Gregor
Only Transients. *Unknown*, Dec 1942

JARDINE, JACK OWEN (1931-   ) *U.S.*
Born: Eaton Rapids, Michigan
as Howard L. Cory [in collaboration with Julie Jardine]
The Sword of Lankor. NY: Ace, [1966], 158pp., paper.
The Mind Monsters. NY: Ace, [1966], 146pp., paper.
as Corrie Howard [in collaboration with Julie Jardine]
When the Spirit Moves You. *Fling*, 1959.
as Larry Maddock
The Disembodied Man. *Imagination*, April 1954
The Flying Saucer Gambit. NY: Ace, [1966], 159pp., paper.
The Golden Goddess Gambit. NY: Ace, [1967], 158pp., paper.
The Emerald Elephant Gambit. NY: Ace, [1967], 158pp., paper.
The Time Trap Gambit. NY: Ace, [1969], paper.
Volar the Mighty. NY: Ace, 1969, paper.
● **Arthur Farmer**

JARDINE, JULIE ANN (1926-   ) *nee* Shohor *U.S.*
Born: Harbin, Manchuria
as Howard L. Cory [in collaboration with Jack Jardine]
The Sword of Lankor. NY: Ace, [1966], 158pp., paper.
The Mind Monsters. NY: Ace, [1966], 146pp., paper.
as Corrie Howard [alone]
stage name as professional dancer and performer
as Corrie Howard [in collaboration with Jack Jardine]
When the Spirit Moves You. *Fling*, 1959
as Mrs. Jack Owen Jardine
title by marriage (1958-1967)

JARRETT, CORA (Hardy) (Mrs.) (1877- ?) *U.S.*
Born: Norfolk, Virginia
as Cora Jarrett
The Ginko Tree. NY: Farrar & Straus, [1935], 339pp.
Strange Houses; A Tale. NY: Farrar & Straus, [1936], 369pp.
□ MYSTERY: *Night Over Fitch's Pond*, 1933; *I Ask No Other Thing*, 1937 (ss col, 1500 cop); *The Silver String*, 1937.
as Faraday Keene
□ *Peccadilloes*, 1929 (ss col); MYSTERY: *The Little Dry Sticks*, short story collected in *Best American Mystery Stories*, 1932; *Pattern In Black and Red*, 1934.

JARVIS, E. K. [house pseudonym]
unattributed
The Man Who Was Two Men. *Amazing*, June 1942
Men Scared of Nothing. *Fantastic Adventures*, July 1942
Giants Beyond Pluto. *Amazing*, Sept 1942
The Infinite Invasion. *Fantastic Adventures*, Sept 1942
Mystery of the Lost Race. *Fantastic Adventures*, Oct 1942
The Fugitive. *Fantastic Adventures*, Feb 1943
The Metal Monster. *Amazing*, March 1943

The Curse of Many Hands. *Fantastic Adventures*, April 1943
Dolls of Death. *Amazing*, Sept 1944
Hickson's Strange Adventure. *Fantastic Adventures*, March 1947
Mystery of the Midgets. *Amazing*, July 1948
The Murder Ray. *Fantastic Adventures*, April 1949
The Wheel From Space. *Fantastic Adventures*, Aug 1949
All Else Is Dust. *Amazing*, March 1950
Let's Do It My Way. *Amazing*, May 1950
"You Can't Escape From Mars." *Amazing*, Sept 1950
Vengeance of the Golden God. *Amazing*, Dec 1950
Rebirth. *Fantastic Adventures*, Feb 1951
Ticket To Venus. *Amazing*, March 1951
The Glory That Was Rome. *Amazing*, April 1951
A Matter of Principle. *Fantastic Adventures*, April 1951
He Knew What He Wanted. *Fantastic Adventures*, Dec 1951
The Chase. *Fantastic Adventures*, April 1952
The Spectre of Suicide Swamp. *Fantastic Adventures*, July 1952
The Talking Cube. *Fantastic Adventures*, Oct 1952
The Man Who Could Not Die. *Fantastic Adventures*, Nov 1952
Death Beyond the Veil. *Amazing*, Jan 1953
The Rim of Faith. *Fantastic Adventures*, Jan 1953
Cast of Characters. *Fantastic Adventures*, Feb 1953
Operation Tombstone. *Amazing*, March 1953
Green Warning. *Amazing*, March 1956
The Rough Rock Road. *Fantastic*, April 1956
Corn-Fed Genius. *Amazing*, Aug 1956
Before Egypt. *Amazing*, Jan 1957
Biddy and the Silver Man. *Fantastic*, Feb 1957
A Home Among the Stars. *Fantastic*, Sept 1957
The Forgetful Celibate. *Amazing*, Nov 1957
Get Out Of Our Skies! *Amazing*, Dec 1957
Cosmic Striptease. *Fantastic*, Jan 1958
I Married A Martian. *Fantastic*, Feb 1958
Two By Two. *Fantastic*, May 1958
A Slight Case of Genius. *Fantastic*, Sept 1958
Intermission. *Fantastic*, Nov 1958
[many of the earlier titles may be by Robert Moore Williams]
by Harlan Ellison
The Moon Stealers. *Fantastic*, Oct 1957
If This Be Utopia. *Fantastic*, Dec 1957
by Paul W. Fairman
Never Trust A Martian. *Amazing*, Jan 1951
by Robert Silverberg
Moon of Death. *Amazing*, Jan 1958

JENKINS, WILL(iam) F(itzgerald) (1896-   ) *U.S.*
Born: Norfolk, Virginia
as William Fitzgerald
The Gregory Circle. *Thrilling Wonder Stories*, April 1947
as Will (F.) Jenkins
Khilit. *Smashing Novels Magazine*, Sept 1936
A Logic Named Joe. *Astounding*, March 1946
The Murder of the U.S.A., NY: Crown, 1946, 172pp.
□ WESTERN: *Fighting Horse Valley*, 1934; *Black Sheep*, 1936.
as Murray Leinster
Oh, Aladdin! *Argosy*, 11 Jan 1919
The Runaway Skyscraper. *Argosy*, 22 Feb 1919
Murder Madness. NY: Brewer & Warren, 1931, 298pp.
The Last Space Ship. NY: Fell, [1949], 239pp.
Fight For Life. NY: Crestwood, [1949], 118pp.
Sidewise In Time. Chicago: Shasta, 1950, 211pp. *ss col*
Space Platform. Chicago: Shasta, [1953], 223pp., ill.
Space Tug. Chicago: Shasta, [1953], 223pp.
Gateway to Elsewhere. NY: Ace, [1954], 139pp., paper. (Ace Double D 53)
The Forgotten Planet. NY: Gnome, [1954], 177pp.

The Brain-Stealers. NY: Ace, [1954], 139pp., paper. (Ace Double D 79)

Operation: Outer Space. Reading, Pennsylvania: Fantasy Press, 1954, 208pp.

The Black Galaxy. NY: Galaxy SF Novel #20, [1954], 127pp. paper.

The Other Side Of Here. NY: Ace, [1955], 134pp., paper. (Ace Double D 94)

City on the Moon. NY: Avalon, [1957], 224pp.

Colonial Survey. NY: Gnome, [1957], 185pp.

Out of This World. NY: Avalon, [1958], 221pp.

War With the Gizmos. Greenwich, Connecticut: Fawcett Gold Medal, [1958], 156pp., paper.

The Monster From Earth's End. Greenwich, Connecticut: Fawcett Gold Medal, [1959], 176pp., paper.

The Mutant Weapon. NY: Ace, [1959], 93pp., paper. (Ace Double D 403)

The Pirates of Zen. NY: Ace, [1959], 163pp., paper. (Ace Double D 403)

Four From Planet 5. Greenwich, Connecticut: Fawcett Gold Medal, [1959], 160pp., paper.

Monsters and Such. NY: Avon, [1959], 174pp., paper.

Twists In Time. NY: Avon, [1960], 160pp., paper. *ss col*

The Wailing Asteroid. NY: Avon, [1960], 143pp., paper.

Men Into Space. NY: Berkley, [1960], 142pp., paper.

The Aliens. NY: Berkley, [1960], 144pp., paper.

Creatures of the Abyss. NY: Berkley, [1961], 143pp., paper.

This World Is Taboo. NY: Ace, [1961], 127pp., paper.

Talents, Inc. NY: Avon, [1962], 159pp., paper.

Operation Terror. NY: Berkley, [1962], 160pp., paper.

Doctor to the Stars. NY: Pyramid, [1964], 176pp., paper.

The Duplicators. NY: Ace, [1964], 143pp., paper. (Ace Double F 275)

The Other Side of Nowhere. NY: Berkley, [1964], 142pp., paper.

Time Tunnel. NY: Pyramid, [1964], 140pp., paper.

The Greks Bring Gifts. NY: Mac Fadden, [1964], 143pp., paper.

Invaders of Space. NY: Berkley, [1964], 144pp., paper.

Space Captain. NY: Ace, [1966], 112pp., paper. (Ace Double M 135)

Get Off My World! NY: Belmont, [1966], 157pp., paper.

Checkpoint Lambda. NY: Berkley, [1967], 143pp., paper.

Miners In the Sky. NY: Avon, [1967], 127pp., paper.

Space Gypsies. NY: Avon, [1967], 128pp., paper.

Timeslip! NY: Pyramid, [1967], 140pp., paper.

S.O.S. from Three Worlds. NY: Ace, [1967], 140pp., paper.

Land of the Giants. NY: Pyramid, [1968], 156pp., paper.

The Hot Spot. NY: Pyramid, [1969], paper.

☐ MYSTERY: *Scalps, A Murder Mystery,* 1930.

JENKS, GEORGE C(harles)   (1850-1929)   *naturalized U.S.*
Born: London

● **as William Wallace Cook** [this may be another real person?]
A Round Trip To the Year 2000. Argosy, July - Nov 1903

Castaway At the Pole. Argosy, March 1904

The Blue Peter Troglydyte. Argosy, Aug 1904

Castaways of the Year 2000. Argosy, Oct 1912 - Jan 1913

A Round Trip to the Year 2000. NY: Street & Smith, 1903, 310pp., paper.

Marooned in 1492. NY: Street & Smith, 1903, 310pp., paper.

Castaway At the Pole. NY: Street & Smith, 1904, 311pp., paper.

Adrift In the Unknown. NY: Street & Smith, 1905, 305pp., paper.

The Eighth Wonder. NY: Street & Smith, 1906, 318pp., paper.

Around the World In Eighty Hours. NY: Chelsea House, 1925, 249pp.

as John Milton Edwards
■ *The Fiction Factory, Being the Experience Of A Writer Who for Twenty-two Years Has Kept A Story Mill Grinding*

Successfully, 1912. [all agree that this was written by George C. Jenks]

as George C. Jenks
☐ *The Demon Doctor,* 1887; (with Anna A. Chapin) *The Deserters,* 1912.

as W. B. Lawson [house pseudonym?]
☐ *The Dalton Boys In California,* 1892; also titles in the "Nick Carter" series.

JOHNS, MARSTON
see **ROBERT LIONEL FANTHORPE**

JOHNSTON(e), CHARLES · (c.1719-c.1800)
as An Adept
Chrysal; or, The Adventures of A Guinea. Wherein Are Exhibited Views of Several Striking Scenes, With Curious and Interesting Anecdotes of the Most Noted Persons of Every Rank of Life, Whose Hand It Passed Through In America, England, Holland, Germany and Portugal. London: T. Becket, 1760, 2 vol.

☐ *The Adventures of Anthony Varnish,* 1786.

as Editor of "The Adventures of A Guinea"
The Reverie; or, A Flight to the Paradise of Fools . . . Dublin: D. Chamberlaine, 1762, 2 vol

☐ *The History of John Juniper, Esq.,* 1781.

JONES, ADRIENNE
as Adrienne Jones
☐ *Where Eagles Fly,* 1957; *Ride the Far Wind,* 1964; *Wild Voyageur; Story of A Canada Goose,* 1966 (juv).

as Gregory Mason [in collaboration with Doris Meek]
☐ *With Soul So Dead,* 1956.

[a real Gregory Mason (1889–   ) wrote a fantasy satire: *The Golden Archer; A Satirical Novel of 1975.* NY: Twayne, 1956, 296pp.]

JONES, ALICE ILGENFRITZ   (? -1906)
as Ferris Jerome
☐ *High-Water-Mark,* 1879.

as Alice Ilgenfritz Jones
☐ *Beatrice of Bayou Teche,* 1895; *The Chevalier of St. Denis,* 1900.

as Two Women of the West [in collaboration with Ella Marchant]
Unveiling A Parallel, A Romance. Boston: Arena Pub Co., 1893, 269pp., paper. [attributed but not confirmed]

JONES, CLARA AUGUSTA
as Clara Augusta
☐ *Aunt Keziah's War Troubles,* 1867; *The Adventures of A Bashful Bachelor,* 1890; *Nobody's Daughter,* 1891; *The Fatal Glove,* 1892.

as Hero Strong
Found Dead; or, the Charles River Mystery. NY: Street & Smith, [1892], 251pp.

☐ *Born to Command,* 1890; *A Beautiful Woman's Sin; or, The Scarred Arm,* 1890.

JONES, FRANCIS
as Milton R. Peril
The Lost City. Amazing, May 1934

JONES, RAYMOND F.   (1915–   )   *U.S.*
Born: Salt Lake City, Utah
as David Anderson
Utility. Astounding, July 1944
as Raymond F. Jones
Test of the Gods. Astounding, Sept 1941

The Toymaker. Los Angeles: FPCI, 1951, 287pp. *ss col*

Renaissance. NY: Gnome, [1951], 255pp.

The Alien. NY: Galaxy SF Novel #6, [1951], 160pp., paper.

This Island Earth. Chicago: Shasta, [1952], 220pp.

Son of the Stars. Philadelphia: Winston, [1952], 210pp. *juv*
Planet of Light. Philadelphia: Winston, [1953], 211pp. *juv*
The Secret People. NY: Avalon, 1956, 224pp.
The Year When Stardust Fell. Philadelphia: Winston, 1958, 203pp.
The Cybernetic Brains. NY: Avalon, 1962, 223pp.
The Non-Statistical Man. NY: Belmont, [1964], 158pp., paper. *4 novellas*
Syn. NY: Belmont, [1969], 141pp., paper.
Moonbase One. NY: Criterion, [1971], 144pp.
Renegades of Time. NY: Laser #1, [1975], 190pp., paper.
The King of Eolim. NY: Laser #12, [1975], paper.
The River and the Dream. NY: Laser #54, [1977], paper.
(with Lester del Rey) *Weeping May Tarry.* NY: Pinnacle, [1978], paper.
■ *Ice Formation On Aircraft*, 1968; *Physicians of Tomorrow*, 1971; *Radar: How It Works*, 1972.

JONES, SUSAN CARLETON   (1864-1926)
as S. Carleton
  The Clasp of Rank. *The Thrill Book*, April 1, 1919
  □ *The La Chance Mine Mystery*, 1920.
as Carleton-Milecete
  □ *The Career of Mrs. Osbourne*, 1903.
as S. Carleton Jones
  □ *Out of Drowning Valley*, 1910.
as Helen Milecete
  □ *A Girl of the North; A Story of London and Canada*, 1900; *A Detached Pirate; the Romance of Gay Vandeleur*, 1903; *The Plague of A Heart*, 1908.

JONES, VERNON
as Raymond A. Young
  A Thief In Time. *Wonder Stories*, July 1935

JORGENSEN, IVAR [house pseudonym]
unattributed
  Whom the Gods Would Slay. *Fantastic Adventures*, June 1951
  A Handful of Dust. *Fantastic Adventures*, Oct 1951
  Rest In Agony! *Fantastic Adventures*, Jan 1952
  Pattern In the Dust. *Fantastic Adventures*, Feb 1952
  The Blessed Assassins. *Amazing*, Oct 1952
  The Missing Symbol. *Fantastic*, Nov-Dec 1952
  The Curse. *Amazing*, Feb 1953
  The Beast. *Fantastic Adventures*, March 1953
  Something For the Woman. *Fantastic*, March-April 1953
  Belly Laugh. *Amazing*, April-May 1953
  The Day the Gods Fell. *Amazing*, June-July, 1953
  The Wishing Stone. *Fantastic*, July-Aug 1953
  The Senator and the Robot. *Amazing*, Aug-Sept 1953
  Secret Weapon. *Fantastic*, Sept-Oct 1953
  The 7th Bottle. *Fantastic*, Aug 1954
  Blessed Are the Murderous. *Amazing*, Nov 1954
  The Vicar of Skeleton Cove. *Fantastic*, Dec 1954
  Plague Planet. *Amazing*, Jan 1955
  Two To the Stars. *Amazing*, March 1955
  The Man Who Talked To Bees. *Amazing*, July 1955
  The Genius. *Amazing*, Sept 1955
  Let's Do It Again. *Amazing*, Nov 1955
  "Madam, I Have Here ——" *Fantastic*, Dec 1955
  Professor Mainbocher's Planet. *Amazing*, Dec 1955
  The Thirty Thousand Stiffs. *Amazing*, Jan 1956
  This Way Out. *Amazing*, Feb 1956
  Meeting At the Summit. *Imagination*, Feb 1956
  The Sore Spot. *Fantastic*, Feb 1956
  Like A Silver Arrow. *Imaginative Tales*, March 1956
  A Trip to Anywhen. *Amazing*, May 1956
  The Case of the Stripped Blonde. *Imaginative Tales*, 1956
  The Mystery At Mesa Flat. *Imagination*, June 1956
  Space Traveler's Revenge. *Imaginative Tales*, July 1956
  Day Of the Comet. *Imagination*, Oct 1956

The Runaway. *Imaginative Tales*, Nov 1956
(with Adam Chase) Quest of the Golden Ape. *Amazing*, Jan-March 1957
Success Story—Complete With Genie. *Dream World*, May 1957
Pause In Battle. *Imaginative Tales*, May 1957
And Then He Was Two. *Fantastic*, June 1957
Dark Miracle. *Fantastic*, July 1957
Tailor-Made Killers. *Fantastic*, Aug 1957
The Penal Cluster. *Amazing*, Sept 1957
Operation Graveyard. *Fantastic*, Oct 1957
Ten From Infinity. NY: Monarch, [1963], 139pp., paper. *ss col*
Rest in Agony. NY: Monarch, [1963], 125pp., paper.
[the two preceding books are possibly by Robert Silverberg]
by Harlan Ellison
  Children of Chaos. *Amazing*, Nov 1957
by Gordon Randall Garret and Robert Silverberg
  Bleekman's Planet. *Imagination*, Feb 1957
  Slaughter On Dornel IV. *Imagination*, April 1957
  Pirates of the Void. *Imaginative Tales*, July 1957
by Robert Silverberg
  O'Captain, My Captain. *Fantastic*, Aug 1956
  New Year's Eve—2000 A. D. *Imaginative Tales*, Sept 1957
  Housemaid No. 103. *Imaginative Tales*, Nov 1957
  Never Trust A Thief! *Imagination*, Feb 1958
  The Lure of Galaxy A. *Imaginative Tales*, March 1958

JORGENSON, ALF A.   *naturalized U.S.*
Born: Norway
as Aaron Arne
  Feet of Clay: A Fantasy. NY: Vantage, 1958, 276pp.

JORGENSON, IVAR   [house pseudonym]
by Paul W. Fairman
  Deadly City. *If*, March 1953
by Robert Silverberg
  This World Must Die! *Science Fiction Adventures*, Aug 1957
  Thunder Over Starhaven. *Science Fiction Adventures*, Oct 1957
  Hunt the Space-Witch! *Science Fiction Adventures*, Jan 1958
  Ozymandias. *Infinity*, Nov 1958
  Starhaven. NY: Avalon, 1958, 220pp.
  Whom The Gods Would Slay. NY: Belmont, [1968], 140pp., paper.
  The Deadly Sky. NY: Pinnacle, [1971], 188pp., paper.

JUDSON, EDWARD ZANE CARROLL (1823-1886) *U.S.*
Born: Stamford, New York
as Ned Buntline
  The Ice King; or, the Fate of the Lost Steamer. A Fanciful Tale of the Far North. Boston: G. H. Williams, 1848, 100pp.
  The Naval Detective's Chase; or, Nick, the Steeple Climber. NY: Street & Smith, 1889.
  □ *The Virgin of the Sun*, 1847; *The White Wizard*, 1858; *Morgan: or, The Knight of the Black Flag*, 1860; *Mermet Ben; or, the Astrologer King*, 1865; *Rose Seymour; or, the Ballet Girl's Revenge*, 1865.

JUDSON, RALPH
as Ralph Stranger
  The Message from Mars. *Wonder Stories*, June 1932

JUNE, HAROLD
● Walter Kateley

KAHLERT, KARL F(riedrich) (1765-1813)
as Lawrence Flammenberg
The Necromancer; or, The Tale of the Black Forest. London: W. Lane, 1794, 2 vol.
as Bernard Stein
□ *Die Waffenbruder,* 1792.

KALER, JAMES OTIS (1848-1912) *U.S.*
Born: Winterport, Maine
as James Otis
The Search for the Silver City. NY: Burt, [1893], 323pp., ill. *juv*
The Aeroplane At Silver Fox Farm. NY: T. Y. Crowell, 1911, 360pp.
□ *Toby Tyler,* 1880; *Left Behind,* 1882; *Mr. Stubb's Brother,* 1883; *Silent Pete,* 1885; *Left Behind; or, Ten Days A Newsboy,* 1885; *Sarah Dillard's Ride,* 1898; *Richard of Jamestown,* 1910; *Ruth of Boston,* 1910.
■ (ed) *Life of John Paul Jones,* 1900.

KAPLAN, M. M.
as Philip Barshofsky
One Prehistoric Night. *Wonder Stories,* Nov 1934
as Philip Jacques Bartel
Twenty-Five Centuries Late. *Wonder Stories,* Nov 1934

KASSON, HELEN WEINBAUM
as Helen W. Kasson
Time and Again. *Weird Tales,* May 1943
as Helen Weinbaum
The Valley of the Undead. *Weird Tales,* Sept 1940

KAVANAGH, HERMINIE TEMPLETON (Mrs.)
as (Mrs.) Herminie Templeton Kavanagh
The Ashes of Old Wishes, and Other Darby O'Gill Tales. Chicago: Jordan Publishing Co., [1926], 246pp. *ss col*
□ *The Color Sergeant,* 1903 (play).
as Herminie Templeton
Darby O'Gill and the Little People. NY: McClure, Phillips, 1903, 294pp.

KAYE, MARX [house pseudonym]
unattributed
Fortean Aspects of the Flying Discs. *Amazing,* June 1948 *article*
by S. J. Byrne
Mystery of the Peruvian Giants. *Amazing,* June 1947 *article*

KAYSER, RONAL
as Dale Clark(e)
The Phantom In The Sky. *Weird Tales,* Jan 1934
The Devil In Hollywood. Avon Fantasy Reader #18, 1952
The Devil In Hollywood. *Fantastic,* Aug 1963
□ MYSTERY: *Focus On Murder,* 1943; *The Narrow Cell,* 1944; *The Red Rods,* 1946; *Death Wore Fins,* 1959.
as Ronal Kayser
The White Prince. *Weird Tales,* Oct 1934

KEIGHTLEY, DAVID N(oel) (1932-   ) *English*
Born: London
as David Noel Keightley

Black Eyes and Truculence. *Cavalier,* Sept 1961
as Noel Keyes
Contact. NY: Paperback Library, 1963, 176pp., paper.

KELLER, DAVID H(enry) (1880-1963) *U.S.*
Born: Philadelphia, Pennsylvania
as Henry Cecil
□ *Songs of A Spanish Lover,* 1924 (50 cop)
as David H. Keller
The Revolt of the Pedestrians. *Amazing,* Feb 1928
The Thought Projector. NY: Stellar Science Fiction Series #2, 1929, 24pp., ill, paper.
The Wolf Hollow Bubbles. Jamaica, New York: Arra Printers, 1934, 20pp.
Les Hypermondes No 1. St. Lo, France: Barbaroux, 1936, 196pp. (2000 cop) *ss col*
The Sign of the Burning Hart. St. Lo, France: Manche, 1938, 164pp., front. (100 cop)
The Thing In the Cellar. Millheim, Pennsylvania: Bizarre Series #2, [1940], 32pp., paper.
The Devil and the Doctor. NY: Simon & Schuster, 1940, 308pp., ill.
Life Everlasting. Newark, New Jersey: Avalon, 1947, 382pp., ill. *ss col*
The Sign of the Burning Hart. Hollywood, California: National Fantasy Fan Foundation, 1948, 166pp. (250cop)
The Solitary Hunters and the Abyss. Philadelphia: New Era Publishing Co., 1948, 265pp., ill.
Full Circle. London: Chapman & Hall, 1948, 235pp.
The Eternal Conflict. Philadelphia: Prime Press, 1949, 191pp. (350 cop, boxed)
The Homunculus. Philadelphia: Prime Press, 1949, 160pp.
The Lady Decides. Philadelphia: Prime Press, 1950, 139pp. (350 cop)
Tales From Underwood. NY: Pellegrini, Cudahy, [1952], 352pp. [published for Arkham House] *ss col*
Figment of A Dream? np: Anthem, 1962, 39pp., ill., paper. (175 cop)
The Folsom Flint and Other Curious Tales. Sauk City, Wisconsin: Arkham House, 1969, 213pp. *ss col*
■ *The Kellers of Hamilton Township; A Study In Democracy,* 1922; *The Sexual Education Series,* 1928 (10 vol); *Know Yourself! Life and Sex Facts, etc.* 1930; *Portfolio of Anatomical Manikins,* 1932; (ed) *Sexology; the Magazine of Sex Science,* Vol 1, 1933.
as Amy Worth
The Garnet Mine. *Ten Story Book,* Nov 1929
A 1950 Marriage. *Paris Nights,* Dec 1929
A Piece of Linoleum. *Ten Story Book,* Dec 1933
● Jacubus Hubelaire

KELLEY, LEO P(atrick) (1928-   ) *U.S.*
Born: Wilkes Barre, Pennsylvania
as Leo F. Kelley
The Counterfeits. NY: Belmont, [1967], 157pp., paper.
as Leo P. Kelley
Dreamtown, U.S.A. *If,* Feb 1955
Odyssey to Earthdeath. NY: Belmont, [1968], 174pp., paper.
The Accidental Earth. NY: Belmont, [1970], 173pp., paper.
The Coins of Murph. NY: Berkley, [1971], 191pp., paper.
Mindmix. Greenwich, Connecticut: Fawcett Gold Medal, [1972], 176pp., paper.
Time 110100. NY: Walker, [1972], 202pp.
Mythmaster. NY: Dell, [1973], 224pp., paper.
The Earth Tripper. Greenwich, Connecticut: Fawcett Gold Medal, [1973], paper.
□ *Brother John,* 1971 (adapted from screenplay)

KELLEY, MARTHA MOTT
as Q. Patrick [in collaboration with Richard Wilson Webb]
● The Red Balloon. *Weird Tales,* Nov 1953

☐ MYSTERY: *Murder At the Woman's City Club*, 1932; *Murder At the 'Varsity*, 1933; *S.S. Murder*, 1933; *The Grindle Nightmare*, 1935; *Return to the Scene*, 1941; *The Girl On the Gallows*, 1954.
[*The Red Balloon* has been attributed by some to a collaboration of Richard W. Webb and Hugh Collinson Wheeler] see **RICHARD WILSON WEBB**.

KELSALL, CHARLES
as Mela Britannicus
■ *Remarks Touching Geography Especially That of the British Isles, Comprising Strictures On the Hierarchy of Great Britain*, 1825.
as Zachary Craft
☐ *The First Sitting of the Committee on the Proposed Monument to Shakespeare*, 1823 (satire).
as Junius Secundus
Constantine and Eugene, or, An Evening at Mount Vernon. Brussels: For the Author, by P.J. de Mat, 1818, 252pp.
as Charles Kelsall
■ *Phantasm of An University with Prolegomena*, 1814; *Remarks On Scholastic and Academic Education, with an Architectural Detail*, 1821.
anonymous
☐ *Idea of A Constitution for Italy*, 1814.

KENNEDY, R. A.
as Author of "Space and Spirit"
The Triuneverse; A Scientific Romance. London: Charles Knight & Co., Ltd., 1962 [really 1912], 221pp.
as R. A. Kennedy
■ *Space and Spirit: A Commentary Upon the Life of Sir Oliver Lodge, entitled "Life and Matter,"* 1909.
The New 'Benedicite;' or Song of Nations, 1915 (2nd edition).

KERNAHAN, JOHN COULSON (1858-1943) *British*
Born: Ilfracombe, Devonshire
as Coulson Kernahan
A Dead Man's Diary, Written After His Decease. London: Ward, Lock, 1890, 218pp.
A Book of Strange Sins. London: Ward, Lock & Bowden, 1893, 195pp. *ss col*
Dead Faces. London: Ward, Lock, 1894, 3pp. [issued in this form to secure copyright, later issued complete as "God and the Ant"]
God and the Ant. London: Ward, Lock, [1895], 60pp.
The Child, The Wise Man and the Devil. London: Bowden, [1896], 69pp., ill.
Visions. London: Hodder & Stoughton, 1905, 299pp., ill.
A World Without A Child; A Story for Women and for Men. London: Hodder & Stoughton, 1905, 91pp.
The Dumpling, A Detective Love Story of the Great Labour Rising. London: Cassell, 1906, 339pp.
The Red Peril. London: Hurst & Blackett, 1908, 329pp.
Visions Old and New. London: Hodder & Stoughton, [c.1921], 240pp.
■ *Wise Men and a Fool*, 1901; *The Reading Girl*, 1925; *Five More Famous Living Poets*, 1928; *Natural History: Begging the Moon's Pardon and Other Nature Fancies and Studies*, 1930; *The Sunlight in the Room*, 1932.

KIDD, MILDRED VIRGINIA *nee* **EMDEN** (?) *U.S.*
as Mrs. James Blish
title by marriage 1947-1963
as Virginia Blish
On the Wall of the Lodge. *Galaxy*, June 1962
as Virginia Kidd
(translator) *The Monster In the Park*, by Gerald Klein, *Magazine of Fantasy & Science Fiction*, Sept 1961.
(co-editor with Roger Elwood) *Saving Worlds*. Garden City:

Doubleday, 1973, 237pp.

KIMBALL, GRACE LUCIA (Atkinson) (Mrs.) (1875-1923)
as Atkinson Kimball [in collaboration with Richard B(owland) Kimball]
The Prince of Mercuria. NY: Hearst's, [1914], 184pp., ill.

KIMBALL, RICHARD B(owland)
as Atkinson Kimball [in collaboration with Grace L. Kimball]
The Prince of Mercuria. NY: Hearst's, [1914], 184pp., ill.

KING, C(harles) DALY (1895-1963) *U.S.*
Born: New York, New York
as C. Daly King
The Curious Mr. Tarrant. London: Collins (Crime Club), [1935], 284pp.
☐ *Obelists At Sea*, 1932; *Obelists en Route*, 1934; *Obelists Fly High*, 1935; *Arrogant Alibi*, 1938.
■ *Beyond Behaviorism*, 1923; *The Psychology of Consciousness*, 1932; *Electrometric Studies of Sleep*, 1946.
as Jeremiah Phelan
The Episode of the Perilous Talisman. *Magazine of Fantasy and Science Fiction*, Feb 1951

KING, WILLIAM (1663-1712) *English*
as Author of "The Journey to London"
Some Remarks On the Tale of A Tub, to Which Are Annexed Mully of Mountown and Orpheus and Euridice. London: A. Baldwin, 1704, 63pp.
as Author of "A Tale of A Tub" and "The Mully of Mountown"
The Fairy Feast. London: 1704, 12pp.
as Dr. King
■ *An Historical Account of the Heathen Gods and Heroes*. [c.1711].
as Monsieur Sorbiere
☐ *A Journey To London, In the Year 1698*, 1698.

KING, (William) (Benjamin) BASIL (1859-1929)
as Basil King
Going West. NY: Harper, [1919], 46pp.
The Spreading Dawn. Stories of the Great Transition. NY: Harper, 1927, 316pp. *ss col*
☐ *Grieselda*, 1900; *The Side of the Angels*, 1916; *The Lifted Veil*, 1917; *The Empty Sack*, 1921; *The Dust-Flower*, 1922; *The Happy Isles*, 1923; *The High Forfeit*, 1925.
■ *The Abolishing of Death*, 1919; *The Conquest of Fear*, 1922; *The Bible and Common Sense*, 1924.

KING-SCOTT, PETER
as Peter Edgar
Cities of the Dead. London: Digit, 1963, 159pp., paper.

KIRWAN, THOMAS (1829-1911)
as Thomas Kirwan
☐ *In Fetters: The Man or the Priest?*, 1893.
■ *Soldiering In North Carolina*, 1864; *Modern Electricity*, 1889; *Ways That Are Dark. Being An Inside History of Some of the Acts and Sayings of Fraudulent Materialisers, Mediums, Pellet Readers, Slate Writers, etc.*, [1902].
as William Wonder
Reciprocity In the Thirtieth Century. NY: Cochrane Publishing Co., 1908, 217pp., front.

KISSLING, DOROTHY HIGHT (Richardson) (Mrs.)
(1904-   ) *U.S.*
as Dorothy Langley
Mr. Bremble's Buttons. NY: Simon & Schuster, 1947, 186pp.
☐ *Wait for Mrs. Willard*, 1944; *Dark Medallion*, 1945; *The Hoogles and Alexander*, 1948; *Tom Sawyer Comes*

Home, 1973.

KLASS, PHILIP J. (1920-   ) *U.S.*
as Philip Klass
■ *UFO's Identified.* NY: Random House, 1968, 290pp.
Secret Sentries In Space, 1971; *UFO's Explained,* 1974.
as Kenneth Putnam
Me, Myself and I. *Planet Stories,* Winter 1947
as William Tenn
Alexander the Bait. *Astounding,* May 1946
(ed) *Children of Wonder.* NY: Simon & Schuster, 1953, 336pp. *ss anthology*
Of All Possible Worlds. NY: Ballantine, [1955], 159pp., paper. *ss col*
The Human Angle. NY: Ballantine, [1956], 152pp., paper. *ss col*
Time In Advance. NY: Bantam, [1958], 153pp., paper. *ss col*
A Lamp for Medusa. NY: Belmont, [1968], 78pp., paper. (Belmont Double)
Of Men and Monsters. NY: Ballantine, [1968], 251pp., paper. *ss col*
The Seven Sexes. NY: Ballantine, [1968], 238pp., paper. *ss col*
The Square Root of Man. NY: Ballantine, [1968], 220pp., paper. *ss col*
The Wooden Stars. NY: Ballantine, [1968], 251pp., paper. *ss col*

KLEINER, RHEINHART
● Randolph St. John

KNAUSS, ROBERT (1892-1955) *German*
as Major Helders
The War In The Air, 1936. London: J. Hamilton, [1932], 254pp., ill. [*Luftkrieg 1936; die Zertrummerung von Paris.* Berlin: W. Kolk, 1932, 150pp.]
as Dr. Robert Knauss
■ *Die Deutsche, Englishe, und Franzosische Kriegsfinanzierung,* 1923; *Im Grossflugzeug nach Peking,* 1927; *Die Welt des Fliegers,* 1950; *Die Armee In Der Demokratie,* 1953.

KNEALE, THOMAS N(igel) (1922-   ) *English*
Born: Lancaster
as Nigel Kneale
Tomato Cain. London: Collins, 1949, 256pp. *ss col*
The Quartermass Experiment. London: Penguin, [1959], 191pp., ill., paper. *teleplay*
Quartermass II. London: Penguin, [1960], 173pp., ill., paper.
Quartermass and the Pit. London: Penguin, [1960], 187pp., ill., paper.
The Year of the Sex Olympics, 1976.
□ TELEVISION SCRIPTS: *The Road,* 1963; *The Stone Tape,* 1972; *The Beasts,* 1976.

KNIGHT, DAMON F(rancis) (1922-   ) *U.S.*
Born: Baker, Oregon
as Stuart Fleming
New Day on Aurora. *Super Science Stories,* May 1943
as Damon Knight
Resilience. *Stirring Science Stories,* Feb 1941
(with F. S. Knight) *The Stencil Duplicated Newspaper.* Hood River, Oregon: [1941]. *fanzine*
Hell's Pavement. NY: Lion, [1955], 192pp., paper.
The People Maker. NY: Zenith, [1959], 159pp., paper.
Masters of Evolution. NY: Ace, [1959], 96pp., paper. (Ace Double D 375)
The Sun Saboteurs. NY: Ace, [1961], 101pp., paper. (Ace Double F 101)
Far Out. NY: Simon & Schuster, 1961, 282pp. *ss col*
In Deep. NY: Berkley, [1963], 158pp., paper.

Beyond the Barrier. Garden City: Doubleday, 1964, 188pp.
Off Center. NY: Ace, [1965], 141pp., paper. (Ace Double M 113) *ss col*
The Rithian Terror. NY: Ace, [1965], 111pp., paper. (Ace Double M 113)
Mind Switch. NY: Berkley, [1965], 144pp., paper. *ss col*
Beyond Tomorrow. NY: Harper & Row, [1965], 332pp. *ss col*
Turning On; Thirteen Stories by Damon Knight. Garden City: Doubleday, 1966, 180pp. *ss col* [British edition has 14 stories]
Three Novels: Rule Golden, Natural State, The Dying Man. Garden City: Doubleday, 1967, 189pp.
The Metal Smile. NY: Belmont, [1968], 158pp., paper.
Two Novels / Damon Knight. London: Gollancz, 1974, 223 pp. (contains "The Sun Saboteurs" [renamed as "The Earth Quarter"] and "Double Meaning")
■ *In Search Of Wonder.* Chicago: Advent, 1956, 180pp., ill. *Charles Fort: Prophet of the Unexplained,* 1970; *The Futurians,* 1977.
as Donald Laverty [in collaboration with James Blish]
No Winter, No Summer. *Thrilling Wonder Stories,* Oct 1948
✔ Ritter Conway

KNIGHT, KATE WILHELM (Mrs. Damon) (1928-   ) *U.S.*
Born: Toledo, Ohio
as Kate Wilhelm
The Mile-Long Spaceship. *Astounding,* April 1957
The Mile-Long Spaceship. NY: Berkley, [1963], 160pp., paper. *ss col*
(with Theodore L. Thomas) *The Clone.* NY: Berkley, [1965], 143pp., paper.
The Nevermore Affair. Garden City: Doubleday, 1966, 236pp.
The Killer Thing. Garden City: Doubleday, 1967, 190pp.
The Downstairs Room and Other Speculative Fiction. Garden City: Doubleday, 1968, 215pp. *ss col*
Let the Fire Fall. Garden City: Doubleday, 1969, 228pp.
(with Theodore L. Thomas) *The Year of the Cloud.* Garden City: Doubleday, 1970, 216pp.
Abyss: Two Novellas (The Plastic Abyss and Stranger in the House). Garden City: Doubleday, 1971, 158pp.
□ MYSTERY: *More Bitter Than Death,* 1963 [1962]; *Margaret and I,* 1971.

KNOWLES, MABEL W(inifred) (1875-   )
as Lester Lurgan
A Message From Mars. London: Greening, 1912, 288pp., ill.
□ *The Mill-Owner,* 1910; *The League of the Triangle,* 1911; *The Wrestler on the Shore,* 1913.
as May Wynne
□ *A Prince of Intrigue,* 1920; *A Terror of the Moor,* 1928; *Peter Rabbit and The Black Crow,* 1930.

KOONTZ, DEAN R(ay) (1945-   ) *U.S.*
as David Axton
□ *Prison of Ice,* 1976.
as Brian Coffey
□ MYSTERY: *Blood Risk,* 1973; *Surrounded,* 1974; *The Wall of Masks,* 1975.
as K. R. Dwyer
□ *Chase,* 1973; *Shattered,* 1973; *Dragonfly,* 1975.
as Dean R. Koontz
Star Quest. NY: Ace, 1968, 127pp., paper. (Ace Double H 70)
The Fall of the Dream Machine. NY: Ace, [1969], 129pp., paper. (Ace Double)
The Dark Symphony. NY: Lancer, [1970], 205pp., paper.
Hell's Gate. NY: Lancer, [1970], 190pp., paper.
Beastchild. NY: Lancer, [1970], 189pp., paper.

Anti-Man. NY: Paperback Library, [1970], 142pp., paper.
The Crimson Witch. NY: Curtis, [1971], 176pp.
The Flesh In the Furnace. NY: Bantam, [1972], 132pp., paper.
A Darkness In My Soul. NY: DAW, [1972], 124pp., paper.
Time Thieves. NY: Ace, [1972], 109pp., paper. (Ace Double)
Warlock. NY: Lancer, [1972], 221pp., paper.
Starblood. NY: Lancer, [1972], 157pp., paper.
Demon Seed. NY: Bantam, 1973, 182pp., paper.
A Werewolf Among Us. NY: Ballantine, [1973], paper.
Hanging On. NY: Evans, 1973, 312pp.
The Haunted Earth. NY: Lancer, [1973], 192pp., paper.
After the Last Race. NY: Atheneum, 1974, 297pp.
Nightmare Journey. NY: Berkley, [1975], 217pp.
Night Chills. NY: Atheneum, 1976, 334pp.

■ (with Gerda Koontz) *The Pig Society,* 1970; *The Underground Lifestyles Handbook,* 1970; *Writing Popular Fiction,* 1973.

KORN, FRIEDRICH (1803-1850)
as F. Nork
Die Seleniten, oder die Mondbewohner wie Sie Sind Aus den Papieren eines Luftseglers. Herausgeben von F. Nork. Leipzig: A.R. Friese, 1835, 238pp.
■ *Die Existenz der Geister und Ihre Einwirkung auf die Sinnenwelt, Psychologisch Erklart und Historisch Begrundet,* 1841; *Die Vampyrbraut oder die Wirkungen des Bosen Blickes,* 1849.
anonymous
Leben Tod und Hollenfahrt des Weltberuhmten Doctor Daus Einaktige Parodie des Goethe schen Faust. Leipzig: J. C. Theile, 1841, 60pp. *play*

KORNBLUTH, CYRIL (1923-1958) *U.S.*
Born: New York, New York
as Gabriel Barclay [house pseudonym]
Hollow of the Moon. *Super Science Stories,* May 1940
as Arthur Cooke [in collaboration with E. Balter, R. W. Lowndes, J. Michel, and Donald A. Wollheim]
The Psychological Regulator. *Comet Stories,* March 1941
as Cecil Corwin
Thirteen O'Clock. *Stirring Science Stories,* Feb 1941
as Walter C. Davies
New Directions. *Cosmic Stories,* March 1941
as Simon Eisner
The Luckiest Man In Denv. *Galaxy,* June 1952
as Kenneth Falconer
Worlds of Guru. *Stirring Science Stories,* June 1941
as S. D. Gottesman [house pseudonym] alone
King Cole of Pluto. *Super Science Stories,* June 1940
as S. D. Gottesman [house pseudonym] [in collaboration with Frederik Pohl]
Before the Universe. *Super Science Stories,* July 1940
Nova Midplane. *Super Science Stories,* Nov 1940
Trouble In Time. *Astonishing,* Dec 1940
Best Friend. *Super Science Stories,* May 1941
Mars-Tube. *Astonishing,* Sept 1941
as S. D. Gottesman [house pseudonym] [in collaboration with Robert W. Lowndes and Frederik Pohl]
The Castle on Outerplanet. *Stirring Science Stories,* April 1941
The Extrapolated Dimwit. *Future,* Oct 1942
as Cyril M. Judd [in collaboration with Judith Merril]
Mars Child. *Galaxy,* May 1951
Gunner Cade. NY: Simon & Schuster, 1952, 218pp.
Outpost Mars. NY: Abelard, [1952], 268pp.
Sin In Space. NY: Beacon, 1956, paper. (Galaxy Novel #46)
as Cyril (M.) Kornbluth
The Only Thing We Learn. *Startling Stories,* July 1949
Take Off. Garden City: Doubleday, 1952, 218pp.
(with Frederik Pohl) *The Space Merchants.* NY: Ballantine, [1953], 179pp., paper/hardback.
The Syndic. Garden City: Doubleday, 1953, 223pp.

(with Frederik Pohl) *Search the Sky.* NY: Ballantine, [1954], 165pp., paper/hardback.
The Explorers. NY: Ballantine, [1954], 145pp., paper. *ss col*
(with Frederik Pohl) *Gladiator-at-law.* NY: Ballantine, [1955], 171pp., paper/hardback.
Not This August. Garden City: Doubleday, 1955, 190pp.
The Mind Worm and Other Stories. London: M. Joseph, 1955, 255pp. *ss col*
A Mile Beyond the Moon. Garden City: Doubleday, 1958, 239pp. *ss col*
The Marching Morons. NY: Ballantine, [1959], 158pp., paper. *ss col*
(with Frederik Pohl) *Wolfbane.* NY: Ballantine, [1959], 140pp., paper. *ss col*
(with Frederik Pohl) *The Wonder Effect.* NY: Ballantine, [1962], 159pp., paper. *ss col*
Thirteen O'Clock and Other Zero Hours. NY: Dell, [1970], 155pp., paper. *ss col*
(with Frederik Pohl) *Critical Mass.* NY: Bantam, [1977], paper. *ss col*
□ (with Frederik Pohl) *Presidential Year,* 1956.
as Paul Dennis Lavond [house pseudonym] [in collaboration with R. W. Lowndes and Frederik Pohl]
Exiles of New Planet. *Astonishing,* April 1941
Einstein's Planetoid. *Science Fiction Quarterly,* Spring 1942
as Paul Dennis Lavond [house pseudonym] [in collaboration with Frederik Pohl]
A Prince of Pluto. *Future,* April 1941
Callistan Tomb. *Science Fiction Quarterly,* Spring 1941
as Scott Mariner [in collaboration with Frederik Pohl]
An Old Neptunian Custom. *Super Science Stories,* Aug 1942
as Jordan Park [in collaboration with Frederik Pohl]
The Man of Cold Rages. NY: Pyramid, [1958], 192pp., paper.
as Martin Pearson [in collaboration with Donald A. Wollheim]
The Embassy. *Astounding,* March 1942
as Ivar Towers [house pseudonym] [in collaboration with Richard Wilson]
Stepsons of Mars. *Astonishing,* April 1940
as Dirk Wylie [in collaboration with Joseph Harold Dockweiler and Frederik Pohl]
Vacant World. *Super Science Stories,* Jan 1941

KORZENIOWSKI, JOSEF KONRAD THEODOR (1857-1924)
naturalized British
[the National Union Catalogue lists full name Joseph Conrad Theodore Korzeniowski]
Born: Berdichev, Ukraine, Russia
as Joseph Conrad
(with Ford Maddox Hueffer) *The Inheritors; An Extravagant Story.* London: Heinemann, 1901, 323pp.
A Set of Six. London: Methuen, 1908, 310pp. *ss col*
The Shadow Line, A Confession. London: Dent, 1917, 197pp. [Garden City: Doubleday, 1917, 197pp.]
□ *Almayer's Folly,* 1895; *An Outcast of the Islands,* 1896; *The Nigger of the "Narcissus,"* 1897; *Tales of Unrest,* 1898; *Lord Jim,* 1900; *Youth,* 1902 (ss col); *Typhoon,* 1903 (ss col); *The Secret Agent,* 1907; *Under Western Eyes,* 1911; *Chance,* 1913; *Victory,* 1915; *The Arrow of Gold,* 1919; *The Rescue,* 1920; *The Rover,* 1922; *Tales of Hearsay,* 1925 (ss col).
■ *London River,* 1904; *Mirror of the Sea,* 1906; *Last Essays,* 1926.

KOSTROWICKI, GUILLAUME APOLLINAIRE ALBERT (1880-1918)
Born: Rome, Italy
as Guillaume Apollinaire
□ *L'heresiarque et Cie.* Paris: Editions Stock, 1910, 254pp. *ss col*
The Heresiarch and Co. Garden City: Doubleday, 1965, 183pp.

KREMER, RAYMOND JEAN MARIE DE (1887-1964)

Belgian
Born: Ghent
as John Flanders
The Graveyard Duchess. *Weird Tales*, Dec 1934
Mystery of the Last Guest. *Weird Tales*, Oct 1935
Vierde Dimensie. Hasselt: Heideland, [1969], 150pp.
Contes D'Horreur et D'Aventures. Paris: Union Generale,
   1972, 311pp.
   □ *Spoken Op de Ruwe Heide,* 1944; *De Zilveren Kaap,*
   1946; *Geheimen van Het Noorden,* 1948.
as Raymond Kremer
Malpertuis, Histoire D'Une Maison Fantastique. Paris:
   Deniel, [1955].
   □ *Les Contes Noirs du Golf,* 1964.
as Jean Ray
Ghouls In My Grave, trans. by L. Blair. NY: Berkley,
   1965, 143pp., paper.
   □ *Griezelen,* 1964; *Le Cite de L'Indicible Peur,* 1965;
   *Les Etoiles de la Mort et 'Autres Aventures de Harry
   Dickson,* 1973.

KREPPS, ROBERT W(ilson) (1919-   ) *U.S.*
Born: Pittsburgh, Pennsylvania
as Robert W. Krepps
A Nickle Saved . . . *Fantastic Adventures,* March 1949
   □ *The Field of Night,* 1948; *The Courts of the Lion,*
   1950; *Tell It On the Drums,* 1955; *Earthshaker,* 1958;
   Gamble My Last Game, 1958; *Baboon Rock,* 1959;
   El Cid, 1961; *Fancy,* 1969.
as Geoff St. Reynard
Through A Dead Man's Eyes. *Fantastic Adventures,*
   Oct 1945

KUBILIUS, WALTER (1918-   ) *U.S.*
as J.S. Klimaris
The Case of the Vanishing Cellars. *Future,* Aug 1942
as Walter Kubilius
Trail's End. *Stirring Science Stories,* June 1941

KUMMER, FREDERIC ARNOLD (Jr.) (1873-1943)
as Arnold Fredericks
   □ *The Ivory Snuff Box,* 1912; *The Blue Lights,* 1915;
   The Film of Fear, 1917; *The Mark of A Rat,* 1929;
   The Spanish Lady, 1933.
as Frederic Arnold Kummer
The Exterminators. *Thrilling Wonder Stories,* Aug 1938
(with Henry P. James) *The Second Coming: A Vision.*
   NY: Dodd, Mead, 1916, 96pp.
Ladies In Hades; A Story of Hell's Smart Set. NY:
   J. Sears, [1928], 272pp., ill.
Gentleman In Hades: The Story of A Damned Debutante.
   NY: J. Sears, [1930], 269pp., ill.
   □ *The Green God,* 1911; *A Lost Paradise,* 1914; *The
   Webb,* 1919; *Plaster Saints,* 1921; *The Golden Piper,*
   1933; *Design for Murder,* 1936; *Death at Eight Bells,*
   1937; *For Flag and Freedom,* 1942; *The Perilous Island,*
   1942; MUSICAL PLAY: *The Magic Melody,* 1919 (music
   by Sigmund Romberg).
   ■ JUVENILE: *The First Days of Man,* 1922; *The First
   Days of Knowledge,* 1923; *The First Days of History,*
   1925.
as Martin Vaeth
After the Plague. *Astounding,* Feb 1940

KUTTNER, C(atherine) L(ucille) MOORE (Mrs. Henry)
   (1911-   ) *U.S.*
Born: Indianapolis, Indiana
[see Henry Kuttner: after 1940 almost all of Henry
Kuttner's work was to a degree a collaboration with his wife
C. L. Moore. Except as herein indicated these collaborations
were uncredited.]

as Keith Hammond [in collaboration with H. Kuttner]
   see **HENRY KUTTNER**
as Hudson Hastings [in collaboration with H. Kuttner]
   see **HENRY KUTTNER**
as Henry Kuttner [in collaboration with Henry Kuttner]
   see **HENRY KUTTNER**
as C. H. Liddell [in collaboration with Henry Kuttner]
   see **HENRY KUTTNER**
as C.L. Moore
Shambleau. *Weird Tales,* Nov 1933
Judgment Night. NY: Gnome, [1952], 344pp. *ss col &
   novel*
Shambleau and Others. NY: Gnome, 1953, 224pp. *ss col*
Northwest of Earth. NY: Gnome, 1954, 212pp. *ss col*
(with Henry Kuttner) *No Boundaries.* NY: Ballantine,
   [1955], 149pp., paper. *ss col*
Doomsday Morning. Garden City: Doubleday, 1957, 216pp.
(with Henry Kuttner) *Earth's Last Citadel.* NY: Ace,
   [1964], 128pp., paper.
Jirel of Joiry. NY: Paperback Library, [1969], paper.
Black God's Shadow. West Kingston, Rhode Island:
   Donald M. Grant, 1977, ill. *ss col*
as Lawrence O'Donnell [alone]
Clash by Night. *Astounding,* March 1943
as Lawrence O'Donnell [in collaboration with Henry Kuttner]
   see **HENRY KUTTNER**
as Lewis Padgett [in collaboration with Henry Kuttner]
   see **HENRY KUTTNER**

KUTTNER, HENRY (1914-1958) *U.S.*
[After 1940 almost all of H. Kuttner's work was in
uncredited collaboration with C. L. Moore.]
   Born: Los Angeles, California
   Bibliography: *Henry Kuttner: A Memorial Symposium,*
   ed. by Karen Anderson.
as Edward J. Bellin [house pseudonym]
The Touching Point. *Stirring Science Stories,* April 1941
as Paul Edmonds
Telepathy Is News. *Science Fiction,* June 1939
as Noel Gardner
The Shining Man. *Fantastic Adventures,* May 1940
as Will Garth [house pseudonym]
Hands Across the Void. *Thrilling Wonder Stories,* Dec 1938
Dr. Cyclops. NY: Phoenix Press, [1940], 255pp.
   □ WESTERN: *Lawless Guns,* 1937.
as James Hall
Dictator of the Americas. *Marvel Science Stories,* Aug 1938
as Keith Hammond
The Invaders. *Strange Stories,* Feb 1939
Valley of the Flame. *Startling Stories,* March 1946
Valley of the Flame. NY: Ace, [1964], 156pp., paper.
as Hudson Hastings
The Big Night. *Thrilling Wonder Stories,* June 1947
as Peter Horn [house pseudonym]
50 Miles Down. *Fantastic Adventures,* May 1940
as Kelvin Kent [alone]
World's Pharaoh. *Thrilling Wonder Stories,* Dec 1939
as Kelvin Kent [in collaboration with Arthur K. Barnes]
Roman Holiday. *Thrilling Wonder Stories,* Aug 1939
Science Is Golden. *Thrilling Wonder Stories,* April 1940
as Robert O. Kenyon
The Dark Heritage. *Marvel Science Stories,* Aug 1938
as Henry Kuttner
The Graveyard Rats. *Weird Tales,* March 1936
Fury. NY: Grosset & Dunlap, 1950, 186pp. [copyright
   listed as Lawrence O'Donnell, a Kuttner pseudonym
   listed below]
Ahead of Time. NY: Ballantine, [1953], 177pp., paper/
   hardback. *ss col*
(with C. L. Moore) *No Boundaries.* NY: Ballantine, [1955],
   149pp., paper. *ss col*

Bypass to Otherness. NY: Ballantine, [1961], 144pp., paper. *ss col*

Return to Otherness. NY: Ballantine, [1962], 240pp., paper. *ss col*

(with C.L. Moore) *Earth's Last Citadel.* NY: Ace, [1964], 128pp., paper.

Best of Kuttner I. London: Mayflower, 1965, 286pp., paper. *ss col*

The Time Axis. NY: Ace, [1965], 142pp., paper.

The Dark World. NY: Ace, [1965], 126pp., paper.

The Last Castle. NY: Ace, [1966], 148pp., paper. (Ace Double H 21)

Best of Kuttner II. London: Mayflower, [1966], 288pp., paper. *ss col*

The Creature From Beyond Infinity. NY: Popular Library, [1968], 125pp., paper.

☐ MYSTERY: *Man Drowning,* 1952; *The Murder of Ann Avery,* 1956; *The Murder of Eleanor Pope,* 1956; *Murder of a Mistress,* 1957; *Murder of a Wife,* 1958.

as C. H. Liddell

The Sky Is Falling. *Planet Stories,* Fall 1950

Carry Me Home. *Planet Stories,* Nov 1950

as Scott Morgan

Trophy. *Thrilling Wonder Stories,* Winter 1944

as Lawrence O'Donnell [alone]

This Is the House. *Astounding,* Feb 1946

as Lawrence O'Donnell [in collaboration with C. L. Moore]

Fury. *Astounding,* May 1947 [see C. L. Moore for one story alone under this name]

as Lewis Padgett

Deadlock. *Astounding,* Aug 1942

A Gnome There Was. NY: Simon & Schuster, 1950, 276pp. *ss col*

Tomorrow and Tomorrow and The Fairy Chessmen. NY: Gnome, [1951], 254pp.

Robots Have No Tails. NY: Gnome, [1952], 224pp. *ss col*

Mutant. NY: Gnome, [1953], 210pp. *ss col*

Well of the Worlds. NY: Galaxy Novel #17, [1953], 127pp., paper.

Line To Tomorrow. NY: Bantam, [1954], 184pp., paper.

(with C.L. Moore) *Beyond Earth's Gates.* NY: Ace, [1954], 138pp., paper. (Ace Double D 69)

The Chessboard Planet. NY: Galaxy Novel #26, [1956], 124pp., paper. [1st book published alone, appeared previously as *The Fairy Chessmen.*]

☐ MYSTERY: *The Brass Ring,* 1946; *The Day He Died,* 1947.

as Woodrow Wilson Smith

Juke Box. *Thrilling Wonder Stories,* Feb 1947

✔ Hugh Maepen, K. H. Maepenn, Charles Stoddard [house pseudonym] [the National Union Catalogue erroneously lists Jack Vance as a Kuttner pseudonym]

see **JOHN HOLBROOK VANCE**

LACH-SZYRMA, WLADISLAW S(omerville) (1814-1915) *British*

as W.S.L.S.

A Voice From Another World. Oxford: Parker, 1874, 68pp.

as (The Rev.) Wladislaw S. Lach-Szyrma

Aleriel; or, A Voyage to Other Worlds. London: Wyman, 1883, 220pp., front., maps of Mars and Venus.

Under Other Conditions. London: Adam & Black, 1892, 229pp.

☐ *Heroes of the Day: Franklin & Garibaldi,* 1860 (poetry).

■ *A Short History of Penzance,* 1878; *Thoughts On Clerical Life,* 1881; *A Church History of Cornwall,* 1887.

LAFOREST-DIVONNE, PHILOMENE DE (Comtesse) (1887-)

as Claude Silve

Eastward In Eden. trans. Evelyn Hatch. NY: Creative Age Press, [1945], 271pp., ill.

☐ *Benediction,* 1936.

LALLI, CELE G(oldsmith) (Mrs.) (1933-) *U.S.*

Born: Scranton, Pennsylvania

as Cele Goldsmith

Asst. Ed. of *Amazing & Fantastic* 1956-1957

Managing Ed. of *Amazing & Fantastic* 1957-1958

Editor of *Amazing & Fantastic* 1958-1965

LAMBERT, LESLIE H(arrison) (? -1940)

as A. J. Alan

Good Evening, Everyone! London: Hutchinson, [1928], 286pp.

☐ *A. J. Alan's Second Book,* 1933; *The Best of A. J. Alan,* 1954.

LAMBURN, RICHMAL CROMPTON (Miss) (1890-1969) *British*

as Richmal Crompton

Dread Dwelling. NY: Boni & Liveright, 1926, 319pp.

Mists and Other Stories. London: Hutchinson, [1928], 287pp. *ss col*

William and the Moon Rocket. London: G. Newnes, 1954, 248pp. *juv*

William and the Space Animal. London: G. Newnes, 1956, 256pp. *juv*

☐ *Just William,* 1922; *The Innermost Room,* 1923; *The Hidden Light,* 1924; *Ladies First,* 1929; *Matty and the Dearingroydes,* 1956 (juv); *The Inheritor,* 1960; *William the Superman,* 1968.

LANCASTER, WILLIAM JOSEPH COSENS (1851-1922) *British*

Born: Weymouth

as Harry Collingwood

The Log of the "Flying Fish." London: Blackie, 1887 [1886], 384pp., ill.

Geoffrey Harrington's Adventures. London: Society for Promoting Christian Knowledge, [1907], 511pp., ill.

With Airship and Submarine. London: Blackie, 1908 [1907], 376pp., ill.

Harry Escombe. London: Blackie, [1910], 303pp., ill.

The Cruise of the "Flying Fish." London: S. Low, [1924], 314pp.

☐ *The Secret of the Sands,* 1888; *The Missing Merchantman,* 1889; *The Cruise of the "Esmeralda,"* 1894;

Overdue; or, the Strange Story of a Missing Ship, 1911;
The First Mate. The Story of a Strange Cruise, 1914.

LANDON, MELVILLE DE LANCY (1839-1910) *U.S.*
Born: New York, New York
as Eli Perkins
Saratoga In 1901. NY: Sheldon, 1872, 249pp., ill.
☐ *The Franco Prussian War, In A Nutshell,* 1871;
Eli Perkins' Wit, Humor, and Pathos, 1883.
■ *Money: Gold, Silver, or Bimetallism?,* 188-.

LANE, JOHN [house pseudonym]
[see **John D. MacDonald**]

LANE, MARY E. BRADLEY (Mrs.)
as Princess Vera Zarovitch
Mizora: A Prophecy. A Mss. [sic.] *Found Among the Private
Papers of the Princess Vera Zarovitch. Being a True
and Faithful Account of Her Journey to the Interior
of the Earth, With a Careful Description of the Country
and Its Inhabitants, Their Customs, Manners and
Government. Written by Herself.* NY: Dillingham, 1890,
312pp.

LANE, SPENCER [house pseudonym]
unattributed
Origin of Thought. *Astounding,* June 1936
Angel In the Dust Bowl. *Astounding,* Dec 1937
Niedbalski's Mutant. *Astounding,* May 1938

LANG, ANDREW (1844-1912) *Scottish*
Born: Selkirk
as A Well Known Author
The Master Sinner. London: Long, 1901, 182pp.
When It Was Light: A Reply to "When It Was Dark."
London: J. Long, 1906, 208pp.
as Andrew Lang
The Princess Nobody. London: Longmans, [1884], 56pp., ill.
In the Wrong Paradise and Other Stories. London: Kegan,
Paul, 1886, 316pp. *ss col*
The Mark of Cain. Bristol: J.W. Arrowsmith, 1886, 198pp.,
paper/hardback. (Bristol Library #13)
Prince Prigio. Bristol: J. W. Arrowsmith, 1889, 144pp., ill.
(with H. Rider Haggard) *The World's Desire.* London:
Longmans, 1890, 316pp., ill.
Prince Ricardo of Pantouflia. Bristol: J. W. Arrowsmith,
[1893], 204pp., ill.
*My Own Fairy Book, Namely Certain Chronicles of Pant-
ouflia, As Notably the Adventures of Prigio, Prince of that
Country, and of His Son, Ricardo, With An Excerpt From
the Annals of Scotland, as Touching Ker of Fairnilee, his
Sojourn with the Queen Faery.* London: Longmans, 1895,
312pp., ill.
A Monk of Fife; A Romance of the Days of Jeanne d'Arc.
London: Longmans, Green, 1895, 335pp.
The Book of Dreams and Ghosts. London: Longmans,
Green, 1897.
The Valet's Tragedy and Other Studies. London: Long-
mans, 1903, 366pp. *ss col*
Adventures Among Books. London: Longmans, 1905,
312pp., front. *essays* [a 50 copy edition was privately
circulated in 1901 in U.S.A.] [contains several essays of
fantasy including "The Supernatural In Fiction."]
☐ *Pickle the Spy,* 1897; *The Mystery of Mary Stuart,*
1901.
■ *Custom and Myth,* 1884; *The Making of a Religion,*
1898; *Crystal Gazing, Its History and Practice,* 1905;
John Knox and the Reformation, 1905; *The Clyde Mystery, A Study In Mystery and Folklore,* 1905; *Dickens'
Last Plot,* 1905.
anonymous [in collaboration with Walter Herries Pollock
(1850-1926)]

He. London: Longmans, Green, 1887, 119pp., paper.
[a burlesque of H. Rider Haggard's *She;* for an American
burlesque of *She* by the same title and published
anonymously see **JOHN DE MORGAN**]
anonymous [in collaboration with May Kendell]
That Very Mab. London: Longmans, Green, 1885, 215pp.

LANGE, JOHN FREDERICK, (Jr.) (1931-) *U.S.*
Born: Chicago, Illinois
as John Lange
■ *The Cognitivity Paradox; An Inquiry Concerning The
Claims of Philosophy.* Princeton, New Jersey: Princeton
University Press, 1970 [ironically the National Union
Catalogue attributes this book to **MICHAEL CRICHTON**,
another Fantasy and Science Fiction author, see note
in **MICHAEL CRICHTON** entry.]
as John Norman
Tarnsman of Gor. NY: Ballantine, [1966], 219pp., paper.
Outlaws of Gor. NY: Ballantine, [1967], 254pp., paper.
Priest Kings of Gor. NY: Ballantine, [1968], 317pp., paper.
Nomads of Gor. NY: Ballantine, [1969], paper.
Assassin of Gor. NY: Ballantine, [1970], 409pp., paper.
Raiders of Gor. NY: Ballantine, [1971], paper.
Captive of Gor. NY: Ballantine, [1972], paper.
Hunters of Gor. NY: DAW #96, [1974], paper.
Marauders of Gor. NY: DAW #141, [1975], paper.
Time Slave. NY: DAW #169, [1975], paper.
Tribesmen of Gor. NY: DAW #185, [1976], paper.
Slave Girl of Gor. NY: DAW #232, [1977], paper.
Beasts of Gor. NY: DAW #280, [1978], paper.

LA SPINA, GREYE BRAGG (Mrs. Robert) (1880-1969) *U.S.*
Born: Wakefield, Massachusetts
as Greye La Spina
Wolf of the Steppes. *The Thrill Book,* Vol 1, No 1,
March 1, 1919
The Tortoise-Shell Cat. *Weird Tales,* Nov 1924
The Devil's Pool. *Weird Tales,* June 1932
Invaders From the Dark. Sauk City, Wisconsin: Arkham
House, 1960, 168pp. (1559 cop)
as Isra Putnam
Broken Idol. *The Thrill Book,* March 15, 1919
The Wax Doll. *The Thrill Book,* Aug 1, 1919
● Baroni di Savuto

LASSER, DAVID (1902-) *U.S.*
as David Lasser
(with David H. Keller, M.D.) The Time Projector. *Wonder
Stories,* July 1931
■ (with C. C. Carr) *Alternating-Current Motor Repair,*
1929; *The Conquest of Space,* 1931; *Old Age Security
$60 at 60; Testimony of David Lasser, National President
of the Workers Alliance of America,* 1939; *Private
Monopoly; the Enemy At Home,* 1945.
as Richard Penny
(with Jerome Gross) Emperors of Space. *Wonder Stories,*
Nov 1931

LAUMER, JOHN KEITH (1925-) *U.S.*
Born: Syracuse, New York
as Keith Laumer
Greylorn. *Amazing,* April 1959
Worlds of the Imperium. NY: Ace, [1962], 133pp., paper.
(Ace Double F 127)
A Trace of Memory. NY: Berkley, [1963], 174pp., paper.
Envoy to New Worlds. NY: Ace, [1963], 134pp., paper.
(Ace Double F 223)
The Great Time Machine Hoax. NY: Simon & Schuster,
1964, 190pp.
A Plague of Demons. NY: Berkley, [1965], 159pp., paper.
Galactic Diplomat. Garden City: Doubleday, 1965, 227pp.
The Other Side of Time. NY: Berkley, [1965], 160pp., paper.

The Time Bender. NY: Berkley, [1966], 160pp., paper.
Retief's War. Garden City: Doubleday, 1966, 208pp., ill.
(with Rosel George Brown) *Earthblood.* Garden City: Doubleday, 1966, 253pp.
Catastrophe Planet. NY: Berkley, [1966], 158pp., paper.
The Monitors. NY: Berkley, [1966], 166pp., paper.
Nine By Laumer. Garden City: Doubleday, 1967, 222pp. ss col
(with Gordon R. Dickson) *Planet Run.* Garden City: Doubleday, 1967, 167pp.
The Invaders. NY: Pyramid, [1967], 142pp., paper. (Invaders No. 1)
Galactic Odyssey. NY: Berkley, [1967], 160pp., paper.
Enemies From Beyond. NY: Pyramid, [1967], 159pp., paper. (Invaders No. 2)
The Day Before Forever and Thunderhead. Garden City: Doubleday, 1968, 164pp.
Greylorn. NY: Berkley, [1968], 192pp., paper.
Assignment In Nowhere. NY: Berkley, [1968], 143pp., paper.
Retief and the Warlords. Garden City: Doubleday, 1968, 188pp.
It's A Mad, Mad, Mad, Galaxy. NY: Berkley, [1968], 160pp., paper.
The Long Twilight. NY: Putnam, [1969], 222pp.
The World Shuffler. NY: Berkley, [1970], 174pp., paper.
The House In November. NY: Putnam, [1970], 192pp.
Time Trap. NY: Putnam, [1970], 150pp.
Retief's Ransom. NY: Putnam, [1971], 189pp.
The Star Treasure. NY: Putnam, [1971], 188pp.
Retief of the CDT. Garden City: Doubleday, 1971, 172pp.
Once There Was A Giant. Garden City: Doubleday, 1971, 252pp.
Deadfall. Garden City: Doubleday, 1971, 204pp.
Dinosaur Beach. NY: Scribner, 1971, 186pp.
The Infinite Cage. NY: Putnam, [1972], 221pp.
The Shape Changer. NY: Putnam, [1972], 189pp.
Timetracks. NY: Ballantine, [1972], 216pp., paper.
The Glory Game. Garden City: Doubleday, 1973, 186pp.
Bolo: The Annals of the Dinochrome Brigade. NY: Putnam, 1976, 179pp.
■ *How To Design and Build Flying Models,* 1960.
as Anthony Le Baron
The Meteor Man. London: Corgi, 1968, 127pp. (Br. ed. of *The Invaders*).

LAUMER, MARCH
● **as Felix Severence**
The Time Machine That Never Got Past First Base: A Laugh — at the Future? Hong Kong, Opium Books, 1968, paper.

LAURENT-CELY, JACQUES (1919-   ) *French*
as Cecil Saint-Laurent
The Inn of Five Lovers. NY: Fiction Library, 1953, 302pp., ill.
□ *Goubon's Folly,* 1951; *The Affairs of Caroline Cherie,* 1954; *The Cautious Maiden,* 1955.

LAVOND, PAUL DENNIS [house pseudonym]
by Cyril Kornbluth, Robert W. Lowndes, and Frederik Pohl
Exiles of New Planet. *Astonishing,* April 1941
Einstein's Planetoid. *Science Fiction Quarterly,* Spring 1942
by Cyril Kornbluth and Frederik Pohl
A Prince of Pluto. *Future,* April 1941
Callistan Tomb. *Science Fiction Quarterly,* Spring 1941
by Robert W. Lowndes
The Doll Master. *Stirring Science Stories,* April 1941
by Robert W. Lowndes, Frederik Pohl and Joseph H. Dockweiler
Something from Beyond. *Future,* Dec 1941
by Frederik Pohl and Joseph H. Dockweiler

Star of the Undead. *Fantasy Book #2,* [c. 1948]

LAYTON, FRANK GEORGE (1872-1941)
as Stephen Andrew
The Serpent and the Cross. London: Greening, 1909, 320pp.
□ *Doctor Grey,* 1911; *Sable and Motley,* 1912.
as F. G. Layton
□ *The Politicians,* 1913 (play); *The Prophet,* 1922 (play).
■ *Behind the Night Bell,* 1938.

LECKIE, PETER MARTIN (1890-   ) *British*
as Peter Martin
Summer in 3000. London: Quality Press, 1946, 184pp.
□ *The Treasure of the Towers,* 1926; *The Quest of the Pirate Gold,* 1927; *Eastern Slave,* 1931; *The Remarkable Andrew,* 1941.

LEE, ARTHUR STANLEY GOULD (1894-   )
Autobiography: *Fly Past: Highlights From A Flyer's Life.* London: Jarrolds, 1974, 222pp.
as Arthur Lee Gould
An Airplane In the Arabian Nights. London: T.W. Laurie, [1947], 239pp.
as Arthur Gould Lee
■ *The Spirit of Air Force Discipline,* 1923; *The Royal House of Greece,* 1948; *Crown Against Sickle,* 1950; *Helen, Queen Mother of Rumania,* 1956; *The Flying Cathedral, The Story of Samuel Franklin Cody, Texas Cowboy . . . and Pioneer British Aviator,* 1965; *No Parachute: A Fighter Pilot in WWI,* 1968.

LEE, HENRY BOYLE
as Henry Boyle Lee
■ *Napoleon Buonaparte,* 1872.
as Theophilus M'Crib
Kennaquhair. A Narrative of Utopian Travel. London: Chapman & Hall, 1872, 335pp.

LEE, MANFRED B. (1905-1971) *ne* Manford Lepofsky *U.S.*
Born: Brooklyn, New York
as Ellery Queen [in collaboration with Frederic Dannay]
see FREDERIC DANNAY
as Barnaby Ross [in collaboration with Frederic Dannay]
see FREDERIC DANNAY

LEE, WAYNE C(yril) (1917-   ) *U.S.*
Born: Lamar, Nebraska
as Lee Sheldon
Project Asteroid. *Teens,* Feb 27, 1966
Doomed Planet. NY: Avalon, 1967, 190pp.

LE FANU, J(oseph) SHERIDAN (1814-1873) *Irish*
Born: Dublin
Biography: *Sheridan Le Fanu,* by Nelson Brown, 1953.
as John Figwood, Barrister-at-Law
■ *The Prelude: Being A Contribution Toward A History of the Election for the University,* 1865.
as J. S(heridan) Le Fanu
The House By the Churchyard. London: Tinsley, 1863, 3 vol.
Wylder's Hand. London: R. Bentley, 1864, 3 vol.
Uncle Silas: A Tale of Bartram-Haugh. London: Tinsley, 1864, 3 vol.
Guy Deverell. London: R. Bentley, 1865, 3 vol.
All In the Dark. London: Guilford printer, 1866, 2 vol.
The Tenants of Malory. London: Tinsley, 1867, 3 vol.
A Lost Name. London: R. Bentley, 1868, 3 vol.
Haunted Lives. London: Tinsley, 1868, 3 vol.
The Wyvern Mystery. London: Tinsley, 1869, 3 vol.
Chronicles of Golden Friars. London: R. Bentley, 1871, 3 vol. ss col
In A Glass Darkly. London: R. Bentley, 1872, 3 vol.

Willing To Die. London: Hurst & Blackett, 1873, 3 vol.

The Purcell Papers. London: R. Bentley, 1880, 3 vol. *ss col*

The Watcher and Other Weird Stories. London: R. Bentley, [1894], 271pp. *ss col*

The Evil Guest. London: Downey, [1894], 3 vol., ill.

Madame Crowl's Ghost and Other Tales. London: G. Bell, 1923, 277pp. *ss col*

Green Tea and Other Ghost Stories. Sauk City, Wisconsin: Arkham House, 1945, 357pp. (2026 cop) *ss col*

A Strange Adventure In the Life of Miss Laura Mildmay. London: Home & Van Thal, 1947, 108pp.

(ed by Bleiler) *Best Ghost Stories.* NY: Dover, 1964, 467pp., paper. *ss col*

□ *Checkmate*, 1871; *The Bird of Passage*, 1878; *The Black Lady of Duva*, 1879; *Poems*, 1904 (poetry).

anonymous

Ghost Stories and Tales of Mystery. Dublin: McGlashan, 1851, 304pp., ill. *ss col*

□ *The Cock and Anchor. Being A Chronicle of Old Dublin City*, 1845 (3 vol); *The Fortunes of Col. Torlogh O'Brien*, 1847; *The Rose and the Key*, 1871 (3 vol).

LEFFINGWELL, ALBERT   (1895-1946)

as Dana Chambers

The Last Secret. NY: Dial Press, 1943 [1944], 289pp.

□ MYSTERY: *Some Day I'll Kill You*, 1939; *She'll Be Dead By Morning*, 1940; *The Blonde Died First*, 1941; *The Frightened Man*, 1942; *Darling, This Is Death*, 1945.

as Giles Jackson

□ *Witch's Moon*, 1941.

as Albert Leffingwell

■ *Toujour's de l'avant.* Paril: Pinaud, 1928, 35pp., ill. (perfumery)

LEGER, RAYMOND ALFRED   (1883-   )

as Raymond McDonald [in collaboration with Edward McDonald]

The Mad Scientist; A Tale of the Future. NY: Cochrane, 1908, 242pp., ill. (with which is incorporated a secret cipher for the best solution of which the publishers offer $1000.00)

LEIPIAR, LOUISE

as L. Major Reynolds

Chrysalis. *Fantastic Adventures*, Dec 1950

LEISK, DAVID JOHNSON   (1906-   )

as Crockett Johnson

Barnaby. NY: Holt, [1943], 361pp., ill.

Barnaby and Mr. O'Malley. NY: Holt, [1944], 327pp., ill.

□ (with Ruth Krauss) *The Carrot Seed*, 1945; (with Ruth Krauss) *Is This You?*, 1955; *Harold and the Purple Crayon*, 1955; *Barkis*, 1956; *Harold's Fairy Tale*, 1956; *Harold's Trip to the Sky*, 1957; *Harold's Circus*, 1959; *Harold's ABC*, 1963; *The Emperor's Gifts*, 1965; *Upside Down*, 1969.

LESLIE, JOSEPHINE AIMEE CAMPBELL   (1898-   )

as R. A. Dick

The Ghost and Mrs. Muir. Chicago: Ziff-Davis, [1945], 174pp.

Witch Errant; An Improbable Comedy In Three Acts. London: Evans, [1959], 79pp., ill. *play*

□ *Unpainted Portrait*, 1954.

LESLIE, MARY ISABEL   (1899-   )

as Temple Lane

The Bands of Orion. London: Jarrolds, [1928], 344pp.

□ *Second Sight*, 1927; *The Little Wood*, 1930; *Full Tide*, 1932; *Friday's Well*, 1943. POETRY: *Fisherman's Wake, Poems*, 1939; *Curlews, Poems*, 1946.

as Mary Isabel Leslie

□ *Full Tide*, 1932.

LESLIE, PETER   (1922-   )   *English*

Born: Launceston, Cornwall

as Peter Leslie

Hell for Tomorrow. London: World Distributors, 1965, 175pp.

The Finger In the Sky Affair. London: 4 Square, 1966, paper. (Man From U.N.C.L.E.)

The Radioactive Camel Affair. London: 4 Square, 1966, 140pp., paper. (Man From U.N.C.L.E.)

The Diving Dames Affair. London: 4 Square, 1967, 139pp., paper. (Man From U.N.C.L.E.)

The Cornish Pixie Affair. London: 4 Square, 1967, paper. (Girl From U.N.C.L.E.)

The Mogul Men. London: Corgi, 1967, 192pp.

The Frighteners. London: 4 Square, 1968, 111pp., paper.

The Splintered Sunglasses Affair. London: 4 Square, 1968, 124pp., paper. (Man From U.N.C.L.E.)

The Night of the Trilobites. London: Corgi, 1968.

The Unfair Fare Affair. London: 4 Square, 1968, 127pp., paper. (Man From U.N.C.L.E.)

as Patrick Macnee

Deadline. London: Hodder & Stoughton, 1965, 188pp.

Dead Duck. London: Hodder & Stoughton, 1967.

LESPERANCE, DAVID

as Gene A. Davidson

The Woodworkers. *10 Story Fantasy*, Spring 1951

LESSER, MILTON   (1928-   )   *U.S.*

as Adam Chase [in collaboration with Paul W. Fairman]

The Final Quarry. *Imaginative Tales*, May 1956

The Golden Ape. NY: Avalon, 1959, 221pp.

as D. J. Granger

Get Out of My World. *Amazing*, June 1957.

as Milton Lesser

All Heroes Are Hated. *Amazing*, Nov 1950

Earthbound. Philadelphia: Winston, 1952, 208pp.

The Starseekers. Philadelphia: Winston, 1953, 212pp.

Recruit for Andromeda. NY: Ace, [1959], 117pp., paper. (Ace Double D 358)

Stadium Beyond the Stars. Philadelphia: Winston, 1960, 206pp.

Spaceman, Go Home. NY: Holt, Rinehart, & Winston, 1961, 221pp.

Secret of the Black Planet. NY: Belmont, [1965], 157pp., paper.

■ *Lost Worlds and the Men Who Found Them*, 1962; *Walt Disney's Strange Animals of Australia*, 1963.

as Stephen Marlowe

You Take the High Road. *Fantastic Adventures*, Oct 1951

□ *Catch The Brass Ring*, 1954; *Turn Left for Murder*, 1955; *The Shining*, 1963; *The Search for Bruno Heidler*, 1966; *Come Over Red Rover*, 1968; *The Summit*, 1970; *Colossus*, 1972; *The Man With No Shadow*, 1974; *Translation*, 1976.

as S. M. Tenneshaw [house pseudonym]

Who's That Knocking at My Door? *Amazing*, Nov 1950

as C(hristopher) (H.) Thames

No Way Out. *Amazing*, Jan 1955

□ *Violence Is Golden*, 1956.

L'ESTRANGE, C. J.

see **GEORGE H. ELY**

LETHABY, JOHN W.

as J. W. L.

Slave Stories In Rubber Seeking. London: W. Scott, [1913], 251pp. *ss col*

as John W. Lethaby
Rubber Romances and Slave Stories. London: W. Scott, 1910, 251pp. (The Evergreen Library) *ss col*

LEVIN, RICHARD
as Cyril Mand [in collaboration with George R. Hahn]
The Fifth Candle. *Weird Tales,* Jan 1939

LEVY, BRIGID ANTONIA BROPHY (Mrs. Michael)
(1929-   ) *English*
Born: London
as Brigid Brophy
Hackenfeller's Ape. London: Hart-Davis, 1953, 122pp.
  ☐ *The Crown Princess,* 1953; *The King of A Rainy Country,* 1956; *Flesh,* 1962; *Black Ship To Hell,* 1962; *The Finishing Touch,* 1963; *The Snow Ball,* 1964.
  ■ *Mozart the Dramatist,* 1964.

LEWANDOWSKI, HERBERT (1896-   )
as Herbert Lewandowski
  ☐ *Das Sexualproblem in der Modernen Litteratur und Kunst,* 1927.
as Lee van Dovski
Eine Reise ins Jahr 3000, Bericht eines Phantastischen Abenteuers. Zurich: Delphi-Verlag, 1951, 300pp.
  ■ *Schweizer Tagebuch eines Internierten,* 1946; *Genie und Eros,* 1947-49 (2 vol); *Eros der Gegenwart,* 1952.

LEWI, CHARLOTTE ARMSTRONG (Mrs. Jack) (1905-1969)
U.S.
Born: Vulcan, Michigan
as Charlotte Armstrong
The Three Day Magic. *Magazine of Fantasy and Science Fiction,* Sept 1952
The Case of the Weird Sisters. NY: Coward-McCann, 1943, 279pp.
  ☐ MYSTERY: *Lay On, MacDuff,* 1942; *The Innocent Flower,* 1945; *A Little Less Than Kind,* 1963; *The Witch's House,* 1963; *Dream of A Fair Woman,* 1966.
as Jo Valentine
  ☐ *The Trouble In Thor,* 1953.

LEWIS, ALETHEA (Brereton) (1749-1827) *English*
as Eugenia de Acton
The Nuns of the Desert; or, The Woodland Witches. London: Lane, 1805, 2 vol.
as Author of "Things By Their Right Names," "Plain Sense," etc.
  ☐ *Rhoda: A Novel,* 1816.
as A Person Without A Name
Things By Their Right Names; A Novel. 1812.
anonymous
  ☐ *Plain Sense,* 1799.

LEWIS, C(live) S(taples) (1898-1963) *Anglo/Irish*
Autobiography: *Surprised by Joy, The Shape of My Early Life.* London: G. Bles, 1955, 224pp.
Bibliography: *Light on C. S. Lewis.,* ed. by Jocelyn Gibb with bibliography by Walter Hooper. NY: 1965.
as N.W. Clerk
A Grief Observed. London: Faber, 1961, 60pp.
as Clive Hamilton
  ☐ POETRY: *Spirits in Bondage: A Cycle of Lyrics,* 1919; *Dymer,* 1926.
as C(live) S(taples) Lewis
The Shoddy Lands. *Magazine of Fantasy and Science Fiction,* Feb 1956
Pilgrim's Regress, An Allegorical Apology for Christianity, Reason, and Romanticism. London: Dent, 1933, 255pp.
Out of the Silent Planet. London: Lane, [1938], 263pp. (black lettering on cover)
The Screwtape Letters. London: Bles, [1942], 160pp.

Perelandra. London: Lane, [1943], 256pp.
That Hideous Strength. London: Lane, [1945], 475pp.
The Great Divorce, A Dream. London: Bles, 1945, 118pp.
The Lion, the Witch, and the Wardrobe. London: Bles, 1950, 172pp., ill.
Prince Caspian. London: Bles, 1951, 194pp., ill.
Voyage of the Dawn Treader. London: Bles, 1952, 223pp., ill.
The Silver Chair. London: Bles, [1953], 217pp., ill.
The Horse and His Boy. London: Bles, [1954], 199pp., ill.
The Magician's Nephew. London: Bles, 1955, 183pp., ill.
The Last Battle. London: Lane, 1956, 184pp.
Till We Have Faces. London: Bles, 1956, 320pp.
Of Other Worlds. Essays and Stories. London: Bles, [1966], 147pp. *col*
  ■ *The Problem of Pain,* 1940; *The Abolition of Man,* 1943; *Mere Christianity,* 1952. LITERARY CRITICISM: *The Allegory of Love,* 1936; *Preface to Paradise Lost,* 1942; *An Experiment In Criticism,* 1961.
as N(at) W(hilk)
  ☐ used on poetry and periodicals from 1926.

LEWIS, ERNEST MICHAEL ROY (1913-   ) *British*
Born: Felixstowe
as Roy Lewis
Birmingham in 1975. *Birmingham Post,* 1933.
What We Did To Father. London: Hutchinson, [1960], 165pp., ill.
  ■ (with Angus Maude) *The British Middle Classes,* 1949;

LEWIS, MARY CHRISTIANNA MILNE (1907-   )
as Christianna Brand
The Three-Cornered Halo. NY: Scribner, [1957], 255pp.
  ☐ MYSTERY: *Death In High Heels,* 1941; *What Dread Hand,* 1968; *Brand X,* 1974 (ss col).
  ■ *Heaven Knows Who,* 1960.
as Mary Roland
  ☐ *The Single Pilgrim,* 1946.
as China Thompson
  ☐ HISTORICAL FICTION: *Starrbelow,* 1958.

LEWIS, M(athew) G(regory) (c.1775-1818) *English*
Born: London
as M. G. Lewis
Ambrosio; or, The Monk. A Romance (4th ed) with considerable additions and alterations. London: J. Bell, 1798, 3 vol. [retitling of *The Monk*]
The Castle of Lindenburg; or, the History of Raymond and Agnes, With the Story of the Bleeding Nun, etc. London: Fisher, 1798, 148pp.
The Castle Spectre; A Drama. London: J. Bell, 1798, 103pp. play.
Tales of Wonder. London: J. Bell, 1801, 2 vol. *ss col*
Feudal Tyrants; or, The Counts of Carlsheim and Sargens, A Romance. London: Hughes, 1806, 4 vol.
Romantic Tales. London: Longman, Hurst, Rees, etc., 1808, 4 vol. *ss col.*
One O'Clock! or, The Knight and the Wood Daemon. London: Lowndes and Hobbs, 1811, 79pp.
  ☐ *The Bravo of Venice,* 1804; *Journal of A West Indian Proprietor,* 1834.
as Monk Lewis
Rosario, or, The Female Monk; A Romance. Chicago: Laird & Lee, 400pp., ill. [revised and edited version of *The Monk*]
anonymous
The Monk. London: J. Bell, 1796, 3 vol.
Tales of Terror. London: J. Bell, 1801, 149pp. *ss col.*

LEY, ROBERT ARTHUR GORDON (1921-1968) *English*
as Ray Luther
Intermind. NY: Banner, 1967.
as Arthur Sellings

The Haunting. *Authentic*, Oct 1953
Time Transfer and Other Stories. London: M. Joseph, 1956, 240pp. *ss col*
Telepath. NY: Ballantine, [1962], 160pp., paper.
The Uncensored Man. London: Dobson, 1964, 183pp.
The Quy Effect. London: Dobson, 1966, 141pp.
The Long Eureka. London: Dobson, 1968, 184pp. *ss col*
The Power of X. London: Dobson, 1968, 156pp.

LEY, WILLY   (1906-1969)   *naturalized U.S.*
Born: Berlin, Germany
as Willy Ley
■ all non-fiction
The Dawn of the Conquest of Space. *Astounding*, March 1937 *article*
Die Fahrt ins Weltall. Leipzig: Hachmeister and Thal, 1926 [1929?], 83pp., ill.
Die Moglichkeit der Weltraumfahrt. 1928.
Grundriss Einer Geschichte der Rakete. Leipzig: Hachmeister and Thal, [1932], 16pp., ill.
The Lungfish and the Unicorn. NY: Modern Age Books, 1941, 305pp.
Rockets. NY: Viking, 1944, 287pp., ill.
Rockets and Space Travel. NY: Viking, 1947, 347pp., ill.
The Lungfish, the Dodo, and the Unicorn. NY: Viking, 1948, 361pp.
The Conquest of Space. NY: Viking, 1949, 160pp., ill.
Dragons In Amber. NY: Viking, 1951, 328pp., ill.
Rockets, Missiles and Space Travel. NY: Viking, 1951, 436pp., ill.
Days of Creation. NY: Viking, 1952, 275pp., ill.
(with L. Sprague de Camp) *Lands Beyond*. NY: Rinehart, 1952, 346pp., ill.
Engineers' Dreams. NY: Viking, 1954, 239pp., ill.
Salamanders and Other Wonders. NY: Viking, 1955, 293pp., ill.
Rockets, Missiles and Space Travel: Revised. NY: Viking, 1957, 528pp., ill.
Satellites, Rockets, and Outer Space. NY: Signet, [1958], 128pp., ill.
Exotic Zoology. NY: Viking, 1959, 468pp.
Watchers of the Skies. NY: Viking, 1963, 528pp., ill.
Beyond the Solar System. NY: Viking, 1964, 108pp., ill.
Missiles, Moonprobes, and Mega Parsecs. NY: Signet, [1964], 189pp., ill.
Our Work In Space. NY: Macmillan, 1964, 143pp., ill.
Ranger to the Moon. NY: Signet, [1965], 127pp., ill.
Mariner IV To Mars. NY: Signet, [1966], 157pp., ill.
On Earth and In the Sky. Garden City: Doubleday, 1967, 249pp.
Rockets, Missiles and Men In Space. NY: Viking, 1968, 557pp., ill.
Events In Space. NY: McKay, [1969], 180pp., ill.
as Robert Willey
At the Perihelion. *Astounding*, Feb 1937

LINEBARGER, PAUL M(yron) A(nthony)   (1913-1966)   *U.S.*
Born: Milwaukee, Wisconsin
Biography: *Exploring Cordwainer Smith*, ed. by John Bangsund. NY: Algol Press, 1975.
as Felix C. Forrest
□ *Ria*, 1947; *Carola*, 1948.
as P(aul) M. A. Linebarger
■ *The Political Doctrines of Sun Yat Sen*, 1937; *The China of Chiang Kai-Shek*, 1941; *Psychological Warfare*, 1948; *Far Eastern Government and Politics*, 1954.
as Carmichael Smith
Atomsk: A Novel of Suspense. NY: Duell, Sloan, and Pearce, [1949], 224pp.
as Cordwainer Smith
Scanners Live In Vain. *Fantasy Book #6*, 1950

You Will Never Be The Same. NY: Regency, [1963], 156pp., paper. *ss col*
The Planet Buyer. NY: Pyramid, [1964], 156pp., paper.
Space Lords. NY: Pyramid, [1965], 206pp., paper. *ss col*
Quest of the Three Worlds. NY: Ace, [1966], 174pp., paper.
The Underpeople. NY: Pyramid, [1968], 159pp., paper.
Under Old Earth, and Other Explorations. NY: Panther, 1970, 184pp.
Stardreamer. NY: Beagle Books, 1971, 185pp.
Norstrilia. NY: Ballantine, [1975], 277pp., paper.
The Best of Cordwainer Smith. NY: Ballantine, [1975], paper. *ss col*

LININGTON, (Barbara) ELIZABETH   (1921-   )
as Anne Blaisdell
Nightmare. London: Longmans, Green, 1960.
□ MYSTERY: *No Evil Angel*, 1965 (Br.); *Date With Death*, 1965 (Br.).
as Lesley Egan
□ MYSTERY: *Against the Evidence*, 1962; *The Borrowed Alibi*, 1962; *Detective's Due*, 1965; *The Nameless Ones*, 1967; *In the Death of A Man*, 1970.
as Elizabeth Linington
Nightmare. NY: Harper, 1961.
□ MYSTERY: *No Evil Angel*, 1964 (U.S.); *Date With Death*, 1966 (U.S.).
■ *Forging An Empire: Queen Elizabeth I*, 1961; *Come To Think Of It*, 1965.
as Egan O'Neill
□ *The Anglophile*, 1957.
as Dell Shannon
□ MYSTERY: *Ace of Spades*, 1961; *Coffin Corner*, 1966; *Chance To Kill*, 1967.

LIVINGSTON, BERKELEY   (1908-   )   *U.S.*
Born: Chicago, Illinois
as H. B. Hickey [all other stories under this name by Herb Livingston]
Hildy Finds His Wings. *Fantastic Adventures*, Sept 1948
as B. E. Liston
A Grave For Gullible. *Fantastic Adventures*, July 1945
as Berkeley Livingston
I'll Be There With Music. *Fantastic Adventures*, June 1943
as Morris J. Steele [house pseudonym]
The Wooden Ham. *Fantastic Adventures*, Dec 1943

LIVINGSTON, HERB   (1916-   )   *U.S.*
as Alexander Blade [house pseudonym]
The Silver Medusa. *Fantastic Adventures*, Feb 1948
as H. B. Hickey
Beyond the Thunder. *Amazing*, Dec 1938

LOBO, GEORGE EDMUND   *British*
as George Edmund Lobo
□ *Golden Desire*, 1926. POETRY: *The Sacrifice of Love and Other Poems*, 1917; *Clay Speaks of The Fire*, 1946.
as Oliver Sherry
Mandrake. London: Jarrolds, [1929], 287pp.

LOCKE, CHARLES F.
as George McLociard
Smoke Rings. *Amazing*, Feb 1928

LOCKE, RICHARD ADAMS   (1800-1871)   *naturalized U.S.*
Born: Somersetshire, England
as Sir John Herschel [hoax]
Discoveries In the Moon Lately Made At the Cape of Good Hope. *New York Sun*, Aug-Sept 1835

Interesting Astronomical Discoveries, Made In the Moon, by Sir John Herschel At the Cape of Good Hope. Pawtucket, Rhode Island, 1835, 9pp.

as Richard Adams Locke

The Moon Hoax; or, A Discovery That the Moon Has a Vast Population of Human Beings. NY: W. Gowans, 1859.

LOCKE, ROBERT DONALD

as Roger Arcot

The Timeless Man. *Other Worlds,* June 1956

as Robert Donald Locke

Demotion. *Astounding,* Sept 1952

☐ *A Taste of Brass,* 1957.

LOFTS, NORAH (Ethel) (Robinson) (Mrs. Robert Jorisch) (1904-   ) *U.S.*

as Juliet Astley

☐ *The Fall of Midas,* 1975.

as Peter Curtis

The Devil's Own. Garden City: Doubleday, 1960, 239pp.

☐ MYSTERY: *Dead March In Three Keys,* 1940; *No Question of Murder,* 1959.

as Norah Lofts

Hauntings! Is There Anybody There. Garden City: Doubleday, 1975 [1974], 181pp. [prior British edition apparently exists]

☐ *I Met A Gipsy,* 1935; *The Golden Fleece,* 1943; *A Calf for Venus,* 1949; *Esther,* 1950; *The Lute Player,* 1951; *Heaven In Your Hand,* 1958 (ss col); *The Concubine,* 1963; *The King's Pleasure,* 1969; *Crown of Aloes,* 1973; *The Homecoming,* 1975.

■ *Women In the Old Testament,* 1949; *Domestic Life In England,* 1976; *Queens of England,* 1977.

LOHRMAN, PAUL [house pseudonym]

unattributed

Let the Gods Decide. *Amazing,* April 1950

The Unremembered. *Amazing,* May 1950

The Man Who Would Not Burn. *Fantastic Adventures,* June 1950

They're Alive On Mars. *Amazing,* July 1950

The Impostor. *Amazing,* March 1953

The Big Tomorrow. *Amazing,* Oct-Nov 1953

by Richard S. Shaver

The World of the Lost. *Fantastic Adventures,* March 1950

LOMBINO, S(alvatore) A. (1926-   ) *U.S.*

Born: New York, New York

as Curt Cannon

☐ MYSTERY: *I Like 'Em Tough,* 1958 (ss col); *I'm Cannon - For Hire,* 1958.

as Hunt Collins

Small Fry. *Future,* Sept 1952

Tomorrow's World. NY: Avalon, [1956], 223pp.

☐ MYSTERY: *Cut Me In,* 1954.

as Evan Hunter

Robert. *Thrilling Wonder Stories,* April 1953

Malice In Wonderland. *If,* Jan 1954

Find The Feathered Serpent. Philadelphia: Winston, [1952], 207pp.

The Last Spin. London: Constable, 1960, 218pp.

Nobody Knew They Were There, 1971.

☐ *Last Summer,* 1968; *The Easter Man* (a play) *and Six Stories,* 1972 (col). SCREENPLAYS: *The Blackboard Jungle,* 1954; *Strangers When We Meet,* 1958; *The Birds, Buddwing,* 1964; *The Paper Dragon,* 1966; *A Horse's Head,* 1967.

as S. A. Lombino

Reaching For the Moon. *Science Fiction Quarterly,* Nov 1951

as Richard Marsten

Delirium on Deneb. *Thrilling Wonder Stories,* April 1953

Rocket To Luna. Philadelphia: Winston, [1953], 211pp.

Danger: Dinosaurs. Philadelphia: Winston, 1953, 209pp.

☐ *Runaway Black,* 1954; *Murder In the Navy,* 1955; *The Spiked Heel,* 1956; *Vanishing Ladies,* 1957.

as Ed McBain

☐ MYSTERY: "87th Precinct" series beginning with: *The Cop Hater,* 1956; *Mugger,* 1956; *Pusher,* 1956.

as Craig Rice [in collaboration with G. A. Randolph]

☐ MYSTERY: *The April Robin Murders,* 1958.

LONG, A(melia) R(eynolds) (1904-   )

as Kathleen Buddington Coxe [in collaboration with Edna McHugh]

☐ MYSTERY: *Murder Most Foul,* 1946.

as Patrick Laing

☐ MYSTERY: *Stone Dead,* 1945; *If I Should Murder,* 1945; *A Brief Case of Murder,* 1949.

as A(melia) Reynolds Long

The Twin Soul. *Weird Tales,* March 1928

The Mystery of the Phantom Shot. *Amazing Detective Tales,* July 1930

The Mechanical Man. NY: Stellar Publishing Co., [1930], 27pp., ill. [Science Fiction Series No. 7, with *The Thought Stealer* by Frank Bourne]

☐ MYSTERY: *The Shakespeare Murders,* 1939; *A Corpse At the Quill Club,* 1940; *Murder to Type,* 1943; *Symphony in Murder,* 1944; *The Leprechaun Murders,* 1950.

as Adrian Reynolds

☐ MYSTERY: *Formula For Murder,* 1947; *The Round Table Murders,* 1952.

as Peter Reynolds

☐ MYSTERY: *Behind the Evidence,* 1936.

as Mordred Weir

Bride of the Antarctic. *Strange Stories,* June 1939.

LONG, FRANK BELKNAP (1903-   ) *U.S.*

Born: New York, New York

as Frank Belknap Long

The Desert Lich. *Weird Tales,* Nov 1924

The Man From Genoa and Other Poems. Athol, Massachusetts: Recluse Press, W. P. Cook, 1926, 31pp. (300 cop) *verse*

The Goblin Tower. Cassia, Florida: Dragon-Fly Press, 1935, 25pp., paper. (100 cop) *verse*

The Hound of Tindalos. Sauk City, Wisconsin: Arkham House, 1946, 316pp. (2602 cop)

John Carstairs, Space Detective. NY: Frederick Fell, 1949, 265pp.

Space Station #1. NY: Ace, [1957], 157pp., paper. (Ace Double D 242)

The Horror Expert. NY: Belmont, [1961], paper.

The Mating Center. NY: Chariot, 1961, 160pp., paper.

Mars Is My Destination. NY: Pyramid, 1962, 158pp., paper.

It Was the Day of the Robot. NY: Belmont, [1963], 141pp., paper.

The Horror From the Hills. Sauk City, Wisconsin: Arkham House, 1963, 110pp. (1997 cop)

Three Steps Spaceward. NY: Avalon, 1963, 192pp.

The Martian Visitors. NY: Avalon, 1964, 192pp.

Mission To A Star. NY: Avalon, 1964, 192pp.

Odd Science Fiction. NY: Belmont, [1964], 141pp., paper.

This Strange Tomorrow. NY: Belmont, [1966], 158pp., paper.

Lest Earth Be Conquered. NY: Belmont, [1966], 144pp., paper.

So Dark A Heritage, 1966.

Journey Into Darkness. NY: Belmont, [1967], 150pp., paper.

. . . And Others Shall Be Born. NY: Belmont, [1968], 172pp., paper. (Belmont Double)

The Three Faces Of Time. NY: Tower, [1969], 156pp., paper.

Monster From Out of Time. NY: Popular Library, [1970], 127pp., paper.

Survival World. NY: Lancer, [1971], 157pp., paper.

The Rim of the Unknown. Sauk City, Wisconsin: Arkham House, 1972, 291pp.

The Night Of the Wolf. NY: Popular Library, [1972], 175pp., paper.

The Early Long. Garden City: Doubleday, 1975, 211pp.

□ POETRY: *On Reading Arthur Machen,* 1949.

■ *Howard Phillips Lovecraft: Dreamer On the Nightside.* Sauk City, Wisconsin: Arkham House, 1975, 237pp., ill.

as Leslie Northern [house pseudonym]

The Purple Dusk. *Thrilling Wonder Stories,* Summer 1945

They Sculp. *Thrilling Wonder Stories,* Winter 1945

LONG, GABRIELLE M(argaret) V(ere) (Campbell) (Mrs. Arthur L.) (1886-1952) *British*

Born: Hayling Island, Hants

Autobiography: *The Debate Continues; Being the Autobiography of Marjorie Bowen,* by Margaret Campbell. London: Heinemann, [1939], 298pp.

as Marjorie Bowen

Black Magic. Tale of the Rise and Fall of Antichrist. London: A. Rivers, 1909, 390pp.

The Cheats, A Romantic Fantasy. London: W. Collins, [1920], 278pp.

The Haunted Vintage. London: Odhams Press, [1921], 320pp.

Seeing Life! And Other Stories. London: Hurst & Blackett, [1923], 285pp. *ss col*

Five Winds. London: Hodder & Stoughton, 1927, 317pp.

Sheep's Head and Babylon, and Other Stories of Yesterday and Today. London: J. Lane, 1929, 344pp. *ss col*

The Last Bouquet. Some Twilight Tales. London: J. Lane, 1933, 348pp. *ss col*

The Bishop of Hell and Other Stories. London: J. Lane, 1949, 230pp. *ss col*

□ *The Viper of Milan,* 1906; *I Will Maintain,* 1910; *Mr. Washington,* 1915; *Crimes Of Old London,* 1919; *Stinging Nettles,* 1923; *Dark Rosaleen,* 1932; *The Man With the Scales,* 1954.

■ *Holland,* 1928; *Mary Queen of Scots,* 1934; *Crowns and Sceptres,* 1937; *Ethics In Modern Art,* 1939; *The Church and Social Progress; An Exposition of Rationalism and Reaction,* 1945; *The Life of John Knox,* 1949.

as Margaret Campbell

autobiography—see above

as Senora Costanza

title by marriage 1912-1917

as Robert Paye

The Devil's Jig. London: J. Lane, 406pp.

Julia Roseling Rave. London: E. Benn, 1933, 223pp.

as George R(unnell) Preedy

The Courtly Charleton. London: Jenkins, 1931, 207pp.

Dr. Chaos, and The Devil Snar'd. London: Cassell, 1933, 280pp. *2 short novels*

□ *General Crack,* 1928; *Violante,* 1932; *Black Man - White Maiden,* 1942.

■ *Child of Checker'd Fortune,* 1939.

as Joseph Shearing

The Fetch. London: Hutchinson, 1942, 184pp.

The Spectral Bride. NY: Smith & Durrell, 1942, 314pp.

□ *Lucile Clery: A Woman of Intrigue,* 1932; *Moss Rose,* 1934; *The Golden Violet,* 1936; *Aunt Beardie,* 1940; *Mignonette,* 1949.

■ *The Angel of the Assassination,* 1935.

✔ **Margaret Vere**

● **John Winch**

LONGUEVILLE, PETER (fl. *c.*1727)

● **as Edward Dorrington**

The Hermit: or, the Unparalleled Sufferings and Surprising

Adventures of Mr. Philip Quarll, an Englishman. Westminster: T. Warner, 1727, 264pp., front. [is ascribed by some authorities to Alexander Bicknell (-1796)]

LOOMIS, NOEL (Miller) (1905-   ) *U.S.*

Born: Wakita, Oklahoma

as Noel Loomis

City of Glass. *Startling Stories,* July 1942

City of Glass. NY: Columbia, 1955, 128pp., paper.

□ *Murder Goes to Press,* 1937; *Rim of the Caprock,* 1952; *West to the Sun,* 1955; *A Time for Violence,* 1960; *Have Gun, Will Travel,* 1960.

■ *The Texan-Santa Fe Pioneers,* 1958; *Wells Fargo,* 1968.

as Benjamin Miller

Date Line. *Thrilling Wonder Stories,* Oct 1948

as Frank Miller

□ *Tejas Country,* 1953

as Silas Water

The Man With Absolute Motion. London: Rich, Cowan, 1955, 206pp.

LOVECRAFT, H(oward) P(hillips) (1890-1937) *U.S.*

Born: Providence, Rhode Island

Bibliography: *The Revised H.P. Lovecraft Bibliography,* by Mark Owings and Jack L. Chalker. Baltimore: 1973. (1500 cop)

Biography: *Autobiography of A Nonentity.* London: Villers Press, 1963 (500 cop); *Lovecraft, A Biography,* by L. Sprague de Camp. NY: 1977.

as Laurence Appleton

Hylas and Myrrah. *The Tryout,* May 1919. *verse*

as Isaac Bickerstaffe, Jr.

articles in *The Providence Evening News,* c.1914-1918.

as John T. Dunne

Lines On Graduation From Rhode Island Hospital School of Nurses. *The Tryout,* Feb 1917 *verse*

● **as Houdini**

Imprisoned With the Pharaohs. *Weird Tales,* May-June 1924

as John J. Jones

The Dead Bookworm. *The United Amateur,* Spring 1919. *verse*

as Humphrey Littlewit

in *United Amateur* publications

as H(oward) P(hillips) Lovecraft

The Alchemist. *The United Amateur,* Nov 1916

Grewsome Tales. (the Story of Herbert West Reanimator). *Home Brew,* Feb 1922 - July 1922 [6 parts]

Dagon. *The Vagrant,* Nov 1919 [*Weird Tales,* Oct 1923]

The Colour Out of Space. *Amazing,* Sept 1927

The Shunned House. Athol, Massachusetts: Recluse Press, 1928, 58pp. (preface by Frank Belknap Long)

The Shadow Over Innsmouth. Everett, Pennsylvania: Visionary Press, 1936, 158pp., ill.

The Notes & Commonplace Book Employed by the Late H. P. Lovecraft. Lakewood, California: Futile Press, 1938, 45pp. (75 cop)

The Outsider & Others. Sauk City, Wisconsin: Arkham House, 1939, 553pp. (1268 cop) *ss col*

Beyond The Wall of Sleep. Sauk City, Wisconsin: Arkham House, 1943, 458pp. (1217 cop) *ss col & poems*

Marginalia. Sauk City, Wisconsin: Arkham House, 1944, 377pp. (2035 cop) *miscellany*

The Dunwich Horror. NY: Bart House, [1945], 136pp., paper. *ss col*

Best Supernatural Stories of H. P. Lovecraft (ed. A. Derleth) Cleveland: World, 1945, 307pp. *ss col*

(with August Derleth) *The Lurker At the Threshold.* Sauk City, Wisconsin: Arkham House, 1945, 196pp. (3041 cop)

The Lurking Fear and Other Stories. NY: Avon, [1947], 223pp., paper. *ss col*

Something About Cats and Other Pieces. Sauk City,

Wisconsin: Arkham House, 1949, 306pp., ill. (2995 cop) *miscellany*

The Case of Charles Dexter Ward. London: Gollancz, 1951, 160pp.

The Haunter of the Dark. London: Gollancz, 1951, 302pp., *ss col*

The Dream Quest of Unknown Kadath. NY: Shroud, 1955, 107pp. (1490 copies in paper, 50 copies hardbound)

(with August Derleth) *The Survivor and Others.* Sauk City, Wisconsin: Arkham House, 1957, 161pp. (2096 cop) *ss col*

The Shuttered Room and Other Pieces. Sauk City, Wisconsin: Arkham House, 1959, 311pp., ill. (2527 cop) *ss col*

The Shunned House. Sauk City, Wisconsin: Arkham House, 1961, 59pp. (100 cop)

Dreams and Fancies. Sauk City, Wisconsin: Arkham House, 1962, 174pp. (2030 cop) *ss col & letters*

The Dunwich Horror and Others. Sauk City, Wisconsin: Arkham House, 1963, 431pp. *ss col*

Collected Poems. Sauk City, Wisconsin: Arkham House, 1963, 134pp., ill. (2000 cop) *poetry*

The Colour Out of Space. NY: Lancer, [1964], 222pp., paper. *ss col*

At the Mountains of Madness and Other Novels. Sauk City, Wisconsin: Arkham House, 1964, 432pp. (3000 cop) *col*

Dagon and Other Macabre Tales. Sauk City, Wisconsin: Arkham House, 1965, 413pp. *ss col*

The Dark Brotherhood. Sauk City, Wisconsin: Arkham House, 1966, 321pp., ill. *ss col*

Three Tales of Horror. Sauk City, Wisconsin: Arkham House, 1967, 134pp., ill. *col*

The Horror In the Museum and Other Revisions. Sauk City, Wisconsin: Arkham House, 1970, 383pp. [collection of pieces extensively revised & rewritten by Lovecraft for other authors]

■ *Supernatural Horror In Literature,* 1945; *Selected Letters,* 1965.

as Archibald Maynwaring [sic: Mainwaring]
The Pensive Swain. *The Tryout,* Oct 1919 *verse*

as H(enry) Paget-Lowe
(with Anna Helen Crofts) Poetry and the Gods. *The United Amateur,* Sept 1920 *verse*
On A Grecian Colonade In A Park. *The Tryout,* Sept 1920 *verse*

as Ward Phillips
Ex Oblivione. *The United Amateur,* March 1921

as Richard Raleigh
probably used in *The United Amateur*

as Ames Dor(r)ance Rowley
Laeta—A Lament. *The Tryout,* Feb 1918 *verse*

as (Theobaldus) Senectissimus, Esq.
Damon—A Monody. *The United Amateur,* May 1919 *verse*

as Edward Softly
Christmas. *The Tryout,* Nov 1920 *verse*
Chloris and Damon. *The Tryout,* June 1923 *verse*

as Augustus T. Swift
Letters to *Argosy* c.1919-1920 e.g. May 22, 1920 issue.

as Theobald
Ye Ballade of Patrick von Flynn. *The Conservative,* April 1916
The Poet's Rash Excuse. *The Tryout,* July 1920 *verse*

as L(ewis) Theobald, (Jr.)
Inspiration. *The Conservative,* Oct 1916 *verse*
Trip of Theobald. *The Tryout,* Sept 1927 *non fiction*
The Convention. *The Tryout,* July 1930 *non fiction*

as Theobaldus
probably used in amateur publications

as Albert Frederic Willie
Nathicana. *The Vagrant,* Spring 1927 *verse*

as Zoilus

The Vivisector. *The Wolverine,* June 1921

LOWNDES, ROBERT AUGUSTINE WARD (1916-   ) *U.S.*
Born: Bridgeport, Connecticut
as Arthur Cooke [in collaboration with E. Balter, C. Kornbluth, J. Michel, and D. A. Wollheim]
The Psychological Regulator. *Comet Stories,* March 1941
as S. D. Gottesman [in collaboration with Frederik Pohl and Cyril Kornbluth]
The Castle On Outerplanet. *Stirring Science Stories,* Apr 1941
The Extrapolated Dimwit. *Future,* Oct 1942
as Carol Grey
Passage to Sharanee. *Future Fiction,* April 1942
as Mallory Kent
Quarry. *Future,* Dec 1941
as Paul Dennis Lavond [house pseudonym]
The Doll Master. *Stirring Science Stories,* April 1941
as Paul Dennis Lavond [house pseudonym] [in collaboration with C. Kornbluth and F. Pohl]
Exiles of New Planet. *Astonishing,* April 1941
Einstein's Planetoid. *Science Fiction Quarterly,* Spring 1942
as Paul Dennis Lavond [house pseudonym] [in collaboration with F. Pohl and J. H. Dockweiler]
Something From Beyond. *Future,* Dec 1941
as Robert (A.) (W.) Lowndes
The Outpost at Altark. *Super Science Stories,* Nov 1940
The Mystery of the Third Mine. Philadelphia: Winston, [1953], 201pp. *juv*
(with James Blish) *The Duplicated Man.* NY: Avalon, [1959], 222pp.
Believer's World. NY: Avalon, [1961], 224pp.
The Puzzle Planet. NY: Ace, [1961], 119pp., paper. (Ace Double D 119)
■ Two Pamphlets Distributed at the 1st World Science Fiction Convention (NYCON 1) in 1939: *An Amazing Story,* 1939; *Dead End, 1938,* 1939. *Three Faces of Science Fiction,* 1973 (A Boskone Book, 500 cop)
as John MacDougal [in collaboration with James Blish]
Chaos, Co-ordinated. *Astounding,* Oct 1946
as Wilfred Owen Morley
A Matter of Philosophy, Sept 1941
as Richard Morrison
The Deliverers. *Science Fiction Quarterly,* Winter 1942
as Robert Morrison
Dead On Arrival. *Amazing,* Aug 1948
as Michael Sherman
Intervention. *Science Fiction Quarterly,* Feb 1952
as Peter Michael Sherman
The Troubador. *Future,* Sept 1951
as Lawrence Woods [in collaboration with Donald A. Wollheim]
Black Flames. *Stirring Science Stories,* April 1941

LUMLEY, B(enjamin) (1812-1875)
as Hermes
Another World; or, Fragments from the Star City of Montalluyah. London: Samuel Tinsley, 1873, 306pp.
as Benjamin Lumley
■ *Reminiscences Of the Opera,* 1864.
anonymous
Sirenia; or, Recollections of a Past Experience. London: Bentley, 1862, 388pp.

LUNN, HUGH (Kingsmill) (1889-1949) *British*
as Hugh Kingsmill
The Dawn's Delay. London: E. Mathews, [1924], 203pp.
The Return of William Shakespeare. London: Duckworth, 1929, 254pp.
The Return of William Shakespeare. Indianapolis: Bobbs-Merrill, [1929], 332pp.
(with Malcolm Muggeridge) *Brave Old World.* London: Eyre & Spottiswoode, 1936, 187pp., ill.

(with Malcolm Muggeridge) *1938—A Preview of Next Year's News*. London: Eyre & Spottiswoode, 1937, 160pp., paper. ill.
□ *The Fall*, 1940.
■ *Matthew Arnold*, 1928; *An Anthology of Invective and Abuse*, 1929; *After Puritanism: 1850-1900*, 1929; *Frank Harris*, 1932; *D. H. Lawrence*, 1938; *Johnson Without Boswell*, 1940; *The Progress of A Biographer*, 1949.
as Hugh Lunn
□ *The Will To Love*, 1919.

LYNCH, JANE GASKELL (1941-   ) *British*
Born: Grange-over-Sands, Lancashire
as Jane Gaskell
Strange Evil. London: Hutchinson, [1957], 255pp.
The King's Daughter. London: Hutchinson, [1958], 279pp.
The Serpent. London: Hodder & Stoughton, [1963], 445pp.
Atlan. London: Hodder & Stoughton, [1965], 286pp.
The City. London: Hodder & Stoughton, [1966], 190pp.
□ *Attic Summer*, 1963; *The Shiny Narrow Grin*, 1964; *The Fabulous Heroine*, 1965; *All Neat In Black Stockings*, 1966; *A Sweet Sweet Summer*, 1969.

LYNDS, DENNIS (1924-   )
as William Arden
□ MYSTERY: *Mystery of the Moaning Cave*, 1968; *A Dark Power*, 1968; *Deadly Legacy*, 1973.
as Michael Collins
Lukan War. NY: Belmont, [1969], 157pp., paper.
The Planets of Death. NY: Berkley, [1970], 159pp., paper.
□ MYSTERY: *Act of Fear*, 1967; *The Brass Rainbow*, 1969; *Night of the Toads*, 1970; *Walk A Black Wind*, 1971; *The Silent Scream*, 1973; *The Blood-Red Dream*, 1976.
as John Crowe
□ MYSTERY: *Another Way To Die*, 1972; *A Touch of Darkness*, 1972; *Bloodwater*, 1974; *Crooked Shadows*, 1975; *When They Kill Your Wife*, 1975.

LYTTON, EDWARD GEORGE EARLE LYTTON BULWER-
(1st Baron Lytton of Knebworth) *ne* Bulwer (1803-1873) *English*
Born: London
as Author of "Night and Morning"
Zanoni. London: Saunders & Otley, 1842, 3 vol.
as Author of "Pelham," "Rienzi," "The Student," etc.
Alice, or the Mysteries. London: Saunders & Otley, 1838, 3 vol.
as Author of "Rienzi," "Eugene Aram," &c., &c.
Night and Morning. London: Saunders & Otley, 1841, 3 vol.
as (Edward) (G.) (Bulwer-) (Lytton) (Lord Lytton)
A Strange Story. Leipzig: Tauchnitz, 1861, 2 vol.
□ *Falkland*, 1827; *The Last Days of Pompeii*, 1834; *Rienzi*, 1835; *The Last of the Barons*, 1843; *Harold*, 1843; *The Caxons*, 1849: MYSTERY: *Pelham*, 1828; *Eugene Aram*, 1832. PLAYS: *The Lady of Lyons*, 1838; *Richelieu*, 1839; *Money*, 1840. POETRY: *The New Timons*, 1846.
as Pisistratus Caxton
The Boatman. Edinburgh: 1864, 16pp.
□ *My Novel*, [c.1852]; *What Will He Do With It, A Novel*, 1859.
anonymous
Godolphin. London: Bentley, 1833, 3 vol.
The Coming Race. Edinburgh: Blackwood, 1871, 292pp.

LYTTON, EDWARD ROBERT BULWER (1st Earl of Lytton) (1831-1891) *English*
Born: London
as Edward Bulwer-Lytton (Lord Lytton)
The Ring of Amasis. From the Papers of A German Physician. NY: Harper, 1863, 301pp.

King Poppy, A Fantasia. London: Longmans, 1892, 306pp., ill.
as Robert Lytton
□ *Julian Fane, A Memoir*, 1872.
as Owen Meredith
The Ring of Amasis. From the Papers of A German Physician, 1863. London: Chapman, Hall, 1863, 3 vol.
□ *Lucile, a novel in verse*, 1860.

MCCLARY, THOMAS CALVERT
as Thomas Calvert McClary
  Rebirth. Astounding, Feb 1934
  Rebirth. When Everyone Forgot. NY: Bart House, [1944], 187pp., paper.
  Three Thousand Years. Reading, Pennsylvania: Fantasy Press, 1954, 224pp.
as Calvin Peregory
  Short-Wave Castle. Astounding, Feb 1934

MCCLELLAND, M(ary) G(reenway) (1853-1895) *U.S.*
Born: Norwood, Virginia
as M.G. McClelland
  Madame Silva and the Ghost of Dred Power. NY: Cassell, [1888], 320pp.
  □ *Oblivion,* 1885; *Princess,* 1886; *Jean Monteith,* 1887; *Burkett's Lock,* 1888; *A Nameless Novel,* 1890; *Mammy Mystic,* 1895; *Sam,* 1906.

MCCOMAS, J(esse) FRANCIS (1910-) *U.S.*
as J. Francis McComas
  (ed. with Raymond J. Healy) *Adventures In Time and Space.* NY: Random House, [1946], 997pp.
  editor of *Magazine of Fantasy and Science Fiction,* 1949-1954
  (ed.) *Special Wonder.* NY: Random House, 1970, 410pp.
as Webb Marlowe
  Flight Into Darkness. Astounding, Feb 1943

MCCOY, JOHN
as Lord Commissioner
  A Prophetic Romance: Mars to Earth. Boston: Arena Publishing Co., 1896, 283pp.
as John McCoy
  ■ *Flowers for Mother's Grave,* 1883; *Consumption or Pulmonary Tuberculosis,* 1900.

MCCUTCHEON, GEORGE BARR (1866-1928) *U.S.*
Born: nr. Lafayette, Indiana
as Richard Greaves
  □ *Brewster's Millions,* 1903.
as George Barr McCutcheon
  Graustark. Chicago: Stone, 1901, 459pp.
  Beverly of Graustark. NY: Dodd, Mead, 1904, 357pp.
  Truxton King. NY: Dodd, Mead, 1909, 369pp.
  The Prince of Graustark. NY: Dodd, Mead, 1914, 394pp.
  The Inn of the Hawk and the Raven. NY: Dodd, Mead, 1920.
  West Wind Drift. NY: Dodd, Mead, 1920, 368pp.
  East of the Setting Sun. NY: Dodd, Mead, 1924, 350pp.
  □ *Nedra,* 1905; *The Flyers,* 1907; *Sherry,* 1919; *Blades,* 1928; *The Merrivales,* 1929.
  ■ *Books Once Were Men,* 1931.

MCDANIEL, DAVID (1939-) *U.S.*
Born: Toledo, Ohio
as David McDaniel
  The Dagger Affair. NY: Ace, [1965], 159pp.
  The Arsenal Out of Time. NY: Ace, [1967], 156pp., paper.
✔ Ted Johnstone

MCDERMOTT, PAUL
as Dennis McDermott [in collaboration with Walter L. Dennis and P. Schuyler Miller]
  The Duel on the Asteroid. Wonder Stories, Jan 1932

MCDONALD, EDWARD RICHARD (1873-)
as Raymond McDonald [in collaboration with Raymond A. Leger]
  The Mad Scientist; A Tale of the Future. NY: Cochrane, 1908, 242pp., ill. (with which is incorporated a secret cipher for the best solution of which the publishers offer $1000.00)

MACDONALD, JOHN D(ann) (1916-) *U.S.*
Born: Sharon, Pennsylvania
as John Wade Farrell
  All Our Yesterdays. Super Science Stories, April 1949
as John D. MacDonald
  Cosmetics. Astounding, Feb 1948
  Wine of the Dreamers. NY: Greenberg, [1951], 219pp.
  Ballroom of the Skies. NY: Greenberg, 1952, 206pp.
  The Girl, the Gold Watch, and Everything. Greenwich, Connecticut: Fawcett Gold Medal, [1962], 207pp., paper.
  □ MYSTERY: *The Brass Cupcake,* 1950; *Dead Low Tide,* 1953; *A Bullet For Cinderella,* 1955; *The Executioners,* 1958; *The Drowner,* 1963; *A Purple Place For Dying,* 1964; *Condominium,* 1977.
  ■ *The House Guests,* 1965 (legends & stories about his cats; some autobiographical material).
as Peter Reed
  Delusion Drive. Super Science Stories, April 1949
✔ John Lane [house pseudonym], Scott O'Hara.

MACDONALD, PHILIP (1896-) *naturalized U.S.*
Born: Great Britain
as Oliver Fleming [in collaboration with Ronald MacDonald]
  □ MYSTERY: *Ambrotox and Limping Duck,* 1920; *The Spandau Quid,* 1923.
as Anthony Lawless
  □ MYSTERY: *Harbour,* 1932 (U.S.); *Moon Fisher,* 1932 (U.S.).
as Philip MacDonald
  Private—Keep Out. Magazine of Fantasy and Science Fiction, Fall 1949.
  □ MYSTERY: *The Rasp,* 1924; *Persons Unknown,* 1931; *The Crime Conductor,* 1931; *Harbour,* 1931 (Br.); *Moon Fisher,* 1931 (Br.).
as Martin Porlock
  □ MYSTERY: *Mystery At Friar's Pardon,* 1931 (Br.); *Mystery In Kensington Gore,* 1932 (Br.); *X vs. Rex,* 1933.

MACDONELL, ARCHIBALD GORDON (1895-1941) *Scottish*
as John Cameron
  □ MYSTERY: *Body Found Stabbed,* 1932.
as Neil Gordon
  The Professor's Poison. NY: Harcourt, Brace, 1928, 280pp.
  □ MYSTERY: *Murder In Earl's Court,* 1931; *The Shakespeare Murders,* 1933.
as A(rchibald) G(ordon) Macdonell
  □ *England, Their England,* 1933; *Autobiography of a Cad,* 1938; *The Spanish Pistol,* 1939.
  ■ *Napoleon and His Marshals,* 1934; *My Scotland,* 1937.

MCGAUGHY, DUDLEY DEAN *U.S.*
Born: Rialto, California
as Dudley Dean
  □ *The Man from Riondo,* 1954; *The Broken Spur,* 1955.
as Dean Owen
  The Brides of Dracula. NY: Monarch, 1960, paper.

End of the World. NY: Ace, [1962], 127pp., paper.
Konga.
Reptilicus.
□ *Guns to the Sunset,* 1948; *Rifle Pass,* 1954; *The Sam Houston,* 1961; *Lone Star Round Up,* 1972.

MCGIVERN, WILLIAM P(eter) (c.1924-   ) *U.S.*
Born: Chicago, Illinois
as Alexander Blade [house pseudonym]
stories unknown
as William P. McGivern
(with David Wright O'Brien) John Brown's Body. *Amazing,* May 1940
The Visible Invisible Man. *Amazing,* Dec 1940
□ MYSTERY: *But Death Runs Faster,* 1945; *The Crooked Frame,* 1952; *The Big Heat,* 1952; *Margin of Terror,* 1953; *Rogue Cop,* 1954; *Night Extra,* 1957; *Caprifoil,* 1972; *Night of the Juggler,* 1975. SCREENPLAYS: *The Wrecking Crew,* 1968; *Brannigan,* 1975.
■ (with Maureen Daly McGivern) *Mention My Name In Mombasa,* 1958.
as Bill Peters
□ MYSTERY: *Blondes Die Young,* 1952.

MACGREGOR, JAMES MURDOCH (1925-   ) *Scottish*
Born: Paisley
as Gregory Francis [in collaboration with Frank Parnell]
Question Mark. *New Worlds,* Winter 1951 (Br.)
as James (M.) MacGregor
The Broken Record. *New Worlds #17,* Sept 1952 (Br.)
□ *A Cry to Heaven,* 1960; *Incident Over the Pacific,* 1960.
as J. T. MacIntosh [also J. T. M'Intosh, J. T. McIntosh]
The Curfew Tolls. *Astounding,* Dec 1950
Safety Margin. *Planet Stories,* Jan 1951
Outpost Zero. *Super Science Stories,* Aug 1951
World Out Of Mind. Garden City: Doubleday, 1953, 222pp.
Born Leader. Garden City: Doubleday, 1954, 221pp.
One In 300. Garden City: Doubleday, 1954, 223pp.
The Fittest. Garden City: Doubleday, 1955, 192pp.
200 Years to Christmas. NY: Ace, [1961], 81pp., paper. (Ace Double F 113)
The Million Cities. NY: Pyramid, [1963], 141pp., paper.
The Noman Way. London: Digit, 1964, 158pp., paper.
Out of Chaos. London: Digit, 1964, 159pp., paper.
Time For A Change. London: M. Joseph, 1967, 183pp.
Six Gates From Limbo. London: M. Joseph, 1968, 174pp.
Snow White And The Giants. NY: Avon, [1968], 159pp., paper.
Transmigration. NY: Avon, [c.1970], 176pp., paper. (1st U.S.)
Flight From Rebirth. NY: Avon, [1971], 160pp., paper.
□ *Take A Pair of Private Eyes,* 1968; *A Coat of Blackmail,* 1971.

MCHARGUE, GEORGESS *U.S.*
Born: Norwalk, Connecticut
as Alice Chase
probably juveniles
as Georgess McHargue
The Baker and the Basilisk. Indianapolis: Bobbs-Merrill, 1970, 31pp., ill. *juv*
The Wonderful Wings of Harold Harrabescu. NY: Delacorte, 1971, 25pp., ill. *juv*
Elidor and the Golden Ball. NY: Dodd, Mead, [1973], 61pp., ill. *juv*
The Mermaid and the Whale. NY: Holt, 1973, 40pp. *juv*
Stoneflight. NY: Viking, 1975, 223pp., ill. *juv*
■ *The Beasts of Never, A History, Natural and Unnatural, of Monsters Mythical and Magical.* Indianapolis: Bobbs-Merrill, 1968, 112pp., ill. (juv); *Facts, Frauds, & Phantasms,* 1972; *The Impossible People,* 1972.

● Margo Seesee Usher

MACHEN, ARTHUR (1863-1947) *British*
Autobiography: *The Autobiography of Arthur Machen.* London: Richards, 1951, 307pp.
Bibliography: *Adrian Goldstone & Wesley Sweetser, A Bibliography of Arthur Machen.* Austin: U. of Texas, [1965], 180pp.
as Arthur Machen
The Great God Pan, and The Inmost Light. London: J. Lane, 1894, 186pp. [Boston: Roberts Brothers, 1894, 234pp.]
The Three Impostors. London: J. Lane, 1895, 290pp. *ss col* [Boston: Roberts Brothers, 1895, 215pp.]
The House of Souls. London: Grant Richards, 1906, 513pp. *ss col*
The Hill of Dreams. London: Grant Richards, 1907, 309pp., front.
The Angels of Mons, the Bowmen, and Other Legends of the War. London: Simpkin, Marshall, 1915, 86pp. *ss col*
The Great Return. London: Faith Press, 1915, 79pp.
The Terror; A Mystery. London: Duckworth, [1917], 190pp.
The Secret Glory. London: Secker, 1922, 309pp.
Strange Roads. London: Classic Press, [1923], 54pp., ill.
The Shining Pyramid. Chicago: Covici-McGee, 1923, 241pp. (875 cop) *ss col*
Ornaments In Jade. NY: Knopf, 1924, 46pp.
The Glorious Mystery. Chicago: Covici-McGee, 1924, 219pp. *essays & ss col*
The Green Round. London: E. Benn, 1933, 218pp.
The Children of the Pool and Other Stories. London: Hutchinson, [1936], 255pp. *ss col*
The Cosy Room. London: Rich & Cowan, 1936, 267pp. *ss col*
The Green Round. Sauk City, Wisconsin: Arkham House, 1968, 218pp. (2058 cop)
■ *Hieroglyphics,* 1902; *Far Off Things,* 1922; *Dog and Duck,* 1924; *The London Adventure,* 1924; *Dreads and Drolls,* 1926.
as Gervase Perrot
The Chronicle of Clemendy; or, the History of IX Joyous Journeys, (trans. by Arthur Machen). London: Society of Pantagruelists, 1888, 314pp., ill.
as Leolinus Siluriensis
■ *The Anatomy of Tobacco*

MCHENRY, JAMES (1785-1845) *naturalized U.S.*
Born: Larne, County Antrim, Ireland
as Author of "The Wilderness"
The Spectre of the Forest; or, Annals of the Housatonic. NY: E. Bliss, 1823, 2 vol.
as James M'Henry
□ *The Antediluvians, or, the World Destroyed,* 1839; *O'Halloran, or, The Insurgent: A Romance of the Irish Rebellion,* 1841.
as Solomon Secondsight
The Wilderness; or, The Youthful Days of Washington. A Tale of the West. London: A. K. Newman, 1823, 3 vol.
A Spectre of the Forest; or, Annals of the Housatonic, A New England Romance. London: A. K. Newman, 1824, 3 vol.

MCILVAINE, CHARLES (1840-1909) *U.S.*
Born: Chester County, Pennsylvania
as Toby Hodge
A Legend of Polecat Hollow. London: Ward, Lock, 1884, 69pp.
as Charles McIlvaine
■ *Toadstools, Mushrooms, Fungi, edible and Poisonous. One Thousand American Fungi,* 1900; *Indoors, Outdoors, Up the Chimney,* 1906 (juv).

MCILWAIN, D(avid)   *(ne* McIlwaine)   (1921-   )
as Charles Eric Maine
   Repulsion Factor. *Authentic #37,* Sept 1953 (Br.)
   Spaceways. London: Hodder & Stoughton, 1953, 191pp.
   Timeliner. London: Hodder & Stoughton, 1955, 192pp.
   Crisis 2000. London: Hodder & Stoughton, [1955], 191pp.
   Escapement. London: Hodder & Stoughton, [1956], 224pp.
   The Isotope Man. London: Hodder & Stoughton, [1957], 189pp.
   High Vacuum. London: Hodder & Stoughton, [1957], 192pp.
   The Tide Went Out. London: Hodder & Stoughton, [1958], 190pp.
   World Without Men. NY: Ace, [1958], 190pp., paper. (Ace Double D 274)
   Count Down. London: Hodder & Stoughton, [1959], 191pp.
   Subterfuge. London: Hodder & Stoughton, [1959], 192pp.
   Calculated Risk. London: Hodder & Stoughton, [1960], 191pp.
   He Owned the World. NY: Avalon, 1960, 224pp.
   The Mind of Mr. Soames. London: Hodder & Stoughton, [1961], 252pp.
   The Darkest of Nights. London: Hodder & Stoughton, [1962], 254pp.
   Never Let Up. London: Hodder & Stoughton, [1964], 191pp.
   B.E.A.S.T. London: Hodder & Stoughton, 1966, 190pp.
as C. E. Maine
   ■ *The World's Strangest Crimes,* 1967.
as Richard Rayner
   □ MYSTERY: *The Trouble With Ruth,* 1960; *Darling Daughter,* 1961; *Stand-In for Danger,* 1963; *Dig Deep for Julie,* 1963.
   ✔ Robert Wade.

MCINTOSH, KENNETH
as Kent Casey
   Flareback. *Astounding,* March 1938

MCINTOSH, KINN HAMILTON   (1930-   )   *British*
   Born: Huddersfield, West Riding, Yorkshire
as Catherine Aird
   □ MYSTERY: *The Religious Body,* 1966; *Henrietta Who?,* 1968; *A Late Phoenix,* 1970; *His Burial Top,* 1973; *Slight Mourning,* 1975.

MCKAY, LEWIS H(ugh)   (1897-   )
as Hugh Matheson
   The Third Force. London: A. Wingate, [1959], 248pp.
   The Balance of Fear. London: Gibbs & Phillips, 1961, 224pp.
   □ *Puritan's Progress,* 1943; *The Expanding Universe and Other Poems,* 1963 (poetry).

MACKAY, MARY   (1855-1924)   *British*
   Born: London
   Biography: *Marie Corelli. The Woman and the Legend,* by Eileen Bigland
as Marie Corelli
   A Romance of Two Worlds. London: Bentley, 1886, 2 vol.
   Vendetta! or, The Story of One Forgotten. London: Bentley, 1886, 2 vol.
   Ardath, The Story of A Dead Self. London: Bentley, 1889, 3 vol.
   The Soul of Lilith. London: Bentley, 1892, 3 vol.
   Barabbas, A Dream of the World's Tragedy. London: Methuen, 1893, 3 vol.
   The Sorrows of Satan; or, the Strange Experience of One Geoffrey Tempest, Millionaire. London: Methuen, 1895, 487pp., front.
   Cameos. London: Hutchinson, [1896], 359pp., front.

   The Distant Voice. A Fact or A Fancy? Philadelphia: Lippincott, 1896, 14pp.
   Ziska, The Problem of A Wicked Soul. Bristol: Arrowsmith, London: Simpkin, Marshall, 1897, 364pp.
   The Song of Miriam and Other Stories. NY: Munro, 1898, 193pp. *ss col*
   Angel's Wickedness; A True Story. NY: W. R. Beers, 1900, 54pp.
   The Master Christian; A Question of Time. London: Methuen, 1900, 632pp.
   A Christmas Greeting of Various Thoughts, Verses and Fancies. London: Methuen, 1901, 133pp.
   The Strange Visitation of Josiah McNason; A Ghost Story. London: Newnes, [1904], 203pp., ill.
   The Devil's Motor; A Fantasy. London: Hodder & Stoughton, [1910], 45pp., ill.
   Life Everlasting; A Reality of Romance. London: Hodder & Stoughton, [1911], 436pp.
   The Young Diana; An Experiment of the Future. London: Hutchinson, 1918, 320pp.
   The Love of Long Ago and Other Stories. London: Methuen, [1920], 271pp. *ss col*
   The Secret Power; A Romance of the Time. London: Methuen, [1921], 332pp., front.
   □ *Wormwood,* 1890; *Poems,* 1925 (poetry).

MCKENNA, RICHARD M(ilton)
as R. M. McKenna
   Casey Agonistes. *Magazine of Fantasy and Science Fiction,* Sept 1958
as Richard McKenna
   Casey Agonistes and Other Science Fiction & Fantasy Stories. NY: Harper, [1973], 150pp.
   □ *The Sand Pebbles,* 1962.

MACKINTOSH, ELIZABETH   (1896-1952)
as Gordon Daviot
   □ *The Man In the Queue,* 1929; *Kif: An Unvarnished History,* 1929; *The Expensive Halo,* 1931; *Claverhouse,* 1937; *The Privateer,* 1952. PLAYS: *Richard of Bordeaux,* 1933; *Queen of Scots,* 1934; *The Laughing Woman,* 1934; *Leith Sands, and Other Short Plays,* 1946.
as Josephine Tey
   □ MYSTERY: *Miss Pym Disposes,* 1947; *The Franchise Affair,* 1948; *Brat Ferrar,* 1949; *To Love and Be Wise,* 1950; *The Daughter of Time,* 1951; *The Singing Sands,* 1952; *A Shilling For Candles,* 1953.

MACLEAN, ALISTAIR STUART   (1922-   )   *British*
as Alistair MacLean
   The Guns of Navarone. Garden City: Doubleday, 1957, 320pp.
   Ice Station Zebra. Garden City: Doubleday, 1963, 276pp.
   Where Eagles Dare. Garden City: Doubleday, 1967, 312pp.
   □ *H. M. S. Ulysses,* 1955; *The Golden Rendezvous,* 1962; *When 8 Bells Toll,* 1966; *Bear Island,* 1971; *Circus,* 1975; *Seawitch,* 1977.
   ■ *Lawrence of Arabia,* 1962; *Captain Cook,* 1972.
as Ian Stuart
   The Satan Bug. NY: Scribner, 1962, 256pp.
   □ *The Black Shrike,* 1961.

MCNEILE, H(erman) C(yril)   (1888-1937)   *English*
as H. C. McNeile
   □ *A Native Superstition,* 1925; *An Act of Providence,* 1927; *The Haunted Rectory,* 1931.
as Sapper
   The Island of Terror. Toronto: Musson Book Co., 1931, 320pp.
   □ MYSTERY: *Bulldog Drummond,* 1920; *The Black Gang,* 1922; *The Female of the Species,* 1928; *When Carruthers Laughed,* 1934.

MCNEILLIE, JOHN
Autobiography: *Around My House*, by Ian Niall, London: Heinemann, 1973, 148pp., ill.
as John McNeillie
☐ *Glasgow Keelie*, 1940.
as Ian Niall
The Boy Who Saw Tomorrow. London: Heinemann, 1952, 259pp.
☐ *No Resting Place*, 1948; *Fox Hollow*, 1949; *The Deluge*, 1951; *A Tiger Walks*, 1960.
■ *The Poacher's Handbook*, 1950; *Fresh Woods*, 1951; *Pastures Now*, 1952; *Trout From The Hills*, 1962; *Country Blacksmith*, 1966.

MCNEILLY, WILFRED (1921-   ) *British*
Born: Scotland
as Martin Gregg
☐ *Dark Amazon*, 1957.
as Errol Lecale
Tigerman of Terrahpur, 1973.
Castledoom, 1974.
The Severed Hand, 1974.
The Death Box, 1974.
Zombie, 1975.
Blood of My Blood, 1975.
as Wilfred McNeilly
☐ *The Break Out*, 1965; *Death In the Top Twenty*, 1965; *No Way Out*, 1968.
as Peter Saxon
The Darkest Night, 1966.
The Torturer. London: Mayflower, 1966, 158pp.
The Disoriented Man. London: Mayflower, 1966, 126pp.
The Killing Bone, 1968.
Through the Dark Curtain. London: H. Baker, [1968], 190pp.
Dark Ways To Death. London: H. Baker, 1968, 175pp.
Black Honey, 1968.
The Haunting of Alan Mars, 1969.
The Vampires of Finisterre, 1970.
☐ *Satan's Child*, 1967; *Corruption*, 1968; *The Enemy Sky*, 1969.
✔ Joe Hunter, Desmond Reid [house pseudonym]
● W. A. Ballinger

MACNIE, J(ohn) (1836-1909)
as Ismar Thiusen
The Diothas; or, A Far Look Ahead. NY: Putnam, 1883, 358pp.

MALLESON, LUCY BEATRICE (1899-1973) *English*
Autobiographical: *Three-a-Penny*, by Anne Meredith. London: Faber, [1940], 296pp.
as Anthony Gilbert
☐ MYSTERY: *The Tragedy At Freyne*, 1927; *The Body On the Beam*, 1932; *Murder by Experts*, 1936; *A Spy for Mr. Crook*, 1944; *Murder Comes Home*, 1950; *And Death Came Too*, 1956; *Out For the Kill*, 1960; *The Visitor*, 1967; *A Nice Little Killing*, 1973.
as J. Kilmeny Keith
☐ *The Sword of Harlequin*, 1927.
as Anne Meredith
☐ *The Coward*, 1934; *The Gambler*, 1937; *The Family Man*, 1942; *The Sisters*, 1948; *A Fig For Virtue*, 1951.

MALLOWAN, AGATHA (Margaret Clarissa Miller) (Dame) (Mrs. Max Edgar Lucien) (1890-1976) *British*
Born: Torquay, Devon
Autobiography: *Come, Tell Me How You Live*, by Agatha Christie Mallowan. London: Collins, 1946, 102pp., ill. [revised edition: London: Collins, 1975, 192pp., ill.]
as Agatha Christie
The Last Seance. *Magazine of Fantasy and Science Fiction*, April 1951

The Mysterious Mr. Quin. London: Collins, 1930, 287pp. *ss col*
The Hound of Death & Other Stories. London: Odham's Press, [1933], 247pp. *ss col*
☐ MYSTERY: *The Mysterious Affair At Styles*, 1920; *The Murder of Roger Ackroyd*, 1926; *Murder On the Orient Express*, 1934; *The A.B.C. Murders*, 1936; *Death On the Nile*, 1937; *Appointment With Death*, 1938; *Funerals Are Fatal*, 1953; *Curtain*, 1975; *Sleeping Murder*, 1976.
as Mrs. Archibald Christie
title by marriage 1914-1928
as Mary Westmacott
☐ *Giant's Bread*, 1930; *The Burden*, 1956.

MALONEY, FRANCIS (Joseph) T(erence) *British*
as Francis T. Maloney
■ *Other Worlds In Space*, 1957; *Telescopes: How To Choose and Use Them*, 1968.
as Terry
signature on art in British science fiction magazines in 1950's, e.g. *New Worlds*.

MALZBERG, BARRY N. *U.S.*
as Barry N. Malzberg
Oracle of the Thousand Hands. NY: Olympia, [1968], 216pp.
The Falling Astronauts. NY: Ace, [1971], paper.
Overlay. NY: Lancer, [1972], 189pp., paper.
Beyond Apollo. NY: Random House, [1972], 138pp.
Revelations. NY: Warner, [1972], paper.
The Men Inside. NY: Lancer, [1973], 175pp., paper.
Phase IV. NY: Pocket Books, [1973], paper.
In the Enclosure. NY: Avon, [1973], 190pp., paper.
Herovit's World. NY: Random House, [1973], 209pp.
Guernica Night: A Science Fiction Masterpiece. Indianapolis: Bobbs-Merrill, 1974, 140pp.
Out From Ganymede. NY: Warner, [1974], paper.
On A Planet Alien. NY: Pocket Books, [1974], 144pp., paper.
The Day of the Burning. NY: Ace, [1974], paper.
Tactics of Conquest. NY: Pyramid, [1974], 172pp., paper.
The Sodom and Gomorrah Business. NY: Pocket Books, [1974], paper.
Underlay. NY: Avon, [1974], paper.
The Destruction of the Temple. NY: Pocket Books, [1974], paper.
The Gamesman. NY: Pocket Books, [1975], paper.
The Many Worlds of Barry Malzberg. NY: Popular Library, 1975, paper. *ss col*
Conversations. Indianapolis: Bobbs-Merrill, [1975], 87pp.
Galaxies. NY: Pyramid, [1975], 128pp., paper.
Down Here In the Dream Quarter. Garden City: Doubleday, 1976, 194pp.
Scop. NY: Pyramid, [1976], paper.
The Best of Barry Malzberg. NY: Pocket Books, [1976], paper.
The Last Transaction. NY: Pinnacle, [1977], paper.
as K. M. O'Donnell
The Empty People. NY: Lancer, [1969], 159pp., paper.
Final War and Other Fantasies. NY: Ace, [1969], paper. *ss col*
Dwellers of the Deep. NY: Ace, [1970], paper.
Universe Day. NY: Avon, [1971], 160pp., paper.
Gather In the Hall of the Planets. NY: Ace, [1971], paper.
In the Pocket and Other Science Fiction. NY: Ace, [1971], paper. *ss col*

MANLEY, MARY DE LA RIVIERE (Mrs. John) (c.1663-1724) *English*
Autobiographical: *Memoirs of the Life of Mrs. Manley (Author of the Atalantis) Containing Not Only the History of Her Adventures But Likewise An Account of the Most*

Considerable Amours In the Court of King Richard the IId. . . To Which Is Added A Compleat Key. 1717, 120pp. [3d edition of *Adventures of Rivella,* listed below]
as Author of "Secret Memoirs and Manners of Several Persons of Quality from the New Atalantis."
Court Intrigues In A Collection of Original Letters from the Island of the New Atalantis. London: Morphew, 1711, 220pp.
as Sir Charles Lovemore
■□ *The Adventures of Rivella; or the History of the Author of the Atalantis.* London: Printed 1714, 120pp. [autobiographical]
anonymous
Secret Memoirs and Manners of Several Persons of Quality of Both Sexes from the New Atalantis. London: Morphew, 1709, 2 vol.
The Secret History of Queen Zarah, and the Zarazians. Albigion [London]: 1705, 2 vol.

MANNING, ADELAIDE FRANCES OKE
as Manning Coles [in collaboration with Cyril Henry Coles]
   see **CYRIL H. COLES**
as Francis Gaite [in collaboration with Cyril Henry Coles]
   see **CYRIL H. COLES**

MARCHANT, ELLA
as Two Women of the West [in collaboration with Alice Ilgenfritz Jones]
   see **ALICE ILGENFRITZ JONES**

MARKS, WINSTON K(itchener)
as Winston K. Marks
   Mad Hatter. *Unknown,* May 1940
   Maniac Perverse. *Astounding,* Oct 1941
as Ken Winney
   Double Take. *Science Fiction Adventures,* Dec 1953

MARNELL, JOSEPH
as Zeno Koomoter
   Visitor From the Planet Phlox. NY: Vantage, 1964, 56pp.

MARSH, JOHN   (1907-   )   *British*
as John Elton
   The Green Plantations. London: Ward, Lock, 1955, 191pp.
as Harrington Hastings [in collaboration with Florence Shepherd]
   □ *Criminal Square,* 1929.
as John Marsh
   Body Made Alive: A Study In the Macabre. London: Stanley Smith, 1936, 232pp.
   □ *The Brain of Paul Moloff,* 1953; *The Hidden Answer,* 1956; *House of Echoes,* 1956.
✔ Julia Davis, John Harley, Irene Lawrence, Joan Marsh, Grace Richmond, Petra Sawley, Monica Ware, Lilian Woodward

MARTIN, R(eginald) A(lec)   (1900-   )
as Brett Cameron
   □ *The Guns of San Rosala,* 1953.
as Rex Dixon
   □ *Pocomoto, Pony Express Rider,* 1953; *Pete of the Wild Grass Country,* 1954; *Pocomoto and the Texas Rangers,* 1968.
as E. C. Elliott
   Kemlo and the Crazy Planet. London: Nelson, 1954.
as Robert Martin
   Beyond Pandora. *Analog,* Sept 1962
   □ *Joey and the River Pirates,* 1954; *Joey and the Mail Robbers,* 1955; *Killer Road,* 1964; *Death of A Ladies' Man,* 1969.
as Scott Martin
   □ *The Claws of the Cougar,* 1951.
✔ Rex Martin

MARTIN, THOMAS HECTOR   (1913-   )   *English*
   Born: Somerset
as Peter Saxon [this title only]
   The Curse of Rathlaw. NY: Lancer, [1968], 190pp., paper.
as Martin Thomas
   The Evil Eye. London: Fleetway, 1958, paper.
   Bred to Kill. London: Fleetway, 1960, paper.
   Assignment Doomsday. London: Fleetway, 1961, paper.
   Beyond the Spectrum. London: Digit, 1964, 157pp., paper.
   Laird of Evil. London: Mayflower, 1965, paper.
   The Mind Killers. London: Mayflower, 1965, paper.
   Such Men Are Dangerous. London: Mayflower, 1965, 139pp., paper.
   Sorcerers of Set. London: Mayflower, 1966, paper.
   The Hands of Cain. London: Mayflower, 1966, 156pp., paper.
   Brainwashed. London: Mayflower, 1968, paper.

MARTYN, EDWARD   (1859-1923)   *Irish*
as Edward Martyn
   The Tale of A Town, and, An Enchanted Sea. Kilkenny: S. O'Grady, 1902, 211pp.
   The Dream Physician. Dublin: Talbot Press, [c.1914], 87pp.
   □ PLAYS: *The Heather Field and Maeve,* 1899; *Grangecolman,* 1912.
as Sirius
   Morgante the Lesser, His Notorious Life and Wonderful Deeds. London: Swan, Sonnenschein, 1890, 329pp.
   □ PLAYS: *The Heather Field,* 1899; *The Dream Physician,* [c.1914].

MASHBURN, W. KIRK (Jr.)   (1900-1968)   *U.S.*
as Kirk Mashburn
   The Sword of Jean Lafitte. *Weird Tales,* Dec 1927
   Placide's Wife. *Weird Tales,* Nov 1931

MASON, C. P.
as C. P. Mason
   Rambling Through the Solar System. *Thrilling Wonder Stories,* Oct 1938
as Epaminondas T. Snooks
   Why the Heavens Fell. *Wonder Stories,* May 1932.

MASON, DOUGLAS R(ankine)   (1918-   )   *English*
   Born: Hawarden, Flint
as Douglas R. Mason
   From Carthage Then I Came. Garden City: Doubleday, 1966, 190pp.
   Landfall Is A State of Mind. London: Hale, 1968.
   Ring of Violence. London: Hale, 1968, 190pp.
   The Tower of Rizwan. London: Hale, 1968, 189pp.
   The Janus Syndrome. London: Hale, 1969.
   Horizon Alpha. NY: Ballantine, [1971], 168pp., paper.
   Satellite 54-Zero. NY: 1971.
   The Resurrection of Roger Diment. NY: Ballantine, [1972], 186pp., paper.
   The End Bringers. NY: Ballantine, [1973], 208pp.
   The Phaeton Condition. NY: Putnam, [1973], 192pp.
as John Rankine
   Two's Company, in *New Writings In SF 1,* edited by John Carnell. London: Dobson, 1964.
   Seventh Moon. *Impulse,* May 1966.
   The Blockage of Sinitron. London: Nelson, 1966. *ss col*
   Interstellar Two-Five. London: Dobson, 1966, 183pp.
   Never the Same Door. London: Dobson, 1968.
   One Is One. London: Dobson, 1968, 176pp.
   Moons of Triopus. London: Dobson, [1968], 176pp.
   Binary Z. London: Dobson, 1969, 190pp.
   The Weisman Experiment, London: 1969.
   Darkside.
   The Plantos Illusion.
   The Garamas Affair.

Operation Umanaq. NY: Ace, [1973], 188pp., paper.
The Bromius Phenomenon. NY: Ace, [1973], paper.
The Fingalman Conspiracy. London: Sidgwick & Jackson, 1973, 190pp.
[books below are based on *Space 1999* TV series]
Moon Odyssey. NY: Pocket Books, 1975, paper.
[London: Dobson, 1975, 144pp.]
Lunar Attack. NY: Pocket Books, 1976, paper.
Astral Quest. NY: Pocket Books, 1976, paper.
Android Planet. NY: Pocket Books, 1976, paper.
Phoenix of Megarion. NY: Pocket Books, 1976, paper.

MASON, F(rancis) VAN WYCK (c.1897-) U.S.
Born: Boston, Massachusetts
as Geoffrey Coffin [in collaboration with H. Brawner]
□ MYSTERY: *Murder In the Senate*, 1935; *The Forgotten Fleet Mystery*, 1936.
as F. V. W. Mason
Phalanxes of Atlans. Astounding, Feb 1931.
as (F.) Van Wyck Mason
□ MYSTERY: *Seeds of Murder*, 1930; *The Washington Legation Murders*, 1935; *The Bucharest Ballerina Murders*, 1940; *The Dardanelles Derelict*, 1949; *Himalayan Assignment. A Colonel North Mystery*, 1952; *Captain Judas*, 1955; *Zanzibar Intrigue*, 1965. HISTORICAL FICTION: *Silver Leopard*, 1955.
as Frank W. Mason
□ *Q Boat*, 1943; *Pilots Man Your Planes!*, 1944; *Flight Into Danger*, 1946.
as Ward Weaver
□ *Hang My Wreath*, 1941; *End of Track*, 1943.

MASON, PAMELA OSTRER (1915-) English
as Pamela Kellino
A Lady Possessed. London: R. Hale, 1943, 269pp. [pub. in U. S. as *Del Palma*, c.1948]
□ *This Little Hand*, 1941; *The Blinds Are Down*, 1944; *Ignoramus, Ignoramus*, 1946.
as (Mrs.) James Mason
title by marriage 1941-1965
as Pamela Mason
■ (with James Mason - the actor) *The Cats In Our Lives*, 1949 (Br.); compiled (with James Mason) *Favorite Cat Stories of Pamela and James Mason*, 1956; *Marriage Is the First Step Toward Divorce*, 1968; *The Female Pleasure Hunt*, 1972.

MATHESON, JOAN
as Jacob Transue
Twilight of the Basilisks. NY: Berkley, [1973], 175pp., paper.

MATHESON, RICHARD (Burton) (1926-) U.S.
Born: Allendale, New Jersey
as Richard Matheson
Born of Man and Woman. Magazine of Fantasy and Science Fiction, Summer 1950
Born of Man and Woman. Philadelphia: Chamberlain, 1954, 252pp. *ss col*
I Am Legend. Greenwich, Connecticut: Fawcett Gold Medal, [1954], 160pp., paper.
The Shrinking Man. Greenwich, Connecticut: Fawcett Gold Medal, [1956], 192pp., paper.
The Shores of Space. NY: Bantam, [1956], 184pp., paper.
A Stir of Echoes. Philadelphia: Lippincott, 1958, 220pp.
Shock! NY: Dell, [1961], 191pp., paper. *ss col*
Shock II. NY: Dell, [1964], 192pp., paper. *ss col*
Shock III. NY: Dell, [1966], 192pp., paper. *ss col*
Shock Waves. NY: Dell, [1970], 190pp., paper. *ss col*
Hell House. NY: Viking, [1971], 279pp.
Bid Time Return. NY: Viking, 1975, 278pp.
□ *Fury On Sunday*, 1954; *Ride the Nightmare*, 1959; *The Beardless Warriors*, 1960. SCREENPLAYS: *The In-credible Shrinking Man*, 1956; *The Pit and the Pendulum*, 1961; *The Raven*, 1963; *The Comedy of Terrors*, 1964; *Legend of Hell House*, 1973.
↙ **Logan Swanson**

MATURIN, CHARLES R(obert) (1782-1824) Irish
Born: Dublin
as Author of "Bertram"
Melmoth the Wanderer. Edinburgh: A. Constable, 1820, 4 vol.
The Albigenses, A Romance. London: Hurst & Robinson, 1824, 4 vol.
□ *Manuel; A Tragedy In Five Acts*, 1817 (play); *Women; or, Pour et contre*, 1818.
as Author of "Montorio", and "The Wild Irish Boy"
□ *The Milesian Chief*, 1812.
as Charles R. Maturin
□ *Bertram; or, The Castle of St. Aldobrand, A Tragedy.* London: Murray, 1816, 83pp.
■ *Five Sermons On the Errors of the Roman Catholic Church*, 1824.
as Rev. C. R. Maturin
□ *Fredolfo; A Tragedy In Five Acts*, 1819 (play).
as Dennis Jasper Murphy
Fatal Revenge; or, The Family of Montorio. London: Longman, Hurst, 1807, 3 vol.
□ *The Milesian Chief*, 1812 (U.S.).

MAXWELL, MARY ELIZABETH (Braddon) (Mrs. John) (1837-1915) British
Born: London
as Author of "Lady Audley's Secret"
Weavers and Weft and Other Tales. London: Maxwell, 1877, 3 vol. *ss col*
The Fatal Three. A Novel. London: Simpkin, Marshall, 1888, 3 vol.
Gerard; or, the World, the Flesh, and the Devil. London: Simpkin, Marshall, 1891, 3 vol.
□ *Phantom Fortune*, 1883.
as (Miss) M(ary) E. Braddon
Ralph the Bailiff and Other Tales. London: Ward, Lock, 1862, 250pp. *ss col*
The Conflict. London: Simpkin, Marshall, 1903, 398pp.
"Beyond These Voices." London: Hutchinson, 1910, 373pp.
□ *Lady Audley's Secret*, 1862; *Eleanor's Victory*, 1863; *A Strange World*, 1875; *Three Times Dead*, 1879; *The Cloven Foot*, 1879; *Wyllard's Weird*, 1885.
● **Babington White**

MEAD, (Edward) SHEPHERD (1914-) U.S.
Born: Saint Louis, Missouri
as Shepherd Mead
The Magnificent McInnes. NY: Farrar & Straus, 1949, 255pp.
Tessie, The Hound of Channel 1. Garden City: Doubleday, 1951, 251pp., ill.
The Big Ball of Wax. NY: Simon & Schuster, 1954, 246pp.
Dudley, There Is No Tomorrow! Then How About This Afternoon. NY: Simon & Schuster, 1963, 288pp.
The Carefully Considered Rape of the World. NY: Simon & Schuster, 1966, 245pp.
□ *How To Succeed In Business Without Really Trying*, 1952.

MEEK, DORIS
as Gregory Mason [in collaboration with Adrienne Jones]
see ADRIENNE JONES

MEEK, S(terner) (St.) P(aul) (1894-) U.S.
Born: Chicago, Illinois
as S. P. Meek [Captain, Major, Col.]

Futility. *Amazing*, July 1929

The Murgatroyd Experiment. *Amazing Stories Quarterly*, Winter 1929

The Monkeys Have No Tails in Zamboanga. NY: Morrow, 1935, 288pp., ill. *ss col*

Arctic Bride. London: Utopian, [1944], 36pp., paper.

The Drums of Tapajos. NY: Avalon, [1961], 224pp.

Troyana. NY: Avalon, [1962], 224pp.

□ *Frog, the Horse That Knew No Master*, 1946.

■ *So You're Going To Get A Puppy*, 1947.

● Sterner St. Paul

MEEKER, NATHAN COOK   (1817-1879)   *U.S.*
as Captain Jacob D. Armstrong
Life and Adventures of Capt. Jacob D. Armstrong. NY: Dewitt & Davenport, 1852, 72pp.
as N. C. Meeker
□ *Life In the West; or, Stories of the Mississippi Valley*, 1868 (ss col).

MEEKER, W. JOHNS
as Willy Johns
The Fabulous Journey of Hieronymous Meeker. Boston: Little, Brown, [1954], 370pp.

MEINHOLD, JOHANN WILHELM   (1797-1851)   *German*
Born: Netzelkow, Usedom Island
as Wilhelm Meinhold
Sidonia, The Sorceress. London: Sims & McIntyre, 1847, 2 vol. [Parlor Library, Vol. 29, Vol. 30]
Sidonia the Sorceress. London: Benn, 1926, 481pp. (225 copies, bound in vellum with slipcase)
as Abraham Schweidler
Maria Schweidler die Bernsteinhexe. Berlin: Dunckerund Humblot, 1843, 296pp.
Mary Schweidler, the Amber Witch (trans. by Lady Duff Gordon). London: Murray, 1844, 171pp.
(ed. by W. Meinhold) *The Amber Witch; The Most Interesting Trial For Witchcraft Ever Known.* (trans. by E. A. Friedlaender). London: H. G. Clark, 1844, 262pp.

MERCER, CECIL WILLIAM   (1885-1960)   *English*
as Dornford Yates
The Stolen March. London: Ward, Lock, 1926, 319pp.
And Berry Came Too. London: Ward, Lock, [1936], 320pp.
□ MYSTERY: *The Courts of Idleness*, 1920; *She Fell Among Thieves*, 1935; *The Devil In Satin*, 1938; *Cost Price*, 1949.

MERRIL, JUDITH (*nee* Josephine Judith Zissman) (1923-   ) *U.S.*
as Cyril (M.) Judd [in collaboration with C. M. Kornbluth]
Mars Child. *Galaxy*, May 1951
Gunner Cade. NY: Simon & Schuster, 1952, 218pp.
Outpost Mars. NY: Abelard, [1952], 268pp.
Sin In Space. NY: Beacon, 1956, paper. (Galaxy Novel #46)
as Judith Merril
That Only A Mother. *Astounding*, July 1948
Shadow On the Hearth. Garden City: Doubleday, 1950, 277pp.
Out of Bounds. NY: Pyramid, [1960], 160pp., paper. *ss col*
Daughters of Earth. Garden City: Doubleday, [1969 (c.1968)], 255pp. *3 novellas*
Survival Ship and Other Stories. Toronto, Canada: Kakabeka Publishing Company, [1973], 229pp. *ss col*
as Mrs. Frederik Pohl
title by marriage
as Rose Sharon
Woman of the World. *Venture*, Jan 1957
The Lady Was A Tramp. *Venture*, March 1957

MERTZ, BARBARA G(ross) (1927-   ) *U.S.*
Born: Canton, Illinois
as Barbara Mertz
■ *Temples, Tombs, and Hieroglyphs*, 1964; *Red Land, Black Land*, 1966.
as Barbara Michaels
Sons of the Wolf. NY: Meredith, 1967, 265pp.
□ *The Master of Black Tower*, 1966; *Prince of Darkness*, 1969; *The Dark On the Other Side*, 1970; *Grey Gallows*, 1972; *Witch*, 1973; *House of Many Shadows*, 1974; *Wings of the Falcon*, 1977.
as Elizabeth Peters
□ *The Jackal's Head*, 1968.

MERWIN, SAM(uel) (Jr.) (1910-   ) *U.S.*
as Matt Lee
A Problem In Astrogation. *Thrilling Wonder Stories*, April 1948
as Sam Merwin
The Scourge Below. *Thrilling Wonder Stories*, Oct 1939
The House of Many Worlds. Garden City: Doubleday, 1951, 216pp.
Killer To Come. NY: Abelard-Schuman, [1953], 251pp.
The White Widows. Garden City: Doubleday, 1953, 224pp.
Three Faces of Time. NY: Ace, [1955], 135pp., paper. (Ace Double D 121)
The Time Shifters. NY: Lancer, 1971, paper. [may be retitling]
Chauvinisto. NY: Major, 1976.
□ HISTORICAL FICTION: (with Leo Margulies) *The Flags Were Three, A Novel of Old New Orleans*, 1945. MYSTERY: *Death In the Sunday Supplement*, 1942; *Knife In My Back*, 1945; "Amy Brewster" Mystery series incl. *Message From A Corpse*, 1945; and *A Matter of Policy*, 1946.
as Sergeant Saturn
in letters section of *Startling Stories* in the mid 1940s.
as Carter Sprague
The Rocket's Red Glare. *Startling Stories*, June 1943
Climate-Disordered. *Startling Stories*, March 1948

METLOVA, MARIA
as Louise Hathaway
The Enchanted Hour. San Francisco: J. J. Newbegin, [1940], 129pp. (500 cop) *ss col*
□ *No Stranger To My Heart*, 1942.

MEYER, DOROTHY QUICK (Mrs. John Adams) (1900-   )
U.S. Born: New York, New York
as Dorothy Quick
The Witch's Mark. *Weird Tales*, Jan 1938
Blue and Silver Brocade. *Unknown*, Oct 1939
Strange Awakening. NY: House of Field, [1938], 266pp.
□ *The Fifth Dagger*, 1947; *One Night In Holyrood*, 1949 (play); *Cry In the Night*, 1957; *Something Evil*, 1958. POEMS: *Threads*, 1927; *Spears Into Life*, 1938; *Laugh While You Can*, 1940; *To What Strange Altar*, 1940; *Variations On A Theme*, 1947; *Interludes*, 1953; *Bold Heart and Other Poems*, 1960.

MICHEL, JOHN B. (1917-   ) *U.S.*
Born: Brooklyn, New York
as Bowen Conway
File 384. *Future*, April 1942
as Arthur Cooke [in collaboration with E. Balter, C. Kornbluth, Robert Lowndes, & Donald A. Wollheim.]
The Psychological Regulator. *Comet Stories*, March 1941
as John Michel
(with Raymond Z. Gallun) The Menace From Mercury. *Science Wonder Quarterly*, Summer 1932
The Goblins Will Get You. *Avon Fantasy Reader #8*
as Hugh Raymond

He Wasn't There! *Astonishing,* Feb 1941

as Lawrence Woods [in collaboration with Donald A. Wollheim]
Earth Does Not Reply. *Science Fiction Quarterly,* Summer 1941

⌐ John Tara

MICHELS, NICHOLAS
as Nicholas Michels
■ *Die Gottwerdung des Menschen,* 1898; *The Rise and Fall of Prohibition In Illinois, 1839-1855,* 1912.
as Nicolai Mikalowitch
Numa's Vision; An Allegory. Chicago: N. Michels, [1899], 173pp.

MIHILAKIS, ULYSSES GEORGE
as Silaki Ali Hassen
Caliph of Yafri. *Unknown,* Sept 1939
as Ulysses George Mihilakis
The Machine of Destiny. *Wonder Stories Quarterly,* Summer 1931

MILKOMANE, ALEXIS MILKOMANOVICH (1903-)
naturalized British
Born: Russia
as George Alexis Bankoff
■ *Plastic Surgery,* 1943; *Operative Surgery,* 1946; *The Conquest Of Pain,* 1946; *The Conquest Of Tuberculosis,* 1946; *The Conquest Of Disease,* 1946; *The Conquest Of Cancer,* 1947; *The Conquest Of The Unknown,* 1947.
as George Borodin
The Book of Joanna. London: Staples Press, 1947, 198pp.
The Pillar of Fire. London: Macdonald, [1947], 320pp.
Spurious Sun. London: T. W. Laurie, [1948], 281pp.
□ *Bastard Angels,* 1942.
■ *Soviet and Tsarist Siberia,* 1944; *Friendly Ocean,* 1946; *The Charm of Ballet,* 1955.
as George Braddon
□ *Judgment Deferred,* 1948; *Murdered Sleep,* 1949.
as Peter Conway
□ *A Dark Side Also,* 1940; *Living Tapestry,* 1946.
as George Sava
□ *Bride of Neptune,* 1946.
■ *The Healing Knife,* 1938; *A Surgeon's Destiny,* 1939; *Valley of Forgotten People,* 1941; *A Tale of Ten Cities,* 1942; *The Boon of the Atom,* 1946; *A Doctor's Odyssey,* 1951.

MILLAR, KENNETH (1915-) U.S.
Born: Los Gatos, California
as John MacDonald
□ *The Moving Target,* 1949.
as John Ross MacDonald
□ MYSTERY: *The Drowning Pool,* 1950; *The Way Some People Die,* 1951; *The Ivory Grin,* 1952; *Meet Me At The Morgue,* 1953; *Find A Victim,* 1954.
as Ross MacDonald
□ MYSTERY: *The Name Is Archer,* 1955 (ss col); *The Doomsters,* 1958; *The Galton Case,* 1959; *The Ferguson Affair,* 1960; *The Zebra Striped Hearse,* 1962; *The Chill,* 1964; *Black Money,* 1966; *The Instant Enemy,* 1968; *The Goodbye Look,* 1969; *The Underground Man,* 1971; *Sleeping Beauty,* 1973.
as Kenneth Millar
Find The Woman. *The Mysterious Traveler Magazine,* Jan 1952
□ MYSTERY: *Dark Tunnel,* 1944; *Trouble Follows Me,* 1946; *Blue City,* 1947; *The Three Roads,* 1948.
■ *The Inward Eye: A Revaluation of Coleridge's Psychological Criticism,* 1952.

MILLER, H. BILLY (1920-1961) U.S.
Born: Garrett, Indiana
as Whit Masterson [in collaboration with Robert A. Wade]
The Dark Fantastic. NY: Avon, [1966], 207pp., paper.
□ *Play Like You're Dead,* 1967.
as Wade Miller [in collaboration with Robert A. Wade]
I Know A Good Hand Trick. *Magazine of Fantasy & Science Fiction,* Nov 1959
How Lucky We Met. *Magazine of Fantasy & Science Fiction,* Oct 1960
□ MYSTERY: *Deadly Weapon,* 1946; *Guilty Bystander,* 1947; *Stolen Woman,* 1950; *Shoot to Kill,* 1951; *Branded Woman,* 1952.
as Dale Wilmer [in collaboration with Robert A. Wade]
□ MYSTERY: *Memo for Murder,* 1951; *Dead Fall,* 1954.

MILLER, P(eter) SCHUYLER (1912-1974) U.S.
as Dennis McDermott [in collaboration with Walter L. Dennis]
The Red Spot of Jupiter. *Wonder Stories,* July 1931
as Dennis McDermott [in collaboration with Walter L. Dennis and Paul McDermott]
The Duel on the Asteroid. *Wonder Stories,* Jan 1932
as P. Schuyler Miller
The Red Plague. *Wonder Stories,* July 1930
(with L. Sprague de Camp) Genus Homo. *Super Science Stories,* March 1941
book reviews in "The Reference Shelf" *Astounding/Analog* Oct 1951 - Jan 1975
(with L. Sprague de Camp) *Genus Homo.* Reading, Pennsylvania: Fantasy Press, 1950, 225pp.
The Titan. Reading, Pennsylvania: Fantasy Press, 1952, 252pp. (1500 cop) *ss col*
as Nihil
Alicia In Blunderland, series in *Science Fiction Digest,* c.1940.

MITCHELL, CLYDE [house pseudonym]
unattributed
The Monster Died At Dawn. *Amazing,* Nov 1956
A Kiss for the Conqueror. *Fantastic,* Feb 1957
by Harlan Ellison
The Wife Factory. *Fantastic,* Nov 1957
by Randall Garrett and Robert Silverberg
The Mummy Takes A Wife. *Fantastic,* Dec 1956
Deadly Decoy. *Amazing,* Feb 1957

MITCHELL, GLADYS MAUDE WINIFRED (1901-)
English
Born: Cowley, Oxford
as Stephen Hockaby
□ *Marsh Hay,* 1933.
as Gladys Mitchell
□ MYSTERY: *The Death In the Wet,* 1934; *Printer's Error,* 1939; *Laurels and Poison,* 1942; *Watson's Choice,* 1955; *Spotted Hemlock,* 1958.

MOLESWORTH, MARY LOUISA (Stewart) (Mrs. R.) (1839-1921) Scottish
Born: Rotterdam, Holland
as Ennis Graham
The Cuckoo Clock. London: Macmillan, 1877, 242pp., ill.
□ *Cicely,* 1874; *Tell Me A Story,* 1882 (juv).
as Mrs. Molesworth
Four Ghost Stories. London: Macmillan, 1888, 255pp.
Uncanny Tales. London: Hutchinson, [1896], 228pp., front.
□ JUVENILES: *Tell Me A Story,* 1875; *Carrots,* 1876; *The Children of the Castle,* 1890; *The Bewitched Lamp,* 1891; *An Enchanted Garden,* 1892; *Hollow Tree House,* 1894; *Fairies of Sorts,* 1908; *Fairies Afield,* 1911.

MONCHO Y GILABERT, ANTONIO
● Miguel Gautisolo

MONROE, DONALD (1888-   ) *U.S.*
as Donald Keith [in collaboration with Keith Monroe]
Butterfly. *Galaxy,* Jan 1957
Mutiny In the Time Machine. NY: Random House, [1963], 181pp., ill. *juv*
Time Machine to the Rescue. NY: Putnam, 1967, 157pp., ill. *juv*

MONROE, KEITH   *U.S.*
see Donald Monroe

MONSELL, MARGARET E(mma) (Irwin) (Mrs. John R.)
as M(argaret) E. Irwin
Still She Wished For Company. London: Heinemann, [1924], 307pp.
These Mortals. London: Heinemann, 1925, 279pp.
Who Will Remember? NY: T. Seltzer, 1925, 293pp.
Madame Fears the Dark; Seven Stories and A Play. London: Chatto & Windus, 1935, 275pp. *col*
Bloodstock and Other Stories. London: Chatto & Windus, 1953, 206pp. *ss col*
☐ *Knock Four Times,* 1927; *Fire Down Below,* 1928; *Young Bess,* 1944 (historical fiction).

MONTGOMERY, ROBERT BRUCE (1921-   ) *English*
Born: Chesham Boris
as Edmund Crispin
edited a best SF of the year series starting in 1955 in England
The Case of the Gilded Fly. London: Gollancz, 1944, 158pp.
☐ MYSTERY: *Holy Disorders,* 1945; *Obsequies At Oxford,* 1945; *The Moving Toyshop,* 1946; *Dead and Dumb,* 1947; *Buried of Pleasure,* 1948; *Frequent Hearses,* 1950; *Beware of the Trains,* 1953.
as Robert Bruce Montgomery
☐ *Four Shakespeare Songs,* 1948; *Concertino for String Orchestra,* 1950; *Concert Waltz, for Two Pianos,* 1952.

MOORCOCK, MICHAEL JOHN (1939-1978) *English*
Born: Mitcham, Surrey
as Michael Barrington [in collaboration with Barrington Bayley]
Peace On Earth. *New Worlds #89,* Dec 1959 (Br.)
as Edward P. Bradbury
Warriors of Mars. London: Compact, 1965, 153pp., paper.
Blades of Mars. London: Compact, 1965, 152pp., paper.
Barbarians of Mars. London: Compact, 1965, 158pp., paper.
as James Colvin
The Deep Fix. *Science Fiction #64,* April 1964 (Br.)
The Deep Fix. London: Compact, 1966, 159pp., paper. *novella & ss col*
as Michael Moorcock
Sojan the Swordsman. *Tarzan Adventures,* May 1957
The Dreaming City. *Science-Fantasy,* June 1961 (Br.)
The Stealer of Souls. London: N. Spearman, 1963, 215pp.
The Sundered Worlds. London: Compact, [1965], 190pp., paper.
The Fireclown. London: Compact, [1965], 189pp., paper.
Stormbringer. London: H. Jenkins, 1965, 192pp.
The Twilight Man. London: Compact, [1966], 190pp., paper.
The Jewel In the Skull. NY: Lancer, [1967], 175pp., paper.
The Wrecks of Time. NY: Ace, [1967], 135pp., paper. (Ace Double H 36)
Sorcerer's Amulet. NY: Lancer, [1968], 190pp., paper.
The Final Programme. NY: Avon, [1968], 191pp., paper.
Sword of the Dawn. NY: Lancer, [1968], 191pp., paper.
The Secret of the Runestaff. NY: Lancer, [1969], 192pp., paper.

The Black Corridor. NY: Ace, [1969], 184pp.
Behold the Man, A Novel. London: Allison & Busby, 1969, 144pp.
The Ice Schooner. NY: Berkley, [1969], 207pp., ill.
The Time Dweller. London: Rupert-Hart Davis, 1969, 176pp.
The Eternal Champion. NY: Dell, [1970], 188pp., paper.
The Singing Citadel. NY: Berkley, [1970], 160pp., paper.
Phoenix In Obsidian. London: Mayflower, [1970], 127pp.
A Cure for Cancer. London: Allison & Busby, [1971].
The Warlord of the Air. NY: Ace, [1971], paper.
The Knight of the Swords. NY: Berkley, [1971], 176pp., paper.
The Sleeping Sorceress. London: New English Library, [1971], 140pp.
The Queen of the Swords. NY: Berkley, [1971], 160pp., paper.
The King of the Swords. NY: Berkley, [1971], 158pp., paper.
The English Assassin; A Romance of Entropy. London: Allison & Busby, [1972], 254pp., ill.
The Dreaming City. NY: Lancer, [1972], 189pp., paper.
An Alien Heat. London: MacGibbon & Kee, 1972, 158pp.
The Dancers At the End of Time. London: MacGibbon & Kee, 1972.
Elric of Melnibone. London: Hutchinson, 1972, 191pp.
Count Brass. London: Mayflower, 1973, 140pp.
The Silver Warriors. NY: Dell, [1973], 220pp., paper.
The Jade Man's Eyes. Brighton: Unicorn Bookshop, 1973, 75pp.
The Champion of Garathorm. 1973.
The Bull and the Spear. London: Allison & Busby, 1973, 168pp.
The Oak and the Ram. London: Allison & Busby, 1973, 168pp.
The Land Leviathan. Garden City: Doubleday, 1974, 150pp.
The Sword and the Stallion. 1974.
The Quest for Tanelorn. 1975.
The Adventures of Una Persson and Catherine Cornelius in the Twentieth Century. London: Quartet, 1976, 216pp.
The End of All Songs. NY: Harper & Row, 1976, 271pp.
The Sailor On the Seas of Fate. London: Quartet, 1976, 170pp.
Legends From the End of Time. NY: Harper & Row, 1976, 182pp., ill.
Lives and Times of Jerry Cornelius. London: Allison & Busby, 1976, 176pp., ill.
(with Michael Butterworth) *The Time of the Hawklords.* Henley-On-Thames: A. Ellis, 1976, 255pp.
The Transformation of Miss Mavis Ming. London: 1977. [US 1st: *A Messiah At the End of Time.* NY: DAW, [1977], 192pp., paper.]
The Condition of Muzak. London: Allison & Busby, [1977]. *Glomana,* 1977.
☐ *The Chinese Agent,* 1970; *Breakfast In the Ruins,* 1971.

MORRIS, RALPH
as John Daniel
A Narrative of the Life and Astonishing Adventures of John Daniel . . . Also A Description of A Most Surprising Engine, Invented by His Son Jacob, On Which He Flew to the Moon, with Some Account of Its Inhabitants, etc., etc. (taken From His Own Mouth by Mr. Ralph Morris). London: M. Cooper, 1751, 319pp., ill.

MORRISON, MARGARET MACKIE (? -1973) *U.S.*
Born: Scotland
as March Cost
A Man Named Luke. London: Collins, [1932], 290pp.

The Dark Glass. London: Collins, [1935], 463pp.
The Dark Star. London: Collins, 1939, 384pp.
The Bespoken Mile. NY: Vanguard, 1959, 448pp.
☐ *The Oldest Wish,* 1928; *The Hour Awaits,* 1952; *Invitation From Minerva,* 1954; *By the Angel, Islington,* 1955; *A Woman of Letters,* 1959; *The Interpreter,* 1960; *Period Pieces,* 1960 (ss col); *The Countess,* 1963; *After the Festival,* 1966; *The Bitter Green of the Willow; Four Fairy Tales,* 1967 (juv).
as Peggy Morrison
☐ *Cosy Chair Stories,* 1924 (juv & ss col)

MORRISSEY, JOSEPH LAURENCE (1905–   )
as Henry Richards
The Hour of the Phoenix. NY: Arcadia, [1965], 191pp.
as Richard Saxon
The Stars Came Down. London: Consul, [1964], 167pp., paper.
The Hour of the Phoenix. London: Consul, [1964], 140pp., paper.
Cosmic Crusade. London: Consul, [1964], 159pp., paper.
Future For Sale. London: Consul, [1964], 151pp., paper.

MORSE, KATHARINE DUNCAN (1888–   ) *U.S.*
as Jerry Doane
☐ *Salt Water In Their Veins,* 1947 (verse).
as Katharine (Duncan) Morse
The Shop of Perpetual Youth, A Playlet In One Scene. NY: S. French, 1922, 14pp. *play*
☐ *Assyrian Sword and Spanish Chalice,* 1951 (poetry); *On the Road to Parnassus,* 1922 (play); *Peter Was A Pirate,* 1939 (juv).
anonymous
■ *The Uncensored Letters Of A Canteen Girl,* 1920 (Personal Narrative).

MUDDOCK, JOYCE E(mmerson) P(reston) (1843–1934) *British*
Born: Southampton, Hants
Autobiography: *Pages From An Adventurous Life,* by Joyce E.P. Muddock, "Dick Donovan," 1907.
as Dick Donovan
Tales of Terror. London: Chatto & Windus, 1899, 328pp.
☐ MYSTERY: *The Man Hunter: Stories From the Notebook of A Detective,* 1888; *Link by Link,* 1893; *Found and Fettered,* 1894.
as J(oyce) (E.) (P.) Muddock
From the Bosom of the Deep. London: Swan & Sonnenschein, 1888, 363pp.
Stories, Weird and Wonderful. London: Chatto & Windus, 1889, 316pp. *ss col*
The Dead Man's Secret, or the Valley of Gold. London: Chatto & Windus, 1889, 270pp.
Kate Cameron of Brux; or, The Feud. A Story of Wild Doings and Strange People, Based on the Legends and Traditions Current In the Locality In Which the Scenes Are Laid. London: Digby & Long, 1900, 335pp.
The Sunless City . . . From the Papers and Diaries of the Late Josiah Flintabbatey Flonatin, esq. London: F. V. White, 1905, 308pp.
☐ *The Golden Idol,* 1899; *Whose Was the Hand,* 1901.
■ *The Romance and History of the Crystal Palace,* 1911.

MULLEN, STANLEY (B.) (1911–1973) *U.S.*
Born: Colorado Springs, Colorado
as Lee Beecher
in his magazine *Gorgon.*
as Stanley Beecher
in the magazine *Fate.*
as John Peter Drummond
some of the Ki-Gor novels in *Jungle Stories* 1939–1954
as Stanley Mullen

Water for Mars. Other Worlds, Jan 1951
Moonfoam and Sorceries. Denver: Gorgon, 1948, 264pp., ill. (100 copies) *ss col*
The Sphinx Child. NY: New Collector, 1948, 24pp., paper.
Kinsmen of the Dragon. Chicago: Shasta, [1951], 336pp.

MULLER, JOHN E.
see **R. LIONEL FANTHORPE**

MUNRO, H(ector) H(ugh) (1870–1916) *British*
Born: Akyob, Burma
as H. H. Munro [often with "Saki"]
The Westminster Alice. London: Westminster Gazette, [1902], 67pp., ill., paper.
Reginald. London: Methuen, 1904, 118pp.
Reginald In Russia and Other Sketches. London: Methuen, 1910, 123pp. *ss col*
The Chronicles of Clovis. London: J. Lane, [1911], 242pp.
When William Came. London: J. Lane, 1914, 322pp.
Beasts and Super-Beasts. London: J. Lane, 1914, 312pp. *col*
The Toys of Peace and Other Papers. London: J. Lane, 1919, 306pp. *col*
The Square Egg and Other Sketches. London: J. Lane, [1924], 318pp., ill. *col*
☐ *The Unbearable Bassington,* 1912.
■ *The Rise of the Russian Empire,* 1900.
as "Saki"
The Westminster Alice. London: Westminster Gazette, [1902], 67pp., ill., paper. [other first editions of this author appear with either "Saki" (H. H. Munro) or H. H. Munro ("Saki") as the author. "Saki" was used alone on magazine articles and some later reprints, especially American editions]

MURFREE, MARY NOAILLES (1850–1922) *U.S.*
Born: Murfreesboro, Tennessee
as Charles Egbert Craddock
The Phantoms of the Foot Bridge, and Other Stories. NY: Harper, 1895, 353pp., ill. *ss col*
The Frontiersman. Boston: Houghton, Mifflin, 1904, 364pp. *ss col*
The Fair Mississippian. Boston: Houghton, Mifflin, 1908, 428pp.
The Raid of the Guerilla and Other Stories. Philadelphia: Lippincott, 1912, 334pp., ill. *ss col*
☐ *In the Tennessee Mountains,* 1884 (ss col); *The Prophet of the Great Smoky Mountains,* 1885; *In the Clouds,* 1886; *In the "Stranger People's" Country,* 1891; *The Amulet,* 1906; *The Ordeal,* 1912.
● **R. Emmet Denbry**

MURRY, COLIN MIDDLETON (1926–   ) *English*
Born: Bridport, Dorsetshire
as Richard Cowper
Breakthrough. London: Dobson, 1967, 214pp.
Phoenix. London: Dobson, 1968, 183pp.
Domino; A Science Fiction Novel. London: Dobson, 1971, 175pp.
Kuldesak. London: Gollancz, 1972, 187pp.
Clone. London: Gollancz, 1972, 190pp.
Time Out of Mind. London: Gollancz, 1973, 159pp.
Worlds Apart. London: Gollancz, 1974, 159pp.
The Twilight of Briareus. London: Gollancz, 1974, 255pp.
The Custodian and Other Stories. London: Gollancz, 1976. *ss col*
The Road to Corlay. London: 1978.
as Colin Murry
The Golden Valley. NY: Hutchinson, [1958], 183pp.
☐ *A Pathos To the Sea,* 1961.

MUSPRATT, ROSALIE HELEN   (1906-1976)   *British*
  Born: Freshfields, Lancashire
as Jasper John
  Sinister Stories. London: H. Walker, 1930, 172pp. *ss col*
as Rosalie Muspratt
  Tales of Terror. London: Old Royalty Book Pub., 1931,
    167pp. *ss col*

NADIR KHAN AL-IDRISI AL DURRANI, AHMADI ABD ALLAH
  (a.k.a. Alexander Nicholayevitch Romanoff)   (1881-1945)
  European
  Born: Kabul, Afghanistan
  Autobiography: *The Cat Had Nine Lives, Adventures and
    Reminiscences,* by Achmed Abdullah. NY: Farrar & Rine-
    hart, 1933, 312pp., ill.
as Achmed Abdullah
  The Red Stain. NY: Hearsts' International Library, 1915,
    309pp.
  The Blue Eyed Manchu. NY: Shores, 1917, 351pp.
  The Honourable Gentleman and Others. NY: Putnam, 1919,
    262pp. *ss col*
  The Mating of the Blades. NY: Mc Cann, 1920, 281pp.
  Wings: Tales of the Psychic. NY: Mc Cann, 1920, 239pp.
    ss col
  Night Drums. NY: Mc Cann, [1921], 329pp., ill.
  Alien Souls. NY: Mc Cann, 1922, 248pp. *ss col*
  The Thief of Baghdad. NY: H. K. Fly, [1924], 319pp.,
    ill.
  The Year of the Wood-Dragon. NY: Brentano's, [1926],
    249pp., ill. *juv*
  Steel and Jade. NY: Doran, 1927, 319pp.
  The Bungalow On the Roof. NY: Mystery League, 1931,
    283pp.
  Mysteries of Asia. London: P. Allen, 1934, 256pp. *ss col*
  (with Anthony Abbot) *The Flower of the Gods.* NY:
    Green Circle, [1936], 254pp.
  Deliver Us From Evil. NY: Putnam, 1939, 248pp.
  (with Anthony Abbot) *The Shadow of the Master.* London:
    Hurst & Blackett, [1940], 224pp.
  (with Anthony Abbot) *These Are Strange Tales.* Philadel-
    phia: Winston, [1948], 212pp. *ss col*
  □ *The Swinging Caravan,* 1925; (with Faith Baldwin)
    Broadway Interlude, 1929; (with Faith Baldwin) *Girl On
    the Make,* 1932.
  ■ (with T. Compton Pakenham) *Dreamers of Empire,*
    1929; (with John Kenny) *For Men Only; A Cook Book,* 1937.
● A. A. Nadir

NEEPER, CAROLYN
as Cary Neeper
  A Place Beyond Man. NY: Scribner, [1975], 270pp.

NELSON, RADELL FARADAY   (1931-   )   *U.S.*
  Born: Schenectady, New York
as Ray Nelson
  Turn Off the Sky. *Magazine of Fantasy and Science
    Fiction,* Aug 1963
  (with Philip K. Dick) *Ganymede Takeover.* NY: Ace,
    1967, 157pp., paper.

NEVILLE, HENRY   (1620-1694)   *English*
as Henry Cornelius van Sloetten
  *The Isle of Pines, or, A late discovery of a fourth Island
    near Terra Australis, Incognita; by Henry Cornelius
    van Sloetten. Wherein is contained. A true relation of
    certain English persons, who in Queen Elizabeths time,
    making a voyage to the East Indies were cast away,
    and wracked near to the coast of Terra Australis,
    Incognita, and all drowned, except one man and four*

women. *And now lately anno Dom. 1667. a Dutch ship making a voyage to the East Indies, driven by foul weather there, by chance have found their posterity (speaking good English) to amount (as they suppose) to ten or twelve thousand persons. The whole relation . . . is here annexed. . .* London: A. Banks & C. Harper, 1668, 31pp. [another edition 1668? states on the title page "one man and four women, whereof one was a negro." This edition also omits the pseudonym and states that it was "written by the man himself." On t.p. is stated "Licensed July 27, 1668. London: Printed in the year 1668. Bound with 3d edition of Defoe's *Robinson Crusoe* in Library of Congress copy"] [see *The Isle of Pines*, 1668; *An Essay in Bibliography*, by W.C. Ford. Boston: The Club of Odd Volumes, 1920]

☐ *Newes from the New-Exchange; or, The commonwealth of ladies*, 1650.

anonymous

■ *Plato Redivivus: or a Dialogue Concerning Government, Wherein, by Observations Drawn from Other Kingdoms and States Both Ancient and Modern, an Endeavor is Used to Discover the Present Politick Distemper of Our Own, With the Causes, and Remedies.* London: 1681, 271pp.

NEVILLE, KRIS OTTMAN (1925-) U.S.
Born: Carthage, Mississippi
as Kris Neville
The Hand From the Stars. *Super Science Stories*, July 1949
The Unearth People. NY: Belmont, [1964], 157pp., paper.
The Mutants. NY: Belmont, [1966], 158pp., paper.
Peril of the Starmen. NY: Belmont, [1967], 72pp., paper. (Belmont Double Novel)
Special Delivery. NY: Belmont, [1967], 84pp., paper. (Belmont Double Novel)
Invaders On the Moon. NY: Belmont, [1970], paper.
■ (with H. Lee) *Epoxy Resins; Their Applications and Technology*, 1957; (with H. Lee) *Handbook of Biomedical Plastics*, 1971.
as Henderson Starke
Dumb Supper. *Magazine of Fantasy and Science Fiction*, Summer 1950

NEWMAN, BERNARD CHARLES (1897-1968) British
Autobiography: *Speaking From Memory.* London: H. Jenkins, [1960], 222pp., ill.
as Don Betteridge
☐ SPY/MYSTERY: *Scotland Yard Alibi*, 1938; *Dictator's Destiny*, 1945; *The Case of the Berlin Spy*, 1954.
as Bernard Newman
The Cavalry Went Through. London: Gollancz, [1930], 288pp.
The Armoured Doves, A Peace Book. London: Jarrolds, [1931], 288pp.
Hosanna. London: Archer, 1933, 287pp.
Secret Weapon. London: Gollancz, 1942, 189pp.
The Flying Saucer. London: Gollancz, 1948, 250pp.
The Wishful Think. London: R. Hale, [1954], 192pp.
The Blue Ants; The First Authentic Accounts of the Russian-Chinese War of 1970. London: R. Hale, [1962], 192pp.
☐ SPY/MYSTERY: *Lady Doctor-Woman Spy*, 1937; *Death To The Spy*, 1939; *Double Menace*, 1954; *The Travelling Executioners*, 1964; *The Spy at No. 10*, 1965; *Evil Phoenix*, 1966; *Draw the Dragon's Teeth*, 1967.
■ *Character Monologues and How To Perform Them*, 1926; *Round-About, Andorra*, 1928; *Albanian Back-Door*, 1936; *I Saw Spain*, 1937; *Danger Spots of Europe*, 1938; *German Secret Service At Work*, 1940; *News From the East*, 1948; *Tito's Yugoslavia*, 1952; *Soviet*

Atomic Spies, 1953; *Morocco Today*, 1953; *Report On Indo-China*, 1954; *Portrait of Poland*, 1959; *The World of Espionage*, 1962; *Spies In Britain*, 1964; *Background to Vietnam*, 1965; *Turkey and the Turks*, 1968.

NEWMAN, JOHN English
as Kenneth Johns [in collaboration with H. Kenneth Bulmer]
Our Invisible Shield. *Authentic SF #59-60*, Aug 1955 *article*
■ *The True Book About Space Travel.* London: Muller, 1960, 143pp., ill. *juv*
as John Newman
Silicones. *New Worlds*, Jan 1953 *article*

NICHOLSON, J(oseph) S(hield) (1850-1927) British
as Author of Thoth
A Dreamer of Dreams. London: Blackwood, 1889, 250pp.
Toxar: A Romance. London: Longmans, 1890, 289pp.
as J(oseph) S(hield) Nicholson
Tales of Ariosto. London: Macmillan, 1913, 297pp. [adapted from L. Ariosto (1474-1533)]
■ *The Silver Question*, 1886; *The Effects of Machinery On Wages*, 1887; *Principles of Political Economy*, 1893-1901; *The Revival of Marxism*, 1920.
anonymous
Thoth: A Romance. Edinburgh: Blackwood, 1888, 209pp.

NICOLL, (Henry) MAURICE (Dunlop) (1884-1953)
as Maurice Nicoll
■ *Dream Psychology*, 1917 (Oxford Medical Publication); *Psychological Commentaries On the Teaching of G. I. Gurdjieff and P.D. Ouspensky*, 1949; *The New Man; An Interpretation of Some Parables and Miracles of Christ*, 1950.
as Martin Swayne
The Blue Germ. NY: Doran, 1918, 288pp.
☐ *Lord Richard In the Pantry*, 1912.
■ *In Mesopotamia*, 1917.

NISOT, MAVIS ELIZABETH (Hocking) (Mrs.) (1893-) British
as Elizabeth Nisot
☐ *Shortly Before Midnight*, 1934; *Twelve To Dine*, 1935.
as William Penmare
The Man Who Could Stop War. London: Hodder & Stoughton, [1929], 308pp.

NOLAN, WILLIAM FRANCIS (1928-) U.S.
Born: Kansas City, Missouri
as Frank Anmar
R. B. A Biographical Sketch. *Ray Bradbury Review*, Jan 1952 *article*
as F. E. Edwards
Bradbury On the Screen: A Saga of Perseverance. *Venture*, Aug 1969 *article*
☐ *Death Is For Losers*, 1968; *The White Cad Cross-Up*, 1969.
as William F. Nolan
The Joy Of Living. *If*, Aug 1954
Impact 20. NY: Paperback Library, [1963], 158pp., paper. *ss col*
(with G. C. Johnson) *Logan's Run.* NY: Dial Press, 1967, 134pp.
Space for Hire. NY: Lancer, 1971, paper.
Alien Horizons. NY: Pocket Books, 1974, paper.
■ *Barney Oldfield; . . . America's Legendary Speed King*, 1961; *Phil Hill: Yankee Champion*, 1962; *Men of Thunder*, 1964; *John Huston, King Rebel*, 1965; *Dashiell Hammett, A Casebook*, 1969; *Steve McQueen, Star On Wheels*, 1972; *The Ray Bradbury Companion*, 1975; *Sinners and Supermen*, 1965 (Biographical Sketches of

Ray Bradbury and Raymond Chandler).
● Mike Cahill

NORTHERN, LESLIE [house pseudonym]
unattributed
Fatal Thoughts. *Startling Stories,* Summer 1945
Skyrover. *Startling Stories,* Winter 1945
by Frank Belknap Long
The Purple Dusk. *Thrilling Wonder Stories,* Summer 1945
They Sculp. *Thrilling Wonder Stories,* Winter 1945

NORTHRUP, EDWIN F(itch)   (1866- ?)
as Edwin F. Northrup
■ *An Experimental Study of Vortex Motions In Liquids,* 1911; *Methods Of Measuring Electrical Resistance,* 1912; *Laws of Physical Science; A Reference Book,* 1917.
as Akkad Pseudoman
Zero to Eighty; Being My Lifetime Doings, Reflections, and Inventions, also My Journey Around the Moon. Princeton, New Jersey: Scientific Publishing Co., 1937, 280pp., ill. (preface signed E. F. Northrup)

NORTON, ANDRE (*nee* Alice Mary Norton)   (1912-   )   *U.S.*
Born: Cleveland, Ohio
as Andrew North
The People of the Crater. *Fantasy Book #1,* 1947
Sargasso of Space. NY: Gnome, [1955], 185pp.
Plague Ship. NY: Gnome, [1956], 192pp.
Voodoo Planet. NY: Ace, [1959], 78pp., paper. (Ace Double D 345)
as Alice Norton
■ *Your Public Library,* 1969; *Public Relations: Information Sources,* 1970.
as Andre Norton
The Prince Commands, Being Sundry Adventures of Michael Karl Sometime Crown Prince & Pretender to the Throne of Morvania. NY: Appleton-Century, 1934, 268pp.
Ralestone Luck. NY: Appleton-Century, 1938, 296pp., ill.
Follow the Drum, Being the Adventures and Misadventures of one Johanna Lovell, Sometime Lady of Catkept Manor in Kent County of Lord Baltimore's Proprietary of Maryland, In the Gracious Reign of King Charles the Second. NY: Wm. Penn Pub. Co., 1942, 312pp.
The Sword Is Drawn. Cambridge, Massachusetts: Houghton-Mifflin, 1944, 178pp.
Rogue Reynard, Being a Tale of the Fortunes and Misfortunes and Divers Misdeeds of that Great Villain, Baron Reynard, The Fox, and How He Was Served With the King's Justice. Based Upon the Beast Saga. Boston: Houghton-Mifflin, 1947.
Scarface, Being the Story of One Justin Polake, Late of the Pirate Isle of Tortuga, and How Fate Did Justly Deal With Him, To His Great Profit. NY: Harcourt, [1948], 263pp., ill.
Sword In Sheath. NY: Harcourt, [1949], 246pp., ill.
Huon of the Horn; Being A Tale of that Duke of Bordeaux Who Came to Sorrow At the Hands of Charlemagne and Yet Won the Favor of Oberon, The Elf King, To His Lasting Fame and Glory. NY: Harcourt, [1951], ill.
Star Man's Son, 2250 A.D. NY: Harcourt, [1952], 248pp., ill.
The Star Rangers. NY: Harcourt, [1953], 280pp.
At Swords' Points. NY: Harcourt, [1954], 279pp.
The Stars Are Ours! Cleveland: World, [1954], 237pp.
Star Guard. NY: Harcourt, [1955], 247pp.
The Crossroads of Time. NY: Ace, [1956], 169pp., paper. (Ace Double D-164)
Star Born. Cleveland: World, [1957], 212pp.
Sea Siege. NY: Harcourt, [1957], 216pp.
Star Gate. NY: Harcourt, [1958], 193pp.

The Time Traders. NY: Harcourt, [1958], 219pp.
The Beast Master. NY: Harcourt, [1959], 192pp.
Secret of the Lost Race. NY: Ace, [1959], 132pp., paper. (Ace Double D 381)
Galactic Derelict. NY: World, [1959], 224pp.
Storm Over Warlock. NY: World, [1960], 251pp.
The Sioux Spaceman. NY: Ace, [1960], 133pp., paper. (Ace Double D 437)
Star Hunter. NY: Ace, [1961], 96pp., paper. (Ace Double D 509)
Catseye. NY: Harcourt, [1961], 192pp.
Eye of the Monster. NY: Ace, [1962], 80pp., paper. (Ace Double F 147)
The Defiant Agents. NY: World, [1962], 224pp.
Lord of Thunder. NY: Harcourt, [1962], 192pp.
Key Out of Time. NY: World, [1963], 224pp.
Witch World. NY: Ace, [1963], 222pp., paper.
Judgment On Janus. NY: Harcourt, [1963], 220pp.
Ordeal In Otherwhere. NY: World, [1964], 221pp.
Web of the Witch World. NY: Ace, [1964], 192pp., paper.
Night of Masks. NY: Harcourt, [1964], 191pp.
Three Against the Witch World. NY: Ace, [1965], 189pp. paper.
The X Factor. NY: Harcourt, [1965], 191pp.
Quest Crosstime. NY: Viking, [1965], 253pp.
Year of the Unicorn. NY: Ace, [1965], 224pp., paper.
Steel Magic. NY: World, [1965], 155pp., ill.
Moon of Three Rings. NY: Viking, [1966], 316pp.
Victory on Janus. NY: Harcourt, [1966], 224pp.
Octagon Magic. NY: World, [1967], 189pp., ill.
Warlock of the Witch World. NY: Ace, [1967], 222pp., paper.
Operation Time Search. NY: Harcourt, [1967], 224pp.
Fur Magic. NY: World, [1968], 174pp., ill.
The Zero Stone. NY: Viking, [1968], 286pp.
Sorceress of the Witch World. NY: Ace, [1968], 221pp., paper.
Dark Piper. NY: Harcourt, 1968, 249pp.
Uncharted Stars. NY: Viking, [1969], 253pp.
Postmarked the Stars. NY: Harcourt, Brace, [1969], 223pp.
Ice Crown. NY: Viking, [1970], 256pp.
High Sorcery. NY: [1970].
Dread Companion. NY: Harcourt, [1970], 234pp.
Android At Arms. NY: Harcourt, [1971], 253pp.
Exiles of the Stars. NY: Viking, [1971], 255pp.
Breed to Come. NY: Viking, [1972], 285pp.
The Crystal Gryphon. NY: Atheneum, 1972, 234pp.
Dragon Magic. NY: Crowell, [1972], 213pp., ill.
Garan the Eternal. Alhambra, California: FPCI, [1972], 199pp. ss col
Spell of the Witch World. NY: DAW #1, [1972], 159pp., ill., paper.
Forerunner Foray. NY: Viking, [1973], 286pp.
Here Abide Monsters. NY: Atheneum, 1973, 215pp.
Iron Cage. NY: Viking, [1974], 288pp.
The Jargoon Pard. NY: Atheneum, 1974, 194pp.
Lavender-Green Magic. NY: Crowell, 1974, 241pp., ill.
Outside. NY: Walker, 1974 [i.e. 1975], 126pp., ill.
(with Michael Gilbert) *The Day of the Ness.* NY: Walker, 1975, 119pp., ill.
Merlin's Mirror. 1975.
No Night Without Stars. NY: Atheneum, 1975, 246pp.
The White Jade Fox. NY: Dutton, [1975], 230pp.
Knave of Dreams. NY: Viking, 1975, 252pp.
Red Hart Magic. NY: Crowell, [1976], 179pp., ill.
(with Dorothy Madlee) *Star Ka'at.* NY: Walker, 1976, 122pp., ill.
Wraiths of Time. NY: Atheneum, 1976, 210pp.
The Opal-Eyed Fan. NY: Dutton, 1977, 212pp.
Quag Keep. NY: Atheneum, 1978, 224pp.
□ (with Bertha Stemm) *Bertie and May,* 1969. HISTORICAL FICTION: *Stand to Horse,* 1956; *Shadow*

Hawk, 1960. WESTERN: *Proud Rebel!*, 1961; *Rebel Spurs*, 1962. GOTHIC: *Snow Shadow*, 1979.

as Allen Weston [in collaboration with Grace Allen Hogarth]
□ *Murders for Sale.* London: Hammond, [1954], 240pp.

NORWAY, NEVIL SHUTE (1899-1960)
Autobiography: *Slide Rule; the Autobiography of An Engineer.* London: Heinemann, [1954], 249pp., ill.

as Nevil Shute
Ordeal. NY: Morrow, 1939, 280pp.
An Old Captivity. NY: Morrow, 1940, 333pp.
In the Wet. London: Heinemann, [1953], 354pp.
On the Beach. NY: Morrow, 1957, 320pp.
□ *Mazaran*, 1926; *So Disdained*, 1928; *Ruined City*, 1938; *Pied Piper*, 1942; *No Highway*, 1948; *A Town Like Alice*, 1950; *Trustee From the Toolroom*, 1960.

NOWLAN, PHIL(ip) (Francis) (1888-1940) *U.S.*
Born: Philadelphia, Pennsylvania

as Philip F. Nowlan
Armageddon—2419 A.D. *Amazing*, Aug 1928
The Airlords of Han. *Amazing*, March 1929
[above stories were the basis for the *Buck Rogers In the 25th Century* comic strip]
Buck Rogers On the Moons of Saturn. Racine, Wisconsin: Whitman, 1934, ill. (by Dick Calkins). (Big Little Book #1143)
Buck Rogers and the Depth Men of Jupiter. Racine, Wisconsin: Whitman, 1935, ill. (by Dick Calkins). (Big Little Book #1169)
(with Dick Calkins) *Buck Rogers, 25th Century featuring Buddy and Allura in "Strange Adventures In the Spider Ship."* Chicago: Pleasure Books, Inc., 1935.
Buck Rogers, 25th Century A.D. In the Interplanetary War With Venus. Racine, Wisconsin: Whitman, [1938]. (Better Little Book #1437)
Armageddon—2419 A.D. NY: Avalon, [1962], 224pp.
Buck Rogers In the 25th Century, Great Classic Newspaper Comic Strips #1. Ann Arbor, Michigan: Ed Aprill, 1964. (500 copies)
Buck Rogers In the 25th Century, Great Classic Newspaper Comic Strips #2. Ann Arbor, Michigan: Ed Aprill, 1965. (500 copies)
Buck Rogers In the 25th Century, Great Classic Newspaper Comic Strips #7. Ann Arbor, Michigan: Ed Aprill, 1967. (500 copies)
Buck Rogers In the 25th Century, Great Classic Newspaper Comic Strips #8. Ann Arbor, Michigan: Ed Aprill, 1968. (500 copies)
(with Dick Calkin, et., al.) *The Collected Works of Buck Rogers In the 25th Century.* NY: Bonanza, 1970, 370pp., ill. *comic strips*

as Frank Phillips
The Onslaught From Venus. *Science Wonder Stories*, Sept 1929

NUETZEL, CHARLES (Alexander) (1934-) *U.S.*
Born: San Francisco, California

as Albert Augustus, Jr.
Slaves of Lomooro. Reseda, California: Powell, 1969.

as Charles English
Lovers: 2075. NY: Scorpion, 1964, paper.

as Charles Nuetzel
(ed) *If This Goes On.* Beverly Hills, California: Book Co. of America, 1965, 256pp.
Queen of Blood. NY: Greenleaf, [c.1967].
Swordsmen of Vistar. Reseda, California: Powell, [1969], 223pp., ill.
Images of Tomorrow. Reseda, California: Powell, [1969], paper. *ss col*
Warrior of Noomas. Reseda, California: Powell, 1969.
Raiders of Noomas. Reseda, California: Powell, 1969.

Last Call For The Stars. Lenox Hill, 1970.

NUTT, CHARLES (1929-1967) *U.S.*
Born: Chicago, Illinois

as Charles Beaumont
"The Devil You Say?" *Amazing*, Jan 1951
The Hunger and Other Stories. NY: Putnam, [1957], 234pp., *ss col*
Yonder. NY: Bantam, [1958], 184pp., paper. *ss col*
Night Ride and Other Journeys. NY: Bantam, [1960], 184pp., paper. *ss col*
The Magic Man and Other Science Fantasy Stories. Greenwich, Connecticut: Fawcett Gold Medal, [1965], 256pp., paper. *ss col*
The Edge. London: Panther, 1966, 143pp., paper. *ss col*
□ SCREENPLAYS: *Queen of Outer Space*, 1958; *The Premature Burial*, 1963; (with Ray Russell) *Masque of the Red Death*, 1964; *Burn, Witch, Burn*, 1964; (with Richard Matheson) *The Seven Faces of Dr. Lao*, 1964.
■ (editor with William F. Nolan) *Omnibus of Speed; An Introduction to the World of Motor Sport*, 1958; *Remember? Remember?*, 1963 (pop culture).
✔ E. J. Beaumont, Keith Grantland, C. B. Lovehill, Charles McNutt, Michael Phillips, S. M. Tenneshaw [house pseudonym]

NUTT, LILY C(live) (1888-)
as Clive Arden
The Enchanted Spring. Indianapolis: Bobbs-Merrill, 1935, 352pp.
□ *Sinners In Heaven*, 1923; *Enticement*, 1924; *The Veil of Glamour*, 1926; *The Spider and the Fly*, 1928; *The Fetters of Eve*, 1931.

O'BRIEN, C(lifford) EDWARD
as Larry Clinton O'Brien
Earth Waits for Dawn. NY: Vantage, [1956], 284pp.

O'BRIEN, DAVID WRIGHT
as Alexander Blade [house pseudonym]
stories unknown see **ALEXANDER BLADE.**
as John York Cabot
The Man the World Forgot. *Fantastic Adventures,* April 1940.
as Bruce Dennis
(with Gerald Vance) The Giant From Jupiter. *Fantastic Adventures,* June 1942
The Incredible Antique. *Fantastic Adventures,* Dec 1942
as Duncan Farnsworth
Twenty-Fifth Century Sherlock. *Fantastic Adventures,* March 1941
as Clee Garson [house pseudonym]
Sharbeau's Startling Statue. *Fantastic Adventures,* Nov 1942
as David Wright O'Brien
Truth Is A Plague. *Amazing,* Feb 1940
as Richard Vardon
Have You Seen Me? *Fantastic Adventures,* June 1943

O'BRIEN, FLORENCE ROMA MUIR WILSON (1891–1930)
as Romer Wilson
The Death of Society; A Novel of Tomorrow. NY: Doran, [1921], 308pp. [British ed: *The Death of Society; Contre de Fee Premier.* London: W. Collins, 1921, 254pp.]
□ *Martin Schuler,* 1917; *The Grand Tour of Alphonse Marichaud,* 1923; *Latterday Symphony,* 1927; *The Hill of Cloves, A Tract On True Love, With A Digression Upon An Invention of the Devil,* 1929 (775 copies).

OFFUTT, ANDREW J. (Jr.)
as Andy Offut
And Gone Tomorrow. *If,* Dec 1954
as Andrew J. Offutt
Blacksword. *Galaxy,* Dec 1959
(with D. Bruce Berry) *Genetic Bomb.* NY: Warner, [1975], 207pp., paper.
✔ John Cleve

O'GRADY, STANDISH JAMES (1846–1928) *Irish*
as Arthur Clive
■ *Boswell and His Enemies,* 1874; *The Trammels of Poetic Expression,* 1875; *Walt Whitman, Poet of Joy,* 1875.
as Luke Netterville
The Queen of the World; or, Under the Tyranny. London: Lawrence & Bullen, 1900, 293pp.
as Standish O'Grady
□ *The Bog of Stars,* 1893 (ss col); *The Chain of Gold,* 1895 (juv); *Ulric, The Ready,* 1896.
■ *All Ireland,* 1898; *Selected Essays and Passages,* 1918.

OLDFIELD, CLAUDE HOUGHTON (1889–   )
as Claude Houghton
The Phantom Host and Other Verses. London: E. Mathews, 1917, 47pp. *poetry*
Neighbours. London: R. Holden, 1926, 277pp.

I Am Jonathan Scrivener. London: Butterworth, 1930, 314pp.
Julian Grant Loses His Way. London: Heinemann, [1933], 332pp.
Three Fantastic Tales. London: Joiner, [1934], 79pp. front. (275 copies) *ss col*
This Was Ivor Trent. London: Heinemann, [1935], 323pp.
The Beast. Belfast: Quota Press, 1936, 44pp., ill. (250 copies)
Six Lives and A Book. London: Collins, 1943, 255pp.
The Man Who Could Still Laugh. London: Todd Publishing Co., 1943, 16pp., paper.
□ *Tavern of Dreams,* 1919 (poetry); *Crisis,* 1929; *A Hair Divides,* 1930; *The Passing of the Third Floor Back,* 1935; *Christina,* 1936; *Passport To Paradise,* 1944; *Transformation Scene,* 1946; *The Enigma of Conrad Stone,* 1952.
■ *The Kingdoms of the Spirit,* 1924.

OLIPHANT, MARGARET OLIPHANT (Wilson) (Mrs. Francis W.) (1828–1897) *Scottish*
Born: Wallyford
Autobiography: *The Autobiography and Letters of Mrs. O.W. Oliphant,* arranged and edited by Mrs. H. Coghill. NY: Dodd, Mead, 1899, 451pp.
as Author of "A Little Pilgrim"
The Open Door and the Portrait. Boston: Roberts Brothers, 1885, 164pp.
as (Mrs.) Oliphant
A Beleaguered City. NY: Munro, 1879, 30pp. (with "The Wakening" by K. S. Macquord)
A Beleaguered City . . . A Story of the Seen and Unseen. London: Macmillan, 1880 [1879], 267pp.
The Wizard's Son. NY: J. W. Lovell, [1883], 454pp.
Stories of the Seen and Unseen. Boston: Roberts Brothers, 1889, 123pp. & 190pp. & 134pp. & 164pp. col
□ *Mrs. Margaret Maitland,* 1849; *Adam Graeme,* 1852; *Zaidee,* 1856; *Chronicles of Carlingford,* 1863-76 (4 novels).
■ *The Makers of Venice,* 1887; *A Literary History of England, 1790–1825,* 1882.
anonymous
A Little Pilgrim. Boston: Roberts Brothers, 1882, 123pp.
The Land of Darkness. London: Macmillan, 1888, 238pp.

OLIVER, AMY ROBERTA (Ruck) (Mrs. George) (1878–   ) *British*
as Mrs. Oliver Onions
appeared along with Berta Ruck on some titles as: Berta Ruck (Mrs. Oliver Onions)
as Berta Ruck
A Wish A Day. NY: Dodd, Mead, [1956], 275pp.
Sherry and Ghosts. London: Hurst & Blackett, [1961], 192pp.
□ *His Official Fiancee,* 1914; *The Immortal Girl,* 1925.

OLIVER, FREDERICK S(penser) (1866–1899)
as Phylos, the Tibetan
A Dweller On Two Planets; or, The Dividing of the Way. Los Angeles: Baumgardt Publishing Co., 1905, 423pp., ill.
An Earth Dweller's Return. Milwaukee, Wisconsin: Lemuria Press, 1940, 509pp., ill. [a rewrite and expansion of "A Dweller on Two Planets"]

OLIVER, GEORGE (*ne* George Oliver Onions) (1873-1961) *British*
Born: Bradford
as Oliver Onions
Tales From A Far Riding. London: Murray, 1902, 312pp.
Back-O'-the Moon, and Other Stories. London: Hurst & Blackett, 1906, 348pp. *ss col*
Widdershins. London: M. Secker, [1911], 315pp. *ss col*

In Accordance With the Evidence. London: M. Secker, [1912], 297pp.

The New Moon, A Romance of Reconstruction. London: Hodder & Stoughton, [1918], 312pp.

The Tower of Oblivion. London: Hodder & Stoughton, 1921, 423pp.

Ghosts In Daylight. London: Chapman, 1924, 236pp. *ss col*

Whom God Hath Sundered. NY: Doran, [1926], 703pp.

The Painted Face. London: Heinemann, 1929, 294pp. *3 novellas*

A Certain Man. London: Heinemann, [1931], 360pp.

The Collected Ghost Stories of Oliver Onions. London: Nicholson & Watson, 1935, 689pp. *ss col*

The Italian Chest and Other Stories. London: M. Secker, 1939, 415pp.

The Hand of Kornelius Voyt. London: Hamilton, [1939], 319pp.

Bells Rung Backwards. London: Staples Press, [1953], 285pp.

□ *The Compleat Bachelor*, 1900; *The Odd-Job Man*, 1903; *Little Devil Doubt*, 1909; *Mushroom Town*, 1914; *A Case In Camera*, 1920; *The Blood Eagle*, 1941.

OLIVER, SYMMES C(hadwick) (1928-   ) *U.S.*
Born: Cincinnati, Ohio
as Chad Oliver

The Land of Lost Content. **Super Science Stories**, Nov 1950

Mists of Dawn. Philadelphia: Winston, [1952], 208pp.

Shadows In The Sun. NY: Ballantine, [1954], 152pp., paper/hardback.

Another Kind. NY: Ballantine, [1955], 170pp., paper/hardback. *ss col*

The Winds of Time. Garden City: Doubleday, 1956, 192pp.

Unearthly Neighbors. NY: Ballantine, [1960], 144pp., paper.

The Wolf Is My Brother. NY: Signet, [1967], 144pp., paper.

The Edge of Forever; Classic Anthropological Science Fiction. Sherbourne Press, 1971, 305pp.

as Symmes C(hadwick) Oliver

■ *Ecology and Cultural Continuity As Contributing Factors In the Social Organization of the Plains Indians*, 1962.

OLSEN, ALFRED JOHANNES (Jr.) (1884-1956) *U.S.*
as Bob Olben

The Superperfect Bride. **Avon Science Fiction Reader** #2, 1951

as Bob Olsen

The Four Dimensional Roller-Press. **Amazing**, June 1927

OLSON, EUGENE E. (1936-   ) *U.S.*
as Brad Steiger

Three Tales for the Horrid At Heart. **Fantastic**, Jan 1963

■ *Strangers From the Skies*, 1966; *ESP Your Sixth Sense*, 1967; *The Mass Murderer*, 1967; *Voices From Beyond*, 1968; *Real Ghosts, Haunted Spirits, and Restless Minds*, 1968; *Sex and the Supernatural*, 1968; *The Mind Travellers*, 1968; (with L. G. Williams) *Other Lives*, 1969; *Judy Garland*, 1969; *Sex and Satanism*, 1969.

O'MALLEY, FRANK (1916-   )
as Frank O'Rourke

The Heavenly World Series and Other Baseball Stories. NY: Barnes, [1952], 192pp. *ss col*

□ *The Team*, 1949; *Bonus Rookie*, 1950; *Gunsmoke Over Big Muddy*, 1952; *Latigo*, 1953.

O'MALLEY, M(ary) D(olling) (Sanders) (Lady) (1889-1974) *British*

as Ann Bridge

The Song of the House. London: Chatto & Windus, 1936, 282pp. *ss col*

And Then You Came. London: Chatto & Windus, 1948, 319pp.

□ *The Ginger Griffin*, 1934; *Illyrian Spring*, 1935; *Enchanter's Nightshade*, 1937; *Singing Waters*, 1946; *House At Kilmartin*, 1951; *The Dark Moment*, 1952.

O'NOLAN, BRIAN (*ne* Brien O'Nuallain) (1911-1966) *Irish*
Born: Northern Ireland
as Myles na gCopaleen

column in the **Dublin Irish Times**, 1940-1966

Faustus Kelly. Dublin: Cahill, 1943, 123pp. *play*

The Best of Myles: A Selection From Cruskeen Lawn. London: Mac Gibbon, 1968, 400pp., ill.

as Flann O'Brien

At Swim-Two-Birds. London: Longmans, 1939, 315pp.

The Dalkey Archive. London: MacGibbon, 1964, 222pp., ill.

The Third Policeman. London: MacGibbon, 1967, 200pp.

□ *The Hard Life*, 1961.

● George Knowall, Brian Nolan

OPPENHEIM, E(dward) PHILLIPS (1866-1946) *English*
Born: Lancaster
Autobiography: *The Pool of Memory.* London: Hodder & Stoughton, 1941, 299pp.
Biography: *The Prince of Story Tellers*, by Robert Standish, 1957.
as E. Phillips Oppenheim

The Great Awakening. London: Ward, Lock, 1902, 320pp.

The Moving Finger. Boston: Little, Brown, 1911. [Brit. title: *The Falling Star*]

The Daughter of Astrea. NY: C. H. Doscher, 1909, 228pp.

The Moving Finger. Boston: Little, Brown, 1911. [Brit. title: *The Falling Star*]

The Double Life of Mr. Alfred Burton. Boston: Little, Brown, 1913, 322pp.

The Great Prince Shan. Boston: Little, Brown, 1922,

The Adventures of Mr. Joseph P. Cray. London: Hodder & Stoughton, [1926], 288pp.

Matorni's Vineyard. Boston: Little, Brown, 1928, 308pp.

Up the Ladder of Gold. Boston: Little, Brown, 1931, 312pp.

The Dumb Gods Speak. London: Hodder & Stoughton, 1937, 319pp.

Mr. Mirakel. Boston: Little, Brown, 1943, 279pp.

□ MYSTERY: *The Mysterious Mr. Sabin*, 1898; *Anna the Adventuress*, 1904; *The Missing Delora*, 1910; *The Mischief-Maker*, 1912; *The Amazing Quest of Mr. Ernest Bliss*, 1919; *The Devil's Paw*, 1920; *Aaron Rodd, Diviner*, 1920; *Miss Brown of XYO*, 1927; *The Million Pound Deposit*, 1930; *Ask Miss Mott*, 1935.

as Anthony Partridge

□ MYSTERY: *The Distributors*, 1908; *The Evil Shepherd*, 1922; *Curious Happenings to the Rooke Legatees*, 1937.

ORDONEZ EDMONDSON Y COTTON, JOSE MARIO GARRY (1922-   ) *naturalized U.S.*
Born: Villa Hersoma de Rascuachitlan, Tabasco, Mexico
as G. C. Edmondson

Blessed Are the Meek. **Astounding**, Sept 1955

The Ship That Sailed the Time Stream. NY: Ace, [1965], 167pp., paper. (Ace Double M 109)

Stranger Than You Think. NY: Ace, [1965], 87pp., paper. (Ace Double M 109)

Chapayeca. Garden City: Doubleday, 1971, 163pp.

OSTRANDER, ISABEL E(genton)   (1885-1924)
as Robert Orr Chippenfield
☐ MYSTERY: *The Second Bullet*, 1919; *Unseen Hands*, 1920; *Above Suspicion*, 1923.
as David Fox
The Man Who Convicted Himself. NY: McBride, 1920, 308pp.
☐ *The Hand Writing On the Wall*, 1916; *The Doom Dealers; An Exploit of the Shadowers, Inc.*, 1923.
as Douglas Grant
☐ *The Fifth Ace*, 1918; *Booty*, 1919; *Anything Once*, 1920.
as Isabel Ostrander
☐ MYSTERY: *At One-Thirty*, 1915; *The Heritage of Cane*, 1916; *The Clue In the Air*, 1917; *The Island of Intrigue*, 1918; *Annihilation*, 1924; *The Black Joker*, 1925.

OURSLER, (Charles) FULTON   (1893-1952)   *U.S.*
Born: Baltimore, Maryland.
Autobiography: *Behold This Dreamer*, 1964.
as Anthony Abbot
(with Achmed Abdullah) *The Flower of the Gods.* NY: Green Circle, [1936], 254pp.
(with Achmed Abdullah) *The Shadow of the Master.* London: Hurst & Blackett, [1940], 224pp.
(with Achmed Abdullah) *These Are Strange Tales.* Philadelphia: Winston, [1948], 212pp. *ss col*
☐ MYSTERY: *The Creeps; Being A Full Statement About the Crimes At Buzzard's Bay*, 1930; *Crime of the Century*, 1931; *The Murder of Geraldine Foster*, 1931; *Murder of A Night Club Lady*, 1932; *Murder of the Circus Queen*, 1933; *About the Murder of A Man Afraid of Women*, 1937.
as Fulton Oursler
☐ *Poor Little Fool*, 1928; *The Great Jasper*, 1930. PLAYS: *The Spider*, 1927; *All the King's Men*, 1929; *The Greatest Story Ever Told*, 1949.
■ *A Skeptic In the Holy Land*, 1936; *Father Flanagan Of Boy's Town*, 1949; *Why I Know There Is A God*, 1950.
● April Armstrong, Samri Frikell

OUSELEY, GIDEON JASPER RICHARD   (1835-1906)
as Theosopho
(with Ellora) *Palingenesia: or, the Earth's New Birth.* by Theosopho, A Minister of the Holies, and Ellora A Seeress of the Sanctuary. Glasgow, Scotland: H. Nisbet, 1884, 359pp.
■ *New Light On Old Truths. A Manual of Doctrine*, 1888.

OWEN, FRANK   (1893-1968)   *U.S.*
as Gerald Abner
Cafeteria Girl.
as Raymond Braithwaite
short stories
as Hung Long Tom
☐ POETRY: *Flower Profiles*, etc.
as Richard Kent
The Desert Woman. Oriental Stories, Oct 1930 – Nov 1930
Divorce Bait.
as Frank Owen
The Man Who Owned the World. Weird Tales, Oct 1923
The Wind That Tramps The World. NY: Lantern Press, 1929, 118pp.
Pictureland. NY: Lantern Press, 1929, 117pp., ill. by 52 children. *juv*
House Mother. NY: Lantern Press, 1929, 300pp.
(with Ethel Owen) *Wind Blown Stories.* NY: The Albingdon Press, 1930.
The Purple Sea. NY: Lantern Press, 1930, 153pp. *ss col*
Rare Earth. NY: Lantern Press, 1931, 292pp.
Della-Wu, Chinese Courtezan; and Other Oriental Love Tales. NY: Lantern Press, 1931, 313pp. *ss col*
A Husband For Kutani. NY: Lee Furman, [1938], 199pp. *ss col*
The Scarlet Hill. NY: Carlyle House, 1941, 367pp.
The Porcelain Magician. NY: Gnome, [1949, c.1948], 256pp., ill. *ss col*
☐ *The Actress*, 1915; (with Ethel Owen) *Coat Tales From the Pockets of the Happy Giant*, 1927; *Between the Covers*, 1938.
as Roswell Williams
The Professional Virgin. NY: Lantern Press, 1931, 281pp.
Three In A Bed. NY: Godwin, 1932, 265pp.
Woman Without Love. NY: G. H. Watt, 1933, 283pp.
The Damned Lover. NY: Macauley, [1933], 256pp.
Vagabond Lady. NY: Macauley, [1934], 252pp.
Hand-Made Lady. NY: Carlyle House, [1934], 281pp.
Madonna of the Damned. NY: Macauley, [1935], 247pp.
Slant Eyed Woman. NY: Regent House, [1935], 246pp.
Loves of Lo-Foh. NY: C. Kendall, [1936], 287pp., ill.
Dark Destiny. NY: R. Speller Pub., [1936], 252pp.
[as the titles may indicate, these may not all be fantasies in the sense commonly meant when used in this book but the information on these books is scarce enough that I have included full entries.]

OWEN, HARRY COLLINSON   (1882-1956)
as Hugh Addison
The Battle of London. London: Jenkins, 1924 [1923], 312pp.
as (H.) Collinson Owen
☐ *The Adventures of Antoine*, 1922; *Zero*, 1927; *An Object Lesson*, 1929 (play).
■ *Salonica and After, The Side Show That Ended The War*, 1919; *The American Illusion*, 1929; *King Crime, An English Study of America's Greatest Problem*, 1931.
● Owen Collinson

PAGE, GERALD W. (1939-   ) *U.S.*
Born: Chattanooga, Tennessee
as Carleton Grindle
The City In the Syrtis. *Spaceway SF,* June 1970
as Gerald W. Page
The Happy Man. *Analog,* March 1963
✔ **Kenneth Pembrooke**

PAGE, NORVELL W. (1904-1961) *U.S.*
Born: Richmond, Virginia
as Randolph Craig
In *The Octopus,* Feb 1939
In *The Scorpion,* April 1939
as Norvell W. Page
Flame Winds. *Unknown,* June 1939
Flame Winds. NY: Berkley, 1969.
Sons of the Bear God, 1969.
as Grant Stockbridge
in *Spider* magazine Oct 1933 – Dec 1943. e.g. The Scourge
of the Yellow Fangs. *The Spider,* April 1937

PAGET, VIOLET (1856-1935) *British*
Born: Chateau St. Leonard, Normandy, France
as Vernon Lee
A Phantom Lover. A Fantastic Story. Edinburgh: Black-
wood, 1886, 116pp.
Hauntings. Fantastic Stories. London: Heinemann, 1890,
237pp. *ss col*
Pope Jacynth & Other Fantastic Tales. London: Grant
Richards, 1904, 200pp. *ss col*
Satan, The Waster, A Philosophic War Trilogy. London:
J. Lane, 1920, 300pp. *plays*
For Maurice, Five Unlikely Stories. London: J. Lane,
1927, 223pp. *ss col*
The Snake Lady and Other Stories. NY: Grove, [1954],
288pp. *ss col*
☐ *Ottilie,* 1883; *Miss Brown,* 1884; *Ariadne In Mantua,*
1903 (play).
■ *Studies of the Eighteenth Century In Italy,* 1880;
*Euphorion: Studies of the Antique and the Medieval
In the Renaissance,* 1882; *Art and Life,* 1896; *Limbo
and Other Essays,* 1897; *The Enchanted Woods and
Other Essays on the Genius of Places,* 1910; *The
Handling of Words and Other Studies In Literary
Psychology,* 1923; *Proteus; or, The Future of Intelligence,*
1925; *Music and Its Lovers, An Empirical Study of
Emotional and Imaginative Responses to Music,*
1932.

PALMER, JOHN LESLIE (1885-1944) *British*
as Francis Beeding [in collaboration with Hilary A. Saunders]
The Hidden Kingdom. Boston: Little, Brown, 1927, 370pp.
The House of Dr. Edwardes. London: Hodder & Stoughton,
1927, 308pp. [basis for film *Spellbound*]
The One Sane Man. Boston: Little, Brown, 1934, 314pp.
☐ MYSTERY: *The Six Proud Walkers,* 1928; *Death Walks
In Eastrepps,* 1931; *The Norwich Victims,* 1935.
as Christopher Hadon
☐ *Under the Long Barrow,* 1939.
as John (Leslie) Palmer
The Hesperides. A Looking Glass Fugue. London: Secker
& Warburg, 1936, 318pp.

☐ *The King's Men,* 1916; *The Happy Fool,* 1922; *Jennifer,*
1926; *Timothy,* 1931; *The Man With Two Names,* 1940.
■ *The Censor and the Theatre,* 1912; *The Comedy of
Manners,* 1913; *Studies In the Contemporary Theatre,*
1927; *Moliere,* 1930; *Ben Jonson,* 1934; *Political Char-
acters of Shakespeare,* 1945.
as David Pilgrim
☐ HISTORICAL FICTION: *So Great A Man,* 1937;
No Common Glory, 1941; *The Grand Design,* 1943;
The Emperor's Servant, 1946.
anonymous
☐ *The Battle of Britain,* 1940 (pamphlet).

PALMER, RAYMOND A(rthur) (1910-   ) *U.S.*
as Henry Gade [house pseudonym]
Pioneer—1957. *Fantastic Adventures,* Nov 1939
Liners of Space. *Amazing,* Dec 1939
The Invincible Crime Buster. *Amazing,* July 1941
as G. H. Irwin [house pseudonym]
The Vengeance of Martin Brand. *Amazing,* Aug 1942
The Justice of Martin Brand. *Other Worlds,* July 1950
as Raymond A. Palmer
(ed.) *Fantastic Adventures* from May 1939 - Dec 1949;
Amazing from June 1938 - Dec 1949; *Other Worlds*
from Nov 1949 - ? ; *Imagination* from Oct 1950 -
Dec 1950.
The Time Ray of Jandra. *Wonder Stories,* June 1930
as Frank Patton [house pseudonym]
The Test Tube Girl. *Amazing,* Jan 1942
Doorway to Hell. *Fantastic Adventures,* Feb 1942
A Patriot Never Dies. *Amazing,* Aug 1943
War Worker. *Amazing,* Sept 1943
Jewels of the Toad. *Fantastic Adventures,* Oct 1943
Mahaffey's Mystery. *Other Worlds,* March 1950
as J(oe) W(alter) Pelkie
King of the Dinosaurs. *Fantastic Adventures,* Oct 1945
as Wallace Quitman
Outlaw of Space. *Amazing,* Aug 1938
as A(lfred) R. Steber [see also **ROGER P. GRAHAM**]
The Blinding Ray. *Amazing,* Aug 1938
[all stories through Sept 1950 under this name are by
Palmer]
as Morris J. Steele [house pseudonym]
Polar Prison. *Amazing,* Dec 1938
The Phantom Enemy. *Amazing,* Feb 1939
Weapon For A Wac. *Amazing,* Sept 1944
as Robert N. Webster
ed. *Fate Magazine*
● **Rae Winters**

PALTOCK, ROBERT (1697-1767) *English*
Born: London
as William Bingfield, Esq.
*The Travels and Adventures of William Bingfield, Esq.
containing as Surprising a fluctuation of Circumstances. . . As Ever Befell One Man, with an accurate
account. . . of that most curious and amazing animal,
the dog-bird.* London: E. Withers & R. Baldwin, 1753,
2 vol., front.
as R. S., a Passenger in the Hector
*The Life and Adventures of Peter Wilkins, a Cornish
Man; Relating particularly, His Shipwreck near the South
Pole . . . His Extraordinary Conveyance to the Country
of Glums and Gawrys, or men and women that fly. . .
Likewise a description of this strange country, with the
laws, custom, and manners of its Inhabitants.* London:
J. Robinson, 1751, 2 vol.

PANGBORN, EDGAR (1909-1976) *U.S.*
Born: New York, New York
as Bruce Harrison
A-100, A Mystery Story. NY: Dutton, [1930], 249pp.

as Edgar Pangborn
Angel's Egg. *Galaxy*, June 1951
West of the Sun. Garden City: Doubleday, 1953, 219pp.
A Mirror for Observers. Garden City: Doubleday, [1954], 222pp.
Davy. NY: St. Martin's Press, [1964], 308pp.
The Judgement of Eve. NY: Simon & Schuster, [1966], 223pp.
□ *Wilderness of Spring*, 1958; *The Trial of Callista Blake*, 1961.

PARCELL, NORMAN H(owe) *English*
as Christopher Fairleigh
□ *In Nursery Rhyme Land*, 1948 (juv).
as John Nicholson
Space Ship to Venus. Bath, England: Venture Books, 1948, 233pp.
Costello, Psychic Investigator. Ilfracombe: A. H. Stockwell, [1954], 238pp.
as Norman Percival
■ *The Demon Bowler and Other Talks to School Boys*, 1945; *The Smoking Mountain, and Other Talks To School Boys*, 1947.

PARGETER, EDITH MAY (1913-   ) *English*
Born: Shropshire
as Edith Pargeter
The City Lies Four Square. NY: Reynal, Hitchcock, [1939], 296pp.
By Firelight. London: Heinemann, 1947, 324pp.
The Lily Hand and Other Stories. London: Heinemann, [1965], 215pp. *ss col*
□ *Hortensius, Friend of Nero*, 1936; *Ordinary People*, 1942; *She Goes To War*, 1942; *The Fair Young Phoenix*, 1948; *Fallen Into A Pit*, 1951; *Holiday With Violence*, 1952; *This Rough Magic*, 1953; *The Heaven Tree*, 1960.
■ *The Coast of Bohemia*, 1950.
as Ellis Peters
□ *Death and the Joyful Woman*, 1961; *Funeral of Figaro*, 1962; *Flight of A Witch*, 1965; *A Nice Derangement of Epitaphs*, 1965; *Black Is the Color of My True Love's Heart*, 1967; *The Grass Widow's Tale*, 1968; *The Knocker On Death's Door*, 1970; *Death To the Landlords*, 1972.

PARNELL, FRANK
as Gregory Francis [in collaboration with James MacGregor]
Question Mark. *New Worlds*, Winter 1951 (Br.)
as Francis Richardson [in collaboration with L. E. Bartle]
The Trojan Way. *Science Fiction #7*, Spring 1954 (Br.)

PARRY, MICHAEL PATRICK (1947-   ) *British*
Born: Brussels, Belgium
as Steve Lee
westerns
✔ Carlos Cassaba, Nick Fury, Linda Lovecraft, Eric Pendragon

PARTRIDGE, EDWARD BELLAMY (1877-   )
Autobiography: *Salad Days*, by Bellamy Partridge. NY: Crowell, [1951], 272pp., ill.
as Thomas Bailey
Long Night. NY: Godwin, [1935], 287pp.
as Bellamy Partridge
□ *A Pretty Pickle*, 1930; *January Thaw*, 1945; *Big Freeze*, 1948; *The Old Oaken Bucket*, 1949.
■ *Sir Billy Howe*, 1932; *The Roosevelt Family In America; An Imperial Saga*, 1936; *Fill 'er Up; The Story of Fifty Years of Motoring*, 1952.
as Edward Bellamy Partridge
□ *Sube Cane*, 1917.

PATTEN, CLINTON A.
● **as James Rock**
Thro' Space. Boston: New England Druggist Publishing Co., 1909, 188pp.

PATTEN, GILBERT (1866-1945)
as Gilbert Patten
□ *Jud and Joe, Printers and Publishers*, 1899; *Bill Bruce of Harvard*, 1910.
as William G. Patten
Aztec Jack, the Desert Nomad; or, The Vulture's Swoop. A Story of Astonishing Adventures In the Buried City of Northern Arizona. NY: Beadle & Adams, 1891, 28pp., ill.
□ *Captain Mystery; or, Five In One*, 1887; *Clear-Grit Cal, The Never-Say-Die Detective*, 1892.
as Burt L. Standish
Frank Merriwell's Air Voyage, or, Heroes Undaunted. NY: Street & Smith, [1907], 315pp.
□ "Frank Merriwell" series
as William West Wilder
□ *Cowboy Chris*, 1897.
✔ Emerson Bell

PATTEN, J. A(lexander)
as Clayton W. Cobb
The Mountaineer Detective. A Thrilling Tale of the Moonshiners. NY: Street & Smith, [1889], 171pp., ill.

PATTON, FRANK [house pseudonym]
unattributed
Astral Assassin. *Amazing*, July 1943
Cloak of Satan. *Fantastic Adventures*, Dec 1943
The Identity of Sue Tenet. *Other Worlds*, Dec 1952
Question Please! *Other Worlds*, April 1953
Sure Thing. *Science Stories*, Feb 1954
The Secret of Pierre Cotreau. *Science Stories*, April 1954
by Raymond A. Palmer
The Test Tube Girl. *Amazing*, Jan 1942
Doorway to Hell. *Fantastic Adventures*, Feb 1942
A Patriot Never Dies. *Amazing*, Aug 1943
War Worker. *Amazing*, Sept 1943
Jewels of the Toad. *Fantastic Adventures*, Oct 1943
Mahaffey's Mystery. *Other Worlds*, March 1950
by Richard S. Shaver
When the Moon Bounced. *Amazing*, May 1949

PAULDING, JAMES KIRKE (c.1778-1860) *U.S.*
Born: New York
as Author of "John Bull In America"
[some of these titles may be anonymous]
The Merry Tales of Three Wise Men of Gotham. NY: G. & C. Carvill, 1826, 324pp. *ss col*
□ *Koningsmarke*, 1823; *The Dutchman's Fireside*, 1831; *Westward Ho!*, 1832; *The Puritan and His Daughter*, 1849.
■ *Lay of A Scotch Fiddle*, 1813; *Letters On Slavery*, 1835.
as "A Doubtful Gentleman"
Tales of A Good Woman. NY: G. & C. Carvill, 1829, 367pp.
as Sampson Fairlamb [signed preface]
□ *A Gift From Fairyland*, 1838.
as Launcelot Langstaff
Salmagundi. Second Series. Philadelphia: M. Thomas, 1819-1820, 3 vol. in 2. [the original series written by Washington Irving, William Irving, & Paulding]
as James K. Paulding
■ *A Life Of Washington*, 1835; *Slavery In the United States*, 1836.

anonymous
John Bull In America; or, The New Munchausen. NY: C. Wiley, 1825, 226pp.

PAYES, RACHEL RUTH COSGROVE (Mrs. Norman M.) (1922-) *U.S.*
Born: Westernport, Maryland
as E.L. Arch
Bridge to Yesterday. NY: Avalon, 1963, 192pp.
The Deathstone. NY: Avalon, 1964, 192pp.
Planet of Death. NY: Avalon, 1964, 192pp.
The First Immortals. NY: Avalon, 1965, 192pp.
The Double Minded Man. NY: Avalon, 1966, 192pp.
The Man With Three Eyes. NY: Avalon, 1967, 190pp.
as Rachel Cosgrove
Hidden Valley of Oz. Chicago: Reilly, 1951.
☐ *The Candy Stripers,* 1954; *Not For Glory,* 1963; *O Charitable Death,* 1968 (mystery).

PAYNE, DONALD GORDON (1924-) *English*
Born: London
as Ian Cameron
The Lost Ones. London: Hutchinson, 1961, 220pp.
☐ *The Midnight Sea,* 1958.
■ *Red Duster, White Ensign; The Story of the Malta Convoys,* 1959.
as Donald Gordon
Star-Raker. London: Hodder & Stoughton, 1962, 256pp.
Flight of the Bat. London: Hodder & Stoughton, [1963], 221pp.
☐ *The Golden Oyster,* 1967.

PECK, GEORGE WASHINGTON (1817-1859) *U.S.*
as Cantell A. Bigly
Aurifodina; or, Adventures In the Gold Region: A Fantastical 49er. Novel. NY: Baker & Scribner, 1849, 103pp.

● **PEEBLES, JOHN EWING** (1928-1968) *British*
[BMC & NUC list real name as James Pebles Ewing Kennaway]
Born: Perthshire, Scotland
as James Kennaway
Tunes of Glory. London: Putnam, 1956, 200pp.
Household Ghosts. London: Longmans, 1961, 187pp.
The Mind Benders. London: Longmans, [1963], 157pp.
The Bells of Shoreditch. London: Longmans, [1963], 211pp.
Some Gorgeous Accident. London: Longmans, 1967, 193pp.

PEMBER-DEVEREUX, MARGARET R(ose) (Roy) (McAdam) (Mrs.) (1877- ?)
as Roy Devereux
When They Came Back. London: Cassell, [1938], 281pp.
☐ *Reprobate Silver,* 1903; *Blue Magic,* 1927; *The Incredible Truth,* 1930.
■ *The Ascent of Woman,* 1896; *Side Lights On South Africa,* 1899; *Aspects of Algeria,* 1912; *Poland Reborn,* 1922; *John Loudon McAdam; Chapters In the History of Highways,* 1936.

PENDLETON, DON (1927-) *U.S.*
Born: Little Rock, Arkansas
as Dan Britain
The God Makers. NY: Pinnacle, [1968], paper.
The Guns of Terra 10. NY: Pinnacle, [1969], paper.
as Stephen Gregory
miscellaneous light fiction
as Don Pendleton
Revolt! NY: Beeline, [1968], paper.
The Olympians. San Diego, California: Greenleaf Classics, [1968], paper.
Cataclysm, The Day the World Ended. NY: Pinnacle, [1969], paper.

1989: Population Doomsday. NY: Pinnacle, [1970], 192pp., pap.
☐ "The Executioner" series, (#1—#35), Pinnacle Books.

PENDRAY, G(eorge) EDWARDS (1901-) *U.S.*
Born: Omaha, Nebraska
as Gawain Edwards
Rescue From Jupiter. Science Wonder Stories, Feb 1930
The Earth Tube. NY: Appleton, 1929, 308pp.
as G. Edward Pendray
Robert Goddard - Space Pioneer. Future, Sept 1958 *article*
☐ (with Kenyon Nicholson) *The Organ,* 1926 (play).
■ *Men, Mirrors, and Stars,* 1935; *The Story of the Time Capsule,* 1939; *The Coming Age of Rocket Power,* 1945.

PERKINS, VIOLET LILIAN
as Lilian Leslie [in collaboration with Archer Leslie Hood]
The Melody From Mars. NY: Authors' International Publishing Company, [1924], 206pp.

PERRY, A. T. (1887-) *naturalized British*
Born: Carpatho - Ukraine
as General Ack-Lak
The Emperor of the World; or, Out of the Steppes. London: J. Starcs, 1912, 73pp., paper.

PETAJA, EMILE (Theodore) (1915-) *U.S.*
Born: Milltown, Montana
as Henry Hasse [in collaboration with Henry Hasse] [one story only]
Don't Come To Mars! Fantastic Adventures, April 1950
as Emil Petaja
Time Will Tell. Amazing, June 1942
Alpha Yes, Terra No! NY: Ace, [1965], 156pp., paper. (Ace Double M 121)
The Caves of Mars. NY: Ace, [1965], 125pp., paper. (Ace Double M 133)
Saga of Lost Earths. NY: Ace, [1966], 124pp., paper. (Ace Double F 392)
The Star Mill. NY: Ace, [1966], 128pp., paper. (Ace Double F 414)
The Stolen Sun. NY: Ace, [1967], 136pp., paper. (Ace Double G 618)
Lord of the Green Planet. NY: Ace, [1967], 118pp., paper. (Ace Double H 22)
Tramontane. NY: Ace, [1967], 119pp., paper. (Ace Double H 36)
The Prism. NY: Ace, [1968], 126pp., paper. (Ace Double H 51)
Doom of the Green Planet. NY: Ace, [1968], 127pp., paper. (Ace Double H 70)
The Time Twister. NY: Dell, [1968], 158pp., paper.
The Path Beyond the Stars. NY: Dell, [1969], 188pp., paper.
The Nets of Space. NY: Berkley, [1969], paper.
Stardrift. Los Angeles: Fantasy Pub. Co., Inc. (FPCI), 1971.
As Dream and Shadow. San Francisco: S.I.S.U., 1972, 118pp., ill. *poetry*
as Theodore Pine [in collaboration with Henry Hasse] this story only
Secret of Satellite Seven. Amazing, Feb 1952
as Theodore Pine [alone]
Mysteries.

PETERSILEA, CARLYLE (1844-1903)
as Ernst von Himmel
The Discovered Country. Boston: E. von Himmel Pub. Co., [1889], 234pp.
Oceanides, A Psychical Novel. Boston: E. von Himmel Pub. Co., [1890], 418pp.

as Carlyle Petersilea

Mary Anne Carew: Wife, Mother, Spirit, Angel. Boston: Colby & Rich, 1893, 252pp.

■ *Technical Studies for Pianoforte,* 1884; *Piano Playing,* 1891 (instruction book); *Letters From the Spirit World. Written through the Mediumship of Carlyle Petersilea,* 1905.

PETERSON, JOHN VICTOR

as John Victor Peterson

Martyrs Don't Mind Dying. *Astounding,* March 1938

as Victor Valding [in collaboration with Allan Ingvald Benson]

Atmospherics. *Astounding,* Sept 1939

PFEIFFER, JOHANN GREGOR (16?–c.1723)

as Grazianus Agricola Auletes

Graziani Agricolae Auletis Sonderbahre Reisen in Unbekandte Lander. Aus Richtig Gehaltenen Diariis, Aufgezeichneten Anmerckungen, und Angmerckten Entdeckungen. Gedruckt zu Hanochia, in der Ophirischen Landschafft Canaan. Hanochia [Bremen?], 1721-1722, 3 pts. in 1 vol.

PFEIL, DON

as William Arrow [house pseudonym]

Escape From Terror Lagoon. NY: Ballantine, [1976], paper.

PHELPS, GEORGE H(amilton) (1854–)

as Patrick Quinn Tangent

The New Columbia; or, The Re-United States. Findlay, Ohio: New Columbia Pub. Co., 1909, 99pp.

PHILIPS, JUDSON P(entecost) (1903–) *U.S.*

Born: Massachusetts

as Hugh Pentecost

Challenge To the Reader. *Mysterious Traveler Magazine,* March 1952

□ MYSTERY: *Cancelled In Red,* 1939; *The 24th Horse,* 1940; *I'll Sing At Your Funeral,* 1942; *Shadow of Madness,* 1950; *Around Dark Corners,* 1970 (ss col); *Birthday, Deathday,* 1972; *The Champagne Killer,* 1972.

as Judson (P.) Philips

(with Thomas M. Johnson) *Red War.* NY: Doubleday, Doran, 1936, 306pp.

□ MYSTERY: *The Death Syndicate,* 1938; *Death Delivers A Post Card,* 1939; *The Fourteenth Trump,* 1942; *The Laughter Trap,* 1964; *The Black Glass City,* 1964; *Dead Woman Of the Year,* 1967; *Escape A Killer,* 1971; *The Vanishing Senator,* 1972.

■ (with R. W. Wood) *Hold 'Em Girls, the Intelligent Woman's Guide to Men and Football,* 1936.

PHILLIFENT, JOHN T(homas) (1916–) *English*

Born: Durham

as John T. Phillifent

Point. *Fantastic,* Dec 1961

The Mad Scientist Affair. London: Four Square, [1966], 118pp., paper. (Man From Uncle #8)

The Corfu Affair. London: Four Square, [1967], 125pp., paper. (Man From Uncle #13)

The Power-Cube Affair. London: Four Square, [1968], 127pp., paper. (Man From Uncle #15) [U.N.C.L.E. volumes numbered differently in U.S.]

Genius Unlimited. NY: DAW #16, [1972], paper.

Hierarchies. NY: Ace, [1973], paper.

Life With Lancelot. NY: Ace, [1973], paper.

King of Argent. NY: DAW #46, [1973], paper.

as John Rackham

Drog. *Science Fantasy #27,* Feb 1958

Space Puppet. London: Pearson, 1954, paper.

Master Weed. London: Pearson, 1954, paper.

Jupiter Equilateral. London: Pearson, 1954, paper.

Alien Virus. London: Pearson, 1955, paper.

The Touch of Evil. London: Digit, [1963], 157pp., paper.

Watch On Peter. London: Jonathan Cape, 1964.

We, The Venusians. NY: Ace, [1965], 138pp., paper. (Ace Double M 127)

Danger From Vega. NY: Ace, [1966], 149pp., paper. (Ace Double G 576)

The Beasts of Kohl. NY: Ace, [1966], 154pp., paper. (Ace Double G 592)

Time To Live. NY: Ace, [1966], 141pp., paper. (Ace Double G 606)

The Double Invaders. NY: Ace, [1967], 120pp., paper. (Ace Double G 623)

Alien Sea. NY: Ace, [1968], 154pp., paper. (Ace Double H 40)

The Proxima Project. NY: Ace, [1968], 149pp., paper. (Ace Double H 91)

Treasure of Tau Ceti. NY: Ace, [1969], paper.

Ipomoea. NY: Ace, [1969], paper.

The Anything Tree. NY: Ace, [1970], paper.

Flower of Doradil. NY: Ace, [1970], paper.

Dark Planet. NY: Ace, [1971], paper.

Beyond Capella. NY: Ace, [1971], paper.

Earthstrings. NY: Ace, [1972], paper.

Beanstalk. NY: DAW #78, [1973], paper.

PHILLIPS, PETER [house pseudonym]

unattributed

Dreams Are Sacred. *Astounding,* Sept 1948

Manna. *Astounding,* Feb 1949

Unknown Quantity. *New Worlds #5,* 1949

P-Plus. *Astounding,* Aug 1949

Plagiarist. *New Worlds,* Summer 1950

"Well I'll Be Hexed." *Fantastic Adventures,* Aug 1950

by Howard Browne

Field Study. *Galaxy,* April 1951

At No Extra Cost. *Marvel,* Aug 1951

She Who Laughs. *Galaxy,* April 1952

Lost Memory. *Galaxy,* May 1952

Criteria. *Planet Stories,* May 1952

University. *Galaxy,* April 1953

Lila. *Startling Stories,* April 1953

Sylvia. *Fantasy Magazine,* June 1953

The Warning. *Magazine of Fantasy and Science Fiction,* Sept 1953

c/o Mr. Makepeace. *Magazine of Fantasy and Science Fiction,* Feb 1954

First Man In the Moon. *Magazine of Fantasy and Science Fiction,* Sept 1954

Variety Agent. *Infinity,* June 1956

Next Stop the Moon. *New Worlds #67,* Jan 1958 (Br.)

PHILLPOTTS, EDEN (1862-1960) *British*

Born: Mt. Aboo, Rajputana Province, India

as Harrington Hext

Number 87. London: T. Butterfield, 1922, 287pp.

The Thing At Their Heels. London: T. Butterfield, 1923, 287pp.

The Monster. NY: Macmillan, 1925, 328pp.

□ MYSTERY: *Who Killed Cock Robin?,* 1924 (U.S.). [*Who Killed Diana?,* 1924 (Br.)]

as Eden Phillpotts

A Deal With the Devil. London: Bliss, Sands & Foster, 1895, 190pp.

Children of the Mist. London: A.D. Innes, 1898, 460pp.

Loup Garou! London: Sands, 1899, 264pp., ill. ss col

Fancy Free. London: Methuen, 1901, 302pp., ill. ss col

The Girl and the Faun. London: Palmer & Hayward, 1916, 78pp., ill.

The Chronicles of St. Tid. London: Skeffington & Son, 1917, 283pp. ss col

Evander. London: Macmillan, 1919, 199pp.

The Grey Room. London: Hurst & Blackett, [1921], 286pp.

Pan and the Twins. London: G. Richards, 1922, 239pp.

Black, White, and Brindled. NY: Macmillan, 1923, 344pp. *ss col*

The Lavender Dragon. London: G. Richards, 1923, 199pp.

The Treasures of Typhon. London: G. Richards, 1924, 249pp.

Circe's Island and The Girl and the Faun. London: G. Richards, 1925, 238pp.

A Voice From the Dark. London: Hutchinson, [1925], 288pp.

Up Hill, Down Dale. London: Hutchinson, [1925], 287pp.

The Miniature. London: Watts, [1926], 125pp.

Peacock House and Other Mystery Stories. London: Hutchinson, [1926], 280pp. *ss col*

Arachne. London: Faber & Gwyer, [1927], 223pp.

The Torch and Other Tales. London: Hutchinson, [1929], 286pp. *ss col*

The Apes. London: Faber, 1929, 182pp.

Alcyone (A Fairy Story). London: E. Benn, [1930], 189pp.

The Owl of Athene. London: Hutchinson, [1936], 198pp.

Lycanthrope: The Mystery of Sir William Wolf. London: T. Butterworth, [1937], 253pp.

Saurus. London: Murray, [1938], 280pp.

Tabletop. NY: Macmillan, 1939, 236pp.

Address Unknown. London: Hutchinson, [1949], 219pp.

□ *Down Dartmoor Way,* 1895; *Lying Prophets,* 1896; *Sons Of the Morning,* 1900; *The American Prisoner; A Romance of the West Country,* 1903; *The Three Brothers,* 1909; *Tales of the Tenements,* 1910 (ss col); *The Beacon,* 1911; *Brother Man,* 1928 (col); *Minions of the Moon,* 1934; *The Changeling,* 1944; *Fall of the House of Heron,* 1949. POETRY: *Sonnets From Nature,* 1935; *The Enchanted Wood,* 1948. PLAYS: *The Farmer's Wife,* 1917; *By a Broom,* 1929; *A Cup Of Happiness,* 1933. MYSTERY: *Miser's Money,* 1920; *The Red Redmaynes,* 1922; *Jig-Saw,* 1926; *The Jury,* 1927; *The Ring Fence,* 1928; *The Anniversary Murder,* 1936.

PHILPOT, JOSEPH HENRY (1850- ?)
as Philip Lafargue
The Forsaken Way; A Romance. London: Hurst & Blackett, 1900, 287pp.
□ *The New Judgment of Paris,* 1888; *The Salt of the Earth,* 1895.
as J. H. Philpot
■ *Maistre Wace, A Pioneer In Two Literatures,* 1925.

PHYSICK, EDWARD HAROLD (1878-1972) *British*
Born: London
as E. H. Visiak
The Haunted Island: A Pirate Romance. London: E. Mathews, 1910, 194pp.
Medusa: A Story of Mystery and Ecstasy, and Strange Horror. London: Gollancz, 1929, 286pp.
□ POETRY: *The Phantom Ship and Other Poems,* 1912; *The Battle Fiends and Other Poems,* 1916.
■ *Milton Agonistes, A Metaphysical Criticism,* 1923; *The Mirror of Conrad,* 1955.

PICTON, NINA
as Laura Dearborn
At the Threshold. NY: Cassell, [1893], 144pp.
as Nina Picton
□ ■ *The Panorama of Sleep; or, Soul and Symbol.* NY: The Philosophic Company, 1903, 160pp., ill.

PIERCE, JOHN R(obinson) (1910-) *U.S.*
as J.J. Coupling
Universes to Order. *Astounding,* Feb 1944 *article*

as J(ohn) (R.) Pierce
The Relics From the Earth. *Science Wonder Stories,* March 1930
■ *Theory and Design of Electron Beams,* 1949; *Travelling Wave Tubes,* 1950; *Electrons, Waves, and Messages,* 1956; (with E.E. Davis) *Man's World of Sound,* 1958; *Symbols, Signals, and Noise,* 1961; (with A.G. Tressler) *The Research State: A History of Science In New Jersey,* 1964; *Quantum Electronics,* 1966; *Science, Art, and Communication,* 1968; *Satellite Communication,* 1968.

PIGGOTT, WILLIAM
as Hubert Wales
Blue Flames. London: J. Long, 1918, 320pp.
□ *Cynthia In the Wilderness,* 1907; *The Spinster,* 1912; *The Rationalist,* 1917.

PILKINGTON, MARY (Hopkins) (Mrs.) (1766-1839) *British*
Born: Cambridge
as Author of "Delia"
The Accusing Spirit; or, DeCourcy and Eglantine. A Romance. London: Lane, 1802, 4 vol., front.
as (Mrs.) (M.S.) Pilkington
□ *Edward Barnard; or, Merit Exalted,* 1797; *The Subterranean Cavern; or, Memoirs of Antoinette de Monflorance,* 1798 (4 vol); *Tales for Young Ladies,* 1802; *The Sorrows of Caesar; or, Adventures of a Foundling Dog,* 1813; *The Shipwreck; or, Misfortune the Inspirer of Virtuous Sentiments,* 1819.
■ *A Mirror for the Female Sex.*

PINCHER, HENRY CHAPMAN (1914-) *British*
Born: Ambala, Punjab, India
as Chapman Pincher
Not With A Bang. London: Weidenfeld, Nicholson, [1965], 302pp.
□ *The Giant Killer,* 1967; *The Penthouse Conspirators,* 1970.
■ *Into the Atomic Age,* 1948; *A Study of Fishes,* 1948; *Evolution,* 1950; *Spotlight on Animals,* 1950; *Sleep, How To Get More Of It,* 1954.

PIRIE-GORDON, C(harles) H(arry) C(linton) (1883-) *British*
as C.H.C. Pirie-Gordon
■ *Innocent the Great, An Essay on His Life and Times,* 1907; (editor) *Burke's Genealogical and Heraldic History of the Landed Gentry (15th) Centenary Edition* ["Burke's Peerage"], 1937.
as Prospero and Caliban [in collaboration with Frederick W. Rolfe]
The Weird of the Wanderer, Being the Papyrus Records of Some Incidents In One Of the Previous Lives of Mr. Nicholas Crabbe. London: Rider, 1912, 298pp.
Hubert's Arthur; Being Certain Curious Documents Found Among the Literary Remains of Mr. N.C., Here Produced by Prospero and Caliban. London: Cassell, [1935], 453pp.

PITTARD, HELENE (Dufour) (Mrs. Eugene) (1874-)
as Noelle Roger
The New Adam. London: S. Paul, 1926, 256pp.
He Who Sees. London: G.G. Harrap, 1935, 295pp.
□ *The Victims' Return,* 1917.

PITCAIRN, JOHN JAMES
as Clifford Ashdown [in collaboration with R. Austin Freeman]
□ MYSTERY: *The Adventures of Romney Pringle,* 1902.
as Ashdown Piers (with R. Austin Freeman)
By The Black Deep. *Winsor Magazine,* May 1903

PLUNKETT, EDWARD JOHN MORETON DRAX (18th Baron Dunsany) (1878-1957) *Irish*

Born: County Kent

as Lord Dunsany

The Gods of Pegana. London: Mathews, 1905, 94pp., ill.

Time and the Gods. London: Heinemann, 1906, 179pp., ill. *ss col*

The Sword of Welleran and Other Stories. London: G. Allen, 1908, 242pp., ill. *ss col*

A Dreamer's Tales. London: G. Allen, 1910, 252pp. *ss col*

The Book of Wonder. London: Heinemann, 1912, 97pp., ill. *ss col*

Five Plays. London: G. Richards, 1914, 111pp. *plays*

Fifty-One Tales. London: Mathews, 1915, 111pp. *ss col*

Tales of Wonder. London: Mathews, 1916, 187pp., ill. *ss col*

A Night At An Inn. NY: Sunwise Turn, Inc., 1916, 34pp. [London: Putnam, [1916?], 15pp.]

Plays of Gods and Men. Dublin: Talbot Press, 1917, 191pp. *plays*

Tales of War. Dublin: Talbot Press, [1918], 155pp.

Tales of Three Hemispheres. Boston: J.W. Luce, [1919], 147pp. *ss col* [London: T. Fisher Unwin, 1920]

If, A Play In Four Acts. London: Putnam, [1921], 160pp. *play*

Don Rodriguez; Chronicles of Shadow Valley. London: Putnam, [1922], 318pp., ill. (500 cop numbered and signed of deluxe edition)

The Queen's Enemies. London: Putnam, [1922], 40pp.

Plays of Near and Far. London: Putnam, [1922], 150pp. (500 cop) *plays*

The Laughter of the Gods. London: Putnam, [1922], 76pp. *play*

The King of Elfland's Daughter. London: Putnam, [1924], 301pp.

Alexander and Three Small Plays. London: Putnam, [1925], 147pp. *col*

The Evil Kettle. London: Putnam, [1925], 117-132 pagination. *play*

The Charwoman's Shadow. London: Putnam, [1926], 339pp.

The Blessing of Pan. London: Putnam, [1927], 287pp., ill. *ss col*

The Old Folks of the Centuries. London: Mathews & Marrot, [1930], 66pp. (900 cop)

The Travel Tales of Mr. Joseph Jorkens. London: Putnam, [1931], 304pp. *ss col*

The Curse of the Wise Woman. London: Heinemann, [1933], 309pp.

Mr. Jorkens Remembers Africa. London: Heinemann, [1934], 298pp. *ss col*

If I Were Dictator; Pronouncements of the Grand Macaroni. London: Methuen, [1934], 107pp.

Up In the Hills. London: Heinemann, [1935], 316pp.

My Talks with Dean Spanley. London: Heinemann, [1936], 137pp.

Rory and Bran. London: Heinemann, [1936], 320pp.

Plays For Earth and Air. London: Heinemann, [1937], 163pp. *plays*

The Story of Mona Sheehy. London: Heinemann, [1939], 334pp. *ss col*

Jorkens Has A Large Whiskey. London: Putnam, [1940], 323pp. *ss col*

The Fourth Book of Jorkens. Sauk City, Wisconsin: Arkham House, 1948, 194pp. (3118 cop) *ss col*

The Man Who Ate the Phoenix. London: Jarrolds, [1949], 223pp. *ss col*

The Strange Journeys of Colonel Polders. London: Jarrolds, 1950, 208pp.

The Last Revolution. London: Jarrolds, 1951, 200pp.

The Little Tales of Smethers and Other Stories. London: Jarrolds, 1952, 232pp. *ss col*

Jorkens Borrows Another Whiskey. London: M. Joseph, 1954, 256pp. *ss col*

☐ PLAYS: *Glittering Gates,* 1909; *The Gods of Mountains,* 1911; *Nowadays,* 1918; *The Laughter of the Gods,* 1933.

■ *Unhappy-Far Off Things,* 1919; *The Art of Playwriting,* 1928 (includes lecture on subject by Dunsany); *My Ireland,* 1937; *The Siren Wakes,* 1945.

POE, EDGAR ALLAN (1809-1849) *U.S.*

Born: Boston, Massachusetts

Bibliography: *Bibliography of the Writings of Edgar A. Poe,* by John W. Robertson, M.D. San Francisco: Russian Hill Private Press, 1934 (350 cop) [Kraus reprint-1969]. *A Bibliography of the First Printing of the Writings of Edgar Allen Poe.* Hattiesburg, Mississippi: Heartman & Canny, 1940.(350 cop)

as A Bostonian

Tamerlane and Other Poems. Boston, Calvin F.S. Thomas. . . Printer, 1827. *poetry*

as Arthur Gordon Pym

The Narrative of Arthur Gordon Pym of Nantucket. Comprising the details of a mutiny and atrocious butchery on board the American brig Grampus, on her way to the South seas in the month of June 1827 . . . with the incredible adventures and discoveries still farther south to which that distressing calamity gave rise. NY: Harper & Bros., 1838, 201pp.

as Edgar A(llan) Poe

(editor) *Southern Literary Messenger* Dec 1835-Jan 1837

(editor) *Burton's Gentleman's Magazine, and Monthly American Review* July 1839-Dec 1840

(editor) *Graham's Magazine* April 1841-May 1842

(editor) *The Broadway Journal* March 8, 1845-Jan 3, 1846

Metzengerstein. *Saturday Courier* (Philadelphia), Jan 14, 1832

The MS Found In A Bottle. *The Saturday Visiter,* Oct 19, 1833

Hans Phaal. *Southern Literary Messenger,* June 1835

Fall of the House of Usher. *Burton's Gentleman's Magazine and American Monthly Review,* Vol V, No 3, Sept 1839

A Descent Into the Maelstrom. *Graham's Monthly,* Vol 18, No 5, May 1841

Al Aaraaf, Tamerlane and Minor Poems. Baltimore: Hatch and Dunning, 1829, 71pp., paper. *poetry*

Poems (second edition). NY: E. Bliss, 1831, 124pp. *poetry*

Tales of the Grotesque and Arabesque. Philadelphia: Lea and Blanchard, 1840, 2 vol. *ss col*

The Prose Romances of Edgar A. Poe. . . No I, Containing The Murders In the Rue Morgue, and The Man That Was Used Up. Philadelphia: William H. Graham, 1843, 48pp., paper. *ss col*

The Raven and Other Poems. NY: Wiley & Putnam, 1845, 100 pp. *poetry*

Tales. NY: Wiley & Putnam, 1845, 228pp. *ss col*

Eureka: A Prose Poem (Eureka: An Essay On the Spiritual and Material Universe). NY: Geo. P. Putnam (of late firm of Wiley & Putnam), 1848, 143pp. *poetry*

The Haunted Palace, in *Gift-leaves of American Poetry,* ed. by R. W. Griswold. NY: J.C. Riker, 1849. *poetry*

■ *The Conchologist's first book, or, A system of Testaceous malacology, arranged expressly for the use of schools, in which the animals, according to Cuvier, are given with the shells, a great number of new species added, and the whole brought up as accurately as possible, to the present condition of the science.* Philadelphia: Pub. for the author, by Haswell, Barrington & Haswell, 1839, 156pp. [acc. to Robertson bibliography, Poe was the "stool-pigeon" who allowed his name to be used on this flagrant theft of a textbook of conchology written by Capt. Thomas Brown and published in Glasgow in 1833. Poe actually wrote the preface and composed the title page to the book above.]

as Quarles

The Raven, in *American Review,* Feb 1845 *poetry*

as Quarles Quickens
  SATIRICAL ESSAY: *English Notes, intended for very extensive circulation.* Boston: Pub. at the Daily Mail Office, 1842, 16pp.; *English Notes: A Rare and Unknown Work, Bieng* [sic] *a reply to Charles Dickens' "American Notes," with critical comments by Joseph Jackson and George H. Sargent.* NY: L.M. Thompson, 1920, 182pp. [100 cop]
anonymous
  The Journal of Julius Rodman (serial). *Burton's,* Jan 1840-June 1840 [uncompleted].

POHL, FREDERIK (1919-   ) *U.S.*
  Born: New York, New York
  Autobiography: *The Way the Future Was: A Memoir.* NY: Ballantine, 1978, 312pp.
as Elton V. Andrews
  Elegy To A Dead Satellite: Luna. *Amazing,* Oct 1937 *poem*
as Paul Flehr
  The Hated. *Galaxy,* Jan 1958
as S. D. Gottesman [in collaboration with Cyril Kornbluth]
  Before the Universe. *Super Science Stories,* July 1940
  Nova Midplane. *Super Science Stories,* Nov 1940
  Trouble In Time. *Astonishing,* Dec 1940
  Best Friend. *Super Science Stories,* May 1941
  Mars-Tube. *Astonishing,* Sept 1941
as S. D. Gottesman [in collaboration with Cyril Kornbluth and Robert Lowndes]
  The Castle on Outerplanet. *Stirring Science Stories,* April 1941
  The Extrapolated Dimwit. *Future,* Oct 1942
as Lee Gregor [in collaboration with Milton A. Rothman]— these stories only
  Heavy Planet. *Astounding,* Aug 1939
  Shawn's Sword. *Astounding,* Oct 1939
as Warren F. Howard
  A Voyage In Time. *Super Science Stories,* April 1941
as Paul Dennis Lavond [house pseudonym] [in collaboration with Cyril Kornbluth]
  The Callistan Tomb. *Science Fiction Quarterly,* Spring 1941
  A Prince of Pluto. *Future,* April 1941
as Paul Dennis Lavond [house pseudonym] [in collaboration with Cyril Kornbluth and Robert W. Lowndes]
  Exiles of New Planet. *Astonishing,* April 1941
  Einstein's Planetoid. *Science Fiction Quarterly,* Spring 1942
as Paul Dennis Lavond [house pseudonym] [in collaboration with Robert W. Lowndes and Joseph H. Dockweiler]
  Something From Beyond. *Future,* Dec 1941
as Paul Dennis Lavond [house pseudonym] [in collaboration with Joseph H. Dockweiler]
  Star of the Undead. *Fantasy Book #2,* [c.1948]
as Edson McCann [in collaboration with R. F. Alvarez-del Rey]
  Preferred Risk. *Galaxy,* June 1955
  Preferred Risk. NY: Simon & Schuster, 1955, 248pp.
as James MacCreigh
  The Dweller In the Ice. *Super Science Stories,* Jan 1941
as Scott Mariner [in collaboration with Cyril Kornbluth]
  An Old Neptunian Custom. *Super Science Stories,* Aug 1942
as Ernst Mason
  The Martian Star-Gazers. *Galaxy,* Feb 1962
as Jordan Park [in collaboration with Cyril Kornbluth]
  The Man of Cold Rages. NY: Pyramid, [1958], 192pp., paper.
as Frederik Pohl
  (with Cyril M. Kornbluth) Gravy Planet. *Galaxy,* June 1952
  (with Cyril M. Kornbluth) *The Space Merchants.* NY: Ballantine, [1953], 179pp., paper/hardback.
  (with Cyril M. Kornbluth) *Search the Sky.* NY: Ballantine, [1954], 165pp., paper/hardback.
  (with Jack Williamson) *Undersea Quest.* NY: Gnome, 1954, 189pp.

  (with Cyril M. Kornbluth) *Gladiator-At-Law.* NY: Ballantine, [1955], 171pp., paper/hardback.
  Alternating Currents. NY: Ballantine, [1956], 154pp., paper/hardback. *ss col*
  (with Jack Williamson) *Undersea Fleet.* NY: Gnome, [1956], 187pp.
  Slave Ship. NY: Ballantine, [1957], 148pp., paper.
  The Case Against Tomorrow. NY: Ballantine, [1957], paper. *ss col*
  (with Jack Williamson) *Undersea City.* NY: Gnome, 1958, 188pp.
  Tomorrow Times Seven. NY: Ballantine, [1959], 160pp., paper. *ss col*
  (with Cyril M. Kornbluth) *Wolfbane.* NY: Ballantine, [1959], 140pp., paper.
  The Man Who Ate the World. NY: Ballantine, [1960], 144pp., paper. *ss col*
  Drunkard's Walk. NY: Ballantine, [1960], 142pp., paper. [NY: Gnome, 1960, 160pp.]
  Turn Left At Thursday. NY: Ballantine, [1961], 159pp., paper. *ss col*
  (with Cyril M. Kornbluth) *The Wonder Effect.* NY: Ballantine, [1962], 159pp., paper. *ss col*
  The Abominable Earthman. NY: Ballantine, [1963], 159pp., paper. *ss col*
  (with Jack Williamson) *The Reefs of Space.* NY: Ballantine, [1964], 188pp., paper.
  A Plague of Pythons. NY: Ballantine, [1965], 158pp., paper.
  (with Jack Williamson) *Starchild.* NY: Ballantine, [1965], 191pp., paper.
  Digits and Dastards. NY: Ballantine, [1966], 192pp., paper. *ss col*
  The Age of the Pussyfoot. NY: Trident, [1969], 191pp.
  (with Jack Williamson) *Rogue Star.* NY: Ballantine, [1969], paper.
  Day Million. NY: Ballantine, [1970], 213pp., paper. *ss col*
  The Gold At Starbow's End. NY: Ballantine, 1972, paper.
  The Best of Frederik Pohl. Garden City: Doubleday, 1975.
  (with Jack Williamson) *Farthest Star.* NY: Ballantine, [1975], paper.
  The Early Pohl. Garden City: Doubleday, [1976], 183pp. *ss col*
  In the Problem Pit. NY: Bantam, [1976], paper. *ss col*
  Man Plus. NY: Random House, 1976.
  (with Cyril M. Kornbluth) *Critical Mass.* NY: Bantam, [1977], paper. *ss col*
  Gateway. NY: St. Martin's, 1977.
  JEM. NY: St. Martin's, [1979], 359pp.
  □ *Edge of the City,* 1957 (novelization of screenplay); (with C.M. Kornbluth) *Presidential Year,* 1956; *Practical Politics, 1972,* 1971.
as Charles Satterfield [house pseudonym] [alone]
  With Redfern on Capella XII. *Galaxy,* Nov 1955
  Third Offense. *Galaxy,* Aug 1958
  Way Up Yonder. *Galaxy,* Oct 1959
as Charles Satterfield [house pseudonym] [in collaboration with R. Alvarez-del Rey]
  No More Stars. *Beyond,* July 1954
as Dirk Wylie [alone]
  Highwayman of the Void. *Planet Stories,* Fall 1944
as Dirk Wylie [in collaboration with Joseph H. Dockweiler]
  Asteroid of the Damned. *Planet Stories,* Summer 1942
  Sky Test. *Super Science Stories,* Nov 1942
  Outpost of the Eons. *Astonishing,* April 1943
as Dirk Wylie [in collaboration with Joseph H. Dockweiler and Cyril Kornbluth]
  Vacant World. *Super Science Stories,* Jan 1941

POLLARD, JOHN X. [house pseudonym]
unattributed
  Call Him Savage! *Amazing,* March 1954
  The Monarch Of Mars. *Fantastic,* April 1956

by Howard Browne
The Strange Mission of Arthur Pendran. *Fantastic Adventures*, June 1944

POLLOCK, JOHN H(ackett) (1887-   )
as A. Philibin
Here Beginneth the Wisdom of the World; A Book of Wonder Tales. Dublin: The Candle Press, 1919, 39pp., ill.
A Tale of Thule, Together With Some Poems. Dublin: Talbot Press, [c.1924], 56pp. col
Mount Kestrel. Dublin: M.H. Gill, 1945, 129pp.
□ *Hills of Dublin*, 1917; *Athens Aflame*, 1923; *Smoking Flax*, [c.1923]; *Irish Ironies*, 1930; *Wild Honey*, 1942; *Autumn Crocus*, 1947 (poetry).
as John H. Pollock
□ *The Valley of the Wild Swans; A Romance*, 1932.
■ *William Butler Yeats*, 1935.

PORGES, ARTHUR (1915-   ) *U.S.*
Born: Chicago, Illinois
as Peter Arthur
The Radio. *Fantastic*, Dec 1960
as Arthur Porges
The Rats. *Magazine of Fantasy and Science Fiction*, Dec 1951
as Pat Rogers
Night Quake. *Fear*, May 1960

PORTER, LINN BOYD (1851-1916) *U.S.*
as Linn Boyd Porter
□ *Caring For No Man*, 1875; *Rainfall*, 1903.
as Albert Ross
Speaking of Ellen. NY: G.W. Dillingham, 1890, 345pp.
□ *The Garston Bigamy*, 1891; *Moulding A Maiden*, 1891; *Out of Wedlock*, 1894; *A Black Adonis*, 1895; *His Foster Sister*, 1896; *Love Gone Astray*, 1896; *That Gay Deceiver*, 1899; *The Naked Truth*, 1899; *A Sugar Princess*, 1900.
anonymous
□ *Thou Shalt Not*, 1899.

PORTER, WILLIAM SYDNEY (1862-1910) *U.S.*
Born: Greensboro, North Carolina
as O. Henry
□ *Waifs and Strays*, 1906 (ss col); *The Four Million*, 1906 (ss col); *Heart of the West*, 1907 (ss col); *The Gentle Grafter*, 1908 (ss col); *The Voice of the City*, 1908 (ss col); *Roads of Destiny*, 1909 (ss col); *Strictly Business*, 1910 (ss col); *Whirligigs*, 1910 (ss col); *Sixes and Sevens*, 1911 (ss col); *Rolling Stones*, 1912 (ss col).

PRAED, ROSA CAROLINE (Mrs. Campbell) (1851-1935)
nee Rosa Caroline Murray-Prior *British*
Born: Bromelton, Queensland, Australia
Biography: *In Mortal Bondage. The Strange Life of Rosa Praed*, by Colin Roderick. Sydney, Australia: Angus & Robertson, 1948, 208pp.
as Mrs. Campbell Praed
The Brother of the Shadow. London: Routledge, 1886, 158pp.
The Soul of Countess Adrian. London: Trischler & Co., 1891, 192pp.
"As A Watch In the Night." London: Chatto & Windus, 1901 [1900], 468pp.
The Insane Root, A Romance of A Strange Country. London: Unwin, [1902], 380pp.
Fugitive Anne. London: J. Long, [1902], 427pp., ill.
The Ghost. London: R. A. Everett, 1903, 304pp.
The Other Mrs. Jacobs: A Matrimonial Complication. London: J. Long, 1903, 309pp.
Nyria. London: Bell, 1904, 432pp.
Stubble Before the Wind. London: J. Long, [1908], 315pp.
By Their Fruits: A Novel. London: Cassell, 1908, 423pp.

Romance of Mlle. Aisse. London: J. Long, [1910], 413pp.
The Body of His Desire; A Romance of the Soul. London: Cassell, 1912, 343pp., ill.
The Mystery Woman. London: Cassell, 1913, 348pp., front.
Lady Bridget In the Never-Never Land. London: Hutchinson, 1915, 336pp.
□ *An Australian Heroine*, 1880; *Moloch*, 1883; *Affinities, A Romance of Today*, 1885; *The Head Station*, 1885; *The Brother of the Shadow, A Mystery of Today*, 1886; (with Justin McCarthy) *The Right Honourable*, 1886; *The Bond of Wedlock*, 1887; (with Justin McCarthy) *The Ladies Gallery*, 1889; *The Lost Earl of Ellan*, 1906; *The Luck of Leura*, 1907.

PRATT, FLETCHER (1897-1956) *U.S.*
Born: Buffalo, New York
as George U. Fletcher
Well of the Unicorn. NY: W. Sloane Associates, [1948], 338pp., maps.
as Irvin Lester
(with Fletcher Pratt) The Octopus Cycle. *Amazing*, May 1928
as Fletcher Pratt
(with Irvin Lester) The Octopus Cycle. *Amazing*, May 1928
The Mad Destroyer. *Wonder Quarterly*, Spring 1930
(with L. Sprague de Camp) *The Incomplete Enchanter.* NY: Holt, [c.1941], 326pp.
(with L. Sprague de Camp) *The Land of Unreason.* NY: Holt, [1942], 260pp.
(with L. Sprague de Camp) *The Carnelian Cube.* NY: Gnome, 1948, 230pp.
(with L. Sprague de Camp) *The Castle of Iron.* NY: Gnome, [1950], 224pp.
Double In Space. Garden City: Doubleday, 1951, 217pp. 2 novels
"The Long View," in *The Petrified Planet.* NY: Twayne, 1952. novella
"The Blue Star," in *Witches Three.* NY: Twayne, 1952, 263pp. novella
Double Jeopardy. Garden City: Doubleday, 1952, 214pp.
(with L. Sprague de Camp) *Tales From Gavagan's Bar.* NY: Twayne, 1953, 228pp., ill.
The Undying Fire. NY: Ballantine, [1953], 148pp., paper/hardback.
(with L. Sprague de Camp) *Wall of Serpents.* NY: Avalon, 1960, 223pp.
Invaders from Rigel. NY: Avalon, 1960, 224pp.
Alien Planet. NY: Avalon, 1962, 224pp.
■ *A Glance At the Public Libraries*, 1928; *The Heroic Years; Fourteen Years of the Republic, 1801 - 1815*, 1934; *The Cunning Mulatto and Other Cases of Ellis Parker, American Detective*, 1935 (U.S.); *Ordeal By Fire; An Informal History of the Civil War*, 1935; *Hail, Caesar!* 1936; *The Navy: A History*, 1938; *Secret and Urgent; the Story of Codes & Ciphers*, 1939; *Fletcher Pratt's Naval War Game*, 1940; *Fighting Ships of the U.S. Navy*, 1941; *The Navy Has Wings*, 1943; *Fleet Against Japan*, 1946; *The Empire and the Glory; Napoleon Bonaparte: 1800-1806*, 1948; *The Third King*, 1950; *Stanton, Lincoln's Secretary of War*, 1953; *All About Rockets & Jets*, 1955.
as B. F. Ruby
The Pellucid Horror. *Amazing*, Aug 1933
(with Fletcher Pratt) The Thing In the Woods. *Amazing*, Feb 1935

PRATT, THEODORE
as Timothy Brace
□ MYSTERY: *Mystery Goes Fishing*, 1936; *Murder Goes In A Trailer*, 1937; *Murder Goes to the Dogs*, 1938.
as Theodore Pratt
Mr. Limpet. NY: Knopf, 1942, 142pp.
Mr. Atom. Fort Lauderdale: Wake-Brook House, 1969,

197pp.
☐ *Spring From Downward*, 1933; *The Barefoot Mailman*, 1943; *The Flame Tree*, 1950; *The Big Bubble*, 1951; *Handsome*, 1951; *Seminole*, 1953; *The Money*, 1965.
■ *The Story of Boca Raton*, 1950; *That Was Palm Beach*, 1968.

PRATT, WILLIAM HENRY (1887-1969) *naturalized U.S.*
Born: England
as Boris Karloff
actor in many horror and science fiction films.
The Frightened. *Tales of the Frightened*, Aug 1957
(ed) *Tales of Terror*. Cleveland: World, 1943, 317pp.

PRICE, E(dgar) HOFFMAN (1898-) *U.S.*
Born: Fowler, California
as Hamlin Daly
The Seven Securities. *Science Fiction Quarterly*, Aug 1952
as E. Hoffman Price
Triangle With Variations. *Droll Stories*, May 1924
The Rajah's Gift. *Weird Tales*, Jan 1925
Strange Gateways. *Unknown*, April 1939
Strange Gateways. Sauk City, Wisconsin: Arkham House, 1967, 208pp. (2007 cop) *ss col*
Far Lands, Other Days. Chapel Hill, North Carolina: Carcosa, 1975.

PRICHARD, H(esketh) (Vernon) HESKETH- (1876-1922)
British
as E. and H. Heron [in collaboration with Mrs. K. Hesketh-Prichard]
Ghosts. Being the Experiences of Flaxman Low. London: C.A. Pearson, 1917, 117pp.
as Hesketh Prichard
☐ *November Joe: Detective of the Woods*, 1913 (ss col).
■ *Where Black Rules White, . . . Hayti*, 1900; *Through the Heart of Patagonia*, 1902; *Hunting Camps*, 1910; *Through Trackless Labrador*, 1911; *Sniping In France*, 1920; *Sport In Wildest Britain*, 1921.
as K. & H. Prichard [in collaboration with Mrs. K. Hesketh-Prichard]
Ghosts. Being the Experiences of Flaxman Low. London: C.A. Pearson, 1899, 300pp., ill.
☐ *The Chronicles of Don Q*, 1904; *Don Q, Son of Zorro*, 1925.

PRICHARD, K(ate) O'BRIEN HESKETH- (Mrs.)
as E. & H. Heron [in collaboration with H. Hesketh-Prichard]
see **H(esketh) (Vernon) HESKETH-PRICHARD**
as K. & H. Prichard [in collaboration with H. Hesketh-Prichard]
see **H(esketh) (Vernon) HESKETH-PRICHARD**

PRITCHARD, WILLIAM THOMAS (1909-) *British*
as William Dexter
World In Eclipse. London: P. Owen, [1954], 195pp.
Children of the Void. London: P. Owen, [1955], 195pp.
◼ *Blue Print for Bill-Ze-Bub; A Sequence of Further Uses for Bill Nord's Ingenious Piece of Magical Apparatus Bill-Ze-Bub*, 1952; *The Riddle of Chung Ling Soo*, 1955.

PRONZINI, BILL
● **as Jack Foxx**
The Jade Figurine.
as Bill Pronzini
Panic! NY: Random House, [1972], 173pp.
☐ *The Snatch*, 1971; *The Stalker*, 1971.
● **as Alan Saxon**
A Run In Diamonds.

PUTNAM, GEORGE H(aven) (1844-1930) *naturalized U.S.*
Born: London, England

as G. H. P.
The Artificial Mother: A Marital Fantasy. NY: Putnam, 1894, 31pp., ill.
☐ *The Little Gingerbread Man*, 1910 (juv).
as George H. Putnam
■ *International Copyright*, 1879; *Authors and Publishers*, 1883; *The Question of Copyright*, 1891; *Authors and Their Public In Ancient Times*, 1893; *Books and Their Makers During the Middle Ages*, 1896-1897 (2 vol); *A Prisoner of War In Virginia, 1864-1865*, 1912.

QUESNEL, PIERRE (1699-1774)
as Hercule Rasiel de Selva
Histoire de l'Admirable Dom Inigo Guipuscoa, Chevalier de la Vierge, Et Fondateur de la Monarchie des Inighistes . . . Par le Sieur Hercule Raisel de Selva. Le Haye [The Hague]: Chez le Veuve Charles Le Vier, 1736, 2 vol in one.
The History of the Wonderful Don Ignatius Loyola de Guysuscoa; Founder of the Order of the Jesuits. With An Account of the Establishment and Government of That Powerful Order. London: Printed for J. Bouquet, 1754, 2 vol.

QUICK, JOHN HERBERT (1861-1925) *U.S.*
Born: Grundy County, Iowa
Autobiography: *One Man's Life,* by Herbert Quick. Indianapolis: Bobbs-Merrill, [1925], 408pp.
as Herbert Quick
In the Fairy Land of America; A Tale of the Pukwudjies. NY: F. A. Stokes, [1901], 190pp., ill.
Aladdin & Co., A Romance of Yankee Magic. NY: Holt, [1904], 337pp.
Virginia of the Air Lanes. Indianapolis: Bobbs-Merrill, [1909], 424pp., ill.
The Invisible Woman. Indianapolis: Bobbs- Merrill, [1924], 488pp.
□ *Double Trouble; or, Every Hero His Own Villain,* 1906; *The Broken Lance,* 1907; *Yellowstone Nights,* 1911; *The Brown Mouse,* 1915; *Vandemark's Folly,* 1922; *The Hawkeye,* 1923; *There Came Two Women,* 1924 (play).

QUILLER-COUCH, A(rthur) T. (Sir) (1863-1944) *British*
Born: Fowey, Cornwall
Autobiography: *Memories & Opinions. An Unfinished Autobiography,* by Q [A. T. Quiller-Couch]. Cambridge U. Press, 1944, 105pp.
as Q
Dead Man's Rock, A Romance. London: Cassell, 1887, 364pp.
Noughts and Crosses: Stories, Studies, and Sketches. London: Cassell, 1891, 263pp. *col*
I Saw Three Ships and Other Winter's Tales. London: Cassell, 1892, 304pp., front. *ss col* [Cassell's Catalogue dated Dec. 1891 at end]
The Delectable Duchy; Stories, Studies & Sketches. London: Cassell, 1893, 320pp. *col*
Wandering Heath. London: Cassell, 1895, 293pp. *ss col*
Fairy Tales Far and Near. Retold by Q. NY: F. A. Stokes, [1895], 196pp., ill. *ss col*
Merry Garden and Other Stories. London: Methuen, [1907], 307pp. *ss col*
Selected Stories by Q. London: Dent, 1921, 240pp. *ss col*
Q's Mystery Stories. London: Dent, 1937, 402pp. *col*
□ *The Astonishing History of Troy Town,* 1888; *The Blue Pavilions,* 1891; *Green Bays, Verses & Parodies,* 1893; *Ia, A Love Story,* 1895; *A Fowley Garland,* 1899 (poetry 300 cop); *Hetty Wesley,* 1903; *Lady Good-For-Nothing,* 1910.
as A(rthur) T. Quiller-Couch
Old Fires and Profitable Ghosts; A Book of Stories. NY: Scribner, 1900, 384pp. [London: Cassell, 1900, 341pp.] *ss col*

The Laird's Luck and Other Fireside Tales. London: Cassell, 1901, 342pp. *ss col*
The White Wolf and Other Fireside Tales. London: Methuen, 1902, 368pp. *ss col*
Two Sides of the Face: Midwinter Tales. Bristol, England: Arrowsmith, 1903, 360pp. *ss col*
Shakespeare's Christmas and Other Stories. London: Smith, Elder, [1904], 335pp. *ss col*
Poison Island. NY: Scribner, 1906, 401pp.
Corporal Sam and Other Stories. London: Smith, Elder, 1910, 291pp. *ss col*
The Sleeping Beauty and Other Fairy Tales, . . . Retold. London: Hodder & Stoughton, [1910], 128pp., (ill. by Edmund Dulac) *ss col*
In Powder and Crinoline; Old Fairy Tales Retold. London: Hodder & Stoughton, [1913], 163pp. (ill. by Kay Nielsen)
Twelve Dancing Princesses and Other Fairy Tales . . . Retold. NY: George H. Doran, [1923], 244pp., ill. [same book as *Powder and Crinoline*] *ss col*
□ *Historical Tales From Shakespeare,* 1899; *The Adventures of Harry Revel,* 1903; *Foe-Farrell,* 1918.
■ (ed) *The Cornish Magazine* July 1898-May 1899; *Adventures In Criticism,* 1896; *On the Art of Writing,* 1916; *Memoir of Arthur John Butler,* 1917; *Shakespeare's Workmanship,* 1918; *On the Art of Reading,* 1920; *Lecture on Lectures,* 1923; *Charles Dickens, and Other Victorians,* 1925; *The Age of Chaucer,* 1926; *Studies In Literature* (1st series, 1918; 2nd series, 1922; 3rd series, 1929).

QUINTON, JOHN P(urcell) (1879- ?) *British*
as Melchoir MacBride
The Story of Glastonbury and the Grail; or, the Light of Avalon, A Mystery Play Concerning the Introduction of Christianity to England by Joseph of Arimathea. London: Hunter & Longhurst, 1909, 101pp., ill. *play*
A Message From the Gods. A Mystery Play. London: Hunter & Longhurst, 1910, 126pp. *play*

RABE, ANN C(rawford) VON (Baroness)
as Von Degen
  A Mystery of the Campagna, and A Shadow On A Wave. NY: Cassell, [1891], 203pp. [The Unknown Library V.3]

RABELAIS, FRANCOIS (c.1494-1553) *French*
  Born near: Chinon
  Biographical and Bibliographical: *Francois Rabelais, the Great Story Teller,* by Paul Eldridge. Cranston, New Jersey: A. S. Barnes, 1971, 215pp.
as Alcofribas Nasier
  Pantagruel. Les Horribles Espouvantables Faictz & Prouesses du Tres nomme Pantagruel Roy des Dipsodes, Filz du Grant Geant Gargatua, composez Nouvellement par Maistre Alcofribas Nasier, Abstracteur de Ou Les Vend Au Palais a Paris en la Gallerie par ou on va a la Chancellerie. [1533], 208pp. [2nd edition] [1st edition 64pp., pub. Lyons, 1533] [This first book, later became the second of the five books of "Gargantua," the second called "Gargantua" became the 1st in the series. For a discussion of the history of the "Gargantua" titles and their publication see the Eldridge volume above. It is a good introductory study.]

RABINOWITZ, SHALOM (1859-1916) *Russian* (to U.S. after 1906)
  Born: Kiev
as Sholom Aleichem
  used in many non-English translations of author's work.
  ☐ *Jewish Children,* 1937; *Wandering Star,* 1952.
as Shalom Rabinowitz
  The Bewitched Tailor (trans. by B. Isaacs). Moscow: Foreign Language Publishing House, 19—, 170pp., ill.
as Solomon (J.) Rabinowitz
  alternate anglicization of name.

RADCLIFFE, ANN WARD (Mrs. William) (1764-1823)
  English
  Born: London
as Authoress of "The Castles of Athlin and Dunbayne"
  A Sicilian Romance. London: T. Hookham, 1790, 2 vol.
as Authoress of "A Sicilian Romance," &c.
  The Romance of the Forest. London: T. Hookham, 1791, 3 vol.
as Ann Radcliffe
  The Mysteries of Udolpho, A Romance. G. G. and J. Robinson, 1794, 4 vol.
  The Italian; or, The Confessional of the Black Penitents. London: T. Cadell, Jun., 1797, 3 vol.
  Gaston de Blondeville; or, The Court of Henry III. London: H. Colburn, 1826, 4 vol.
anonymous
  The Castles of Athlin and Dunbayne. London: T. Hookham, 1789, 280pp.

RANDOLPH, GEORGIANA ANN (1908-1957) *U.S.*
  Born: Chicago, Illinois

as Gypsy Rose Lee [ghost writer]
  ☐ *The G-String Murders.* NY: Simon & Schuster, 1941, 305pp., ill. (mystery)
  ☐ *Mother Finds A Body.* NY: Simon & Schuster, 1942, 312pp. (mystery)
as Craig Rice [alone]
  Telefair; The House On the Island. Indianapolis: Bobbs-Merrill, [1942], 287pp.
  ☐ MYSTERY: *Eight Faces At Three,* 1939; *The Corpse Steps Out,* 1940; *The Thursday Turkey Murders,* 1943; *Home, Sweet Homicide,* 1944.
as Craig Rice [in collaboration with S.A. Lombino]
  ☐ MYSTERY: *The April Robin Murders,* 1958.
as Daphne Sanders
  ☐ MYSTERY: *To Catch A Thief,* 1943.
as George Sanders [ghost writer]
  ☐ MYSTERY: *Crime On My Hands,* 1944.
as Michael Venning
  ☐ MYSTERY: Melville Fairr series incl. *The Man Who Slept All Day,* 1942; *Murder Through the Looking Glass,* 1943; *Jethro Hammer,* 1944.

RANKIN, HUGH DOAK *U.S.*
as Doak
  art in *Weird Tales* c.1928-c.1936

RAPPOPORT, SOLOMON (1863-1920)
as S. Ansky [variously rendered as An-Ski, Anski, An-Sky, etc. on other editions]
  The Dybbuk; A Play In Four Acts. NY: Boni & Liveright, 1926, 145pp. *play*

RASPE, RUDOLPH E(rich) (1737-1794) *German*
as Baron Munchausen
  (ed. by Raspe) *Baron Munchausen's Narrative of His Marvellous Travels and Campaigns In Russia.* Oxford: Printed for the Editor, 1786, 49pp.
  The Surprising Travels of Baron Munchausen, . . . A Voyage Into the Moon and Dog Star. London: Published for the Booksellers, [c.1792], 162pp.
as R. Raspe
  ■ *An Account of Some German Volcanoes,* 1776; *A Descriptive Catalogue of A Collection of Ancient and Modern Gems, etc.,* 1791; *A Critical Essay on Oil Painting,* 1801.
as H. J. Sarratt [theft and impostoring]
  ☐ *Koenigsmark the Robber; or, The Terror of Bohemia; In Which is Introduced Stella, or, The Maniac of the Wood, A Pathetic Tale,* 1803.

RAYMOND, RENE BRABAZON (1906-   ) *British*
as James Hadley Chase
  Miss Shumway Waves A Wand. London: Jarrolds, [1944], 169pp.
  ☐ MYSTERY: *No Orchids For Miss Blandish,* 1939; *The Dead Stay Dumb,* 1939; *Twelve Chinks and A Woman,* [c.1940]; *Eve,* 1945; *Last Page,* 1947 (play); *You're Lonely When You're Dead,* 1949; *The Flesh of the Orchid,* 1950; *Figure It Out For Yourself,* 1950; *The Double Shuffle,* 1952; *The Fast Buck,* 1952; *I'll Bury My Dead,* 1953; *Tiger By the Tail,* 1954; *This Is For Real,* 1965; *You Have Yourself A Deal,* 1966.
as Ambrose Grant
  ☐ MYSTERY: *More Deadly Than the Male,* 1946.
as Raymond Marshall
  ☐ MYSTERY: *Blondes' Requiem,* 1945; *Mallory,* 1950; *In A Vain Shadow,* 1951; *Why Pick On Me?,* 1951; *Mission To Venice,* 1954.
  ⌐ James L. Docherty

REED, LILIAN CRAIG (1932-   ) *U.S.*
Born: San Diego, California
as Kit Reed
  The Wait. *Magazine of Fantasy and Science Fiction*,
    April 1958
  Mister Da V. and Other Stories. London: Faber, 1967,
    222pp. ss col
  □ *Mother Isn't Dead, She's Only Sleeping*, 1961; *At War
    As Children*, 1964; *The Better Part*, 1967; *Armed Camps*,
    1969; *Cry of the Daughter*, 1971.

REEDS, F. ANTON
as F. Anton Reeds
  Sunset for Pawns. *Vortex #1*, 1953
as Anthony Riker
  The Time Contraption. *Vortex #1*, 1953

REEVE, CLARA (1729-1807) *English*
Born: Ipswich, East Suffolk
as The Editor of "The Phoenix"
  The Champion of Virtue, A Gothic Story. Colchester,
    England: Printed for the Author by W. Keymer, 1777,
    190pp., front. [2nd edition, 1778, retitled *The Old
    English Baron*]
as C. R.
  □ *The Two Mentors*, 1783; *The Exiles; or, Memoirs of
    Count de Cronstadt*, 1788; *The School for Widows*,
    1791.
  ■ *The Progress of Romance, Through Times, Countries,
    and Manners*, 1785.

REEVES, HELEN BUCKINGHAM MATHERS (Mrs. Henry A.)
    (1853-1920) *British*
Born: Somerset
as David Lyall
  [Note: Helen Reeves wrote a book entitled *David Lyall's
    Love Story.* London: Hodder & Stoughton, 1897, 302pp.
    as "Author of the Land O' the Leal"; in the same
    period Annie S. Swan (later Smith), another British
    writer, was using David Lyall as a pseudonym. The
    N.U.C. lists these novels (by Swan) under Reeves and
    also lists an edition of *The Land of the Leal* as by
    David Lyall (pub. in Toronto)]
as Helen Mathers
  The Juggler and the Soul. London: Skeffington, 1896,
    220pp.
  □ MYSTERY: *Murder or Manslaughter?*, 1885.
anonymous or as "by the Author of ———"
  □ *Comin Thru the Rye*, 1875; *Cherry Ripe*, 1877; *Land
    O' The Leal*, 1878; *The Story of A Sin*, 1882; *A Man
    of To-Day*, 1894.

REEVES, JUSTIN
as Aladra Septama
  The Beast Men of Ceres. *Amazing Stories Quarterly*,
    Winter 1929

REHM, WARREN S.
as Omen Nemo
  *The Practical City. A Future City Romance, or, A Study
    In Environment.* Lancaster, Pennsylvania: Lancaster
    County Magazine, [1898], 35pp., front.

REIZENSTEIN, ELMER L. (1892-1967) *U.S.*
Born: New York, New York
    [possibly legally changed name to Rice]
as Elmer Rice
  A Voyage To Purilla. NY: Cosmopolitan, 1930, 297pp.
  Imperial City. NY: Coward-McCann, 1937, 554pp.
  □ PLAYS: *On Trial*, 1914; *Home Of the Free*, 1917;
    (with Dorothy Parker) *Close Harmony*, 1924; *Cock
    Robin*, 1927; *Street Scene*, 1929; *We, The People*,

1933; *Between Two Worlds*, 1934.

REPP, ED(ward) EARL (*c.*1900-   ) *U.S.*
as Bradner Buckner
  Revolution On Venus. *Amazing*, April 1939
as John Cody
  □ *Empty Holsters*, 1936.
as Peter Field
  □ WESTERN: *Dry-Gulch Adams*, 1934; *Mustang Mesa*,
    1937; *Canyon of Death*, 1938; *Doctor Two-Guns*, 1939;
    (etc., over 50 westerns under this name.)
as Ed Earl Repp
  The Radium Pool. *Science Wonder Stories*, Aug 1929
  The Radium Pool. Los Angeles: FPCI, 1948, 188pp.
  The Stellar Missiles. Los Angeles: FPCI, 1949, 192pp.
    3 novellas
  □ *Cyclone Jim*, 1935; *Gun Hawk*, 1936; *Hell In the Saddle*,
    1937. SCREENPLAY: *Devil's Saddle Legion*, 1937
    (Warner Bros.); *Prairie Thunder*, 1937 (Warner Bros.).

RESNICK, MICHAEL D. (1942-   ) *U.S.*
as Michael Resnick
  The Goddess of Ganymede. West Kingston, Rhode Island:
    Donald Grant, 1967, 246pp., ill.
  Pursuit On Ganymede. NY: Paperback Library, 1968,
    144pp., paper.

RESNIER, ANDRE GUILLAUME (1729-1811)
as Reinser III
  *Republique Universelle, ou, l'Humanite Ailee, Reunie
    Sous l'Empire de la Raison.* [Geneva?] l'an Premier
    de la Raison, [1788], 398pp., 2 folded plates.

RESSICH, JOHN (1877-   )
as Gregory Baxter [in collaboration with Eric de Banzie]
  The Narrowing Lust. London: Selwyn & Blount, 1928,
    287pp.
  □ MYSTERY: *Blue Lightning*, 1926; *The Ainceworth
    Mystery*, 1930; *Death Strikes At Six Bells*, 1930; *Murder
    Could Not Kill*, 1932.
as John Ressich
  □ *Voices In the Wilderness*, 1924; *The Triumph Of A Fool*,
    1926; *Gallop!*, 1932.

REYNOLDS, DALLAS MCCORD (1917-   ) *U.S.*
Born: Corcoran, California
as Mark Mallory
  Posted. *Space SF*, Spring 1957
as Mack Reynolds
  Isolationist. *Fantastic Adventures*, April 1950
  The Case of the Little Green Men. NY: Phoenix Press,
    [1951], 224pp.
  The Earth War. NY: Pyramid, [1963], 141pp., paper.
  Planetary Agent X. NY: Ace, [1965], 133pp., paper.
    (Ace Double M 131)
  Time Gladiator. London: 4 Square, 1966, 157pp., paper.
  Of Godlike Power. NY: Belmont, [1966], 174pp., paper.
  Dawnman Planet. NY: Ace, [1967], 123pp., paper.
  Space Pioneer. London: 4 Square, 1967, 160pp., paper.
  The Rival Rigellians. NY: Ace, [1967], 132pp., paper.
    (Ace Double G 632)
  Computer War. NY: Ace, [1967], 111pp., paper. (Ace
    Double H-34)
  After Some Tomorrow. NY: Belmont, [1967], 158pp.
    paper.
  Mercenary From Tomorrow. NY: Ace, [1968], 131pp.,
    paper. (Ace Double H-65)
  Code Duello. NY: Ace, [1968], 141pp., paper. (Ace
    Double H-103)
  Star Trek—Mission to Horatius. Racine, Wisconsin:
    Whitman, 1968, 210pp.

The Space Barbarians. NY: Ace, [1969], paper.

The Cosmic Eye. NY: Belmont, [1969], 157pp., paper.

Once Departed. NY: Curtis, 1970.

Computer World. NY: Curtis, 1970.

Black Man's Burden. NY: Ace, [1972], paper. (Ace Double 06612)

Border, Breed, Nor Birth. NY: Ace, [1972], paper. (Ace Double 06612)

Looking Backward From the Year 2000. NY: Ace, [1973], paper.

Commune 2000 AD. NY: Bantam, [1974], paper.

Depression or Bust. NY: Ace, [1974], paper.

Ability Quotient. NY: Ace, [1975], paper.

Amazon Planet. NY: Ace, [1975], paper.

Satellite City. NY: Ace, [1975], paper.

Tomorrow Might Be Different. NY: Ace, [1975], paper.

The Towers of Utopia. NY: Bantam, [1975], paper.

Day After Tomorrow. NY: Ace, [1976], paper.

The Five Way Secret Agent. NY: Ace, [1976], paper.

Galactic Medal of Honor. NY: Ace, [1976], paper.

Rolltown. NY: Ace, [1976], paper.

Section G. United Planet. NY: Ace, [1976], paper.

The Best of Mack Reynolds. NY: Pocket Books, [1976], paper. *ss col*

After Utopia. NY: Ace, [1977], paper.

Equality In the Year 2000. NY: Ace, [1977], paper.

Perchance To Dream. NY: Ace, [1977], paper.

Police Patrol 2000 A.D. NY: Ace, [1977], paper.

Space Visitor. NY: Ace, [1977], paper.

The Best Ye Breed. NY: Ace, [1978], paper.

■ *The Expatriates,* 1963; *Puerto Rican Patriot; The Life of Luis Munoz Rivera,* 1969.

as Dallas Ross
You Might Say Virginia Dared. *Amazing,* Sept 1950

REYNOLDS, WALTER D(oty)   (1860- ?)
as Lord Prime, Esq., Librarian To the State Library of Pennsylvania, A.D. MMXVI
Mr. Jonnemacher's Machine. The Port to Which We Drifted. Philadelphia: Knickerbocker Book Co., [1898], 255pp., ill.

RICE, JANE
as Mary Austin [used only on this verse]
Night Thought. *Magazine of Fantasy and Science Fiction,* Sept 1959 *verse*
as Jane Rice
The Dream. *Unknown,* July 1940
✔ Allison Rice [in collaboration with Ruth Allison]

RICHARD, FRANCOIS   *French*
as F. Richard-Bessiere [in collaboration with Richard Bessiere]
see RICHARD BESSIERE

RICHARDSON, R(obert) S(hirley)   (1902-   )   *U.S.*
as Philip Latham
N Day. *Astounding,* Jan 1946
Five Against Venus. Philadelphia: Winston, [1952], 214pp.
Missing Men of Saturn. Philadelphia: Winston, [1953], 215pp.
as R(obert) S(hirley) Richardson
The Other Side of Astronomy. *Astounding,* Sept 1939 *article*
Second Satellite. NY: McGraw-Hill, 1956, 191pp., ill.
■ *An Investigation of Molecular Spectra In Sun Spots,* 1931; *Hydrocarbon Bands In the Solar Spectrum,* 1933; *The Nature of Solar Hydrogen Vortices,* 1941; *Sunspot Groups of Irregular Magnetic Polarity,* 1948; *Exploring Mars,* 1954; *The Fascinating World of Astronomy,* 1960; *Man and the Moon,* 1960; *Mars,* 1964; *Getting Acquainted With Comets,* 1967.

RICHTER, ERNST H.   (1901-1959)   *German*
✔ **William Brown, Ernest Terridge**

RIDDELL, CHARLOTTE ELIZA(beth) L(awson) (Cowan)   (1832-1906) (Mrs. J.H.)   *Irish*
Born: Antrim
as Rainey Hawthorne
☐ *The Ruling Passion,* 1857; *The Rich Husband,* 1858.
as Charlotte Elizabeth L. Riddell
■ *A Mad Tour; or, A Journey Undertaken At An Insane Moment Through Central Europe On Foot,* 1891.
as (Mrs.) J.H. Riddell
Fairy Water. A Christmas Story. London: Routledge's Christmas Annual, 1866.
Frank Sinclair's Wife and Other Stories. London: Tinsley, 1874, 3 vol. *ss col*
The Uninhabited House. London: Routledge's Christmas Annual, [1876], 96pp.
The Disappearance of Mr. Jeremiah Redworth. London: Routledge, [1879], 96pp.
Weird Stories. London: J. Hogg, [1884], 314pp. *ss col*
Idle Tales. London: Ward & Downey, 1887, 288pp. *ss col*
Princess Sunshine and Other Stories. London: Ward & Downey, 1889, 2 vol. *ss col*
The Banshee's Warning & Other Tales. London: Remington, 1894, 277pp. *ss col*
Handsome Phil and Other Stories. London: F.V. White, 1899, 320pp. *ss col*
☐ *The Moors and the Fen,* 1858; *The Race For Wealth,* 1866; *Far Above Rubies,* 1867; *Above Suspicion,* [c.1876]; *The Prince of Wales's Garden Party and Other Stories,* 1882 (ss col); *The Nun's Curse,* 1888; *Football of Fate,* 1900.
as F. G. Trafford
☐ *George Geith of Fen Court,* 1865.

RIDEAUX, CHARLES DE BALZAC   (1900-   )
as John Chancellor
☐ MYSTERY: *The Mystery of Norman Court,* 1924; *The Dark God,* 1928; *Frass,* 1929; *Mystery At Angel's End,* 1930; *The Return of Frass,* 1930.

RIDLEY, JAMES   (1736-1765)
as Charles Morell
The Tales of the Genii. London: J. Wilkie, 1764, 2 vol., ill. [an original work modeled on the Arabian Nights]
● **as Helter Van Scelter**
☐ *The Schemer; or, Universal Satirist,* 1763.
anonymous
☐ *The History of James Lovegrove, Esq.,* 1761, 2 vol.

RILEY, JAMES WHITCOMB   (1849-1916)   *U.S.*
Born: Greenfield, Indiana
as Benjamin F. Johnson, of Boone
Poems in Indiana newspapers.
☐ *The Old Swimmin' Hole and 'Leven More Poems.* Indianapolis: George C. Hitt & Co., 1883, 50pp. (1000 cop) (poetry)
as James Whitcomb Riley
The Boss Girl, A Christmas Story, and Other Sketches. Indianapolis: Bowen-Merrill, 1886, 263pp.
The Flying Islands of the Night. Indianapolis: Bowen-Merrill, 1892, 88pp. *play in verse*
Eccentric Mr. Clark. NY: New York Book Co., [1901], 189pp.
☐ POETRY: *Rhymes of Childhood,* 1890; *The Raggedy Man,* 1907; *The Orphant Annie Book,* 1908; *When the Frost Is On the Punkin,* 1911.

RITCHIE, LEWIS ANSELM DA COSTA (*ne* L.A. da Costa Ricci)
   British
as Bartimeus
   Overlooked. London: E. Benn, 1933, 223pp.
   ☐ *Naval Occasions*, 1914; *The Long Trick*, 1917; *Unreality;
      A Romance*, 1920; *Seaways*, 1923 (ss col); *An Off
      Shore Wind*, 1936; *Under Sealed Orders*, 1938.
   ■ *The Turn of the Road*, 1946.

ROACH, ROBERT W. A. (1933-   ) *English*
   Born: Chipping Sodbury, Glouchestershire
as A.K. Jorgensson
   Coming-Of-Age Day. *Science Fantasy #76*, Sept 1965

ROBBINS, CLARENCE AARON   (1888-1949)   *U.S.*
   Born: Brooklyn, New York
as C. A. Robbins ("Tod" Robbins)
   The Unholy Three. NY: J. Lane, 1917, 310pp.
as Tod Robbins
   The Terrible Three. *All Story Weekly*, July 14, 1917
   The Bibulous Baby. *The Thrill Book*, July 1, 1919
   Mysterious Martin. NY: J. S. Olgilvie, [1912], 153pp.
   Silent, White and Beautiful. NY: Boni & Liveright, [1920],
      256pp. *ss col*
   Who Wants A Green Bottle. London: P. Allen, [1926],
      280pp.
   The Master of Murder. London: P. Allen, 1933, 198pp.
   ☐ *The Scales of Justice and Other Poems*, 1915 (poetry);
      Red of Surley, 1919; *In the Shadow*, 1929.

ROBERTS, KEITH JOHN KINGSTON   (1935-   ) *English*
   Born: Kettering, Northamptonshire
as Keith Roberts
   Anita. *Science Fantasy*, Sept/Oct 1964 (Br.)
   Escapism. *Science Fantasy*, Sept/Oct 1964 (Br.)
   The Furies. London: Hart-Davis, 1966, 254pp.
   Pavane. London: Hart-Davis, 1968, 224pp. [Garden City:
      Doubleday, 1968, 279pp.]
   The Inner Wheel. London: Hart-Davis, 1970, 203pp.
      [Garden City: Doubleday, 1970, 207pp.]
   ☐ HISTORICAL FICTION: *The Boat of Fate*, 1971.
   ↙ **John Kingston, David Stringer**

ROBERTSON, ALICE A(lberthe)   (1871- ?)   *U.S.*
as K. David
   The Sun Bird. NY: H. Vinal, Ltd., 1927, 241pp.
   White Madness. NY: H. Vinal, Ltd., 1928, 189pp. *ss col*
as Berthe St. Luz
   Tamar Curze. NY: R. F. Fenno, [1908], 206pp., ill.
   ☐ *Black Butterflies*, 1905.

ROBERTSON, FRANK C(hester)   (1890-   )   *U.S.*
   Autobiography: *A Ram In the Thicket.* NY: Abelard Press,
      1950, 357pp.
as Robert Crane [This pseudonym was used by Bernard
      Glemser in the science fiction field]
   see BERNARD GLEMSER
   ☐ WESTERN: *Thunder In the West*, 1934; *Stormy
      Range*, 1936.
as Frank Chester Field
   ☐ *The Rocky Road to Jerico*, 1935.
as Frank C(hester) Robertson
   ☐ WESTERN: *The Boss of the Tumbling H*, 1927;
      Branded Men, 1936; *Cowman's Jack-Pot*, 1942;
      Boomerang Jail, 1947; *Rope Crazy*, 1948.
   ↙ **King Hill**

ROBINETT, STEPHEN
as Tak Hallus
   Minitalent. *Astounding*, March 1969
as Stephen Robinett
   Stargate. NY: St. Martin's, 1976.

The Man Responsible. NY: Ace, [1977], paper.

ROBINSON, MARY (Darby) (Mrs. Thomas) (1758-1800)
   English
   Born: Bristol, Gloucestershire
   Autobiography: *Memoirs of the Late Mrs. Robinson,
      Written by Herself, with Some Posthumous Pieces.*
      London: Phillips, 1801, 4 vol. (vol. 1 & 2 printed by
      Wilkes & Taylor, vol. 3 & 4 printed by T. Gillet)
as Mary Darby
   name used as actress
as A Friend to Humanity
   ☐ *Impartial Reflections On the Present Situation of the
      Queen of France*, 1791.
as Laura Maria
   ☐ *Ainsi ve le Monde, a Poem*, 1790 (poetry).
as Perdita
   wrote for periodicals and possibly some books under this
   name—it often appeared with Mrs. Robinson on her
   books.
as Mrs. M(ary) Robinson
   Vancenza; or, The Dangers of Credulity. London: Bell,
      1792, 2 vol. [Mrs. Robinson, an actress, was a great
      beauty—painted by Gainsborough, Reynolds, etc.—
      she was secretly married to a London clerk at the age
      of sixteen. She was then seduced into becoming the
      mistress of the Prince of Wales (later George IV) by
      the receipt of his personal note for £20,000. The Prince
      deserted her and then *welshed* (as it were) on the note.
      An expert on credulity, indeed.]
   ☐ *Sapho and Phaon. In A Series of Legitimate Sonnets
      With Thoughts On Poetical Subjects and Anecdotes
      of the Grecian Poetess*, 1769 (poetry); *Poems By Mrs.
      Robinson*, 1775 (poetry); *The Widow*, 1794; *Hubert de
      Sevrac, A Romance*, 1796; *The Natural Daughter, A
      Novel*, 1799; *The False Friend*, 1799; *The Poetical Works
      of the Late Mrs. Mary Robinson*, 1806.
   ■ *Thoughts On the Condition of Women, and On the
      Injustice of Mental Insubordination (2d ed)*, 1799
      (contains a list of women literary figures living in the
      eighteenth century].

ROCHA, ADOLPHO   (1907-   )   *Portuguese*
as Miguel Torga
   . . .*Farrusco the Blackbird, and Other Stories from the
      Portuguese*, trans. by D. Brass. NY: Arts, Inc., [1951],
      93pp., ill. (Golden Griffin Books No. 5)

ROCKEN, KURT WALTER   (1906-   )   *German*
as C. V. Rock
   ☐ MYSTERY: *Die Mordende Geist*, 1937; *Goldkette In
      Hollywood*, 1940; *Moch Doch Mit!*, 1942.
as Walter Rocken
   ☐ *Zwischen Wolkenkratzern*, 1943.
as Henry Walter
   Der Ruf vom Mond; Utopischer Roman. Linz: Pittsburgh
      Ibis-Verlag, [1947], 320pp.
   Mondsender LB11, Utopischer Roman. Linz: Pittsburgh
      Ibis-Verlag, [1948], 239pp.
   Mondstation Ovillon, Utopischer Roman. Bischofswiesen/
      Obb: Delta Verlag, [1950], 319pp.

ROCKLYNNE, ROSS   (1913-   )   *U.S.*
   [Real name possibly R. L. Rocklin]
as H. F. Cente
   Sales Talk. *Planet Stories*, July 1953
as Ross Rocklynne
   Man of Iron. *Astounding*, Aug 1935
   The Men and the Mirror. NY: Ace, [1973], paper.
   The Sun Destroyers. NY: Ace, [1973], paper. (Ace Double)

ROE, IVAN (1917-) *British*
Born: London
as Ivan Roe
The Salamander Touch. London: Hutchinson, [1952], 224pp.
□ *The Green Tree and the Dry,* 1950.
■ *The Breath of Corruption; An Interpretation of Dostoievsky,* 1946; *Shelley: The Last Phase,* 1953.
as Richard Savage
When the Moon Died. London: Ward, Lock, 1955, 189pp.

ROE, WILLIAM J(ames) (1843-1915) *U.S.*
as Hudor Genone
Inquirendo Island. NY: Putnam, 1886, 347pp.
Bellona's Husband. Philadelphia: Lippincott, 1887, 332pp.
The Last Tenet Imposed Upon the Khan of Tomathoz. Chicago: C.H. Kerr, 1892, 165pp., ill.
■ *A Dikastery of One (in Reply to Corvinus) A Plea for the Religion of Science,* 1905.
as G. I. Cervus
□ *A Model Wife. A Novel,* 1885; *"White Feathers,"* 1885; *Cut: A Story of West Point,* 1886.
as William J. Roe
□ *The Song For the Songs' Sake,* 1913 (poetry).
■ *An Inn For Journeying Thoughts,* 1912.

ROHR, WOLF DETLEF *German*
● Geff Caine; Wayne Coover; Allan Reed.

ROLFE, FREDERICK W(illiam) SERAFINO AUSTIN LEWIS MARY (1860-1913)
as Prospero and Caliban [in collaboration with C. H. C. Pirie-Gordon]
The Weird of the Wanderer: Being the Papyrus Records of Some Incidents In One of the Previous Lives of Mr. Nicholas Crabbe. London: Rider, 1912, 298pp.
Hubert's Arthur: Being Certain Curious Documents Found Among the Literary Remains of Mr. N. C., Here Produced by Prospero and Caliban. London: Cassell, [1935], 453pp.
as Fr(ederick) (W.) Rolfe, (Baron Corvo)
Hadrian the Seventh. London: Chatto & Windus, 1904, 413pp.
Don Tarquinio. London: Chatto & Windus, 1905, 257pp.
□ *Don Renato, In Ideal Content,* 1909 (1 cop); *Three Tales of Venice,* 1913; *The Desire and Pursuit of the Whole,* 1934.
as (Frederick) Baron Corvo
□ *Amico di Sandro; A Fragment of A Novel,* 1951.
■ *Chronicles of the House of Borgia,* 1901; *A History of the Borgias,* 1910; *The Bull Against The Enemy of the Anglican Race,* 1929.
anonymous
□ *Tarcissus: The Boy Martyr of Rome, In the Diocletian Persecution. AD CCCIII,* 1880 (poetry).

ROPES, ARTHUR R(eed) (1859-1933) *British*
Born: London
as A(rthur) R. Ropes
□ *Poems,* 1884 (poetry).
■ *A Sketch of the History of Europe,* 1888; *Frederick the Great's Invasion of Saxony,* 1891; *The Causes of the Seven Years War,* 1899.
as Adrian Ross
The Holt of the Pit. London: Edward Arnold, 1914, 300pp.
□ MUSICAL COMEDY: *The Messenger Boy,* 1900; *The Merry Widow,* 1907; *Monsieur Beaucaire,* 1919; *Lilac Time,* 1922.

ROSENBERG, ELINOR BLAISDELL (Mrs. Melrich) (1904-) *U.S.*
as Anne Blaisdell
Nightmare. NY: Lancer, [1967], paper. [Not the same book as the British title *Nightmare* by Anne Blaisdell which

is the pseudonym of **ELIZABETH LININGTON**.]
as Elinor Blaisdell
(ed.) *Tales of the Undead.* NY: T. Crowell, 1947, 372pp.
Nightmare. London: Corgi, 1964, paper.
□ *Falcon Fly Back,* 1939.
Illustrator for many books, esp. juveniles and classics of literature.

ROSEWATER, FRANK (1856- ?) *U.S.*
as Marian and Franklin Mayoe
Doomed: A Startling Message to the People of Our Day, Interwoven In An Antediluvian Romance of Two Old Worlds and Two Young Lovers, by Queen Metel and Prince Loab of Atlo, Re-Incarnated In Its Editors Marian and Franklin Mayoe; By the Atlan Calendar 14,009; by Our Calendar, the Year 1920. NY: F. Rosewater, 1920, 282pp., ill.
as Frank Rosewater
'96 A Romance of Utopia. Omaha, Nebraska: Utopia Co., 1894; 268pp.
The Making of A Millennium; The Story of A Millennial Realm and Its Law. Chicago[?]: Century Pub. Co., [1908], 183pp., ill. [place of pub. possibly Omaha, Neb.]
■ *No More Free Rides on This Jackass; or, Protection Forever and Everywhere,* 1882; *The Light of Centrism; the Forecast of A Practical Millennium,* 1908; *The Coming Golden Age,* 1917.

ROSS, ALBERT HENRY (1881-)
as Frank Morison
Sunset. NY: Century Pub. Co. [1932]. 281pp., ill.
■ *J. H. Jowett, M.A., D.D.; A Character Study,* 1911; *Who Moved the Stone?,* 1930; *War On Great Cities, A Study of the Facts,* 1937; *And Pilate Said—A New Study of the Roman Procurator,* 1939.

ROTHMAN, MILTON A. (1919-) *U.S.*
as Lee Gregor [alone]
Asteroid. Astonishing, Feb 1940
as Lee Gregor [in collaboration with Frederik Pohl]
Heavy Planet. Astounding, Aug 1939
Shawn's Sword. Astounding, Oct 1939
as Milton A. Rothman
Book Reviews. Astounding, Sept 1948-Feb 1950
Probabilities and Punctures. Astounding, April 1951 article

ROTSLER, WILLIAM
as William Arrow [house pseudonym]
Visions of Nowhere. NY: Ballantine, [1976], paper. (Return to Planet of the Apes #1)
Man, the Hunted Animal. NY: Ballantine, [1976], paper. (Return to Planet of the Apes #3)
as John Ryder Hall
Futureworld. NY: Ballantine, [1976], paper.
Sinbad and the Eye of the Tiger. NY: Pocket Books, [1977], paper.
as William Rotsler
Patron of the Arts. NY: Ballantine, [1974], paper.
To the Land of the Electric Angel. NY: Ballantine, [1976], paper.
Zandra. Garden City: Doubleday, 1978.

RUBEN, WILLIAM S.
as William S. Ruben
Dionysus: The Ultimate Experiment. NY: Manor, 1977.
as Fred Shannon
Weightless In Gaza. NY: Tower, [1970], paper.

RUMBALL, CHARLES
as Charles Delorme
The Marvellous and Incredible Adventures of Charles

Thunderbolt In [the] Moon. London: T. Gunn, 1851, 391pp.
□ *The Pedlar. A Tale of Emigration,* 1857.

RUSSELL, (Mrs. J. W.)
as I. H. Leney
Shadowland In Ellan Vannin; or Folk Tales of the Isle of Man. London: Elliot Stock, 1890, 150pp.

RUSSELL, ERIC FRANK (1905-   ) *British*
as Webster Craig
Homo Saps. *Astounding,* Dec 1941
as Maurice G. Hugi
The Mechanical Mice. *Astounding,* Jan 1941
as Duncan H. Munro
Muten. *Astounding,* Oct 1948
as Eric Frank Russell
The Saga of Pelican West. *Astounding,* Feb 1937
Sinister Barrier. *Unknown,* March 1939
Sinister Barrier. Surrey: World's Work, 1943, 135pp.
Sinister Barrier. Reading, Pennsylvania: Fantasy Press, 1948, 253pp., ill.
Sinister Barrier. NY: Galaxy Novel #1, [1950], 158pp., paper.
Dreadful Sanctuary. Reading, Pennsylvania: Fantasy Press, 1951, 276pp.
Sentinels From Space. NY: Bouregy & Curl, [1953], 256pp.
Deep Space. Reading, Pennsylvania: Fantasy Press, 1954, 259pp. *ss col*
Men, Martians, and Machines. London: Dobson, 1955, 191pp. *ss col*
Three to Conquer. NY: Avalon, [1956], 224pp.
Wasp. NY: Avalon, [1957], 223pp.
Six Worlds Yonder. NY: Ace, [1958], 128pp., paper. (Ace Double D 315) *ss col*
The Space Willies. NY: Ace, [1958], 131pp., paper. (Ace Double D 315)
Far Stars. London: Dobson, 1961, 191pp. *ss col*
The Great Explosion. London: Dobson, 1962, 203pp.
Dark Tides. London: Dobson, [1962], 183pp.
With A Strange Device. London: Dobson, [1964], 182pp.
Somewhere A Voice. London: Dobson, 1965, 184pp. *ss col*
■ *Great World Mysteries,* 1957; *The Rabble Rousers,* 1963.

RUSSELL, GEORGE WILLIAM (1867-1935) *Irish*
Born: Lurgan, County Armagh
as A. E.
The Mask of Apollo and Other Stories. Dublin: Whaley, [1904], 53pp. *ss col*
The Avatars: A Futurist Fantasy. London: Macmillan, 1933, 188pp.
□ *Collected Poems by A. E.,* 1913 (poetry).
as George Russell Williams [often with "A.E." on title page]
□ *Deirdre,* 1907 (play); *Collected Poems,* 1926 (poetry); *House of the Titans and Other Poems,* 1934 (poetry).
■ *Irish Essays,* 1906; *The National Being, some Thoughts on an Irish Policy,* 1917; *England's War on Ireland's Industry,* 1920.

RYMER, JAMES MALCOLM
as Author of "Grace Rivers"
Varney the Vampyre; or, The Feast of Blood. London: E. Lloyd, [1847], parts.
as Malcolm J. Errym
□ *The Renegade; or, Secrets of the Gulf Mill,* 1859; *Sea-Drift; or, The Wreckers of the Channel,* 1860.
as James Malcolm Rymer
□ *Grace Rivers; or, The Merchant's Daughter,* 1844.

anonymous
The Black Monk; or, The Secret of the Grey Turret. London: E. Lloyd, [1844], parts.

RYNAS, STEPHEN A.
as Stephen Arr
The Apprentice Sorcerer. *Fantasy Fiction Magazine,* Nov 1953
Mr. President. *Galaxy,* Nov 1953
The Ball. *Vortex #2,* 1953

SABEN, GERTRUDE CHETWYND SHALLCROSS
as Author of "The Terror by Night" [in collaboration with Frederick E. Burkitt]
□ *The Co-Respondent*, 1912.
as Gregory Saben [in collaboration with Frederick E. Burkitt]
The Terror by Night. London: Newnes, [1912], 316pp.
The Sorcerer. London: J. Richmond, [1918], 316pp.
□ *Born of A Woman*, 1913.

ST. CLAIR, MARGARET (Mrs.) (1911-) *U.S.*
Born: Kansas
as Margaret St. Clair
Rocket To Limbo. *Fantastic Adventures*, Nov 1946
Agent Of the Unknown. NY: Ace, [1956], 128pp., paper. (Ace Double D 150)
The Green Queen. NY: Ace, [1956], 128pp., paper. (Ace Double D 176)
The Games of Neith. NY: Ace, [1960], 149pp., paper. (Ace Double D 453)
Sign of the Labrys. NY: Bantam, [1963], 139pp., paper.
Message From the Eocene. NY: Ace, [1964], 114pp., paper. (Ace Double M 105)
Three Worlds of Futurity. NY: Ace, [1964], 142pp., paper. (Ace Double M 105)
The Dolphins of Altair. NY: Dell, [1967], 188pp., paper.
The Shadow People. NY: Dell, [1969], paper.
The Dancers of Noyo. NY: Ace, [1973], paper.
Change The Sky and Other Stories. NY: Ace, [1974], paper. *ss col*
as Idris Seabright
The Listening Child. *Magazine of Fantasy and Science Fiction*, Dec 1950
● William Hazel

SAMACHSON, JOSEPH (1906-) *U.S.*
Born: Trenton, New Jersey
as William Morrison
Bad Medicine. *Thrilling Wonder Stories*, Feb 1941
Mel Oliver and Space Rover On Mars. NY: Gnome, [1954], 191pp. *2 novels*
as Joseph Samachson
"The Science Stage," in *Magazine of Fantasy and Science Fiction* beginning with March 1957 issue.
as Brett Sterling [house pseudonym]
Worlds To Come. *Captain Future*, Spring 1943
Days of Creation. *Captain Future*, Spring 1944

SAMPLINER, LOUIS H.
as Alexander Blade [house pseudonym]
Dr. Loudon's Armageddon. *Amazing*, Sept 1941

SAMUELS, PHILIP FRANCIS (1881-)
as Samuels-Bacon
Bensalem and New Jerusalem. Boston: Samuels-Bacon Pub. Co., [1936], 154pp.
■ Bacon/Shakespeare Controversy: *Man v. Ape In the Play of Ear-ce-rammed*, 1932; *Five Lectures On "Shakespeare,"* 1937; *Shylock vs. The Merchant of Venice*, 1937.

SANDERS, LEONARD M., JR. (1929-) *U.S.*
Born: Denver, Colorado
as Leonard M. Sanders, Jr.
sometime book page editor of *Ft. Worth Star-Telegram*.
as Dan Thomas
The Seed. NY: Ballantine, [1968], 252pp., paper.

SANDERSON, IVAN T(erence) (1911-1973) *naturalized U.S.*
Born: Scotland
as Terence Roberts
Report On the Status Quo. NY: Merlin, [1955], 66pp., ill.
as Ivan T. Sanderson
An Introduction to Ufology. *Fantastic Universe*, Feb 1957 *article*
■ *Things*, 1967; *Uninvited Visitors*, 1967.

SANDS, DAVE [house pseudonym]
see **Bryce Walton**

SAUNDERS, HILARY A(iden) (St. George) (1898-1951) *British*
as Francis Beeding [in collaboration with John Palmer]
The Hidden Kingdom. Boston: Little, Brown, 1927, 370pp.
The House of Dr. Edwardes. London: Hodder & Stoughton, 1927, 308pp. [basis for film *Spellbound*].
The One Sane Man. Boston: Little, Brown, 1934, 314pp.
□ MYSTERY: *The Six Proud Walkers*, 1928; *Death Walks In Eastrepps*, 1931; *The Norwich Victims*, 1935.
as Hilary A. Saunders
■ *Combined Operations, The Official Story of the Commandos*, 1943; *Ford At War*, 1946; *The Left Hand Shake, The Boy Scout Movement During the War*, 1949.
anonymous
■ *The Battle of Britain*, 1940 (pamphlet).

SAVINKOV, BORIS (Viktorovich) (1879-1925) *Russian*
as Ropshin
What Never Happened. trans. by T. Seltzer, NY: Knopf, 1917, 448pp.
□ *The Pale Horse*, 1909.
as Boris Savinkov
□ *The Black Horse*, 1924.
■ *Memoirs of A Terrorist*, 1931.

SAYLER, HARRY LINCOLN (1863- ?) *U.S.*
as Ashton Lamar (all juveniles)
The Boy Aeronaut's Club; or, Flying for Fun. Chicago: Reilly & Britton, [c.1910], 265pp., front.
The Aeroplane Express; or, The Boys [sic] *Aeronaut's Grit.* Chicago: Reilly & Britton, [1910], 246pp., ill.
In the Clouds For Uncle Sam; or, Morey Marshall of the Signal Corps. Chicago: Reilly & Britton, [1910], 216pp.
The Stolen Aeroplane; or, How Bud Wilson Made Good. Chicago: Reilly & Britton, [1910], 223pp., ill.
Battling the Bighorn; or, The Aeroplane In the Rockies. Chicago: Reilly & Britton, [1911], 280pp.
A Cruise In the Sky; or, The Legend of the Great Pink Pearl. Chicago: Reilly & Britton, 1911, 218pp.
When Scout Meets Scout; or, The Aeroplane Spy. Chicago: Reilly & Britton, [1912], 249pp.
On the Edge of the Arctic; or, An Aeroplane In Snowland. Chicago: Reilly & Britton, [1913], 256pp., ill.
as Gordon Stuart
All as follows: Reilly & Britton, [1912].
The Boy Scouts of the Air In Northern Wilds.
The Boy Scouts of the Air In Indian Land.
The Boy Scouts of the Air At Greenwood School.
The Boy Scouts of the Air At Eagle Camp.
as H. L. Sayler
The Airship Boys; or, The Quest of the Aztec Treasure. Chicago: Reilly & Britton, [1909], 315pp., ill.

The Airship Boys Adrift; or, Saved By An Aeroplane.
Chicago: Reilly & Britton, [1909], 312pp., ill.
The Airship Boys Due North; or, By Balloon To the Pole.
Chicago: Reilly & Britton, [1910], 335pp.
The Airship Boys In the Barren Lands; or, The Secret of the White Eskimos. Chicago: Reilly & Britton, [1910], 326pp.
The Airship Boys In France; or, the Flight of the Flying Cow. Chicago: Reilly & Britton, [1911], 295pp., ill.
The Airship Boys' Ocean Flyer; or, New York to London In Twelve Hours. Chicago: Reilly & Britton, [1911], 327pp., ill.
□ *Terrible Teddy and Peaceful Bill; or, The Quest of the Treasure Box,* 1908.
■ *American Romance of the South. Recent Search For the Lost Capital of the Powerful Nation of Creek Indians, Who Were Ruled by the Shrewd Hand of A Scion of the Rich Scotch McGillivrays At the Time of the American Revolution. The Refuge of Princess Charlotte, the Daughter-In-Law of Peter the Great,* 1908 [excerpt from *Journal of American History*].
● as **Elliott Whitney** [in collaboration with H. Bedford-Jones]
□ *The Blind Lion of the Congo,* 1912; *The White Tiger of Nepal,* 1912; *The King Bear of Kadiak* [sic] *Island,* 1912.

SCHACHNER, NAT(han) (1895-1955)   *U.S.*
as **Chan Corbett**
When the Sun Dies. *Astounding,* March 1935
as **Walter Glamis**
The Orange God. *Astounding,* Oct 1933
as **Nat(han) Schachner**
(with Leo Zagat) The Tower of Evil. *Wonder Stories Quarterly,* Summer 1930
Pirates of the Gorm. *Astounding,* May 1932
Space Lawyer. NY: Gnome, [1953], 222pp.
□ HISTORICAL FICTION: *By The Dim Lights,* 1941; *The King's Passenger,* 1942; *The Sun Shines West,* 1943; *The Wanderer, A Novel of Dante and Beatrice,* 1944.
■ *The Medieval Universities,* 1938; *The Price of Liberty, A History of the American Jewish Committee,* 1948. BIOGRAPHY: *Aaron Burr,* 1937; *Alexander Hamilton,* 1946; *Thomas Jefferson,* 1951.

SCHEER, KARL HERBERT (1928-   )   *German*
Born: Frankfort
as **Alexej Turbojew**
● *Der Mann von Oros; Technisch-Utopischer Roman.* Balve/Westfalen: Balowa-Verlag, [c.1959], 254pp.

SCHERR, MARIE
as **Marie Cher**
The Immortal Gymnasts. London: Heinemann, [1915], 309pp.
The Inner Room. Oxford: Blackwell, 1937, 116pp.
□ *The Door Unlatched,* 1927; *Up At the Villa,* 1929.
■ *Charlotte Corday and Certain Men of the Revolutionary Torment,* 1929; *Poison At Court; Certain Figures of the Reign of Louis the Fourteenth,* 1931.

SCHMIDT, WILLY (1896-   )   *German*
as **German Gerhold**
Das Letzte Gesetze, der Durchbruch zum Weltbild der Kommenden Epoche. Stuttgart: Kulturaufbau-Verlag, 1946, 402pp., ill.
■ *Jahrmarkt am Dom; Hundert Kleine Geschichten,* 1946.

SCHNABEL, JOHANN GOTTFRIED (c.1692-c.1750)
   German
as **(Eberhard Julius?) Gisander**
Wunderliche Fata Einiger See-Fahrer. . .Absonderlich

Alberti Julili, Eines Gebohrnen Sachsens. . .Entworffen von Dessen Bruders-Sohnes-Sohnes-Sohne, mons. Eberhard Julio auch par commission dem Drucke Ubergeben von Gisandern. Nordhausen, Bey: J. H. Gross, [c.1736], 608pp., 4 vol. [later editions are often titled *Die Insel Felsenburg*]

SCHNEIDER, ISADOR (1896-   )
as **I.S.**
Doctor Transit. NY: Boni & Liveright, 1925, 285pp. [may have author's complete name on the book]
as **Isador Schneider**
□ *The Temptation of Anthony; A Novel In Verse, and Other Poems,* 1928 (poetry); *From the Kingdom of Necessity,* 1935; *The Judas Time,* 1947.
■ (with T. M. Bayer, A. Brody, and Jessica Smith) *War and Peace in Finland, A Documented Survey,* 1940; *Traitor or Holy Idiot? The Case of Ezra Pound,* 1945.

SCHNITTKIND, HENRY THOMAS (1886-   ) [at some point apparently changed name legally to Thomas]
as **Henry (T.) Schnittkind**
Giuseppe, and Laughter Wins; Fairy Tales for Workingmen's Children, containing the Hymn Cosmopolitan. Boston: Stratford Pub. Co., 1914, 61pp.
Alice and the Stork; A Fairy Tale for Workingmen's Children. Boston: R.G. Badger, [1915], 95pp.
■ *A Guide To Aeschylus,* 1924.
as **Henry Thomas**
Cleopatra's Private Diary. Boston: Stratford Pub. Co., 1927, 306pp.
The Prince and the Pauper (Adapted for Young People From Mark Twain). Boston: W.H. Baker Co., 1938, 27pp.
A Midsummer Night's Dream (Adapted for Young People from Shakespeare). Boston: Baker's Plays, 1944, 25pp. play
■ *The Complete Book of English,* 1938; *The Modern Self Educator,* 1940; *Mathematics Made Easy,* 1940; *Living Biographies of Famous Women,* 1942; *The Living World of Philosophy,* 1946; *50 Great Americans,* 1948; *Forty Famous Composers,* 1948; *Life Stories of the Great Inventors,* 1948; *Better English Made Easy— The Henry Thomas Method,* 1954; (with Dana Lee Thomas) *Living Adventures In Philosophy,* 1954.

SCHOEPFLIN, HAROLD VINCENT (1893-   )   *U.S.*
as **Harl Vincent**
The Golden Girl of Munan. *Amazing,* June 1928
The Doomsday Planet. NY: Tower, [1966], 141pp., paper.

SCHOPFER, JEAN (1868-1931)   *French*
as **Claude Anet**
La Fin d'un Monde. Paris: B. Grasset, 1925, 274pp., ill.
The End of the World. NY: Knopf, 1927, 268pp., ill.
□ *Petite Ville,* 1901; *Le Bergeries,* 1904; *Ariane,* 1920 (Fr.); *Mademoiselle Bourrat,* 1923 (play); *La Fille Perdue,* 1924 (play); *Ariane,* 1927 (U.S.); *Mayerling,* 1930.
■ *Through Persia In A Motor Car, by Russia and the Caucasus,* 1907; *Through the Russian Revolution: Notes of an Eye Witness, From 12th March—30th May, 1917; La Revolution Russe, 1917-1919* (4 vol.); *While the Earth Shook,* 1927.

SCHWARTZ, JOZUA M(arius) W(illen) VAN DER POORTEN (1858-1915)
as **Maarten Maartens**
The Sin of Joost Avelingh. London: Remington & Co., 1889, 2 vol.
□ *An Old Maid's Love,* 1891; *God's Fool; A Koopstad Story,* 1892; *Some Women I Have Known,* 1899; *Eve: An Incident of Paradise Regained,* 1912.

SCOTT, PEG O'NEILL SCOTT   *U.S.*
as Barton Werper
Tarzan and the Snake People. NY: Gold Star, 1964, paper.

SCOTT, PETER T.   *U.S.*
as Barton Werper
Tarzan and the Silver Globe. NY: Gold Star, 1964, paper.
Tarzan and the Cave City. NY: Gold Star, 1964, paper.
Tarzan and the Abominable Snowman. NY: Gold Star, 1965, paper.
Tarzan and the Winged Invaders. NY: Gold Star, 1965, paper.

SCOTT, ROBERT   *British*
as "Blue Wolf"
Dwifa's Curse; A Tale of the Stone Age. London: R. Scott, [1921], 253pp.

SCOTT, WALTER (Sir)   (1771-1832)   *Scottish*
Born: Edinburgh
as Author of "Waverley"
The Monastery. Edinburgh: Constable, 1820, 3 vol.
The Pirate. Edinburgh: Constable, 1822, 3 vol.
Red Gauntlet: A Tale of the Eighteenth Century. Edinburgh: Constable, 1824, 3 vol.
The Black Dwarf. A Legend of Montrose. Edinburgh: R. Cadell, 1841, 315pp.
as Jedediah Cleishbotham
Tales of My Landlord. Edinburgh: Blackwood, 1816, 4 vol.
Tales of My Landlord, Second Series. Edinburgh: Constable, 1818, 4 vol.
Tales of My Landlord, Third Series. Edinburgh: Constable, 1819, 4 vol.
Tales of My Landlord, Fourth and Last Series. London: Cadell, 1832, 4 vol.
as Sir Walter Scott
■ *The Border Antiquities of England and Scotland,* 1814-1817, 2 vol.
anonymous
□ *The Caldonian Comet,* 1810; *Tales of A Grandfather,* 1829.
✔ **Chrystal Croftangry**
● **Peter Pattieson**

SCOTTI, GIULIO CLEMENTE   (1602-1669)
as Lucius Cornelius Europaeus [also rendered Lucii Cornelii Europaei]
Monarchia Solipsorum ad Leonem Allatium. Venice: 1645, 144pp. [a satire against the Jesuits, also attributed to one Melchior Inchofer whose name is also sometimes treated as a pseudonym of G. Scotti]

SEARLS, HENRY HUNT   (1922-   )   *U.S.*
Born: San Francisco, California
as Hank Searls
Martyr's Flight. Imagination, Dec 1955
The Big X. NY: Harper, 1959, 241pp.
The Crowded Sky. NY: Harper, [1960], 274pp.
The Astronaut. NY: Pocket Books, [1962], 149pp., paper.
The Pilgrim Project. NY: McGraw-Hill, [1964], 274pp.
The Hero Ship. NY: World, 1969, 304pp.
□ *Pentagon,* 1971.
■ *The Lost Prince: Young Joe, The Forgotten Kennedy; the Story of the Oldest Brother,* 1969.

SENARENS, LUIS P.   (c.1863-1939)   *U.S.*
as Noname [sometimes rendered as No Name]

Frank Reade, Jr. and His Queen Clipper of the Clouds. NY: F. Tousey, 1893, 2pts., ill. [one of the continuation of the original series by Harry Enton which began with *Frank Reade and His Steam Man of the Plains, c.*1876].
Jack Wright and His Electric Air Rocket; or, The Boy Exile of Siberia. NY: F. Tousey, 1893, 30pp.
Jack Wright and His Prairie Privateer; or Fighting the Western Road-Agents. NY: F. Tousey, 1893, 28pp., ill.
as Lu Senarens
■ *How To Become A West Point Cadet,* 1891.
● **Cecil Burleigh, Kit Clyde, Frank Doughty, W. J. Earle, Gaston Garne, Capt. Howard, Ned Sparling**

SERNER, MARTIN G(unnar)   (1886-1947)   *Swedish*
as Frank Heller
The Thousand and Second Night; An Arabesque. NY: Crowell, [1925], 333pp.
□ *Storhertigens Finanser,* 1919; *The Emperor's Old Clothes,* 1923; *The Marriage of Yussuf Khan,* 1923; *Mr. Collin,* 1924 (Br.); *The Perilous Transactions of Mr. Collin,* 1924 (Br.); *The London Adventures of Mr. Collin,* 1924 (Br.); *Mr. Collin Is Ruined,* 1925 (U.S.); *The Strange Adventures of Mr. Collin,* 1926 (U.S.); *Doktor Z,* 1926; *Herr Collin Contra Napoleon,* 1927; *Odysseus; Oder, die Sieben Menus,* 1927; *Lead Me Into Temptation,* 1927; *Die Debatte um Atlantis, Kriminalroman,* 1944.
■ *Twilight of the Gladiators; Italy and the Italians, 1939-1943,* 1944.
as Gunnar Serner
■ *On the Language of Swinburne's Lyrics and Epics, A Study,* 1910.

SEWELL, MARGARET ELIZABETH   (1919-   )   *U.S.*
Born: Coonoor, India
as Elizabeth Sewell
The Dividing of Time. London: Chatto & Windus, 1951, 249pp.
□ *The Singular Hope,* 1955.
■ *The Structure of Poetry,* 1951; *Paul Valery, the Mind In the Mirror,* 1952; *The Field of Nonsense,* 1952.

SEYMOUR, FREDERICK H(enri)   (1850-1913)
as Lord Gilhooley
The God Yutzo of B.C. 763. Detroit, Michigan: Bornman, 1896, 181pp., ill.
Mangis, ye Sorcerer (from ye Ancient French). NY: F.T. Neeley, [1898], 252pp. [Neeley's Universal Lib. #43]
Ye Wisdom of Confucius; or, Ye Mummyfyed Fynger; Ye Strange Relation of a Vysyt of Ye Spiryt of Yen Hui Ye Dyscyple of Confucius to Sir Patrick Gilhoolye, bart., At His Chambers At Ye Inner Temple, London, and Ye Strange Circumstances Connected Therewyth. In A.D. 1604. NY: Stokes, [1900], 192pp.
□ *Dennis Foggarty, The Irish Yutzo and His Wife Honora,* 1903; *Gilhooleyisms,* 1904.

SHARKEY, JOHN MICHAEL   (1931-   )   *U.S.*
Born: Chicago, Illinois
as Jack Sharkey
The Captain of His Soul. Fantastic, March 1959
The Obvious Solution. Fantastic, March 1959
The Secret Martians. NY: Ace, [1960], 132pp., paper. (Ace Double D 471)
Ultimatum in 2050 A.D. NY: Ace, [1965], 120pp., paper. (Ace Double M 117)
The Addams Family. NY: Pyramid, 1965, paper.
□ MYSTERY: *Murder Maestro Please,* 1960; *Death For Auld Lang Syne,* 1962.

SHARP, WILLIAM (*c.*1855-1905)   *Scottish*
Born: Paisley
as W.H. Brooks
The Pagan Review, No. 1, Aug., 1892. Rudgwick, England: W. H. Brooks, 64pp. [Written completely by William Sharp under various pseudonyms and published by him as W. H. Brooks]
as Fiona MacLeod
Pharais; A Romance of the Isles. Derby, England: Harpur & Murray, 1894, 171pp.
Vistas. Derby, England: F. Murray, 1894, 184pp.
Ecce Puella and Other Fantasies. London: E. Mathews, 1895, 124pp. *col*
The Mountain Lovers. London: J. Lane, 1895, 222pp., ill.
The Sin Eaters and Other Tales & Episodes. Edinburgh: P. Geddes, [1895], 294pp. *ss col*
Green Fire, A Romance. Westminster: A. Constable, 1896, 294pp.
The Washer of the Ford and Other Legendary Moralities. Edinburgh: P. Geddes, [1896], 320pp., ill. *ss col*
Barbaric Tales. Edinburgh: P. Geddes, [1897], 202pp. *ss col*
The Laughter of Peterkin. "A Retelling of Old Tales of the Celtic Underworld." London: A. Constable, 1897, ill. *ss col*
The Dominion of Dreams. Westminster: A. Constable, 1899, 327pp.
The Divine Adventure; Iona; By Sundown Shores: Studies In Spiritual History. London: Chapman & Hall, 1900, 323pp.
The Hills of Ruel, and Other Stories. London: Heinemann, 1921, 92pp., ill. *ss col*
□ *From the Hills of Dream; Mountain Songs and Island Runes,* 1896; *Bride of the Islands,* 1914.
■ *The Winged Destiny; Studies in the Spiritual History of Gael,* 1904; *When the Forest Murmurs, Nature Essays,* 1906; *At the Turn of the Year,* 1913 (essays).
as W(illiam) Sharp
Romantic Ballads and Poems of Phantasy, 1888. *poetry*
Children of To-Morrow; A Romance. London: Chatto & Windus, 1889, 312pp.
The Gypsy Christ and Other Tales. Chicago: Stone & Kimball, 1895, 282pp. *ss col*
Vistas, The Gypsy Christ, and Other Prose Imaginings. NY: Duffield, 1912, 484pp. *plays & ss col*
□ *Earth's Voices,* 1884 (poetry); *The Sport of Chance,* 1888; *Wives In Exile,* 1896; *Silence Farm,* 1899.
■ *Dante Gabriel Rosetti,* 1882; *Life of Heinrich Heine,* 1888; *Life of Robert Browning,* 1890; *Fair Women In Painting and Poetry,* 1894; *Progress of Art In the Century,* 1902; *Literary Geography,* 1904; *Papers Critical and Reminiscent,* 1912.

SHAVER, RICHARD S(harpe)   (1907-1975)   *U.S.*
as Wes Amherst
Sons of the Serpent. *Other Worlds,* Jan 1950
as Edwin Benson [name of real author—used this story only]
Marai's Wife. *Other Worlds,* March 1950
as Alexander Blade [house pseudonym]
Flesh Against Spirit. *Amazing,* March 1948
as Peter Dexter
The Gamin. *Other Worlds,* March 1950
as Richard Dorset
She Was Sitting In the Dark. *Science Stories,* Dec 1953
as Richard English
The Heart of the Game. *Orbit #1,* 1953
as G. H. Irwin [house pseudonym]
Lair of the Grimalkin. *Fantastic Adventures,* April 1948
Where No Foot Walks. *Other Worlds,* Nov 1949
Glass Woman Of Venus. *Other Worlds,* Jan 1951
as Paul Lohrman [house pseudonym]
The World of the Lost. *Fantastic Adventures,* March 1950

as Frank Patton [house pseudonym]
When the Moon Bounced. *Amazing,* May 1949
as Stan Raycraft
Pillars of Delight. *Amazing,* Dec 1949
as D. Richard Sharpe
First Rocket. *Amazing,* Aug 1947
as Richard Shaver
I Remember Lemuria. *Amazing,* March 1945
I Remember Lemuria. Evanston, Illinois: Venture Books, 1948, 215pp., ill.
● **Edwin Dexter, Peter Dorot, Mollie Elclair**

SHECKLEY, ROBERT   (1928-   )   *U.S.*
Born: New York, New York
as Phillips Barbee
The Leech. *Galaxy,* Dec 1952
as Finn O'Donnevan
Feeding Time. *Fantasy Fiction,* Feb 1953
as Robert Sheckley
Final Examination. *Imagination,* May 1952
Untouched by Human Hands. NY: Ballantine, [1954], 169pp., paper/hardback. *ss col*
Citizen In Space. NY: Ballantine, [1955], 200pp., paper/hardback. *ss col*
Pilgrimage To Earth. NY: Bantam, [c.1957], 167pp., paper. *ss col*
Immortality Delivered. NY: Avalon, 1958, 221pp.
Store of Infinity. NY: Bantam, [1960], 151pp., paper. *ss col*
Notions: Unlimited. NY: Bantam, [1960], 170pp., paper. *ss col*
The Status Civilization. NY: Signet, [1960], 127pp., paper.
Shards of Space. NY: Bantam, [1962], 152pp., paper. *ss col*
Journey Beyond Tomorrow. NY: Signet, [1962], 144pp., paper.
Mindswap. NY: Delacorte, 1966, 216pp.
Dimension of Miracles. NY: Dell, [1968], 190pp., paper.
The People Trap. NY: Dell, [1968], 204pp., paper. *ss col*
Can You Feel Anything When I Do This? Garden City: Doubleday, 1971, 191pp. *ss col*
□ MYSTERY: *Dead Run,* 1961; *White Death,* 1963; *The Game of X,* 1965.

SHEEHAN, PERLEY POORE   (1875-1943)   *U.S.*
Born: Cincinnati, Ohio
as Paul Regard
Haunted Legacy. *All Story Weekly,* May 2, 1914
as Perley Poore Sheehan
Monsieur De Guise. *The Scrap Book,* Jan 1911
The Woman of the Pyramid. *All Story Magazine,* March 1914
The Ghost Mill. *All Story Weekly,* April 4, 1914
The Prophet. London: T. F. Unwin, 1913, 312pp.
The Whispering Chorus. NY: G. H. Watt, 1927, 316pp.
The Abyss of Wonders. Reading, Pennsylvania: Polaris Press, 1953, 190pp., ill. (1500 cop, boxed)
□ *The Passport Invisible,* 1917; *Those Who Walk In Darkness,* 1917; *Believe It, It's So,* 1919; *The House With A Bad Name,* 1920; *Three Sevens, A Detective Story,* 1927. PLAYS: (with R. H. Davis) *We Are French,* 1915; *Lola Montez,* 1936. SCREENPLAYS: *The Hunchback of Notre Dame,* 1923; *King Arthur,* 1936; *Blennerhassett,* 1937; *Five Little Peppers and How They Grew,* 1939.

SHELDON, ALICE BRADLEY   *U.S.*
as Alice Bradley
The Lucky Ones. *The New Yorker,* Nov 16, 1946 *article*
as Raccoona Sheldon
Angel Fix. *If,* Aug 1974
as James Tiptree, Jr.
Birth of A Salesman. *Analog,* March 1968

Ten Thousand Light Years From Home. NY: Ace, [1973], 319pp., paper. *ss col*
Warm Worlds & Otherwise. NY: Ballantine, [1975], 222pp., paper. *ss col*
Up the Walls of the World. NY: Berkley/Putnam, 1978.
Star Songs of An Old Primate. NY: Ballantine/Del Rey, [1978], 270pp., paper.

SHELDON, WALT
as Walt Sheldon
Perfect Servant. *Startling Stories,* July 1948
as Sheldon Walters
"All You Do Is Tranz the Framis!," *Amazing,* July 1950

SHELLABARGER, SAMUEL (1888-1954)
as John Esteven
Voodoo. A Murder Mystery. Garden City: Doubleday, 1930, 317pp.
☐ MYSTERY: *The Door of Death,* 1928; *By Night At Dinsmore,* 1935; *Graveyard Watch,* 1938.
as Samuel Shellabarger
☐ *The Black Gale,* 1929. HISTORICAL FICTION: *Captain From Castile,* 1945; *Prince of Foxes,* 1947; *The King's Cavalier,* 1950; *Lord Vanity,* 1953; *The Token,* 1955.
■ *A Thesaurus of Figures of Speech In Anglo-Saxon and the Edda,* 1917; *The Chevalier Bayard; A Study In Fading Chivalry,* 1928.

SHELLEY, MARY WOLLSTONECRAFT (Godwin) (Mrs. Percy B.) (1797-1851) *English*
Born: London
as Author of "Frankenstein"
The Last Man. London: H. Colburn, 1826, 3 vol.
☐ *The Fortunes of Perkin Warbeck,* 1830; *Lodore,* 1835; *Falkner, A Novel,* 1837 (3 vol).
as Mary W. Shelley
Tales & Stories. London: W. Paterson, 1891, 386pp. *col*
Proserpine & Midas; Two Unpublished Mythological Dramas. London: H. Milford, 1922, 89pp.
anonymous
Frankenstein; or, The Modern Prometheus. London: Lackington, Hughes, 1818, 3 vol.

SHELLEY, PERCY B(ysshe) (1792-1822) *English*
Born: Warnham, Sussex
as A Gentleman of the University of Oxford
St. Irvyne; or, the Rosicrucian. London: Printed for J. J. Stockdale, 1811, 236pp.
as P.B.S.
Zastrozzi, A Romance. London: G. Wilkie & J. Robinson, 1810, 252pp.
as Percy Bysshe Shelley
The Witch of Atlas. 1820.
The Assassins. A Fragment of A Romance, in *Essays, Letters from Abroad, Translations and Fragments.* London: E. Moxon, 1840, 2 vol.
☐ POETRY: *Queen Mab,* 1813; *Prometheus Unbound,* 1818; *Ode To the West Wind,* 1819. PLAY: *Oedipus Tyrannus,* 1820.
■ *In Defense of Poetry,* 1821.

SHERMAN, FRANK DEMPSTER (1860-1916) *U.S.*
Born: Peekskill, New York
as Frank Dempster Sherman
☐ POETRY: *Madrigals and Catches,* 1887; *Lyrics for a Lute,* 1890; *Lyrics of Joy,* 1904; *The Poems of Frank Dempster Sherman,* 1917.
as Two Wags [in collaboration with John Kendrick Bangs]
New Waggings of Old Tales. Boston: Ticknor, 1888, 165pp., ill. *ss col*

SHIEL, M(atthew) P(hipps) (1865-1947) *British*
Born: Monserrat, West Indies
Bibliography: *The Works of M.P. Shiel. A Study In Bibliography,* by A. Reynolds Morse. Los Angeles: F.P.C.I., 1948, 170pp., ill. (1000 copies numbered)
as Gordon Holmes [in collaboration with Louis Tracy]
☐ MYSTERY: *A Mysterious Disappearance,* 1905; *The Late Tenant,* 1906; *By Force of Circumstance,* 1909; *The de Bercy Affair,* 1910; *The House of Silence,* 1911; *The House 'Round the Corner,* 1917.
as M.P. Shiel
Prince Zaleski. London: J. Lane, 1895, 163pp. *col*
The Rajah's Sapphire. London: Ward, Lock & Bowden, 1896, 119pp., ill.
Shapes In the Fire. London: J. Lane, 1896, 324pp. *ss col*
The Yellow Danger. London: G. Richards, 1898, 348pp.
The Lord of the Sea. London: G. Richards, 1901, 496pp.
The Purple Cloud. London: Chatto & Windus, 1901, 463pp.
The Yellow Wave. London: Ward, Lock, 1905, 320pp., ill. (last 2 pages adv.)
The Last Miracle. London: T.W. Laurie, 1906, 320pp.
The Isle of Lies. London: T.W. Laurie, [1909], 250pp.
The Pale Ape and Other Pulses. London: T.W. Laurie, [1911], 339pp. *ss col*
The Dragon. London: G. Richards, [1913], 356pp. [reissued as *The Yellow Peril* in 1929]
Children of the Wind. London: G. Richards, 1923, 302pp.
Here Comes the Lady. London: G. Richards, [1928], 335pp. *ss col*
Dr. Krasinski's Secret. NY: Vanguard, [1929], 337pp.
This Above All. NY: Vanguard, [1933], 304pp.
The Invisible Voices. London: G. Richards, [1935], 304pp. *ss col*
The Young Men Are Coming. London: G. Allen & Unwin, [1937], 375pp.
Xelucha and Others. Sauk City, Wisconsin: Arkham House, [1975]. *ss col*
☐ *Contraband of War,* 1899 (historical fiction); *The Man Stealers,* 1900 (historical fiction); *The Weird O'It,* 1902; *The Evil That Men Do,* 1904; *The Lost Viol,* 1905; *How The Old Woman Got Home,* 1927; *The Black Box,* 1930 (mystery); *Say Au R'Voir But Not Goodbye,* 1933.
■ *Science, Life, and Literature,* 1950.

SHIPLEY, MIRIAM ALLEN DE FORD (1888-1975) (Mrs. Maynard) *U.S.*
Born: Philadelphia, Pennsylvania
as Miriam Allen de Ford
The Last Generation. *Harper's,* Nov 1946
(ed) *Space, Time, and Crime.* NY: Paperback Library, [1964], paper. *ss col*
Xenogenesis. NY: Ballantine, [1969], paper. *ss col*
Elsewhere, Elsewhen, Elsehow. NY: Walker, [1971], 180pp. *ss col*
☐ *Children of the Sun,* 1939 (poetry); *Shaken With the Wind,* 1942.
■ *The Cosmopolitanism of Lafcadio Hearn,* 1916; *The Augustan Poets,* 1925; *The Life and Poems of Catullus,* 1925; *Latin Self Taught,* 1926; *The Facts About Fascism,* 1926; *Love-Children; A Book of Illustrious Illegitimates,* 1931; *Cicero As Revealed In His Letters,* 1939; *Who Was When?, A Dictionary of Contemporaries,* 1940; *They Were San Franciscans,* 1941; *The Meaning of All Common Given Names,* 1943; *The Facts About Basic English,* 1944; *Facts You Should Know About California,* 1945; *Making A Book Contract,* 1946; *Psychologist Unretired; the Life Pattern of Lillian J. Martin,* 1948; *Up-Hill All The Way; The Life of Maynard Shipley,* 1956; *The Overbury Affair; The Murder Trial That Rocked The Court of King James I,* 1960;

Stone Walls; Prisons From Fetters to Furloughs, 1962; *Murderers Sane and Mad; Case Histories In the Motivation and Rationale of Murder,* 1965; *Thomas More,* 1967; *The Real Ma Barker,* 1970.

SHIRAS, WILMAR H. (1908-   ) *U.S.*
Born: Boston, Massachusetts
as Jane Howes
■ *Slow Dawning,* 1946.
as Wilmar H. Shiras
In Hiding. *Astounding,* Nov 1948
Children of the Atom. NY: Gnome, [1953], 216pp.

SILBERBERG, LESLIE F(rances) STONE (Mrs. William) (1905-   ) *U.S.*
Born: Philadelphia, Pennsylvania
as Leslie F. Stone
Men Without Wings. *Air Wonder Stories,* July 1929
When the Sun Went Out. NY: Stellar Pub. Co., [1929], 24pp., ill. (SF Series #4)
Out of the Void. NY: Avalon, 1967, 191pp.

SILVANI ANITA
as A. F. S.
The Strange Story of Ahrinziman. Chicago: R. R. Donnelley, 1906, 284pp.
as Anita Silvani
□ *The Silver Gauntlet.*

SILVERBERG, ROBERT (1936-   ) *U.S.*
Born: New York, New York
as Gordon Aghill [in collaboration with Gordon Randall Garrett]
Gambler's Planet. *Amazing,* June 1956
as Robert Arnette [house pseudonym]
Cosmic Kill. *Amazing,* April/May 1957
as T. D. Bethlen
Invasion Vanguard. *SF Stories,* May 1958
as Alexander Blade [house pseudonym] [alone]
The Android Kill. *Imaginative Tales,* Nov 1957
3117 Half-Credit Uncirculated. *Science Fiction Adventures,* June 1958
as Alexander Blade [house pseudonym] [in collaboration with Gordon Randall Garrett]
The Alien Dies At Dawn. *Imagination,* Dec 1956
Wednesday Morning Sermon. *Imaginative Tales,* Jan 1957
The Ambassador's Pet. *Imagination,* Oct 1957
as Ralph Burke [alone]
Stay Out of My Grave. *Amazing,* July 1956
as Ralph Burke [in collaboration with Gordon Randall Garrett]
No Trap For the Keth. *Imaginative Tales,* Nov 1956
The Incomplete Theft. *Imagination,* Feb 1957
as Walker Chapman
■ *The Loneliest Continent; The Story of Antarctic Discovery,* 1964; *Kublai Khan, Lord of Xanadu,* 1966; *The Golden Dream Seekers of El Dorado,* 1967.
as Walter Chapman
■ (ed) *Antarctic Conquest,* 1966.
as Dirk Clinton
Planet of the Angry Giants. *Super Science Fiction,* Aug 1959
as Richard Greer [house pseudonym] [in collaboration with Gordon Randall Garrett]
The Great Kladnar Race. *Amazing,* Dec 1956
as E. K. Jarvis [house pseudonym]
Moon of Death. *Amazing,* Jan 1958
as Ivar Jorgensen [house pseudonym] [alone]
O' Captain, My Captain. *Fantastic,* Aug 1956
New Year's Eve - 2000 A.D. *Imaginative Tales,* Sept 1957
Housemaid No. 103. *Imaginative Tales,* Nov 1957
Never Trust A Thief! *Imagination,* Feb 1958
The Lure of Galaxy A. *Imaginative Tales,* March 1958

as Ivar Jorgensen [house pseudonym] [in collaboration with Gordon Randall Garrett]
Bleekman's Planet. *Imagination,* Feb 1957
Slaughter on Dornel IV. *Imagination,* April 1957
Pirates of the Void. *Imaginative Tales,* July 1957
as Ivar Jorgenson [house pseudonym]
This World Must Die! *Science Fiction Adventures,* Aug 1957
Thunder Over Starhaven. *Science Fiction Adventures,* Oct 1957
Hunt the Space-Witch! *Science Fiction Adventures,* Jan 1958
Ozymandias. *Infinity,* Nov 1958
Starhaven. NY: Avalon, [1958], 220pp.
Whom the Gods Would Slay. NY: Belmont, [1968], 140pp., paper.
The Deadly Sky. NY: Pinnacle, [1971], 188pp., paper.
as Warren Kastel [this story only]
The Dead World. *Imaginative Tales,* Sept 1957
as Calvin M. Knox
Look Homeward, Spaceman. *Amazing,* Aug 1956
Lest We Forget Thee, Earth. NY: Ace, [1958], 126pp., paper. (Ace Double D 291)
The Plot Against Earth. NY: Ace, [1959], 138pp., paper. (Ace Double D 358)
One of Our Asteroids Is Missing. NY: Ace, [1964], 124pp., paper. (Ace Double F 253)
● **as Ray Mc Kenzie**
stories in *Trapped* and *Guilty* magazines
as Dan Malcolm
Castaways of Space. *Super Science Stories,* Oct 1958
as Webber Martin
Spacerogue. *Infinity,* Nov 1958
as Alex Merriman
The Horror In the Attic. *Super Science Fiction,* Aug 1959
as Clyde Mitchell [house pseudonym] [in collaboration with Gordon Randall Garrett]
The Mummy Takes A Wife. *Fantastic,* Dec 1956
Deadly Decoy. *Amazing,* Feb 1957
as David Osborne
The Moon Is New. *Future,* April 1959
Invisible Barriers. NY: Avalon, [1958], 223pp.
Aliens From Space. NY: Avalon, [1958], 223pp.
as George Osborne
The Isolationists. *Science Fiction Stories,* Nov 1958
as Robert Randall [in collaboration with Gordon Randall Garrett]
Vanishing Act. *Imaginative Tales,* Jan 1956
The Shrouded Planet. NY: Gnome, 1957, 188pp.
The Dawning Light. NY: Gnome, [1959], 191pp.
as Eric Rodman
Slaves of the Tree. *Super Science Fiction,* June 1958
as Lee Sebastian
■ JUVENILE: *Rivers,* 1966; *The South Pole,* 1968.
as Robert Silverberg
"Fanmag Department." *Science Fiction Adventures,* Dec 1953
Gorgon Planet. *Nebula #7,* Feb 1954 (Br.)
Revolt On Alpha C. NY: Crowell, [1955], 148pp.
The 13th Immortal. NY: Ace, [1957], 129pp., paper. (Ace Double D 223)
Master of Life and Death. NY: Ace, [1957], 163pp., paper. (Ace Double D 237)
Invaders From Earth. NY: Ace, [1958], 169pp., paper. (Ace Double D 286)
Starman's Quest. Hicksville, New York: Gnome, [1958], 185pp.
Stepsons of Terra. NY: Ace, [1958], 158pp., paper. (Ace Double D 311)
The Planet Killers. NY: Ace, [1959], 131pp., paper. (Ace Double D 407)
Lost Race of Mars. Philadelphia: Winston, [1960], 120pp.

Collision Course. NY: Avalon, [1961], 224pp.

The Seed of Earth. NY: Ace, [1962], 139pp., paper. (Ace Double F 145)

Next Stop the Stars. NY: Ace, [1962], 114pp., paper. *ss col* (Ace Double F 145)

Recalled to Life. NY: Lancer, [1962], 144pp., paper.

The Silent Invaders. NY: Ace, [1963], 117pp., paper. (Ace Double F 195)

Regan's Planet. NY: Pyramid, [1964], 141pp., paper.

Godling, Go Home! NY: Belmont, [1964], 157pp., paper. *ss col*

Time of the Great Freeze. NY: Holt, [1964], 192pp.

Conquerors From the Darkness. NY: Holt, [1965], 192pp.

To Worlds Beyond; Stories of Science Fiction. Philadelphia: Chilton, [1965], 170pp. *ss col*

Needle In a Timestack. NY: Ballantine, [1966], 190pp., paper. *ss col*

The Gate of Worlds. NY: Holt, [1967], 244pp.

The Time Hoppers. Garden City: Doubleday, [1967], 182pp.

Those Who Watch. NY: Signet, [1967], 143pp., paper.

To Open the Sky. NY: Ballantine, [1967], 222pp., paper.

Thorns. NY: Ballantine, [1967], 222pp., paper.

Planet of Death. NY: Holt, [1967], 125pp.

Hawksbill Station. Garden City: Doubleday, 1968, 166pp.

The Masks of Time. NY: Ballantine, [1968], 252pp., paper.

Across A Billion Years. NY: Dial Press, [1969], 249pp.

The Calibrated Alligator, and Other Science Fiction Stories. NY: Holt, [1969], 224pp. *ss col*

Dimension 13. NY: Ballantine, [1969], paper. *ss col*

To Live Again. Garden City: Doubleday, 1969, 231pp.

The Man In the Maze. NY: Avon, [1969], 192pp., paper.

Nightwings. NY: Walker, 1970 [c.1969], 190pp.

Three Survived. NY: Holt, [1969], 117pp.

Up the Line. NY: Ballantine, [1969], paper.

The Cube Root of Uncertainty. NY: Macmillan, [1970], 239pp. *ss col*

Downward To the Earth. Garden City: Doubleday, [1970], 180pp.

Parsecs and Parables. Garden City: Doubleday, 1970, 203pp. *ss col*

Tower of Glass. NY: Scribner, [1970], 247pp.

World's Fair, 1992. Chicago: Follett, [1970], 248pp.

Moonferns and Starsongs. NY: Ballantine, [1971], 244pp., paper. *ss col*

A Time Of Changes. Garden City: Doubleday, [1971], 183pp.

The World Inside. Garden City: Doubleday, [1971], 201pp.

Beyond Control; Seven Stories of Science Fiction. Nashville, Tennessee: T. Nelson, [1972], 219pp.

The Book of Skulls. NY: Scribner, [1972], 222pp.

Dying Inside. NY: Scribner, [1972], 245pp.

The Reality Trip and Other Implausibilities. NY: Ballantine, [1972], 210pp., paper. *ss col*

The Second Trip. Garden City: Doubleday SF Book Club, [1972], 185pp.

Unfamiliar Territory. NY: Scribner, [1973], 212pp. *ss col*

Valley Beyond Time. NY: Dell, [1973], paper. *ss col*

Born With the Dead. NY: Random House, [1974], 267pp. *ss col*

Sundance and Other S.F. Stories. Nashville, Tennessee: T. Nelson, [1974], 192pp. *ss col*

Earth's Other Shadow. NY: Signet, [1975], paper. *ss col*

The Feast of St. Dionysus. NY: Scribner, [1975], 255pp., *ss col*

The Stochastic Man. NY: Harper & Row, [1975], 229pp.

Sunrise On Mercury and Other S.F. Stories. Nashville, Tennessee: T. Nelson, [1975], 175pp. *ss col*

The Best of Robert Silverberg. NY: Pocket Books, [1976], 258pp., paper. *ss col*

Capricorn Games. NY: Random House, 1976, 180pp. *ss col*

Shadrach In the Furnace. Indianapolis: Bobbs-Merrill, 1976.

The Shores of Tomorrow. Nashville, Tennessee: T. Nelson, [1976]. *ss col*

☐ *The Mask of Akhnaten,* 1965.

■ *Treasures Beneath the Sea,* 1960; *First Men Into Space,* 1961; *Lost Cities and Vanished Civilizations,* 1962; *The Fabulous Rockefellers,* 1963; *15 Battles That Changed the World,* 1963; *Home of the Red Man; Indian North America Before Columbus,* 1963; *Sunken History, the Story of Underwater Archaeology,* 1963; *Akhnaten, The Rebel Pharaoh,* 1964; *Great Adventures In Archeology,* 1964; *The Great Doctors,* 1964; *Man Before Adam,* 1964; *The Man Who Found Nineveh; the Story of Austen Henry Layard,* 1964; *The Great Wall of China,* 1965; *Men Who Mastered the Atom,* 1965; *Niels Bohr; The Man Who Mapped the Atom,* 1965; *The Old Ones: Indians of the American Southwest,* 1965; *Scientists and Scoundrels; A Book of Hoaxes,* 1965; *Socrates,* 1965; *The World of Coal,* 1965; *The Dawn of Medicine,* 1966; *Forgotten By Time; A Book of Living Fossils,* 1966; *Frontiers In Archeology,* 1966; *To The Rock of Darius; the Story of Henry Rawlinson,* 1966; *The Adventures of Nat Palmer, Antarctic Explorer,* 1967; *The Auk, The Dodo, and the Oryx,* 1967; *Bridges,* 1967; *Light for the World; Edison and the Power Industry,* 1967; *Men Against Time; Salvage Archaeology In the U.S.,* 1967; *The Morning of Mankind,* 1967; *The World of the Rain Forest,* 1967; *Four Men Who Changed the Universe,* 1968; *Ghost Towns of the American Midwest,* 1968; *The Mound Builders of Ancient America, the Archaeology of A Myth,* 1968; *Stormy Voyager, The Story of Charles Wilkes,* 1968; *The World of the Ocean Depths,* 1968; *The Challenge of Climate: Man and His Environment,* 1969; *Vanishing Giants; The Story of the Sequoias,* 1969; *Wonders of Ancient Chinese Science,* 1969; *The World of Space,* 1969; *If I Forget Thee, O Jerusalem: American Jews and the State of Israel,* 1970; *Mammoths, Mastodons and Man,* 1970; *The Pueblo Revolt,* 1970; *The Seven Wonders of the Ancient World,* 1970; *Before the Sphinx,* 1971; *Bruce of the Blue Nile,* 1971; *John Muir, Prophet Among the Glaciers,* 1972; *The Longest Voyage; Circumnavigators In the Age of Discovery,* 1972; *The Realm of Prester John,* 1972; *The World Within the Ocean Wave,* 1972; *The World Within the Tide Pool,* 1972; *Drug Themes In Science Fiction,* 1974.

as Leonard G. Spencer [house pseudonym] [in collaboration with Gordon Randall Garrett]

The Beast With 7 Tails. *Amazing,* Aug 1956

as S. M. Tenneshaw [house pseudonym] [alone]

The Old Man. *Imagination,* April 1957

as S. M. Tenneshaw [house pseudonym] [in collaboration with Gordon Randall Garrett]

The Ultimate Weapon. *Imaginative Tales,* Jan 1957

The Man Who Hated Noise. *Imaginative Tales,* March 1957

House Operator. *Imagination,* Dec 1957

as Hall Thornton

Freak Show. *Fantastic,* March 1957

as Gerald Vance [house pseudonym] [in collaboration with Gordon Randall Garrett]

The Judas Valley. *Amazing,* Oct 1956

as Richard F. Watson

A Planet All My Own. *Super Science Fiction,* Aug 1958

● Ellis Robertson [in collaboration with Harlan Ellison]

SILVETTE, HERBERT (1906-   ) *U.S.*

as Barnaby Dogbolt

Eve's Second Apple. NY: Dutton, 1946, 318pp.

The Goose's Tale. NY: Dutton, 1947, 317pp.

☐ *Bomb of Gilead,* 1946; *Maiden Voyage,* 1950; *Grave Example,* 1953.

as Herbert Silvette
- ■ *The Doctor On the Stage. Medicine and Medical Men In Seventeenth Century English Drama,* 1936-1937; *The Making of Anatomies In Seventeenth Century England,* 1936; *Catalogue of the Works of Philemon Holland of Coventry, Doctor of Physicke, 1600-1940,* 1940; *Manual of Experimental Pharmacology,* 1945.

SIMPSON, WILLIAM - of Alameda, California
as Thomas Blot
The Man From Mars. His Morals, Politics, and Religion. San Francisco: Bacon & Company, 1891, 173pp.
as William Simpson
The Man From Mars; His Morals, Politics, and Religion, 3d. *Revised and Enlarged by An Extended Preface and A Chapter On Women's Suffrage.* San Francisco: Press of E.D. Beattie, [c.1900], 281pp.

SIMSON, ERIC ANDREW (1895-   )
as Laurence Kirk
The Gale of the World. London: Cassell, [1948], 187pp.
- □ *Dangerous Crossroads; A Romance of the African Jungle,* 1927; *One More River,* 1929; *Rings On Her Fingers,* 1936; *Three Minute Murder,* 1936 (play); *Mushrooms On Toast,* 1938; *Red Herrings Ltd.,* 1940.

SINCLAIR, BERTHA M(uzzy) (1874-1940)
as B. M. Bower
The Adam Chasers. Boston: Little, Brown, 1927, 274pp.
- □ *Cabin Fever,* 1918; *The Bellehelen Mine,* 1924. WESTERN: *Chip of the Flying U.,* 1906; *Good Indian,* 1912; *The Gringos,* 1913; *Cow-Country,* 1921; *Desert Brew,* 1925; *Fool's Goal,* 1930; *The Haunted Hills,* 1934; *The Dry Ridge Gang,* 1935.

SINHOLD VON SCHUTZ, PHILIPP BALTHASAR (1657-1742)
as Amadei Creutzbergs
Seelen-Erquickende Himmels-Lust auf Erde. Nurnberg: Monath, 1728, 852[92]pp.
as Irenico Ehrenkron
- □ *Schesische Kirchen-Historie,* [c.1709].
as Ludwig Ernst von Faramond
later editions of *"Die Gluckseeligste Insul..."*
as Constantino von Wahrenberg
Die Gluckseeligste Insul auf der Gantzen Welt, Oder das Land der Zufriedenheit, Dessen Regierungs-Art, Beschaffenheit, Fruchtbarkeit, Sitten der Einwohner, Religion, Kirchen-Verfassung und Dergleichen, Samt der Gelegenheit, wie Solches Land, Entdecket Worden Ausfuhrlich Erzehlet Wird. Konigsberg [Brandenburg-Prussia]: G. F. Frommann, 1723, 340pp., ill.
anonymous
Der Fliehende Passagier Durch Europa. Freystadt [Leipzig: Gleditsch], 1700-1702, 3 vol.
- □ *Das Curieuse Caffe - Hauss zu Venedig,* 1698; *Der Teutsche Esop,* 1733.

SINIAVSKII, ANDREI DONATEVICH
as Abram Tertz
Fantastic Stories. NY: Pantheon, 1963, 213pp. *ss col*
The Makepeace Experiment, (trans. - M. Harari). NY: Pantheon, 1965, 192pp.

SKINNER, CONRAD A(rthur) (1889-   )
as Michael Maurice
Not In Our Stars. London: T. F. Unwin, [1923], 288pp.
Marooned. A Romance. London: S. Low, [1932], 278pp.
- □ *The Final Sentence,* 1926; *The Permanent Eclipse,* 1926; *Blind Vision,* 1929; *Luther Wing,* 1930.

as Conrad (A.) Skinner
- ■ *Concerning the Bible,* 1927; *An Approach to Church Membership,* 1946.

SKINNER, JUNE O'GRADY (1922-   ) *Canadian*
Born: Vancouver, British Columbia
as Rohan O'Grady
Pippin's Journal. NY: Macmillan, 1962, 230pp., ill.

SLADEK, JOHN T(homas) (1937-   ) *U.S.*
as Thom Demijohn [in collaboration with Thomas M. Disch]
Black Alice. Garden City: Doubleday, 1968.
as John T. Sladek
The Poets of Millgrove, Iowa. *New Worlds,* Nov 1966 (Br.)
The Reproductive System. London: Gollancz, 1968, 192pp.
The Muller-Fokker Effect. London: Hutchinson, [1970].
- □ (co-editor, with Pamela Zoline) *Ronald Reagan; The Magazine of Poetry,* 1968 (pub. London).

SLATER, ERNEST
as Paul Gwynne
Nightshade. London: Constable, 1910, 431pp.
- □ *Marta,* 1902; *The Pagan At the Shrine,* 1903; *The Bandolero,* 1904; *Peggy Gets the Sack,* 1926.
- ■ *The Guadalquivir, Its Personality, Its People, and Its Associations,* 1912.

SLESAR, HENRY (1927-   ) *U.S.*
as Sley Harson [in collaboration with Harlan Ellison]
- □ He Disappeared! *Guilty,* March 1957
as O.H. Leslie
Death Rattle. *Fantastic,* Dec 1956
Marriages Are Made In Detroit. *Amazing,* Dec 1956
as Henry Slesar
The Bloodless Laws. *Fantastic Universe,* May 1956

SLOTKIN, JOSEPH (? -1929) *British*
as Joseph Slotkin
The Gingerbread House. *Startling Stories,* March 1953
Too Bad You Died. *Fantastic Story Magazine,* March 1953
- ● Oliver Spie, Nick Tolz

SMALL, AUSTIN J.
as Seamark
The Avenging Ray. London: Hodder & Stoughton, [1930], 314pp.
Out of the Dark. London: Hodder & Stoughton, [1931], 319pp. *ss col*
- □ MYSTERY: *The Master Mystery,* 1928 (Br.); *The Vantine Diamonds,* 1929 (Br.).
as Austin J. Small
The Man They Couldn't Arrest. London: Hodder & Stoughton, [1925], 320pp.
Master Vorst. London: Hodder & Stoughton, [1926], 303pp.
The Avenging Ray. Garden City: Doubleday, 1930, 287pp.
The Seamark Omnibus of Thrills. London: Hodder & Stoughton, 1937, 512pp. *ss col*
- □ MYSTERY: *The Frozen Trail,* 1924; *Pearls of Desire,* 1924; *The Silent Six,* 1924 (U.S.); *The Death Maker,* 1926; *The Web of Murder,* 1929; *The Vantine Diamonds,* 1930 (U.S.).

SMITH, ELIZABETH THOMASINA (Meade) (1854-1914) *British*
as Laura T. Meade
- □ *The Colonel's Conquest,* 1907.
as L.T. Meade
(with Clifford Halifax) *Stories From the Diary of A Doctor (1st series).* London: G. Newnes, 1894, 370pp. *ss col*
(with Clifford Halifax) *Stories From the Diary of A Doctor (2d series).* London: Bliss, Sands, 1896, 357pp. *ss col*

(with Robert Eustace) *A Master of Mysteries.* London: Ward, Lock, [1898], 279pp.

(with Robert Eustace) *The Brotherhood of the Seven Kings.* London: Ward, Lock, 1899, 373pp., ill.

(with Robert Eustace) *The Sanctuary Club.* London: Ward, Lock, 1900, 300pp., ill.

The Sorceress of the Strand. London: Ward, Lock, 1903, 312pp., ill.

Belinda Treherne. London: J. Long, 1910, 318pp.

The Great Lord Masareene. London: F.V. White, 1912, 312pp.

□ *Daddy's Boy,* 1889; *Polly; A New Fashioned Girl,* 1889; *Bashful Fifteen,* 1892; (with Robert Eustace) *The Lost Square,* 1898; *An Adventuress,* 1899; (with Robert Eustace) *The Golden Star Line,* 1899; *On the Brink of A Chasm,* 1899; *The Oracle of Maddox Street,* 1904.

SMITH, ERNEST BRAMMAH (1868-1942) *British*
Born: Manchester
as Ernest Bramah
The Wallet of Kai Lung. London: G. Richards, 1900, 337pp.
What Might Have Been, The Story of A Social War. London: J. Murray, 1907, 380pp. [also pub. as *The Secret of the League.* London: Nelson, 1907, 287pp.]
The Transmutation of Ling. London: G. Richards, 1911, 80pp. (500 cop)
Kai Lung's Golden Hours. London: G. Richards, 1922, 311pp.
The Specimen Case. London: Hodder & Stoughton, 1924, 320pp.
Kai Lung Unrolls His Mat. London: G. Richards, [1928], 343pp.
The Moon of Much Gladness, Related by Kai Lung. London: Cassell, [1932], 316pp.
The Return of Kai Lung. NY: Sheridan House, [1937], 319pp.
Kai Lung Beneath the Mulberry Tree. London: Richard's Press, 1940, 320pp.
□ MYSTERY: *Max Carrados,* 1914; *The Eyes of Max Carrados,* 1923.
■ *English Farming and Why I Turned It Up,* 1894; *A Guide to the Varieties and Rarity of English Regal Copper Coins, Charles II to Victoria, 1671-1860,* 1929.
anonymous
What Might Have Been. The Story of A Social War. London: J. Murray, 1907, 380pp.

SMITH, FREDERICK E(dwin) (1st Earl of Birkenhead) (1872-1930) *British*
Biography: *The First Phase,* 1933; *The Last Phase,* 1935, both by F.W.F. Smith.
as The Earl of Birkenhead
The World of 2030 AD. NY: Brewer & Warren, 1930, 215pp., ill. *non fiction*
■ *Judgements Delivered by Lord Chancellor Birkenhead, 1919-1922,* 1923; *Famous Trials of Fiction,* [c.1926]; *Fourteen English Judges,* 1926.
as Rt. Honorable Sir Frederick Smith
■ *International Law,* 1900; *Essay On the Philosophy of the Licensing Bill,* 1908; *The Destruction of Merchant Ships Under International Law,* 1917.

SMITH, GEORGE H(enry) (1922-) *U.S.*
Born: Vicksburg, Mississippi
as M.J. Deer [in collaboration with Mary J. Deer Smith]
A Place Named Hell. NY: France, 1963, paper.
Flames of Desire. NY: France, 1963, paper.
as Jerry Jason
The Psycho Masters. NY: Tempo, 1965, paper.
as G(eorge) H. Smith
The Last Spring. Startling Stories, Aug 1953

1976. Year of Terror. NY: Epic, [1961], paper.
Scourge of the Blood Cult. NY: Epic, [1961?], paper.
The Coming Of the Rats. NY: Pike, [1961], 158pp., paper.
Doomsday Wing. NY: Monarch, [1963], 124pp., paper.
The Unending Night. NY: Monarch, [1964], 128pp., paper.
The Forgotten Planet. NY: Avalon, [1965], 189pp., paper.
The Four Day Weekend. NY: Belmont, 1966, 157pp., paper.
Druid's World. NY: Avalon, 1967, 192pp.
Kar Kaballa. NY: Ace, [1969], paper.
Witch Queen of Lochlann. NY: Signet, [1969], paper.
The Second War of the Worlds. NY: DAW #215, [1978], paper.
The Island Snatchers. NY: DAW #298, [1978], paper.
■ *The Sex and Savagery of Hell's Angels,* 1967; *Who Is Ronald Reagan?,* 1968.

SMITH, GEORGE O. (1911-) *U.S.*
as Wesley Long
Circle of Confusion. *Astounding,* March 1944
as George O. Smith
Calling the Empress. *Astounding,* June 1943
Venus Equilateral. Philadelphia: Prime Press, [1947], 455pp., ill.
Pattern for Conquest. NY: Gnome, [1949], 252pp.
Nomad. Philadelphia: Prime Press, [1950], 286pp.
Operation Interstellar. NY: Century, [1950], 127pp., paper.
Hellflower. NY: Abelard, [1953], 264pp.
Highways In Hiding. NY: Gnome, [c.1955], 223pp.
Troubled Star. NY: Avalon, [1957], 220pp.
Fire In the Heavens. NY: Avalon, [1958], 224pp.
The Path of Unreason. Hicksville, New York: Gnome, 1958, 185pp.
Lost In Space. NY: Avalon, [1959], 224pp.
The Fourth "R." NY: Ballantine, [1959], 160pp., paper.
■ *Mathematics: The Language of Science,* 1961 (juv); *Scientists' Nightmares,* 1972.

SMITH, L. H. (1916-)
as Speedy Williams
Journey Through Space. NY: Exposition Press, 1958, 108pp.

SMITH, M(ary) J. DEER (Mrs. George H.) *U.S.*
as M. J. Deer [in collaboration with George H. Smith]
see **GEORGE H. SMITH**

SMITH, ORMOND G. (1860-1933) *U.S.*
as Nick Carter [in collaboration with John R. Coryell]
Nick Carter series, first installment only: *New York Weekly,* Sept 18, 1886.

SMITH, RICHARD R.
as Richard E. Smith
Top Secret Boomerang. *Fantastic Universe,* Sept 1954
as Richard R. Smith
The Tormented One. *Fantastic Universe,* Nov 1954

SMITH, RON(ald) L(oran) (1936-) *U.S.*
Born: Hermit, California
as Martin Loran [in collaboration with John Baxter]
An Ounce of Dissension. *Analog,* July 1966
as Ron Smith
I Don't Mind. *Magazine of Fantasy and Science Fiction,* Oct 1956

SOHL, GERALD ALLEN (1913-) *U.S.*
Born: Los Angeles, California
as Jerry Sohl
The 7th Order. *Galaxy,* March 1952
The Haploids. NY: Rinehart, [1952], 248pp.
The Transcendent Man. NY: Rinehart, [1953], 244pp.

Costigan's Needle. NY: Rinehart, [1953], 250pp.

The Altered Ego. NY: Rinehart, [1954], 248pp.

Point Ultimate. NY: Rinehart, [1955], 244pp.

The Mars Monopoly. NY: Ace, [1956], 183pp., paper. (Ace Double D 162)

Prelude to Peril. NY: Rinehart, [1957], 247pp.

The Time Dissolver. NY: Avon, [1957], 158pp., paper.

The Odious Ones. NY: Rinehart, [1959], 245pp.

One Against Herculum. NY: Ace, [1959], 124pp., paper. (Ace Double D 381)

Night Slaves. Greenwich, Connecticut: Fawcett Gold Medal, [1965], 174pp., paper.

□ *The Lemon Eaters,* 1967; *The Spun Sugar Hole,* 1971.

SOLER, ANTONIO JOAQUIN ROBLES (1897-)
Spanish

[uses Antonio Robles in daily life]

as Antoniorrobles

Tales of Living Playthings. NY: Modern Age, [1938], 119pp., ill. *ss col*

Merry Tales From Spain. Philadelphia: Winston, [1939], 141pp., ill. *ss col*

The Refugee Centaur. NY: Twayne, [1952], 245pp., ill.

SOUTHWOLD, STEPHEN (ne Stephen H. Critten) *British*
Born: Southwold, Suffolk

Autobiography: *My Writing Life,* by Neil Bell. London: A. Redman, [1955], 264pp.

as Neil Bell

Precious Porcelain. London: Gollancz, 1931, 351pp.

The Disturbing Affair of Noel Blake. London: Gollancz, 193-, 280pp.

The Lord of Life. London: Collins, 1933, 320pp.

Mixed Pickles. London: Collins, 1935, 314pp. *ss col*

One Came Back. London: Collins, 1938, 416pp.

Alpha and Omega. London: Hale, [1946], 326pp. *ss col*

Life Comes To Seathorpe. London: Eyre & Spottiswoode, [1946], 301pp.

Who Was James Carey? London: Eyre & Spottiswoode, [1949], 384pp.

The Dark Page. London: Eyre & Spottiswoode, [1951], 285pp.

The Secret Life of Miss Lottinger. London: Redman, 1953, 320pp.

Who Walk In Fear. London: Redman, 1953, 310pp. *3 novellas*

□ *Life and Andrew Otway,* 1932; *Bredon & Sons,* 1933; *The Day's Dividing,* 1935; *Crocus,* 1936; *The Abbot's Heel,* 1939; *The Tower of Darkness,* 1942; *Child Of My Sorrow,* 1944; *I Am Legion,* 1950.

as S. H. Lambert

Portrait of Gideon Power. London: Jarrolds, 1944, 168pp.

as Paul Martens

Death Rocks the Cradle. A Strange Tale. London: Collins, 1933, 254pp.

as "Miles"

The Seventh Bowl. London: E. Partridge, 1930, 253pp. (500 cop)

The Gas War of 1940. London: E. Partridge, 1931, 302pp.

as Stephen Southwold

The Tales of Joe Egg. London: Collins, 1936, 224pp., ill. *ss col*

□ *Twilight Tales,* 1925 (ss col); *The Book of Animal Tales,* 1929 (juv - ss col); *A Romance In Lavender,* 1946.

SOUTHWORTH, E(mma) D(orothy) E(liza) N(evitte) (Mrs. Frederick) (1819-1899) *U.S.*
Born: Washington, D.C.

as (Mrs.) E.D.E.N. Southworth

The Haunted Homestead and Other Novelettes. Philadelphia: T.B. Peterson, [1860], 292pp.

□ *Retribution,* 1849; *The Mother-In-Law; or, The Isle of Rays,* 1851; *The Missing Bride,* 1855; *The Hidden Hand,* 1859; *The Fatal Marriage,* 1869; *The Maiden Widow,* 1870; *The Phantom-Wedding,* 1878.

SPENCER, LEONARD G. [house pseudonym]
unattributed

The Girl From Bodies, Inc. *Fantastic,* Oct 1956

The Man With the X-Ray Eyes. *Dream World,* Feb 1957

by Gordon Randall Garrett and Robert Silverberg

The Beast With 7 Tails. *Amazing,* Aug 1956

SPENCER, WILLIAM
as Bill Spencer

The Watchtower. *New Worlds #97,* Aug 1960

as William Spencer

Getaway. *New Worlds,* March 1964

SPICKLER, CHARLES A(braham) (1880-) *U.S.*
as Brogan the Scribe

Outline of Heaven. Yardley, Pennsylvania: Horus & Co., [1933], 263pp.

SPILLANE, FRANK MORRISON (1918-) *U.S.*
Born: Brooklyn, New York

as Mickey Spillane

The Veiled Woman. *Fantastic,* Nov-Dec 1952

□ MYSTERY: *I, the Jury,* 1947; *Vengeance Is Mine,* 1950; *Kiss Me Deadly,* 1952; *The Girl Hunters,* 1962; *Death of the Guns,* 1964; *The By-Pass Control,* 1966; *Delta Factor,* 1967; *The Erection Set,* 1972.

SPOTSWOOD, DILLON JORDAN
as Nuverbis

Out of the Beaten Track. A Story of the Old South, Love, Hypnotism, and Adventure. NY: Abbey Press, [1901], 212pp., ill.

as Dillon Jordan Spotswood

■ *Yellow Fever and the Absence of Quarantine In the South During the Epidemic of 1897,* 1898.

SQUIRE, JOHN COLLINGS (1884-1958) *British*
Born: Plymouth

Autobiography: *The Honeysuckle and the Bee.* NY: E.P. Dutton, 1938, 282pp.

as Solomon Eagle

■ *Books In General,* 1917.

as J. C(ollings) Squire

(with John L. Balderston) *Berkeley Square, a Play in Three Acts.* NY: S. French, 1928, 96pp., ill. *play*

(with Alexander Pope) Poem and Reply. *If,* March 1961 *verse*

(ed) *If It Had Happened Otherwise.* London: Longmans, 1931, 281pp. [U.S. title: *If; or, History Rewritten.*]

□ *Imaginary Speeches,* 1912; *The Three Hills and Other Poems,* 1913 (poetry); *The Birds and Other Poems,* 1919 (poetry); *Collected Parodies,* 1921; *Apes and Parrots,* 1928; *Sunday Mornings,* 1930; *Water Music,* 1939.

■ *Essays on Poetry,* 1924.

STEARNS, EDGAR FRANKLIN (1879-) *U.S.*
as Edgar Franklin

Mr. Hawkins' Humorous Adventures. NY: Dodge, [1904], 323pp., ill.

□ *In and Out,* 1917; *The Comeback,* 1928.

as Albert Stearns

Chris and the Wonderful Lamp. NY: Century, 1895, 253pp., ill.

Sindbad, Smith & Co. NY: Century, 1896, 271pp., ill.

STEELE, MARY QUINTARD (Mrs. William O.) (1922-   )
Born: Chattanooga, Tennessee
as Wilson Gage
Secret of the Fiery Gorge. NY: World, [1960], 185pp., ill. *juv*
  □ JUVENILE: *Secret of the Indian Mound*, 1958; *The Secret of Crossbone Hill*, 1959; *A Wild Goose Tale*, 1961; *Dan and the Miranda*, 1962; *Miss Osborne-of-the Mop*, 1963; *Big Blue Island*, 1964; *The Ghost of Five-Owl Farm*, 1966.

STEELE, MORRIS J. [house pseudonym]
unattributed
The Martian's Masterpiece. *Amazing*, March 1945
by Berkeley Livingston
The Wooden Ham. *Fantastic Adventures*, Dec 1943
by Raymond A. Palmer
Polar Prison. *Amazing*, Dec 1938
The Phantom Enemy. *Amazing*, Feb 1939
Weapon For A Wac. *Amazing*, Sept 1944

STEINER, GEROLF   *German*
as Gerolf Steiner
  ■ *Wort-Elemente der Wichtigsten Zoologischen Fachaus-druke. . .* 1962; *Das Zoologische Laboratorium*, 1963.
as Harold Stumpke
SATIRE: *The Snouters: Form and Life of the Rhinogrades* (trans. Leigh Chadwick). Garden City: Doubleday, 1967, 92pp., ill.

STERLING, BRETT [house pseudonym]
by Ray Bradbury
Referent. *Thrilling Wonder Stories*, Oct 1948
by Edmond Hamilton
The Star of Dread. *Captain Future*, Summer 1943
Magic Moon. *Captain Future*, Winter 1944
Red Sun of Danger. *Startling Stories*, Spring 1945
Never the Twain Shall Meet. *Thrilling Wonder Stories*, Fall 1946
Danger Planet. NY: Popular Library, 1968, paper.
by Joseph Samachson
Worlds To Come. *Captain Future*, Spring 1943
Days of Creation. *Captain Future*, Spring 1944

STEVENS, L(awrence) STERNE   *U.S.*
as Lawrence
artist in *genre* magazines
as Steven Lawrence
artist in *genre* magazines

STEVENSON, JOHN (1853- ?) *U.S.*
as Stephen Jackson
The Magic Mantle and Other Stories. NY: M.S. Greene, [1903], 333pp., ill. *ss col*

STEWART, ALFRED W(alter) (1880-1947) *British*
Autobiography: *Alias J. J. Connington.* London: Hollis & Carter, 1947, 279pp.
as J(ohn) J(ervis) Connington
Nordenholt's Million. London: Constable, 1923, 303pp.
  □ MYSTERY: *Death At Swaythling Court*, 1926; *The Dangerous Talisman*, 1926; *The Eye In the Museum*, 1929; *The Boat-House Riddle*, 1931; *The Castleford Cunundrum*, 1932; *Nemesis At Raynham-Parva*, 1934; *In Whose Dim Shadow*, 1935; *The Counsellor*, 1939; *No Past Is Dead*, 1942.
as Alfred Walter Stewart
  ■ *Stereochemistry*, 1907; *Recent Advances In Physical and Organic Chemistry*, 1908; *Chemistry and Its Border-land*, 1914; (with Hugh Graham) *Recent Advances In Organic Chemistry*, 7th Edition, 1948.

STINE, G. HARRY (1928-   ) *U.S.*
as Lee Correy
". . . and A Star to Steer Her By." *Astounding*, June 1953
Starship Through Space. NY: Holt, [1954], 241pp., ill. *juv*
Rocket Man. NY: Holt, [1955], 224pp., ill. *juv*
Contraband Rocket. NY: Ace, [1956], 141pp., paper. (Ace Double D 146)
as G. Harry Stine
Galactic Gadgeteer. *Astounding*, May 1951
  ■ *Rocket Power and Space Flight*, 1957; *Earth Satellites and the Race For Space Superiority*, 1957; *Man and the Space Frontier*, 1962; *Handbook of Model Rocketry*, 1965; *The Model Rocketry Manual*, 1970.

STINE, HENRY EUGENE (1945-   ) *U.S.*
Born: Sikeston, Mississippi
as Hank Stine
  ● A Love Called This Thing. *Bait Magazine*, date unknown
Season of the Witch. NY: Essex, [1968], paper.
as Sibley Whyte
  ● Dark of Night. *Baracuda Magazine*, date unknown

STOCKBRIDGE, GRANT
see **NORVELL W. PAGE**

STODDARD, CHARLES [house pseudonym]
unattributed
The Atom Smashers. *Thrilling Wonder Stories*, June 1941 *article*
Martian Menu. *Captain Future*, Summer 1941
Rule of Thumb. *Thrilling Wonder Stories*, Dec 1941 *article*
Rule of Math. *Thrilling Wonder Stories*, Aug 1942 *article*
Atlantis Here We Come. *Thrilling Wonder Stories*, April 1943 *article*
The Invisible Vandals. *Startling Stories*, Fall 1944

STOKER, ABRAHAM (1847-1912) *Irish*
Born: Dublin
as Bram Stoker
Under the Sunset. London: S. Low, 1882 [c.1881], 190pp., ill. *ss col*
Dracula. London: Constable, 1897, 390pp.
The Mystery of the Sea. London: Heinemann, 1902, 454pp.
The Jewel of Seven Stars. London: Heinemann, 1903, 337pp.
Lady Athlyne. London: Heinemann, 1908, 333pp.
The Lady of the Shroud. London: Heinemann, 1909, 367pp.
The Lair of the White Worm. London: W. Rider & Son, [1911], 324pp.
Dracula's Guest and Other Weird Stories. London: Routledge, [1914], 200pp. *ss col*
  □ *Crooken Sands*, 1894; *The Man From Shorrox's*, 1894; *The Watter's Mou'*, 1894; *The Man*, 1905.
  ■ *The Duties of Clerks of Petty Sessions In Ireland*, 1879; *Famous Impostors*, 1910.

STOKES, MANNING LEE
as Bernice Ludwell
Haunted Spring. NY: Arcadia House, [1956], 219pp.
  □ *Love Without Armor*, 1955; *Moon of Hope*, 1956.
as Lee Manning
  □ *Scarlet Angel*, 1950; *Season For Passion*, 1950.
as Manning Lee Stokes
  □ MYSTERY: *The Wolf Howls "Murder,"* 1945; *The Dying Room*, 1947; *The Lady Lost Her Head*, 1950; *Hang the Hangman*, 1956.

STORY, A. M. SOMMERVILLE
as Frankfort Sommerville

The Face of Pan: A Romance of the Ages, and Other Stories. London: Macgregor, Reid & Shaw, 1907, 118pp., ss col

☐ *A Parisian Princess,* 1911.

as Sommerville Story

■ *The Battlefields of France,* 1919–1920; *Dining In Paris, A Guide,* 1924.

STOWE, (Mrs. H. M.) *U.S.*
as Eleve

The Elixir of Life, or, Robert's Pilgrimage. An Allegory. Chicago: no pub. given, 1890, 124pp.

■ *Life Is Worth Living,* 1889.

as Mrs. H. M. Stowe

☐ *Easter Island,* 1892; *Giants In Those Days,* 1892; *The Land of Fair Men,* 1892.

■ *Spiritual Law In the Natural World,* 1901; *The Wonderful Kingdom,* 1915.

STRATEMEYER, EDWARD (1862-1930) *U.S.*
Born: Elizabeth, New Jersey

as Victor Appleton

"Tom Swift" series, see **HOWARD GARIS**

as Capt. Ralph Bonehill

☐ *Boys of the Fort; or, A Young Captain's Pluck,* 1901; "Flag of Freedom" series, 1899-1902; "Mexican War" series, 1900-1902; "Frontier" series, 1903-1907.

as Roy Rockwood

Through Space To Mars, or, The Longest Journey On Record. NY: Cupples & Leon Co., [1910], 248pp., ill.

Lost On the Moon, or, In Quest of the Field of Diamonds. NY: Cupples & Leon Co., [1911], 248pp., ill.

On A Torn Away World, or, The Captives of the Great Earthquake. NY: Cupples & Leon, [1913], 246pp., ill.

as Edward Stratemeyer

The Last Cruise of the Spitfire; or, Luke Foster's Last Voyage. Boston: Lee & Shepard, 1900, 245pp.

The Aircraft Boys of Lakeport; or, Rivals of the Skies. Boston: Lothrop, Lee & Shepard, [1912], 320pp.

☐ *Bound to Be An Electrician; or, Franklin Bell's Success,* 1903; "Working Upward" series; "Dave Porter" series.

■ *American Boy's Life of William McKinley,* 1901; *American Boy's Life of Theodore Roosevelt,* 1904.

as Arthur M. Winfield

☐ "The Rover Boys" series, 1899-1926; "Putnam Hall" series.

● Henry Abbott, Allen Chapman, Theodore Edison, "Frank," Harvey Hicks, "Jack," W.B. Lawson, Allen Winfield

STREET, C(ecil) J(ohn) C(harles) (1884-1964) *British*
as Miles Burton

The Secret of High Eldersham. NY: Mystery League, 1931, 286pp.

Devil's Reckoning. London: Collins, [1948], 191pp.

☐ MYSTERY: *The Hardway Diamonds Mystery,* 1930; *The Charabanc Mystery,* 1934; *The Clue of the Silver Brush,* 1936; *Dead Stop,* 1943; *A Crime In Time,* 1955.

as F. O. O.

■ *With the Guns,* 1916.

as John Rhode

☐ MYSTERY: *A. S. F.,* 1924; *The Paddington Mystery,* 1925; *Tragedy At the Unicorn,* 1928; *The Murders On Praed Street,* 1928; *Dead Men At the Folly,* 1932; *The Claverton Mystery,* 1933; *The Corpse In the Car,* 1935; *The Tower of Evil,* 1938; *Dead of the Night,* 1942; *Death At the Dance,* 1952; "Dr. Priestley" series.

as C. J. C. Street

■ *Ireland In 1921,* 1922; *Hungary and Democracy,* 1923; *Rhineland and Ruhr,* 1923; *Lord Reading,* 1928.

STUBBS, HARRY C(lement) (1922-) *U.S.*
Born: Somerville, Massachusetts

as Hal Clement

Proof. Astounding, June 1942

Needle. Garden City: Doubleday, 1950, 222pp.

Iceworld. NY: Gnome, [1953], 216pp.

Mission of Gravity. Garden City: Doubleday, 1954, 224pp.

The Ranger Boys In Space. Boston: L. C. Page, [1956], 257pp.

Cycle of Fire. NY: Ballantine, [1957], 185pp., paper.

Some Notes on Xi Bootis. Chicago: Advent, 1959, paper.

Close to Critical. NY: Ballantine, [1964], 190pp., paper.

Natives of Space. NY: Ballantine, [1965], 156pp., paper.

Small Changes. Garden City: Doubleday, 1969, 230pp.

Starlight. NY: Ballantine, [1971], 279pp., paper.

Ocean On Top. NY: DAW #57, [1973], paper.

STURGEON, THEODORE (*ne* Edward Hamilton Waldo) (1918-) *U.S.* [possibly legally changed name to Sturgeon—unconfirmed]
Born: New York, New York

as Frederick R. Ewing

☐ *I, Libertine.* NY: Ballantine, [1956], paper.

as Theodore Sturgeon

The Ether Breather. Astounding, Sept 1939

Without Sorcery. NY: Prime Press, 1948, 355pp., ill. ss col

The Dreaming Jewels. NY: Greenberg, [1950], 217pp.

More Than Human. NY: Farrar, Straus, Young, [1953], 233pp.

E Pluribus Unicorn. NY: Abelard, [1953], 276pp.

A Way Home. NY: Funk & Wagnalls, 1955, 333pp. ss col

Caviar. NY: Ballantine, [1955], 167pp., paper. ss col

The Cosmic Rape. NY: Dell, [1958], 160pp., paper.

A Touch of Strange. Garden City: Doubleday, 1958, 262pp. ss col

Aliens 4. NY: Avon, [1959], 224pp., paper. ss col

Venus Plus X. NY: Pyramid, [1960], 160pp., paper.

Beyond. NY: Avon, [1960], 157pp., paper. ss col

Some Of Your Blood. NY: Ballantine, [1961], 143pp., paper.

Voyage To the Bottom of the Sea. NY: Pyramid, [1961], 159pp., paper.

. . . And My Fear Is Great and Baby Is Three. NY: Magnabook 3, [1963], paper.

Sturgeon In Orbit. NY: Pyramid, [1964], 159pp., paper. ss col

The Joyous Invasions. London: Gollancz, 1965, 208pp. 3 novellas

Starshine. NY: Pyramid, [1966], paper.

Sturgeon Is Alive and Well. NY: Putnam, [1971], 221pp. ss col

The Worlds of Theodore Sturgeon. NY: Ace, [1972], paper. ss col

Case and the Dreamer. Garden City: Doubleday, 1974, paper. col

☐ WESTERN: *A King and Four Queens,* 1956.

as E. Hunter Waldo

The Ultimate Egoist. Unknown, Feb 1941

as Billy Watson

The Man Who Told Lies. Magazine of Fantasy and Science Fiction, Sept 1959

● E. Waldo Hunter

STURGIS, MEL(vin)
as Colin Sturgis [in collaboration with Lester Cole]

Conversion Factor. Magazine of Fantasy and Science Fiction, Nov 1957

as Mel(vin) Sturgis
  The Gift. *Imagination,* Nov 1951

STURTZEL, HOWARD ALLISON
as Paul Annixter
  Black Sorcery. *Weird Tales,* Jan 1924
  □ *Swiftwater,* 1950; *Brought to Cover,* 1951.
  ■ *Wilderness Ways,* 1930.

STURTZEL, JANE LEVINGTON (Comfort) (Mrs. Howard A.)
as Jane Levington Comfort
  □ *From These Beginnings,* 1937; *Time Out for Eternity,* 1938.
⌐ Jane Annixter

SUDDABY, (William) Donald (1900-   ) *British*
Born: Leeds
as Alan Griff
  Lost Men In the Grass. London: Oxford U. Press, [1940], 192pp., ill. [N.U.C. lists 1945 edition, otherwise the same]
as Donald Suddaby
  The Star Raiders. Oxford: Oxford U. Press, 1950, 232pp., ill.
  Village Fanfare; or, The Man From the Future. Oxford U. Press, 1954, 195pp., ill.
● *Prisoners of Saturn.* London: Lane, 1957, 190pp., ill.
  □ *New Tales of Robin Hood,* 1950; *The Death of Metal,* 1952; *Merry Jack Jugg—Highwayman,* 1954.

SUTTON, ERIC GRAHAM SUTTON (1892-   ) *British*
as Anthony Marsden
  Salter's Folly. London: Jarrolds, [1927], 287pp.
  □ *Death On the Downs,* 1929; *The Mercenary,* 1931; *Death Strikes From the Rear,* 1934; *The Mycroft Murder Case,* 1935.
as Graham Sutton
  Damnation of Mr. Zinkler. London: Jonathan Cape, [1935], 347pp.
  □ *Fish and Actors,* 1924; *The Great Permanence,* 1929; *Fell Days,* 1948; *North Star,* 1949.

SWAIN, DWIGHT V(reeland) (1915-   ) *U.S.*
Born: Michigan
as Clark South
  The Devil's Lady. *Fantastic Adventures,* Oct 1942
as Dwight V. Swain
  Henry's Super-Solvent. *Fantastic Adventures,* Nov 1941
  The Transposed Man. NY: Ace, [1955], 97pp., paper. (Ace Double D 113)

SWIFT, JONATHAN (1667-1745) *Irish-English*
Born: Dublin
  Bibliography: *Contributions Toward A Bibliography of Gulliver's Travels,* by Lucius L. Hubbard. Chicago: 1922 (200 copies).
As Author of The Tale of a Tub
  Baucis and Philemon: a poem on the.ever-lamented loss of the two yew-trees, in the parish of Chilthorne, near the count-town of Somerset, etc, 1709.
as Isaac Bickerstaff, Esq., Student in Astrology, Commentator on the Occult Sciences and One of the Eighth Order of Poets In the Cities of London and Westminster
  Bickerstaff's Almanac: or a vindication of the stars, from all the false imputations and erroneous assertions of the late John Partridge, and all other mistaken astrologers whatever. For the Year 1710. London: 1710, octavo.
as M.B. Drapier
  ■ *Drapier's Letters,* 1724-1725.
as Lemuel Gulliver
  Travels Into Several Remote Nations of the World. In Four Parts By Lemuel Gulliver, First A Surgeon, and Then A Captain of Several Ships. London: B. Motte, 1726, 2 vol., octavo.
as J.S.D.S.P.
  The Beast's Confession to the Priest On Observing How Most Men Mistake Their Own Talents. Dublin; London: Reprinted, 1738 by T. Cooper, octavo. [1st ed. Dublin 1738]
as Dr. S_____t.
  □ *The Blunderful Blunder of Blunders; Being An Answer To The Wonderful Wonder of Wonders,* 1721; *Cadenus and Vanessa,* 1726 (poetry).
anonymous
  The Tale of a Tub. 1704. *allegorical satire* (published with two related works, *The Battle of the Books* and *Discourse Concerning the Mechanical Operation of the Spirit)*
⌐ Cadenus, Presto

SWINTON, ERNEST D(unlop) (Sir) (1868-1951) *British*
  Autobiography: *Over My Shoulder.* Oxford: G. Ronald, 1951, 282pp., ill.
as Backsight-Forethought
  The Defence of Duffer's Drift. London: W. Clowes, 1911, 39pp., maps. [Reprinted from the United Service Magazine]
as O'le Luk-Oie (Olaf Shut-eye)
  The Green Curve and Other Stories. Edinburgh: Blackwood, [1909], 318pp. *ss col*
  The Great Tab Dope, and Other Stories. Edinburgh: Blackwood, 1915, 368pp. *ss col*
as Ernest D. Swinton
  ■ *The Russian Army and the Japanese War,* 1909; *Eye Witness's Narrative of the War,* 1915; *The Study of War,* 1926; *An Eastern Odyssey,* 1935.

SYMMES, JOHN CLEVES (1780-1829) *U.S.*
Born: Southwold, Long Island, New York
as (Captain) Adam Seaborn
  Symzonia: A Voyage of Discovery. NY: J. Seymour, 1820, 248pp.
  ■ *The Symmes Theory of Concentric Spheres, Demonstrating That the Earth Is Hollow, Habitable Within, and Widely Open About the Poles. Compiled by Americus Symmes from the Writings of His Father.* Louisville, Kentucky: Bradley & Gilbert, 1878, 69pp.

TABORI, PAUL (1908-1974) *naturalized British*
[sometimes rendered Paul Tabor]
Born: Budapest, Hungary
as Paul Tabori
Private Gallery. London: Sylvan Press, [1944], 128pp., ill.
The Talking Tree. London: Sampson Low, 1950, 246pp.
The Survivors. London: Consul, 1959, 170pp., paper.
The Green Rain. NY: Pyramid, [1961], 192pp., paper.
The Doomsday Brain. London: Tandem, [1967], 190pp., paper.
The Invisible Eye. NY: Pyramid, [1967], 173ppp., paper.
The Cleft. NY: Pyramid, [1969], paper.
The Torture Machine. NY: Pyramid, [1969], paper.
The Demons of Sandora. NY: Award, 1970, paper.
☐ *Japanese Jeopardy,* 1942; *The Ragged Guard,* 1942; *They Came to London,* 1943; *Bricks Upon Dust,* 1945; *The Leaf of A Lime Tree,* 1946; *Solo,* 1948; *Salvatori,* 1951; *A Story of Crime,* 1952. SCREENPLAY: *Star of My Night.*
■ *The Nazi Myth; The Real Face of the Third Reich,* 1939; *The Real Hungary,* 1939; *Epitaph for Europe,* 1942; *Harry Price, the Biography of A Ghost Hunter,* 1950; *Alexander Korda,* 1959; *The Natural Science of Stupidity,* 1959; *The Book of the Hand,* 1962; *The Art of Folly,* 1962; *A Pictorial History of Love,* 1966; *Dress and Undress: The Sexology of Fashion,* 1969; *The Humor and Technology of Sex,* 1969; *Maria Theresa,* 1969; *Beyond the Senses,* 1971; *The Anatomy of Exile,* 1972; *Pioneers of the Unseen,* 1972.
● Peter Stafford, Christopher Stevens

TAIT, GEORGE B.
as Alan Barclay
Welcome Stranger. *New Worlds,* Autumn 1951 (Br.)
Information. *Astounding,* Feb 1952
as G. B. Tait
Down In Our Village In Somerset. *Authentic #60,* Aug 1955 (Br.)

TEED, CYRUS REED *U.S.*
as Lord Chester
The Great Red Dragon; or, The Flaming Devil of the Orient. Estero, Florida: Guiding Star Publishing House, 1909, 148pp.
as Cyrus
■ *Emanuel Swedenborg, His Mission,* 1895.
as Koresh
■ *The Cellular Cosmogony; or, The Earth A Concave Sphere,* 1899; *The Immortal Manhood; The Laws and Processes of Its Attainment,* 1902; *The Mystery of the Gentiles,* 1926; *Fundamentals of Koreshan Universality,* 1927.
as Cyrus R. Reed
☐ *The Koreshan Unity, Co-operative; The Solution of Industrial Problems,* 19 ? .

TELUCCINI, MARIO (fl. 1566-1568)
as Il Bernia
Artemidoro di Mario Teluccini Sopranominato Il Bernia. Doue si Contengono le Grandezze de Gli Antipodi. Venetia: Domenico & Guerra, 1566, 467pp.

TENNESHAW, S. M. [house pseudonym]
unattributed
Come Along With Me. *Fantastic Adventures,* Sept 1947
Who Sups With the Devil. *Fantastic Adventures,* April 1948
Doom Globe. *Amazing,* May 1948
The Pied Piper of Space. *Amazing,* June 1948
The Tavern Knight. *Fantastic Adventures,* June 1948
The Holey Land. *Amazing,* Aug 1948
The Magician of Misty Cave. *Fantastic Adventures,* Feb 1949
The Monster. *Amazing,* April 1949
The Outcast. *Amazing,* June 1949
Queen of the Ice Men. *Fantastic Adventures,* Nov 1949
Diana and the Golden Ring. *Fantastic Adventures,* March 1950
The Lunar Point of View. *Fantastic Adventures,* April 1950
Beyond the Walls of Space. *Amazing,* Nov 1951
Let Space Be Your Coffin. *Imagination,* Nov 1954
Four Hours to Eternity. *Imaginative Tales,* March 1955
The Doormen Of Space. *Imaginative Tales,* March 1956
It Fell From the Sky. *Imaginative Tales,* May 1956
The Obedient Servant. *Imagination,* June 1956
Juggernaut From Space. *Imaginative Tales,* Sept 1956
Trouble On Sun-Side. *Imagination,* Oct 1956
The Friendly Killers. *Imagination,* June 1958
Nine Shadows At Doomsday. *Space Travel,* Nov 1958
by Gordon Randall Garrett
Kill Me If You Can. *Imagination,* June 1957
by Gordon Randall Garrett and Robert Silverberg
The Ultimate Weapon. *Imaginative Tales,* Jan 1957
The Man Who Hated Noise. *Imaginative Tales,* March 1957
House Operator. *Imagination,* Dec 1957
by Edmond Hamilton
Last Call for Doomsday! *Imagination,* Dec 1956
by Milton Lesser
Who's That Knocking At My Door? *Amazing,* Nov 1950
by Robert Silverberg
The Old Man. *Imagination,* April 1957

TERHUNE, ALBERT PAYSON (*c.*1872-1942) *U.S.*
Biography: *To the Best of My Memory.* NY: Harper, 1930, 272pp.
as David Belasco [ghost written, see **DAVID BELASCO**]
The Return of Peter Grimm. NY: Dodd, Mead, 1912, 344pp., ill.
as Albert Payson Terhune
In the Lion's Mouth. *Argosy,* Feb 1906
The Man Who Shivered. *Argosy,* Dec 1913
Unseen! NY: Harper, 1937, 280pp.
Around the World In 30 Days. NY: Street & Smith, [1914], 313pp.
☐ *Lad A Dog,* 1919; *Bruce,* 1920; *The Tiger's Claw,* 1924; *Treasure,* 1926; *Blundell's Last Guest, A Detective Story,* 1927; *Lad of Sunnybank,* 1928; *Water!,* 1928; *The Way of a Dog,* 1934.
■ *Syria From the Saddle,* 1896.
as Albert Payson Terhune [in collaboration with Sinclair Lewis]
☐ "Dad." *All Story Cavalier Weekly,* July 4-25, 1914

TETERNIKOV, FEDOR KUZ'MICH (1863-1927) *Russian*
[Fedor sometimes rendered Theodor]
Born: St. Petersburg
as Fedor Sologub
The Sweet Scented Name and Other Fairy Tales, Fables, and Stories. London: Constable, 1915, 239pp. *ss col*
The Old House and Other Tales. London: M. Secker, [1915], 294pp. *ss col*

The Little Demon. London: M. Secker, [1916], 349pp.
[originally appeared in 1905 in the magazine *Vop
Rosi Zhizni*, (Russia); first Russian Book pub., 1907]
The Created Legend. London: M. Secker, [1916], 318pp.
[orig. pub. 1908]
Ortruda.
Drops of Blood.

THIBAULT, JACQUES ANATOLE FRANCOIS   (1844-1924)
French
Born: Paris
as Anatole France
Thais. Chicago: N.C. Smith, [1891], 205pp.
Tales From A Mother of Pearl Casket. NY: G. H.
Richmond, 1896, 247pp.
The Well of Santa Clara. Paris: Clark & Bishop, 1903,
427pp., ill. [500 cop]
The Well of St. Clare. London: J. Lane, 1909, 302pp.
Penguin Island. London: J. Lane, 1909, 345pp. [*L'Ile des
Pingouins.* Paris: Calmann-Levy, 1908, 419pp.]
The White Stone. London: J. Lane, 1910, 239pp.
Bee The Princess of the Dwarfs. London: Dent, [1912],
127pp.
The Revolt of the Angels. London: J. Lane, 1914, 348pp.
[*La Revolte des Anges.* Paris: Calmann-Levy, 1914,
416pp.]
☐ *Poems,* 1873 (poetry); *Corinthian Revels,* 1876; *Jocaste
and the Lean Cat,* 1876; *Sylvester Bonnard,* 1881; *The
Yule Log,* 1881; *The Wishes of Jean Servien,* 1881;
Opinions of the Abbe Jerome Coignard, 1893.

THISTED, V(aldemar) ADOLPH   (1815-1887)
as L.W.J.S.
Letters from Hell. London: Bentley, 1884, 348pp. (with
introduction by George Macdonald)
as M. Rowel
Letters from Hell. London: R. Bentley, 1866, 2 vol.

THOMAS, ELIZABETH (Mrs.) of Tidenham   (fl. *c.*1805-1820)
English
[a.k.a. Wife of the Vicar of Tidenham]
as (Mrs.) Bridget Bluemantle
● *The Vindictive Spirit.* London: Newman, 1812?, 4 vol.
☐ *Monte Video; or, The Officer's Wife and Her Sister,* 1809;
Mortimer Hall; or, The Labourer's Hire, 1811; *The Prison
House; or, The World We Live In,* 1814 (4 vol); *The Baron
of Falconberg, or, Child Harolde In Prose,* 1815 (3 vol);
Claudine, 1817 (3 vol); *Woman; or, Minor Maxims,* 1818.

THOMAS, THEODORE L.   (1920-   )   *U.S.*
as Leonard Lockhard
Improbable Profession. Astounding, Sept 1952 *article*
as Theodore L. Thomas
The Revisitor. Space, Sept 1952
(with Kate Wilhelm) *The Clone.* NY: Berkley, [1965], 143pp.
(with Kate Wilhelm) *The Year of the Cloud.* Garden City:
Doubleday, 1970, 216pp.

THOMPSON, ANTHONY ALBERT   *English*
as Anthony Alban
Catharsis Central. London: Dobson, 1968, 192pp.
as Anthony A. Thompson
■ *Big Brother In Britain Today,* 1970.

THOMSON, W(illiam) (Dr.)   (1746-1817)   *British*
as The Man In the Moon
*Mammuth; or, Human Nature Displayed On A Grand
Scale: In A Tour with the Tinkers Into the Inland
Parts of Africa.* London: J. Murray, 1789, 2 vol.
as The Man of the People
*The Man In the Moon: or, Travels Into the Lunar
Regions.* London: Printed for J. Murray, 1783, 2 vol.

as Thomas Newte
■ *Observations On the Importance of the East-India
Fleet,* 1795.
as An Officer In Col. Baillie's Detachment
■ *Memoirs of the War In Asia,* 1780-1784.
as Charles Stedman
■ *The History of the Origin, Progress, and Termination of
the American War,* 1794 (2 vol.).
as William Thomson
■ *The History of Great Britain from the Revolution of
1688 to the Accession of George the First,* 1787.

TIECK, JOHANN LUDWIG   (1773-1853)   *German*
Born: Berlin, Brandenburg-Prussia
as Peter Leberecht
Abdallah, Eine Erzahlung. Berlin: C.A. Nicolai, 1795,
356pp.
*Phantasus; Eine Sammlung von Marchen Erzahlungen,
Schuspielen, und novellen.* Berlin: Realschulbuch-
Landlung, 1810-1816, 3 vol.
The Elves. tr. by Thomas Carlyle, with *Other Tales &
Sketches.* NY: Harper, 1846, 152pp.
The Midsummer Night; or, Shakespeare and the Fairies.
London: Whittingham, 1854, 35pp.
☐ *Puss In Boots,* 1797 (juv. play); *Folk Tales,* 1797 (ss col);
The Runenberg, 1804; *The Pictures; The Betrothing,*
1825; *Gedichte,* 1834 (poetry).

TILLOTSON, JOE W.
as Robert Fuqua
art work for SF magazines - illustrator in late 1930's
and 1940's; also books, e.g. *The Sleepy Village* by
Naomi Zimmerman.

TODD, RUTHVEN   (1914-   )
as R. T. Campbell
☐ MYSTERY: *Unholy Dying,* 1945; *Bodies In A Bookshop,*
1946.
as Ruthven Todd
Over the Mountain. London: Falcon, [*c.*1939], 208pp.
[London: Harrap, [1939], 281pp.]
The Lost Traveller. London: Grey Walls, [1943], 159pp.,
ill.
Space Cat. NY: Scribner, [1952], 69pp., ill. *juv.*
Space Cat Visits Venus. NY: Scribner, [1955], 87pp., ill.
juv
Space Cat Meets Mars. NY: Scribner, 1957, ill. *juv.*
Space Cat and the Kittens. NY: Scribner, 1958, ill. *juv.*
☐ *Loser's Choice,* 1953. POETRY: *Until Now,* 1940; *Ten
Poems,* 1940; *The Acreage of the Heart,* 1944; *The Planet
In My Hands,* 1944; *A Mantelpiece of Shells,* 1954.
■ *The Laughing Mulatto; The Story of Alexandre Dumas,*
1940; *A Checklist of Books Concerning William Blake
and Those Associated With Him,* 1941; *A Catalogue of
the Drawings and Paintings of William Blake,* 1942;
*Tracks In the Snow: Studies In English Science and
Art,* 1946; *The Tropical Fish Book,* 1953; *Trucks,
Tractors, and Trailers,* 1954.

TOOKER, RICHARD   (1902-   )   *U.S.*
as Henry E. Lemke
The Last of the Swarm. Wonder Stories, Oct 1933
as Richard Tooker
Tyrant of the Red World. Wonder Stories, Aug 1932
The Day of the Brown Horde. NY: Payson & Clarke,
1929, 309pp.
The Dawn Boy. Philadelphia: Penn Pub. Co., [1932],
284pp., ill.
Inland Deep. Philadelphia: Penn Pub. Co., [1936], 267pp.,
ill.

TOURGEE, ALBION W(inegar) (1838-1905) *U.S.*
Born: Williamsfield, Ohio
as Henry Churton
☐ *Toinette,* 1874.
as Edgar Henry
☐ *'89. Edited from the Original Manuscript.* NY: Cassell, 1891 [1888], 498pp.
as Wm. Penn Nixon [copyright holder]
■ *The Veteran and His Pipe.* Chicago: Bedford, Clarke, 1886, 269pp. [non-fiction essays - later editions have the author's name]
as Albion W. Tourgee
☐ *Figs and Thistles,* 1879; *A Fool's Errand,* 1879; *Bricks Without Straw,* 1880; *Black Ice,* 1884; *Button's End,* 1887; *Pactolus Prime,* 1890; *Out of the Sunset,* 1893; *An Outing With the Queen of Hearts,* 1894.
■ *Code of Civil Procedure of North Carolina,* 1878; *An Appeal to Caesar,* 1884; *The War of the Standards; coin and credit versus coin without credit,* 1896.

TOWERS, IVAR [house pseudonym]
unattributed
The Man Without A Planet. *Super Science Stories,* Nov 1942
by Cyril Kornbluth and Richard Wilson
Stepsons of Mars. *Astonishing,* April 1940

TOWLE, ? (Mrs. Arthur Edwards) *British*
Born: Shropshire
as Margery (H.) Lawrence
Nights of the Round Table: A Book of Strange Tales. London: Hutchinson, [1926], 283pp. ss col
The Terraces of Night. Being Further Chronicles of the Club of the Round Table. London: Hurst & Blackett, [1932], 287pp. ss col
The Floating Cafe and Other Stories. London: Jarrolds, 1936, 303pp. ss col
The Bridge of Wonder. London: R. Hale, [1939], 479pp.
Strange Caravan. London: R. Hale, [1941], 304pp.
Number 7 Queer Street. London: R. Hale, 1945, 350pp.
Rent In the Veil. London: R. Hale, 1951, 391pp.
Master of Shadows. London: R. Hale, 1959, 188pp. 4 novellas
The Tomorrow of Yesterday. London: R. Hale, 1966, 190pp.
Bride of Darkness. London: R. Hale, 1967, 189pp.
☐ *Songs of Childhood,* 1913 (poetry); *Miss Brandt, Adventuress,* 1923; *Red Heels,* 1925; *Bohemian Glass,* 1928; *Fine Feathers,* 1928; *Drums of Youth,* 1929; *The Madonna of Seven Moons,* 1933; *Madame Holle,* 1934; *The Crooked Smile,* 1935; *Step Light Lady,* 1942; *Ferry Over Jordan,* 1944; *Emma of Alkistan,* 1953.

TRACY, LOUIS (1863-1928) *British*
as Gordon Holmes [alone]
☐ MYSTERY: *The Arncliff Puzzle,* 1906.
as Gordon Holmes [in collaboration with M.P. Shiel]
☐ MYSTERY: *A Mysterious Disappearance,* 1905; *The Late Tenant,* 1906; *By Force of Circumstance,* 1909; *The de Bercy Affair,* 1910; *The House of Silence,* 1911; *The House 'Round the Corner,* 1917.
as Louis Tracy
● *A Japanese Revenge.* Cleveland, Ohio: A. Wesbrook, 188-?, 199pp.
The Final War, A Story of the Great Betrayal. London: C.A. Pearson, 1896, 372pp., ill.
The American Emperor; The Story of the Fourth Empire of France. London: C.A. Pearson, 1897, 336pp., ill.
The Lost Provinces; How Vansittart Came Back to France. London: C.A. Pearson, 1898, 380pp., ill.

The Invaders: A Story of Britain's Peril. London: C.A. Pearson, 1901, 428pp., ill.
The King of Diamonds. London: F.V. White, 1904, 312pp.
Karl Grier, the Strange Story of A Man With A Sixth Sense. London: Hodder & Stoughton, 1906, 277pp.
The House 'Round the Corner. London: Ward, Lock, 1914, 304pp.
The Turning Point. NY: Clode, [1923], 362pp.
The Gleave Mystery. NY: Clode, 1926, 318pp.
☐ *The Wings of the Morning,* 1903; *The Pillar of Light,* 1904; *The Albert Gate Affair,* 1904; *The Sirdar's Sabre,* 1904; *A Story of An Opal and Three Diamonds,* 1904; *At the Court of the Maharaja,* 1906; *The Captain of the Kansas,* 1906; *Minkie,* 1907; *The Red Year. A Story of the Indian Mutiny,* 1907; *The Message,* 1908; *A Son of the Immortals,* 1909; *Fennell's Tower,* 1910; *The Silent House,* 1911; *Mirabel's Island,* 1912; *Diana of the Moorland,* 1918; *The Bartlett Mystery,* 1919; *Number Seventeen,* 1919; *The Strange Case of Mortimer Fenley,* 1919; *The Pelham Affair,* 1923; *The Black Cat,* 1925.

TRACY, ROGER S(herman) (1841-1926)
as T. Shirley Hodge
The White Man's Burden; A Satirical Forecast. Boston: Gorham Press, [1915], 225pp.
as R(oger) S. Tracy
■ *The Essentials of Anatomy, Physiology, and Hygiene,* 1884; *Handbook of Sanitary Information for House-holders,* 1884.

TRALINS, STANLEY ROBERT (1926-   ) *U.S.*
Born: Baltimore, Maryland
as Robert (S.) Tralins
The Cosmoids. NY: Belmont, [1966], 143pp., paper.
● Sean O'Shea

TREMAINE, F(rederick) ORLIN (1899-   ) *U.S.*
as Arthur Lane
Editorial Assoc., *Marvel Science Stories,* Nov 1950-Feb 1951
Assoc. Editor, *Marvel Science Stories,* May 1951-May 1952
as F. Orlin Tremaine
The Golden Girl of Kalendar. *Fantastic Adventures,* Sept 1939
■ *Short Story Writing,* 1949.
as Warner Van Lorne [this story only]
The Upper Level Road. *Astounding,* Aug 1935
● Anne Beale, Guthrie Paine, Warren B. Sand, Alfred Santos

TREMAINE, NELSON
as Warner Van Lorne
Liquid Power. *Astounding,* July 1935

TRENERY, GLADYS GORDON (1885-1938) *British*
as G. G. Pendarves
The Devil's Graveyard. *Weird Tales,* Aug 1926

TREVOR, ELLESTON (*ne* Trevor Dudley-Smith) (1920-   )
English
Born: Bromley, Kent
as Mansell Black
☐ MYSTERY: *Chorus of Echoes,* 1950; *Dead On Course,* 1951.
as Adam Hall
☐ *The Volcanoes of San Domingo,* 1964. MYSTERY/SPY: *The Berlin Memorandum,* 1965; *The Quiller Memorandum,* 1965; *The Ninth Directive,* 1966; *A Place For the Wicked,* 1968; *The Striker Portfolio,* 1969; *Bury Him Among Kings,* 1970; *The Warsaw Document,* 1971; *The Tango Briefing,* 1973; *The Mandarin Cypher,* 1975.

as Simon Rattray
  ☐ MYSTERY: "Hugo Bishop" series, incl. *Knight Sinister*, 1951; *Queen In Danger*, 1952; *Bishop In Check*, 1953.

as Warwick Scott
  Domesday Story. London: Davies, 1952, 255pp.
  The Short. London: Heinemann, 1966.

as Caesar Smith
  ☐ MYSTERY: *Heat Wave*, 1957.

as Elleston Trevor
  The Chicken Switch. *Science Fantasy #71*, April 1965
  The Immortal Error. London: Swan, 1946, 189pp.
  ☐ *Deep Wood*, 1947; *Sweethallow Valley*, 1950 (juv.); *Mole's Castle*, 1950; *Red Fern's Miracle*, 1951; *Tiger Street*, 1951; *A Blaze of Roses*, 1952; *The Passion and the Pity*, 1953; *Squadron Airborne*, 1955; *The Killing Ground*, 1956; *The Pillars of Midnight*, 1957 (mystery); *Badger's Moon*, 1959 (juv.); *The Billboard Madonna*, 1960; *The Flight of the Phoenix*, 1964 (mystery).
  ↳ Peter Fitzalan, Howard North.

TRIPLETT, W.
● Terry Bull

TUBB, E(dwin) C(harles)   (1919-   )   *English*
Born: London

as Anthony Armstrong
  Illusion. *Vargo Statten Magazine*, May 1954 (Br.)

as Alice Beecham
  Lover, Where Art Thou? *Authentic*, March 1955 (Br.)

as Anthony Blake
  When He Died. *Authentic #66*, Feb 1956 (Br.)

as Julian Carey
  Repair Job. *Authentic #57*, May 1956 (Br.)

as Morley Carpenter
  Test Piece. *Vargo Statten Magazine*, Feb 1954 (Br.)

as Norman Dale
  The Veterans. *New Worlds*, March 1955 (Br.)

as R. H. Godfrey
  No Place For Tears. *New Worlds*, April 1955 (Br.)

as Charles Gray
  Precedent. *New Worlds*, May 1952 (Br.)

as Charles Grey
  Honour Bright. *Futuristic Science Fiction Stories #12*, 1953 (Br.)
  The Wall. London: Milestone, [1953], 128pp., paper.
  Dynasty of Doom. London: Milestone, [1953], 126pp., paper.
  Tormented City. London: Milestone, [1953], 126pp., paper.
  Space Hunger. London: Milestone, [1953], 128pp., paper.
  I Fight For Mars. London: Milestone, [1953], 128pp., paper.
  The Extra Man. London: Milestone, [1954], 128pp., paper.
  Hand of Havoc. London: Milestone, [1954], 116pp., paper.
  Enterprise 2115. London: Milestone, [1954], 160pp., paper.

as Vorsted Gridban
  Alien Universe. London: Scion, [1952], paper.
  Reverse Universe. London: Scion, [1952], 128pp., paper.
  De Bracy's Drug. London: Scion, [1953], 127pp., paper.
  Planetoid Disposals Ltd. London: Milestone, [1953], 128pp., paper.
  Fugitive of Time. London: Milestone, [1953], 160pp., paper.

as Alan Guthrie
  Samson. *New Worlds*, May 1955 (Br.)

as George Holt
  Emergency Exit. *British SF Magazine*, Sept 1954 (Br.)

as Gill Hunt
  Planet Fall. London: Curtis, 1952.

as Alan Innes
  The Long Journey. *Authentic*, March 1956 (Br.)

as Gordon Kent
  Heroes Don't Cry. *New Worlds*, Jan 1953 (Br.)

● as Gregory Kern [E.C. Tubb is probably author of many, if not all, of the DAW "Cap Kennedy" series listed below]
  Galaxy of the Lost. NY: DAW, [1973], paper.
  Slave Ship From Sergan. NY: DAW, 1973, paper.
  Monster of Metelaze. NY: DAW, 1973, paper.
  Enemy Within the Skull. NY: DAW, 1974, paper.
  Jewel of Jarhen. NY: DAW, 1974, paper.
  Seetee Alert. NY: DAW, 1974, paper.
  The Gholan Gate. NY: DAW, 1974, paper.
  The Eater of Worlds. NY: DAW, 1974, paper.
  Earth Enslaved. NY: DAW, 1974, paper.
  Planet of Dread. NY: DAW, 1974, paper.
  Spawn of Laban. NY: DAW, 1974, paper.
  The Genetic Buccaneer. NY: DAW, 1974, paper.
  A World Aflame. NY: DAW, 1974, paper.
  The Ghosts of Epidoris. NY: DAW, 1975, paper.
  Mimics of Dephene. NY: DAW, 1975, paper.
  Beyond the Galactic Lens. NY: DAW, 1975, paper.

as Duncan Lamont
  The Editor Regrets. *Science Fantasy*, Nov 1955 (Br.)

as King Lang
  Saturn Patrol. London: Curtis, 1951.

as Carl Maddox
  Menace From the Past. London: C.A. Pearson, 1953.
  The Living World. London: C.A. Pearson, 1954.

as Phillip Martyn
  Forgetfulness. *New Worlds*, April 1955 (Br.)

as Carl Moulton
  Man In Between. *Authentic*, March 1956 (Br.)

as Gavin Neal
  Short Circuit. *New Worlds*, Jan 1955 (Br.)

as John Seabright
  The Moron. *Nebula*, March 1956 (Br.)

as Brian Shaw
  Argentis. London: Curtis, 1952.

as Roy Sheldon
  Gold Men of Aureus. *Authentic #3*, Feb 1951 (Br.)
  The Metal Eater. London: Panther, 1954.

as Eric Storm
  Sword of Tormain. *Planet Stories*, March 1954

as E.C. Tubb
  No Short Cuts. *New Worlds*, Summer 1951 (Br.)
  Alien Impact. London: Hamilton, 1952, paper.
  Atom War On Mars. London: Hamilton, 1952.
  The Mutants Rebel. London: Panther, 1953, paper.
  Alien Life. London: Paladin, 1953, paper.
  Venusian Adventure. London: Comyns, [1953], paper.
  World At Bay. London: Panther, [1954], 159pp., paper.
  City of No Return. London: Scion, [1954], 144pp., paper.
  Journey to Mars. London: Scion, [1954], paper.
  The Stellar Legion. London: Scion, [1954], 144pp., paper.
  The Hell Planet. London: Scion, [1954], 143pp., paper.
  The Resurrected Man. London: Scion, [1954], 120pp., paper.
  Alien Dust. London: Boardman, 1955, 223pp.
  The Space-Born. NY: Ace, [1956], 158pp., paper. (Ace Double D 193)
  Moon Base. London: Jenkins, 1964.
  Ten From Tomorrow. London: Hart-Davis, 1966. *ss col*
  Death Is A Dream. London: Hart-Davis, 1967.
  The Winds of Gath. NY: Ace, [1967], paper.
  C.O.D. Mars. NY: Ace, [1968], paper.
  Derai. NY: Ace, [1968], paper.
  S.T.A.R. Flight. NY: Paperback Library, [1969], paper.
  Toyman. NY: Ace, [1969], paper.
  Kalin. NY: Ace, [1969], paper.
  The Jester At Scar. NY: Ace, [1970], paper.
  Lallia. NY: Ace, [1971], paper.
  Technos. NY: Ace, [1972], paper.
  A Scatter of Stardust. NY: Ace, [1972], paper.
  Century of the Manikin. NY: DAW, [1972], paper.

Veruchia. NY: Ace, [1973], paper.
Mayenne. NY: DAW, [1973], paper.
Jondelle. NY: DAW, [1973], paper.
Zenya. NY: DAW, [1974], paper.
Eloise. NY: DAW, [1975], paper.
Eye of the Zodiac. NY: DAW, [1975], paper.
Space 1999: Breakaway. NY: Pocket Books, 1975, paper.
Jack of Swords. NY: DAW, [1976], paper.
Space 1999: Collision Course. NY: Pocket Books, 1976, paper.
Space 1999: Alien Seed. NY: Pocket Books, 1976, paper.
Space 1999: Rogue Planet. NY: Pocket Books, 1976, paper.
Spectrum of A Forgotten Sun. NY: DAW, [1976], paper.
Haven of Darkness. NY: DAW, [1977], paper.
Prison of Night. NY: DAW, [1977], paper.
Incident On Ath. NY: DAW, [1978], paper.
The Quillian Sector. NY: DAW, 1978, paper.

as Ken Wainwright
  Sleeve of Care. *Authentic,* Feb 1956 (Br.)
as Frank Weight
  Prime Essential. *New Worlds #42,* Dec 1955 (Br.)
as Douglas West
  The Dogs of Hannoie. *Science Fantasy,* Sept 1955 (Br.)
as Eric Wilding
  Death-Wish. *Authentic #54,* Feb 1955 (Br.)
as Frank Winnard
  First Impression. *Authentic,* Feb 1956 (Br.)

TUCKER, ARTHUR WILSON (1914-   ) *U.S.*
as Hoy Ping Pong
  founder of Society for the Prevention of Wire Staples
    In Scientifiction Magazines (SPWSSTM)
  How to Write an Stf Story. *The Fantasy Fan,* Nov
    1933 (Br.)
as Bob Tucker
  Interstellar Way-Station. *Super Science Stories,* May 1941
as Wilson Tucker
  The Job Is Ended. *Other Worlds,* Nov 1950
  City In the Sea. NY: Rinehart, [1951], 250pp. [NY:
    Galaxy, [1951], 159pp., paper.]
  The Long Loud Silence. NY: Rinehart, [1952], 217pp.
  The Time Masters. NY: Rinehart, [1953], 249pp.
  Wild Talent. NY: Rinehart, [1954], 250pp.
  The Science Fiction Subtreasury. NY: Rinehart, [1954],
    240pp. *ss col*
  Time Bomb. NY: Rinehart, [1955], 246pp.
  The Lincoln Hunters. NY: Rinehart, 1958, 221pp.
  To the Tombaugh Station. NY: Ace, [1960], 145pp.,
    paper. (Ace Double D 479)
  The Year of the Quiet Sun. NY: Ace, [1970], paper.
  ☐ MYSTERY: *The Chinese Doll,* 1946; *To Keep or Kill,* 1947;
    The Dove, 1948; *The Stalking Man,* 1949; *The Man In
    My Grave,* 1956; *Last Stop,* 1963; *A Procession of the
    Damned,* 1965; *The Warlock,* 1967; *This Witch,* 1971.

TUCKER, GEORGE (1775-1861) *U.S.*
  Born: Bermuda
  As Professor of Moral Philosophy at U. of Virginia (1825-
  1845) influenced Edgar Allan Poe
as Joseph Atterley
  *A Voyage to the Moon: with Some Account of the
    Manners and Customs, Science and Philosophy, of the
    People of Morosofia, and other Lunarians.* NY: E. Bliss,
    1827, 264pp.
  "*A Century Hence: or, A Romance of 1941*" [an unpub-
    lished manuscript in U. of Virginia Library].
as George Tucker
  ☐ *The Valley of the Shenandoah; or, Memoirs of the
    Graysons,* 1824.
  ■ *Speech of Mr. Tucker of Virginia on the Restriction
    of Slavery In Missouri,* 1820; *Principles of Rent, Wages,
    and Profits,* 1837; *Life of Jefferson,* 1837 (2 vol); *The*

Theory of Money and Banks Investigated, 1839;
Political Economy for the People, 1859.

TUCKER, NATHANIEL BEVERLEY (1784-1851) *U.S.*
  [do not confuse with nephew of the same name (1820-1890)]
  Born: Chesterfield County, Virginia
as Edward William Sidney
  The Partisan Leader; A Tale of the Future. J. Caxton,
    1856, [really Washington, D.C.: D. Green, 1836], 2 vol.
  ■ *An Essay on the Moral and Political Effect of the
    Relation Between the Caucasian Master, and the African
    Slave,* 1839; *A Series of Lectures On the Science of
    Government,* 1845; *The Principles of Pleading,* 1846.
anonymous
  ☐ *George Balcombe, A Novel,* 1836.

TURNBULL, DORA A(my) (Dillon) (Mrs.) *British*
as Patricia Wentworth
  The Red Lacquer Case. London: Andrew Melrose, 1924,
    284pp.
  ☐ *Marriage Under the Terror,* 1910; *Little More Than
    Kin,* 1911; *Devil's Wind,* 1912. MYSTERY: *Simon
    Heriot,* 1914; *The Astonishing Adventures of Jane
    Smith,* 1923; *Hue and Cry,* 1927; *Nothing Ventured,*
    1932; *Walk With Care,* 1933; *In the Bride's Mirror,*
    1934; *Run!,* 1938; *Miss Silver Deals With Death,* 1943;
    The Key, 1946; *Pilgrims' Rest,* 1946; *Wicked Uncle,*
    1947; *The Case of William Smith,* 1948.

TURNER, EILEEN ARBUTHNOT ROBERTSON (Mrs. Henry E.)
  (1903-   ) *English*
as E(ileen) Arnot Robertson
  Three Came Unarmed. Garden City: Garden City
    Publishing Co., [1929], 328pp.
  ☐ *Cullum,* 1928; *Four Frightened People,* 1931; *Ordinary
    Families,* 1933; *Thames Portrait,* 1937; *Summer's Lease,*
    1940; *The Signpost,* 1943; *Devices and Desires,*
    1954.

TURNERELLI, EDWARD T(racy) (? -c. 1891) *British*
  Autobiography: *Memories of A Life of Toil.* London: Field,
    1884, 251pp.
as Author of "Kazan"
  A Night In A Haunted House. A Tale of Facts. (Christmas
    Tales for Christmas Charities No. 2) London: [1859],
    octavo.
  Two Nights In A Haunted House In Russia. London:
    [1873], octavo.
as Edward Tracy Turnerelli
  ■ *Russia On the Borders of Asia. Kazan, The Ancient
    Capital of the Tartar Khans,* 1854; *What I Know of the
    Late Emperor Nicholas [II] and His Family,* 1855; *Sixty
    Years of Conservative Work,* 1891.

TYSSOT DE PATOT, SIMON (1655-1728?)
as James Masse
  Voyages et Avantures de Jacques Masse. A Cologne:
    Chez Jacques Kainkus [really The Hague: H. Scheurleer],
    1710, 508pp.
as James Massey [often rendered in German: Jakob Massens]
  The Travels and Adventures of James Massey (trans. by
    Stephen Whatley). London: J. Watts, 1733, 318pp.
as Reverend Pierre Cordelier Pierre de Mesange
  *La Vie, les Avantures, & le Voyage de Groenland du
    Reverend Pierre Cordelier Pierre de Mesange. Avec une
    Relation Bien Circonstanciee de l'Origine, de l'Histoire,
    des Moeurs, & du Paradis des Habitans de Pole
    Arctique.* Amsterdam: E. Roger, 1720, 2 vol.

UNWIN, DAVID STORR   (1918-   )
as David Severn
>*The Future Took Us.* London: Bodley Head, 1957, 173pp., ill. *juv*
>☐ *Rick Afire,* 1942; *A Cabin For Crusoe,* 1943; *The Cruise of the Maiden Castle,* 1948; *Dream Gold,* 1949; *Treasure For Three,* 1950; *Foxy-Boy,* 1959; *Three At the Sea,* 1959.

UPCHURCH, BOYD BRADFIELD   (1919-   )   *U.S.*
>Born: Atlanta, Georgia
as John Boyd
>*The Last Starship From Earth.* London: Weybright & Talley, 1968, 182pp.
>*The Pollinators of Eden.* London: Weybright & Talley, [1969], 212pp.
>*The Rakehells of Heaven.* London: Weybright & Talley, [1969], 184pp.
>*Sex and the High Command.* London: Weybright & Talley, [1970], 212pp.
>*The Organ Bank Farm.* London: Weybright & Talley, [1970], 216pp.
>*The I.Q. Merchant.* London: Weybright & Talley, 1972.
>*The Gorgon Festival.* London: Weybright & Talley, [1972], 184pp.
>*The Doomsday Gene.* London: Weybright & Talley, 1973.
>*Andromeda Gun.* NY: Berkley/Putnam, 1974.
>*Barnard's Planet.* NY: Berkley/Putnam, 1975.
>*The Girl With the Jade Green Eyes.* NY: Viking, 1978.
>☐ *The Slave Stealer,* 1970.

URNER, NATHAN D.
as Burke Brentford
>*Gold-Dust Darrell; or, The Wizard of the Mines.* NY: Street & Smith, 1890, 230pp., paper.
>☐ *Florence Falkland; or, The Shrouded Life,* 1888; *Rocky Mountain Sam,* 1890; *Lost In New York; or, Meta's Misfortunes,* 1891.
as O.N. Looker
>☐ *Naughty New York; or, The Apronstrings Relaxed. A Novel of the Period.* NY: The American News Company, 1882, 192pp.
as Mentor
>■ *Never: A Handbook For the Uninitiated and Inexperienced Aspirants to Refined Society's Giddy Heights and Glittering Attainments,* 1883; *Always: A Manual of Etiquette for the Guidance of Either Sex Into the Empurpled Penetralia of Fashionable Life,* 1884; *Stop! A Handy Monitor, Pocket Conscience and Portable Guardian Against the World, The Flesh, and the Devil,* 1884.

VAIL, KAY BOYLE (Mrs. Laurence) (1903–)
as Kay Boyle

Monday Night. NY: Harcourt, [1938], 274pp.

☐ *Short Stories,* 1929 (ss col); *Plagued By the Nightingale,* 1931; *The First Lover and Other Stories,* 1933 (ss col); *White Horses of Vienna and Other Stories,* 1936 (ss col); *Death of A Man,* 1936; *Avalanche,* 1944; *Thirty Stories,* 1946 (ss col); *The Smoking Mountain,* 1951 (ss col); *The Sea Gull On the Step,* 1955.

VAIRASSE, DENIS (1630–1700)
as Captain Siden

The History of the Sevarites or Sevarambi: A Nation Inhabiting Part of the Third Continent, Commonly Called, Terrae Australes Incognitae (trans. by A. Roberts) London: H. Brome, 1675, 114pp.

VANCE, GERALD [house pseudonym]
unattributed [many probably by Chester S. Geier]

The Science of Suckers. *Amazing,* Nov 1941
Double In Death. *Fantastic Adventures,* April 1942
Captain Stinky. *Amazing,* June 1942
(with Bruce Dennis) The Giant From Jupiter. *Fantastic Adventures,* June 1942
Captain Stinky's Luck. *Amazing,* Sept 1942
Plot of Gold. *Fantastic Adventures,* Nov 1942
Monsoons of Death. *Amazing,* Dec 1942
Larson's Luck. *Amazing,* Jan 1943
The Needle Points to Death. *Amazing,* Jan 1944
Double-Cross on Mars. *Amazing,* Sept 1944
Reggie and the Vampire. *Fantastic Adventures,* Sept 1948
The Happy Death of Algernon Applenod. *Fantastic Adventures,* Nov 1948
The Psyche Steps Out. *Amazing,* May 1950
Time of My Life. *Amazing,* June 1950
Brothers Under the Skin. *Amazing,* Nov 1950
The Devil In a Box. *Amazing,* Nov 1950
Vanguard Of the Doomed. *Amazing,* Feb 1951
Flight To Dishonor. *Amazing,* June 1951
We, The Machine. *Amazing,* July 1951
The Laughter of Shiru. *Fantastic Adventures,* Oct 1951
The Perfect Hideout. *Amazing,* Oct 1951
C'Mon—A. . . My Planet. *Amazing,* Jan 1952
Monkey In the Ice Box. *Amazing,* May 1952
Strictly Formal. *Fantastic Adventures,* May 1952
Deadly Dust. *Amazing,* Oct 1952
Too Many Worlds. *Amazing,* Dec 1952
The Yellow Needle. *Fantastic,* Oct 1954
Conception: Zero. *Fantastic,* June 1956
Vital Ingredient. *Amazing,* Sept 1956
Equation of Doom. *Amazing,* Feb 1957
Heads You Lose. *Fantastic,* July 1957
Too Old For Space. *Fantastic,* Dec 1957
Earth Specimen. *Fantastic,* Feb 1958
The Lavender Talent. *Fantastic,* March 1958
Somebody Up There Typed Me. *Fantastic,* Aug 1958

by Gordon Randall Garrett and Robert Silverberg

The Judas Valley. *Amazing,* Oct 1956

by Roger P. Graham

The Cosmic Trap. *Fantastic,* Nov 1957

VANCE, JOHN HOLBROOK (1916–) *U.S.*
Born: San Francisco, California
Biography & Bibliography: *Jack Vance: Science Fiction Stylist,* by Richard Tiedman with bibliography by R. Briney.

as John Holbrook

Ultimate Quest. *Super Science Stories,* Sept 1950

as Jack Vance

The World-Thinker. *Thrilling Wonder Stories,* Summer 1945.
The Dying Earth. NY: Hillman, [1950], 176pp., paper. *ss col*
The Space Pirate. NY: Toby Press, 1953, 129pp., paper.
Vandals of the Void. Philadelphia: Winston, [1953], 213pp.
To Live Forever. NY: Ballantine, [1956], 185pp., paper.
Big Planet. NY: Avalon, [1957], 223pp.
Slaves of the Klau. NY: Ace, [1958], 129pp., paper. (Ace Double D 295)
The Languages of Pao. NY: Avalon, [c.1958], 223pp.
The Dragon Masters. NY: Ace, [1962], 102pp., paper. (Ace Double F 185)
Son of the Tree. NY: Ace, [1964], 111pp., paper. (Ace Double F 265)
The Houses of Iszm. NY: Ace, [1964], 112pp., paper. (Ace Double F 265)
The Star King. NY: Berkley, [1964], 158pp., paper.
Future Tense. NY: Ballantine, [1964], 160pp., paper. *4 novelettes*
The Killing Machine. NY: Berkley, [1964], 158pp., paper.
Valley of the Flame. NY: Ace, [1964], 156pp., paper.
Space Opera. NY: Pyramid, [1965], 143pp., paper.
Monsters In Orbit. NY: Ace, [1965], 119pp., paper. (Ace Double)
The World Between & Other Stories. NY: Ace, [1965], 134pp., paper. (Ace Double) *ss col*
The Brains of Earth. NY: Ace, [1966], 108pp., paper. (Ace Double M 141)
The Many Worlds of Magnus Randolph. NY: Ace, [1966], paper. (Ace Double M 141)
The Blue World. NY: Ballantine, [1966], 190pp., paper.
The Eyes of the Overworld. NY: Ace, [1966], 189pp., paper. (Ace Double M 149)
The Last Castle. NY: Ace, [1967], paper.
The Palace of Love. NY: Berkley, [1967], 189pp., paper.
City of the Chasch. NY: Ace, [1968], 157pp., paper.
Servants of the Wankh. NY: Ace, [1969], paper.
Eight Fantasms and Magics; A Science Fiction Adventure. NY: Macmillan, [1969], 288pp.
The Dirdir. NY: Ace, [1969], paper.
Emphyrio. Garden City: Doubleday, 1969, 261pp.
The Pnume. NY: Ace, [1970], paper.
The Anome. NY: Dell, [1973], paper.
The Brave Free Men. NY: Dell, [1973], paper.
Trullion: Alastor 2262. NY: Ballantine, [1973], paper.
The Asutra. NY: Dell, 1974, paper.
The Gray Prince. Indianapolis: Bobbs-Merrill, 1974.
The Worlds of Jack Vance. NY: Ace, [1974], paper.
Marune: Alastor 933. NY: Ballantine, [1975], paper.
"The Dogtown Tourist Agency." in *Epoch.* NY: Berkley/Putnam, 1975.
Showboat World. NY: Pyramid, [1975], paper.
Maske: Thaery. NY: Berkley/Putnam, 1976.
The Best of Jack Vance. NY: Pocket Books, 1976, paper.
Ruling Machine. NY: DAW, 1978, paper.
Wyst: Alastor 1716. NY: DAW, 1978, paper.

as John Holbrook Vance

☐ MYSTERY: *The Man In the Cage,* 1960; *The Fox Valley Murders,* 1966; *The Pleasant Grove Murders,* 1967; *The Deadly Isles,* 1969.

as Alan Wade

☐ MYSTERY: *Isle of Peril,* 1957.

VANCEL, DORIS
as Doris Thomas
   The Bracelet. *Fantastic Adventures,* April 1943

VAN RENSSELAER, FREDERICK
as Marmaduke Dey
   Muertalma; or, The Poisoned Pin. A Detective Story.
   NY: Street & Smith, 1890.

VAN TUYL, ROSEALTHEA (1901-   ) *U.S.*
   Born: Lynch, Nebraska
as Zaara Van Tuyl
   From the Book of Shadows. Las Vegas, Nevada: C.
   Beaconsfield, [1967], 138pp.
   Skyways for Doorian. Las Vegas, Nevada: C. Beacons-
   field, [1967], 144pp.

VAN VOGT, EDNA MAYNE HULL (Mrs. A.E.) (1905-1975)
   naturalized U.S.
as E. M(ayne) Hull
   The Flight That Failed. *Astounding,* Dec 1942
   (with A. E. Van Vogt) *Out of the Unknown.* Los
   Angeles: FPCI, [1948], 141pp.
   Planets for Sale. NY: Frederick Fell, [1954], 192pp.
   (with A. E. Van Vogt) *The Winged Man.* Garden City:
   Doubleday, 1966, 190pp.

VAN ZELLER, (Claude) HUBERT (Dom) (1905-   )
   British
   Born: Suez, Egypt
   Autobiography: *Willingly to School.* London: Sheed &
   Ward, [1952], 262pp., ill. and *One Foot In the Cradle; An
   Autobiography.* London: J. Murray, [1965], 282pp., ill.
as Brother Choleric
   ☐ HUMOR: *Cracks In the Cloister,* 1954; *Further Cracks
   In Fabulous Cloisters,* 1957 (US); *Last Cracks In Legend-
   ary Cloisters,* 1960 (Br.); *Posthumous Cracks In the
   Cloisters,* 1962.
as Hugh Venning
   The End: A Projection, Not A Prophecy. London: Douglas
   Organ, 1947, 298pp.
as Hubert Van Zeller
   ■ *Isaias, Man of Ideas,* 1951; *The Choice of God,* 1956;
   The Inner Search, 1957; *Approach to Penance,* 1958;
   Approach to Prayer, 1958; *Approach to Christian
   Sculpture,* 1959; *Approach to Monasticism,* 1960.

VARLEY, JOHN
● Herb Boehm

VAUGHAN, AURIEL R. (Lady)
as Oriel Malet
   My Bird Sings. London: Faber, 1946, 185pp.

VAUGHAN, OWEN
as Owen Rhoscomyl
   The Shrouded Face. London: C. A. Pearson, 1898, 366pp.
   The Lady of Castell March. NY: Doubleday, Mc Clure,
   1898, 338pp.
   ☐ *The Jewel of YNYS Galon,* 1895; *Battlement and Tower,*
   1896; *For the White Rose of Arno,* 1896; *A Scout's
   Story,* 1910 (US).
as Owen Vaughan
   ☐ *Vronina,* 1907; *Isle Raven,* 1908; *A Scout's Story,*
   1908 (Br.).

VAULET, CLEMENT (1876-   ) *French*
as Clement Vautel
   Voyage au Pays des Snobs. Paris: 1928, 296pp.

VAUX, PATRICK
as Navarchus [in collaboration with James Woods]
   The World's Awakening. London: Hodder & Stoughton,
   1908, 463pp.
as Patrick Vaux
   (with Lionel Yexley) *When the Eagle Flies Seaward.*
   London: Hurst & Blackett, 1907, 343pp.
   ☐ *The Shock of Battle,* 1906; *Thews of England,* 1906
   (ss col); *Sea-Salt and Cordite,* 1914; *Salt Sea Patrols,*
   1929 (ss col).

VENABLE, CLARKE (1892-   )
as Covington Clarke
   The Mystery Flight of the Q2. Chicago: Reilly & Lee,
   [1932], 270pp.
   ☐ *The Lost Canyon,* 1925; *The Phantom of Paradise
   Valley,* 1926; *For Valor,* 1928; *Aces Up,* 1929; *Desert
   Wings,* 1930; *Mosby's Night Hawk,* 1931; *Sky Caravan,*
   1931.
as Clark(e) Venable
   ☐ *"Aw Hell,"* 1927; *All the Brave Rifles,* 1929.
   ■ *Fleetfin, An Idyll of A Little River,* 1925 (animal
   legends and stories).

VERN, DAVID (1924-   ) *U.S.*
as Alexander Blade [house pseudonym]
   stories unknown *see* **ALEXANDER BLADE**
as Craig Ellis [house pseudonym]
   Dr. Varsag's Second Experiment. *Amazing,* Aug 1943
as Peter Horn [house pseudonym]
   Vagabonds of the Void. *Amazing,* March 1940
   Giants Out of the Sun. *Amazing,* May 1940
as David V. Reed
   Where Is Roger Davis? *Amazing,* May 1939
   The Whispering Gorilla. London: World, 1950, 160pp.,
   paper.
   The Thing That Made Love. NY: Universal, nd., 160pp.,
   paper.
   Murder In Space. NY: Galaxy Novel #23, 1954, 127pp.,
   paper.
as Clyde Woodruff
   The Man With Five Lives. *Fantastic Adventures,* Jan 1943

VERNON, GEORGE S(hirra) G(ibb) (1885-   )
as Vernon George
   The Crown of Asia. London: S. Paul, [1939], 286pp.,
   front.

VERRILL, A(lpheus) HYATT (1871-1954) *U.S.*
   Autobiographical: *Thirty Years In the Jungle.* London:
   J. Lane, [1929], 281pp.
as Ray Ainsbury
   When the Moon Ran Wild. London: Consul, 1962, 158pp.
as A. Hyatt Verrill
   Beyond the Pole. *Amazing,* Oct 1926
   Uncle Abner's Legacy. NY: Holt, 1915, 243pp.
   The Golden City. NY: Duffield, 1916, 272pp. *juv*
   The Trail of the Cloven Hoof. NY: Dutton, [1918], 260pp.,
   ill.
   The Trail of the White Indians. NY: Dutton, [1920],
   197pp., ill. *juv*
   The Boy Adventurers In the Land of the Monkey Men.
   NY: Putnam, 1923, 284pp., ill. *juv*
   The Bridge of Light. Reading, Pennsylvania: Fantasy
   Press, 1950, 248pp.
   ☐ JUVENILES: *The American Crusoe,* 1914; *The Cruise
   of the Cormorant,* 1915; *In Morgan's Wake,* 1915;
   Marooned In the Forest, 1916; *The Boy Adventurers
   In the Forbidden Land,* 1922; *The Radio Detectives,*
   1922; *The Radio Detectives Under the Sea,* 1922; *The
   Boy Adventurers In the Land of El Dorado,* 1923; *The*

Boy Adventurers In the Unknown Land, 1924; *The Incas' Treasure House*, 1932; *The Treasure of Bloody Gut*, 1937.

■ *Gasolene Engines; Their Operation, Use and Care*, 1912; *Knots, Splices and Rope Work*, 1912; *Harper's Wireless Book*, 1913; *Harper's Aircraft Book*, 1913; *Porto Rico Past and Present*, 1914; *The Amateur Carpenter*, 1915; *A.B.C. of Automobile Driving*, 1916; *The Real Story of the Whaler*, 1916; *The Ocean and Its Mysteries*, 1916; *The Book of Camping*, 1917; *Islands and Their Mysteries*, 1920; *Panama Past and Present*, 1921; *The Home Radio*, 1922; *Rivers and Their Mysteries*, 1922; *Smugglers and Smuggling*, 1924; *Lost Treasure*, 1930; *Under Peruvian Skies*, 1930; *The Inquisition*, 1931; *Before the Conquerors*, 1935; *Strange Insects and Their Stories*, 1936; *My Jungle Trails*, 1937; *Strange Reptiles and Their Stories*, 1937; *Strange Birds and Their Stories*, 1938; *Strange Fish and Their Stories*, 1938; *Minerals, Metals and Gems*, 1939; *Strange Animals and Their Stories*, 1939; *Wonder Plants and Plant Wonders*, 1939; *Perfumes and Spices*, 1940; *Wonder Creatures of the Sea*, 1940; *Prehistoric Animals and Their Stories*, 1948; *America's Ancient Civilizations*, 1952; *The Strange Story of Our Earth*, 1952.

VERSACK, MARIA TERESA RIOS   (1917-   )   U.S.
Born: Brooklyn, New York
as Tere Rios
The Fifteenth Pelican. Garden City: Doubleday, 1965, 118pp., ill.

VETSCH, JAKOB
as Jakob Mundus
Die Sonnenstadt; ein Roman aus der Zukunft, von Mundus. Zurich: Selbstverlag der Verfassers, 1922, 406pp., ill.
as Jakob Vetsch
■ *Die Laute de Appenzeller Mundarten*, 1910; *Die Umgehung des Gesetzes*, 1917.

VIARD, HENRI   (1912-   )   French
as Henry Ward
Hell's Above Us. trans. by A. Neame. London: Sidgwick & Jackson, 1960, 319pp.
The Green Suns. trans. by A. Neame. London: Sidgwick & Jackson, 1961, 206pp.
□ (with B. Zacharias) *Le Roi des Mirmidous*, 1966; *Les Mytheux*, 1967.

VICKERS, JOHN
as Jaido Morata
The New Koran of the Pacifican Friendhood: or, Textbook of Turkish Reformers, In the Teaching and Example of their Esteemed Master, Jaido Morata. London: G. Mainwaring, 1861, 573pp., front.

VICKERS, ROY   (1889-1965)   English
as David Durham
□ MYSTERY: *The Woman Accused*, 1923; *The Exploits of Fidelity Dove*, 1924.
as Roy Vickers
□ *Ishmael's Wife*, 1924; *The Hawk*, 1930.
□ MYSTERY: *A Murder for A Million*, 1924; *The Girl In the News*, 1938; *Eight Murders In the Suburbs*, 1954; *Double Image*, 1955; *Find the Innocent*, 1961.
● Sefton Kyle

VIDAL, GORE   (1925-   )   U.S.
as Edgar Box
□ MYSTERY: *Death In the Fifth Position*, 1952; *Death Before Bedtime*, 1953; *Death Likes It Hot*, 1954.

as Gore Vidal
Visit To A Small Planet. *Magazine of Fantasy and Science Fiction*, March 1957 *play*
Messiah. NY: Dutton, 1954, 254pp.
Visit To A Small Planet and Other Television Plays. Boston: Little, Brown, [1956], 278pp. *plays*
Kalki. NY: Random House, 1978.
□ *Williwaw*, 1946; *The City and the Pillar*, 1948; *The Judgement of Paris*, 1952; *Julian*, 1964; *Washington, D.C.*, 1967; *Myra Breckinridge*, 1968; *Burr*, 1973; *1876. A Novel*, 1976; PLAYS: *The Best Man*, 1960; *Suddenly Last Summer*, 1960 (screenplay).
■ *Rocking the Boat*, 1962; *Matters of Fact & of Fiction: Essays 1973-1976*, 1977.

VILLENEUVE
as Mr. de Listonai
Le Voyageur Philosophe dans un Pais Inconnu aux Habitants de la Terre. Multa Incredibilia Vers. Multa Credibilia Falsa. Par Mr. de Listonai. Amsterdam: 1761, 2 vol.

VIVIAN, E(velyn) CHARLES (H.)   (1882-1947)   British
Born: Norfolk
as Charles Cannell
□ *Broken Couplings*, 1923; *A Guarded Woman*, 1923; *Barker's Drift*, 1924; *Ash*, 1925; *The Guardian of the Cup*, 1925; *The Moon and Chelsea*, 1925; *The Passionless Quest*, 1926; *And the Devil*, 1931.
as Jack Mann
Coulson Goes South. London: Wright & Brown, [1933], 288pp.
Dead Man's Chest. NY: Godwin, 1934, 288pp.
Gee's First Case. London: Wright & Brown, 1936, 286pp.
Nightmare Farm. London: Wright & Brown, [1937], 288pp.
Grey Shapes. London: Wright & Brown, 1938, 286pp.
The Kleinert Case. London: Wright & Brown, 1938, 288pp.
The Maker of Shadows. London: Wright & Brown, 1938, 288pp.
The Ninth Life. London: Wright & Brown, [1939], 282pp.
Her Ways Are Death. London: Wright & Brown, [c.1939], 288pp.
The Glass Too Many. London: Wright & Brown, [1940], 284pp.
as E. Charles Vivian
Count Gaspar. *Golden Fleece*, May 1939
Passion-Fruit. London: Heinemann, 1912, 312pp.
The City of Wonder. London: Hutchinson, [1922], 287pp.
Fields of Sleep. London: Hutchinson, [1923], 288pp.
People of the Darkness. London: Hutchinson, 1924, 288pp.
The Lady of the Terraces. London: Hodder & Stoughton, [1925], 319pp.
Stardust. London: Hutchinson, [1925], 286pp.
A King There Was. London: Hodder & Stoughton, [1926], 320pp.
Woman Dominant. London: Ward, Lock, [1929], 311pp.
□ MYSTERY: *Delicate Fiend*, 1930; *Innocent Guilt*, 1931; *Ladies In the Case*, 1933; *Girl In the Dark*, 1933; *Accessory After*, 1934; *The Capsule Mystery*, 1935; *.38 Automatic*, 1937; *She Who Will Not*, 1945.
■ *The British Army From Within*, 1914; *A History of Aeronautics*, 1921.

VLASTO, JOHN A(lexander)   (1877-1958)
as John Remenham
The Lurking Shadow. London: Macdonald, [1946], 192pp.
The Peacemaker. London: Macdonald, 1947, 256pp.
□ MYSTERY: *The Canal Mystery*, 1928; *Arsenic*, 1930; *The Dump*, 1931; *The Crooked Bough*, 1948.

as John A. Vlasto
- ☐ (with Stephen Field) *"Marina," or, The Priest of Tenochtitban,* 1903.
- ■ *The Popular Pekingese,* 1926.

VONNEGUT, KURT JR. (1922-   )*U.S.*
Born: Indianapolis, Indiana
Autobiographical/Bibliographical/Criticism: *The Vonnegut Statement. Original Essays on the Life and Work of Kurt Vonnegut, Jr., with a Bibliography,* ed. by Jerome Klinkowitz & John Somer. NY: Delacorte, 1973.
as Ferdinand [variously rendered Ferdy or Ferdinandanilland] "Bull Session," column in *Shortridge Daily Echo,* Shortridge High School, Indianapolis, Indiana, Sept 1939-May 1940.
as Kurt Vonnegut, Jr.
Unready To Wear. *Galaxy,* April 1953
Player Piano. NY: Scribner, 1952, 295pp.
The Sirens of Titan. NY: Dell [1959], 319pp., paper.
Canary In A Cat House. Greenwich, Connecticut: Fawcett Gold Medal, [1961], 160pp., paper. *ss col*
Mother Night. Greenwich, Connecticut: Fawcett Gold Medal, [1962], 174pp., paper.
Cat's Cradle. NY: Holt, Rinehart, & Winston, 1963, 233pp.
God Bless You, Mr. Rosewater; or, Pearls Before Swine. NY: Delacorte, [1965], 217pp.
Welcome To The Monkey House. NY: Delacorte, [1968], 298pp. *ss col*
Slaughterhouse-Five; or, the Children's Crusade. NY: Delacorte, [1969], 186pp.
Happy Birthday, Wanda June. NY: Delacorte, [1971], 199pp., ill. *play*
Between Time and Timbuktu, or Prometheus-5. NY: Delacorte, [1972]. *play*
Breakfast of Champions. NY: Delacorte, 1973.
Slapstick; or, Lonesome No More! NY: Delacorte, [1976].
- ■ *Wampeters, Foma & Granfalloons (Opinions),* 1976, (essays).

VOSE, REUBEN
as Invisible Sam
Despotism; or, The Last Days of the American Republic. NY: 1856, 463pp.

WADE, ROBERT ALLISON (1920-   ) *U.S.*
Born: San Diego, California
as Whit Masterson [alone]
- ☐ *All Through the Night,* 1955.
as Whit Masterson [in collaboration with H. Billy Miller]
The Dark Fantastic. NY: Avon, [1966], 207pp., paper.
- ☐ *Play Like You're Dead,* 1967.
as Wade Miller [in collaboration with H. Billy Miller]
I Know A Good Hand Trick. *Magazine of Fantasy and Science Fiction,* Nov 1959
- ☐ MYSTERY: *Deadly Weapon,* 1946; *Guilty Bystander,* 1947; *Stolen Woman,* 1950; *Shoot To Kill,* 1951.
as Robert Wade
- ☐ *Knave of Eagles,* 1969.
as Dale Wilmer [in collaboration with H. Billy Miller]
- ☐ MYSTERY: *Memo For Murder,* 1951; *Dead Fall,* 1954.

● **WALKER, RICHARD** (1791-1870)
[has been ascribed but is unconfirmed]
as A Sub-Utopian
Oxford In 1888, A Fragmentary Dream by A Sub-Utopian, Published from the Original MS. by the Editor, R.P. with A Map of Architectural and Other Improvements. Oxford: 1838, octavo.

WALL, JOHN W. *British*
as Sarban
Ringstones and Other Stories. London: P. Davies, 1951, 283pp.
The Sound of His Horn. London: P. Davies, 1952, 154pp.
The Doll Maker, and Other Tales of the Uncanny. London: P. Davies, 1953, 247pp.

WALLACE, (Richard Horatio) EDGAR *ne* Walter Wallace (1875-1932) *British*
Born: Greenwich, London
as Richard "Dick" Freeman
name as adopted son of G. Freeman - used as child
as Edgar Wallace
Sanders of the River. London: Ward, Lock, 1911, 304pp.
Private Selby. London: Ward, Lock, 1912, 319pp.
The People of the River. London: Ward, Lock, 1912, 318pp.
Bosambo of the River. London: Ward, Lock, 1914, 304pp.
Bones. London: Ward, Lock, 1915, 304pp.
1925. The Story of A Fatal Peace. London: G. Newnes, 1915, 128pp., paper.
Keepers of the King's Peace. London: Ward, Lock, 1917, 303pp., ill. *col*
Lieutenant Bones. London: Ward, Lock, 1918, 320pp.
The Green Rust. London: Ward, Lock, 1919, 319pp.
Bones In London. London: Ward, Lock, 1921, 316pp.
Sandi The King Maker. London: Ward, Lock, 1922, 304pp.
Captains of Souls. Boston: Small, Maynard, [1922], 362pp. [London: J. Long, 1923, 318pp.]
The Day of Uniting. London: Hodder & Stoughton, [1926], 314pp.
Again Sanders. London: Hodder & Stoughton, [1928], 315pp.
Planetoid 127-and-The Sweizer Pump. London: Reader's Library Pub. Co., 1929, 252pp. *2 novels*
The Ghost of Down Hill-and-The Queen of Sheba's Belt. London: Reader's Library Pub. Co., [1929], 188pp.

Mr. Commissioner Sanders. NY: Doubleday, Doran, 1930, 320pp.

(with Merian C. Cooper) *King Kong.* NY: Grosset & Dunlap, 1933, 249pp. (ill. from film)

☐ MYSTERY: *The Four Just Men,* 1905; *"Smithy,"* 1905; *Angel Esquire,* 1908; *The Council of Justice,* 1908; *The Tomb of T"s,* 1916; *The Just Men of Cordova,* 1917; *Clue of the Twisted Candle,* 1918; *The Book of All-Power,* 1921; *The Law of the Four Just Men,* 1921; *The Angel of Terror,* 1922; *The Flying Fifty-Five,* 1922; *The Clue of the New Pin,* 1923; *Bones of the River,* 1923; *The Sinister Man,* 1924; *The Daughters of the Night,* 1925; *Barbara On Her Own,* 1926; *The Black Abbot,* 1926; *Big Foot,* 1927; *Again The Ringer,* 1929; *Again the Three Just Men,* 1929; *The Calendar,* 1930.

WALLER, LESLIE (1923-   ) *U.S.*
Born: Chicago, Illinois
as C.S. Cody
The Witching Night. Cleveland: World, [1952], 255pp.
☐ *Lie Like A Lady,* 1955.
as Leslie Waller
(with Louise Waller) *Take Me To Your Leader.* NY: Putnam, [1961], paper., ill. *humor*
☐ *The Bed She Made,* 1951; *Phoenix Island,* 1958; *The Banker,* 1963; *Overdrive,* 1967; *A Change In the Wind,* 1969.
■ *Time,* 1959; *Weather,* 1959; *Numbers,* 1960; *Electricity,* 1961; *Explorers,* 1961; *Our American Language,* 1961; *American Inventions,* 1963; *The American West,* 1966; *Plants,* 1967.

WALLIS, G(eraldine) MCDONALD (1925-   ) *U.S.*
as Hope Campbell
stage name as actress
☐ *Liza,* 1965; *Home to Hawaii,* 1967; *Why Not Join The Giraffes,* 1968; *Meanwhile, Back At the Castle,* 1970; *No More Trains To Tottenville,* 1971; *There's A Pizza Back In Cleveland,* 1972.
as G. McDonald Wallis
The Light of Lilith. NY: Ace, [1961], 123pp., paper. (Ace Double F 108)
Legend of Lost Earth. NY: Ace, [1963], 133pp., paper. (Ace Double F 187)

WALLIS, GEORGE C.
as John Stanton
name used in writing for comics
as B. Wallis
From Time's Dawn. Fantastic Novels, May 1950
as G(eorge) C. Wallis
The Orbit Jumper. Tales of Wonder, Winter 1938
The Children of the Sphinx. Bristol, England: The Cosmopolitan Printing Pub. & Adv., Co. [c.1907]. [*The Children of the Sphinx. A Romance of Egypt.* London: Simpkin, Marshall, [1924], 203pp.]
The Call of Peter Gaskell. Surrey: World's Work, 1948 [c.1947], 130pp.
☐ *Paquita the Pearl,* 1924.
as B. & G.C. Wallis
The World At Bay. Amazing, Nov 1928

WALPOLE, HORACE (4th Earl of Orford) (*ne* Horatio Walpole) (1717-1797) *English*
Born: London
as Onuphrio Muralto
The Castle of Otranto. London: T. Lownds, 1765, 200pp. (pub. as if trans. from Italian by William Marshal)
as S.T.
An Account of the Giants Lately Discovered; In A Letter to A Friend In the Country. London: 1866, 31pp., octavo.
as H. W.

Hieroglyphic Tales. England: Strawberry Hill Press, 1785, Vol. I, (7 cop).
as Horace Walpole
☐ *The Mysterious Mother,* 1768 (verse).
■ *Anecdotes of Painting In England,* 1762-1771; *Catalogue of Engravers In England,* 1763; *Historic Doubts on Richard III,* 1768.

WALSH, J(ames) M(organ) (1897-1952) *British*
Born: Geelong, Victoria, Australia
as H. Haverstock Hill
The Terror Out of Space. Amazing, Feb 1934
The Secret of the Crater. London: Hurst & Blackett, [1930], 287pp.
☐ *The Golden Isle,* 1928.
as Stephen Maddock
A Woman of Destiny. London: Collins, 1933, 252pp.
as J.M. Walsh
Vandals of the Void. Wonder Stories Quarterly, Summer 1931
Vandals of the Void. London: Hamilton, [1931], 288pp.
Vanguard to Neptune. London: Kemsley, 1952, 190pp., paper.
☐ THRILLER/MYSTERY: *The Hand of Doom,* 1927; *The White Mask,* 1927; *The Crimes of Cleopatra's Needle,* 1928; *The Purple Stain,* 1928; *The Silver Greyhound,* 1928; *The Black Ghost,* 1930; *Exit Simeon Hex,* 1930; *The Company of Shadows,* 1931; *Lady Incognito,* 1932; *The League of Missing Men,* 1932; *The Secret Service Girl,* 1933; *Chalk-Face,* 1937; *Black Dragon,* 1938; *Dial 999,* 1938; *King's Enemies,* 1939; *Death At His Elbow,* 1941; *Spies from the Skies,* 1941; *The Mystery of the Green Caterpillars,* 1944.

WALTON, BRYCE (1918-   ) *U.S.*
as Kenneth O'Hara
The Difference. Marvel Science Stories, Feb 1951
as Bryce Walton
The Ultimate World. Planet Stories, Winter 1945
Sons of the Ocean Deeps. Philadelphia: Winston, [1952], 216pp.
☐ *Cave of Danger,* 1967; *Harpoon Gunner,* 1968; *Hurricane Reef,* 1970.
✔ Paul Franklin
● Dave Sands [house pseudonym?]

WALTON, HARRY
as Harry Collier
A Suitor by Proxy. Wonder Stories, April 1935
as Harry Walton
Quicksilver, Unlimited. Astounding, July 1937

WANDREI, HOWARD ELMER (1909-1965) *U.S.*
as Robert Coley
Don't Go Haunting. Unknown, June 1939
as H.W. Guernsey
Macklin's Little Friend. Astounding, Nov 1936
Here Lies. Weird Tales, Oct 1937
The Hexer. Unknown, June 1939
as Howard Von Drey
The God Box. Astounding, April 1934
✔ Robert A. Garron, Howard Graham

WARD, ARTHUR HENRY S(arsfield) (1883-1959) *British*
Born: Birmingham
Biography: *Master of Villainy: A Biography of Sax Rohmer,* by Cay Van Ash and Elizabeth S. Rohmer. Bowling Green Ohio: Bowling Green Univ. Press.
as Michael Furey
Wulfheim. London: Jarrolds, 1950, 208pp.
as (A.) Sarsfield Ward
☐ *The Secret of the Holm Peel,* (magazine story).

as Sax Rohmer

The Insidious Dr. Fu-Manchu. NY: McBride, 1913, 383pp.

The Sins of Severac Bablon. London: Cassell, 1914, 342pp.

The Yellow Claw. NY: McBride, 1915, 427pp.

The Return of Dr. Fu-Manchu. NY: McBride, 1916, 332pp.

The Hand of Fu-Manchu. NY: McBride, 1917, 308pp.

The Brood of the Witch Queen. London: C.A. Pearson, 1918, 212pp.

The Orchard of Tears. London: Methuen, 1918, 250pp.

Tales of Secret Egypt. London: Methuen, 1918, 312pp. ss col

The Quest of the Sacred Slipper. NY: Doubleday, Page, 1919, 293pp.

The Golden Scorpion. London: Methuen, 1919, 250pp.

The Dream Detective. London: Jarrolds, 1920, 256pp., ill.

The Haunting of Low Fennel. London: C.A. Pearson, 1920, 252pp. ss col

The Green Eyes of Bast. London: Cassell, 1920, 314pp.

Bat Wing. London: Cassell, 1921, 306pp.

Fire-Tongue. London: Cassell, 1921, 306pp.

Tales of Chinatown. London: Cassell, 1922, 322pp. ss col

Grey Face. Garden City: Doubleday, 1924, 331pp.

Moon of Madness. Garden City: Doubleday, 1927, 233pp.

She Who Sleeps. Garden City: Doubleday, 1928, 332pp.

The Emperor of America. Garden City: Doubleday, 1929, 310pp.

The Day the World Ended. Garden City: Doubleday, 1930, 306pp.

Daughter of Fu Manchu. Garden City: Doubleday, 1931, 316pp.

Tales of East and West. London: Cassell, 1932, 288pp.

Yu'an Hee See Laughs. Garden City: Doubleday, 1932, 312pp.

The Mask of Fu Manchu. Garden City: Doubleday, 1932, 330pp., ill.

Fu Manchu's Bride. Garden City: Doubleday, 1933, 319pp.

The Trail of Fu Manchu. Garden City: Doubleday, 1934, 329pp.

The Bat Flies Low. Garden City: Doubleday, 1935, 314pp.

President Fu Manchu. Garden City: Doubleday, 1936, 342pp.

Salute to Bazarada and Other Stories. London: Cassell, 1939, 311pp. ss col

The Drums of Fu-Manchu. Garden City: Doubleday, 1939, 308pp.

The Island of Fu-Manchu. Garden City: Doubleday, 1941, 299pp.

Seven Sins. NY: McBride, 1943, 328pp.

The Shadow of Fu-Manchu. Garden City: Doubleday, 1948, 190pp.

Nude In Mink. Greenwich, Connecticut: Fawcett Gold Medal, 1950, 174pp., paper. [British title *Sins of Sumuru*]

Sumuru. Greenwich, Connecticut: Fawcett Gold Medal, 1951, 179pp., paper. [British title: *Slaves of Sumuru.* London: Jenkins, 1952, 190pp.—different ending than U.S. version]

The Fire Goddess. Greenwich, Connecticut: Fawcett Gold Medal, 1952, 192pp., paper.

The Moon Is Red. London: Jenkins, 1954, 188pp.

Return of Sumuru. Greenwich, Connecticut: Fawcett Gold Medal, 1954, 172pp., paper.

Sinister Madonna. London: Jenkins, 1956, 187pp.

Re-Enter Fu-Manchu. Greenwich, Connecticut: Fawcett Gold Medal, 1957, 144pp., paper.

Emperor Fu-Manchu. London: Jenkins, 1959, 221pp.

■ *The Romance of Sorcery,* 1914.

anonymous

(with George Robey) *Pause!,* 1910 (ss col).

WARD, ELIZABETH STUART (Phelps) (Mrs. Herbert D.) (1844-1911) *U.S.*

Born: Andover, Massachusetts

Autobiography: *Chapters From A Life,* by Elizabeth Stuart Phelps. Boston: Houghton, Mifflin, 1896, 278pp.

as Mary Adams

□ *Confessions of A Wife,* 1902.

as Elizabeth Stuart Phelps

The Gates Ajar. Boston: Fields, Osgood, 1869, 248pp.

Men, Women, and Ghosts. Boston: Fields, Osgood, 1869, 334pp. ss col

Sealed Orders. Boston: Houghton & Osgood, 1879, 345pp.

Beyond the Gates. Boston: Houghton, Mifflin, 1883, 196pp.

The Gates Between. Boston: Houghton, Mifflin, 1887, 222pp.

(with Herbert D. Ward) *The Master of the Magicians.* Boston: Houghton, Mifflin, 1890, 324pp.

Within the Gates. Boston: Houghton, Mifflin, 1901, 150pp.

The Oath of Allegiance & Other Stories. Boston: Houghton, Mifflin, 1909, 373pp. ss col

□ *Gypsy Breynton,* 1866; *Gypsy's Cousin Joy,* 1866; *Gypsy's Sowing and Reaping,* 1866; *Gypsy's Year at the Golden Crescent,* 1868; *Hedged In,* 1870; *The Trotty Book,* 1870; *The Silent Partner,* 1871; *The Story of Avis,* 1877; *Old Maid's Paradise,* 1879; *Doctor Zay,* 1882; *Poetry Studies,* 1885 (poetry); *Songs of the Silent World,* 1885 (poetry); *Burglars In Paradise,* 1886; *A Chariot of Loveliness,* 1899; *Avery,* 1902; *The Man In the Case,* 1906; *Walled In,* 1907; *The Empty House and Other Stories,* 1910 (ss col); *Fire,* 1910; *Comrades,* 1911; *Fourteen to One,* 1911 (ss col).

■ *The Struggle for Immortality,* 1889; *Austin Phelps; A Memoir,* 1891.

WARD, ROSE ELIZABETH KNOX (Mrs. Arthur S.) (1886-) *U.S.*

as Elizabeth (S.) Rohmer

□ MYSTERY: *Bianca in Black,* 1958.

↗ **Lisbeth Knox**

WARDE, BEATRICE LAMBERTON (Becker) (Mrs.) (1900-) *U.S.* [possibly became naturalized British]

as Paul Beaujon

Peace Under Earth, Dialogues From the Year 1946. NY: Dodd, Mead, 1939, 46pp., front.

□ *Unjustified Lives. A Volume of Rhymes About Printers and Their Ancestors,* 1935 (verse).

■ *Pierre S. Fournier, 1712-1768 and XVIIIth Century French Typography,* 1926.

as B(eatrice) (L.) Warde

The Shelter In Bedlam. A Story In Dialogue. London: Privately Printed for B.L.W., 1937-38 [1937], 43pp.

■ *The Nature of the Book,* 1930; *Enjoying England, A Book About An Enchanted Island,* by B.L. Warde, An American In London, 1931; *Type Faces Old and New,* 1935; *Printing Should Be Invisible,* 1936; *Bombed But Unbeaten,* 1941; *The Crystal Goblet, Sixteen Essays On Typography,* 1955.

WARNER, K(enneth) L(ewis) (1918-) *English*

as Dighton Morel

Moonlight Red. London: S. Warburg, 1960, 287pp.

WASSERBURG, JOSEPH

as Adam Bradford

Lilliput Revisited. *Fantastic,* Dec 1963

WASSERBURG, PHILIPP (1827-1897)
as Philipp Laicus
Etwas Spater! Forsetzung von Bellamy's Ruckblick aus dem Jahre 2000. Mainz: F. Kirchheim [?], 1891, 208pp.
☐ *Liberale Phrasen*, 1871.

WATSON, HENRY CROCKER MARRIOTT
as H.C.M.W.
The Decline and Fall of the British Empire; or, The Witch's Cavern. London: Trischler & Co., 1890, 291pp.
anonymous
Erchomenon; or, The Republic of Materialism. London: S. Low, 1879, 226pp.

WAYNE, CHARLES STOKES (1858- ?) *U.S.*
Born: Philadelphia, Pennsylvania
as Horace Hazeltine
☐ *The Snapdragon*, 1912; *The King Pin*, 1923.
as Charles Stokes Wayne
Mr. Lord's Moonstone and Other Stories. Philadelphia: Wynne & Wayne, 1888, 142pp. *ss col*
A Witch of To-Day and Other Selections. NY: Town Topics Pub. Co., [1898], 248pp. (Tales From Town Topics No. 30) *ss col*
The Marriage of Mrs. Merlin. NY: G.W. Dillingham, 1907, 262pp.
A Prince To Order; A Novel. NY: J. Lane, 1905, 317pp. [possibly appeared under the pseudonym of Horace Hazeltine]
☐ *Anthony Kent*, 1893; *The Lady and Her Tree*, 1895.

WEAVER, GERTRUDE (Renton) (Mrs.)
as G. Colmore
A Brother of the Shadows. London: N. Douglas, 1926, 320pp.
☐ *A Daughter of Music*, 1894; *The Strange Story of Hester Wynne*, 1899; *The Thunder Bolt*, 1919; *The Guardian*, 1923.
as Gertrude (C.) Dunn
Unholy Depths. London: Butterworth, 1926, 319pp.
The Mark of the Bat: A Tale of Vampires Living and Dead. London: Butterworth, 1928, 302pp.
And So Forever. London: Butterworth, 1929, 286pp.

WEBB, RICHARD WILSON
as Q. Patrick [in collaboration with Martha Mott Kelley]
● The Red Balloon. *Weird Tales*, Nov 1953 [this story has been attributed to R.W. Webb & Hugh Collinson Wheeler in collaboration]
☐ MYSTERY: *Murder At the Woman's City Club*, 1932; *Murder At the 'Varsity*, 1933; *S.S. Murder*, 1933; *The Grindle Nightmare*, 1935; *Return to the Scene*, 1941; *The Girl On the Gallows*, 1954.
as Patrick Quentin [in collaboration with Hugh Collinson Wheeler]
☐ MYSTERY: *A Puzzle For Fools*, 1936; *Puzzle For Wantons*, 1945; *Puzzle For Fiends*, 1946; *Puzzle for Players*, 1946; *Run To Death*, 1948; *Black Widow*, 1952; *The Man With Two Wives*, 1955.
as Jonathan Stagge [in collaboration with Hugh Collinson Wheeler]
☐ MYSTERY: *Murder Gone To Earth*, 1936; *Murder or Mercy*, 1937; *Murder by Prescription*, 1938; *The Stars Spell Death*, 1939; *Call A Hearse*, 1942; *Death My Darling Daughter*, 1945; *The Three Fears*, 1949.

WEEKLEY, MAURICE ARDEN
[often rendered Weekly]
as Rice Arden
Food For Thought. Vortex #2, 1953

WEINBAUM, STANLEY G(rauman) (1900-1935) *U.S.*
Born: Louisville, Kentucky
as John Jessel
The Adaptive Ultimate. *Astounding*, Nov 1935
as Stanley G. Weinbaum
A Martian Odyssey. *Wonder Stories*, July 1954
Dawn of Flame and Other Stories. The Weinbaum Memorial Volume. Jamaica, New York: Conrad W. Ruppert, [1936], 313pp. (500 cop) *ss col*
The New Adam. Chicago: Ziff-Davis, 1939, 262pp.
The Black Flame. Reading, Pennsylvania: Fantasy Press, 1948, 240pp., ill.
A Martian Odyssey and Others. Reading, Pennsylvania: Fantasy Press, 1949, 289pp. *ss col*
The Dark Other. Los Angeles: F.P.C.I., 1950, 256pp.
The Red Peri. Reading, Pennsylvania: Fantasy Press, 1952, 270pp. *ss col*
A Martian Odyssey and Other Classics of Science Fiction. NY: Lancer, 1962, 159pp., paper. *ss col*
● **Marge Stanley**

WEINSTEIN, AARON (1898-1967) *U.S.*
as A.A. Wyn
As a publisher he started A.A. Wyn, Inc. and inaugurated "Ace" paperbacks and "Ace Doubles" (two different books, bound as one, and upside down in relation to each other). Ace was a mainstay of the nascent SF book publishing industry in the 1950's and 1960's.

WEISINGER, MORT(imer) (1915-) *U.S.*
Born: New York, New York
as Will Garth [house pseudonym]
Turnabout. *Startling Stories*, March 1939
Incident On Titan. *Thrilling Wonder Stories*, June 1941
as Tom Erwin Geris
Lever of Destruction. *Science Fiction*, Dec 1939
as Ian Rectez
article in the magazine *Science Fiction* in 1933
as Mort Weisinger
The Price of Peace. *Amazing*, Nov 1933
■ *1001 Valuable Things You Can Get Free*, 1955.

WEISS, EHRICH (1874-1926) *U.S.*
Born: Appleton, Wisconsin
as Harry Houdini [possibly ghost written by H.P. Lovecraft]
The Hoax of the Spirit Lover. *Weird Tales*, April 1924

WEISS, GEORGE HENRY (1898-1946) *U.S.*
as Francis Flagg
The Machine Man of Ardathia. *Amazing*, Nov 1927
The Night People. Los Angeles: F.P.C.I., 1947, 32pp.

● **WELCH, EDGAR L(uderne)** (1855- ?)
● **as J. Drew Gay**
The Mystery of the Shroud, A Tale of Socialism. Bristol: J.W. Arrowsmith, [1887], 134pp.
■ *From Pall Mall to Punjab*, 1876; *Plevna, the Sultan, and the Porte Reminiscences of the War In Turkey*, 1878.
● **as GRIP**
How John Bull Lost London; or, The Capture of the Channel Tunnel, Fourth Edition. London: S. Low, 1882, 127pp.
The Monster Municipality; or, Gog and Magog Reformed. A Dream. London: S. Low, 1882, 128pp.
■ "Grip's" Historical Souvenir series, e.g. *Grip's Historical Souvenir of Clyde, New York*, 1905 - series dates are between 1894 and 1905.

[Some bibliographies list these authors as above. The NUC lists only the series of souvenir guides for "Grip" and lists his real name as Edgar L. Welch. The BMC lists the two titles of fiction as by Grip and acknowledges it as a pseudonym of an unknown author. The BMC and the NUC also list J. Drew Gay as a real author with the books above ascribed to him. Possibilities are as follows in order of likelihood:

1. J. Drew Gay is a real author who wrote under that name and there is another real author named Edgar L. Welch who wrote a series of souvenir guides under the name GRIP. There is a third author, real name unknown, who used the name GRIP on the fiction books, under that name above.

2. Number 1 is correct, but the British "Grip" is really J. Drew Gay.

3. Edgar L. Welch is the British GRIP who moved to America and used his British pseudonym twenty years later to write souvenir books in New York.

4. J. Drew Gay used the "Grip" pseudonym in England, moved to America, changed his name to Edgar L. Welch, and later used the GRIP pseudonym on his souvenir guides.

5. The entry as it stands is correct. It is probable that the options 1 through 5 decrease in probability at a geometric rather than arithmetic rate.]

WELLMAN, BERT J.
as A Law Abiding Revolutionist
The Legal Revolution of 1902. Chicago: C.H. Kerr, 1898, 334pp. (Library of Progress No. 27)

WELLMAN, MANLY WADE (c.1903-   ) U.S.
Born: Kamundongo, Portuguese West Africa
as Gabriel Barclay [house pseudonym]
Elephant Earth. Astonishing, Feb 1940
as Levi Crow
Young-Man-With-Skull-At-His-Ear. Magazine of Fantasy and Science Fiction, May 1953
as Gans T. Field
The Hairy Ones Shall Dance. Weird Tales, Jan 1938
Romance In Black. London: Utopian Publications, 1946, 64pp., ill.
as Will Garth [house pseudonym]
stories unknown - see **WILL GARTH**
as Manly Wade Wellman
Back To The Beast. Weird Tales, Nov 1927
The Invading Asteroid. NY: Stellar, 1932, paper.
Sojarr of Titan. NY: Prestwood, [1949], 120pp., paper.
The Devil's Planet. London: World Distributors, 1951, 128pp., paper.
Twice In Time. NY: Avalon, [1957], 222pp.
Giants From Eternity. NY: Avalon, [1959], 223pp.
The Dark Destroyers. NY: Avalon, 1959, 224pp.
Island In the Sky. NY: Avalon, [1961], 223pp.
Who Fears the Devil. Sauk City, Wisconsin: Arkham House, 1963, 213pp. (2058 cop)
The Solar Invasion. NY: Popular Library, 1968, 126pp., paper.
Worse Things Waiting. Chapel Hill, North Carolina: Carcosa, [1973], 352pp. ss col
(with Wade Wellman) Sherlock Holmes' War of the Worlds. NY: Warner, 1975, paper.
The Beyonders. NY: Warner, [1977], paper.
☐ MYSTERY: Star For A Warrior, 1946; Knife Between Brothers, 1947; Find My Killer, 1947; The Sleuth Patrol, 1947. HISTORICAL FICTION: Gray Riders: Jeb Stuart and His Men, 1954; Flag On the Levee, 1955; Fort Sun Dance, 1955.

■ Dead and Gone, Classic Crimes of North Carolina, 1954; Rebel Boast: First At Bethel-Last At Appomattox, 1956; Fastest On the River, 1957; Harper's Ferry, Prize of War, 1960; Winston-Salem In History, 1966.
↙ John Cotton, Manuel Ferney, Juan Perez, Hampton Wells, Wade Wells

WELLS, BASIL
as Gene Ellerman
Raiders of the Second Moon. Planet Stories, Summer 1945
"Crusader," Fantasy Book #5, 1949
as Basil Wells
Queen of the Blue World. Planet Stories, Winter 1941
Planets of Adventure. Los Angeles: F.P.C.I., 1949, 280pp. ss col
Doorways To Space. Los Angeles: F.P.C.I., 1951, 206pp. ss col

WERTENBAKER, G. PEYTON (1907-   ) U.S.
as Green Peyton
☐ Black Cabin, 1933; Rain On the Mountain, 1934.
■ 5,000 Miles Towards Tokyo, 1945; San Antonio, City In the Sun, 1946; For God and Texas; The Life of P.B. Hill, 1947.
as G. Peyton Wertenbaker
The Man From the Atom. Science and Invention, Aug 1923

WESSOLOWSKI, HANS W. (1882-   ) naturalized U.S.
Born: Germany
as H. Wesso
artist in Amazing and other magazines in the late '20's through the early '30's

WEST, GEORGE WALLACE (1900-   ) U.S.
Born: Walnut Hills, Kentucky
as Wallace West
Loup Garou. Weird Tales, Oct 1927
The Bird of Time. NY: Gnome, 1959, 256pp.
Lords of Atlantis. NY: Avalon, 1960, 220pp.
The Memory Bank. NY: Avalon, 1961, 221pp.
Outposts of Space. NY: Avalon, 1962, 224pp.
River of Time. NY: Avalon, 1963, 221pp.
The Time Locker. NY: Avalon, 1964, 190pp.
The Everlasting Exiles. NY: Avalon, 1967, 190pp.
☐ NOVELIZATIONS OF SCREEN PLAYS: Jimmy Allen In the Sky Parade, 1936; Thirteen Hours By Air, 1936.
■ Men With Admiral Byrd In Little America, 1934 (Paramount Newsreel); Our Good Neighbors In Latin America, 1942; Our Good Neighbors In Soviet Russia, 1945; Down to the Sea In Ships, 1947.

WESTLAKE, DONALD E(dwin) (1933-   ) U.S.
Born: Brooklyn, New York
as Curt Clark
Nackles. Magazine of Fantasy and Science Fiction, Jan 1964
Anarchaos. NY: Ace, [1967], 143pp., paper.
as Tucker Coe
☐ MYSTERY: Kinds of Love, Kinds of Death, 1966; Murder Among Children, 1968 [c.1967]; Wax Apple, 1970; A Jade In Aries, 1971; Don't Lie To Me, 1972.
as Timothy J. Culver
Ex Officio.
as Richard Stark
Birth of A Monster. Super Science Fiction, Aug 1959
☐ The Man With the Getaway Face, 1963; The Damsel, 1967; Green Eagle Score, 1967; The Dame, 1969; Deadly Edge, 1971; Lemons Never Lie, 1971; Slayground, 1971.

as D.E. Westlake
children's books
as Donald E. Westlake
Or Give Me Death. *Universe #8,* Nov 1954
The Curious Facts Preceding My Execution and Other
Fictions. NY: Random House, [1968], 211pp. *ss col*
☐ MYSTERY: *Killing Time,* 1961; *The Fugitive Pigeon,*
1965; *The Busy Body,* 1966; *The Spy In the Ointment,*
1966; *God Save the Mark,* 1967; *Adios Scheherazade,*
1970; *The Hot Rock,* 1970; *Bank Shot,* 1972; *Cops and*
Robbers, 1972; *Jimmy the Kid,* 1974; *Enough,* 1977.
■ *Under An English Heaven,* 1972.
✔ J. Morgan Cunningham

WHEELER, HUGH COLLINSON *English*
as Patrick Quentin [in collaboration with Richard Wilson
Webb]
see **RICHARD WILSON WEBB**
as Jonathan Stagge [in collaboration with Richard Wilson
Webb]
see **RICHARD WILSON WEBB**

WHITE, JAMES, ESQ.
as J.W.
Earl Strongbow; or, The History of Richard de Clare and
Beautiful Geralda. London: J. Dodsley, 1789, 2 vol.,
12 mo.

WHITE, THEODORE EDWARD (1938-   ) *U.S.*
Born: Washington, D.C.
as Ron Archer
(with David Van Arnam) *Lost in Space.* NY: Pyramid,
[1967], 157pp., paper.
as Norman Edwards [in collaboration with Terry Carr]
Invasion From 2500. NY: Monarch, [1964], 126pp., paper.
as Ted White
(with Forrest J. Ackerman, et. al.) The Detroit Convention.
Fantastic Universe, Jan 1960 *article*
(with Marion Zimmer Bradley) Phoenix. *Amazing,* Feb 1963
Android Avenger. NY: Ace, [1965], 113pp., paper. (Ace
Double M123)
Phoenix Prime. NY: Lancer, [1966], 188pp., paper.
Sorceress of Qar. NY: Lancer, [1966], 191pp., paper.
The Jewels of Elsewhen. NY: Belmont, [c.1967], 172pp.,
paper.
The Secret of the Marauder Satellite. Philadelphia:
Westminster, [1967], 171pp. *juv*
(with David Van Arnam) *Sideslip.* NY: Pyramid, [1968],
188pp., paper.
The Great Gold Steal. NY: Bantam, [1968], paper.
(Captain America)
The Spawn of the Death Machine. NY: Paperback Library,
1968, 175pp., paper.
No Time Like Tomorrow. NY: Crown, [1969], 152pp.
By Furies Possessed. NY: Signet, paper.
Trouble On Project Ceres. Philadelphia: Westminster,
[1971], 157pp.
(with M. Woldman) *The Oz Encounter.* NY: Pyramid,
paper.

WHITE, WILLIAM ANTHONY PARKER (1911-1968) *U.S.*
as Anthony Boucher
On A Limb. *Unknown,* Oct 1941
Snulbug. *Unknown,* Dec 1941
Far and Away. NY: Ballantine, [1955], 166pp., paper.
ss col
The Compleat Werewolf. NY: Simon & Schuster, [1969],
256pp. *ss col*
☐ MYSTERY: *The Case of the Seven of Calvary,* 1937;
The Case of the Crumpled Knave, 1939; *The Case of*
The Baker Street Irregulars, 1940; *The Case of the*
Solid Key, 1941; *The Case of the Seven Sneezes,*

1942.
as H. H. Holmes
Q. U. R. *Astounding,* March 1943
Rocket To The Morgue. NY: Duell, Sloan, & Pearce, [1942],
279pp.
☐ MYSTERY: *Nine Times Nine,* 1940.
■ Book reviews in *New York Herald Tribune,* 1951-1968
as Herman W. Mudgett
There Was A Young Man of Cape Horn. *Magazine of*
Fantasy and Science Fiction, Aug 1951 *verse*
as William A(nthony) P(arker) White
Ye Goode Olde Ghoste Storie. *Weird Tales,* Jan 1927
✔ Parker White

WHITELOCK, LOUISE (Clarkson) (Mrs.) (1865- ?)
as L. Clarkson
The Shadow of John Wallace. NY: White, Stokes, & Allen,
1884, 417pp.
☐ *Violet, With Eyes of Blue!,* 1876 (poetry); *Little Stay*
At Home and Her Friends, 1879 (juv); *The Rag Fair*
and Other Reveries, 1879 (poetry); *Indian Summer;*
Autumn Poems and Sketches, 1881 (poetry); *Violet*
Among the Lilies, 1885 (poetry).
as L. Clarkson Whitelock
A Mad Madonna and Other Stories. Boston: J. Knight,
1895, 203pp. *ss col*

WHITING, SYDNEY
as S. W.
Helionde; or, Adventures In the Sun. London: Chapman &
Hall, 1855, 424pp.

WHITMORE, H.
as Lemuel Gulliver, Junior
Modern Gulliver's Travels. Lilliput: Being a New Journey
to that Celebrated Island. . . From the Year 1702
(When They Were First Discovered and Visited by
Captain Lemuel Gulliver, the Father of the Compiler
of This Work) to the Present Aera 1796. London: T.
Chapman, 1796, 226pp.

WIBBERLEY, LEONARD (Francis) (Patrick) *ne* Leonard Francis
Patrick O'Conner-Wibberley (1915-   ) *naturalized U.S.*
Born: Dublin, Ireland
as Leonard Holton
☐ MYSTERY: "Father Joseph Bredder" series incl.: *The*
Saint Maker, 1959; *The Secret of the Doubting Saint,*
1961; *A Problem In Angels,* 1970.
as Patrick O'Conner
☐ *The Black Tiger,* 1956; *Gunpowder for Washington,* 1956
(juv); *Black Tiger At Le Mans,* 1958; *The Five Dollar*
Watch Mystery, 1959; *Black Tiger At Indianapolis,*
1962.
as Leonard Wibberley
Mrs. Searwood's Secret Weapon. Boston: Little, Brown,
1954, 294pp., ill.
The Mouse That Roared. Boston: Little, Brown, [1955],
279pp.
McGillicuddy McGotham. Boston: Little, Brown, [1956],
111pp., ill.
Take Me To Your President. NY: Putnam, 1957, 186pp.
Beware of the Mouse. NY: Putnam, [1958], 189pp., ill.
The Coming of the Green. NY: Holt, 1958, 184pp.
The Quest of Excalibur. NY: Putnam, 1959, 190pp., ill.
The Mouse on the Moon. NY: Morrow, 1962, 191pp.
Feast of Freedom. NY: Morrow, 1964, 186pp.
Encounter Near Venus. NY: Farrar, Straus & Giroux,
1967, 214pp., ill. *juv*
Attar of the Ice Valley. NY: Farrar, Straus & Giroux,
1968, 160pp.
One In Four. NY: Morrow, 1976.
Homeward To Ithaka. NY: Morrow. 1978.

☐ *The Wound of Peter Wayne*, 1955; *Yesterday's Land, A Baja California Adventure*, 1961; *The Ballad of the Pilgrim Cat*, 1962; *The Island of the Angels*, 1965; *The Centurion*, 1966.

● **Christopher Webb**

WICKER, THOMAS GREY   (1926-   ) *U.S.*
Born: North Carolina
    associate editor of *The New York Times*
as Paul Connolly [sometimes rendered Connelly]
● *The Devil Must.* NY: Harper, 1957, 280pp.
    ☐ *So Fair, So Evil*, 1955.
as Tom Wicker
    ☐ *The Judgment*, 1961.
    ■ *Kennedy Without Tears, The Man Beneath the Myth*, 1964; *J.F.K. and L.B.J.; The Influence of Personality Upon Politics*, 1968.

WIDNER, ARTHUR L.
as Arthur Lambert
    The Perfect Incinerator. *Science Fiction Quarterly*, Winter 1942

WIENER, NORBERT   (1894-1964) *U.S.*
Autobiography: *Ex-Prodigy: My Childhood and Youth*, 1953, 309pp.; *I Am A Mathematician*. Garden City: Doubleday, 1956, 380pp.
as W. Norbert
    The Miracle of the Broom Closet. *Magazine of Fantasy and Science Fiction*, Feb 1954
as Norbert Wiener
    ☐ *The Tempter*, 1959.
    ■ *The Fourier Integral and Certain of Its Applications*, 1933; *Cybernetics*, 1948; *The Human Use of Human Beings*, 1950; *Nonlinear Problems In Random Theory*, 1958; *God and the Golem, Inc; A Comment On Certain Points Where Cybernetics Impinges On Religion*, 1964; (et. al.) *Differential Space, Quantum Systems, and Prediction*, 1966; *General Harmonic Analysis, and Tauberian Theorems*, 1966.

WILCOX, DON   (1908-   ) *U.S.*
as Buzz-Bolt Atomcracker
    Confessions of A Mechanical Man. *Amazing*, May 1947
as Alexander Blade [house pseudonym]
    The Eye of the World. *Fantastic Adventures*, June 1949
as Cleo Eldon
    The Sapphire Enchantress. *Fantastic Adventures*, Dec 1945
as Max Overton
    Robotcycle for TWO. *Amazing*, Sept 1942
    The Deadly Yappers. *Fantastic Adventures*, Sept 1942
as Miles Shelton
    Whirlpool In Space. *Amazing*, Nov 1939
as Don Wilcox
    Pit of Death. *Amazing*, July 1939
    ☐ JUVENILE: *David's Ranch*, 1954; *Basketball Star*, 1955; *Joe Sunpool*, 1956; *Castle On the Campus*, 1959.

WILCOX, MARRION   (1858-1926)
as Author of "Real People"
    The Devil Is Dead and Scenes in General Dayton's Garden. London: Gilbert & Rivington, 1889, 382pp.
    ☐ *Senora Villena and Gray: An Oldhaven Romance*, 1887.
as Marrion Wilcox
    ☐ *Real People*, 1886; *The Paradise In Hyde Park*, 1890; *Vengeance of the Female*, 1899.
    ■ *A Short History of the War With Spain*, 1898; (ed) *Encyclopedia of Latin America*, 1917.

WILDING, PHILIP   *English*
as John Robert Haynes
    Scream From Outer Space. London: Rich, Cowan, 1955, 176pp.
as Logan Stewart
    ☐ WESTERN: *War Bonnet Pass*, 1959; *Black Horse Canyon*, 1964; *Gunhawk*, 1964.
as Philip Wilding
    Spaceflight Venus. London: Hennel, Locke, 1954, 190pp.
    Shadow Over the Earth. London: Hennel, Locke, 1956, 160pp.
● **Jefferson Fraser, Lloyd Marshall, Erle Russell, Borden Stanton, Logan Stuart**

WILEY, CARL A.
as Russell Saunders
    Clipper Ships of Space. *Astounding*, May 1951

WILKINSON, LOUIS UMFREVILLE   (1881-   ) *British*
as Louis Marlow
    The Devil in Crystal. London: Faber, 1944, 113pp.
    ☐ *Mr. Amberthwaite*, 1928; *Two Made Their Bed*, 1929; *Love By Accident, A Tragi-Farce*, 1929; *The Lion Took Fright*, 1930; *Fool's Quarter Day*, 1935; *Forth, Beast!*, 1946.
    ■ *Welsh Ambassadors (Powys Lives and Letters)*, 1936.
as Louis U(mfreville) Wilkinson
    ☐ *The Buffoon*, 1916; *Brute Gods*, 1919.
    ■ *Syllabus Of A Course of Six Lectures On Poets of the English Romantic Revival*, 1906.

WILLIAMS, DAVID RHYS
as Gan "Index"
    Y dyn oddimewn; neu, Am dro i fyd y tumewn-ogiaid. Utica, New York: Swyddfa Y Drych, 1913, 163pp.

WILLIAMS, HAROLD   (1853- ?)
as George Afterem
    ☐ *Silken Threads, A Detective Story*, 1885.
anonymous
    ☐ *Mr. & Mrs. Morton, A Novel*, 1883.

● **WILLIAMS, R.F.**
as Author of "Mephistopheles in London"
    Eureka: A Prophecy of the Future. London: Longman, 1837, 3 vol.

WILLIAMS, ROBERT MOORE   (1907-   ) *U.S.*
Born: Farmington, Missouri
as John S. Browning
    Burning Bright. *Astounding*, July 1948
as H. H. Harmon
    Secret of the Lightning. *Fantastic Adventures*, Sept 1949
    Swamp Girl of Venus. *Amazing*, Sept 1949
as E.K. Jarvis [house pseudonym] [Robert Moore Williams wrote most, if not all, stories under this name up to 1950]
● The Man Who Was Two Men. *Amazing*, June 1942
as Robert Moore
    Zero As A Limit. *Astounding*, July 1937
as Russell Storm
    Thunor Flees the Devils. *Fantastic Adventures*, Feb 1940
as Robert Moore Williams
    Beyond That Curtain. *Thrilling Wonder Stories*, Dec 1937
    The Chaos Fighters. NY: Ace, [1955], 160pp., paper.
    Conquest of the Space Sea. NY: Ace, [1955], 151pp., paper. (Ace Double D 99)
    Doomsday Eve. NY: Ace, [1957], 138pp., paper. (Ace Double D 215)
    The Blue Atom. NY: Ace, [1958], 124pp., paper. (Ace Double D 322)
    The Void Beyond and Other Stories. NY: Ace, [1958], 130pp., paper. *ss col* (Ace Double D 322)

To the End of Time. NY: Ace, [1960], 108pp., paper. *ss col* (Ace Double D 427)

World of the Masterminds. NY: Ace, [1960], 148pp., paper. (Ace Double D 427)

The Day They H-Bombed Los Angeles. NY: Ace, [1961], 128pp., paper. (Ace Double D 530)

The Darkness Before Tomorrow. NY: Ace, [1962], 118pp., paper. (Ace Double F 141)

King of the Fourth Planet. NY: Ace, [1962], 128pp., paper. (Ace Double F149)

Walk Up the Sky. NY: Avalon, [1962], 221pp.

The Star Wasps. NY: Ace, [1963], 126pp., paper. (Ace Double F 177)

Flight From Yesterday. NY: Ace, [1963], 120pp., paper. (Ace Double F 223)

The Lunar Eye. NY: Ace, [1964], 115pp., paper. (Ace Double F 261)

The Second Atlantis. NY: Ace, [1965], 123pp., paper.

Vigilante—21st Century. NY: Lancer, [1967], 189pp., paper.

Zanthar of the Many Worlds. NY: Lancer, [1967], 192pp., paper.

Zanthar At the Edge of Never. NY: Lancer, [1968], 285pp., paper.

The Bell From Infinity. NY: Lancer, [1968], 189pp., paper.

Zanthar At Moon's Madness. NY: Lancer, [1968], 189pp., paper.

Zanthar At Trip's End. NY: Lancer, [1969], paper.

Beachhead Planet. NY: Dell, 1970, paper.

Love Is Forever, We Are For Tonight. NY: Curtis, [1970], paper.

When Two Worlds Meet. NY: Curtis, 1970.

Jongor of Lost Land. NY: Popular Library, 1970, paper.

The Return of Jongor. NY: Popular Library, 1970, paper.

Jongor Fights Back. NY: Popular Library, 1970, paper.

Now Comes Tomorrow. NY: Curtis, 1971.

WILLIAMS, THOMAS LANIER (1914-   ) U.S.
as Tennessee Williams
Hard Candy, A Book of Stories. NY: New Directions, [1954], 220pp. *ss col*

WILLIAMS-ELLIS, MARY AMABEL NASSAU STRACHEY
(Mrs.) (1894-   ) British
as A(mabel) (S.) Williams-Ellis
Fairies and Enchanters. NY: T. Nelson, [1933], 342pp.
☐ *Noah's Ark*, 1925; *The Wall of Glass*, 1927; *Learn To Love First*, 1939.
■ *An Anatomy of Poetry*, 1922; *The Tragedy of John Ruskin*, 1928; *Men Who Found Out*, 1930; *A History of English Life, Political and Social*, 1936; *Women In War Factories*, 1943; *Laughing Gas and Safety Lamp; the Story of Sir Humphrey Davy*, 1954.

WILLIAMSON, ETHEL
as Jane Cardinal
The Living Idol. London: S. Paul, [1933], 288pp.
as Cherry Veheyne
☐ *The Journal of Henry Bulver*, 1921; *The Devil Is Sick*, 1930.

WILLIAMSON, JOHN STEWART (1908-   ) U.S.
Born: Bisbee, Arizona
as Will Stewart
Collision Orbit. Astounding, July 1942
Seetee Shock. NY: Simon & Schuster, 1950, 238pp.
Seetee Ship. NY: Gnome, 1951, 255pp.
as Jack Williamson
The Metal Man. Amazing, Dec 1928
(with Miles J. Breuer) *The Girl From Mars.* NY: Stellar, [1929], 24pp., ill., paper. (S.F. Series No. 1)
Lady In Danger. NY: Utopian, 1945, paper.

The Legion of Space. Reading, Pennsylvania: Fantasy Press, 1947, 259pp., ill.

Darker Than You Think. Reading, Pennsylvania: Fantasy Press, 1948, 310pp., ill.

The Humanoids. NY: Simon & Schuster, 1949, 239pp.

The Green Girl. NY: Avon, 1950, 125pp., paper.

The Cometeers. Reading, Pennsylvania: Fantasy Press, 1950, 310pp., ill. *2 novellas (includes One Against The Legion)*

Dragon's Island. NY: Simon & Schuster, 1951, 246pp.

The Legion of Time. NY: Fantasy Press, 1952, 252pp. *2 novellas (includes After World's End)*

(with Frederik Pohl) *Undersea Quest.* NY: Gnome, 1954, 189pp.

Dome Around America. NY: Ace, [1955], 133pp., paper. (Ace Double D 118)

(with James E. Gunn) *Starbridge.* NY: Gnome, 1955, 221pp.

(with Frederik Pohl) *Undersea Fleet.* NY: Gnome, 1956, 187pp.

(with Frederik Pohl) *Undersea City.* NY: Gnome, 1958, 188pp.

The Trial of Terra. NY: Ace, [1962], 159pp., paper.

Golden Blood. NY: Lancer, [1964], 157pp., paper.

(with Frederik Pohl) *The Reefs of Space.* NY: Ballantine, [1964], 188pp., paper.

The Reign of Wizardry. NY: Lancer, [1964], 142pp., paper.

(with Frederik Pohl) *Starchild.* NY: Ballantine, [1965], 191pp., paper.

Bright New Universe. NY: Ace, [1967], 158pp., paper.

One Against the Legion. NY: Pyramid, [1967], 220pp., paper.

Trapped In Space. Garden City: Doubleday, 1968, 144pp., ill.

(with Frederik Pohl) *Rogue Star.* NY: Ballantine, 1969, 213pp., paper.

The Pandora Effect. NY: Ace, [1969], paper. *ss col*

People Machines. NY: Ace, [1971], paper. *ss col*

The Moon Children. NY: Putnam, [1972], 190pp.

The Early Williamson. Garden City: Doubleday, 1975. *ss col*

(with Frederik Pohl) *Farthest Star.* NY: Ballantine, [1975], paper.

The Power of Blackness. NY: Berkley/Putnam, 1976.

The Best of Jack Williamson. NY: Ballantine, [1978], paper. *ss col*

■ *H.G. Wells—Critic of Progress.*

WILLIS, GEORGE ANTHONY ARMSTRONG (1897-   )
British
as A.A.
☐ Humorous pieces written for *Punch* and *The New Yorker.*
The Secret Trail (a Jimmy Rezaire Story), 1928.
as Anthony Armstrong
Lure of the Past. London: S. Paul, 1920, 256pp.

The Love of Prince Raameses. London: S. Paul, 1921, 256pp.

The Wine of Death. London: S. Paul, [1925], 288pp.

The Prince Who Hiccupped & Other Tales. London: E. Benn, 1932, 216pp., ill. *ss col*

The Pack of Pieces. London: M. Joseph, 1942, 180pp., ill.

(with Bruce Graeme) *When the Bells Rang.* London: Harrap, 1943, 240pp.

The Strange Case of Mr. Pelham. London: Methuen, 1957, 224pp.

☐ *The Trail of Fear*, 1927; *No Dragon: No Damsel*, 1928; *In the Dentist's Chair, A One Act Thriller*, 1931 (play); *The Trail of the Black King*, 1931; *Well Caught*, 1932 (play); *Ten Minute Alibi*, 1933; *Mile-Away Murder*, 1937; *Spies In Amber*, 1956; HISTORICAL FICTION: *The Heart of A Slave Girl*, 1922; *When The Nile Was Young*, 1923.

■ *Taxi!*, 1930.

WILSON, DORIS MARIE CLAIRE BAUMGARDT POHL
as Leslie Perri
Space Episode. *Future*, Dec 1941
as Mrs. Frederik Pohl
title by marriage 1940-1942
as Mrs. Richard Wilson
title by marriage

WILSON, JOHN (Anthony) B(urgess) (1917-   ) *English*
Born: Manchester, Lancashire
as Anthony Burgess
The Doctor Is Sick. London: Heinemann, [1960], 260pp.
Devil of A State. London: Heinemann, [1961], 282pp.
A Clockwork Orange. London: Heinemann, [1962], 196pp.
The Wanting Seed. London: Heinemann, [1962], 285pp.
The Eve of Saint Venus. London: Sidgwick & Jackson, [1964], 138pp., ill.
☐ *Time For A Tiger*, 1956; *Enemy In the Blanket*, 1958; *The Right To An Answer*, 1960; *Honey For the Bears*, 1963; *Nothing Like the Sun; A Story of Shakespeare's Life*, 1964; *A Vision of Battlements*, 1965; *Beds In the East*, 1968; *The Worm and the Ring*, 1970; *MF*, 1971.
■ *Language Made Plain*, 1964; *Here Comes Everybody, An Introduction to James Joyce*, 1965; *The Novel Now; A Guide to Contemporary Fiction*, 1967; *Urgent Copy; Literary Studies*, 1968; *Shakespeare*, 1970.
as Joseph Kell
☐ *One Hand Clapping*, 1961; *Inside Mr. Enderby*, 1963.

WILSON, RICHARD (1920-   ) *U.S.*
Born: Huntington, New York
as Ivar Towers [house pseudonym] [in collaboration with Cyril M. Kornbluth]
Stepsons of Mars. *Astonishing*, April 1940
as Richard Wilson
Murder From Mars. *Astonishing*, April 1940
The Girls From Planet 5. NY: Ballantine, [1955], 184pp., paper/hardback.
Those Idiots From Earth. NY: Ballantine, [1957], 160pp., paper. ss col
And Then the Town Took Off. NY: Ace, [1960], 123pp., paper. (Ace Double D 437)
30-Day Wonder. NY: Ballantine, [1960], 158pp., paper.
Time Out For Tomorrow. NY: Ballantine, [1962], 159pp., paper.

WILSON, ROBIN S(cott)
as Robin Scott
Third Alternative. *Astounding*, March 1964
as Robin Scott Wilson
(ed) *Clarion: An Anthology of Speculative Fiction and Criticism*, 1971, paper. stories & crit.

WINTERBOTHAM, RUSS(ell) (Robert) (1904-1971) *U.S.*
Born: Salina, Kansas
as J. Harvey Bond
The Other World. NY: Avalon, 1963, 191pp.
as Franklin Hadley
Planet Big Zero. NY: Monarch, 1964, paper.
as R.R. Winterbotham
Joyce of the Secret Squadron, A Captain Midnight Adventure. Racine, Wisconsin: Whitman, [1942], 251pp., ill.
☐ *Red Ryder and the Mystery of the Whispering Walls*, 1941.
as Russ Winterbotham
The Star That Would Not Behave. *Astounding*, Aug 1935
The Space Egg. NY: Avalon, [1958], 224pp.
The Red Planet. NY: Monarch, [1962], 140pp., paper.

The Men From Arcturus. NY: Avalon, [1963], 192pp.
The Puppet Planet. NY: Avalon, [1964], 189pp.
The Lord of Nardos. NY: Avalon, 1966, 192pp.
☐ "Big Little Books:" *Maximo, The Amazing Superman*, etc.
■ *Lindbergh, Hero of the Air*, 1928.

WISE, ARTHUR (1923-   ) *English*
Born: York
as John McArthur
Days In the Hay. London: Cassell, 1960, 185pp.
as Arthur Wise
The Little Fishes. London: Gollancz, 1961, 191pp.
The Day the Queen Flew to Scotland for the Grouse Shooting, A Document. Dublin: Cavalier, [1968], 189pp.
☐ MYSTERY: *The Death's Head*, 1962; *Who Killed Enoch Powell?*, 1970.
■ *Communication In Speech*, 1965; *Weapons In the Theatre*, 1968; *The Art and History of Personal Combat*, 1971; *Talking For Management, A Practical Course In Oral Communication*, 1971.

● WOLFF, CECIL DRUMMOND
as Cedric Dane Waldo
The Ban of the Gubbe. Edinburgh: Blackwood, 1896, 195pp.

WOLLHEIM, DONALD A. (1914-   ) *U.S.*
Born: New York, New York
Long time editor for Ace Books, recently founded DAW books, publishing original science fiction in paper.
as Arthur Cooke [in collaboration with E. Balter, Cyril Kornbluth, Robert Lowndes, and John Michel]
The Psychological Regulator. *Comet Stories*, March 1941
as Millard Verne Gordon
The Space Lens. *Wonder Stories*, Sept 1935
as David Grinnell
Top Secret. *Magazine of Fantasy and Science Fiction*, Fall 1950
Across Time. NY: Avalon, 1957, 223pp.
The Edge of Time. NY: Avalon, 1958, 221pp.
The Martian Missile. NY: Avalon, 1959, 224pp.
Destiny's Orbit. NY: Avalon, 1962, 224pp.
(with Lin Carter) Destination Saturn. NY: Avalon, 1967, 192pp.
To Venus; To Venus. NY: Ace, [1970], paper.
as Martin Pearson [alone]
So You Want To Be A Space-Flier. *Cosmic Stories*, May 1941
as Martin Pearson [in collaboration with Cyril Kornbluth] [this story only]
The Embassy. *Astounding*, March 1942
as Allen Warland
Baby Dreams. *Science Fiction Quarterly*, Winter 1941-1942
as Donald A. Wollheim
The Man From Ariel. *Wonder Stories*, Jan 1934
(ed) *The Pocket Book of SF*. NY: Pocket Books, [1943], 310pp., paper. ss col
The Secret of Saturn's Rings. Philadelphia: Winston, [1954], 207pp.
The Secret of the Martian Moons. Philadelphia: Winston, [1955], 206pp.
One Against the Moon. Cleveland: World, [1956], 220pp.
The Secret of the Ninth Planet. Philadelphia: Winston, [1959], 203pp.
Mike Mars, Astronaut. Garden City: Doubleday, 1961, 188pp., ill. (1st of *juv* series)
Mike Mars At Cape Canaveral. Garden City: Doubleday, 1961, 186pp., ill. *juv*
Mike Mars Flies the X-15. Garden City: Doubleday, 1961, 187pp., ill. *juv*

Mike Mars In Orbit. Garden City: Doubleday, 1961, 188pp., ill. *juv*

Mike Mars Flies the Dyna-Soar. Garden City: Doubleday, 1962, 188pp., ill. *juv*

Mike Mars South Pole Spaceman. Garden City: Doubleday, [1962], 190pp., ill. *juv*

Mike Mars and the Mystery Satellite. Garden City: Doubleday, [1963], 190pp., ill. *juv*

Mike Mars Around the Moon. Garden City: Doubleday, [1964], ill. *juv*

Two Dozen Dragon Eggs. NY: Powell, [1969], paper. *ss col*

as Lawrence Woods [alone]
Strange Return. *Stirring Science Stories*, Feb 1941

as Lawrence Woods [in collaboration with Robert Lowndes]
Black Flames. *Stirring Science Stories*, April 1941

as Lawrence Woods [in collaboration with John Michel]
Earth Does Not Reply. *Science Fiction Quarterly*, Summer 1941

as "X"
"!!!" *Stirring Science Stories*, April 1941

WOOD, ELLEN PRICE (Mrs. Henry) (1814-1887)   *English*
as Mrs. (Henry) Wood
Told In the Twilight. London: R. Bentley, 1875, 3 vol. *ss col*

☐ *East Lynne*, 1861; *The Channings*, 1862; *The Shadow of Ashlydyat*, 1863; *Gervase Castonel; or, the Six Gray Powders*, 1863; *Anne Hereford*, 1868; *Castle Wafer; or, the Plain Gold Ring*, 1868; *Dene Hollow*, 1871; *Within the Maze*, 1872; *Edina*, 1876; *The Haunted Tower*, 1877; *A Tale of Sin and Other Tales*, 1881 (ss col); *The Mystery of Jesse Page and Other Tales*, 1885 (ss col); *The Unholy Wish*, 1885; *The Mystery*, 1887.

WOODS, JAMES
as Navarchus [in collaboration with Patrick Vaux]
The World's Awakening. London: Hodder & Stoughton, 1908, 463pp.

as James Woods
Editor of the *Fleet* magazine

as Lionel Yexley
(with Patrick Vaux) *When the Eagle Flies Seaward*. London: Hurst & Blackett, 1907, 343pp.

☐ editor of many books of "yarns" about life at sea.

■ *The Inner Life of the Navy: Being An Account of the Inner Social Life Led by Our Naval Seamen on Board Ships of War*, 1908.

● **WOODWARD, WAYNE** (*c*.1911-1964)   *U.S.*
Born: Minnesota
as Hannes (Vajn) Bok
artist
The Alien Vibration. *Future*, Feb 1942
(with A. Merritt) *The Black Wheel*. NY: New Collectors Group, 1947, 115pp.
Bokanalia Memorial Folder #1. Bokanalia Foundation, 1968. *art portfolio*
The Sorcerer's Ship. NY: Ballantine, [1969], paper.
Beyond the Golden Stair. NY: Ballantine, [1970], paper.
Spinner of Silver and Thistle. San Francisco: Sisu, 1972.

as Dolbokov [in collaboration with Boris Dolgov]
on artwork

WOOLFOLK, JOSIAH PITTS (1894-1971)   *U.S.*
as Sappho Henderson Britt
☐ *Love In Virginia*, 1935.

as Howard Kennedy
☐ *Lady Killer*, 1935; *Lady Mislaid*, 1936; *Proxy Princess*, 1937.

as Gordon Sayre
☐ *Rented Wife*, 1933; *Unwilling Sinner*, 1933; *Fiddler's Fee*, 1934; *Male and Female*, 1934; *Assistant Wife*,

1935; *Wife to Trade*, 1936; *Ecstasy Girl*, 1937.

as Jack Woodford
The Band of Gold. *Weird Tales*, March 1925
☐ *Evangelical Cockroach*, 1929 (ss col); *Here Is My Body*, 1931; *Illegitimate*, 1933; *She Liked the Man*, 1936; EROTICA: *Sin and Such*, 1930; *White Meat*, [c.1934]; *Temptress*, 1935.
■ *Trial and Error, A Dithyramb on the Subject of Writing and Selling*, 1933; *Plotting; How To Have A Brain Child*, 1939.

WOOLRICH, CORNELL (1906-1968)   *U.S.*
Born: New York, New York
as George Hopley
The Night Has A Thousand Eyes. NY: Farrar & Straus, 1945, 301pp.

as William Irish
The Phantom Lady. Philadelphia: Lippincott, 1942, 291pp.
After Dinner Story. Philadelphia: Lippincott, 1944, 209pp.
The Blue Ribbon. London: Hutchinson, 1951, 208pp.
The Night I Died. London: Hutchinson, 1951, 259pp.

as Cornell Woolrich
Speak to Me of Death. *Fantasy Fiction*, May 1950
Beyond the Night. NY: Avon, [1959], 160pp., paper.
The Doom Stone. NY: Avon, [1960], 159pp., paper.
☐ *Cover Charge*, 1926; *Children of the Ritz*, 1927; *Times Square*, 1929; *The Bride Wore Black*, 1940; *The Black Curtain*, 1941. ADAPTED TO SCREENPLAYS: *No Man of Her Own*, 1950; *Rear Window*, 1954; *The Bride Wore Black*, 1967.

WORLEY, FREDERICK U.
as Benefice
Three Thousand Dollars a Year. Moving Forward, or How We Got There. The Complete Liberation of All the People. Abridged From the Advance Sheets of A History of Industrial and Governmental Reforms In the United States, To Be Published In the Year 2001. Washington, D.C.: J.P. Wright, [1890], 104pp.

WORRELL, EVERIL (1893-1969)   *U.S.*
Born: Nebraska
● **as O.M. Cabral**
Tiger! Tiger! *Strange Stories*, June 1940
as Lireve Monett
Norn. *Weird Tales*, Feb 1936
as Everil Worrell
The Bird of Space. *Weird Tales*, Sept 1926

WORTH, PETER [house pseudonym]
unattributed
Lunar Holiday. *Fantastic Adventures*, Nov 1949
Typewriter From the Future. *Amazing*, Feb 1950
Read It and Weep. *Amazing*, June 1950
[above titles possibly by **CHESTER S. GEIER**]
by Roger P. Graham
The Robot and the Pearly Gates. *Amazing*, Jan 1949
I Died Tomorrow. *Fantastic Adventures*, May 1949
Window To the Future. *Amazing*, May 1949
Lullaby. *Amazing Annual*, 1950
Null F. *Fantastic Adventures*, Feb 1950
The Master Ego. *Fantastic Adventures*, March 1951
The Imitators. *Amazing*, June 1951

WORTS, GEORGE F(rank) (1892-   )   *U.S.*
as Loring Brent
The Return of George Washington. London: Hodder & Stoughton, [1928], 320pp.
No More A Corpse, An Astounding Story. NY: A.H. King, [1932], 311pp.

as George F. Worts
The Return of George Washington. *Argosy*, Oct 15, 1927

Peter the Brazen. A Mystery Story of Modern China. Philadelphia: Lippincott, 1919, 379pp.

The Phantom President. NY: J. Cape & R. Ballou, [1932], 363pp.

The House of Creeping Horror. NY: A.H. King, [1934], 256pp.

The Monster of the Lagoon. London: Swan, 1947, 96pp., paper.

□ MYSTERY: *The Silver Fang,* 1930; *The Blue Lacquer Box,* 1939; *Dangerous Young Man,* 1940; *Laughing Girl,* 1941; *Overboard,* 1943; *Five Who Vanished,* 1945.

WRIGHT, FARNSWORTH (1888-1940) U.S.
Born: California
as Francis Hard
The Great Panjandrum. Weird Tales, Nov 1924
as Farnsworth Wright
The Closing Hand. Weird Tales, March 1923

WRIGHT, LIONEL PERCY (1923-) English
Born: Walford, Hertfordshire
as Lan Wright
Who Speaks of Conquest. NY: Ace, [1957], 160pp., paper. (Ace Double D 205)
A Man Called Destiny. NY: Ace, [1958], 128pp., paper. (Ace Double D 311)
Assignment Luther. London: Digit, 1963, 158pp., paper.
Exile from Xanadu. NY: Ace, [1964], 137pp., paper. (Ace Double M 103)
The Last Hope of Earth. NY: Ace, [1965], 159pp., paper. (Ace Double F 347)
The Creeping Shroud. London: Compact, 190pp., paper.
The Pictures of Pavanne. NY: Ace, [1968], 139pp., paper. (Ace Double H-48)

WRIGHT, MABEL OSGOOD (Mrs. James) (1859-1934) U.S.
as Barbara
The Open Window; Tales of the Months. NY: Macmillan, 1908, 381pp., ill. *ss col*
□ *People of the Whirlpool,* 1903 (possibly anon.); *The Woman Errant,* 1904; *At the Sign of the Fox, A Romance,* 1905.
as Mabel Osgood Wright
□ *Tommy-Anne and the Three Hearts,* 1896; *Webeno the Magician,* 1899; *The Dream Fox Story Book,* 1900 (ss col); *Dogtown,* 1902; *Aunt Jimmy's Will,* 1903; *The Stranger At the Gate,* 1913; *Eudora's Men,* 1931.
■ *Birdcraft,* 1895; *Citizen Bird,* 1897; *Four Footed Americans and Their Kin,* 1898; *Flowers and Ferns In Their Haunts,* 1901; *My New York,* 1926.

WRIGHT, MARY M. (Dunn) (Mrs.) (1894-) U.S.
Born: Corpus Christi, Texas
as Lilith Lorraine
Into the 28th Century. Wonder Stories Quarterly, 1930
The Brain of the Planet. NY: Stellar Publishing Co., [1929], 23pp., ill., paper. (Science Fiction Series No. 5)
□ POETRY: *Banners of Victory,* 1937; *The Day Before Judgment,* 1944; *Let the Patterns Break,* 1947; *Not For Oblivion,* 1956.
■ *Let Dreamers Wake, A Text Book for Poets,* 1945.

WRIGHT, NOEL (1890-)
as Nigel Worth
The Man In the Box; A Tale of Adventure. London: Mills & Boon, [1923], 252pp.
The Arms of Phaedra: A Tale of Wonder and Adventure. London: Mills & Boon, 1924, 284pp.
□ *Roger Sinclair's Treasure,* 1927.
■ *Glimpses of South Africa,* 1929.

WRIGHT, SEWELL PEASLEE (1897-1970) U.S.
Born: Buler, Pennsylvania
as Sewell Peaslee Wright
The Thing In the Glass Box. Weird Tales, Feb 1926
From the Ocean's Depth. Astounding, March 1930
□ *Childless Women,* 1937.
■ *Ethical Advertising for Funeral Directors,* 1924.
● **Thomas Andrews, Leigh Cameron, Parke Spencer**

WRIGHT, S(idney) FOWLER (1874-1965) British
as Sidney Fowler
The Bell Street Murders. London: Harrap, [1931], 255pp.
□ MYSTERY: *By Saturday,* 1931; *Was Murder Done?,* 1936.
as Anthony Wingrave
Vengeance of Gwa. London: T. Butterworth, 1935, 280pp.
as S. Fowler Wright
The Rat. Weird Tales, March 1929
The Amphibians, A Romance of 500,000 Years Hence. London: Merton Press, [1925 (c.1924)], 279pp.
The Amphibians. Leeds: Swan Press, 1925, 279pp. (1000 cop, buckram)
Deluge. A Romance. London: F. Wright, 1927, 320pp.
The Island of Captain Sparrow. London: Gollancz, 1928, 254pp.
Dawn. NY: Cosmopolitan, 1929, 349pp.
The World Below. London: Collins, 1929, 314pp.
Power. London: Jarrolds, [1933], 381pp.
Dream; or, The Simian Maid. London: Harrap, [1931], 251pp.
The New Gods Lead. London: Jarrolds, 1932, 288pp. *ss col*
Beyond the Rim. London: Jarrolds, 1932, 318pp.
David (An Imaginative Romance). London: Harrap, 1934, 318pp.
Prelude In Prague. A Story of the War of 1938. London: Newnes, [1935], 317pp. [issued in U.S. as *The War of 1938*]
Four Day's War. London: R. Hale, 1936, 288pp.
Meggido's Ridge. London: R. Hale, 1937, 284pp.
The Screaming Lake. London: R. Hale, [1937], 288pp.
The Adventure of Wyndam Smith. London: Jenkins, [1938], 284pp.
The Hidden Tribe. London: R. Hale, [1938], 284pp.
The Witchfinder & Other Tales. London: Books of Today, [1946], 218pp. *ss col*
The Adventures In the Blue Room. London: Rich, 1948, 192pp.
The World Below. Chicago: Shasta, 1949, 344pp.
The Throne of Saturn. Sauk City, Wisconsin: Arkham House, 1949, 186pp. (3062 cop)
The Spider's War. NY: Abelard-Schuman, 1954, 256pp.
□ (ed.) *Poetry* mag., 1920-1932; *The Ballad of Elaine,* 1926; *The Case of Anne Bickerton,* 1930; *Elfwin, A Romance of History,* 1930.
■ *Police and Public,* 1929; *The Life of Sir Walter Scott,* 1932; *Should We Surrender Colonies,* 1939.

WRIGHT, WILLARD HUNTINGTON (1888-1939) U.S.
Born: Charlottesville, Virginia
as S.S. Van Dine
The Bishop Murder Case. Scientific Detective Monthly, Jan 1930
The Bishop Murder Case. NY: Scribner, 1929, 349pp.
□ MYSTERY: *The Canary Murder Case,* 1927; *The Dragon Murder Case,* 1933; *The Casino Murder Case,* 1934; *The Gracie Allen Murder Case,* 1938; *The Winter Murder Case,* 1939.
as Willard Huntington Wright
□ *The Man of Promise,* 1930.

■ Literary critic: *Town Topics*, 1910-1914; Art critic: *The Forum*, 1915-1916; *Modern Painting, Its Tendency and Meaning*, 1915; *The Creative Will: Studies In the Philosophy and the Syntax of Aesthetics*, 1916; *Informing A Nation*, 1917; *Misinforming A Nation*, 1917; *The Future of Painting*, 1923.

WRZOS, JOSEPH (1929-   ) *U.S.*
as Joseph Ross
   Managing editor, *Amazing*, Aug 1965-Oct 1967.
   Managing editor, *Fantastic*, Sept 1965-Oct 1967.
   (ed.) *The Best of Amazing*. Garden City: Doubleday, 1967, 222pp.

WYBRANIEC, PETER F(rank) (1882-   )
as Dr. Raphael W. Leonhart
   Speratia, the Land of Hope. Boston: Meador Pub. Co., 1935, 271pp.

YERKE, T(heodore) B(ruce)
as Carlton J. Fassbinder
   Reflections On Falling Over Backwards In A Swivel Chair. *Infinity*, Nov 1957
● **as Theodore B. Yerke**
   ■ *Report on Subject Classification of Forestry Literature*, 1962.

YERXA, LEROY (1915-1946)
as Alexander Blade [house pseudonym]
   Is This The Night? *Amazing*, March 1945
as Leroy Yerxa
   Death Rides At Night. *Amazing*, Aug 1942

YOUD, C(hristopher) S. (1922-   ) *English*
   Born: Knowsley
as John Christopher
   Tree of Wrath. *Worlds Beyond*, Jan 1951
   The Twenty-Second Century. London: Grayson, 1954, 239pp. *ss col*
   The Year of the Comet. London: M. Joseph, 1955, 270pp.
   The Death of Grass. London: M. Joseph, 1956, 231pp. [U.S. title: *No Blade of Grass*]
   The Long Winter. NY: Simon & Schuster, 1962, 253pp.
   Sweeney's Island. NY: Simon & Schuster, 1964, 218pp.
   The Possessors. NY: Simon & Schuster, 1964, 252pp.
   The Ragged Edge. NY: Simon & Schuster, 1965, 254pp.
   The Little People. NY: Simon & Schuster, [c.1966], 224pp.
   The White Mountains. London: H. Hamilton, 1967, 151pp.
   The City of Gold and Lead. London: H. Hamilton, 1967, 159pp.
   The Pendulum. NY: Simon & Schuster, [1968], 254pp.
   The Pool of Fire. NY: Macmillan, [1968], 178pp.
   The Lotus Caves. NY: Macmillan, [1969], 154pp.
   The Guardians. NY: Macmillan, 1970.
   The Prince In Waiting. NY: Macmillan, [1970], 182pp.
   Wild Jack. NY: Macmillan, [1970], 168pp.
   Beyond the Burning Lands. NY: Macmillan, [1971], 170pp.
   Sword of the Spirits. NY: Macmillan, [1972], 162pp.
as William Vine
   The Rather Improbable History of Hillary Kiffer. *Avon Science Fiction and Fantasy Reader*, April 1953
as C.S. Youd
   Christmas Tree. *Astounding*, Feb 1949
as Samuel Youd
   □ *Giant's Arrow*, 1960; *The Choice*, 1961; *Messages of Love*, 1961; *The Summers At Accorn*, 1963.
● **Peter Graaf**

ZACHARIE DE LISIEUX - PERE (1582-1661)

as Petri Firmiani

☐ *Opuscula, quibus continentur Gyges Gallus. Somnnia sapientis & Saeculi genius,* 1686.

as Louis Fontaines

Relation du Pays de Jansenie, ou Il Est Traitte des Singularitez Qui S'y Trouvent des Coustumes Moeurs et Religion des Habitans. Paris: 1660, 118pp.

A Relation of the Country of Jansenia. . . Composed In French by L. Fontaines, Esq., and Newly Translated by P.B. London: 1668.

ZACHARY, HUGH

as Zach Hughes

The Book of Rack the Healer. NY: Award, [1973], paper.

The Legend of Mairee. NY: Ballantine, [1974], paper.

Seed of the Gods. NY: Berkley, [1974], paper.

Tide. NY: Berkley/Putnam, [1974].

The Stork Factor. NY: Berkley, [1975], paper.

For Texas and Zed. NY: Popular Library, [1976], paper.

The St. Francis Effect. NY: Berkley, [1976], paper.

Tiger In the Stars. NY: Laser, [1976], paper.

ZACHERLE, JOHN (1919-   )

as Zacherley

(ed.) *Zacherley's Midnight Snacks.* NY: Ballantine, [1960], paper. *ss col*

(ed.) *Zacherley's Vulture Stew.* NY: Ballantine, [1960], 160pp., paper. *ss col*

ZAGAT, ARTHUR LEO (1895-1948) *U.S.*

as Arthur Leo Zagat

(with Nat(han) Schachner) The Tower of Evil. *Wonder Stories Quarterly,* Summer 1930

The Great Dome On Mercury. *Astounding,* April 1932

Seven Out of Time. Reading, Pennsylvania: Fantasy Press, 1949, 240pp.

● **Grendon Alzee**

ZELAZNY, ROGER (Joseph) (1937-   ) *U.S.*

Born: Euclid, Ohio

as Harrison Denmark

The Stainless Steel Leech. *Amazing,* April 1963

A Thing of Terrible Beauty. *Fantastic,* April 1963

as Roger Zelazny

Horseman! *Fantastic,* Aug 1962

Passion Play. *Amazing,* Aug 1962

This Immortal. NY: Ace, [1966], 174pp., paper.

The Dream Master. NY: Ace, [1966], 155pp., paper.

Four For Tomorrow. NY: Ace, [1967], 191pp., ill., paper. *col*

Lord of Light. Garden City: Doubleday, 1967, 257pp.

Creatures of Light and Darkness. Garden City: Doubleday, 1969.

Damnation Alley. NY: Putnam, [1969], 157pp.

Isle of the Dead. NY: Ace, [1969], 190pp., paper.

Nine Princes In Amber. Garden City: Doubleday, 1970, 188pp.

The Doors of His Face: The Lamps of His Mouth, and Other Stories. Garden City: Doubleday, 1971, 229pp. *ss col*

Jack of Shadows. NY: Walker, [1971], 207pp.

Guns of Avalon. Garden City: Doubleday, 1972, 180pp.

Today We Choose Faces. NY: Signet, [1973], paper.

To Die In Italbar. Garden City: Doubleday, 1973.

The Sign of the Unicorn. Garden City: Doubleday, 1975.

(with Philip K. Dick) *Deus Irae.* Garden City: Doubleday, 1976.

The Hand of Oberon. Garden City: Doubleday, 1976.

Bridge of Ashes. NY: Signet, [1976], paper.

Doorways In the Sand. NY: Harper & Row, 1976.

My Name Is Legion. NY: Ballantine, [1976], paper.

The Illustrated Roger Zelazny. NY: Baronet, 1978, ill.

ZIEGLER, EDWARD WILLIAM (1932-   ) *U.S.*

Born: New York, New York

as Theodore Tyler

The Man Whose Name Wouldn't Fit; or, The Case of Cartwright-Chickering. Garden City: Doubleday, 1968, 262pp.

as Edward Ziegler

■ *Men Who Make Us Rich,* 1962; *Vested Interests; Their Origins, Development, and Behavior,* 1964.

INDEX

ARMSTRONG, CHARLES WICKSTEED 5
ARMSTRONG, CHARLOTTE see Charlotte Armstrong Lewi 88
ARMSTRONG, GEOFFREY see John Russell Fearn 50
ARMSTRONG, CAPT. JACOB D. see Nathan Cook Meeker 100
ARMSTRONG, T(erence) I(an) F(ytton) 5
ARMSTRONG, WARREN see W. E. Bennett 13
ARNE, AARON see Alf A. Jorgenson 78
ARNETTE, ROBERT [house pseudonym] 5-6
ARNOLD, BIRCH see Alice Elinor Bowen Bartlett 10
ARONIN, BEN see Edna Herron 69
AROUET, FRANCOIS-MARIE 6
ARR, STEPHEN see Stephen A. Rynas 126
ARROW, WILLIAM [house pseudonym] 6
ARTHUR, PETER see Arthur Porges 118
ARTHUR, ROBERT see Robert Arthur Feder 51
ARZHAK, NIKOLAI see Yuli M. Daniel 38
ASH, FENTON see Frank Atkins 7
ASH, PAUL see Pauline Ashwell 6
ASHBEE, C(harles) R(obert) 6
ASHBY, R(ubie) C(onstance) 6
ASHDOWN, CLIFFORD
    see R(ichard) Austin Freeman 54
    see John James Pitcairn 115
ASHE, GORDON see John Creasey 36
ASHKENAZY, IRWIN 6
ASHLEY, FRED see Frank Atkins 7
ASHTON, WINIFRED 6
ASHTON-GWATKIN, FRANK T(relawny) A(rthur) 6
ASHWELL, PAULINE 6
ASIMOV, ISAAC 6-7
ASKHAM, FRANCIS see Julia Eileen Courtney Greenwood 60
ASTLEY, JULIET see Norah Lofts 90
ATHANAS, VERNE see William Verne Athanas 7
ATHANAS, W(illiam) V(erne) 7
ATHELING, WILLIAM, JR. see James Blish 16
ATKEY, PHILIP 7
ATKINS, FRANK 7
ATOMCRACKER, BUZZ-BOLT see Don Wilcox 155
ATTERLEY, JOSEPH see George Tucker 144
AUBREY, FRANK see Frank Atkins 7
AUGUSTA, CLARA see Clara Augusta Jones 77
AUGUSTUS, ALBERT JR. see Charles Nuetzel 107
AUSTIN, FRANK see Frederick Faust 49
AUSTIN, MARY see Jane Rice 123
AUSTIN, MARY H(unter) (Mrs. Stafford W.) 7
AUTHOR OF "ADVENTURES OF JOHN JOHNS" see
    Frederic Carrel 28
AUTHOR OF "BERTRAM" see Charles R. Maturin 99
AUTHOR OF "DARNLEY" see G. P. R. James 75
AUTHOR OF "DELIA" see Mary Pilkington 115
AUTHOR OF "FRANKENSTEIN" see Mary W. Shelley 131
AUTHOR OF "GEORGE BATEMAN" see Elizabeth Blower 17
AUTHOR OF "GRACE RIVERS" see James Malcolm Rymer 126
AUTHOR OF "THE HAUNTED PRIORY" see Stephen Cullen 37
AUTHOR OF "HE" see John De Morgan 41
AUTHOR OF "HOMER TRAVESTIE" see Thomas Bridges
    (of Hull) 20
AUTHOR OF "JOHN BULL IN AMERICA" see James K.
    Paulding 112
AUTHOR OF "JOHN HALIFAX, GENTLEMAN" see Dinah
    M. Craik 35
AUTHOR OF "THE JOURNEY TO LONDON" see William
    King 80
AUTHOR OF "KAZAN" see Edward T. Turnerelli 144
AUTHOR OF "KING SOLOMON'S WIVES" see John De
    Morgan 41
AUTHOR OF "LADY AUDLEY'S SECRET" see Mary Elizabeth
    Braddon Maxwell 99
AUTHOR OF "A LITTLE PILGRIM" see Margaret O. W.
    Oliphant 108
AUTHOR OF "THE LOVER'S OPERA" see William Rufus
    Chetwood 30

AUTHOR OF "MADELEINE" see Isabella Kelly Hedgeland 67
AUTHOR OF "MADEMOISELLE IXE" see Mary Elizabeth
    Hawker 67
AUTHOR OF "MARGARET DUNBAR" see Anne Cox 35
AUTHOR OF "MASTERING FLAME" see Ruth Cranston 35
AUTHOR OF "MEPHISTOPHELES IN LONDON" see R. F.
    Williams 155
AUTHOR OF "MILES WALLINGFORD," ETC. see James
    Fenimore Cooper 34
AUTHOR OF "MONTORIO," AND "THE WILD IRISH BOY"
    see Charles R. Maturin 99
AUTHOR OF "NIGHT AND MORNING" see Edward George
    Bulwer-Lytton 93
AUTHOR OF "OLIVE" see Dinah M. Craik 35
AUTHOR OF "OUR NEIGHBORHOOD" see Mary Griffith 61
AUTHOR OF "PELHAM," "RIENZI," "THE STUDENT," ETC.
    see Edward George Bulwer- Lytton 93
**AUTHOR OF "THE PRAIRIE," "THE RED ROVER," "THE
    PILOT," ETC.** see James Fenimore Cooper 34
AUTHOR OF "REAL PEOPLE" see Marrion Wilcox 155
AUTHOR OF "THE REJUVENATION OF MISS SEMAPHORE"
    see Charlotte O. Eccles 45
AUTHOR OF "RIENZI," "EUGENE ARAM," &C., &C. . .
    see Edward George Bulwer-Lytton 93
AUTHOR OF "THE RISING SUN," &C. see Edward Du Bois 44
AUTHOR OF "SAINT BERNARD'S PRIORY" see Mrs. Harley 65
**AUTHOR OF "SECRET MEMOIRS AND MANNERS OF
    SEVERAL PERSONS. . . FROM THE NEW ATALANTIS"**
    see Mary de la Riviere Manley 98
AUTHOR OF "SPACE AND SPIRIT" see R. A. Kennedy 80
AUTHOR OF "THE SPY," "THE PILOT," ETC. see James
    Fenimore Cooper 34
**AUTHOR OF "A TALE OF A TUB," AND "THE MULLY OF
    MOUNTOWN"** see William King 80
AUTHOR OF "THE TALE OF A TUB" see Jonathan Swift 139
AUTHOR OF "THE TERROR BY NIGHT"
    see Frederick Evelyn Burkitt 25
    see G. C. S. Saben 127
AUTHOR OF "THINGS BY THEIR RIGHT NAMES" see
    Alethea Lewis 88
AUTHOR OF "THOTH" see J. S. Nicholson 105
AUTHOR OF "A TIME OF TERROR" see D(ouglas) M. Ford 53
AUTHOR OF "UNCENSORED RECOLLECTIONS" see Julian
    Osgood Field 51
AUTHOR OF "VIVIAN GREY" see Benjamin Disraeli 42
AUTHOR OF "WAVERLEY" see Sir Walter Scott 129
AUTHOR OF "THE WILDERNESS" see James McHenry 95
**AUTHORESS OF "THE CASTLES OF ATHLIN AND DUN-
    BAYNE"** see Ann Radcliffe 121
AUTHORESS OF "A SICILIAN ROMANCE" &C. see Ann
    Radcliffe 121
AVALLONE, MICHAEL (Angelo), JR. 7-8
AVERY, RICHARD see Edmund Cooper 33
AVICE, CLAUDE 8
AXTON, DAVID see Dean R. Koontz 81
AYCOCK, ROGER D(ee) 8
AYRE, THORNTON see John Russell Fearn 50
AYSCOUGH, JOHN see Monsignor Count Francis B. Bicker-
    staffe-Drew 14

B.,F. see Richard Francis Burton 26
B., M. see Frederick Faust 49
**B., R., AUTHOR OF "THE HISTORY OF THE WARS OF
    ENGLAND, &C."** see Nathaniel Crouch 37
BACHELDER, JOHN 8
BACKSIGHT-FORETHOUGHT see Ernest D. Swinton 139
BADGER, RICHARD C. see Eric Temple Bell 13
BAHL, FRANKLIN [house pseudonym] 8
BAILEY, THOMAS see Edward Bellamy Partridge 112
BAKER, RACHEL MADDUX (Mrs. King) 8
BALCHIN, NIGEL MARLIN 8
BALDERSTON, JOHN L. see J. C(ollings) Squire 136

BALDWIN, EDWARD see William Godwin 58
BALDWIN, FAITH see Nadir Khan 104
BALDWIN, OLIVER RIDSDALE 8
BALFORT, NEIL see R. Lionel Fanthorpe 47
BALFOUR, FREDERIC H(enry) 8
BALFOUR, M. MELVILLE see Margaret M. Balfour 8
BALFOUR, MARGARET MELVILLE 8
BALL, B(rian) N. 9
BALLARD, K. G. see Holly Roth Fanta 47
BALLINGER, BILL S. see William S. Ballinger 9
BALLINGER, W. A. see Wilfred McNeilly 97
BALLINGER, WILLIAM S(anborn) 9
BALTER, E. 9
BANAT, D. R. see Ray Bradbury 19
BANCROFT, LAURA see L. Frank Baum 11
BANGS, F. H. see John Kendrick Bangs 9
BANGS, JOHN KENDRICK 9
BANIM, JOHN 9
BANIM, MICHAEL 9
BANKOFF, GEORGE ALEXIS see Alexis Milkomane 101
BANKS, EDWARD see Ray Bradbury 19
BANSHUCK, GREGO see Hugo Gernsback 57
BARBARA see Mabel Osgood Wright 159
BARBEE, PHILLIPS see Robert Sheckley 130
BARBER, MARGARET FAIRLESS 9
BARBET, PIERRE see Claude Avice 8
BARCLAY, ALAN see George B. Tait 140
BARCLAY, FLORENCE LOUISA CHARLESWORTH (Mrs.) 9
BARCLAY, GABRIEL [house pseudonym] 9-10
BARCYNSKA, COUNTESS see Marguerite F. Evans 47
BARFIELD, ARTHUR OWEN 10
BARFIELD, OWEN see Arthur Owen Barfield 10
BARGONE, FREDERIC CHARLES PIERRE EDOUARD 10
BARHAM, RICHARD H(arris) 10
BARKER, GRANVILLE see Harley G. Granville-Barker 60
BARKER, LEONARD N(oel) 10
BARLAY, BENNET see Kendell F. Crossen 37
BARLOW, JAMES WILLIAM 10
BARNABY, HUGO see Ernest H. Fitzpatrick 52
BARNARD, MARJORIE FAITH 10
BARNES, ARTHUR KELVIN 10
BARNES, DAVE see Arthur K. Barnes 10
BARON CORVO see Frederick (W.) Rolfe 125
BARON MUNCHAUSEN see Hugo Gernsback 57
BARON MUNCHAUSEN see Rudolph E. Raspe 121
BARONTI, (Princess) GERVE(e) see Baronte Gerve(e) 57
BARR, ROBERT 10
BARRETT, A. W. see William E. Clery 31
BARRETT, ALFRED W(alter) 10
BARRETTON, GRANDAL(l) see Gordon Randall Garrett 56
BARRETTON, GRANDELL see Gordon Randall Garrett 56
BARRINGTON, E. see Eliza Adams Beck 12
BARRINGTON, MICHAEL
  see Barrington J. Bayley 12
  see Michael Moorcock 102
BARRY, B. X. see R. A. Giles 58
BARSHOFSKY, PHILIP see M. M. Kaplan 79
BARSTOW, EMMUSKA ORCAY (Mrs. Montagu W.) 10
BARTEL, PHILIP JACQUES see M. M. Kaplan 79
BARTIMEUS see Lewis Ritchie 124
BARTLE, L. E. 10
BARTLETT, ALICE ELINOR BOWEN 10
BARTLETT, MRS. J. M. D. see Alice Elinor Bowen Bartlett 11
BARTON, ERLE see R. Lionel Fanthorpe 47
BARTON, EUSTACE ROBERT (Dr.) 11
BARTON, LEE see R. Lionel Fanthorpe 48
BARTON, OTHELLO see R. Lionel Fanthorpe 48
BARUCH, HUGO 11
BASS, T. J. see Thomas J. Bassler 11
BASSETT, EDWARD BARNARD 11
BASSLER, THOMAS J. 11
BATES, HARRY 11

BATES, H(erbert) E(rnest) 11
BATH, OLIVER see Hardinge Goulburn Giffard 58
BAUM, L(yman) FRANK 11
BAXTER, GEORGE OWEN see Frederick Faust 49
BAXTER, GREGORY
  see Eric de Banzie 39
  see John Ressich 122
BAXTER, JOHN (Martin) 11
BAYER, T. M. see Isador Schneider 128
BAYLEY, B(arrington) J. 12
BEACH, TOM see Larry Mark Harris 65
BEAL, NICK see Forrest J. Ackerman 1
BEALE, ANNE see F. Orlin Tremaine 142
BEAN, NORMAN see Edgar Rice Burroughs 25
BEARD, JAMES H. 12
BEAUJON, PAUL see Beatrice Lamberton Warde 151
BEAUMONT, CHARLES see Charles Nutt 107
BEAUMONT, E. J. see Charles Nutt 107
BEAUMONT, EDGAR (Dr.) 12
BECHDOLT, JACK see John Ernest Bechdolt 12
BECHDOLT, JOHN ERNEST 12
BECK, ALLEN see Hugh B. Cave 29
BECK, CHRISTOPHER see Thomas C. Bridges 20
BECK, ELIZA LOUISA (Moresby) ADAMS (Mrs.) 12
BECK, L(ily) ADAMS see Eliza Adams Beck 12
BEDFORD, DONALD F.
  see H. Bedford-Jones 12
  see Kenneth Fearing 50
BEDFORD-JONES, H(enry) (James O'Brien) 12
BEDROD-FORAN, CAPT.
  see H. Bedford-Jones 12
  see Capt. W. Robert Foran 52
BEECHAM, ALICE see E. C. Tubb 143
BEECHER, LEE see Stanley Mullen 103
BEECHER, STANLEY see Stanley Mullen 103
BEEDING, FRANCIS
  see John Palmer 111
  see Hilary A. Saunders 127
BEESLEY, DOROTHY GLADYS SMITH (Mrs. Alec Macbeth) 12
BEFFROY DE REIGNY, LOUIS ABEL 12
BEGBIE, HAROLD 12
BEITH, JOHN HAY 12
BELASCO, DAVID 12
  see Albert Payson Terhune (ghostwriter) 140
BELDONE, PHIL "CHEECH" see Harlan Ellison 46
BELFOUR, HUGO JOHN 13
BELL, ACTON see Anne Bronte 21
BELL, CURRER see Charlotte Bronte 21
BELL, ELLIS see Emily J. Bronte 21
BELL, EMERSON see Gilbert Patten 112
BELL, ERIC TEMPLE 13
BELL, JOHN KEBLE 13
BELL, NEIL see Stephen Southwold 136
BELL, THORNTON see R. Lionel Fanthorpe 48
BELLIN, EDWARD J. [house pseudonym] 13
BENEDICT, STEVE 13
BENEFICE see Frederick U. Worley 158
BENJAMIN, LEWIS SAUL 13
BENNET, ROBERT A(mes) see F. G. Browne 22
BENNETT, GEOFFREY MARTIN 13
BENNETT, GERTRUDE BARROWS 13
BENNETT, W(illiam) E(dward) 13
BENSON, ALLAN INGVALD 13
BENSON, EDWIN [house pseudonym] 13
  see Richard Shaver 130
BENSON, STELLA see Stella Benson Anderson 5
BERCKMAN, EVELYN (Domenica) 13
BERESFORD, LESLIE 13
BERINGTON, SIMON 14
BERKELEY, ANTHONY see A(nthony) B(erkeley) Cox 35
IL BERNIA see Mario Teluccini 140
BERRY, BRYAN 14

BERRY, D. BRUCE see Andrew J. Offutt 108
BERTIN, EDDIE C. see Eddy C. Bertin 14
BERTIN, EDDY C. 14
BESSIERE, RICHARD 14
BESTER, ALFRED 14
BETA see Edward Barnard Bassett 11
BETHLEN, T. D. see Robert Silverberg 132
BETTERIDGE, DON see Bernard Newman 105
BEYNON, JOHN see John B(eynon) Harris 65
BICKERSTAFF, ISAAC see Jonathan Swift 139
BICKERSTAFFE, ISAAC JR. see H. P. Lovecraft 91
BICKERSTAFFE-DREW, FRANCIS BROWNING (Monsignor Count) 14
BIERCE, AMBROSE (Gwinnett) 14
BIGLY, CANTELL A. see George Washington Peck 113
BIGNON, JEAN PAUL, ABBE 14
BILBO, JACK see Hugo Baruch 11
BINDER, EANDO
   see Earl Andrew Binder 14
   see Otto Oscar Binder 15
BINDER, EARL ANDREW 14
BINDER, OTTO OSCAR 15
BINGFIELD, WILLIAM see Robert Paltock 111
BINGHAM, CARSON see Bruce Cassiday 29
BIRD, C. see Harlan Ellison 45
BIRD, CORDWAINER see Harlan Ellison 45
BIRD, CORTWAINER see Harlan Ellison 45
BIRKIN, CHARLES L(loyd) 15
BIRKENHEAD, EARL OF see Frederick E. Smith 135
BIRON, CHARTRES see Henry C. Biron 15
BIRON, HENRY CHARTRES 15
BISHOP, ZEALIA BROWN REED (Mrs. D. W.) 15
BIXBY, DREXEL JEROME LEWIS 15
BIXBY, JEROME see Drexel Jerome Bixby 15
BLACK, MANSELL see Elleston Trevor 142
BLADE, ALEXANDER [house pseudonym] 15-16
BLAINE, JOHN
   see H. L. Goodwin 59
   see Peter J. Harkins 64
BLAIR, ANDREW 16
BLAIR, ANDREW J(ames) F(raser) 16
BLAIR, ERIC ARTHUR 16
BLAIR, HAMISH see Andrew J. F. Blair 16
BLAISDELL, ANNE see (Barbara) Elizabeth Linington 89
BLAISDELL, ANNE see Elinor Blaisdell Rosenberg 125
BLAISDELL, ELINOR see Elinor Blaisdell Rosenberg 125
BLAKE, ANTHONY see E. C. Tubb 143
BLAKE, NICHOLAS see C. Day-Lewis 39
BLAND, EDITH NESBIT 16
BLAND, FABIAN see Edith Nesbit Bland 16
BLASSINGAME, WYATT RAINEY 16
BLAUSTEIN, ALBERT P(aul) 16
BLAYN, HUGO see John Russell Fearn 50
BLAYRE, CHRISTOPHER see Edward Heron-Allen 69
BLISH, JAMES (Benjamin) 16
BLISH, MRS. JAMES see Mildred Virginia Kidd 80
BLISH, VIRGINIA see Mildred Virginia Kidd 80
BLISS, ADAM
   see Eve Burkhardt 25
   see Robert F. Burkhardt 25
BLIXEN, KAREN see Karen Blixen-Finecke 17
BLIXEN, TANIA see Karen Blixen-Finecke 17
BLIXEN-FINECKE, KAREN CHRISTENTZE DINESEN 17
BLOCH, ROBERT (Albert) 17
BLOODSTONE, JOHN see Stuart J. Byrne 26
BLOT, THOMAS see William Simpson 134
BLOW, MARYA MANNES (Mrs. Richard) 17
BLOWER, ELIZABETH 17
"BLUE WOLF" see Robert Scott 129
BLUEMANTLE, (Mrs.) BRIDGET see Elizabeth Thomas 141
BLYTH, HARRY 17
BOAISTUAL, PIERRE see Pierre Boaistual de Launay 17

BOAISTUAL DE LAUNAY, PIERRE 17
BOEHM, HERB see John Varley 147
BOEX, JOSEPH HENRI HONORE 18
BOEX, SERAPHIN JUSTIN FRANCOIS 18
BOISGILBERT, EDMUND (M.D.) see Ignatius Donnelly 43
BOK, HANNES (Vajn) see Wayne Woodward 158
BOLAND, BERTRAM J(ohn) 18
BOLAND, JOHN see Bertram J. Boland 18
BOLDREWOOD, ROLFE see Thomas A. Browne 22
BOLITHO, HECTOR see Henry Hector Bolitho 18
BOLITHO, HENRY HECTOR 18
BOLT, LEE see Frederick Faust 49
BOND, J. HARVEY see Russell R. Winterbotham 157
BOND, NELSON S(lade) 18
BOND, STEPHEN 18
BONEHILL, CAPT. RALPH see Edward Stratemeyer 138
BOREL, MARGUERITE (Appell) 18
BORODIN, GEORGE see Alexis Milkomane 101
"A BOSTONIAN" see Edgar A(llan) Poe 116
BOTT, HENRY 18
BOTTSFORD, LORD see James D. Hird 70
BOUCHER, ANTHONY see William Anthony Parker White 154
BOULT, S. KYE see William E. Cochran 32
BOUNDS, SYDNEY JAMES 18
BOWEN, ELIZABETH see Elizabeth Cameron 27
BOWEN, MARJORIE see Gabrielle M. V. Long 91
BOWER, B. M. see Bertha M. Sinclair 134
BOWER, JOHN G(raham) 18
BOX, EDGAR see Gore Vidal 148
BOYCE, MORTON see John Russell Fearn 50
BOYD, E. see Ray Bradbury 19
BOYD, FELIX see Harry Harrison 65
BOYD, JOHN see Boyd Bradfield Upchurch 145
BOYD, LYLE G(ifford) (Mrs. William C.) 18
BOYD, WILLIAM C(louser) 18
BOYLE, KAY see Kay Boyle Vail 146
BOYLE, CAPT. ROBERT see William Rufus Chetwood 30
BRACE, TIMOTHY see Theodore Pratt 118
BRACKETT, LEIGH see Leigh Brackett Hamilton 64
BRADBURY, EDWARD P. see Michael Moorcock 102
BRADBURY, RAY (Douglas) 19
BRADDON, GEORGE see Alexis Milkomane 101
BRADDON, M(ary) E(lizabeth) see Mary Elizabeth Braddon Maxwell 99
BRADEN, WALTER see Walter Braden Finney 51
BRADFORD, ADAM see Joseph Wasserburg 151
BRADLEY, ALICE see Alice Bradley Sheldon 130
BRADLEY, MARION ZIMMER see Marion Zimmer Bradley Breen 20
BRAINERD, CHAUNCEY COREY 19
BRAINERD, EDITH RATHBONE (Jacobs) 19
BRAITHWAITE, RAYMOND see Frank Owen 110
BRA[I]THWAIT[E], RICHARD 19
BRAMAH, ERNEST see Ernest Brammah Smith 135
BRAND, CHRISTIANNA see Mary Christianna (Milne) Lewis 88
BRAND, MAX see Frederick Faust 49
BRANDON, CARL see Terry Carr 28
BRANSBY, EMMA LINDSAY SQUIER (Mrs. John) 20
BRASH, MARGARET MAUD 20
BRAWNER, H. see F. Van Wyck Mason 99
BREBNER, PERCY 20
BREEN, MARION ELEANOR ZIMMER BRADLEY (Mrs. Walter) 20
BREHAT, ALFRED (de) see Alfred Guezenec 61
BRENDALL, EDITH see Eddy C. Bertin 14
BRENGLE, WILLIAM [house pseudonym] 20
BRENT, LORING see George F. Worts 158
BRENTFORD, BURKE see Nathan D. Urner 145
BRETNOR, REGINALD 20
BRETT, LEO see R. Lionel Fanthorpe 48
BREUER, MILES J. see John Stewart Williamson 156
BRIARTON, GRENDEL see Reginald Bretnor 20
BRIDGE, ANN see Mary D. O'Malley 109

"CARLETON-MILECETE" see Susan Carleton Jones 78
CARNAC, LEVIN see George Griffith-Jones 61
CARPENTER, MORLEY see E. C. Tubb 143
CARR, JOHN DICKSON 28
CARR, TERRY 28
CARREL, FREDERIC 28
CARRINGTON, HEREWARD HUBERT LAVINGTON 28
CARROLL, LEWIS see Charles L. Dodgson 42-43
CARTER, BRUCE see Richard (Alexander) Hough 71
CARTER, JOHN FRANKLIN 28
CARTER, JOHN L(ouis) J(ustin) 28
CARTER, LIN(wood) (Vrooman) 28
CARTER, MARGERY LOUISE ALLINGHAM (Mrs. Phillip Y.) 29
CARTER, NICHOLAS see John Russell Coryell 34
CARTER, NICK [house pseudonym]
    see John Russell Coryell 34
    see Ormond G. Smith 135
CARTER, PAUL A. 29
CARTER, PHILIP see Paul A. Carter 29
CARTMELL, ROBERT 29
CARTMILL, CLEVE 29
CASE, JUSTIN see Hugh B. Cave 29
CASELEYR, CAMILLE AUGUST MARIE 29
CASEY, KENT see Kenneth McIntosh 96
CASEY, RICHARD [house pseudonym] 29
CASSABA, CARLOS see Michael Patrick Parry 112
CASSIDAY, BRUCE BINGHAM 29
CASSIDAY, DORIS see Bruce Cassiday 29
"CASSIUS" see Michael Foot 52
CASTLE, ROBERT see Edmond Hamilton 63
CASTLETOWN, LORD see Bernard E. Fitzpatrick 52
CASWELL, EDWARD A. 29
CAVE, HUGH B(arnett) 29
CAVENDISH, PETER see Sydney Horler 71
CAXTON, PISISTRATUS see Edward George Bulwer-Lytton 93
CECIL, HENRY see David H. Keller 79
CENTE, H. F. see Ross Rocklynne 124
CERVANTES see William Henry Ireland 74
CERVUS, G. I. see William J. Roe 125
CHABER, M. E. see Ken(dell) F. Crossen 37
CHAIN, JULIAN see Julian Chain May Dikty 42
CHALLIS, GEORGE see Frederick Faust 49
CHAMBERS, DANA see Albert Leffingwell 87
CHANCELLOR, JOHN see Charles de Balzac Rideaux 123
CHANDLER, A. BERTRAM 29
CHANDLER, BERTRAM A. see A. Bertram Chandler 30
CHANDLER, LAWRENCE see Howard Browne 22
CHAPIN, ANNA A. see George C. Jenks 77
CHAPMAN, ALLEN see Edward Stratemeyer 138
CHAPMAN, MARGARET STORM (Jameson) (Mrs. Guy P.) 30
CHAPMAN, WALKER see Robert Silverberg 132
CHAPMAN, WALTER see Robert Silverberg 132
CHAPNIK, MORRIS see Forrest J. Ackerman 1
CHARBY, JAY see Harlan Ellison 45
CHARLES-HENNEBERG, NATHILIE
    see Nathilie Henneberg zu Irmelshausen Wasungen 68
    see Charles Henneberg 68
CHASE, ADAM
    see Paul W. Fairman 47
    see **Ivar Jorgensen** 78
    see Milton Lesser 87
CHASE, ALICE see Georgess McHargue 95
CHASE, CLEVELAND B. see H. Bedford-Jones 12
CHASE, JAMES HADLEY see Rene Raymond 121
CHATRIAN, ALEXANDRE 30
CHAUCER, DANIEL see Ford Maddox Ford 53
CHER, MARIE see Marie Scherr 128
CHESNEY, WEATHERBY see C. J. Cutliffe Hyne 73
CHESTER, LORD see Cyrus Reed Teed 140
CHETWOOD, WILLIAM RUFUS 30
CHILDERS, ERSKINE see Robert Erskine Childers 30
CHILDERS, ROBERT ERSKINE 30

CHILDS, EDMUND BURTON 30
CHINWELL, WALTER see Forrest J. Ackerman 1
CHIPPENFIELD, ROBERT ORR see Isabel E. Ostrander 110
CHOATE, LOWELL see Alice K. Hopkins 71
CHOLERIC, BROTHER see Hubert Van Zeller 147
CHRISTIE, AGATHA see Agatha Mallowan 97
CHRISTIE, MRS. ARCHIBALD see Agatha Mallowan 97
CHRISTOPHER, JOHN see C. S. Youd 160
CHURTON, HENRY see Albion W. Tourgee 142
CIARDI, JOHN 30
CLARK, CHARLES H(eber) 30
CLARK, CURT see Donald E. Westlake 153
CLARK, CYNTHIA CHARLOTTE (Moon) 30
CLARKE, A. V. see H. Kenneth Bulmer 24
CLARKE, ARTHUR C(harles) 30
CLARKE, COVINGTON see Clarke Venable 147
CLARK(e), DALE see Ronal Kayser 79
CLARKE, F(rancis) H. 31
CLARKE, GEORGE S(ydenham) (1st Baron Sydenham of Combe) 31
CLARKSON, L. see Louise Whitelock 154
CLAY, BERTHA M. see John Russell Coryell 35
CLAY, CHARLES M. see Cynthia Clark 30
CLAYTON, RICHARD HENRY MICHAEL 31
CLEISHBOTHAM, JEDEDIAH see Sir Walter Scott 129
CLEMENS, SAMUEL L(anghorne) 31
CLEMENT, HAL see Harry Clement Stubbs 138
CLERK, N. W. see C(live) S(taples) Lewis 88
CLERY, WILLIAM E. 31
CLEVE, JOHN see Andrew J. Offutt 108
CLIFFORD, CHARLES see William Henry Ireland 74
CLINTON, DIRK see Robert Silverberg 132
CLINTON, ED(win) M. JR. 31
CLIVE, ARTHUR see Standish James O'Grady 108
CLIVE, DENNIS see John Russell Fearn 50
CLOUKEY, CHARLES see Charles Cloutier 31
CLOUTIER, CHARLES 31
CLYDE, KIT see Lu(is) (P.) Senarens 129
COBB, CLAYTON W. see J. A. Patten 112
COBBE, FRANCES POWER 31
COCHRAN, WILLIAM E. 32
COCKBURN, CLAUDE see Francis Claude
    Cockburn 32
COCKBURN, FRANCIS CLAUDE 32
CODY, C. S. see Leslie Waller 150
CODY, JOHN see Ed Earl Repp 122
COE, TUCKER see Donald E. Westlake 153
COFFEY, BRIAN see Dean R. Koontz 81
COFFIN, GEOFFREY see F. Van Wyck Mason 99
COHEN, CHESTER 32
COLE, LES(ter) 32
COLERIDGE, JOHN
    see Earl Andrew Binder 14
    see Otto Oscar Binder 15
COLES, CYRIL HENRY 32
COLES, MANNING
    see Cyril Henry Coles 32
    see Adelaide F. O. Manning 98
COLEY, ROBERT see Howard Wandrei 150
COLLIER, HARRY see Harry Walton 150
COLLIN DE PLANCY, J. see Jacques Simon Collin de Plancy 32
COLLIN DE PLANCY, J. A. S. see Jacques Simon Collin
    de Plancy 32
COLLIN DE PLANCY, JACQUES SIMON 32
COLLINGWOOD, HARRY see William C. Lancaster 84
COLLINS, EDWARD JAMES MORTIMER 32
COLLINS, HUNT see S. A. Lombino 90
COLLINS, J. L. 32
COLLINS, MABEL C. see Mabel C. Cook 33
COLLINS, MICHAEL see Dennis Lynds 93
COLLINS, MORTIMER see Edward James Mortimer Collins 32
COLLINS, WILKIE see (William) Wilkie Collins 32
COLLINS, (William) WILKIE 32

COLLINSON, OWEN see Harry Collinson Owen 110
COLLINSON, PETER see (Samuel) Dashiell Hammett 64
COLMORE, G. see Gertrude Weaver 152
COLODNY, ROBERT see (Samuel) Dashiell Hammett 64
COLSON, BILL see William Verne Athanas 7
COLT, WINCHESTER REMINGTON see L. Ron Hubbard 72
COLVIN, JAMES see Michael Moorcock 102
COMBE, WILLIAM 32
COMFORT, JANE LEVINGTON see Jane Levington Comfort
        Sturtzel 139
COMFORT, MONTGOMERY see John Ramsey Campbell 27
COMPTON, D(avid) G(uy) 33
COMRADE, ROBERT W. see Edwy S. Brooks 21
CONANT, CHESTER B. see Chester Cohen 32
CONKLIN, EDWARD GROFF 33
CONKLIN, GROFF see Edward Groff Conklin 33
CONN, ALAN see Alan Connell 33
CONNELL, ALAN 33
CONNINGTON, J(ohn) J(ervis) see Alfred Walter Stewart 137
CONNOLLY, PAUL see Thomas Grey Wicker 155
CONQUEST, (George) ROBERT (Acworth) 33
CONQUEST, JOAN see Joan Conquest Cooke 33
CONQUEST, ROBERT see (George) Robert (Acworth) Conquest 33
CONRAD, GREGG see Roger P. Graham 59
CONRAD, JOSEPH see Josef Konrad Theodor Korzeniowski 82
CONWAY, BOWEN see John B. Michel 100
CONWAY, GERARD (F.) 33
CONWAY, HUGH see Frederick J. Fargus 48
CONWAY, PETER see Alexis Milkomane 101
CONWAY, RITTER see Damon Knight 81
CONWAY, TROY see Michael Avallone Jr. 8
COOK, CHRISTINE CAMPBELL THOMSON (Mrs. Oscar) 33
COOK, DON see H(arold) L(eland) Goodwin 59
COOK, MABEL C(ollins) (Mrs. Kenningsgate) 33
COOK, WILLIAM WALLACE
    see George C. Jenks 77
COOKE, ARTHUR
    see E. Balter 9
    see Cyril Kornbluth 82
    see Robert W. Lowndes 92
    see John Michel 100
    see Donald A. Wollheim 157
COOKE, JOAN CONQUEST (Mrs. Leonard) 33
COOKE, JOHN ESTES see L. Frank Baum 11
COOKE, MARGARET see John Creasey 36
COOMB, WILLIAM see William Combe 33
COOPER, EDMUND 33
COOPER, HENRY ST. JOHN see John Creasey 36
COOPER, JAMES FENIMORE 34
COOPER, JEFFERSON see Gardner F. Fox 53
COOPER, MERIAN C. see Edgar Wallace 150
COOVER, WAYNE see Wolf Detlef Rohr 125
COPPEL, ALFRED see Alfredo Coppel, Jr. 34
COPPEL, ALFREDO JOSE DE MARINI Y, JR. 34
CORBETT, CHAN see Nathan Schachner 128
CORBETT, E(lizabeth) B(urgoyne) (Mrs. George) 34
CORBETT, G. see Elizabeth B. Corbett 34
CORBIN, MICHAEL see Cleve Cartmill 29
CORD, BARRY see Peter B. Germano 57
CORELLI, MARIE see Mary MacKay 96
CORLEY, ERNEST see H. Kenneth Bulmer 25
CORNING, KYLE see Erle Stanley Gardner 55
CORNWELL, DAVID JOHN MOORE 34
CORREY, LEE see G. Harry Stine 137
CORSTON, GEORGE see Michael George Corston 34
CORSTON, MICHAEL GEORGE 34
CORTES, DIANA see Winifred Ashton 6
CORVAIS, ANTHONY see Ray Bradbury 19
CORVO, BARON see Frederick (W.) Rolfe 125
CORWIN, CECIL see Cyril Kornbluth 82
CORY, HOWARD L.
    see Jack Owen Jardine 76

    see Julie Ann Jardine 76
CORY, MATILDA WINIFRED MURIEL (Graham) (Mrs.) 34
CORY, VIVIAN 34
CORYELL, JOHN RUSSELL 34
CORYMBOEUS see Richard Braithwaite 20
COSGROVE, RACHEL see Rachel Cosgrove Payes 113
COST, MARCH see Margaret Mackie Morrison 102
COSTANZA, SENORA see Gabrielle M. V. Long 91
COSTELLO, P. F. [house pseudonym] 35
COTES, MAY see Charles Grant Allen 2
COTTERELL, BRIAN see Aylward Edward Dingle 42
COTTON, JOHN see John Russell Fearn 50
COTTON, JOHN see Manly Wade Wellman 153
COTTON, JUNIOR see Thomas Bridges (of Hull) 20
COTTON, ROBERT TURNER see Edward James Mortimer
        Collins 32
COUCH, A. T. Q. see Arthur T. Quiller-Couch 120
COULSON, JUANITA RUTH WELLONS (Mrs. Robert S.) 35
COULSON, ROBERT S. 35
COUPLING, J. J. see J(ohn) (R.) Pierce 115
COURTNEY, ROBERT see Harlan Ellison 45
COUSIN-JACQUES see Louis Abel Beffroy de Reigny 12
COVE, JOSEPH WALTER 35
COWPER, RICHARD see John Middleton Murry 103
COX, ANNE 35
COX, A(nthony) B(erkeley) 35
COX, ARTHUR JEAN 35
COX, JEAN see Arthur Jean Cox 35
COXE, EDWARD D. 35
COXE, KATHLEEN BUDDINGTON see A(melia) R(eynolds)
        Long 90
COXON, MURIEL (Hine) (Mrs. Sidney) 35
CRACKEN, JAEL see Brian W. Aldiss 2
CRADDOCK, CHARLES EGBERT see Mary N. Murfree 103
CRAFT, ZACHARY see Charles Kelsall 80
CRAIG, A. A. see Poul Anderson 5
CRAIG, RANDOLPH see Norvell W. Page 111
CRAIG, WEBSTER see Eric Frank Russell 126
CRAIGIE, DAVID see Dorothy M. Craigie 35
CRAIGIE, DOROTHY M. 35
CRAIK, DINAH MARIA MULOCK (Mrs. George L.) 35
CRANE, ROBERT see Bernard Glemser 58
CRANE, ROBERT see Frank Chester Robertson 124
CRANSTON, RUTH (Mrs.) 35
CRAWFORD, MARGARET (Mrs. William L.) 36
CRAWFORD, WILLIAM L. 36
CRAYON, DIEDRICK, Jr. see Kenneth Bruce 22
CRAYON, GEOFFREY see Washington Irving 74
CREASEY, JOHN 36
CRELLIN, H. N. see Horatio (Nelson) Crellin 36
CRELLIN, HORATIO (Nelson) 36
CREUTZBERGS, AMADEI see Philipp Balthasar Sinhold von
        Schutz 134
CRICHTON, DOUGLAS see Michael Crichton 36
CRICHTON, MICHAEL 36
CRISPIN, EDMUND see Robert Bruce Montgomery 102
CRISTABEL see Christine Abrahamsen 1
CRITCHIE, ESTIL see Arthur J. Burks 25
CRITTEN, STEPHEN H. see Stephen Southwold 136
CROCKER, SAMUEL 36
CROFTANGRY, CHRYSTAL see Sir Walter Scott 129
CROFTS, ANNA HELEN see H. P. Lovecraft 92
CROLY, HERBERT DAVID 36
CROMPTON, RICHMAL see Richmal Crompton Lamburn 84
CRONIN, BERNARD CHARLES 36
CROOK, COMPTON N. 36
CROSBY, HARRY C. 36
CROSS, AMANDA see Carolyn G. Heilbrun 68
CROSS, JOHN KEIR 36
CROSS, POULTON see John Russell Fearn 50
CROSS, VICTORIA see Vivian Cory 34
CROSSE, VICTORIA see Vivian Cory 34

CROSSEN, KENDELL F(oster) 37
CROUCH, NATHANIEL 37
CROW, LEVI see Manly Wade Wellman 153
CROWE, JOHN see Dennis Lynds 93
CROWN, PETER J. 37
CROWNINSHIELD, MARY BRADFORD (Mrs. Schuyler) 37
CROWNINSHIELD, (Mrs. Schuyler) see Mary Bradford
    Crowninshield 37
CRUGER, JULIA GRINNELL (Storrow) (Mrs. Van Rensselaer) 37
CULLEN, STEPHEN 37
CULVER, TIMOTHY J. see Donald E. Westlake 153
CUMMINGS, M(onette) A. 37
CUMMINGS, (Mrs. Ray) 37
CUMMINGS, RAY(mond) KING 37
CUNNINGHAM, CECIL CLAYBOURNE see Ray Bradbury 19
CUNNINGHAM, E. see Ray Bradbury 19
CUNNINGHAM, E. V. see Howard Fast 49
CUNNINGHAM, J. MORGAN see Donald E. Westlake 154
CURTIES, T. J. HORSLEY 37
CURTIS, PETER see Norah Lofts 90
CURTIS, PRICE see Harlan Ellison 45
CURZON-HERRICK, (Maud) KATHLEEN (Cairnes) (Plantagenet)
    (Lady) 38
CUSTANCE, LEO see (C.) Ranger Gull 62
CYRUS see Cyrus Reed Teed 140

D., W. J. see Walter J. de la Mare 40
DAHLGREN, MADELEINE see Sarah Madeleine (Vinton)
    Dahlgren 38
DAHLGREN, SARAH MADELEINE (Vinton) (Mrs. John A.) 38
DAKERS, ELAINE KIDNER (Mrs. Andrew) 38
DALE, GEORGE E. see Isaac Asimov 7
DALE, NORMAN see E. C. Tubb 143
DALEY, BERNARD JOHN 38
DALEY, JOHN BERNARD see Bernard John Daley 38
DALTON, PRISCILLA see Michael Avallone Jr. 8
DALY, HAMLIN see E. Hoffman Price 119
DAMON, GENE see Marion Zimmer Bradley Breen 20
DANBY, FRANK see Julia Frankau 54
DANE, CLEMENCE see Winifred Ashton 6
DANE, MARK see Michael Avallone Jr. 8
DANE, W.N. see Wendayne Ackerman 1
DANIEL, GLYN E(dmund) 38
DANIEL, JOHN see Ralph Morris 102
DANIEL, YULI MARKOVICH 38
DANIELS, LOUIS G see Daniel F. Galouye 55
DANNAY, FREDERIC 38
DANRIT, CAPTAIN see Emile A. Driant 43
DANRIT, CAPTAINE see Emile A. Driant 43
DANVERS, JACK see Camille August Marie Caseleyr 29
DANZELL, GEORGE see Nelson S. Bond 18
DANZIGER, ADOLPHE see Gustaf Adolf Danziger de Castro 40
DANZIGER, G(ustav) A. see Gustaf Adolf Danziger de Castro 40
D'APERY, HELEN (Burrell) (Mrs.) 39
DARBY, MARY see Mrs. M(ary) Robinson 124
DARE, ALAN see George Goodchild 59
DARE, HOWARD see Stuart J. Byrne 26
DARLTON, CLARK see Walter Ernsting 46
DARYL, PHILLIPE see Paschal Grousset 61
DASHIELL, SAMUEL see (Samuel) Dashiell Hammett 64
DAUKES, S(idney) H(erbert) 39
DAVID, K. see Alice A. Robertson 124
DAVIDSON, GENE A. see David Lesperance 87
DAVIDSON, HUGH see Edmond Hamilton 63
DAVIDSON, MARION see Howard Roger Garis 55
DAVIES, FREDERICK see Ron(ald) D. Ellik 45
DAVIES, HOWELL 39
DAVIES, M(ary) C(atherine) 39
DAVIES, WALTER C. see Cyril Kornbluth 82
DAVIOT, GORDON see Elizabeth MacKintosh 96
DAVIS, CHAN see Horace Chandler Davis 39
DAVIS, E. E. see John R. Pierce 115

DAVIS, HORACE CHANDLER 39
DAVIS, JAMES 39
DAVIS, JULIA see John Marsh 98
D'AVOI, PAUL see Paul Erie 46
DAWSON, PETER see Frederick Faust 49
DAY, EMILY FOSTER (Mrs. Frank R.) 39
DAY, MAX see Bruce Cassiday 29
DAY-LEWIS, C(ecil) 39
DE ACTON, EUGENIA see Alethea Lewis 88
DEAN, DUDLEY see Dudley Dean McGaughy 94
DEANE, NORMAN see John Creasey 36
DEARBORN, LAURA see Nina Picton 115
DE BANZIE, ERIC(h) 39
DE BURY, F. BLAZE (Mademoiselle) 39
DE CAMP, CATHERINE CROOK (Mrs. L. Sprague) 39
DE CAMP, L(yon) SPRAGUE 39
DE CASTRO, ADOLF see Gustaf Adolf Danziger de Castro 40
DE CASTRO, GUSTAF ADOLF DANZIGER 40
DEE, NICHOLAS see Joan Aiken 1
DEE, ROGER see Roger D. Aycock 8
DEEMING, RICHARD see Richard Deming 41
DEER, M. J.
    see George H. Smith 135
    see M(ary) J. Deer Smith 135
DE FORD, MIRIAM ALLEN see Miriam Allen de Ford Shipley 131
DE GLANAVILLE, BARON see Jacques Simon Collin de Plancy 32
DE GRAEFF, ALLEN see Albert P(aul) Blaustein 16
DEGRAEFF, W. B. see Edward Groff Conklin 33
DEHAN, RICHARD see Clotilde I. M. Graves 60
DE LA MARE, WALTER J(ohn) 40
DELARO, SELINA see Edward Heron-Allen 69
DE LAUTREAMONT, COMPTE see Isidore L. Ducasse 44
DE LISTONAI, MR. see Villeneuve 148
DELL, DUDLEY see Horace L. Gold 58
DEL MARTIA, ASTRON see John Russell Fearn 50
DELORME, CHARLES see Charles Rumball 125
DEL REY, LESTER see R. Alvarez-del Rey 3
DEL REY, LESTER
    see R. Alvarez-del Rey 3
    see Paul W. Fairman 47
DE LUNATICO, F. see G. P. R. James 75
DE MESANGE, REV. PIERRE CORDELIER PIERRE see Simon
    Tyssot de Patot 144
DEMIJOHN, THOM
    see Thomas M. Disch 42
    see John T. Sladek 134
DE MILLE, JAMES 40
DEMING, RICHARD 41
DEMOCRITUS JUNIOR see Robert Burton 26
DE MORGAN, JOHN 41
DE MOURANT, GEORGE SOULI see H. Bedford-Jones 12
DEMPSEY, HANK see Harry Harrison 65
DENBRY, R. EMMET see Mary Noailles Murfree 103
DENHOLM, MARK see John Russell Fearn 50
DE NILINSE, BARON see Jacques Simon Collin de Plancy 32
DENMARK, HARRISON see Roger Zelazny 161
DENNIS, BRUCE see David Wright O'Brien 108
DENNIS, WALTER L. 41
DENT, LESTER 41
DE PRE, JEAN-ANNE see Michael Avallone Jr. 8
DE REYNA, DIANE DETZLER (Mrs.) 41
DE REYNA, JORGE see Diane Detzler De Reyna 41
DERING, ROSS GEORGE see Frederic H. Balfour 8
DERLETH, AUGUST W(illiam) 41
DE SAINT-ALBIN, J. S. C. see Jacques Simon Collin de Plancy 32
DE SAINT LEON, COUNT REGINALD see Edward Du Bois 44
DE SANDISSON, M. see Jean Paul Bignon 14
DE SELVA, HERCULE RASIEL see Pierre Quesnel 120
D'ESME, JEAN see Jean D'Esmenard 46
DEVEREUX, ROY see Margaret R. Pember-Devereux 113
DE WEESE, GENE 41
DE WEESE, JEAN see Gene De Weese 41

DE WEINDECK, WINTELER 42
DE WREDER, PAUL see N(ora) K(athleen) Hemming 68
DEXTER, EDWIN see Richard Shaver 130
DEXTER, MARTIN see Frederick Faust 49
DEXTER, PETER see Richard Shaver 130
DEXTER, WILLIAM see William Thomas Pritchard 119
DEY, MARMADUKE see Frederick Van Rensselaer 147
DICK, PHILIP K.
   see Radell Nelson 104
   see Roger Zelazny 161
DICK, R. A. see Josephine A. Leslie 87
DICKBERRY, F. see F. Blaze DeBury 39
DICKSON, CARR see John Dickson Carr 28
DICKSON, CARTER see John Dickson Carr 28
DICKSON, GORDON R.
   see Poul Anderson 4
   see (John) Keith Laumer 86
DIFFIN, C(harles) W(illard) 42
DIKTY, JULIAN CHAIN MAY (Mrs. Theodore) 42
DI LUCCA, SIGNOR GAUDENTIO see Simon Berington 14
DINESEN, ISAK see Karen Blixen-Finecke 17
DINGLE, AYLWARD EDWARD 42
DINGLE, CAPT. see Aylward Edward Dingle 42
DIOSCORIDES, DR. see Pieter Harting 66
DIPLOMAT see John Franklin Carter 28
DI SAVUTO, BARONI see Greye La Spina 85
DISCH, THOMAS M. 42
DISRAELI, BENJAMIN (1st Earl of Beaconsfield) 42
DITO UND IDEM
   see Elisabeth Queen-Consort of Charles 1 King of Rumania 45
   see Mme. Mite Kremnitz 45
DITZEN, RUDOLF 42
DIVER, KATHERINE HELEN MAUDE (Marshall) (Mrs.) 42
DIVER, MAUDE see Katherine Helen Maude Diver 42
DIVINE, ARTHUR D(urham) 42
DIVINE, DAVID see Arthur Durham Divine 42
DIXON, REX see R. A. Martin 98
DOAK see Hugh Doak Rankin 121
DOANE, JERRY see Katherine Duncan Morse 103
DOCHERTY, JAMES L. see Rene Raymond 121
DOCKWEILER, JOSEPH HAROLD 42
DODD, DOUGLAS see John Russell Fearn 50
DODGSON, CHARLES L(utwidge) 42
DOGBOLT, BARNABY see Herbert Silvette 133
DOLBOKOV
   see Boris Dolgov 158
   see Wayne Woodward 158
DOLGOV, BORIS see Wayne Woodward 158
DOMINIC, R. B.
   see Martha Hennissart 68
   see Mary J. Latis 68
DONNELLY, IGNATIUS 43
DONOVAN, DICK see Joyce E. P. Muddock 103
DOROT, PETER see Richard Shaver 130
DORRINGTON, EDWARD see Peter Longueville 91
DORSET, RICHARD see Richard Shaver 130
DORSET, ST. JOHN see Hugo J. Belfour 13
"A DOUBTFUL GENTLEMAN" see James K. Paulding 112
DOUGHTY, FRANK see Lu(is) (P.) Senarens 129
DOUGLAS, GEORGE BRISBANE SCOTT (5th Baronet) 43
DOUGLAS, GEORGE NORMAN 43
DOUGLAS, GERTRUDE (Lady) see George Brisbane Scott
   Douglas 43
DOUGLAS, HUDSON see Robert Aitken 2
DOUGLAS, JULIA see Mrs. H. D. Everett 47
DOUGLAS, LEONARD see Ray Bradbury 19
DOUGLAS, MICHAEL see Michael Crichton 36
DOUGLAS, NORMAN see George Norman Douglas 43
DOUGLAS, THEO see Mrs. H. D. Everett 47
DOUGLASS, ELLSWORTH 43
DOWDING, A. L. 43
DOWNES, QUENTIN see Michael Harrison 66

DOWNEY, EDMUND 43
DOYLE, ADRIAN CONAN see John Dickson Carr 28
DOYLE, JOHN see Harlan Ellison 45
DRAPER, WARWICK HERBERT 43
DRAPIER, M. B. see Jonathan Swift 139
DRAX, PETER see Eric Eldrington Addis 1
DREADSTONE, CARL see John Ramsey Campbell 27
DREW, SHERIDAN see John Russell Fearn 50
DREXEL, JAY B. see Drexel Jerome Bixby 15
DRIANT, EMILE A(ugustin) (Cyprien) 43
DRUMMOND, JOHN PETER see Stanley Mullen 103
DRUSSAI, GAREN 43
DUANE, ANDREW see Robert E. Briney 21
DUANE, TOBY see W. Paul Ganley 55
DU BOIS, EDWARD 44
DUCASSE, ISIDORE L(ucien) 44
DUCHACEK, IVO MARIA RUDOLF (Duka) 44
THE "DUCHESS" see Margaret W. Hungerford 73
DUDLEY-SMITH, TREVOR see Elleston Trevor 142
DUKA, IVO see Ivo Duchacek 44
DU MAURIER, DAPHNE see Daphne du Maurier Browning 22
DUNCAN, C. T. see Albert P. Blaustein 16
DUNKERLEY, WILLIAM A(rthur) 44
DUNN, GERTRUDE (C.) see Gertrude Weaver 152
DUNNE, JOHN T. see H. P. Lovecraft 91
DUNSANY, LORD see Edward John Moreton Drax Plunkett 116
DUNSTAN, ANDREW see A. Bertram Chandler 30
D'URFEY, THOMAS 44
DURHAM, DAVID see Roy Vickers 148
DWIGGENS, ELMER see Ellsworth Douglass 43
DWYER, K. R. see Dean R. Koontz 81

E., A. see George W. Russell 126
E.M.F. see Mrs. E. M. Foster 53
E., T. see Thomas Erskine 46
EAGLE, SOLOMON see John C(ollings) Squire 136
EARL OF HALSBURY see Hardinge Goulburn Giffard 58
EARLAND, ARTHUR see Edward Heron-Allen 69
EARLE, W. J. see Lu(is) (P.) Senarens 129
ECCLES, CHARLOTTE O'CONOR 45
ECKMAN, J. FORREST see Forrest J. Ackerman 1
EDEN, ROB
   see Eve Burkhardt 25
   see Robert F. Burkhardt 25
EDGAR, ALFRED 45
EDGAR, PETER see Peter King-Scott 80
EDISON, THEODORE see Edward Stratemeyer 138
EDITOR OF "THE ADVENTURES OF A GUINEA" see Charles
   Johnston(e) 77
EDITOR OF "THE PHOENIX" see Clara Reeve 122
EDMONDS, HELEN WOODS (Mrs. Stuart) 45
EDMONDS, PAUL see Henry Kuttner 83
EDMONDSON, WALLACE see Harlan Ellison 45
EDMONDSON, G. C. see Jose M. G. Ordonez Edmondson
   y Cotton 109
EDWARDS, CHARMAN see Frederick A. Edwards 45
EDWARDS, F. E. see William F. Nolan 105
EDWARDS, FREDERICK A(nthony) 45
EDWARDS, GAWAIN see G(eorge) Edwards Pendray 113
EDWARDS, HAMM see Thelma D. Hamm Evans 47
EDWARDS, JOHN MILTON see George C. Jenks 77
EDWARDS, JULIA see John Russell Coryell 35
EDWARDS, NORMAN
   see Terry Carr 28
   see Theodore Edward White 154
EGAN, LESLEY see (Barbara) Elizabeth Linington 89
EGBERT, H. M. see Victor R. Emanuel 46
EGERTON, GEORGE see Mary C. Bright 21
EGREMONT, MICHAEL see Michael Harrison 66
EHRENKRON, IRENICO see Philipp Balthasar Sinhold von
   Schutz 134
EIDE, EDITH 45

EISNER, SIMON see Cyril Kornbluth 82
ELCLAIR, MOLLIE see Richard Shaver 130
ELDERSHAW, FLORA SYDNEY PATRICIA 45
ELDERSHAW, M. BARNARD
    see Marjorie Faith Barnard 10
    see Flora Sydney Patricia Eldershaw 45
ELDON, CLEO see Don Wilcox 155
ELDRED, BRIAN see Ray Bradbury 19
ELEVE see (Mrs. H. M.) Stowe 138
ELISABETH, QUEEN-CONSORT OF CHARLES I KING OF
    RUMANIA 45
ELIZABETH, QUEEN OF R(o)UMANIA see Elisabeth Queen-
    Consort of Charles I King of Rumania 45
ELLANBEE, BOYD
    see Lyle G. Boyd 18
    see William C. Boyd 19
ELLANBY, BOYD
    see Lyle G. Boyd 18
    see William C. Boyd 19
ELLERMAN, GENE see Basil Wells 153
ELLET, ELIZABETH FRIES (Lummis) (Mrs.) 45
ELLIK, RON(ald) (D.) 45
ELLIOTT, E. C. see R. A. Martin 98
ELLIOTT, WILLIAM see Ray Bradbury 19
ELLIS, CRAIG [house pseudonym] 45
ELLIS, LANDON see Harlan Ellison 45
ELLIS, S. M. see G. P. R. James 75
ELLISON, HARLAN (Jay) 45
ELLSON, HAL see Harlan Ellison 46
ELRON see L. Ron Hubbard 72
ELSTAR, DOW see Raymond Z. Gallun 55
ELTON, JOHN see John Marsh 98
ELTON, MAX see John Russell Fearn 50
ELWOOD, ROGER see Mildred Virginia Kidd 80
ELY, GEORGE H(erbert) 46
EMANUEL, V(ictor) R(ousseau) 46
EMERSIE, JOHN 46
EMSH see Ed(mund) Emshwiller 46
EMSHWILLER, ED(mund) (Alexander) 46
EMSLER see Ed(mund) Emshwiller 46
ENACRYOS see J. H. H. Boex 18
ENGELHARDT, FREDERICK see L. Ron Hubbard 72
ENGLISH, CHARLES see Charles Nuetzel 107
"AN ENGLISH MERCURY" see Joseph Hall 63
ENGLISH, RICHARD see Richard Shaver 130
ENSENADA, LE DOCTEUR see Jacques Simon Collin de Plancy 32
ERCKMANN, EMILE 46
ERCKMANN-CHATRIAN
    see Alexandre Chatrian 30
    see Emile Erckmann 46
ERICSON, WALTER see Howard Fast 49
ERIE, PAUL 46
ERMAN, JACQUES DE FORREST see Forrest J. Ackerman 1
ERMANN, JACK see Forrest J. Ackerman 1
ERNST, PAUL FREDERICK 46
ERNSTING, WALTER 46
ERRYM, MALCOLM J. see James Malcolm Rymer 126
ERSKINE, DOUGLAS see John Buchan 23
ERSKINE, THOMAS (1st Baron Erskine of Restormel) 46
ERWIN, PATRICK see Robert E. Howard 72
ESMENARD, JEAN D'(Vicomte) 46
ESTERBROOK, TOM see L. Ron Hubbard 72
ESTEVEN, JOHN see Samuel Shellabarger 131
"ESTIVAL" see Ivan Leon Estival 47
ESTIVAL, IVAN LEON 47
THE ETTRICK SHEPHERD see James Hogg 70
EUROPAEI, LUCII CORNELII see Giulio Clemente Scotti 129
EUROPAEUS, LUCIUS CORNELIUS see Giulio Clemente
    Scotti 129
EUSTACE, ROBERT see Eustace Robert Barton 11
EVAN, EVIN see Frederick Faust 49
EVANS, BILL see Ron(ald) D. Ellik 45

EVANS, E. E(verett) 47
EVANS, EVAN see Frederick Faust 49
EVANS, JOHN see Howard Browne 22
EVANS, MARGUERITE FLORENCE HELENE JERVIS (Mrs.
    Caradoc) 47
EVANS, T(helma) D. HAMM (Mrs. E. Everett) 47
EVERETT, H. D. (Mrs.) 47
EWING, FREDERICK R. see Theodore Sturgeon 138
EX-PRIVATE X see A. M. Burrage 25
EXCELLMANS, BARON KARLO see William Henry Ireland 74

F.B. see Richard Francis Burton 26
F., E. M. see Mrs. E. M. Foster 53
F.G. see Francis Godwin 58
F., L. see Mary Elizabeth Hawker 67
F. O. O. see C. J. C. Street 138
FAIR, A. A. see Erle Stanley Gardner 55
FAIRBAIRN, ROGER see John Dickson Carr 28
FAIRBURN, EDWIN 47
FAIRLAMB, SAMPSON see James K. Paulding 112
FAIRLEIGH, CHRISTOPHER see Norman H(owe) Parcell 112
FAIRLESS, MICHAEL see Margaret F. Barber 9
FAIRMAN, PAUL W. 47
FAIRWAY, SIDNEY see Sidney Daukes 39
FALCONER, KENNETH see Cyril Kornbluth 82
FALCONER, LANOE see Mary Elizabeth Hawker 67
FALLADA, HANS see Rudolf Ditzen 42
FANE, BRON see R. Lionel Fanthorpe 48
FANTA, HOLLY ROTH (Mrs. Joseph) 47
FANTHORPE, R(obert) L(ionel) 47
FARGUS, FREDERICK J(ohn) 48
FARJEON, J(oseph) J(efferson) 48
FARLEY, RALPH MILNE see Roger Sherman Hoar 70
FARMER, ARTHUR see Jack Owen Jardine 76
FARMER, PHILIP JOSE 48
FARNESE, A. 49
FARNINGHAM, MARIANNE see Mary Anne Hearne 67
FARNOL, JEFFERY see John Jeffery Farnol 49
FARNOL, JOHN JEFFERY 49
FARNSWORTH, DUNCAN see David Wright O'Brien 108
FARRELL, JOHN WADE see John D. MacDonald 94
FARRERE, CLAUDE see Frederic Charles Bargone 10
FASSBINDER, CARLTON J. see T. B. Yerke 160
FAST, HOWARD MELVIN 49
FAULKNER, DOROTHEA M. 49
FAUST, ALEXANDER see Harry Altshuler 3
FAUST, FREDERICK (Schiller) 49
FAWCETT, FRANK D(ubrez) 49
FAWKES, F(rank) A(ttfield) 50
FEARING, KENNETH 50
FEARN, JOHN RUSSELL 50
FECAMPS, ELISE see John Creasey 36
FEDER, ROBERT ARTHUR 51
FEDOR, A. see Henry Hasse 66
FENTON, E. see Pierre Boaistual de Launay 18
"FERDINAND" see Kurt Vonnegut, Jr. 149
FERGUSON, HELEN see Helen Woods Edmonds 45
FERNEY, MANUEL see Manly Wade Wellman 153
FERRARS, E. X. see Morna Doris Brown 21
FERRARS, ELIZABETH see Morna Doris Brown 21
FERVAL, PAUL see H. Bedford-Jones 12
FIELD, FRANK CHESTER see Frank Chester Robertson 124
FIELD, GANS T. see Manly Wade Wellman 153
FIELD, JULIAN OSGOOD 51
FIELD, PETER see Ed Earl Repp 122
FIELD, STEPHEN see John A. Vlasto 149
FIELDING, HOWARD see Charles W. Hooke 71
FIGGIS, DARRELL 51
FIGHTON, CAPT. GEORGE Z. see Winteler de Weindeck 42
FIGWOOD, JOHN, BARRISTER-AT-LAW see J. S(heridan)
    Le Fanu 86
FINN, HUCK see Samuel L. Clemens 31

FINNEY, JACK see Walter Braden Finney 51
FINNEY, WALTER BRADEN 51
FIRMIANI, PETRI see Zacharie de Lisieux-pere 161
FIRTH, VIOLET M(ary) 51
FISCHER, MARGARET ANN PETERSON (Mrs. A. O.) 52
FISH, ROBERT L. 52
FISHER, CLAY see Henry Wilson Allen 3
FISHER, GENE 52
FISHER, STEPHEN (Gould) 52
FISHER, STEVE see Stephen (Gould) Fisher 52
FISKE, TARLETON see Robert Bloch 17
FITZALAN, PETER see Elleston Trevor 143
FITZGERALD, HUGH see L. Frank Baum 11
FITZGERALD, WILLIAM see Will F. Jenkins 76
FITZPATRICK, BERNARD (Edward) (Barnaby) (2nd Baron Castletown) 52
FITZPATRICK, ERNEST H(ugh) 52
FLACK, ISAAC H(arvey) 52
FLAGELLUM see William Henry Ireland 74
FLAGG, FRANCIS see George Henry Weiss 152
FLAMMENBERG, LAWRENCE see Karl F. Kahlert 79
FLANDERS, JOHN see Raymond Kremer 83
FLAVIUS see Edward Heron-Allen 69
FLEHR, PAUL see Frederik Pohl 117
FLEMING, GERALDINE see John Russell Coryell 35
FLEMING, OLIVER see Philip MacDonald 94
FLEMING STUART see Damon Knight 81
FLETCHER, BARRIE see William Charles Anderson 5
FLETCHER, GEORGE U. see Fletcher Pratt 118
FLETCHER, JOHN see Thomas D'Urfey 44
FLETCHER, J(oseph) S(mith) 52
FLONATIN, JOSIAH FLINTABBATEY see Joyce E. P. Muddock 103
FLYING OFFICER "X" see Herbert Ernest Bates 11
FODOR, NANDOR see Hereward Carrington 28
FOIGNY, GABRIEL DE 52
FOLEY, DAVE 52
FONTAINES, LOUIS see Zacharie de Lisieux-pere 161
FOOT, MICHAEL (Mackintosh) 52
FORAN, W(illiam) ROBERT (Capt.) 52
FORBUSH, ZEBINA see Francis H. Clarke 31
FORD, D(ouglas) M(orley) 53
FORD, FORD MADDOX 53
FORD, GARRET [house pseudonym] 53
    see Margaret Crawford 36
    see William L. Crawford 36
FORD, LESLIE see Zenith Jones Brown 22
FORD, W. C. see Henry Neville 105
"A FORMER RESIDENT OF THE HUB" see John Bachelder 8
FORREST, FELIX C. see Paul M. A. Linebarger 89
FORTUNE, DION see Violet M. Firth 51
FOSSE, HAROLD C. see Horace L. Gold 58
FOSTER, E. M. (Mrs.) 53
FOSTER, GEORGE C(ecil) 53
FOSTER, RICHARD see Kendell F. Crossen 37
FOULDS, ELFRIDA VIPONT (Brown) 53
4E see Forrest J. Ackerman 1
FOWLER, SIDNEY see S. Fowler Wright 159
FOX, DAVID see Isabel E. Ostrander 110
FOX, GARDNER F(rancis) 53
FOXX, JACK see Bill Pronzini 119
FRANCE, ANATOLE see Jacques Anatole Thibault 141
FRANCHEZZO see A. Farnese 49
FRANCIS, GREGORY
    see James MacGregor 95
    see Frank Parnell 112
FRANCIS, LEE [house pseudonym] 53-54
"FRANK" see Edward Stratemeyer 138
FRANK, PAT see Harry Hart 66
FRANKAU, JULIA (Davis) (Mrs.) 54
FRANKLIN, EDGAR see Edgar Franklin Stearns 136
FRANKLIN, JAY see John Franklin Carter 28

FRANKLIN, MAX see Richard Deming 41
FRANKLIN, PAUL see Bryce Walton 150
FRASER, JEFFERSON see Philip Wilding 155
FRAZEE, CHARLES S(tephen) 54
FRAZEE, STEVE see Charles S(tephen) Frazee 54
FRAZER, ROBERT CAINE see John Creasey 36
FREDERICK, JOHN see Frederick Faust 49
FREDERICKS, ARNOLD see Frederic Arnold Kummer 83
FREEMAN, R(ichard) AUSTIN 54
FREEMAN, RICHARD "DICK" see (Richard) Edgar Wallace 149
FRENCH, ALICE 54
FRENCH, PAUL see Isaac Asimov 7
FREUGON, RUBY see R. C. Ashby 6
FREYER, FREDERICK see William S. Ballinger 9
FRIEDE, DONALD
    see H. Bedford-Jones 12
    see Kenneth Fearing 50
FRIEDMAN, DAVID GERROLD 54
FRIEND, OSCAR J(erome) 54
A FRIEND TO HUMANITY see Mrs. M(ary) Robinson 124
FRIKELL, SAMRI see Charles Fulton Oursler 110
FROME, DAVID see Zenith Jones Brown 22
FROST, FREDERICK see Frederick Faust 49
FRYERS, AUSTIN see William E. Clery 31
A FUGITIVE see Edward D. Coxe 35
FUQUA, ROBERT see J. W. Tillotson 141
FUREY, MICHAEL see Arthur S. Ward 150
FURTH, CARLTON see Joe Gibson 58
FURY, NICK see Michael Patrick Parry 112
FYFE, HORACE B(rowne) 54

G., F. see Francis Godwin 58
G. H. P. see George H. Putnam 119
GADE, HENRY [house pseudonym] 55
GAGE, WILSON see Mary Quintard Steele 137
GAITE, FRANCIS
    see Cyril Henry Coles 32
    see Adelaide F. O. Manning 98
GALAXAN, SOL see Alfredo Coppel, Jr. 34
GALBRAITH, ALEXANDER 55
GALLISTER, MICHAEL see H. Bedford-Jones 12
GALLOWAY, JAMES M. 55
GALLUN, RAYMOND Z. 55
GALOUYE, DANIEL F(rancis) 55
GALSWORTHY, JOHN 55
GAN "INDEX" see David Rhys Williams 155
GANLEY, W. PAUL 55
GANPAT see Martin L. Gompertz 58
GARDENER, HENRY see E. Everett Evans 47
GARDNER, E. D. 55
GARDNER, ERLE STANLEY 55
GARDNER, JEFFREY see Gardner F. Fox 53
GARDNER, NOEL see Henry Kuttner 83
GARDNER, ROLF see Bryan Berry 14
GARIS, HOWARD ROGER 55
GARNE, GASTON see Lu(is) (P.) Senarens 129
GARNET, G. see Irwin Ashkenazy 6
GARRETT, EILEEN J(eanette) (Lyttle) 56
GARRETT, (Gordon) RANDALL (Philip) (David) 56
GARRETT, RANDALL see Gordon Randall Garrett 56
GARRISON, CHARLES M. 56
GARRON, ROBERT A. see Howard Wandrei 150
GARSON, CLEE [house pseudonym] 56
GARTH, WILL [house pseudonym] 56
GARTMANN, HEINZ 57
GASHBUCK, GRENO see Hugo Gernsback 57
GASKELL, JANE see Jane Lynch 93
GASKO, GORDON 57
GAUL, GILBERT see James De Mille 40
GAUTISOLO, MIGUEL see Antonio Moncho y Gilabert 102
GAWSWORTH, JOHN see T. I. F. Armstrong 5
GAY, J. DREW see Edgar L. Welch 152

GEIER, CHESTER S. 57
GEISEL, THEODOR SEUSS 57
GENERAL X see Roger Sherman Hoar 70
GENONE, HUDOR see William J. Roe 125
GENTLEMAN, FRANCIS 57
A GENTLEMAN OF THE UNIVERSITY OF OXFORD
    see Percy B(ysshe) Shelley 131
GEORGE, JONATHAN see John Frederick Burke 25
GEORGE, PETER BRYAN 57
GEORGE, VERNON see George S. G. Vernon 147
GERAHTY, DIGBY GEORGE 57
GERHOLD, GERMAN see Willy Schmidt 128
GERIS, TOM ERWIN see Mort(imer) Weisinger 152
GERMANO, PETER B. 57
GERNSBACK, HUGO 57
GERRARE, WIRT see William O. Greener 60
GERROLD, DAVID see David Gerrold Friedman 54
GERVE(e), BARONTE(i?) 57
GIBBS, LEWIS see Joseph Walter Cove 35
GIBSON, AMANDA MELVINA THORLEY 57
GIBSON, JOE 58
GIBSON, MRS. WALTER B. 58
GIBSON, WALTER B(rown) 58
GIDDY, ERIC CAWOOD GWYDDN 58
GIFFARD, HARDINGE GOULBURN (2nd Earl of Halsbury) 58
GIFT, THEO see Theodora Havers 67
GILBERT, ANTHONY see Lucy Beatrice Malleson 97
GILBERT, MICHAEL see Andre Norton 106
GILES, GEOFFREY
    see Forrest J. Ackerman 1
    see Walter Gillings 58
GILES, GORDON A. see Otto Oscar Binder 15
GILES, R. A. 58
GILHOOLEY, LORD see Frederick H. Seymour 129
GILL, PATRICK see John Creasey 36
GILLINGS, WALTER 58
GILLMORE, INEZ HAYNES see Inez Haynes Gillmore Irwin 75
GILMAN, ROBERT CHAM see Alfredo Coppel, Jr. 34
GILMORE, ANTHONY
    see Harry Bates 11
    see D(esmond) W(inter) Hall 63
GISANDER, (Eberhard Julius?) see Johann Gottfried Schnabel 128
GLAMIS, WALTER see Nathan Schachner 128
GLANAVILLE, BARON DE see Jacques Simon Collin de Plancy 32
GLEMSER, BERNARD 58
GODFREY, HAL see Charlotte O. Eccles 45
GODFREY, R. H. see E. C. Tubb 143
GODWIN, FRANCIS (Bishop of Hereford) 58
GODWIN, WILLIAM 58
    see Edward Du Bois 44
GOETCHIUS, MARIE LOUISE see Marice R. G. Hale 63
GOLD, EVELYN PAIGE (Mrs. Horace L.) 58
GOLD, H(orace) L(eonard) 58
GOLDSMITH, CELE see Cele Lalli 84
GOMPERTZ, MAJOR M. L. A. see Martin L. Gompertz 59
GOMPERTZ, MARTIN LOUIS ALAN 58
GONSALES, DOMINGO see Francis Godwin 58
GOODCHILD, GEORGE 59
GOODRICH, SAMUEL GRISWOLD 59
GOODWIN, HAL see H(arold) L(eland) Goodwin 59
GOODWIN, H(arold) L(eland) 59
GOODWIN, JOHN see Sidney F. Gowing 59
GORDON, DAVID see Gordon Randall Garrett 56
GORDON, DONALD see Donald Gordon Payne 113
GORDON, JULIEN see Julia Grinnell Cruger 37
GORDON, MILLARD VERNE see Donald A. Wollheim 157
GORDON, NATHANIEL see Gordon Gasko 57
GORDON, NEIL see Archibald Gordon Macdonell 94
GORDON, REX see S(tanley) B(ennett) Hough 71
GOTTESMAN, S. D.
    see Cyril Kornbluth 82
    see Robert Lowndes 92

see Frederik Pohl 117
GOULD, ARTHUR LEE see Arthur Gould Lee 86
GOULD, STEPHEN see Stephen (Gould) Fisher 52
GOWING, SIDNEY F(loyd) 59
GRAAF, PETER see Christopher S. Youd 160
GRAHAM, ENNIS see Mary Louisa Molesworth 101
GRAHAM, FELIX see Fredric Brown 21
GRAHAM, HARVEY see Isaac H. Flack 52
GRAHAM, HOWARD see Howard Wandrei 150
GRAHAM, ROBERT see Joe Haldeman 63
GRAHAM, ROGER P(hillips) 59
GRAHAM, WINIFRED see Matilda Cory 34
GRAINGER, FRANCIS E(dward) 60
GRANGER, D. J. see Milton Lesser 87
GRANT, AMBROSE see Rene Raymond 121
GRANT, DOUGLAS see Isabel Ostrander 110
GRANT, MARGARET see John Russell Coryell 35
GRANT, MAXWELL see Walter B. Gibson 58
GRANTLAND, KEITH see Charles Nutt 107
GRANVILLE-BARKER, HARLEY G(ranville) 60
GRAUTOFF, FERDINAND H(einrich) 60
GRAVES, CLOTILDE INEZ MARY 60
GRAY, ANNABEL see Anne Cox 35
GRAY, BERKELEY see Edwy S. Brooks 21
GRAY, CHARLES see E. C. Tubb 143
GRAYDON, ROBERT MURRAY 60
GREAVES, RICHARD see George Barr McCutcheon 94
GREBANIER, FRANCES (Vinciguerra) (Mrs. Bernard D. N.) 60
GREEN, CHARLES M. see Erle Stanley Gardner 55
GREEN, GLINT see Margaret Peterson Fischer 52
GREEN, ROGER L. see Edmund Cooper 34
GREEN, ROLAND C. 60
GREENER, WILLIAM O(liver) 60
GREENWOOD, JULIA EILEEN COURTNEY 60
GREER, RICHARD [house pseudonym] 60
GREGG, MARTIN see Wilfred McNeilly 97
GREGOR, LEE see Milton A. Rothman 125
GRENDON, STEPHEN see August W. Derleth 41
GRENNELL, DEAN A. 60
GREY, CAROL see Robert W. Lowndes 92
GREY, CHARLES see E. C. Tubb 143
GREYSUN, DORIAC see Eddy C. Bertin 14
GRIBBON, WILLIAM LANCASTER 60
GRIDBAN, VORSTED see John Russell Fearn 50
GRIDBAN, VORSTED see E. C. Tubb 143
GRIFF, ALAN see Donald Suddaby 139
GRIFFIN, ANTHONY JEROME 61
GRIFFITH, GEORGE see George Griffith-Jones 61
GRIFFITH, MARY (Mrs.) 61
GRIFFITH-JONES, GEORGE CHETWYND 61
GRIGSBY, ALCANOAN O. 61
GRILE, DOD see Ambrose Bierce 14
GRINDLE, CARLETON see Gerald W. Page 111
GRINNELL, DAVID see Donald A. Wollheim 157
GRIP see Edgar L. Welch 152
GROSS, JEROME see David Lasser 85
GROUSSET, PASCHAL 61
GUERNSEY, H.W. see Howard Wandrei 150
GUEZENEC, ALFRED 61
GUILDFORD, JOHN see Bluebell M. Hunter 73
GUIN, WYMAN WOODS 61
GUINTA, JOHN see Gardner F. Fox 53
GULL, C(yril) A(rthur) RANGER 62
GULLIVER, LEMUEL see Jonathan Swift 139
GULLIVER, LEMUEL JUNIOR see H. Whitmore 154
GUNN, JAMES E(dwin) 62
GUNN, VICTOR see Edwy S. Brooks 21
GUTHRIE, ALAN see E. C. Tubb 143
GUTHRIE, THOMAS A(nstey) 62
GUY, L. 62
GWYNNE, PAUL see Ernest Slater 134

J. S. D. S. P. see Jonathan Swift 139
J.T. see Eric Temple Bell 13
J.W. see James White 154
J. W. L. see John W. Lethaby 87
"JACK" see Edward Stratemeyer 138
JACKSON, GILES see Albert Leffingwell 87
JACKSON, JOHN 75
JACKSON, SHIRLEY see Shirley Jackson Hyman 73
JACKSON, STEPHEN see John Stevenson 137
JACOB, PIERS ANTHONY DILLINGHAM 75
JAFFE, HYMAN 75
JAMES, EDWIN see James E. Gunn 62
JAMES, G(eorge) P(ayne) R(ainsford) 75
JAMES, HENRY P. see Frederic Arnold Kummer 83
JAMES, PHILIP
    see R. Alvarez-del Rey 3
    see James H. Beard 12
JAMESON, ANNIE EDITH (Foster) 75
JAMESON (M.) STORM see Margaret Storm Jameson
    Chapman 30
JAMESON, MALCOLM 76
JANIFER, LAURENCE, M. see Larry Mark Harris 65
JANVIER, IVAN see Algirdas Jonas Budrys 24
JANVIER, PAUL see Algirdas Jonas Budrys 24
JARDIN, REX
    see Eve Burkhardt 25
    see Robert F. Burkhardt 25
JARDINE, JACK OWEN 76
JARDINE, JULIE ANN 76
JARRETT, CORA (Hardy) (Mrs.) 76
JARVIS, E. K. [house pseudonym] 76
JARVIS, LEE see Albert Hernhuter 69
JASON, JERRY see George Henry Smith 135
JAY, MEL see R. Lionel Fanthorpe 48
JEFFRIES, HUGH Geoffrey Hewelcke 69
JENKINS, WILL(iam) F(itzgerald) 76
JENKS, GEORGE C(harles) 77
JENNINGS, DEAN see Charles S(tephen) Frazee 54
JEROME, FERRIS see Alice Ilgenfritz Jones 77
JEROME, OWEN FOX see Oscar J. Friend 54
JESSEL, JOHN see Stanley G. Weinbaum 152
JOHANNESSON, OLOF see Hannes Alfven 2
JOHN, JASPER see Rosalie Muspratt 104
JOHNHETT see John Hettinger 69
JOHNS, KENNETH
    see H. Kenneth Bulmer 24
    see John Newman 105
JOHNS, MARSTON see R. Lionel Fanthorpe 48
JOHNS, WILLY see W. Johns Meeker 100
JOHNSON, BENJAMIN F., OF BOONE see James Whitcomb
    Riley 123
JOHNSON, CROCKETT see David J. Leisk 87
JOHNSON, G. C. see William F. Nolan 105
JOHNSON, THOMAS M. see Judson (P.) Philips 114
JOHNSTON(e), CHARLES 77
JOHNSTONE, TED see David McDaniel 94
JONES, ADRIENNE 77
JONES, ALICE ILGENFRITZ 77
JONES, CLARA AUGUSTA 77
JONES, FRANCIS 77
JONES, FRANK see John Russell Fearn 50
JONES, JOANNA see John Frederick Burke 25
JONES, JOHN J. see H. P. Lovecraft 91
JONES, RAYMOND. F. 77
JONES, S. CARLETON see Susan Carleton Jones 78
JONES, SUSAN CARLETON 78
JONES, VERNON 78
JONQUIL see J. L. Collins 32
JORGENSEN, IVAR [house pseudonym] 78
JORGENSON, ALF A. 78
JORGENSON, IVAR [house pseudonym] 78

JORGENSSON, A. K. see Robert W. A. Roach 124
JUDD, CYRIL (M.)
    see Cyril Kornbluth 82
    see Judith Merril 100
JUDSON, EDWARD ZANE CARROLL 78
JUDSON, RALPH 78
JULIA see Mrs. H. D. Everett 47
JUNE, HAROLD 78
JUNIOR SUBALTERN see John Hay Beith 12
JUNIUS SECUNDUS see Charles Kelsall 80
"A JUSTIFIED SINNER" see James Hogg 70

K(1), THE JUNIOR SUBALTERN see John Hay Beith 12
KAEMPFERT, WADE see R. Alvarez-del Rey 3
KAHLERT, KARL F(riedrich) 79
KALER, JAMES OTIS 79
KANE, JIM see Peter B. Germano 57
KANE, WILSON see Robert Bloch 17
KAPLAN, M. M. 79
KARAGEORGE, MICHAEL see Poul Anderson 5
KARISHKA, PAUL see David P. Hatch 66
KARLOFF, BORIS see William Henry Pratt 119
KASSON, HELEN WEINBAUM 79
KASTEL, WARREN
    see Chester S. Geier 57
    see Robert Silverberg 132
KATELEY, WALTER see Harold June 78
KAVAN, ANNA see Helen Woods Edmonds 45
KAVANAGH, HERMINIE TEMPLETON (Mrs.) 79
KAYE, MARX [house pseudonym] 79
KAYNE, MARVIN see John Russell Fearn 50
KAYSER, RONAL 79
KEENE, FARADAY see Cora Jarrett 76
KEIGHTLEY, DAVID N(oel) 79
KEITH, DONALD
    see Donald Monroe 102
    see Keith Monroe 102
KEITH, J. KILMENY see Lucy Beatrice Malleson 97
KELL, JOSEPH see John Anthony Burgess Wilson 157
KELLER, DAVID H(enry) 79
KELLEY, LEO F. see Leo P. Kelley 79
KELLEY, LEO P(atrick) 79
KELLEY, MARTHA MOTT 79
KELLINO, PAMELA see Pamela O. Mason 99
KELLY, ISABELLA see Isabella Kelly Hedgeland 67
KELSALL, CHARLES 80
KEMP, H. see Harold Hersey 69
KENDALL, JOHN see Margaret M. Brash 20
KENDELL, MAY see Andrew Lang 85
KENDRAKE, CARLETON see Erle Stanley Gardner 55
KENDRICKS, JAMES see Gardner F. Fox 53
KENNAWAY, JAMES see John Ewing Peebles 113
KENNEDY, HOWARD see Josiah Pitts Woolfolk 158
KENNEDY, P. see Harold Hersey 69
KENNEDY, R. A. 80
KENNY, CHARLES J. see Erle Stanley Gardner 55
KENNY, JOHN see Nadir Khan 104
KENT, GORDON see E. C. Tubb 143
KENT, KELVIN
    see Arthur K. Barnes 10
    see Henry Kuttner 83
KENT, MALLORY see Robert W. Lowndes 92
KENT, PHILIP see H. Kenneth Bulmer 24
KENT, RICHARD see Frank Owen 110
KENYON, ROBERT O. see Henry Kuttner 83
KERBY, SUSAN (Alice) see Alice Elizabeth Burton 26
KERN, GREGORY see E. C. Tubb 143
KERNAHAN, COULSON see John Coulson Kernahan 80
KERNAHAN, JOHN COULSON 80
KEYES, NOEL see David N. Keightley 79
KEYNE, GORDON see H. Bedford-Jones 12
KIDD, MILDRED VIRGINIA 80

KIMBALL, ATKINSON
    see Grace L. Kimball 80
    see Richard B. Kimball 80
KIMBALL, GRACE LUCIA (Atkinson) (Mrs.) 80
KIMBALL, RICHARD B(owland) 80
KING, C(harles) DALY 80
KING, DR. see William King 80
KING, WILLIAM 80
KING, (William) (Benjamin) BASIL 80
KING-SCOTT, PETER 80
KINGSMILL, HUGH see Hugh Lunn 92
KINGSTON, JOHN see Keith Roberts 124
KINSEY-JONES, BRIAN see Brian N. Ball 9
KIPPAX, JOHN see John Charles Hynam 73
KIPROY, C. see Harold Hersey 69
KIRK, ELEANOR see Eleanor M. Ames 4
KIRK, LAURENCE see Eric Andrew Simson 134
KIRKMAN, MILO see Garen Drussai 44
KIRWAN, THOMAS 80
KISSLING, DOROTHY HIGHT (Richardson) (Mrs.) 80
KLASS, PHILIP J. 81
KLAXON see John G. Bower 18
KLEIN, GERALD see Mildred Virginia Kidd 80
KLEINER, RHEINHART 81
KLIMARIS, J. S. see Walter Kubilius 83
KLIMIUS, NICOLAS see Ludwig Holberg 70
KNAUSS, ROBERT 81
KNEALE, NIGEL see Thomas N(igel) Kneale 81
KNEALE, THOMAS N(igel) 81
KNICKERBOCKER, DIEDRICH see Washington Irving 74
KNIGHT, DAMON F(rancis) 81
KNIGHT, F. S. see Damon Knight 81
KNIGHT, KATE WILHELM (Mrs. Damon) 81
KNIGHT, KOBOLD (W.) see Eric Cawood Gwyddn Giddy 58
KNIGHT, NORMAN L. see James Blish 16
KNOWALL, GEORGE see Brian O'Nolan 109
KNOWLES, MABEL W(inifred) 81
KNOX, CALVIN M. see Robert Silverberg 132
KNOX, LISBETH see Rose Elizabeth Knox Ward 151
KOIZUMI YAKUMO see Patricios Lafcadio T. C. Hearn 67
KOLDA, HELENA see Ivo Duchacek 44
KOOMOTER, ZENO see Joseph Marnell 98
KOONTZ, DEAN R(ay) 81
KOONTZ, GERDA see Dean R. Koontz 82
KORESH see Cyrus Reed Teed 140
KORN, FRIEDRICH 82
KORNBLUTH, CYRIL 82
KORZENIOWSKI, JOSEF KONRAD THEODOR 82
KOSTROWICKI, GUILLAUME APOLLINAIRE ALBERT 82
KOUYOUMDJIAN, DIKRAN see Michael Arlen 5
KRAUSS, RUTH see David J. Leisk 87
KREMER, RAYMOND JEAN MARIE DE 82
KREMNITZ, MITE (Mme.) see Elisabeth, Queen-Consort of
    Charles I King of Rumania 45
KREPPS, ROBERT W(ilson) 83
KUBILIUS, WALTER 83
KUMMER, FREDERIC ARNOLD (Jr.) 83
    see Joseph Harold Dockweiler 42
KUPPORD, SKELTON see J. Adams 1
KUTTNER, C(atherine) L(ucille) Moore (Mrs. Henry) 83
KUTTNER, HENRY 83
KUTTNER, HENRY
    see C. L. Moore Kuttner 83
    see Henry Kuttner 83
KYLE, SEFTON see Roy Vickers 148

L. F. see Mary Elizabeth Hawker 67
L., J. W. see John W. Lethaby 87
L. S., W. S. see Wladislaw S. Lach-Szyrma 84
L. W. J. S. see V. Adolph Thisted 141
L., X. see Julian Osgood Field 51
LACH-SZYRMA, WLADISLAW S(omerville) 84

LAFARGUE, PHILIP see J. H. Philpot 115
LAFAYETTE, RENE see L. Ron Hubbard 72
LAFOREST-DIVONNE, PHILOMENE DE (Comtesse) 84
LAICUS, PHILIPP see Philipp Wasserburg 152
LAING, PATRICK see A(melia) R(eynolds) Long 90
LALLI, CELE G(oldsmith) (Mrs.) 84
LAMAR, ASHTON see H(arry) L(incoln) Sayler 127
LAMARQUE, A. see Eileen J. Garrett 56
LAMBERT, ARTHUR see Arthur L. Widner 155
LAMBERT, LESLIE H(arrison) 84
LAMBERT, S. H. see Stephen Southwold 136
LAMBURN, RICHMAL CROMPTON (Miss) 84
LAMONT, DUNCAN see E. C. Tubb 143
LAMPREY, A. C. see Robert L. Fish 52
LANCASTER, WILLIAM JOSEPH COSENS 84
LANCING, GEORGE see Bluebell M. Hunter 73
LANCOUR, GENE see Gene Fisher 52
LANDON, MELVILLE DE LANCY 85
LANE, ARTHUR see F. Orlin Tremaine 142
LANE, GRANT see Stephen (Gould) Fisher 52
LANE, JANE see Elaine Kidner Dakers 38
LANE, JOHN see John D. MacDonald 94
LANE, MARY E. BRADLEY (Mrs.) 85
LANE, SPENCER [house pseudonym] 85
LANE, TEMPLE see Mary Isabel Leslie 87
LANG, ANDREW 85
LANG, KING see E. C. Tubb 143
LANG, SIMON see Darlene Hartman 66
LANGART, DARREL(l) T. see Gordon Randall Garrett 56
LANGE, JOAN see Michael Crichton 36
LANGE, JOHN see Michael Crichton 36
LANGE, JOHN (Frederick), (Jr.) 85 [see Michael Crichton 36]
LANGLEY, DOROTHY see Dorothy H. Kissling 80
LANGRENUS, MANFRED see Friedrich Hecht 67
LANGSTAFF, LAUNCELOT see James K. Paulding 112
LANGSTAFF, LAUNCELOT see Washington Irving 74
LARA see George Griffith-Jones 61
LASKI, MARGHANITA see Marghanita Laski Howard 72
LA SPINA, GREYE (Bragg) (Mrs. Robert) 85
LASSER, DAVID 85
LASSEZ, M. see H. Bedford-Jones 12
LATHAM, PHILIP see R(obert) S(hirley) Richardson 123
LATHEN, EMMA
    see Martha Hennissart 68
    see Mary J. Latis 68
LATIS, MARY J. see Martha Hennissart 68
LATROON, M. see Richard Head 67
LAUMER, (John) KEITH 85
LAUMER, KEITH see (John) Keith Laumer 85
LAUMER, MARCH 86
LAURA MARIA see Mary Darby Robinson 124
LAURENT-CELY, JACQUES 86
LAURIE, A(ndre) see Paschal Grousset 61
LAUTREAMONT, COMPTE DE see Isidore L. Ducasse 44
LAVERTY, DON(ald)
    see James Blish 17
    see Damon Knight 81
LAVINGTON, HUBERT see Hereward Carrington 28
LAVOND, PAUL DENNIS [house pseudonym] 86
A LAW ABIDING REVOLUTIONIST see Bert J. Wellman 153
LAWLESS, ANTHONY see Philip MacDonald 94
LAWRENCE see L(awrence) Sterne Stevens 137
LAWRENCE, IRENE see John Marsh 98
LAWRENCE, MARGERY (H.) see (Mrs.) A. E. Towle 142
LAWRENCE, RICHARD see L. E. Bartle 10
LAWRENCE, STEVEN see L(awrence) Sterne Stevens 137
LAWSON, DENNIS see Frederick Faust 49
LAWSON, W. B.
    see George C. Jenks 77
    see Edward Stratemeyer 138
LAWTON, DENNIS see Frederick Faust 49
LAYTON, F(rank) G(eorge) 86

LYTTON, ROBERT
see Edward R. Bulwer Lytton 93

M. B. see Frederick Faust 49
MAARTENS, MAARTEN see Jozua M. W. Schwartz 128
MACAPP, C. C. see Carroll M. Capps 27
MACARTHUR, BURKE see Arthur J. Burks 25
MCARTHUR, JOHN see Arthur Wise 157
MACAULEY, C. R. see John Kendrick Bangs 9
MCBAIN, ED see S. A. Lombino 90
MACBRIDE, MELCHOIR see John P. Quinton 120
MCCANN, ARTHUR see John W. Campbell, Jr. 27
MCCANN, EDSON
    see R. Alvarez-del Rey 3
    see Frederik Pohl 117
MCCARTHY, JUSTIN see Rosa Caroline Praed 118
MCCLARY, THOMAS CALVERT 94
MCCLELLAND, M(ary) G(reenway) 94
MCCOMAS, J(esse) FRANCIS 94
MCCOY, JOHN 94
MACCREIGH, JAMES see Frederik Pohl 117
M'CRIB, THEOPHILUS see Henry Boyle Lee 86
MCCULLOCH, JOHN TYLER see Edgar Rice Burroughs 26
MCCUTCHEON, GEORGE BARR 94
MACDANIEL, CHARLES see Charles M. Garrison 56
MCDANIEL, DAVID 94
MCDERMOTT, DENNIS see Walter L. Dennis 41
    see Paul McDermott 94
    see P. Schulyer Miller 101
MCDERMOTT, PAUL 94
MCDONALD, ANSON see Robert A. Heinlein 68
MCDONALD, EDWARD RICHARD 94
MACDONALD, JOHN see Kenneth Millar 101
MACDONALD, JOHN D(ann) 94
MACDONALD, JOHN ROSS see Kenneth Millar 101
MACDONALD, PHILIP 94
MCDONALD, RAYMOND
    see Raymond A. Leger 87
    see Edward McDonald 94
MACDONALD, RONALD see Philip MacDonald 94
MACDONALD, ROSS see Kenneth Millar 101
MACDONELL, ARCHIBALD GORDON 94
MACDOUGAL, JOHN
    see James Blish 17
    see Robert W. Lowndes 92
MACDUFF, ANDREW see Horace B. Fyfe 54
MACFARLANE, STEPHEN see John Keir Cross 37
MCGAUGHY, DUDLEY DEAN 94
MCGIVERN, MAUREEN DALY see William P. McGivern 95
MCGIVERN, WILLIAM P(eter) 95
MCGOWAN, INEZ see Roger P. Graham 59
MACGREGOR, JAMES MURDOCH 95
MACGREGOR, MARY see Malcolm Jameson 76
MCHARGUE, GEORGESS 95
MACHEN, ARTHUR 95
MCHENRY, JAMES 95
M'HENRY, JAMES see James McHenry 95
MCHUGH, EDNA see A(melia) R(eynolds) Long 90
MCILVAINE, CHARLES 95
MCILWAIN, D(avid) 96
MCINTOSH, J. T. see James M. MacGregor 95
MACINTOSH, J(ames) (T.) see James M. MacGregor 95
MCINTOSH, KENNETH 96
MCINTOSH, KINN HAMILTON 96
MCKAY, LEWIS H(ugh) 96
MACKAY, MARY 96
MCKENNA, R(ichard) (Milton) 96
MCKENZIE, RAY see Robert Silverberg 132
MACKINTOSH, ELIZABETH 96
MACLEAN, ALISTAIR STUART 96
MACLEOD, FIONA see W(illiam) Sharp 130
MCLOCIARD, GEORGE see Charles F. Locke 89
MCNAUGHTON, BRIAN G. see Robert E. Briney 21

MACNEE, PATRICK see Peter Leslie 87
MCNEILE, H(erman) C(yril) 96
MCNEILLIE, JOHN 97
MCNEILLY, WILFRED 97
MACNIE, J(ohn) 97
MCNUTT, CHARLES see Charles Nutt 107
MACQUORD, K. S. see Margaret Oliphant 108
MACPATTERSON, F. see Walter Ernsting 46
MADDERN, AL see Harlan Ellison 46
MADDOCK, LARRY see Jack Owen Jardine 76
MADDOCK, STEPHEN see J. M. Walsh 150
MADDOX, CARL see E. C. Tubb 143
MADDUX, RACHEL see Rachel Maddux Baker 8
MADLEE, BERTHA see Andre Norton 106
MAEPEN, HUGH see Henry Kuttner 84
MAEPENN, K. H. see Henry Kuttner 84
MAGILL, RORY see Dorothea M. Faulkner 49
MAGNUS, JOHN see Harlan Ellison 46
MAGRISKA, COUNTESS HELENE see Enid Florence Brockies 21
MAINE, C. E. see D(avid) McIlwain 96
MAINE, CHARLES ERIC see D(avid) McIlwain 96
MAINE, DAVID see Claude Avice 8
MAITIN, RICHARD see John Creasey 36
MAJORS, SIMON see Gardner F. Fox 53
MALCOLM, DAN see Robert Silverberg 132
MALET, LUCAS see Mary Harrison 66
MALET, ORIEL see Auriel R. Vaughan 147
MALLESON, LUCY BEATRICE 97
MALLORY, MARK see Dallas McCord Reynolds 122
MALLOWAN, AGATHA (Margaret Clarissa Miller) (Mrs. Max
    Edgar Lucien) 97
MALONEY, FRANCIS (Joseph) T(erence) 97
MALZBERG, BARRY N. 97
THE MAN IN THE MOON see William Thomson 141
THE MAN OF THE PEOPLE see William Thomson 141
MAND, CYRIL
    see George R. Hahn 63
    see Richard Levin 88
MANDERS, HARRY see Philip Jose Farmer 49
MANLEY, MARY DE LA RIVIERE (Mrs. John) 97
MANN, ABEL see John Creasey 36
MANN, JACK see E. Charles Vivian 148
MANNES, MARYA see Marya Mannes Blow 17
MANNING, ADELAIDE F(rances) O(ke) 98
MANNING, DAVID see Frederick Faust 49
MANNING, LEE see Manning Lee Stokes 137
MANTON, PETER see John Creasey 36
MAO see Hazel Iris Wilson Addis 1
MARAS, KARL see H. Kenneth Bulmer 24
MARBO, CAMILLE see Marguerite Borel 18
MARCHANT, ELLA 98
MARCLIFFE, THEOPHILUS see William Godwin 58
MARGROFF, R. see Piers Anthony Dillingham Jacob 75
MARGULIES, LEO see Sam Merwin, Jr. 100
MARIA, LAURA see Mrs. M(ary) Robinson 124
MARIN, A. C. see Alfredo Coppel, Jr. 34
MARIN, ALFRED see Alfredo Coppel, Jr. 34
MARINER, SCOTT
    see Cyril Kornbluth 82
    see Frederik Pohl 117
MARION, HENRY see R. Alvarez-del Rey 3
MARIUS see Steve Benedict 13
MARKHAM, ROBERT see Kingsley Amis 4
MARKHAM, RUSS see Steve Hall 63
MARKS, WINSTON K(itchener) 98
MARLOW, LOUIS see Louis U(mfreville) Wilkinson 155
MARLOWE, STEPHEN see Milton Lesser 87
MARLOWE, WEBB see J. Francis McComas 94
MARNELL, JOSEPH 98
MARNER, ROBERT see Algirdas Jonas Budrys 24
MARRIC, J. J. see John Creasey 36
MARRIOTT, RONALD see Hazel Iris Wilson Addis 1

MARSDEN, ANTHONY see Eric Graham Sutton Sutton 139
MARSDEN, JAMES see John Creasey 36
MARSH, JOAN see John Marsh 98
MARSH, JOHN 98
MARSHAL, JAMES see Sydney James Bounds 18
MARSHALL, LLOYD see Philip Wilding 155
MARSHALL, RAYMOND see Rene Raymond 121
MARSTEN, RICHARD see S. A. Lombino 90
MARTENS, PAUL see Stephen Southwold 136
MARTIN, PETER see Peter Martin Leckie 86
MARTIN, R(eginald) A(lec) 98
MARTIN, REX see R. A. Martin 98
MARTIN, ROBERT see R. A. Martin 98
MARTIN, SCOTT see R. A. Martin 98
MARTIN, THOMAS HECTOR 98
MARTIN, WEBBER see Robert Silverberg 132
MARTYN, EDWARD 98
MARTYN, PHILLIP see E. C. Tubb 143
MARVELL, ANDREW see Howell Davies 39
MASHBURN, KIRK see W. Kirk Mashburn, Jr. 98
MASHBURN, W. KIRK (Jr.) 98
MASON, C. P. 98
MASON, DOUGLAS R(ankine) 98
MASON, ERNST see Frederik Pohl 117
MASON, F. V. W. see F. Van Wyck Mason 99
MASON, F(rancis) VAN WYCK 99
MASON, FRANK W. see F. Van Wyck Mason 99
MASON, GREGORY
    see Adrienne Jones 77
    see Doris Meek 99
MASON, JAMES see Pamela O. Mason 99
MASON, JAMES (Mrs.) see Pamela O. Mason 99
MASON, PAMELA OSTRER 99
MASON, TALLY see August W. Derleth 41
MASON, VAN WYCK see F. Van Wyck Mason 99
MASSE, JAMES see Simon Tyssot de Patot 144
MASSENS, JAKOB see Simon Tyssot de Patot 144
MASSEY, JAMES see Simon Tyssot de Patot 144
MASTERSON, WHIT
    see H. Billy Miller 101
    see Robert Wade 149
MATHERS, HELEN see Helen Mathers Reeves 122
MATHESON, HUGH see Lewis H. McKay 96
MATHESON, JOAN 99
MATHESON, RICHARD (Burton) 99
    see Charles Nutt 107
MATHESON, RODNEY see John Creasey 36
MATHIESON, UNA COOPER see Amanda Melvina Thorley
    Gibson 57
MATURIN, CHARLES R(obert) 99
MATURIN, REV. C. R. see Robert C. Maturin 99
MAURICE, MICHAEL see Conrad (A.) Skinner 134
MAUROIS, ANDRE see Emile S. W. Herzog 69
MAVITY, HUBERT see Nelson S. Bond 18
MAXWELL, JOSLYN see M. J. Ireland 74
MAXWELL, MARY ELIZABETH (Braddon) (Mrs. John) 99
MAY, J. C. see Julian Chain May Dikty 42
MAY, JULIAN (C.) see Julian Chain May Dikty 42
MAYNWARING, ARCHIBALD see H.P. Lovecraft 92
MAYOE, MARIAN AND FRANKLIN see Frank Rosewater 125
MEAD, (Edward) SHEPHERD 99
MEAD, SHEPHERD see (Edward) Shepherd Mead 99
MEADE, L. T. see Elizabeth Thomasina Meade Smith 134
MEADE, LAURA T. see Elizabeth Thomasina Meade Smith 134
MEEK, DORIS 99
MEEK, S. P. [Captain, Major, Col.] see Sterner St. Paul Meek 99
MEEK, S(terner) (St.) P(aul) 99
MEEKER, N(athan) C(ook) 100
MEEKER, W. JOHNS 100
MEINHOLD, JOHANN WILHELM 100
MEINHOLD, WILHELM see Johann Wilhelm Meinhold 100
MELA BRITANNICUS see Charles Kelsall 80

MELVILLE, LEWIS see Lewis Saul Benjamin 13
MENASCO, NORMAN see Wyman Guin 61
MENDICANT, ARCH see Brian W. Aldiss 2
MENTOR see Nathan D. Urner 145
MERCER, CECIL WILLIAM 100
MERCHANT, PAUL see Harlan Ellison 46
MERCURIO BRITANNICO see Joseph Hall 63
MEREDITH, ANNE see Lucy Beatrice Malleson 97
MEREDITH, HAL see Harry Blyth 17
MEREDITH, OWEN see Edward Robert Bulwer Lytton 93
MERLYN, ARTHUR see James Blish 17
MERRIL, JUDITH 100
MERRILL, P. J. see Holly Roth Fanta 47
MERRIMAN, ALEX see Robert Silverberg 132
MERRIMAN, PAT see Philip Atkey 7
MERRITT, AIME see Forrest J. Ackerman 1
MERTZ, BARBARA G(ross) 100
MERWIN, SAM(uel) (Jr.) 100
MESANGE, REV. PIERRE CORDELIER PIERRE DE see Simon
    Tyssot de Patot 144
METCALF, SUZANNE see L. Frank Baum 11
METLOVA, MARIA 100
MEYER, DOROTHY QUICK (Mrs. John Adams) 100
MIALL, ROBERT see John Frederick Burke 25
MICHAELS, BARBARA see Barbara Mertz 100
MICHAELS, STEVE see Michael Avallone, Jr. 8
MICHEL, JOHN B. 100
MICHELS, NICHOLAS 101
MIHILAKIS, ULYSSES GEORGE 101
MIKALOWITCH, NICOLAI see Nicholas Michels 101
MILECETE, HELEN see Susan Carleton Jones 78
"MILES" see Stephen Southwold 136
MILKOMANE, ALEXIS MILKOMANOVICH 101
MILLAR, KENNETH 101
MILLER, BENJAMIN see Noel Loomis 91
MILLER, FRANK see Noel Loomis 91
MILLER, H. BILLY 101
MILLER, MARJORIE see Isaac Asimov 6
MILLER, P(eter) Schuyler 101
MILLER, WADE
    see H. Billy Miller 101
    see Robert Wade 149
M'INTOSH, J. T. see James M. MacGregor 95
MITCHELL, CLYDE [house pseudonym] 101
MITCHELL, GENE see H. Hoadley 70
MITCHELL, GLADYS (Maude Winifred) 101
MOHOAO SEE Edwin Fairburn 47
MOLBECH, CHRISTIAN see Poul Anderson 4
MOLESWORTH, MARY LOUISA (Stewart) (Mrs. R.) 101
MONCHO Y GILABERT, ANTONIO 102
MONDELLE, WENDAYNE see Wendayne Ackerman 1
MONETT, LIREVE see Everil Worrell 158
MONIG, CHRISTOPHER see Kendell F. Crossen 37
MONROE, DONALD 102
MONROE, KEITH 102
MONROE, LYLE see Robert A. Heinlein 68
MONSELL, MARGARET E(mma) (Irwin) (Mrs. John R.) 102
MONTGOMERY, ROBERT BRUCE 102
MOORCOCK, MICHAEL JOHN 102
MOORE, ANON see James M. Galloway 55
MOORE, C. L. see Catherine Lucille Moore Kuttner 83
MOORE, ROBERT see Robert Moore Williams 155
MOORE, WALLACE see Gerard Conway 33
MORATA, JAIDO see John Vickers 148
MORE, ANTHONY see Edwin M. Clinton, Jr. 31
MOREL, DIGHTON see Kenneth (L.) Warner 151
MORELL, CHARLES see James Ridley 123
MORESBY, L(ouis) see Eliza Adams Beck 12
MORGAN, JANE see James Fenimore Cooper 34
MORGAN, DAN see John Charles Hynam 73
MORGAN, SCOTT see Henry Kuttner 84
MORICH, STANTON see George Griffith-Jones 61

MORISON, FRANK see Albert Henry Ross 125
MORLAND, PETER (Henry) see Frederick Faust 49
MORLEY, BRIAN see Marion Zimmer Bradley Breen 20
MORLEY, SUSAN see John Keir Cross 37
MORLEY, WILFRED OWEN see Robert W. Lowndes 92
MORRIS, RALPH 102
MORRIS, SARA see Jonathan Frederick Burke 25
MORRISON, MARGARET MACKIE 102
MORRISON, PEGGY see Margaret Mackie Morrison 103
MORRISON, RICHARD see Robert W. Lowndes 92
MORRISON, ROBERT see Robert W. Lowndes 92
MORRISON, WILLIAM see Joseph Samachson 127
MORRISSEY, JOSEPH LAURENCE 103
MORSE, KATHERINE (Duncan) 103
MORTON, ANTHONY see John Creasey 36
MOSES, MONTROSE J. see David Belasco 12
MOULTON, CARL see E. C. Tubb 143
MOURANT, GEORGE SOULI DE see H. Bedford-Jones 12
MUDDOCK, JOYCE E(mmerson) P(reston) 103
MUDGETT, HERMAN W. see William Anthony Parker White 154
MULLEN, STANLEY (B.) 103
MULLER, JOHN E. see R. Lionel Fanthorpe 48
MULOCK, MISS see Dinah M. Craik 35
MUNCHAUSEN, BARON see Hugo Gernsback 57
MUNCHAUSEN, BARON see R(udolph) (Erich) Raspe 121
MUNDUS, JAKOB see Jakob Vetsch 148
MUNDY, TALBOT see William Lancaster Gribbon 60
MUNRO, DUNCAN H. see Eric Frank Russell 126
MUNRO, H(ector) H(ugh) 103
MURALTO, ONUPHRIO see Horace Walpole 150
MURFREE, MARY NOAILLES 103
MURPHY, DENNIS JASPER see Charles R. Maturin 99
MURRAY-PRIOR, ROSA CAROLINE see Rosa Caroline Praed 118
MURRY, COLIN (Middleton) 103
MUSAEUS PALATINUS see Richard Braithwaite 20
MUSPRATT, ROSALIE 104
MYSELF AND ANOTHER see Edward A. Caswell 29

N. W. see C(live) S(taples) Lewis 88
NADIR, A. A. see Nadir Khan 104
NADIR KHAN AL-IDRISI AL DURRANI, AHMADI ABD ALLAH 104
NA GCOPALEEN, MYLES see Brian O'Nolan 109
NAPIER, GEOFFREY see Bernard Glemser 58
NAPIER, GERALDINE see Bernard Glemser 58
NASIER, ALCOFRIBAS see Francois Rabelais 121
NATHAN, DANIEL see Frederic Dannay 38
NAVARCHUS
     see Patrick Vaux 147
     see James Woods 158
NEAL, GAVIN see E. C. Tubb 143
NEAL, HARRY see Drexel Jerome Bixby 15
NEEF, ELTON T. see R. Lionel Fanthorpe 48
NEEPER, CAROLYN 104
NEEPER, CARY see Carolyn Neeper 104
NELSON, RADELL FARADAY 104
NELSON, RAY see Radell Faraday Nelson 104
NEMO, OMEN see Warren S. Rehm 122
NESBIT, E(dith) see Edith Nesbit Bland 16
NETTERVILLE, LUKE see Standish James O'Grady 108
NEVILLE, HENRY 104
NEVILLE, KRIS OTTMAN 105
NEWMAN, BERNARD CHARLES 105
NEWMAN, JOHN 105
NEWTE, THOMAS see William Thomson 141
NIALL, IAN see John McNeillie 97
NICHOLSON, JOHN see Norman H(owe) Parcell 112
NICHOLSON, J(oseph) S(hield) 105
NICHOLSON, KENYON see G(eorge) Edwards Pendray 113
NICOLL, (Henry) Maurice (Dunlop) 105
NICOLL, MAURICE see (Henry) Maurice Nicoll 105
NIHIL see P. Schuyler Miller 101
NILE, DOROTHEA see Michael Avallone, Jr. 8

NILINSE, BARON DE see Jacques Simon Collin de Plancy 32
NISOT, ELIZABETH see (Mrs.) (Mavis) Elizabeth Nisot 105
NISOT, MAVIS ELIZABETH (Hocking) (Mrs.) 105
NIVEN, LARRY see David Gerrold Friedman 54
NIXON, WM. PENN see Albion W. Tourgee 142
NOBEL, PHIL see R. Lionel Fanthorpe 48
NOEL, L. see Leonard N. Barker 10
NOLAN, BRIAN see Brian O'Nolan 109
NOLAN, WILLIAM FRANCIS 105
     see Charles Nutt 107
NONAME see Lu(is) (P.) Senarens 129
NOONE, EDWINA see Michael Avallone, Jr. 8
NORBERT, W. see Norbert Wiener 155
NORK, F. see Friedrich Korn 82
NORMAN, JOHN see John Frederick Lange, Jr. 85
NORMYX see George Norman Douglas 43
NORTH, ANDREW see Andre Norton 106
NORTH, ERIC see Bernard Cronin 36
NORTH, HOWARD see Elleston Trevor 143
NORTHERN, LESLIE [house pseudonym] 106
NORTHRUP, CAPT. B. A. see L. Ron Hubbard 72
NORTHRUP, EDWIN F(itch) 106
NORTON, ALICE MARY see Andre Norton 106
NORTON, ANDRE 106
NORWAY, NEVIL SHUTE 107
NOSILLE, NALRAH see Harlan Ellison 46
NOSTRADAMUS, MERLIN see Frances Power Cobbe 32
NOWLAN, PHIL(ip) (Francis) 107
NUETZEL, CHARLES (Alexander) 107
NUTT, CHARLES 107
NUTT, LILY C(live) 107
NUVERBIS see Dillon Jordan Spotswood 136

O'BRIEN, C(lifford) EDWARD 108
O'BRIEN, DAVID WRIGHT 108
     see William P. McGivern 95
O'BRIEN, DEAN D.
     see Earl Andrew Binder 15
     see Otto Oscar Binder 15
O'BRIEN, DEE see Marion Zimmer Bradley Breen 20
O'BRIEN, E. G. see Arthur C. Clarke 31
O'BRIEN, FLANN see Brian O'Nolan 109
O'BRIEN, FLORENCE ROMA MUIR WILSON 108
O'BRIEN, LARRY CLINTON see C(lifford) Edward O'Brien 108
O'CONNER, PATRICK see Leonard Wibberley 154
O'CONNER-WIBBERLEY, LEONARD FRANCIS PATRICK see
     Leonard Wibberley 154
O'DONNELL, K. M. see Barry N. Malzberg 97
O'DONNELL, LAWRENCE
     see Henry Kuttner 84
     see C. L. Moore 83
O'DONNEVAN, FINN see Robert Sheckley 130
AN OFFICER IN COL. BAILLIE'S DETACHMENT see William
     Thomson 141
OFFUT, ANDY see Andrew J. Offutt, Jr. 108
OFFUTT, ANDREW J. (Jr.) 108
O'FLINN, PETER see R. Lionel Fanthorpe 48
O'GRADY, ROHAN see June O'Grady Skinner 134
O'GRADY, STANDISH JAMES 108
O'HARA, KENNETH see Bryce Walton 150
O'HARA, SCOTT see John D. MacDonald 94
O'HARA FAMILY, THE
     see John Banim 9
     see Michael Banim 9
OLBEN, BOB see Alfred Johannes Olsen, Jr. 109
OLDFIELD, CLAUDE HOUGHTON 108
OLD SLEUTH see Harlan Page Halsey 63
O'LE LUK-OIE see Ernest D. Swinton 139
OLIPHANT, (Mrs.) see Margaret O. Oliphant 108
OLIPHANT, MARGARET OLIPHANT (Wilson) (Mrs.
     Francis W.) 108
OLIVER, AMY ROBERTA (Ruck) (Mrs. George) 108

OLIVER, CHAD see Symmes C(hadwick) Oliver 109
OLIVER, FREDERICK S(penser) 108
OLIVER, GEORGE 108
OLIVER, SYMMES C(hadwick) 109
OLSEN, ALFRED JOHANNES (Jr.) 109
OLSEN, BOB see Alfred Johannes Olsen, Jr. 109
OLSON, EUGENE E. 109
O'MALLEY, FRANK 109
O'MALLEY, M(ary) D(olling) (Sanders) (Lady) 109
OMEGA see Ray Bradbury 19
O'NEILL, EGAN see (Barbara) Elizabeth Linington 89
ONIONS, GEORGE OLIVER see George Oliver 108
ONIONS, MRS. OLIVER see Amy Roberta Oliver 108
ONIONS, OLIVER see George Oliver 108
O'NOLAN, BRIAN 109
O'NUALLAIN, BRIEN see Brian O'Nolan 109
OPPENHEIM, ANSEL (Mrs.) see John Emersie 46
OPPENHEIM, E(dward) PHILLIPS 109
ORCZY, BARONESS see Emmuska Orcay Barstow 10
ORDONEZ EDMONDSON Y COTTON, JOSE MARIO GARRY 109
O'ROURKE, FRANK see Frank O'Malley 109
ORTH, BENNINGTON see Roger Sherman Hoar 70
ORWELL, GEORGE see Eric Arthur Blair 16
OSBORNE, DAVID see Robert Silverberg 132
OSBORNE, GEORGE see Robert Silverberg 132
OSCEOLA see Karen Blixen-Finecke 17
O'SHEA, SEAN see Stanley Robert Tralins 142
OSTRANDER, ISABEL E(genton) 110
OTIS, JAMES see James Otis Kaler 79
OURSLER, (Charles) FULTON 110
OURSLER, FULTON see (Charles) Fulton Oursler 110
OUSELEY, GIDEON JASPER RICHARD 110
OVERTON, MAX see Don Wilcox 155
OWEN, COLLINSON see Harry Collinson Owen 110
OWEN, DEAN see Dudley Dean McGaughy 94
OWEN, ETHEL see Frank Owen 110
OWEN, FRANK 110
OWEN, HARRY COLLINSON 110
OWEN, HUGH see Frederick Faust 49
OWENS, A. see Harold Hersey 69
OXENHAM, JOHN see William A. Dunkerley 44

P. B. S. see Percy B(ysshe) Shelley 131
P., G. H. see George H. Putnam 119
PADGETT, LEWIS
  see Henry Kuttner 84
  see C. L. Moore 83
PAGE, GERALD W. 111
PAGE, NORVELL, W. 111
PAGET, VIOLET 111
PAGET-LOWE, H(enry) see H. P. Lovecraft 92
PAIG, EVELYN see Evelyn Paige Gold 58
PAIGE, EVELYN see Evelyn Paige Gold 58
PAINE, GUTHRIE see F. Orlin Tremaine 142
PAKENHAM, T. COMPTON see Nadir Khan 104
PALATINUS, MUSAEUS see Richard Braithwaite 20
PALMER, JOHN LESLIE 111
PALMER, RAYMOND A(rthur) 111
PALTOCK, ROBERT 111
PAMJEAN, LOUIS see H. Bedford-Jones 12
PAMPHILUS, HESYCHIUS see Richard Braithwaite 20
"PAN" see Leslie Beresford 13
PANEDONIUS, PHILOGENES see Richard Braithwaite 20
PANGBORN, EDGAR 111
PARABELLUM see Ferdinand H. Grautoff 60
PARCELL, NORMAN H(owe) 112
PARGETER, EDITH MAY 112
PARIS, JOHN see Frank T. A. Ashton-Gwatkin 6
PARK, JORDAN
  see Cyril Kornbluth 82
  see Frederik Pohl 117
PARKER, BERT see Harlan Ellison 46

PARKER, DOROTHY see Elmer L. Reizenstein 122
PARKES, LUCAS see John B(eynon) Harris 65
PARKES, WYNDHAME see John B(eynon) Harris 65
PARLEY, PETER see Samuel Griswold Goodrich 59
PARNELL, FRANK 112
PARR, ROBERT see Erle Stanley Gardner 55
PARRY, MICHAEL PATRICK 112
PARTRIDGE, ANTHONY see E. Phillips Oppenheim 109
PARTRIDGE, BELLAMY see Edward Bellamy Partridge 112
PARTRIDGE, EDWARD BELLAMY 112
PASSANTE, DOM see John Russell Fearn 50
PASTOR, TONY see Harlan Page Halsey 63
PATER, (Philip) ROGER see Gilbert Roger Hudleston 72
PATRICK, JOHN see Michael Avallone, Jr. 8
PATRICK, Q.
  see Martha Mott Kelley 79
  see Richard Wilson Webb 152
A PATRIOT see L. Guy 62
PATTEN, CLINTON A. 112
PATTEN, GILBERT 112
PATTEN, J. A(lexander) 112
PATTEN, WILLIAM G. see Gilbert Patten 112
PATTIESON, PETER see Sir Walter Scott 129
PATTON, FRANK [house pseudonym] 112
PAUL, F. W. see Paul W. Fairman 47
PAULDING, JAMES KIRKE 112
PAYE, ROBERT see Gabrielle M. V. Long 91
PAYES, RACHEL RUTH COSGROVE (Mrs. Norman M.) 113
PAYNE, DONALD GORDON 113
PEARSON, MARTIN
  see Cyril M. Kornbluth 82
  see Donald A. Wollheim 157
PEASE, LT. JOHN see Roger Sherman Hoar 70
PECK, GEORGE WASHINGTON 113
PEEBLES, JOHN EWING 113
PELKIE, J(oe) W(alter) see Raymond A. Palmer 111
PEMBER-DEVEREUX, MARGARET R(ose) (Roy) (McAdam) (Mrs.) 113
PEMBROOKE, KENNETH see Gerald W. Page 111
PENDARVES, G. G. see Gladys Gordon Trenery 142
PENDLETON, DON 113
PEN-DRAG-ON, ARSER see William Henry Ireland 74
PENDRAGON, ERIC see Michael Patrick Parry 112
PENDRAY, G(eorge) EDWARDS 113
PENMARE, WILLIAM see (Mrs.) (Mavis) Elizabeth Nisot 105
PENNY, RICHARD see David Lasser 85
PENTECOST, HUGH see Judson (P.) Philips 114
PERCIVAL, NORMAN see Norman H(owe) Parcell 112
PERDITA see Mrs. M(ary) Robinson 124
PEREGORY, CALVIN see Thomas Calvert McClary 94
PEREZ, JUAN see Manly Wade Wellman 153
PERIL, MILTON R. see Francis Jones 77
PERKINS, ELI see Melville De Lancy Landon 85
PERKINS, VIOLET LILIAN 113
PEROWNE, BARRY see Philip Atkey 7
PERRI, LESLIE see Doris Baumgardt Wilson 157
PERROT, GERVASE see Arthur Machen 95
A PERSON WITHOUT A NAME see Alethea Lewis 88
PETAJA, EMIL (Theodore) 113
PETERS, BILL see William P. McGivern 95
PETERS, BRYAN see Peter George 57
PETERS, ELIZABETH see Barbara Mertz 100
PETERS, ELLIS see Edith Pargeter 112
PETERSILEA, CARLYLE 113
PETERSON, JOHN VICTOR 114
PETERSON, MARGARET see Margaret Peterson Fischer 52
PEYTON, GREEN see G. Peyton Wertenbaker 153
PFEIFFER, JOHANN GREGOR 114
PFEIL, DON 114
PHELAN, JEREMIAH see C. Daly King 80
PHELPS, ELIZABETH STUART see Elizabeth Stuart Phelps Ward 151

PHELPS, GEORGE H(amilton) 114
PHILIBIN, A. see John H. Pollock 118
PHILIPS, JUDSON P(entecost) 114
PHILLIFENT, JOHN T(homas) 114
PHILLIPS, FRANK see Philip F. Nowlan 107
PHILLIPS, MARK
   see Gordon Randall Garrett 56
   see Larry Mark Harris 65
PHILLIPS, MICHAEL see Charles Nutt 107
PHILLIPS, PETER [house pseudonym] 114
PHILLIPS, ROG see Roger P. Graham 60
PHILLIPS, WARD see H. P. Lovecraft 92
PHILLPOTTS, EDEN 114
PHILOGENES PANEDONIUS see Richard Braithwaite 20
PHILPOT, JOSEPH HENRY 115
PHIZ see Hablot Knight Browne 22
PHYLOS, THE TIBETAN see Frederick S. Oliver 108
PHYSICK, EDWARD HAROLD 115
PICA, PETER see Brian W. Aldiss 2
PICTON, NINA 115
PIERCE, JOHN R(obinson) 115
PIERS, ASHDOWN see John James Pitcairn 115
PIGGOTT, WILLIAM 115
PIKE, ROBERT L. see Robert L. Fish 52
PILGRIM, DAVID see John (Leslie) Palmer 111
PILKINGTON, (Mrs.) (M.S.) see Mary (Hopkins) Pilkington 115
PILKINGTON, MARY (Hopkins) (Mrs.) 115
PINCHER, CHAPMAN see Henry Chapman Pincher 115
PINCHER, HENRY CHAPMAN 115
PINE, THEODORE
   see Henry Hasse 66
   see Emil Petaja 113
PIRIE-GORDON, C(harles) H(arry) C(linton) 115
PITCAIRN, FRANK see Francis Claude Cockburn 32
PITCAIRN, JOHN JAMES 115
PITTARD, HELENE (Dufour) (Mrs. Eugene) 115
PLANET PRINCE, THE see J. Harvey Haggard 63
PLATT, CHARLES see Thomas M. Disch 42
PLUNKETT, EDWARD JOHN MORETON DRAX (18th Baron Dunsany) 115
POE, EDGAR ALLAN 116
POHL, FREDERIK 117
POHL, FREDERIK (Mrs.) see Judith Merril 100
POHL, FREDERIK (Mrs.) see Doris Baumgardt Wilson 157
POLLARD, JOHN X. [house pseudonym] 117
POLLOCK, JOHN H(ackett) 118
POLLOCK, WALTER HERRIES see Andrew Lang 85
POMERANO, CASTALIO see Richard Braithwaite 20
POPE, ALEXANDER see John C(ollings) Squire 136
PORGES, ARTHUR 118
PORJES, TILLY see Wendayne Ackerman 1
PORLOCK, MARTIN see Philip MacDonald 94
PORTER, C. O. see Albert P. Blaustein 16
PORTER, LINN BOYD 118
PORTER, WILLIAM SYDNEY 118
POWELL, SONNY see Alfred Bester 14
POWERS, CECIL see Charles Grant Allen 3
PRAED, MRS. CAMPBELL see Rosa Caroline Praed 118
PRAED, ROSA CAROLINE (Mrs. Campbell) 118
PRATT, FLETCHER 118
PRATT, THEODORE 118
PRATT, WILLIAM HENRY 119
PREEDY, GEORGE R(unnell) see Gabrielle M. V. Long 91
PRESTO see Jonathan Swift 139
PRICE, E(dgar) HOFFMAN 119
PRICHARD, HESKETH see H. Hesketh-Prichard 119
PRICHARD, H(esketh) (Vernon) HESKETH- 119
PRICHARD, K. AND H.
   see H. Hesketh-Prichard 119
   see Mrs. K. Hesketh-Prichard 119
PRICHARD, K(ate) O'BRIEN HESKETH- 119
PRIESTLEY, MRS. J. B. see Jacquetta Hawkes 67

PRIME, LORD see Walter D. Reynolds 123
PRINCE OF WALES (later George IV) see Mrs. M(ary) Robinson 124
PRINCESS OF WIED see Elisabeth, Queen-Consort of Charles I King of Rumania 45
PRITCHARD, WILLIAM THOMAS 119
PRONZINI, BILL 119
PROPHET JAMES, THE see James S. Buck 24
PROSPERO AND CALIBAN
   see C. H. C. Pirie-Gordon 115
   see Frederick (W.) Rolfe 125
PRUNING KNIFE see Henry F. Allen 3
PSEUDOMAN, AKKAD see Edwin F. Northrup 106
PUTNAM, GEORGE H(aven) 119
PUTNAM, ISRA see Greye La Spina 85
PUTNAM, KENNETH see Philip Klass 81
PYM, ARTHUR GORDON see Edgar A(llan) Poe 116

Q see A(rthur) Quiller-Couch 120
QUARLES see Edgar A(llan) Poe 116
QUEEN, ELLERY
   see Frederic Dannay 38
   see Manfred B. Lee 86
QUENTIN, PATRICK
   see Richard Wilson Webb 152
   see Hugh Collinson Wheeler 154
QUESNEL, PIERRE 120
QUICK, DOROTHY see Dorothy Quick Meyer 100
QUICK, HERBERT see John Herbert Quick 120
QUICK, JOHN HERBERT 120
QUICKENS, QUARLES see Edgar A(llan) Poe 117
¿QUIEN SABE? see Harry Bates 11
QUILLER-COUCH, A(rthur) T. (Sir) 120
QUINTON, JOHN P(urcell) 120
QUITMAN, WALLACE see Raymond A. Palmer 111

R. B., AUTHOR OF "THE HISTORY OF THE WARS OF ENGLAND, &C." see Nathaniel Crouch 37
R., C. see Clara Reeve 122
R. S. see Robert Paltock 111
RABE, ANN C(rawford) VON (Baroness) 121
RABELAIS, FRANCOIS 121
RABINOWITZ, SHALOM 121
RABINOWITZ, SOLOMON (J.) see Shalom Rabinowitz 121
RACKHAM, JOHN see John T. Phillifent 114
RADCLIFFE, ANN WARD (Mrs. William) 121
RAGGED, HYDER see Henry C. Biron 15
RAINEY, W. B. see Wyatt Rainey Blassingame 16
RASIEL DE SELVA, HERCULE see Pierre Quesnel 120
RALEIGH, RICHARD see H. P. Lovecraft 92
RALPH, MR. LE DOCTEUR see Francois-Marie Arouet 6
RAMAL, WALTER see Walter J. de la Mare 40
RAME, DAVID see Arthur Durham Divine 42
RAMSDEN, LEWIS see A. L. Dowding 43
RANDALL, ROBERT
   see Gordon Randall Garrett 56
   see Robert Silverberg 132
RANDOLPH, G. A. see S. A. Lombino 90
RANDOLPH, GEORGIANA ANN 121
RANGER, KEN see John Creasey 36
RANKIN, HUGH DOAK 121
RANKINE, JOHN see Douglas R. Mason 98
RAPPOPORT, SOLOMON 121
RASPE, RUDOLPH E(rich) 121
RATH, E. J.
   see Chauncey Brainerd 19
   see Edith Brainerd 19
RATTRAY, SIMON see Elleston Trevor 143
RAY, JEAN see Raymond Kremer 83
RAYCRAFT, STAN see Richard Shaver 130
RAYMOND, E. V. see Raymond Z. Gallun 55
RAYMOND, HUGH see John B. Michel 100

RAYMOND, LITZKA see Mrs. Walter B. Gibson 58
RAYMOND, RENE BRABAZON 121
RAYMOND, ROBERT see Robert Alter 3
RAYNER, OLIVE PRATT see Charles Grant Allen 3
RAYNER, RICHARD see D(avid) McIlwain 96
RECOUR, CHARLES see Henry Bott 18
RECTEZ, IAN see Mort(imer) Weisinger 152
REED, ALLAN see Wolf Detlef Rohr 125
REED, DAVID V. see David Vern 147
REED, KIT see Lilian Craig Reed 122
REED, LILIAN CRAIG 122
REED, LILIAN CRAIG 122
REED, PETER see John D. MacDonald 94
REEDS, F. ANTON 122
REES, DILWYN see Glyn E(dmund) Daniel 38
REEVE, CLARA 122
REEVES, HELEN BUCKINGHAM MATHERS (Mrs. Henry A.) 122
REEVES, JUSTIN 122
REGARD, PAUL see Perley Poore Sheehan 130
REHM, WARREN S. 122
REID, DESMOND see Wilfred McNeilly 97
REID, WALLACE Q. see George Goodchild 59
REINSER III see Andre Guillaume Resnier 122
REIZENSTEIN, ELMER L. 122
REMENHAM, JOHN see John A. Vlasto 148
REPP, ED(ward) EARL 122
RESNIER, ANDRE GUILLAUME 122
RESSICH, JOHN 122
RETLA, ROBERT see Robert Alter 3
REYNOLDS, ADRIAN see A(melia) R(eynolds) Long 90
REYNOLDS, DALLAS MCCORD 122
REYNOLDS, L. MAJOR see Louise Leipiar 87
REYNOLDS, MACK see Dallas McCord Reynolds 122
REYNOLDS, PETER see A(melia) R(eynolds) Long 90
REYNOLDS, RON see Ray Bradbury 19
REYNOLDS, WALTER D(oty) 123
RHODE, JOHN see C. J. C. Street 138
RHOSCOMYL, OWEN see Owen Vaughan 147
RICCI, L. A. DA COSTA see Lewis Ritchie 124
RICCI, LEWIS see Lewis Ritchie 124
RICE, ALLISON
   see Ruth Allison 123
   see Jane Rice 123
RICE, CRAIG see Georgiana Ann Randolph 121; S.A. Lombino 90
RICE, ELMER see Elmer L. Reizenstein 122
RICE, JANE 123
RICHARD, FRANCOIS 123
RICHARD, KENT see Kendell F. Crossen 37
RICHARD-BESSIERE, F.
   see Richard Bessiere 14
   see Francois Richard 123
RICHARDS, CLAY see Kendell F. Crossen 37
RICHARDS, FRANK see Charles Hamilton 63
RICHARDS, HENRY see Joseph Laurence Morrissey 103
RICHARDSON, FLAVIA see Christine Campbell Thomson Cook 33
RICHARDSON, FRANCIS
   see L. E. Bartle 10
   see Frank Parnell 112
RICHARDSON, R(obert) S(hirley) 123
RICHMOND, GRACE see John Marsh 98
RICHTER, ERNST H. 123
RIDDELL, CHARLOTTE ELIZA L(awson) (Cowan) (Mrs. J. H.) 123
RIDDELL, J. H. (Mrs.) see Charlotte Elizabeth L. Riddell 123
RIDEAUX, CHARLES DE BALZAC 123
RIDLEY, JAMES 123
RIKER, ANTHONY see F. Anton Reeds 122
RILEY, JAMES WHITCOMB 123
RILEY, TEX see John Creasey 36
RILEY, WILLIAM K. see John Creasey 36
RIOS, TERE see Maria Teresa Rios Versack 148
RITCHIE, LEWIS ANSELM DA COSTA 124
RIVERSIDE, JOHN see Robert A. Heinlein 68

ROACH, ROBERT W. A. 124
ROBBINS, CLARENCE AARON 124
ROBBINS, TOD see Clarence Aaron Robbins 124
ROBERTS, KEITH JOHN KINGSTON 124
ROBERTS, KENNETH see Lester Dent 41
ROBERTS, LIONEL see R. Lionel Fanthorpe 48
ROBERTS, MURRAY see Robert Murray Graydon 60
ROBERTS, TERENCE see Ivan T. Sanderson 127
ROBERTSON, ALICE A(lberthe) 124
ROBERTSON, E(ileen) Arnot see Eileen Arbuthnot Robertson
   Turner 144
ROBERTSON, ELLIS
   see Harlan Ellison 46
   see Robert Silverberg 133
ROBERTSON, FRANK C(hester) 124
ROBESON, KENNETH
   see Lester Dent 41
   see Paul F. Ernst 46
ROBEY, GEORGE see Arthur S. Ward 151
ROBINET, LEE see F. G. Browne 22
ROBINETT, STEPHEN 124

ROBINSON, MARY (Darby) (Mrs. Thomas) 124
ROBLES, ANTONIO see Antonio Robles Soler 136
ROCHA, ADOLPHO 124
ROCK, C. V. see Kurt Walter Rocken 124
ROCK, JAMES see Clinton A. Patten 112
ROCKEN, KURT WALTER 124
ROCKEN, WALTER see Kurt Walter Rocken 124
ROCKLIN, R. L. see Ross Rocklynne 124
ROCKLYNNE, ROSS 124
ROCKWOOD, ROY see Edward Stratemeyer 138
RODMAN, ERIC see Robert Silverberg 132
ROE, IVAN 125
ROE, WILLIAM J(ames) 125
ROEDER, PAT see Harlan Ellison 46
ROGER, NOELLE see Helene Pittard 115
ROGERS, DOUG see Ray Bradbury 19
ROGERS, MELVA see Roger P. Graham 60
ROGERS, PAT see Arthur Porges 118
ROHMER ELIZABETH (S.) see Rose Elizabeth Knox Ward 151
ROHMER, SAX see Arthur S. Ward 151
ROHR, WOLF DETLEF 125
ROLAND, MARY see Mary Christianna Milne Lewis 88
ROLANT, RENE see R. Lionel Fanthorpe 48
ROLFE, FREDERICK W(illiam) SERAFINO AUSTIN LEWIS
   MARY 125
ROMANOFF, ALEXANDER NICHOLAYEVITCH see Nadir
   Khan 104
ROME, ALGER
   see Drexel J. Bixby 15
   see Algirdas Jonas Budrys 24
ROPES, ARTHUR R(eed) 125
ROPSHIN see Boris Savinkov 127
ROSE, LAURENCE, F. see John Russell Fearn 50
ROSE, FRANCIS (Frank) see John Russell Fearn 50
ROSENBERG, ELINOR BLAISDELL (Mrs. Melrich) 125
ROSEWATER, FRANK 125
ROSNY, J. H.
   see J. H. H. Boex 18
   see S. J. F. Boex 18
ROSNY-AINE, J. H. see J. H. H. Boex 18
ROSNY-JEUNE, J. H. see S. J. F. Boex 18
ROSS, ADRIAN see A(rthur) R. Ropes 125
ROSS, ALBERT see Linn Boyd Porter 118
ROSS, ALBERT HENRY 125
ROSS, BARNABY
   see Frederic Dannay 39
   see Manfred B. Lee 86
ROSS, DALLAS see Dallas McCord Reynolds 123

STANTON, EDWARD see Edward S. Huntington 73
STANTON, JOHN see G(eorge) C. Wallis 150
STANTON, VANCE see Michael Avallone, Jr. 8
STARK, RICHARD see Donald E. Westlake 153
STARKE, HENDERSON see Kris Neville 105
STARR, JOHN see Roger D. Aycock 8
STATTEN, VARGO see John Russell Fearn 51
STAUNTON, SCHUYLER see L. Frank Baum 11
STEARNS, ALBERT see Edgar Franklin Stearns 136
STEARNS, EDGAR FRANKLIN 136
STEBER, A(lfred) R.
    see Roger P. Graham 60
    see Raymond A. Palmer 111
STEDMAN, CHARLES see William Thomson 141
STEELE, MARY QUINTARD (Mrs. William O.) 137
STEELE, MORRIS J. [house pseudonym] 137
STEIGER, BRAD see Eugene E. Olson 109
STEIN, BERNARD see Karl F. Kahlert 79
STEINER, GEROLF 137
STERLING, BRETT [house pseudonym] 137
STERN, PAUL FREDERICK see Paul F. Ernst 46
STEVENS, CHRISTOPHER see Paul Tabori 140
STEVENS, FRANCIS see Gertrude Barrows Bennett 13
STEVENS, L(awrence) STERNE 137
STEVENSON, JOHN 137
STEWART, ALFRED W(alter) 137
STEWART, LOGAN see Philip Wilding 155
STEWART, WILL see John Stewart Williamson 156
STINE, G. HARRY 137
STINE, HANK see Henry Eugene Stine 137
STINE, HENRY EUGENE 137
STOCKBRIDGE, GRANT see Norvell W. Page 111
STODDARD, CHARLES [house pseudonym] 137
STOKER, ABRAHAM 137
STOKER, BRAM see Abraham Stoker 137
STOKES, MANNING LEE 137
STOKES, SIMPSON see Frank D. Fawcett 50
STONE, LESLIE F. see Leslie Stone Silberberg (Mrs. William) 132
STORM, ERIC see E. C. Tubb 143
STORM, MALLORY see Paul W. Fairman 47
STORM, RUSSELL see Robert Moore Williams 155
STORY, A. M. SOMMERVILLE 138
STOVER, LEON see Harry Max Harrison 66
STOWE, (Mrs. H. M.) 138
STRANG, HERBERT see George H(erbert) Ely 46
STRANGER, RALPH see Ralph Judson 78
STRATEMEYER, EDWARD 138
STRATFORD, H. PHILIP see H. Kenneth Bulmer 24
STRATTON, THOMAS
    see Robert Coulson 35
    see Gene DeWeese 41
STREET, C(ecil) J(ohn) C(harles) 138
STRINGER, DAVID see Keith Roberts 124
STRONG, HERO see Clara Augusta Jones 77
STRONG, SPENCER see Forrest J. Ackerman 1
STRONGI'TH'ARM, CHARLES see Charles Wicksteed Armstrong 5
STROUD, ALBERT see Algirdas Jonas Budrys 24
STRUGATSKI, ARKADI see Wendayne Ackerman 1
STRUGATSKI, BORIS see Wendayne Ackerman 1
STUART, DON A. see John W. Campbell, Jr. 27
STUART, GORDON
    see H. Bedford-Jones 12
    see H(arry) L(incoln) Sayler 127
STUART, IAN see Alistair MacLean 96
STUART, LOGAN see Philip Wilding 155
STUART, SIDNEY see Michael Avallone, Jr. 8
STUBBS, HARRY C(lement) 138
"A STUDENT OF OCCULTISM" see Franz Hartmann 66
STUMPKE, HAROLD see Gerolf Steiner 137
STURGEON, THEODORE 138

STURGIS, COLIN
    see Les(ter) Cole 32
    see Mel(vin) Sturgis 138
STURGIS, MEL(vin) 138
STURTZEL, HOWARD ALLISON 139
STURTZEL, JANE LEVINGTON (Comfort) (Mrs. Howard A.) 139
A SUB-UTOPIAN see Richard Walker 149
SUDDABY (William) DONALD 139
SUTTON, ERIC GRAHAM SUTTON 139
SUTTON, GRAHAM see Eric Graham Sutton Sutton 139
SWAIN, DWIGHT V(reeland) 139
SWAN, ANNIE S. see Helen Mathers Reeves 122
SWANSON, LOGAN see Richard Matheson 99
SWAYNE, MARTIN see (Henry) Maurice Nicoll 105
SWEVEN, GODFREY see J. Macmillan Brown 21
SWIFT, ANTHONY see J(oseph) J(efferson) Farjeon 48
SWIFT, AUGUSTUS T. see H. P. Lovecraft 92
SWIFT, JONATHAN 139
SWINTON, ERNEST D(unlop) (Sir) 139
SYDENHAM, LORD see George S. Clarke 31
SYLVA, CARMEN see Elisabeth, Queen-Consort of Charles I King of Rumania 45
SYMMES, JOHN CLEVES 139
SYNTAX, DR. see William Combe 33

T. E. see Thomas Erskine 46
T., J. see Eric Temple Bell 13
T., S. see Horace Walpole 150
TABOR, PAUL see Paul Tabori 140
TABORI, PAUL 140
TAINE, JOHN see Eric Temple Bell 13
TAIT, G(eorge) B. 140
TALL, STEPHEN see Compton N. Crook 36
TANGENT, PATRICK QUINN see George H. Phelps 114
TARA, JOHN see John B. Michel 101
TARNACRE, ROBERT see Robert Cartmell 29
TARNE, ROSINA see John Russell Fearn 51
TATE, ROBIN see R. Lionel Fanthorpe 48
TAVERAL, JOHN see Robert E. Howard 72
TAYLOR, JUDSON R. see Harlan Page Halsey 63
TEED, CYRUS R(eed) 140
TELUCCINI, MARIO 140
TEMPLE, JAMES see Eric Temple Bell 13
TEMPLE, RALPH see R. W. Alexander 2
TEMPLETON, HERMINIE see Herminie Templeton Kavanaugh 79
TEMPLETON, JESSE see George Goodchild 59
TENN, WILLIAM see Philip Klass 81
TENNESHAW, S. M. [house pseudonym] 140
TENTH PRESIDENT OF THE WORLD REPUBLIC see Andrew Blair 16
TERHUNE, ALBERT PAYSON 140
TERRIDGE, ERNEST see Ernst H. Richter 123
TERRY see Francis T. Maloney 97
TERTZ, ABRAM see Andrei Donatevich Siniavskii 134
TETERNIKOV, FEDOR KUZ'MICH 140
TEY, JOSEPHINE see Elizabeth MacKintosh 96
THAMES, C(hristopher) (H.) see Milton Lesser 87
THANET, NEIL see R. Lionel Fanthorpe 48
THANET, OCTAVE see Alice French 54
THEOBALD see H. P. Lovecraft 92
THEOBALD, L(ewis), (Jr.) see H. P. Lovecraft 92
THEOBALDUS see H. P. Lovecraft 92
THEOSOPHO see Gideon Ouseley 110
THIBAULT, JACQUES ANATOLE FRANCOIS 141
THISTED, V(aldemar) ADOLPH 141
THIUSEN, ISMAR see J. MacNie 97
THOMAS, DAN see Leonard M. Sanders, Jr. 127
THOMAS, DANA LEE see Henry (T.) Schnittkind 128
THOMAS, DORIS see Doris Vancel 147
THOMAS, ELIZABETH (Mrs.) of TIDENHAM 141
THOMAS, HENRY see Henry (T.) Schnittkind 128
THOMAS, K. see John Russell Fearn 51

WHITLEY, GEORGE see A. Bertram Chandler 30
WHITMORE, H. 154
WHITNEY, ELLIOTT
   see H. Bedford-Jones 12
   see H(arry) L(incoln) Sayler 128
WHITNEY, REID see R. Coutts Armour 5
WHITNEY, SPENCER see Arthur J. Burks 25
WHYTE, SIBLEY see Henry Eugene Stine 137
WIBBERLEY, LEONARD (Francis) (Patrick) 154
WICKER, THOMAS GREY 155
WICKER, TOM see Thomas Grey Wicker 155
WIDNER, ARTHUR L. 155
WIENER, NORBERT 155
WILCOX, DON 155
WILCOX, MARRION 155
WILDE, JIMMY see John Creasey 36
WILDER, WILLIAM WEST see Gilbert Patten 112
WILDING, ERIC see E. C. Tubb 144
WILDING, PHILIP 155
WILEY, CARL A. 155
WILEY, JOHN see Roger P. Graham 60
WILHELM, KATE see Kate Wilhelm Knight 81
WILKINSON, LOUIS U(mfreville) 155
WILLER see Ed(mund) Emshwiller 46
WILLEY, ROBERT see Willy Ley 89
WILLIAMS, DAVID RHYS 155
WILLIAMS, GEORGE RUSSELL see George W. Russell 126
WILLIAMS, HAROLD 155
WILLIAMS, L. G. see Eugene E. Olson 109
WILLIAMS, MASON see Dean A. Grennell 60
WILLIAMS, R. F. 155
WILLIAMS, ROBERT MOORE 155
WILLIAMS, ROSWELL see Frank Owen 110
WILLIAMS, SPEEDY see L. H. Smith 135
WILLIAMS, TENNESSEE see Thomas Lanier Williams 156
WILLIAMS, THOMAS LANIER 156
WILLIAMS-ELLIS, A. S. see Mary A. N. S. Williams-Ellis 156
WILLIAMS-ELLIS, MARY AMABEL NASSAU STRACHEY (Mrs.) 156
WILLIAMSON, ETHEL 156
WILLIAMSON, JACK see John Stewart Williamson 156
WILLIAMSON, JOHN STEWART 156
WILLIE, ALBERT FREDERIC see H. P. Lovecraft 92
WILLIS, CHARLES see Arthur C. Clarke 31
WILLIS, GEORGE ANTHONY ARMSTRONG 156
WILMER, DALE
   see H. Billy Miller 101
   see Robert Wade 149
WILSON, DORIS MARIE CLAIRE BAUMGARDT POHL 157
WILSON, GABRIEL
   see Ray Cummings 37
   see Mrs. Ray Cummings 37
WILSON, J. ARBUTHNOT see Charles Grant Allen 3
WILSON, JOHN (Anthony) B(urgess) 157
WILSON, RICHARD 157
WILSON, RICHARD (Mrs.) see Doris Baumgardt Wilson 157
WILSON, ROBIN S(cott) 157
WILSON, ROMER see Florence Roma Muir Wilson O'Brien 108
WILSON, SANDY see Alexander Galbraith 55
WINCH, JOHN see Gabrielle M. V. Long 91
WINFIELD, ALLEN see Edward Stratemeyer 138
WINFIELD, ARTHUR M. see Edward Stratemeyer 138
WINGRAVE, ANTHONY see S. Fowler Wright 159
WINIKI, EPHRIAM see John Russell Fearn 51
WINNARD, FRANK see E. C. Tubb 144
WINNEY, KEN see Winston K. Marks 98
WINSLOW, THYRA SAMTER see (Mrs. Nelson Waldorf) Hyde 73
WINTER, H. G.
   see Harry Bates 11
   see D(esmond) W(inter) Hall 63
WINTERBOTHAM, R. R. see Russell R. Winterbotham 157

WINTERBOTHAM, RUSS(ell) (Robert) 157
WINTERS, RAE see Raymond A. Palmer 111
WINWAR, FRANCES see Frances Grebanier 60
WISE, ARTHUR 157
WITHERUP, ANNE WARRINGTON see John Kendrick Bangs 9
WOLDMAN, M. see Theodore Edward White 154
WOLFF, CECIL DRUMMOND 157
WOLLHEIM, DONALD A. 157
WONDER, WILLIAM see Thomas Kirwan 80
WOOD, ELLEN PRICE (Mrs. Henry) 158
WOOD, MRS. (Henry) see Ellen Price Wood 158
WOOD, R. W. see Judson (P.) Philips 114
WOODCOTT, KEITH see John Brunner 23
WOODFORD, JACK see Josiah Pitts Woolfolk 158
WOODRUFF, CLYDE see David Vern 147
WOODS, JAMES 158
WOODS, LAWRENCE
   see Robert Lowndes 92
   see John Michel 101
   see Donald A. Wollheim 158
WOODWARD, LILIAN see John Marsh 98
WOODWARD, WAYNE 158
WOOLFOLK, JOSIAH PITTS 158
WOOLRICH, CORNELL 158
WORLEY, FREDERICK U. 158
WORRELL, EVERIL 158
WORTH, AMY see David H. Keller 79
WORTH, NIGEL see Noel Wright 159
WORTH, PETER [house pseudonym] 158
WORTS, GEORGE F(rank) 158
WRAY, REGINALD see W. B. Home-Gall 70
WRIGHT, FARNSWORTH 159
WRIGHT, KENNETH see R. Alvarez-del Rey 4
WRIGHT, LAN see Lionel Percy Wright 159
WRIGHT, LIONEL PERCY 159
WRIGHT, MABEL OSGOOD (Mrs. James) 159
WRIGHT, MARY M. (Dunn) (Mrs.) 159
WRIGHT, NOEL 159
WRIGHT, SEWELL PEASLEE 159
WRIGHT, S(idney) FOWLER 159
WRIGHT, WEAVER see Forrest J. Ackerman 1
WRIGHT, WILLARD HUNTINGTON 159
WRZOS, JOSEPH 160
WURMSAAM, VERMELIO see Franz Callenbach 27
WYBRANIEC, PETER F(rank) 160
WYCLIFFE, JOHN see H. Bedford-Jones 12
WYLIE, DIRK
   see Joseph Harold Dockweiler 42
   see Cyril Kornbluth 82
   see Robert W. Lowndes 92
   see Frederik Pohl 117
WYN, A. A. see Aaron Weinstein 152
WYNDHAM, JOHN see John B(eynon) Harris 65
WYNNE, MAY see Mabel W. Knowles 81

X see Frank Attfield Fawkes 50
"X" see Donald A. Wollheim 158
X, GENERAL see Roger Sherman Hoar 70
X. L. see Julian Osgood Field 51

YATES, DORNFORD see Cecil William Mercer 100
YERKE, T(heodore) B(ruce) 160
YERXA, LEROY 160
YEXLEY, LIONEL see James Woods 158
YORK, JEREMY see John Creasey 36
YORK, SIMON see Robert A. Heinlein 68
YOUD, C(hristopher) S. 160
YOUD, SAMUEL see C. S. Youd 160
YOUNG, COLLIER see Robert Bloch 17
YOUNG, RAYMOND A. see Vernon Jones 78

ZACHARIAS, B. see Henri Viard 148
ZACHARIE DE LISIEUX-PERE 161
ZACHARY, HUGH 161
ZACHERLE, JOHN 161
ZACHERLEY see John Zacherle 161
ZAGAT, ARTHUR LEO 161
ZAROVITCH, PRINCESS VERA see Mary E. Bradley Lane 85
ZEIGFIELD, KARL see R. Lionel Fanthorpe 48
ZELAZNY, ROGER (Joseph) 161
ZETFORD, TULLY see H. Kenneth Bulmer 25
ZIEGLER, EDWARD WILLIAM 161
ZISSMAN, JOSEPHINE JUDITH see Judith Merril 100
ZOILUS see H. P. Lovecraft 92

NOTES ON COLLECTING

In this section the reader will find illustrations with comments designed to give a visual referent to some of the entries in the text. This section also contains notes on collecting science fiction and fantasy. In contrast to the rest of the book, there is no tight structuring in this section and one illustrative arrangement may serve several purposes.

Collecting science fiction and fantasy was, until recently, a moderately inexpensive proposition; the relatively few collectors tended to be young and impecunious. Their effective demand was not great enough to drive the market or even the most desirable items in the field to stratospheric prices. Recent years have changed the collecting picture drastically. Institutions with large budgets and grown-up fans with inflated salaries have combined with the phenomenal growth of interest in the fields to send prices on many traditional collector's items out of sight and out of the price range of many of the traditional collectors in the field. Small press books such as those of Arkham House, Gnome, and Shasta and first editions of authors who are "in" lead the field in terms of prices while a number of new small presses are creating collectibles which are snapped up and become prohibitive in price almost before they are bound.

This situation has created a problem for the new collector who is interested in science fiction and fantasy and who would like to build an interesting collection of worthwhile material at a moderate price. In a sense, this entire dictionary is meant as an answer to that problem. Among the more than thirteen hundred authors listed are literally thousands of opportunities for collection which can be satisfying and which will not send a new collector to the poor house. In this guide I will present a number of ideas on areas of collecting which I believe have been overlooked by the many collectors in the field, and which, although not fashionable (and therefore not expensive) are areas in which exciting collecting can still be accomplished on a moderate budget.

Before we embark upon a perusal of these areas, let us have a word about book collecting in general. In the pages of this dictionary are many books which you, as a collector, are not likely to run across on your own. If you are serious about collecting some of the more esoteric authors, or are interested in authors whose original editions are either foreign or rather old, searches through random used book stores will eventually bring you to the desire for a personal dealer who will help you to find your needed volumes through what is known as a "book search." This service is performed by many dealers as a free service, or as one requiring a nominal fee to defray expenses. It should be noted that only books of a certain value, i.e. over three or four dollars, should be searched. A bookseller will not search a seventy-five cent book, and if he does he will often charge you three or four dollars for it! If you want a seventy-five cent paperback, and only want to pay seventy-five cents for it, find a dealer who has a large inflow of books in the area in which your interests lie and who is willing to put your name on what is known as a "want" list. He will then drop you a line or call you if he obtains the book in his regular course of acquisition; and he will sell it to you without adding a surcharge for having actually searched for the book.

Let us assume that you are having a book searched. When the dealer finds the book he will send you a "quote" on the book. The quote will include a description of the particular book, more detailed as the price increases; a general statement of condition, and a price. To evaluate the price, you must understand the description and the statement of condition. There follows a glossary of the most common terms used in describing books. These terms are almost universally understood by dealers and will also help you to describe the book you want to buy or, perhaps, to sell to a dealer.

a.e.g. all edges gilt

association copy A copy of a book which has belonged to the author or one of the author's close associates (sometimes extended to include extensively inscribed books in the author's own hand).

dust wrapper The paper wrapper, usually printed, which protects a hard cover book. Relatively uncommon in the 19th century, these wrappers are considered a necessary part of books from post World War I on. The absence of a dust wrapper, when one originally existed, will decrease the price of a collectible book by as much as fifty-percent.

paper wrapper (also rendered wraps) Indicates that the book was bound in a stiff paper cover. Commonly referred to as paperbacks,

these books are designated by the term **paper** in all my entries.

contemporary binding This term means contemporary with the publishing of the book and indicates that it is probable that the book has not been *rebound*. The term is used mostly with regard to older books which were published without bindings and then bound to order for the original owner.

antique binding This is a *new* binding made to look contemporary with the book it is on, or made to make a new book look like a period piece.

foxed/foxing This refers to brownish spots which discolor the paper or plates in a book. Usually caused by imperfect bleaching of the paper used in the book. Foxing can be removed, but only by an expert.

points A term referring to differences in the physical aspect of one *state* of a printing of a book and another. These points define the *state*. Thus a printer may run a number of copies of a book, notice an error, correct it, and run the rest of the edition. The two variations are *states* of the edition and the inclusion or exclusion of the error from a given book is a *point* which indicates the *state*. Points may be created by a change in paper, a piece of type that breaks in mid-print run, or any of a hundred different ways. Knowing points will help the collector from being charged the going rate for an earlier state, while receiving a later state of the same edition. Some limited editions are numbered and signed by the author, artist, etc. The presence of these signatures and identifying numbers are, in a sense, points, and having them can drastically raise the price of a book.

plates & illustrations Both terms refer to pictures in the book. Plates are generally on a separate, often heavier, leaf of paper with no printing on the reverse. Illustrations generally refer to pictures printed on the same stock as the book and with text on the opposite side.

leaf A sheet in the book each side of which is a page. The front side is called the *recto*, the back side the *verso*.

uncut and untrimmed Terms which refer to the three outer edges of the leaves. An untrimmed book has not been trimmed and has uneven edges to the paper. The outer folds of the paper will be intact and must be cut open to reveal the pages. If this has not been done the book is termed uncut (sometimes described as unopened).

SIZES

Books are often described by size according to a system which has nothing to do with size. This system is a description of the number of *folds* that the original sheet of paper used in manufacturing has in it and the number of pages produced from one sheet of paper by folding it a given number of times. Size varies depending, obviously, on the original sheet.

Elephant Folio or Folio: A book made from sheets folded once forming two leaves and having four pages. Elephant Folios are those made from the largest sheets.

Quarto (4to): Made from sheets folded twice giving four leaves and eight pages. This dictionary is an average size quarto.

Octavo (8vo): Made with four folds, eight leaves, sixteen pages. The standard hardback book size is an octavo.

duodecimo (12mo): A small size book, about the size of a mass market paperback.

mass market paperback: A paperback size developed in recent years to accomodate a standard rack. Older mass markets are approx. 6½ × 4¼, while in recent years they have been taller, approx. 7 1/8 × 4¼.

trade paperbacks (or quality paperbacks): All other modern paperbacks, usually of a larger size.

CONDITION

MINT - like new in every respect

VERY FINE - almost mint, some leeway accorded for age, but not much.

FINE - almost like new, perhaps has been read by a very careful reader.

VERY GOOD - clean, binding tight, no discernable wear, but obviously not quite new—an average used book.

GOOD - sound copy, binding tight, may show some wear—a slightly below average used book.

FAIR - soiled, perhaps minor tears in dust jacket, but still sound.

POOR - soiled, worn, but intact with all parts of the book still there.

READING COPY - all text still there and still in binding.

BINDING COPY - disbound but all interior leaves present.

NOTE: Each dealer will vary in his estimate of what constitutes "fine" or "good." In recent years there has been a type of quotation inflation, such that a number of dealers will quote books as much as two grades higher than the guide above would suggest. There has also been an increase in the practice of quoting with an "otherwise," as in "small tear at base of spine, *otherwise* very good." In moderation this is a legitimate practice but quotes such as "missing dust jacket, binding has two inch tear at top of spine, title page stamped with previous owner's name, missing page 37 and 38, *otherwise*, fine," are the mark of a, shall we say, overeager book seller. If you are contemplating using a dealer, order a couple of books from his catalogue which he has marked FINE. If you would be proud to show the books you get to a friend, you'll be happy with the dealer. If the books *look* like *used books*, shop around.

The foregoing information is supplemented by the abbreviation list and the guide to usage of the dictionary. A more thorough treatment may be found in the *A B C For Book-Collectors* by John Carter.

The most popular areas of collecting in recent years have been: 1. small press editions; 2. original art work; 3. special interest collecting, i.e. "Star Wars" memorabilia, etc.; 4. hardcover 1st editions of specific authors who have a large personal following. For those interested in these areas there are a number of sources for further information, many of which are listed in the bibliography at the end of this book. The dictionary provides 1st edition information and includes a number of small press publications by the authors covered. In addition, most specialist dealers are interested in and knowledgeable about these collecting areas. The remainder of this guide will deal with those areas not in fashion among collectors and dealers.

Collecting by its nature is dualistic. On the one hand, it is an idiosyncratic phenomenon with each collector deciding for his own reasons to collect just this particular type of book. On the other hand, modern collecting partakes of the "social," in that fads develop and it becomes "in" to collect just this type of material. When the fads begin the intelligent idiosyncratic collector may ponder his wounded exchequer and look for the modestly priced finds that the market is overlooking. A few suggestions follow:

The real "original" is on the left. The book on the right is a reprint (notice difference in logo). Only the copyright page indicates that the book on the right is a 1961 second printing. No price change in eight years—now *that* seems like science fiction.

Ballantine pioneered the "simultaneous" publication of paper and hardback editions in the early 1950s. While the hardbacks are more expensive items today, they were not necessarily published earlier than the paperbacks. Only the points will tell (see *points* above). As the paperbacks become more scarce they will rise in price. Now is the time to collect a set of these classics.

The "original" John Wyndam book *Out of the Deeps* is really an American 1st (with some textual differences) of *The Kracken Wakes*, first published in England. At right, Poul Anderson's first "serious" science fiction novel, *Brainwave*.

Andre Norton, one of science fiction's most prolific and best selling authors, has written A LOT of books. Most of her first editions are paperbacks and have not been heavily collected. Many are Ace Doubles, which *are* often collected as a set, but are still not prohibitively expensive.

Above: the first use of Andre Norton's **Andrew North** pseudonym, appearing in the 1947 Fantasy Book No. 1. Below: two of her Ace Double 1st editions, *The Sioux Spaceman* (1960) as Andre Norton, and *Voodoo Planet* (1959), as **Andrew North**.

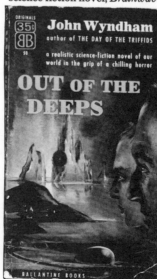

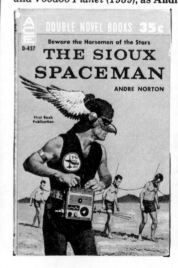

GALAXY NOVELS   In the fall of 1950 one of the best and most successful of science fiction magazines was launched. *Galaxy Magazine* was an instant success from its first issue in October 1950. Soon after the inception of this magazine the publishers began issuing a series of novels. At first these novels were in the same format as the magazine, a digest sized book. Later titles were issued in the regular mass market paperback size. Neither a magazine nor a standard book publishing venture, these books have been largely ignored by collectors, despite their many desirable characteristics.

Galaxy novels included both original first editions by major authors and reprints of classic stories. The most bibliographically significant of the line is *Galaxy Novel #3* issued in either December of 1950 or January of 1951. It is *Prelude To Space* by Arthur C. Clarke and constitutes the first edition of his *first* published novel. I have seen it in a dealer's catalogue recently for twenty-five dollars. It is, at that price, one of the most moderately priced 1st editions of a first book by a first ranked author in the field of science fiction.

Paperback 1st editions are generally moderately priced relative to other 1st edition prices in the field. This is due partly to the prejudice of libraries, which constitute a large part of the market for collectors, and which historically disdain paperback acquisitions. It is this type of disdain which in the past has led to the lamentable loss of a number of turn-of-the-century paperbacks in both the mystery and science fiction fields. No one ever bothered to collect them, so today some titles are simply no longer extant.

Paperback 1st editions are often "put down" as collectibles because they are fragile. I have even seen dealers make this point. To anyone interested in collecting as a means of preserving artifacts which have been important to the development of the field, the very fragility of the paperback is a reason to collect it. In the hands of a careful collector, paperback books can be carefully handled and preserved for the future. Left on the market, these books are indeed fragile and with the death of each book, a piece of the history of the development of the fantasy and science fields is lost.

In addition to containing several important first editions and a number of classic reprints, Galaxy Novels drew from the best artists in the field for their covers, which are, overall, excellent. Galaxy novels are bibliographically interesting as novels, they represent a unique publishing venture by a *genre* magazine, they are scarce but findable, they are moderately priced, and they are worth preserving as a body. Gathering together a set for one's personal library should provide a great deal of collecting pleasure and, as they are generally well bound, for paperbacks, many hours of reading enjoyment at a moderate price.

GALAXY NOVEL CHECKLIST

1. SINISTER BARRIER by Eric Frank Russell (reprint)
2. THE LEGION OF SPACE by Jack Williamson (reprint)
3. PRELUDE TO SPACE by Arthur C. Clarke (1st edition)
4. THE AMPHIBIANS by S. Fowler Wright (reprint)
5. THE WORLD BELOW by S. Fowler Wright (reprint)
6. THE ALIEN by Raymond F. Jones (1st edition)
7. EMPIRE by Clifford Simak (1st edition)
8. ODD JOHN by Olaf Stapledon (reprint)
9. FOUR SIDED TRIANGLE by William F. Temple (reprint)
10. RAT RACE by Jay Franklin (reprint)
11. THE CITY IN THE SEA by Wilson Tucker (reprint)
12. THE HOUSE OF MANY WORLDS by Sam Merwin, Jr. (reprint)
13. SEEDS OF LIFE by John Taine (reprint)
14. PEBBLE IN THE SKY by Isaac Asimov (reprint)
15. THREE GO BACK by J. Leslie Mitchell (reprint)
16. THE WARRIORS OF DAY by James Blish (1st edition?)
17. WELL OF THE WORLDS by Lewis Padgett (1st edition)
18. CITY AT WORLD'S END by Edmond Hamilton (reprint)
19. JACK OF EAGLES by James Blish (reprint)
20. THE BLACK GALAXY by Murray Leinster (1st edition)
21. THE HUMANOIDS by Jack Williamson (reprint)
22. KILLER TO COME by Sam Merwin, Jr. (reprint)
23. MURDER IN SPACE by David V. Reed (1st edition)
24. LEST DARKNESS FALL by L. Sprague de Camp (reprint)
25. THE LOST SPACESHIP by Murray Leinster (reprint)
26. CHESSBOARD PLANET by Lewis Padgett (1st separate ed.)
27. TARNISHED UTOPIA by Malcolm Jameson (1st edition)
28. DESTINY TIMES THREE by Fritz Leiber (reprint)
29. FEAR by L. Ron Hubbard (1st separate ed.?)
30. DOUBLE JEOPARDY by Fletcher Pratt (reprint)
31. SHAMBLEAU by C.L. Moore (1st separate ed.)
32. ADDRESS: CENTAURI by F. L. Wallace (reprint)
33. MISSION OF GRAVITY by Hal Clement (reprint)
34. TWICE IN TIME by Manley (sic.) WADE WELLMAN (reprint)
35. THE FOREVER MACHINE by Mark Clifton & Frank Riley (reprint of THEY'D RATHER BE RIGHT)
36. THE DEVIATES by Raymond F. Jones (reprint of THE SECRET PEOPLE)

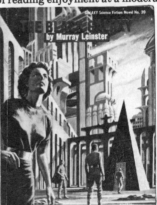

At left and below
Three 1st editions in the Galaxy Novels series.

At right and below
Four of the reprints in the series, including a Wally Wood cover on *The Forever Machine* by Clifton & Riley, and one by Emsh on *The House of Many Worlds* by Sam Merwin, Jr.

First Appearance - Before the First Edition

Science fiction and fantasy have a history of carrying two tendencies to such extremes that they are almost identifying characteristics of the *genres*. The number of novels which first appeared in magazine form is probably larger than for any other body of literature since the 19th century British penchant for issuing novels in parts reached its peak. There are also probably more variant forms, edited, expanded, re-thought, and abridged, of the average science fiction and fantasy novel than exist in any other field of literature.

Thus, in science fiction and fantasy, more than in any other field, the first book publication is often far removed in form and content from the author's original conception. Often a good novelette has been pumped up to a bad novel. Sometimes a good novel that ran as a serial in magazine form has been reduced to the bone to fit a book publisher's format, or, an author with second thoughts has gone back to tinker here and adjust a little there . . .

Only one thing is constant, the magazine version is the father of the book. The original story as read by the public, reviewed by the fanzines, and ultimately bought by the book publisher is the one contained in the magazine. These magazine novels are the sinews from which the publishing houses have built their science fiction lines. From the end of World War II until the early 1960's, almost all science fiction book publishers drew from the magazines. There are hundreds of these first appearances by practically every major writer in the field. They are bibliographically important, they are fascinating and they are unbelievably reasonably priced.

Magazine collectors in the field have long simply regarded all of the issues of a given magazine as part of a run. Price for the first issue of one or two post war magazines may have reached fifteen or twenty dollars, but for the vast majority of magazines, dealers' prices are geared to collectors of long runs. Single issues of all but a

few post war magazines hardly ever top $5.00, regardless of the contents. As a case in point, Vol. I of *Galaxy* magazine is generally priced in 1978 catalogues as follows: Vol. I No. 1, $15; Vol I No. 2, $7.50; Vol. I No. 3-6, $5 each. Prices are for fine copies. Now it just so happens that the cover story for Vol. I No. 5, the February 1951 edition of *Galaxy* was a novella by Ray Bradbury called "The Fireman." This is the original version of *Fahrenheit 451*, preceding the Ballantine 1st edition by almost two years, and it can be had for a fraction of the price of the book version, which has been extensively revised.

This temporary, I am sure, set of circumstances should give the creative collector much to ponder. Perhaps a collection of all the variant forms of each of your ten favorite books. Perhaps the original version of the fifty most important novels of the 1950's or the best 100 from the postwar period (you choose the best, of course). Perhaps a collection of short stories that were later turned into novels. Perhaps the first appearance of all of the stories from your favorite anthology, or anthologies. Perhaps a collection of *all* of the magazine appearances of your favorite author. The possibilities are endless and as a bonus you'll be collecting, in most cases, illustrated versions done by the best artists in the field.

Note: Tracing back from book to magazine will require access to an index of the magazines. See bibliography on page 199 for *The Index to the Science Fiction Magazines 1926-1950*, by Donald B. Day and *The Index to the Science Fiction Magazines 1951-1965* by Norm Metcalf. Frequently there are title changes from magazine to book. The more conscientious publishers will credit the original magazine publication, usually on the copyright page.

It should also be noted that in recent years, with the decline of the magazine as a force in the fantasy and science fiction field and the growth of paperback book publishing, novels are often bought for book publication first, with magazine rights as an afterthought. Care must be taken in each case to determine precedence.

Above *Seetee Shock* by Jack Williamson writing as Will Stewart, Astounding, Feb 1949ff

Against the Fall of Night, by Arthur C. Clarke, Startling Stories, Nov 1948

Above *The Fireman*, Galaxy, Feb 1951—1st published version of Bradbury's *Fahrenheit 451*

Gravy Planet, in Galaxy (1952) retitled *The Space Merchants* in its 1953 Ballantine 1st ed.

Below both in Galaxy
The Demolished Man by Alfred Bester, Jan 1952ff

The Caves of Steel by Isaac Asimov, Oct 1953ff

Below . . . *And Now You Don't* Astounding, Nov 1949ff, the first appearance of Asimov's *Second Foundation*

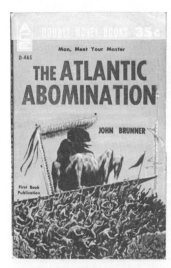

Above: Poul Anderson called his first Nicholas Van Rijn novel, *The Man Who Counts*, in Astounding, Feb 1958. In the Ace book 1st edition it became *War of the Wing-Men*. Recent editions have restored the original title. **Below:** *Earthman, Go Home!* (1960), and *We Claim These Stars!* (1959).

R. Alvarez-del Rey, better known as Lester del Rey, was everywhere but on the cover of the 1st issue of *Science Fiction Adventures*. He appears with an article as **Lester del Rey** and as **R. Alvarez** (Publisher); **Philip St. John** (Editor); and **John Vincent** (Associate Editor).

ILLUSTRATIONS BY LEHR • ORBAN • BAYMOND • SCHOENHERR • VAN DONGEN
R. ALVAREZ   Publisher   PHILIP ST. JOHN   Editor
BILL BRADLEY • Circulation Mgr.   MICHAEL SHAARA • Assoc. Editor
DAVID GELLER • Advertising Mgr.   JOHN VINCENT • Assoc. Editor
M. L. MITCHELL • West Coast Office   M. BERWIN   Art Director
SCIENCE FICTION ADVENTURES is published bi-monthly by Science Fiction Publications, Inc., 175 Fifth Avenue, New York 10, N. Y. Copyright 1952 by Science Fiction Publications, Inc. All rights, including translation reserved. Entry as second-class matter applied for at the Post Office at New York, N. Y. Subscriptions $3.00 per year in the United States and Possessions; $3.50 per year in Canada; $3.50 elsewhere. All stories in this issue are new and have not previously been published. No actual persons are designated in works of fiction, either by name or characters, any similarity is coincidental. Not responsible for unsolicited manuscripts of art work. All submissions must include return postage to expedite the return of manuscripts not acceptable.
PRINTED IN U. S. A.   175   35c per copy

Above left column: John Brunner's output of book length science fiction has been impressive. Best known for *Stand on Zanzibar* (1968), and its sequel, *The Sheep Look Up* (1972), he has a long list of earlier paperback 1st editions, including *The Atlantic Abomination* (1960), and *Slavers of Space* (1960). Brunner is another top writer whose output is important, but whose earlier works are not "collected," and are therefore moderately priced.

Above right: Robert Silverberg writes and writes and writes. Both cover stories of the December, 1957, Science Fiction Adventures above are his: *Valley Beyond Time* as Silverberg, and *Earth Lives Again*, writing as **Calvin Knox**. The novel, *The Dawning Light*, one of his many collaborations with Gordon Randall Garrett, this time writing as **Robert Randall**, first appeared in Astounding, March 1957ff. *Lest We Forget Thee, Earth* (1958), written as **Calvin M. Knox**, is one of his many paperback 1st editions. Assembling a collection of all of Silverberg's writings, including his many, many non-fiction works, would keep a collector busy for many a pleasant moon. Again, his early works are not "in" and his non-ficiton is almost unknown among collectors—so, the price is right.

Alex Schomberg, March 1955

Alejandro, Dec 1947

Van Dongen, May 1954

Earle Begley, March 1951

Hannes Bok, Nov 1951

Bert Tanner, April 1968

Chesley Bonestell, Oct 1952

Jeff Jones, April 1970

Mel Hunter, Sept 1970

Lawrence, Feb 1949

Vaughn Bode, May 1969

Kelly Freas, Feb 1959

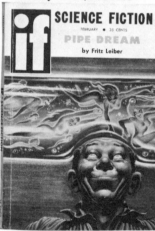

Gray Morrow, March 1966

Virgil Finlay, March 1958

Ed Emshwiller, April 1954

Artwork is one of the most popular areas of collecting. Here are fifteen of the most prolific artists. Their work is available inexpensively, on the magazines their work was produced for. Interior illustrations are interesting to collect and most have never been reproduced in any other form.

Happy Hunting!

Literally thousands of magazines and books have been used in the compilation of *Who Goes There*. Each book entry has been checked against the *National Union Catalogue* and the *British Museum Catalogue* when the actual book was not physically available. Below are those books, actually in my possession, which were read during the search for information in compiling *Who Goes There*. The editions cited are from my personal library and are not necessarily first editions. It goes almost without saying, that without the efforts of the authors, editors, and publishers listed below my task would have been impossible. [One book which I did not use, but which deserves to be mentioned is Barry McGhan's, *Science Fiction Pseudonyms*, available from Howard de Vore, 4705 Weddel St., Dearborn, Michigan. I ran across this book a few months ago and it contains many *fan* pseudonyms, which are not included in my book due to my inability to find two independent references attributing these pseudonyms to the authors cited by McGhan.]

Adams, Donald K., ed. *et. al. The Mystery & Detection Annual 1973*. Beverly Hills, California: Donald Adams, 1973 [1974], 337pp., ill.

Aldiss, Brian W. *Billion Year Spree: The True History of Science Fiction*. Garden City: Doubleday, 1973, 339pp.

Aldiss, Margaret. *Item Eighty-Three: Brian W. Aldiss: A Bibliography 1954-1972*. [Oxford]: SF Horizons, [1972], no pagination, [35], paper.

Amis, Kingsley. *New Maps of Hell*. NY: Ballantine, [1960], 140pp., paper.

The Armchair Detective, Vol. II, No. 4, Oct 1978. White Bear Lake, Minnesota: Allen J. Hubin, ed.

The Armchair Detective, Vol. II, No. 3, 1978.

Ash, Brian, ed. *The Visual Encyclopedia of Science Fiction*. New York: Harmony Books, [1977], 352pp., ill., paper.

Ash, Brian. *Who's Who in Science Fiction*. New York: Taplinger, [1978], 219pp., paper.

Ashley, Michael, ed. *The History of the Science Fiction Magazine, Part 1, 1926-1935*. [London]: New English Library, [1974], 239pp., ill.

Ashley, Michael, ed. *The History of the Science Fiction Magazine: Vol. 2, 1936-1945*. Chicago: Regnery, 298pp., ill., paper.

Ashley, Michael, ed. *The History of the Science Fiction Magazine: Vol. 3, 1946-1955*. Chicago: Contemporary Books, [1976], 349pp., ill., paper.

Ashley, Mike. *Who's Who in Horror & Fantasy Fiction*. New York: Taplinger, [1978], 240pp.

Asimov, Isaac. *Asimov's Biographical Encyclopedia of Science and Technology: The Lives and Achievements of 1,195 Great Scientists from Ancient Times to the Present Chronologically Arranged*. [New York]: Avon, [1976], 805pp., ill., paper.

Atheling, William, Jr. (James Blish). *The Issue At Hand*. Chicago: Advent, 1964 [1970], 136pp.

Atheling, William, Jr. (James Blish). *More Issues At Hand*. Chicago: Advent, 1970 [1971], 154pp.

Baird, Newton. A Fredric Brown Checklist, in *The Armchair Detective*, 1978.

Barron, Neil. *Anatomy of Wonder: Science Fiction*. New York: R. R. Bowker, 1976 [1977], 471pp., paper.

Barzun, Jacques and Taylor, Wendell Hertig. *A Catalogue of Crime*. New York: Harper & Row, [1976], 831pp.

Benet, William Rose. *The Reader's Encyclopedia: Second Edition*. New York: Crowell, [1965], 1,118pp., ill.

Benet, William Rose. *The Reader's Encyclopedia: Second Edition*. New York: Crowell, [1965], 2 vol., ill.

Bleiler, Everett F. and Dikty, T. E., eds. *The Best Science Fiction Stories: 1949*. New York: Frederick Fell, [1949], 314pp., *ss col*

Bleiler, Everett F. and Dikty, T. E., eds. *The Best Science ☆ Fiction Stories: 1950*. New York: Frederick Fell, [1950], 347pp. *ss col*

Bleiler, Everett F. and Dikty, T. E., eds. *The Best Science ☆ Fiction Stories: 1951*. New York: Frederick Fell, [1951], 351pp. *ss col*

Bleiler, Everett F. *The Checklist of Fantastic Literature: A Bibliography of Fantasy, Weird, and Science Fiction Books Published in the English Language*. Chicago: Shasta, 1948, 452pp.

Bleiler, Everett F. *The Checklist of Fantastic Literature: A Bibliography of Fantasy, Weird and Science Fiction Books Published in the English Language*. Naperville, Illinois: Fax Collector's Editions, [1972], 455pp.

Bleiler, Everett F. *The Checklist of Science Fiction and Supernatural Fiction*. Glen Rock, New Jersey: Firebell Books, [1978], 266pp. plus ads.

Boucher, Anthony, ed. (William Parker White). *The Best From Fantasy and Science Fiction: Seventh Series*. Garden City: Doubleday, [1958], 264pp.

Bretnor, Reginald, ed. *Science Fiction, Today and Tomorrow*. Baltimore, Maryland: Penguin, [1974], 342pp., paper.

Bretnor, Reginald, ed. *Science Fiction, Today and Tomorrow*. New York: Harper & Row, [1974], 342pp.

Briney, Robert E. and Wood, Edward. *SF Bibliographies: An Annotated Bibliography of Bibliographical Works on Science Fiction and Fantasy Fiction*. Chicago: Advent, 1972, 49pp.

Carter, Paul A. *The Creation of Tomorrow: Fifty Years of Magazine Science Fiction*. New York: Columbia Univ. Press, 1977, 318pp., ill.

[Carlson, Kaymar?] *Fantasy-Pseudonyms*. (no city): National Fantasy Fan Federation and Benefits Committee, April 1956, 13pp., paper.

Clareson, Thomas. *Science Fiction Criticism: An Annotated Checklist*. (no city): Kent State Univ. Press, [1973], 225pp.

Cockcroft, Thomas G. L. *Index To The Weird Fiction Magazines, Vols. I & II*. New York: Arno Press, 1975 [1974], 100pp.

Connes, G. A. *A Dictionary of the Characters and Scenes in the Novels, Romances and short Stories of H. G. Wells*. Dijon: Maurice Darantiere, 1926, 489pp.

Currey, L. W., compiler. *Fantasy and Science Fiction Catalogue 47*, Fall/Winter 1979. Elizabethtown, New York: L. W. Currey, 1978, 232pp., ill., paper.

Dann, Jack, ed. *Wandering Stars: An Anthology of Jewish Fantasy and Science Fiction*. New York: Harper & Row, [1974], 243pp. *ss col*

Dann, Jack and Dozois, Gardner, eds. *Future Power: A Science Fiction Anthology*. [New York: Random House, 1976], 256pp. *ss col*

Day, Bradford M. *The Checklist of Fantastic Literature in Paperbound Books*. New York: Arno Press, 1975 [1974], 128pp.

Day, Bradford M., ed. *The Supplemental Checklist of Fantastic Literature*. New York: Arno Press, 1975, 155pp.

Day, Donald B. *Index to the Science Fiction Magazines 1926-1950*. Portland, Oregon: Perri Press, [1952], 184pp.

de Camp, L. Sprague. *Lovecraft: A Biography*. Garden City: Doubleday, 1975, 510pp., ill.

de Camp, L. Sprague and Crook, Catherine. *Science Fiction Handbook, Revised: A Guide To Writing Imaginative Literature*. New York: McGraw-Hill, [1977], 220pp., paper.

de la Mare, Walter. *Eight Tales*. Sauk City, Wisconsin: Arkham House, 1971, 108pp.

de la Ree, Gerry, ed. *Fantasy Collector's Annual - 1974*. Saddle River, New Jersey: Gerry de la Ree, 1974, 64pp., ill., paper.

de la Ree, Gerry, ed. *Fantasy Collector's Annual - 1975*. Saddle River, New Jersey: Gerry de la Ree, 1974, 80pp., ill., paper.

del Rey, Lester (R. Alvarez-del Rey). *The Early del Rey: Vol. I.* New York: Ballantine, [1976], 337pp., paper.

Derleth, August. *Thirty Years of Arkham House 1939-1969: A History and Bibliography.* Sauk City, Wisconsin: Arkham House, 1970, 99pp., ill.

Dikty, T. E.. ed. *The Best Science Fiction Stories and Novels, 1956.* New York: Frederick Fell, [1956], 256pp.

Dozois, Gardner. *The Fiction of James Tiptree, Jr.* [New York]: Algol Press, [1977], no pagination, [36], paper.

Ellison, Harlan, ed. *Again Dangerous Visions, Vol. II.* [New York]: New American Library, [1973], 449pp., ill., paper.

Eshbach, Lloyd Arthur, ed. *Of Worlds Beyond: The Science of Science Fiction Writing—A Symposium.* Chicago: Advent, 1964 [1970], 104pp.

Evans, Christopher (Dr.). *Cults of Unreason.* New York: Dell, [1975], 252pp., paper.

[no editor given] *Exploring Cordwainer Smith.* New York: Algol Press. [1975], 33pp., paper.

Farmer, Philip Jose. *Doc Savage: His Apocalyptic Life.* New York: Bantam, [1975], 269pp., paper.

Franklin, H. Bruce. *Future Perfect: American Science Fiction of the Nineteenth Century.* New York: Oxford University Press, 1966, 402pp.

Gerber, Richard. *Utopian Fantasy: A Study of English Utopian Fiction Since the End of the Nineteenth Century.* New York: McGraw-Hill, [1973], 168pp., paper.

Gibb, Jocelyn, ed. *Light On C. S. Lewis, w/Bibliography by Walter Hooper.* NY: Harcourt, [1965], 160pp.

Goble, Neil. *Asimov Analyzed.* Baltimore, Maryland: Mirage, 1972, 174pp.

Griffith, George. *The Raid of 'Le Vengeur' w/Critical Biography by Sam Moskowitz and Annotated Bibliography by George Locke.* [London]: Ferret Fantasy Ltd., 1974, 144pp., ill., paper. *ss col*

Gunn, James. *Alternate Worlds: The Illustrated History of Science Fiction.* [no city]: A & W Visual Lib., [1975], 256pp., ill., paper.

Haining, Peter, ed. *The Fantastic Pulps.* New York: Vintage, [1976], 418pp., ill., paper. *ss col*

Halkett, Samuel and Laing, John, Rev. *A Dictionary of the Anonymous and Pseudonymous Literature of Great Britain Including the Works of Foreigners Written in, or Translated Into the English Language.* Boston, Massachusetts: Lockwood, Brooks & Co., 1882, 4 vol.

Handley-Taylor, Geoffrey and Smith, Timothy D'Arch. *C. Day-Lewis: The Poet Laureate; A Bibliography.* Chicago: St. James Press, 1968, 42pp., ill.

Hart, James D. *The Oxford Companion To American Literature.* New York: Oxford Univ. Press, 1956 [1962], 890pp.

Hedman, Iwan. *Deckare Och Thrillers Pa Svenska 1864-1973.* Sweden: Dast Dossier Nr. 3, [1974], 377pp., ill.

Hudgens, Betty Lenhardt. *Kurt Vonnegut, Jr.: A Checklist.* Detroit, Michigan: Gale Research, 1972, 67pp., ill.

[no editor given] *Index To The Science Fiction Magazines 1966-1970.* [West Hanover, Massachusetts]: New England Science Fiction Association, 1971, 82pp.

[no editor given] *Index to Fantasy & Science Fiction In Munsey Publications.* [no city, no date given], 36pp., paper.

Katz, Harvey A., *et. al. Introductory Psychology Through Science Fiction.* Chicago: Rand McNally, [1974], 510pp., paper.

[Knapp, Lawrence]. *The First Editions of Philip Jose Farmer: Science Fiction Bibliographies—2.* [Menlo Park, California: David G. Turner, Bookman, 1976], 8 pp., paper.

Knight, Damon. *In Search of Wonder: Essays On Modern Science Fiction.* Chicago: Advent, 1967 [revised 1968], 306pp., ill.

Knight, Damon, ed. *Science Fiction of the Thirties.* Indianapolis, Indiana: Bobbs-Merrill, [1975], 464pp., ill.

Knight, Damon, ed. *Turning Points: Essays On The Art of Science Fiction.* New York: Harper & Row, [1977], 303pp.

Kronenberger, Louis, ed. *et. al. Atlantic Brief Lives: A Biographical Companion To The Arts.* Boston, Massachusetts: Little, Brown, [1971], 900pp.

Lazarus, A. L. *The Indiana Experience: An Anthology.* Bloomington, Indiana: Indiana Univ. Press, [1977], 426pp., paper.

Lepper, Gary M. *A Bibliographical Introduction to Seventy-Five Modern American Authors.* Berkeley, California: Serendipity Books, 1976, 428pp.

Locke, George, ed. *Ferret Fantasy's Christmas Annual For 1972.* London: Ferret Fantasy, 1972, 76pp., ill., paper.

Locke, George, ed. *Ferret Fantasy's Christmas Annual For 1973.* London: Ferret Fantasy, 1974, 54pp., paper.

Locke, George. *Science Fiction First Editions: A Select Bibliography and Notes For the Collector.* [London]: Ferret [Fantasy], [1978], 96pp., paper.

Locke, George. *Voyages In Space: A Bibliography of Interplanetary Fiction 1801-1914.* [London]: Ferret Fantasy, 1975, 80pp.

Lord, Glen. *The Last Celt. A Bio-bibliography of Robert E. Howard.* NY: Berkley, [1976], 415pp., paper.

Lundwall, Sam J. *Science Fiction: What It's All About.* New York: Ace, [1971], 256pp., ill., paper.

MacDougall, Curtis D. *Hoaxes.* New York: Ace, [1958], 320pp.

Manuel, Frank E. and Fritzie P. *French Utopias: An Anthology of Ideal Societies.* New York: Schocken Books, [1971], 426pp., ill., paper.

Metcalf, Norm. *The Index of Science Fiction Magazines 1951-1965.* El Cerrito, California: Stark, [1968], 249pp.

Moskowitz, Sam. *The Immortal Storm: A History of Science Fiction Fandom.* Westport, Connecticut: Hyperion Press, [1974], 269pp., ill., paper.

Moskowitz, Sam. *Seekers of Tomorrow: The Masters of Modern Science Fiction.* New York: Ballantine, [1967], 450pp., paper.

Moskowitz, Sam. *Strange Horizons: The Spectrum of Science Fiction.* New York: Scribner's, [1976], 298pp.

Moskowitz, Sam, ed. *Under The Moons of Mars: A History and Anthology of "The Scientific Romance" in the Munsey Magazines, 1912-1920.* New York: Holt, Rinehart, [1970], 433pp.

Mullen, R. D. and Suvin, Darko, eds. *Science-Fiction Studies #6, Vol. 2, Part 2, July 1975.* [Terre Haute, Indiana: Dept. of English, Indiana State University], [pagination 102-199].

Mullen, R. D. and Suvin, Darko, eds. *Science-Fiction Studies #5, Vol. 2, Part 1, March 1975.* [Terre Haute, Indiana: Dept. of English, Indiana State University], 99pp.

Negley, Glenn. *Utopian Literature: A Bibliography With A Supplementary Listing of Works Influential in Utopian Thought.* Lawrence, Kansas: Regents Press, [1977], 228pp.

Nolan, William F. *The Ray Bradbury Companion: A Life and Career History, Photolog, and Comprehensive Checklist of Writings with Facsimiles From Ray Bradbury's Unpublished and Uncollected Work in All Media.* Detroit, Michigan: Gale Research, 1975, 339pp., ill.

Nowell-Smith, Simon. *International Copyright Law and the Publisher in the Reign of Queen Victoria.* Oxford: Clarendon Press, 1968, 109pp.

Owings, Mark and Chalker, Jack L. *The Revised H. P. Lovecraft Bibliography.* Baltimore, Maryland: Mirage Press, 1973, 43pp., paper.

Owings, Mark (introduction by Janet Kagan). *James H. Schmitz: A Bibliography.* Baltimore, Maryland: Croatan House, [1973], no pagination [32], paper.

Panshin, Alexei (introduction by James Blish). *Heinlein in Dimension.* Chicago: Advent, 1968, 204pp.

Penzler, Otto and Steinbrunner, Chris, eds., *et. al. Detectionary: A Biographical Dictionary of Leading Characters in Detective and Mystery Fiction, Including Famous and Little-Known Sleuths, Their Helpers, Rogues Both Heroic* and Sinister, and Some of Their Most Memorable Adventures, as Recounted in Novels, Short Stories, and Films. [Woodstock, New York: Overlook Press, 1977], 299pp., ill.

Pizor, Faith K. and Comp, T. Allan, eds. *The Man In the Moone: and Other Lunar Fantasies.* New York: Praegar, [1971], 230pp.

Pohl, Frederik. *The Early Pohl.* Garden City: Doubleday, [1976], 183pp. [S. F. Book Club Edition]

Pohl, Frederik. *The Way The Future Was: A Memoir.* New York: Ballantine, [1978], 312pp., ill.

Pollard, Arthur, ed. *et. al. Webster's New World Companion to English and American Literature.* New York: World, [1973], 850pp.

Quayle, Eric. *The Collector's Book of Books.* New York: C. Potter, [1971], 144pp., ill.

Rabkin, Eric S. *The Fantastic In Literature.* Princeton, New Jersey: Princeton Univ. Press, [1977], 234pp., paper.

Reginald, R., ed. *Contemporary Science Fiction Authors.* (orig. title *Stella Nova*) New York: Arno Press, 1975, 365pp.

Resnick, Michael. *The Official [Price] Guide To Fantastic Literature: Pulps: Digests: Hardcovers: Paperbacks: Star Trek: Radio Premiums: Fanzines: Original Art: Edgar Rice Burroughs.* [Florence, Alabama: House of Collectibles, 1976], 212pp., ill., paper.

Rogers, Alva. *A Requiem for Astounding.* Chicago: Advent, 1964, 224pp., paper.

Rose, Stephen and Lois. *The Shattered Ring: Science fiction and the quest for meaning.* Richmond, Virginia: John Knox Press, [1970], 127pp., paper.

Scholes, Robert and Rabkin, Eric S. *SF: Science Fiction: History ● Science ● Vision.* London: Oxford Univ. Press, 1977, 258pp., paper.

[no editor given] *The Science Fiction Novel: Imagination and Social Criticism.* Chicago: Advent, 1969 [1971], 128pp.

Slusser, George Edgar. *Harlan Ellison: Unrepentant Harlequin.* San Bernardino, California: Borgo Press, 1977, 63pp.

Spelman, Dick. *A Preliminary Checklist of Science Fiction and Fantasy Published by Ballantine Books (1953-1977).* 76pp., paper.

Steinbrunner, Chris and Penzler, Otto, eds. *Encyclopedia of Mystery and Detection.* New York: McGraw-Hill, [1976], 436pp., ill.

Strauss, Erwin T. *The M.I.T. Science Fiction Society's Index To the S-F Magazines, 1951-1965.* Cambridge, Massachusetts: [1966], (no title page), 207pp.

Svendsen, Clara and Lasson, Frans. *The Life and Destiny of Isak Dinesen.* Chicago: Univ. of Chicago Press, [1976], 227pp., ill., paper.

Talman, Wilfred B. *The Normal Lovecraft.* Saddle River, New Jersey: Gerry de la Ree, 1973, 30pp., ill., paper.

Tuck, Donald H. *The Encyclopedia of Science Fiction and Fantasy Through 1968. Vol. I & Vol. II. A Bibliographic Survey of the Fields of Science Fiction, Fantasy, and Weird Fiction through 1968.* Chicago: Advent, [1974-1978], 2 vol.

Warner, Charles Dudley, ed. *et. al. Biographical Dictionary of Authors.* New York: J. A. Hill, [1902], 2 vol.

Warner, Harry, Jr. *All Our Yesterdays: An Informal History of Science Fiction Fandom in the Forties.* Chicago: Advent, 1969 [1971], 336pp., ill., paper.

Webster's Biographical Dictionary. Springfield, Massachusetts: G. & C. Merriam, [1958], 1,697pp.

Webster's Geographic Dictionary. Springfield, Massachusetts: G. & C. Merriam, [1949], 1,293pp.

Weinberg, Robert, ed. *WT50: A Tribute To Weird Tales.* [Oak Lawn: Robert Weinberg, 1974], 135pp., ill., paper.

Wells, Geoffrey H. *The Works of H. G. Wells 1887-1925: A Bibliographic Dictionary and Subject Index.* London: George Routledge & Sons, Ltd., 1926, 274pp.

Wells, Stuart W., III. *The Science Fiction and Heroic Fantasy Author Index.* Duluth, Minnesota: Purple Unicorn Books, [1978], 186pp.

Whispers, Vol. 2, Number 2-3, June 1975, 131pp., paper.

Winn, Dilys. *Murder Ink: The Mystery Reader's Companion.* New York: Workman Publishing, [1977], 522pp., ill., paper.

Xenophile. No. 20, March 1977.

Who Goes There was set in Univers and Century
Textbook on a Compugraphic 88 photo typesetter, and
printed on sixty lb. offset white paper by
White Arts, Inc., in Spencer, Indiana

Two thousand copies of *Who Goes There* have been
printed, fifteen hundred of which are bound in paper
wrappers and five hundred of which have been
case bound.

This is copy number